James Patterson first took the bestseller lists by storm with his phenomenally successful international No 1 bestseller '*Along Came a Spider*' in 1993. It introduced homicide detective Alex Cross, his highly popular hero who has also appeared in *Kiss the Girls*, *Jack & Jill*, *Cat & Mouse*, *Pop Goes the Weasel*, *Roses are Red*, *Violets are Blue*, *Four Blind Mice* and *The Big Bad Wolf*. James Patterson lives in Palm Beach County, Florida, with his wife and their young son.

JAMES PATTERSON

ALONG CAME A SPIDER

HarperCollins*Publishers*

HarperCollins*Publishers*
77–85 Fulham Palace Road,
Hammersmith, London W6 8JB

www.harpercollins.co.uk

This paperback edition 2004
37

First published in Great Britain by
HarperCollins*Publishers* in 1993

ISBN 0-00-647615-5

Set in Berkeley

Printed and bound in Great Britain by
Clays Limited, St Ives plc

Acknowledgments

I WOULD LIKE TO THANK Peter Kim, who helped me learn about the private lives, the secrets, and the taboos that still exist all across America. Anne Pough-Campbell, Michael Ouweleen, Holly Tippett, and Irene Markocki gave me more of a feeling for Alex and his life in the Southeast section of D.C. Liz Delle and Barbara Groszewski kept me honest. Maria Pugatch (my Lowenstein) and Mark and MaryEllen Patterson put me back in touch with my half-dozen years working psych at McLean Hospital. Carole and Brigid Dwyer and Midgie Ford helped tremendously with Maggie Rose. Richard and Artie Pine ran with this like the banshees they can be. Finally, Fredrica Friedman was my partner in crime from beginning to end.

Let's Play Make-Believe
(1932)

New Jersey, near Princeton; March 1932

The Charles Lindbergh farmhouse glowed with bright, orangish lights. It looked like a fiery castle, especially in that gloomy, fir-wooded region of Jersey. Shreds of misty fog touched the boy as he moved closer and closer to his first moment of real glory, his first kill.

It was pitch-dark and the grounds were soggy and muddy and thick with puddles. He had anticipated as much. He'd planned for everything, including the weather.

He wore a size nine man's work boot. The toe and heel of the boots were stuffed with torn cloth and strips of the *Philadelphia Inquirer*.

He *wanted* to leave footprints, plenty of footprints. A man's footprints. Not the prints of a twelve-year-old boy. They would lead from the county highway called the Stoutsburg Wertsville Road, up to, then back from, the farmhouse.

He began to shiver as he reached a stand of pines, not thirty yards from the sprawling house. The mansion was just as grand as he'd imagined: seven bedrooms and four baths on the second floor alone. Lucky Lindy and Anne Morrow's place in the country.

Cool beans, he thought.

The boy inched closer and closer toward the dining-room window. He was fascinated by this condition known as *fame.* He thought a lot about it. Almost all the time. What was *fame* really like? How did it smell? How did it taste? What did *fame* look like close up?

"The most popular and glamorous man in the world" was right there, sitting at the table. Charles Lindbergh *was* tall, elegant, and fabulously golden haired, with a fair complexion. "Lucky Lindy" truly seemed above everyone else.

So did his wife, Anne Morrow Lindbergh. Anne had short hair. It was curly and black, and it made her skin look chalky white. The light from the candles on the table appeared to be dancing around her.

Both of them sat very straight in their chairs. Yes, they certainly looked superior, as if they were God's special gifts to the world. They kept their heads high, delicately eating their food. He strained to see what was on the table. It looked like lamb chops on their perfect china.

"I'll be more famous than either of you pitiful stiffs," the boy finally whispered. He promised that to himself. Every detail had been thought through a thousand times, at least that often. He very methodically went to work.

The boy retrieved a wooden ladder left near the garage by workingmen. Holding the ladder tightly against his side, he moved toward a spot just beyond the library window. He climbed silently up to the nursery. His pulse was racing, and his heart was pounding so loud he could hear it.

Light cast from a hallway lamp illuminated the baby's room. He could see the crib and the snoozing little prince in it. Charles Jr., "the most famous child on earth."

On one side, to keep away drafts, was a colorful screen with illustrations of barnyard animals.

He felt sly and cunning. "Here comes Mr. Fox," the boy whispered as he quietly slid open the window.

Then he took another step up the ladder and was inside the nursery at last.

Standing over the crib, he stared at the princeling. Curls of golden hair like his father's, but *fat*. Charles Jr. was gone to fat at only twenty months.

The boy could no longer control himself. Hot tears streamed from his eyes. His whole body began to shake, from frustration and rage — only mixed with the most incredible joy of his life.

"*Well, daddy's little man. It's our time now,*" he muttered to himself.

He took a tiny rubber ball with an attached elastic band from his pocket. He quickly slipped the odd-looking looped device over Charles Jr.'s head, just as the small blue eyes opened.

As the baby started to cry, the boy plopped the rubber ball right into the little drooly mouth. He reached down into the crib and took Baby Lindbergh into his arms and went swiftly back down the ladder. All according to plan.

The boy ran back across the muddy fields with the precious, struggling bundle in his arms and disappeared into the darkness.

Less than two miles from the farmhouse, he buried the spoiled-rotten Lindbergh baby — *buried him alive*.

That was only the start of things to come. After all, he was only a boy himself.

He, not Bruno Richard Hauptmann, was the Lindbergh baby kidnapper. He had done it all by himself.

Cool beans.

Part One

Maggie Rose and Shrimpie Goldberg

(1992)

CHAPTER 1

EARLY ON THE MORNING of December 21, 1992, I was the picture of contentment on the sun porch of our house on 5th Street in Washington, D.C. The small, narrow room was cluttered with mildewing winter coats, work boots, and wounded children's toys. I couldn't have cared less. This was home.

I was playing Gershwin on our slightly out-of-tune, formerly *grand* piano. It was just past 5 A.M., and cold as a meat locker on the porch. I was prepared to sacrifice a little for "An American in Paris."

The phone jangled in the kitchen. Maybe I'd won the D.C., or Virginia, or Maryland lottery and they'd forgotten to call the night before. I play all three games of misfortune regularly.

"Nana? Can you get that?" I called from the porch.

"It's for you. You might as well get it yourself," my testy grandmother called back. "No sense me gettin' up, too. No sense means nonsense in my dictionary."

That's not exactly what was said, but it went something like that. It always does.

I hobbled into the kitchen, sidestepping more toys on morning-stiff legs. I was thirty-eight at the time. As the saying goes, if I'd known I was going to live that long, I would have taken better care of myself.

The call turned out to be from my partner in crime, John Sampson. Sampson knew I'd be up. Sampson knows me better than my own kids.

"Mornin', brown sugar. You up, aren't you?" he said. No other I.D. was necessary. Sampson and I have been best friends since we were nine years old and took up shoplifting at Park's Corner Variety store near the projects. At the time, we had no idea that old Park would have shot us dead over a pilfered pack of Chesterfields. Nana Mama would have done even worse to us if she'd known about our crime spree.

"If I wasn't up, I am now," I said into the phone receiver. "Tell me something good."

"There's been another murder. Looks like our boy again," Sampson said. "They're waitin' on us. Half the free world's there already."

"It's too early in the morning to see the meat wagon," I muttered. I could feel my stomach rolling. This wasn't the way I wanted the day to start. "Shit. Fuck me."

Nana Mama looked up from her steaming tea and runny eggs. She shot me one of her sanctimonious, lady-of-the-house looks. She was already dressed for school, where she still does volunteer work at seventy-nine. Sampson continued to give me gory details about the day's first homicides.

"Watch your language, Alex," Nana said. "Please watch your language so long as you're planning to live in this house."

"I'll be there in about ten minutes," I told Sampson. "I own this house," I said to Nana.

She groaned as if she were hearing that terrible news for the first time.

"There's been another bad murder over in Langley Terrace. It looks like a thrill killer. I'm afraid that it is," I told her.

"That's too bad," Nana Mama said to me. Her soft brown eyes grabbed mine and held. Her white hair looked like one of the doilies she puts on all our living-room chairs. "That's such a bad part of what the politicians have let become a deplorable city. Sometimes I think we ought to move out of Washington, Alex."

"Sometimes I think the same thing," I said, "but we'll probably tough it out."

"Yes, black people always do. We persevere. We always suffer in silence."

"Not always in silence," I said to her.

I had already decided to wear my old Harris Tweed jacket. It was a murder day, and that meant I'd be seeing white people. Over the sport coat, I put on my Georgetown warm-up jacket. It goes better with the neighborhood.

On the bureau, by the bed, was a picture of Maria Cross. Three years before, my wife had been murdered in a drive-by shooting. That murder, like the majority of murders in Southeast, had never been solved.

I kissed my grandmother on the way out the kitchen door. We've done that since I was eight years old. We also say good-bye, just in case we never see each other again. It's been like that for almost thirty years, ever since Nana Mama first took me in and decided she could make something of me.

She made a homicide detective, with a doctorate in psychology, who works and lives in the ghettos of Washington, D.C.

CHAPTER 2

I AM OFFICIALLY a Deputy Chief of Detectives, which, in the words of Shakespeare and Mr. Faulkner, is a lot of sound and fury, signifying *nada*. The title should make me the number-six or -seven person in the Washington Police Department. It doesn't. People wait for my appearance at crime scenes in D.C., though.

A trio of D.C. Metro blue-and-whites were parked helter-skelter in front of 41-15 Benning Road. A crime-lab van with blackened windows had arrived. So had an EMS ambulance. MORTUARY was cheerfully stenciled on the door.

There were a couple of fire engines at the murder house. The neighborhood's ambulance-chasers, mostly eye-fucking males, were hanging around. Older women with winter coats thrown over their pajamas and nightgowns, and pink and blue curlers in their hair, were up on their porches shivering in the cold.

The row house was dilapidated clapboard, painted a gaudy Caribbean blue. An old Chevette with a broken, taped-up side window looked as if it had been abandoned in the driveway.

"Fuck this. Let's go back to bed," Sampson said. "I just

remembered what this is going to be like. I hate this job lately."

"I love my work, love Homicide," I said with a sneer. "See that? There's the M.E. already in his plastic suit. And there are the crime-lab boys. And who's this coming our way now?"

A white sergeant in a puffy blue-black parka with a fur collar came waddling up to Sampson and me as we approached the house. Both his hands were jammed in his pockets for warmth.

"Sampson? Uh, Detective Cross?" The sergeant cracked his lower jaw the way some people do when they're trying to clear their ears in airplanes. He knew exactly who we were. He knew we were S.I.T. He was busting our chops.

"Wuz up, man?" Sampson doesn't like his chops being busted very much.

"*Senior* Detective Sampson," I answered the sergeant. "I'm Deputy Chief Cross."

The sergeant was a jelly-roll-belly Irish type, probably left over from the Civil War. His face looked like a wedding cake left out in the rain. He didn't seem to be buying my tweed jacket ensemble.

"Everybody's freezin' their toches off," he wheezed. "That's wuz up."

"You could probably lose a little of them toches," Sampson advised him. "Might give Jenny Craig a call."

"Fuck you," said the sergeant. It was nice to meet the white Eddie Murphy.

"Master of the riposte." Sampson grinned at me. "You hear what he said? Fuck you?"

Sampson and I are both physical. We work out at the gym attached to St. Anthony's — St. A's. Together, we weigh about five hundred pounds. We can intimidate, if we want to. Sometimes it's necessary in our line of work.

I'm only six three. John is six nine and growing. He always wears Wayfarer sunglasses. Sometimes he wears a raggy Kangol hat, or a yellow bandanna. Some people call him "John-John" because he's so big he could be two Johns.

We walked past the sergeant toward the murder house. Our elite task force team is supposed to be above this kind of confrontation. Sometimes we are.

A couple of uniforms had already been inside the house. A nervous neighbor had called the precinct around four-thirty. She thought she'd spotted a prowler. The woman had been up with the night-jitters. It comes with the neighborhood.

The two uniformed patrolmen found three bodies inside. When they called it in, they were instructed to wait for the Special Investigator Team. S.I.T. It's made up of eight black officers supposedly slated for better things in the department.

The outside door to the kitchen was ajar. I pushed it all the way open. The doors of every house have a unique sound when they open and close. This one whined like an old man.

It was pitch-black in the house. Eerie. The wind was sucked through the open door, and I could hear something rattling inside.

"We didn't turn on the lights, sir," one of the uniforms said from behind me. "You're Dr. Cross, right?"

I nodded. "Was the kitchen door open when you came?" I turned to the patrolman. He was white, baby-faced, growing a little mustache to compensate for it. He was probably twenty-three or twenty-four, real frightened that morning. I couldn't blame him.

"Uh. No. No sign of forced entry. It was unlocked, sir."

The patrolman was very nervous. "It's a real bad mess in there, sir. It's a family."

One of the patrolmen switched on a powerful milled-aluminum flashlight and we all peered inside the kitchen.

There was a cheap Formica breakfast table with matching lime green vinyl chairs. A black Bart Simpson clock was on one wall. It was the kind you see in the front windows of all the People's drugstores. The smells of Lysol and burnt grease melded into something strange to the nose, though not entirely unpleasant. There were a lot worse smells in homicide cases.

Sampson and I hesitated, taking it all in the way the murderer might have just a few hours earlier.

"He was right here," I said. "He came in through the kitchen. He was here, where we're standing."

"Don't talk like that, Alex," Sampson said. "Sound like Jeane Dixon. Creep me out."

No matter how many times you do this kind of thing, it never gets easier. You don't want to have to go inside. You don't want to see any more horrible nightmares in your lifetime.

"They're upstairs," the cop with the mustache said. He filled us in on who the victims were. A family named Sanders. Two women and a small boy.

His partner, a short, well-built black man, hadn't said a word yet. His name was Butchie Dykes. He was a sensitive young cop I'd seen around the station.

The four of us entered the death house together. We each took a deep breath. Sampson patted my shoulder. He knew that child homicide had me shook.

The three bodies were upstairs in the front bedroom, just off the top of the stairs.

There was the mother, Jean "Poo" Sanders, thirty-two. Even in death, her face was haunting. She had big brown eyes, high cheekbones, full lips that had already turned purplish. Her mouth was stretched open in a scream.

Poo's daughter, Suzette Sanders, fourteen years on this earth. She was just a young girl but had been prettier than her mother. She wore a mauve ribbon in her braided hair and a tiny nose earring to prove she was older than her years. Suzette was gagged with dark blue panty hose.

A baby son, Mustaf Sanders, three years old, was lying faceup, and his little cheeks seemed stained with tears. He was wearing a "pajama bag" like my own kids wear.

Just as Nana Mama had said, it was a bad part of what somebody had let become a bad city. In this big bad country of ours. The mother and the daughter were bound to an imitation brass bedpost. Satin underwear, black and red mesh stockings, and flowery bed sheets had been used to tie them up.

I took out the pocket recorder I carry and began to put down my first observations. "Homicide cases H234 914 through 916. A mother, teenage daughter, little boy. The women have been slashed with something extremely sharp. A straight razor, possibly.

"Their breasts have been cut off. The breasts are nowhere to be found. The pubic hair of the women has been shaved. There are multiple stab wounds, what the pathologists call 'patterns of rage.' There is a great deal of blood, fecal matter. I believe the two women, both the mother and daughter, were prostitutes. I've seen them around."

My voice was a low drone. I wondered if I'd be able to understand all the words later.

"The little boy's body seems to have been casually tossed aside. Mustaf Sanders has on hand-me-down pajamas that are covered with Care Bears. He is a tiny, incidental pile in the room." I couldn't help grieving as I looked down at the little boy, his sad, lifeless eyes staring up at me. Everything was very noisy inside my head. My heart ached. Poor little Mustaf, whoever you were.

"I don't believe he wanted to kill the boy," I said to Sampson. "He or she."

"Or it." Sampson shook his head. "I vote for it. It's a Thing, Alex. The same Thing that did Condon Terrace earlier this week."

CHAPTER 3

SINCE SHE HAD BEEN THREE OR FOUR years old, Maggie Rose Dunne was always *watched* by people. At nine, she was used to special attention, to strangers gawking at her as if she was Maggie Scissorhands, or Girl Frankenstein.

That morning she was being watched, but she didn't know it. This one time, Maggie Rose would have cared. This one time, it mattered very much.

Maggie Rose was at Washington Day School in Georgetown, where she was trying to blend in with the other hundred and thirty students. At that moment, they were all singing enthusiastically at assembly.

Blending in wasn't easy for Maggie Rose, even though she desperately wanted to. She was the nine-year-old daughter of Katherine Rose, after all. Maggie couldn't walk past a mall video store without seeing a picture of her mother. Her mother's movies seemed to be on the tube about every other night. Her mom got nominated for Oscars more often than most actresses got mentioned in *People* magazine.

Because of all that stuff, Maggie Rose tried to disappear into the woodwork a lot. That morning she had on a beat-up Fido

Dido sweatshirt with strategic holes front and rear. She'd picked out grungy, wrinkled Guess jeans. She wore old pink Reebok sneakers — her "trusty dusties" — and Fido socklets picked out from the bottom of her closet. She purposely hadn't washed her long blond hair before school.

Her mom's eyes had bugged when she'd spotted the getup. She said, "Quadruple yuk," but she let Maggie go to school that way anyway. Her mom was cool. She really understood the tough deal Maggie had to live with.

The kids in the crowded assembly, first- through sixth-grade classes, were singing "Fast Car" by Tracy Chapman. Before she played the folk/rock song on the auditorium's gleaming black Steinway, Ms. Kaminsky had tried to explain the message of it for everybody.

"This moving song, by a young black woman from Massachusetts, is about being dirt poor in the richest country in the world. It's about being black in the nineteen nineties."

The petite, rail-thin music and visual arts teacher was always so intense. She felt it was a good teacher's duty not only to inform, but to persuade, to mold the important young minds at the prestigious Day School.

The kids liked Ms. Kaminsky, so they tried to imagine the plight of the poor and disadvantaged. Since the tuition at Washington Day was twelve thousand dollars, it took some imagination on their part.

"*You got a fast car,*" they sang along with Ms. K. and her piano.

"*And I got a plan to get us out of here.*"

As Maggie sang "Fast Car," she really tried to imagine what it would be like to be poor like that. She'd seen enough poor people sleeping in the cold on Washington streets. If she concentrated, she could visualize terrible scenes around Georgetown and Dupont Circle. Especially the men with dirty rags who washed your windshield at every stoplight. Her mother always gave them a dollar, sometimes more. Some of the beggars recognized her mom and went apeman crazy. They smiled like their day had been made, and Katherine Rose always had something nice to say to them.

"*You got a fast car*," Maggie Rose sang out. She felt like letting her voice really get up there.

"*But is it fast enough so we can fly away*
"*We gotta make a decision*
"*We leave tonight or live and die this way.*"

The song finished to loud applause and cheers from all the kids at assembly. Ms. Kaminsky took a queer little bow at her piano.

"Heavy duty," Michael Goldberg muttered. Michael was standing right next to Maggie. He was her best friend in Washington, where she'd moved less than a year ago, coming from L.A. with her parents.

Michael was being ironic, of course. As always. That was his East Coast way of dealing with people who weren't as smart as he was — which meant just about everybody in the free world.

Michael Goldberg was a genuine brainiac, Maggie knew. He was a reader of everything and anything; a gonzo collector; a doer; always funny *if* he liked you. He'd been a "blue baby," though, and he still wasn't big or very strong. That had gotten him the nickname "Shrimpie," which kind of brought Michael down off his brainiac pedestal.

Maggie and Michael rode to school together most mornings. That morning they'd come in a real Secret Service town car. Michael's father was the secretary of the treasury. As in *the* secretary of the treasury. Nobody was really just "normal" at Washington Day. Everybody was trying to blend in, one way or another.

As the students filed out of morning assembly, each of them was asked who was picking them up after school. Security was tremendously important at Washington Day.

"Mr. Devine —," Maggie started to tell the teacher-monitor posted at the door from the auditorium. His name was Mr. Guestier and he taught languages, which included French, Russian, and Chinese, at the school. He was nicknamed "Le Pric."

"And Jolly Chollie Chakely," Michael Goldberg finished for her. "Secret Service Detail Nineteen. Lincoln town car. License number SC-59. North exit, Pelham Hall. They're assigned to *moi* because the Colombian cartel has made death threats against my father. *Au revoir, mon professeur.*"

It was noted in the school log for December 21. *M. Goldberg and M.R. Dunne — Secret Service pickup. North exit, Pelham, at three.*

"C'mon, Dweebo Dido." Michael Goldberg poked Maggie Rose sharply in her rib cage. "I got a fast car. Uh huh, uh huh. And I got a plan to get us out of here."

No wonder she liked him, Maggie thought. Who else would call her a dweebo? Who else but Shrimpie Goldberg?

As they walked out of the assembly hall, the two friends were being watched. Neither of them noticed anything wrong, anything out of the ordinary. They weren't supposed to. That was the whole idea. It was the master plan.

CHAPTER 4

At NINE O'CLOCK that morning, Ms. Vivian Kim decided to re-create Watergate in her Washington Day School classroom. She would never forget it.

Vivian Kim was smart, pretty, and a stimulating American history teacher. Her class was one of the students' favorites. Twice a week Ms. Kim acted out a history skit. Sometimes she let the children prepare one. They got to be really good at it, and she could honestly say her class was never boring.

On this particular morning, Vivian Kim had chosen Watergate. In her third-grade class were Maggie Rose Dunne and Michael Goldberg. The classroom was being *watched*.

Vivian Kim alternately played General Haig, H. R. Haldeman, Henry Kissinger, G. Gordon Liddy, President Nixon, John and Martha Mitchell, and John and Maureen Dean. She was a good mimic and did an excellent job on Liddy, Nixon, General Haig, and especially the Mitchells and Mo Dean.

"During his annual State of the Union message, President Nixon spoke to the entire nation on television," Ms. Kim told the children. "Many people feel that he lied to us. When a high government official lies, he commits a horrible crime. We've put our trust in that person, based on his solemn word, his integrity."

"Hiss." "Boo!" A couple of kids in class participated in the lesson. Within reason, Vivian Kim encouraged this kind of involvement.

"Boo is absolutely right," she said. "Hiss, too. Anyway, at this moment in our history, Mr. Nixon stood before the nation, before people like you and me." Vivian Kim arranged herself as if she were at a speaking podium. She began to do her version of Richard Nixon for the class.

Ms. Kim made her face dark and gloomy. She shook her head from side to side. "I want you to know . . . that I have no intention whatever of ever walking away from the job that the American people elected me to do for the people of the United States." Vivian Kim paused on the actual words from Nixon's infamous speech. It was like a held note in a bad but powerful opera.

The classroom of twenty-four children was silent. For the moment, she had completely won their attention. It was a teacher's nirvana, however short-lived. Nice, Vivian Kim thought to herself.

There was a brittle tap, tap, tap on the glass pane of the classroom door. The magical mood was broken.

"Boo! Hiss," Vivian Kim muttered. "Yes? Who's there? Hello? Who is it?" she called.

The glass and polished mahogany door slowly opened. One of the kids hummed from the score of *Nightmare on Elm Street*. Mr. Soneji, hesitantly, almost shyly, stepped inside. Nearly every child's face in the classroom brightened instantly.

"Anybody home?" Mr. Soneji piped in a thin squeaky voice. The children erupted with laughter. "Ohhh! Look. Everybody's home," he said.

Gary Soneji taught mathematics, and also computer science — which was even more popular than Vivian Kim's class.

He was balding, with a droopy mustache, and English schoolboy glasses. He didn't look like a matinee idol, but he was one at the school. In addition to being an inspired teacher, Mr. Soneji was the grand master of Nintendo video games.

His popularity, and the fact that he was a computer wizard, had earned him the nickname "Mr. Chips."

Mr. Soneji greeted a couple of the students by name as he quickly made his way to Ms. Kim's desk.

The two teachers then spoke privately at the front desk. Ms. Kim had her back to the class. She was nodding a lot, not saying much. She seemed tiny standing next to Mr. Soneji, who was over six feet tall.

Finally, Ms. Kim turned to the children. "Maggie Rose and Michael Goldberg? Could the two of you please come up front? Bring your things if you would."

Maggie Rose and Michael exchanged puzzled glances. What was this all about? They gathered their belongings, and then headed to the front to find out. The other kids had begun whispering, even talking out loud in the classroom.

"Okay. Put a lock on it. This isn't recess," Ms. Kim quieted them. "This is still class. Please have some respect for the rules we've all agreed to live by here."

When they got to the front of the classroom, Mr. Soneji crouched down to talk privately to Maggie and Michael. Shrimpie Goldberg was at least four inches shorter than Maggie Rose.

"There's a little problem, but it's nothing to worry about." Mr. Soneji was calm and very gentle with the children. "Everything is basically fine. There's just a little glitch, that's all. Everything is okay, though."

"I don't think so," Michael Goldberg said, shaking his head. "What's this little so-called glitch all about?"

Maggie Rose didn't say anything yet. She was feeling afraid

for some reason. Something had happened. Something was definitely wrong. She could feel it in the pit of her stomach. Her mom always told her she had too active an imagination, so she tried to look cool, act cool, *be* cool.

"We just received a phone call from the Secret Service," said Ms. Kim. "They've gotten a threat. It concerns both you and Maggie. It's probably a crank call. But we're going to hustle you both home as a precaution. Just a safety precaution. You guys know the drill."

"I'm sure you'll both be back before lunch," Mr. Soneji added in support, though he didn't sound too convincing.

"What kind of threat?" Maggie Rose asked Mr. Soneji. "Against Michael's father? Or does it have to do with my mom?"

Mr. Soneji patted Maggie's arm. Time and again, the teachers at the private school were amazed at how grown-up most of these kids were.

"Oh, the usual kind we get now and then. Big talk, no action. Just some jerk looking for attention, I'm sure. Some creep." Mr. Soneji made an exaggerated face. He showed just the right amount of concern, but he made the kids feel secure.

"Then why do we have to go all the way home to Potomac, for crying out loud?" Michael Goldberg grimaced and gesticulated like a miniature courtroom lawyer. In many ways he was a cartoon version of his famous father, the secretary.

"Just to be on the safe side. Okay? Enough said. I'm not going to have a debate with you, Michael. Are we ready to travel?" Mr. Soneji was nice, but firm.

"Not really." Michael continued to frown and shake his head. "No way, José Canseco. Seriously, Mr. Soneji. This isn't fair. It isn't right. Why can't the Secret Service come here and stay till school's over?"

"That's not the way they want to do it," Mr. Soneji said. "I don't make up the rules."

"I guess we're ready," said Maggie. "C'mon, Michael. Stop arguing. This is a done deal."

"It's a done deal." Ms. Kim offered a helpful smile. "I'll send over your homework assignments."

Both Maggie Rose and Michael started to laugh. "*Thank you, Ms. Kim!*" they said in unison. Leave it to Ms. Kim to have a good joke to fit the situation.

The halls outside the classroom were nearly empty, and very quiet. A porter, a black man named Emmett Everett, was the only person who saw the trio as they left the school building.

Leaning on his broom, Mr. Everett watched Mr. Soneji and the two children walk the length of the long hallway. He was the last person to see them all together.

Once outside, they hurried across the school's cobblestoned parking lot, which was framed by elegant birch trees and shrubbery. Michael's shoes made clicking noises against the stones.

"Dork shoes." Maggie Rose leaned into him and made a joke. "Look like dork shoes, act like dork shoes, sound like dork shoes."

Michael had no argument. What could he say? His mother and father still bought his clothes at freaking Brooks Brothers. "What am I *supposed* to be wearing, Miss Gloria Vanderbilt? Pink sneakers?" he offered lamely.

"Sure, *pink* sneakers." Maggie beamed. "Or lime green Airouts. But not shoes for a funeral, Shrimpster."

Mr. Soneji led the children to a late-model blue van parked under elm and oak trees that went the length of the administration building and school gym. Nonsynchronous bouncing basketballs echoed from inside the gym.

"The two of you can jump right in back here. Upsy-daisy. There we go," he said. The teacher helped boost them up and into the back of the van. His eyeglasses kept slipping down his nose. Finally, he just took them off.

"You're driving us home?" Michael asked.

"I know it's no Mercedes stretch, but it'll have to do, Sir Michael. I'm just following the instructions we got on the phone. I spoke to a Mr. Chakely."

"Jolly Chollie." Michael used his nickname for the Secret Service agent.

Mr. Soneji climbed inside the blue van himself. He pulled the sliding door shut with a bang.

"Just be a sec. Make a little room for you guys here."

He rummaged through cardboard boxes stacked toward the front of the van. The van was a mess. It was the antithesis of the orderly, almost compartmentalized, math teacher's style in school. "Sit anywhere, kids." He kept talking while he looked for something.

When he turned again, Gary Soneji was wearing a scary, rubbery-looking black mask. He held some kind of metal implement in front of his chest. It looked like a miniature fire extinguisher, only it was more sci-fi than that.

"Mr. Soneji?" Maggie Rose asked, her voice rising in pitch. "Mr. Soneji!" She threw her hands in front of her face. "You're frightening us. Stop kidding around!"

Soneji was pointing the small metal nozzle right at Maggie Rose and Michael. He took a fast step toward them. He planted both of his rubber-soled black brogans firmly.

"What's that thing?" Michael said, not even sure why he said it.

"Hey, I give up. Take a whiff, boy genius. You tell me."

Soneji hit them with a blast of chloroform spray. He kept his finger on the trigger for a full ten seconds. Both children were covered with mist as they collapsed into the back seat of the van.

"Out, out, bright lights," Mr. Soneji said in the quietest, gentlest voice. "Now no one will ever know." That was the beauty of it. No one would ever know the truth.

Soneji climbed into the front and fired up the blue van. As he drove from the parking area, he sang "Magic Bus" by The Who. He was in an awfully good mood today. He was planning to be America's first serial kidnapper, among other things.

CHAPTER 5

I GOT an "emergency" call at the Sanders house at about quarter to eleven. I didn't want to talk to anybody with more emergencies.

I had just spent ten minutes with the news folks. At the time of the project murders, some of the newsies were my buddies. I was a press pet. I'd even been featured in the *Washington Post's* Sunday magazine section. I talked about the murder rate among black people in D.C. once again. This past year there had been nearly five hundred killings in our capital. Only eighteen victims were white. A couple of reporters actually made a note on that. Progress.

I took the phone from a young, smart S.I.T. detective, Rakeem Powell. I was absently palming a biddy basketball that must have belonged to Mustaf. The ball gave me a funny feeling. Why murder a beautiful little boy like that? I couldn't come up with an answer. Not so far, anyway.

"It's The Jefe, the chief." Rakeem frowned. "He's concerned."

"This is Cross," I said into the Sanders telephone. My head was still spinning. I wanted to get this conversation over with real fast.

The mouthpiece smelled of cheap musk perfume. Poo's or Suzette's fragrance, maybe both of theirs. On a table near the phone were photos of Mustaf in a heart-shaped frame. Made me think of my own two kids.

"This is Chief of Detectives Pittman. What's the situation over there?"

"I think we have a serial killer. Mother, daughter, a little boy. Second family in less than a week. Electricity was shut off in the house. He likes to work in the dark." I ticked off a few gory details for Pittman. That was usually enough for him. The chief would leave me alone with this one. Homicides in Southeast don't count for much in the greater scheme.

A beat or two of uneasy silence followed. I could see the Sanders family Christmas tree in the TV room. It had been decorated with obvious care: tinsel, shiny dime-store decorations, strings of cranberries and popcorn. There was a homemade tinfoil angel on top.

"I heard it was a dealer got hit. Dealer and two prostitutes," The Jefe said.

"No, that's not true," I said to Pittman. "They've got a nice Christmas tree up."

"Sure it is. Don't bullshit me, Alex. Not today. Not right now."

If he was trying to get a rise out of me, he got one. "One victim is a three-year-old little boy in his pajamas. He may have been dealing. I'll check into it."

I shouldn't have said that. I shouldn't say a lot of things. Lately, I'd been feeling I was on the edge of exploding. Lately means for about three years or so.

"You and John Sampson hustle over to Washington Day," Pittman said. "All hell has broken loose here. I'm serious."

"I'm serious, too," I said to the chief of detectives. I tried to keep my voice down. "I'm sure this is a signature killer. It's bad here. People are crying in the streets. It's almost Christmas."

Chief Pittman ordered us to come to the school in Georgetown, anyway. All hell had broken loose, he kept repeating.

Before I left for Washington Day, I phoned the serial-killer unit inside our own department; then the "super unit" at the FBI's Quantico base. The FBI has computer files of all known cases of serial killings, complete with psychiatric profiles matching M.O.'s up with a lot of unpublished serial-killing details. I was looking for a match on age, sex, type of disfigurement.

One of the techies handed me a report to sign as I left the Sanders house. I signed my usual way — with a ✝.

Cross.

Tough guy from the tough part of town, right.

CHAPTER 6

THE PRIVATE-SCHOOL SURROUNDINGS were a little intimidating for Sampson and me. This was a long, long way from the schools and people of Southeast.

We were two of only a few blacks inside the Washington Day School lobby. I'd heard there were supposed to be African kids, the children of diplomats, at the private school, but I didn't see any. Just clusters of shocked teachers, children, parents, police. People were crying openly on the front lawns and inside the school's lobby.

Two little kids, two little babies had been kidnapped from one of Washington's most prestigious private schools. I understood that it was a sad, tragic day for everybody involved. *Leave it at that*, I told myself. *Just do your job.*

We went about our police business. We tried to suppress the fury we were feeling, but it wasn't easy. I kept seeing the sad eyes of little Mustaf Sanders. A uniform told us we were wanted in the headmaster's office. Chief of Detectives Pittman was there waiting for us.

"Be cool," Sampson advised. "Live to fight another day."

George Pittman usually wears a gray or blue business suit on the job. He favors pin-striped dress shirts and striped silver-and-blue neckties. He's a Johnson & Murphy shoe and belt man. His gray hair is always slicked back so it fits his bullet head like a tight helmet. He is known as The Jefe, the Boss of Bosses, Il Duce, Thee Pits, Georgie Porgie . . .

I think I know when my trouble with Chief of Detectives Pittman began. It was after the *Washington Post* ran that story on me in the Sunday magazine section. The piece detailed how I was a psychologist, but working Homicide and Major Crimes in D.C. I had told the reporter why I continued to live in Southeast. "It makes me feel good to live where I live. Nobody's going to drive me out of my own house."

Actually, I think it was the title chosen for the article that pushed Chief Pittman (and some others in the department) over the edge. The young journalist had interviewed my grandmother while researching the piece. Nana had been an English teacher, and the impressionable writer ate that up. Nana had proceeded to fill his head with her notion that because black people are basically traditionalists, they would logically be the very last people in the South to give up religion, morals, and even formal manners. She said that I was a true Southern man, having been born in North Carolina. She also questioned why it was that we idolize near-psychotic detectives in films, TV, books, and newspaper articles.

The title of the piece, which ran over my brooding photograph, was "The Last Southern Gentleman." The story caused big problems inside our very uptight department. Chief Pittman especially took offense. I couldn't prove it, but I believed the story had been placed by someone in the mayor's office.

I gave a one-two-three rap on the door of the headmaster's office and Sampson and I walked in. Before I could say a word, Pittman held up his right hand. "Cross, you just listen to what

I have to say," he said as he came over to us. "There's been a kidnapping at this school. It's a major kidnapping —"

"That's a real bad thing," I butted in immediately. "Unfortunately, a killer has also struck the Condon Terrace and Langley neighborhoods. The killer's hit two times already. Six people are *dead* so far. Sampson and I are the senior people on that case. Basically, we're *it*."

"I'm apprised of the situation in the Condon and Langley projects. I've already made contingencies. It's taken care of," Pittman said.

"Two black women had their breasts sliced off this morning. Their pubic hair was shaved while they were tied up in bed. Were you apprised of that?" I asked him. "A three-year-old boy was murdered, in his pajamas." I was shouting again. I glanced at Sampson and saw him shaking his head.

A group of teachers in the office looked our way. "Two young black women had their breasts sliced off," I repeated for their benefit. "Someone's wandering around D.C. this morning with breasts in his pocket."

Chief Pittman gestured toward the headmaster's inner office. He wanted the two of us inside the room. I shook my head. I wanted to have witnesses when I was around him.

"I know what you're thinking, Cross." He lowered his voice and spoke very close to my face. The odor of stale cigarettes billowed out at me. "You think I'm out to get you, but I'm not. I know you're a good cop. I know your heart's usually in the right place."

"No, you don't know what I'm thinking. Here's what I'm thinking! Six black people are dead already. A crazed, homicidal killer is out there. He's in heat. He's sharpening his eyeteeth. Now two white kids have been kidnapped, and that's a horrible thing. Horrible! But I'm already on a fucking case!"

Pittman suddenly jabbed his index finger at me. His face was very red. "*I* decide what cases you're on! *I* decide! You're experienced as a hostage negotiator. You're a psychologist. We have other people to send into Langley and Condon. Besides, Mayor Monroe has specifically asked for you."

So that was it. Now I understood everything. Our mayor had intervened. It was all about me.

"What about Sampson? At least leave him on the project murders," I said to the chief of detectives.

"You got any complaints, take them up with the mayor. You're both working on this kidnapping. That's all I have to say to you at this time."

Pittman turned his back on us and walked away. We were on the Dunne-Goldberg kidnapping case, like it or not. We didn't like it.

"Maybe we should just go back to the Sanders house," I said to Sampson.

"Nobody miss us here," he agreed.

CHAPTER 7

A GLEAMING, black BMW K-1 motorcycle squeezed between the low fieldstone gates of the Washington Day School. The driver was I.D.'d, then the bike sped down a long narrow road toward a gray cluster of school buildings. It was eleven o'clock.

The BMW K-1 streaked to sixty in the few seconds it took to get to the administration building. The motorcycle then braked easily and smoothly, barely throwing gravel. The rider slid it in behind a pearl-gray Mercedes stretch limousine with diplomat's plates DP101.

Still seated on the bike, Jezzie Flanagan pulled off a black helmet to reveal longish blond hair. She looked to be in her late twenties. Actually, she'd turned thirty-two that summer. Life was threatening to pass her right by. She was a relic now, ancient history, she believed. She had come straight to the school from her lake cottage, not to mention her first vacation in twenty-nine months.

That latter fact helped to explain her style of dress that morning: the leather bike jacket, the faded black jeans with leg warm-ers, thick leather belt, the red-and-black checkered lumberman's shirt, and the worn engineering boots.

Two D.C. policemen rushed up on either side of her. "It's okay, officers," she said, "here's my I.D." After eyeing the identification, they backed away quickly and became solicitous. "You can go right in," one of them said. "There's a side door just around those high hedges, Ms. Flanagan."

Jezzie Flanagan managed a friendly smile for the two harried-looking policemen. "I don't exactly look the part today, I know. I was on my vacation. I race the bike. I raced it here."

Jezzie Flanagan took the shortcut across a pristine lawn that was lightly coated with frost. She disappeared inside the school's administration building.

Neither of the D.C. policemen took his eyes off her until she was gone. Her blond hair blew like streamers in the stiff winter wind. She was definitely stunning to look at, even in dirty jeans and work boots. And she had a very powerful job. They both knew that from her I.D. She was a player.

As she made her way through the front lobby, someone grabbed at her. Someone caught a piece of Jezzie Flanagan, which was typical of her life in D.C.

Victor Schmidt had hooked onto her arm. Once upon a time, and this was difficult for Jezzie to imagine now, Victor had been her partner. Her first, in fact. Now he was assigned to one of the students at the Day School.

Victor was short and balding. A stylish *GQ* sort of dresser. Confident for no particularly good reason. He'd always struck her as misplaced in the Secret Service, maybe better suited for lower rungs of the diplomatic corps.

"Jezzie, how's it going?" he half whispered, half spoke. He never seemed to go all the way on anything, she remembered. That had always bugged her.

Jezzie Flanagan blew up. Later, she realized she had really been on edge when Schmidt stopped her. Not that she needed an excuse for the flare-up. Not that morning. Not under the circumstances.

"Vic, do you know that two children have been taken from this school, maybe kidnapped?" she snapped. "One is the secretary of the treasury's son? The other is Katherine Rose's little girl? The actress Katherine Rose Dunne. How do you think I'm doing? I'm a little sick to my stomach. I'm angry. I'm also petrified."

"I just meant hello. Hello, Jezzie? I know what the hell has happened here."

But Jezzie Flanagan had already walked away, at least partly to keep from saying anything else to Victor. She did feel nervous. And ill. And mostly, wired as hell. She wasn't so much looking for familiar faces in the crowded school lobby, as the right faces. There were two of them now!

Charlie Chakely and Mike Devine. Her agents. The two men she had assigned to young Michael Goldberg, and also Maggie Rose Dunne, since they traveled back and forth to school together.

"How could this happen?" Her voice was loud. She didn't care that the talk nearby had stopped and people were staring. A black hole was cut into the noise and chaos of the school lobby. Then she lowered her voice to a whisper as she questioned the agents about what had happened so far. She listened quietly as she let them explain. Apparently, she didn't like what they had to say.

"Get the hell out of here," she exploded a second time. "Get out right now. Out of my sight!"

"There was nothing we could have done," Charlie Chakely tried to protest. "What could we have done? Jesus Christ!" Then he and Devine skulked away.

Those who knew Jezzie Flanagan might have understood her emotional reaction. Two children were missing. It had happened on her watch. She was an immediate supervisor of the Secret

Service agents who guarded just about everyone other than the president: key cabinet members and their families, about a half-dozen senators, including Ted Kennedy. She reported to the secretary of the treasury himself.

She had worked unbelievably hard to get all that trust and responsibility, and she *was* responsible. Hundred-hour weeks; no vacation year after year; no life to speak of.

She could hear the upcoming scuttlebutt before it happened. Two of her agents had royally screwed up. There would be an investigation — an old-fashioned witch-hunt. Jezzie Flanagan was on the hot seat. Since she was the first woman ever to hold her job, the fall, if it came, would be steep and painful, and very public.

She finally spotted the one person she'd been looking for in the crowd — and hoping not to find. Secretary of the Treasury Jerrold Goldberg had already arrived at his son's school.

Standing with the secretary were Mayor Carl Monroe, an FBI special agent she knew named Roger Graham, and two black men she didn't recognize right off. Both of the blacks were tall; one of them extremely so, *huge*.

Jezzie Flanagan took a deep breath and walked quickly over to Secretary Goldberg and the others.

"I'm very sorry, Jerrold," she said in a whisper as she arrived. "I'm sure the children will be found."

"A teacher" was all Jerrold Goldberg could manage. He shook his head of close-cropped white curls. His eyes were wet and shiny. "A teacher of children, little babies. How could this happen?"

He was clearly heartbroken. The secretary looked ten years older than his actual age, which was forty-nine. His face was as white as the school's stucco walls.

Before coming to Washington, Jerrold Goldberg had been at Salomon Brothers on Wall Street. He'd made twenty or thirty million in the prosperous, thoroughly crazy 1980s. He was bright, worldwise, and tested on his wisdom. He was as pragmatic as they came.

On this day, though, he was just the father of a kidnapped little boy, and he looked extremely fragile.

CHAPTER 8

I WAS TALKING to Roger Graham from the FBI when the Secret Service supervisor, Jezzie Flanagan, joined our group. She said what she could to comfort Secretary Goldberg. Then the talk quickly turned back to the apparent kidnapping, and the next steps to be taken.

"Are we a hundred percent sure it was this math teacher who took the children?" Graham asked the group. He and I had worked closely together before. Graham was extremely smart, and had been a star in the Bureau for years. He'd co-written a book about busting up organized crime in New Jersey. It had been made into a hit movie. We respected and liked each other, which is rare between the Bureau and local police. When my wife had been killed in Washington, Roger had gone out of his way to involve the Bureau in the investigation. He'd given me more help than my own department.

I decided to try to answer Roger Graham's question. I'd calmed down enough to talk by then, and I told them what Sampson and I had picked up so far.

"They definitely left the school grounds together," I said. "A porter saw them. The math teacher, a Mr. Soneji, went to Ms.

Kim's class. He lied to her. Said there was a telephone threat and that he was supposed to take the kids to the headmaster's office to be driven home. Said the Secret Service hadn't specified whether the threat involved the boy or girl. He just kept on going with them. The kids trusted him enough to go along."

"How could a potential kidnapper possibly get on the teaching staff of this kind of school?" the special agent asked. A pair of sunglasses peeked from the breast pocket of his suit. Winter shades. Harrison Ford had played him in the movie made from his book. It wasn't bad casting, really. Sampson called Graham "Big Screen."

"That, we don't know yet," I told Graham. "We will soon."

Sampson and I were finally introduced to Secretary Goldberg by Mayor Monroe. Monroe did a little bit on how we were one of D.C.'s most decorated detective teams and so on and so forth. Then the mayor ushered the secretary inside the headmaster's office. Special Agent Graham trailed along. He rolled his eyes at Sampson and me. He wanted us to know it wasn't his show.

Jezzie Flanagan stayed behind. "I've heard about you, Detective Cross, now that I think of it. You're the psychologist. There was an article in the *Washington Post*." She smiled nicely, a demi-smile.

I didn't smile back. "You know newspaper articles," I told her. "Usually a pack of half-truths. In that case, definitely some tall tales."

"I'm not so sure about that," she said. "Nice to meet you, anyway." Then she walked into the office behind Secretary Goldberg, the mayor, and the star FBI agent. Nobody invited me — the psychologist-detective of magazine fame. Nobody invited Sampson.

Monroe did poke his head out. "Stick around, you two. Don't make any waves. Don't get pissy, either. We need you here. I need to talk with you, Alex. Stay put. *Don't* get pissy."

Sampson and I tried to be good cops. We stood around outside the headmaster's office for another ten minutes. Finally, we left our posts. We were feeling pissy.

I kept seeing the face of little Mustaf Sanders. Who was going to go and find his killer? No one. Mustaf had already been forgotten. I knew that would never happen with the two private-school children.

A little later that morning, Sampson and I were lying across the natural pine floor of the Day School "playroom" with a few of the children.

We were there with Luisa, Jonathan, Stuart, Mary-Berry, and her "big" sister Brigid. No one had been able to pick these kids up yet, and they were frightened. Some of the children at the school had wet their pants, and there was one case of severe vomiting. There was the possibility of crisis trauma, a condition I had some experience treating.

Also down on the polished wood floor with us was the teacher, Vivian Kim. We'd wanted to talk to her about Soneji's visit to her class, and Soneji, in general.

"We're new kids in your school," Sampson joked with the children. He had actually taken his sunglasses off, though I wasn't sure if he had to. Kids usually take to Sampson. He fits into their "friendly monster" grouping.

"No you're not!" said Mary-Berry. Sampson had gotten her to smile already. A good sign.

"That's right, we're really policemen," I told the kids. "We're here to make sure everybody's okay now. I mean, phew, what — a — morning!"

Ms. Kim smiled at me from across the floor. She knew I was trying to give the kids some reassurance. The police were there and it was safe again. No one could hurt them now; order had been restored.

"Are you a good policeman?" Jonathan asked me. He seemed very serious and earnest for such a small boy.

"Yes, I am. So is my partner here, Detective Sampson."

"You're big. You're awfully big," said Luisa. "Big, big, BIG as my house!"

"So we can protect everybody better," Sampson said to the little girl. Sampson had caught on fast.

"Do you have any kids?" Brigid asked me. She'd carefully observed us both before speaking. She was wonderfully bright-eyed, and I liked her already.

"I have two children," I said. "A boy and a girl."

"And what are their names?" asked Brigid. She had neatly reversed our roles.

"Janelle and Damon," I told her. "Janelle's four and Damon's six."

"What's your wife's name?" asked Stuart.

"I don't have a wife," I told him.

"My, my, my, Mr. Rogers," Sampson said under his breath.

"Are you divorced?" Mary-Berry asked me. "Is that the deal?"

Ms. Kim laughed out loud. "What a question to ask our nice friend, Mary."

"Are they going to hurt Maggie Rose and Michael Goldberg?" Jonathan the Serious wanted to know. It was a good, fair question. It deserved an answer.

"I hope they won't, Jonathan. I will tell you one thing. Nobody will hurt you. Detective Sampson and I are here just to make sure."

"We're tough, in case you couldn't tell." Sampson grinned. "Grrr. Nobody will ever hurt these kids. Grrr."

Luisa started to cry a few minutes later. She was a cute kid. I wanted to hug her, but I couldn't.

"What's the matter, Luisa?" Ms. Kim asked. "Your mom or your dad will be here soon."

"No, they won't." The little girl shook her head. "They won't come. They never pick me up at school."

"Someone will come," I said in a quiet voice. "And tomorrow, everything will be fine again."

The door to the playroom slowly opened. I looked away from the children. It was Mayor Carl Monroe come for a visit to our city's schools for the advantaged.

"You keeping out of trouble, Alex?" Mr. Mayor nodded and smiled as he took in the unusual playroom scene. Monroe was in his mid-forties, and ruggedly handsome. He had a full head of hair and a thick black mustache. He looked businesslike in a navy blue suit, white shirt, and bright yellow tie.

"Oh, yeah. I'm just trying to do something worthwhile with my spare time here. Both Sampson and I are."

That got a mayoral chuckle. "Looks like you've succeeded. Let's take a ride. Come with me, Alex. We've got to talk over a few things."

I said good-bye to the kids and Ms. Kim and walked with Monroe out of the school building. Maybe I'd find out what was really going on now, and why I was on the kidnapping instead of my homicide cases. And if I had any choice in the matter.

"You come in your own car, Alex?" Monroe asked as we jogged down the school's front steps.

"Mine and HFC Finance's," I said.

"We'll take your car. How's the S.I.T. group working out for you? The concept's strong," he said as we continued toward the parking area. He had apparently already sent his own driver and car ahead. A man of the people, our mayor.

"What exactly is the concept for S.I.T.?" I asked him. I'd been pondering my current job situation, especially reporting in to George Pittman.

Carl Monroe smiled broadly. He can be very slick with people, and he's actually very smart. He always appears to be caring and benevolent, and maybe he is. He can even listen when he needs to.

"The main idea is to make sure that the strongest black men and women in the Metro police force rise to the top, as they should. Not just the ass-kissers, Alex. That hasn't always happened in the past."

"I think we'd be all right without too much affirmative action. You heard about the murders in Condon and Langley Terrace?" I asked Monroe.

He nodded, but didn't say anything more about the signature murders. They were not a priority with the mayor today.

"Mother, daughter, three-year-old little boy," I persisted, starting to get angry again. "Nobody gives a shit about them."

"So what's new, Alex? Nobody cared about their lives. Why should anybody care about their deaths?"

We had gotten to my car, a '74 Porsche that has seen much better days. The doors creaked and there was a faint odor of past fast-food lunches. I drove it during the three years I was in private practice. We both got in.

"You know, Alex, Colin Powell is head of the Joint Chiefs now. Louis Sullivan was our secretary of Health and Human Services. Jesse Jackson helped to get me this job," Monroe said as we got onto Canal Road and headed downtown. He stared at his reflection in the side window as he talked.

"And now you're helping me?" I said. "Without even being asked. That's real nice, real thoughtful."

"That's right," he agreed. "You're so damn quick, Alex."

"Then *help* me out here. I want to solve the murders in the projects. I'm sorry as hell about those two white children, but their kidnapping won't go wanting for attention or help. Fact is, that's going to be a problem. Too much goddamned help."

"Of course it is. We both know that." Monroe nodded agreement. "Those dumb bastards will be tripping all over one another. Listen to me, Alex. Will you just listen?"

When Carl Monroe wants something from you, he'll talk you

into submission if he has to. I had seen this before and now he started up with me again.

"As the legend of Alex Cross has it, you're broke now."

"I'm doing fine," I said. "Roof over our heads. Food on the table."

"You stayed in Southeast, when you could easily have gotten out," he continued with this broken record I'd heard before. "You still working over at St. A's?"

"Yeah. Soup brigade. Some free therapy sessions. The Black Samaritan."

"You know, I saw you in a play once at St. A's. You can act, too. You have real presence."

"Athol Fugard's *The Blood Knot*." I remembered the time. Maria had lured me into her theater group. "The play is powerful. It can make anybody look all right."

"You follow what I'm saying? You listening to me at all?"

"You want to marry me." I laughed out loud at Monroe. "You want to go out on a date with me first, though."

"Something like that," Monroe roared back.

"You're doing it just the right way, Carl. I like to be sweet-talked before I get fucked."

Monroe laughed some more, a little harder than he should have. He could be buddies with you, then stare right through you the next time you met. Some people called him "Coconut" around the department. I was one of them. "Brown on the outside, white inside." I had the feeling that he was actually a lonely man. I still wondered exactly what he wanted from me.

Monroe was quiet for a moment. He spoke again as we turned onto the Whitehurst Freeway. Traffic was heavy, and slushy streets didn't help.

"This is a tragic, tragic situation we're facing. This kidnapping is also important for us. Whoever solves it will be important. I want you to help solve it, to be a player. I want you to establish a reputation with this case."

"I don't want a reputation," I said flat out to Monroe. "Don't want to be a fucking player."

"I know you don't. And that's one of the reasons you should be. I'll tell you something that is the truth. You're smarter than us, and you are going to be a big deal in this city. Stop being such a stubborn bastard about it. Let the walls come down now."

"I don't agree. Not if I can help it. Not if I can get in the way of it. Your idea of being a success isn't mine."

"Well, I know what's right here. For both of us," he said. This time Carl Monroe didn't smile one bit. "You keep me up to date on the progress of this case. You and I are in this one together, Alex. This is a career-making case."

I nodded at Monroe. *Sure thing*, I thought. "Whose career, Carl?"

I had stopped in front of the District Building with all its fancy trimmings. Monroe slid out of his seat. He looked down at me from outside the car. "This case is going to be enormously important, Alex. It's yours."

"No, thanks," I said.

But Monroe was already gone.

CHAPTER 9

AT TWENTY-FIVE MINUTES PAST TEN, well within the range he'd set during his dry runs from Washington, Gary Soneji turned his van onto an unmarked drive. The side road was badly potholed and densely overgrown with weeds. A blackberry bramble was on either shoulder.

Less than fifty yards in from the main highway, he couldn't see anything but the dirt road and a mess of overhanging bushes. No one could see his van from the highway.

The van bumped along past a ramshackle, faded white farmhouse. The building looked as if it were shrinking, collapsing right back into its foundation. No more than forty yards past the house was what remained of an equally run-down storage barn.

Soneji drove the van inside. He'd done it; he'd pulled it off.

A black 1985 Saab was parked in the barn. Unlike the rest of the deserted farm, the barn had a lived-in feel.

It had a dirt floor. Cheesecloth was taped over three broken windows in the hayloft. There were no rusting tractors or other farm machinery. The barn had the smell of damp earth and gasoline.

Gary Soneji pulled two Cokes from a cooler on the passenger seat. He polished off both sodas, letting out a satisfied belch after downing the second cold one.

"Either of you guys want a Coke?" he called out to the drugged, comatose children. "No? Okay then, but you're going to be real thirsty soon."

There were no sure things in life, he was thinking, but he couldn't imagine how any policeman could get him now. Was it foolish and dangerous to be this confident? he wondered. Not really, because he was also being realistic. *There was no way to trace him now.* There wasn't a single clue for them to follow.

He had been planning to kidnap somebody famous since — well, since forever. Who that someone was had changed, and changed again, but never the clear, main objective in his mind. He'd been working at Washington Day School for months. This moment, right now, proved it had been worth every sucky minute.

"Mr. Chips." He thought of his nickname at the school. Mr. Chips! What a lovely, lovely bit of play-acting he'd done. Real Academy Award stuff. As good as anything he'd seen since Robert De Niro in *The King of Comedy*. And that performance was a classic. De Niro himself had to be a psychopath in real life.

Gary Soneji finally pulled open the van's sliding door. Back to work, work, work his fingers to the bone.

One body at a time, he hauled the children out into the barn. First came Maggie Rose Dunne. Then little boy Goldberg. He laid the unconscious boy and girl beside each other on the dirt floor. He undressed each child, leaving them in their underwear. He carefully prepared doses of secobarbital sodium. Just your friendly local pharmacist hard at work. The dose was somewhere between a sleeping pill and a hospital anesthetic. It would last for about twelve hours.

He took out preloaded one-shot needles called Tubex. This

was a closed injection system that came prepackaged, complete with dose and needle. He set out two tourniquets. He had to be very careful. The exact dosage could be tricky with small children.

Next, he pulled the black Saab forward about two yards. This move exposed a five-by-four-foot plot in the floor of the barn.

He'd dug the hole during several previous visits to the deserted farm. Inside the open cavity was a homemade wooden compartment, a kind of shelter. It had its own oxygen tank supply. Everything but a color TV for watching reruns.

He placed the Goldberg boy inside the wooden compartment first. Michael Goldberg weighed next to nothing in his arms, which was exactly what he felt about him. Nothing. Then came the little princess, the little pride and joy, Maggie Rose Dunne. All the way from La-la-land originally.

He slid the Tubex needles into each child's arm. He was extra careful to give each dose slowly, over a three-minute period.

The doses were measured by weight, .25 milligrams per kilogram of body weight. He checked the breathing of each child. Sleep tight, my multimillion-dollar babies.

Gary Soneji shut the trapdoor with a bang. Then he buried the wooden compartment under half a foot of fresh soil. Inside the deserted storage barn. In the middle of godforsaken Maryland farm country. Just like little Charlie Lindbergh, Jr., had been buried sixty years before.

No one would find them out here. Not until he wanted them found. *If* he wanted them found. Big *if*.

Gary Soneji trudged back up the dirt road to what remained of the ancient farmhouse. He wanted to wash up. He also wanted to start to enjoy this a little. He'd even brought a Watchman to see himself on TV.

CHAPTER 10

NEWS BULLETINS were flashing on the television screen every fifteen minutes or so. Gary Soneji was right there on the high and mighty tube. He saw photographs of "Mr. Chips" on every news bulletin. The news reports didn't offer a clue about what was really going on, though.

So this was fame! This was how fame felt. He liked it a lot. This was what he'd been practicing for all these years. "*Hi, Mom! Look who's on TV. It's the Bad Boy!*"

There was only one glitch all afternoon, and that was the press conference given by the FBI. An agent named Roger Graham had spoken, and Agent Graham obviously thought he was hot shit. He wanted some fame for himself. "You think this is your movie, Graham? Wrong, baby!" Gary Soneji shouted at the TV. "I'm the only star here!"

Soneji had been prowling around inside the farmhouse for several hours, watching the night slowly fall outside. He felt the different textures of darkness as they blanketed the farm. It was now seven o'clock and time to get on with his plan.

"Let's do it." He pranced around the farmhouse like a prize-fighter before a bout. "Let's get it on."

For a while, he thought about Charles and Anne Morrow Lindbergh, his all-time favorite couple. That calmed him some. He thought about Baby Charles; and about that poor fool, Bruno Hauptmann, who had obviously been framed for the brilliantly conceived and executed crime. He was convinced that the Lindbergh affair was the century's most elegant crime, not just because it remained unsolved — many, many crimes went unsolved — but *because it was important and unsolved*.

Soneji was confident, realistic, and, most of all, pragmatic about his own masterpiece. A "fluke" was always possible. A "lucky accident" by the police could occur. The actual exchange of money would be tricky. It meant contact, and contact was always highly dangerous in life.

To his knowledge, and his knowledge was encyclopedic, no modern kidnapper had satisfactorily solved the ransom-exchange problem. Not if they wanted to be paid for their labors, and he needed a huge payday for his multimillion-dollar kids.

Wait until they hear how much money.

The thought brought a smile to his lips. Of course, the world-beater Dunnes and the all-powerful Goldbergs could, and would, pay. It was no accident he had chosen those two families — with their pampered little snotnosed brats, and their unlimited supply of wealth and power.

Soneji lit one of the white candles he kept in a side pocket of his jacket. He sniffed a pleasant whiff of beeswax. Then he made his way to the small bathroom off the kitchen.

He was remembering an old Chambers Brothers song, "Time." It was time . . . time . . . time to pull the rug out from under everybody's feet. Time . . . time . . . time for his first little surprise, the first of many. Time . . . time . . . time to start to build his own legend. This was his movie.

The room, the whole house, was freezing cold in late December. Gary Soneji could see his breath wisping out as he set up shop in the bathroom.

Fortunately, the abandoned house had well water, which was still running in the bathroom. Very cold water indeed. Gary Soneji lit some candles, and began to work. It would take him a full half-hour before he was through.

First, he removed the dark brown, balding half-wig. He'd purchased it three years before, at a theatrical costume store in New York City. That same night, he'd gone to see *Phantom of the Opera*. He'd loved the Broadway musical. He identified with the Phantom so much that it frightened him. It sent him off to read the original novel, first in French, then in English.

"Well, well, what do we have here?" he spoke to the face in the mirror.

With the glue and other schmutz off, a full head of blond hair was revealed. Long and wavy blond curls.

"Mr. Soneji? Mr. Chips? Is that you, fella?"

Not a bad-looking sort, actually. Good prospects? On a roll, maybe? Clearly on a roll, yes.

And nothing at all like Chips. Nothing like our Mr. Soneji!

Away came the thick mustache that Gary Soneji had worn since the day he'd arrived to interview at the Washington Day School. Then the contact lenses were removed. His eyes changed from green back to chestnut brown.

Gary Soneji held the dwindling candle up to the dingy, cracked bathroom mirror. He rubbed one corner of the glass clean with the sleeve of his jacket.

"There. Just look at you. Look at you now. Genius is in the details, right?"

That insipid nerd from the private school was almost completely eradicated. The wimp and the do-gooder. Mr. Chips was dead and gone forever.

What a wondrous farce it had been. What a daring plan of action, and how well executed. A shame no one would ever know what had really happened. But whom could he tell?

Gary Soneji left the farmhouse around 11:30 P.M., right on

his schedule. He walked to a detached garage that was north of the house.

In a special place in the garage, very special, he hid five thousand dollars from his savings, his secret cache, money he'd stolen over the years. That was part of the plan, too. Long-range thinking.

Then he headed down to the barn, and his car. Once he was inside the barn, he checked on the kids again. So far, so great.

No complaints from the kiddies.

The Saab started right up. He drove out to the main road, using only the dimmers.

When he finally reached the highway, he flicked on the headlights. He still had work to do tonight. Masterpiece Theatre continued.

Cool beans.

CHAPTER 11

FBI SPECIAL AGENT ROGER GRAHAM lived in Manassas Park, midway between Washington and the FBI Academy in Quantico. Graham was tall and physically impressive, with short, sandy brown hair. He'd worked on several major kidnappings, but nothing quite as disturbing as this current nightmare.

At a little past one that morning, Graham finally got home. Home was a sprawling Colonial, on an average street in Manassas Park. Six bedrooms, three baths, a big yard that covered nearly two acres.

Unfortunately, this had not been a normal day. Graham was drained and beaten up and bone-tired. He often wondered why he didn't just settle down and write another book. Take early retirement from the Bureau. Get to know his three children before they fled from the house.

The street in Manassas Park was deserted. Porch lights glowed down the line of the road, and they were a comforting, friendly sight. Lights appeared in the rearview mirror of Graham's Ford Bronco.

A second car had stopped on the street in front of his house, its headlamps gleaming. A man got out, and waved a notepad that was clutched in his hand.

"Agent Graham? Martin Bayer, New York Times," the man called out as he walked up the driveway. He flashed a press credential.

Jesus Christ. Son-of-a-bitching New York Times, Graham thought to himself. The reporter wore a dark suit, pin-striped shirt, rep tie. He was your basic up-and-coming New York yuppie on assignment. All these assholes from the Times and the Post looked the same to Graham. Not a real reporter among them anymore.

"You've come a long way at this hour for a 'no comment,' Mr. Bayer. I'm sorry," Roger Graham said. "I can't give you anything on the kidnapping. Frankly, there isn't anything to give."

He wasn't sorry, but who needed enemies at the New York Times. Those bastards could stick their poison pens in one of your ears and out the other.

"One question, and one question only. I understand that you don't have to answer, but it's that important to me — for me. For me to be here at one in the morning."

"Okay. Let's have it. What's your question?" Graham shut the door of his Bronco. He locked up for the night, flipped the car keys, and caught them.

"Are all of you this incredibly insipid and stupid?" Gary Soneji asked him. "That's my question, Grahamcracker."

A long, sharp knife flashed forward once. Then flashed again. The blade sliced back and forth across Roger Graham's throat.

The first slashing motion pinned him back against his Ford Bronco. The second slashed his carotid artery. Graham dropped dead in his driveway. There had been no time to duck, run, or even say a prayer.

"You're supposed to be a freaking star, Roger. You wanted to be the star, right? I see no evidence of that. None, zero," Soneji said. "You're supposed to be way better than this. I need to be challenged by the best and the brightest."

Soneji bent low and slid a single index card into the breast pocket of Agent Graham's white shirt. He patted the dead man's chest. "Now, would a *New York Times* reporter really be here at one in the morning, you arrogant fuck? Just to talk to your sorry ass?"

Then Soneji drove away from the murder scene. The death of Agent Graham wasn't a big deal to him. Not really. He'd killed over two hundred people before this one. Practice makes perfect. It wouldn't be the last time, either.

This one would wake everybody up, though. He just hoped they had somebody better waiting in the wings.

Otherwise, where was the fun? The challenge? How could this get bigger than the Lindbergh kidnapping?

CHAPTER 12

I WAS ALREADY BECOMING emotionally involved with the kidnapped children. My sleep was restless and agitated that first night. In my dreams, I replayed several bad scenes at the school. I saw Mustaf Sanders again and again. His sad eyes stared out at me, asking for help, getting none from me.

I woke to find both my kids in bed with me. At some time during the early morning, they must have snuck aboard. It's one of their favorite tricks, their little jokes on "Big Daddy."

Damon and Janelle were fast asleep on top of a patchwork quilt. I'd been too wasted to pull it off the bed the night before. We must have looked like two resting angels — and a fallen plowhorse.

Damon is a beautiful little boy of six who always reminds me of how special his mother was. He has Maria's eyes. Jannie is the other apple of my eye. She's four, going on fifteen. She likes to call me "Big Daddy," which sounds like some black slang she's managed to invent. Maybe she knew the football star "Big Daddy" Lipscomb in some other life.

Also on the bed was a copy of William Styron's book on his depression, *Darkness Visible*, which I'd been reading. I was hoping it might give me some clue to help me get over my own depression — which had plagued me ever since Maria's murder. Three years now, felt like twenty.

What actually woke me that morning were headlights fanning across the window blinds. I heard a car door bang and the fast crunch of feet on gravel in the driveway. Careful not to wake the kids. I slipped over to the bedroom window.

I peered down on two Metro D.C. patrol cars parked behind the old Porsche in our drive. It looked miserably cold outside. We were just entering the deepest hollow of D.C.'s winter.

"Give me a break," I mumbled into the chilly window blinds. "Go away."

Sampson was heading for the back door to our kitchen. It was twenty to five on the clock next to the bed. Time to go to work.

Just before five that morning, Sampson and I pulled up in front of a crumbling prewar brownstone in Georgetown, a block west of M Street. We had decided to check out Soneji's apartment ourselves. The only way to get stuff done right is to do it yourself.

"Lights are all on. Looks like somebody's home," Sampson said as we climbed out of the car. "Now who could it be?"

"Three guesses. The first two don't count," I mumbled. I was suffering from early-morning queasiness. A visit to the monster's den wasn't going to help.

"The FBI. Maybe Efrem Zimbalist, Jr., is up there," Sampson guessed. "Maybe they're filming *Real Stories from the FBI*."

"Let's go see."

We entered the building and took the narrow winding stairway up. On the second floor, yellow crime-scene tape had been placed in a crisscross pattern across the doorway to Soneji's apartment. It didn't look like the place where a "Mr. Chips" would live. More like a Richard Ramirez or a Green River killer.

The scarred wooden door was open. I could see two FBI techies working inside. A local deejay called The Greaseman was screeching from a radio on the floor.

"Hey, Pete, what's doin'?" I called inside. I knew one of the FBI techies on the job, Pete Schweitzer. He looked up at the sound of my voice.

"Well, look who's here. Welcome to the Inner Sanctum."

"We came over to bother you. See how it's done," Sampson said. We'd both worked with Pete Schweitzer before, liked and trusted him as much as you could any FBI personnel.

"Come in and make yourselves at home at Casa Soneji. This is my fellow flyshit finder and bagger, Todd Toohey. Todd likes to listen to The Greaseman in the A.M. These two are ghouls like us, Toddie."

"The best," I told Todd Toohey. I had already started to nose around the apartment. Everything was feeling unreal again. There was this cold, damp spot inside my head. Eerie-time.

The small studio apartment was a mess. There wasn't much furniture — a bare mattress on the floor, an end table and lamp, a sofa that looked as if it had been picked up off the street — but the floor was covered with things.

Wrinkled sheets and towels and underwear were a large part of the general chaos. Two or three loads of laundry were spilled out on the floor. Most of the clutter was books and magazines, though. Several hundred books, and at least that many magazines, were piled in the single small room.

"Anything interesting so far?" I asked Schweitzer. "You look through his library?"

Schweitzer talked to me without looking up from a pile of books he was dusting. "Everything is interesting. Check out the books along the wall. Also, consider the fact that our fine-feathered friend *wiped down this whole fucking apartment* before he split."

"He do a good job? Up to your standards?"

"Excellent job. I couldn't have done much better myself. We haven't found a partial print anywhere. Not even on any of those goddamn books."

"Maybe he reads with plastic gloves on," I offered.

"I think he might. I shit you not. Place was dusted by a pro, Alex."

I was crouched near several stacks of the books now. I read the titles on several of the spines. Most of it was nonfiction from the last five years or so.

"True-crime fan," I said.

"Lots and lots of kidnapping stories," Schweitzer said. He looked up and pointed. "Right side of the bed, near the reading lamp. That's the kidnapping section."

I walked over and looked at the volumes. Most of the books had been stolen from the library at Georgetown. I figured he must have had an I.D. to get into the stacks there. Was he a past student? Maybe a professor?

Several computer printouts were taped to the bare wall over his private library on kidnapping. I started to read down the lists.

Aldo Moro. Kidnapped in Rome. Five bodyguards killed during abduction. Moro's body found in a parked car.

Jack Teich, released after payment of $750,000.

J. Reginald Murphy, editor of the Atlanta Constitution, *released after payment of $700,000.*

J. Paul Getty 3rd, released in southern Italy after $2.8 million ransom paid.

Mrs. Virginia Piper of Minneapolis, released after her husband paid $1,000,000.

Victor E. Samuelson, released in Argentina after payment of $14.2 million ransom.

I whistled as I spotted the amounts on his list. What was he going to ask for Maggie Rose Dunne and Michael Goldberg?

It was a really small place, and there hadn't been much room for Soneji to wipe off fingerprints. Still, Schweitzer said he hadn't left anything. I wondered if Soneji could have been a cop. That was one way to plan a crime, and maybe improve your chances of getting away with it.

"Come in here for a minute." Sampson was in the bathroom that was off to one side of the tiny studio.

The walls were papered with photos from magazines, newspapers, record albums, book jackets.

He'd left a final surprise for us. There were no fingerprints, but he had scrawled a message.

Just over the mirror was a type-set headline: *I WANT TO BE SOMEBODY!*

Up on the walls was an exhibition. I saw River Phoenix. And Matt Dillon. There were photos from Helmut Newton books. I recognized Lennon's murderer, Mark David Chapman. And Axl Rose. Pete Rose was up on the wall, too. And Neon Deon Sanders. Wayne Williams was there. And newspaper stories. The Happy Land Social Club fire in New York City. A *New York Times* story of the Lindbergh kidnapping. A story about the kidnapping of Samuel Bronfman, the Seagram's heir, and a story about the missing child Etan Patz.

I thought about Soneji the kidnapper, all alone in his desolate apartment. *He had carefully wiped every inch of space for fingerprints. The room itself was so small, so monkish. He was a reader, or at least liked to have books around. Then there was his photo gallery. What did it tell us? Leads? Misdirections?*

I stood in front of the mirror that was over the sink and stared into it as I knew he had many, many times. What was I supposed to see? What had Gary Soneji seen?

"This was *his* picture on the wall — the face in this mirror," I offered a theory to Sampson. "It's the key picture here, the central one. He wants to be the star of all this."

Sampson was leaning against a wall of photos and news clippings. "Why no fingerprints, Dr. Freud?"

"He must know we have his fingerprints on file somewhere. Makes me think he may have been wearing some kind of disguise at the school. Maybe he put on makeup right here before he went off to school. He could be a stage actor. I don't think we've seen his face yet."

"I think the boy has big plans. He definitely wants to be a star," Sampson said.

I want to be somebody!

CHAPTER 13

MAGGIE ROSE DUNNE had awoken from the strangest sleep of her life. Horrible and indescribable bad dreams.

She felt as if everything around her were moving in slow motion. She was thirsty. She needed to pee awfully bad.

I'm too tired this morning, Mom. Please! I don't want to get up. Don't want to go to school today. Please, Mom. I don't feel so good. Honest, I really don't, Mommy.

Maggie Rose opened her eyes. At least she thought she had opened her eyes, but she couldn't see anything. Nothing at all.

"Mommy! Mommy! Mommy!" Maggie finally screamed, and couldn't stop screaming.

For an hour after that, at least that long, she floated in and out of consciousness. She felt weak all over. She floated like a leaf on the hugest river. The currents just took her wherever they wanted.

She thought about her mom. Did she know Maggie was gone? Was she looking for her now? She had to be looking for her.

Maybe someone took her arms and legs off. She couldn't feel them. It must have been long ago.

It was black. She must be buried in the ground. She must be rotting and becoming a skeleton. Was that why she couldn't feel her arms and legs?

Am I going to be like this forever? She couldn't stand that, and she was crying again. She was so confused. She couldn't think at all.

Maggie Rose *could* open and close her eyes, though. At least she *thought* she could. But there was just no difference with her eyes open or closed. Everything was darkness. Either way.

If she did it over and over, opened and closed her eyes real fast, she saw color.

Now, inside the blackness, she saw streaks and tears of color. Mostly red and bright yellow.

Maggie wondered if she might be strapped or tied down. Was that what they really did to you inside a casket? Did they strap you down? Why would they do that? To stop you from getting out of the ground? To keep your spirit under the earth forever and ever?

Suddenly, she remembered something. Mr. Soneji. A little of the fog that swirled around her cleared away for a second.

Mr. Soneji had taken her out of school. When had it happened? Why? Where was Mr. Soneji now?

And Michael! What had happened to Michael? They had left school together. She remembered that much.

She moved then, and the most amazing thing happened. She discovered that *she could roll herself over*.

That's what Maggie Rose did. She rolled over, and was suddenly up against something.

She could feel her whole body again. She still had a body to feel. She was absolutely certain she had her body and that she wasn't a skeleton.

And Maggie screamed!

She had rolled into *someone* or *something*.

Someone else was there in the dark with her.

Michael?

It had to be Michael.

"*Michael?*" Maggie's voice was so low it was barely a whisper. "Michael? Is that you?"

She waited for an answer.

"Michael?" she whispered louder.

"Michael, c'mon. Please talk to me."

Whoever it was wouldn't answer. It was more terrifying than being alone.

"Michael . . . It's me. . . . Don't be afraid. . . . It's Maggie. . . . Michael, please wake up.

"Oh, Michael, please . . . Please, Shrimpie. I was just kidding about your dopey school shoes. C'mon, Michael. Talk to me, Shrimpie. It's Dweebo Dido."

CHAPTER 14

THE DUNNE HOUSE was what local real-estate mavens might call Lutyens-style neo-Elizabethan. Neither Sampson nor I had seen too many of those in Southeast D.C.

Inside, the house had the serenity and diversity I guess might be common among the rich. There were a lot of expensive "things." Art Deco plaques, and oriental screens, a French sun-dial, a Turkestan rug, what looked like a Chinese or Japanese altar table. I remembered something Picasso had once said: "Give me a museum, and I'll fill it."

There was a small bathroom off one of the formal sitting rooms. Chief of Detectives George Pittman grabbed me and pulled me in there minutes after I arrived. It was around eight o'clock. Too early for this.

"What do you think you're doing?" he asked me. "What are you up to, Cross?"

The room was really cramped, no place for two good-sized, grown-up men to be. It wasn't your average toilet, either. The floor was covered with a William Morris rug. A designer chair sat in one corner.

"I thought I would get some coffee. Then I was going to sit in on the morning briefing," I said to Pittman. I wanted to get out of that bathroom so bad.

"Don't fuck around with me." He started to raise his voice. "Do *not* fuck with me."

Oh, don't do that, I wanted to say to him. *Don't make a big, awful scene in here.* I thought about putting his head underwater in the toilet bowl, just to keep him quiet.

"Lower your voice, or I'm leaving," I said. I try to act in a reasonable and considerate manner most of the time. It's one of my character flaws.

"Don't tell me to lower my voice. Who the fuck told you to go home last night? You and Sampson. Who told you to go to the Soneji apartment this morning?"

"Is that what this is all about? Is that why we're in here together now?" I asked.

"You bet it is. I'm running this investigation. That means if you want to tie your shoe, you talk to me first."

I grinned. I couldn't help it. "Where'd you get that line? Did Lou Gossett say that in *An Officer and a Gentleman*?"

"You think this is a lot of fun and games, Cross?"

"No, I don't. I don't think it's any fun. Now *you* keep the fuck out of my face, or you won't have one," I warned him.

I walked out of the bathroom. Chief of Detectives Pittman didn't follow me. *Yes,* I can be provoked. *No,* that little turd shouldn't fuck with me.

At a little past eight, the Hostage Rescue Team was finally gathered together in a large, exquisitely decorated sitting room. Right away I sensed something was wrong. Something was up for sure.

Jezzie Flanagan from the Secret Service had taken the floor. I remembered her from the morning before at the Day School. She stood in front of a working fireplace.

The mantel was strung with holly boughs, tiny white lights, and Christmas cards. Several nontraditional cards were obviously from friends of the Dunnes in California — photographs of decorated palm trees, of Santa's sleigh in the sky over Malibu. The Dunnes had recently moved to Washington, after Thomas Dunne took a job as director of the Red Cross.

Jezzie Flanagan looked more formal than she had at the school. She wore a loose gray skirt, with a black turtleneck sweater, and small gold earrings. She looked like a Washington lawyer, an attractive and very successful one.

"Soneji contacted us at midnight, last night. Then again around one o'clock. We didn't expect him to contact us so soon. None of us did," she started things off.

"The initial phone call was made from the Arlington area. Soneji made it clear he had nothing to say about the children, except that both Maggie Dunne and Michael Goldberg are doing well. What else would he say? He wouldn't allow us to speak to either of the children, so we don't know that for sure. He sounded lucid and very much in control."

"Has the voice tape been analyzed yet?" Pittman asked from his seat near the front. If Sampson and I had to be on the outside looking in, it was good to know Pittman was right there with us. Apparently, nobody was talking to him, either.

"It's being done," Flanagan answered the question politely. She gave it just about the attention it deserved, I thought, but she avoided any condescension. She was real good at keeping control.

"How long was he actually on the line?" the Justice lawyer, Richard Galletta, asked next.

"Not very long, unfortunately. Thirty-four seconds to be exact," Flanagan answered him with the same efficient courtesy. Cool, but pleasant enough. Smart.

I studied her. She was obviously comfortable being up in

front of people. I'd heard that she'd gotten credit for some strong moves at Service in the past few years — which meant that she took a lot of credit.

"He was long gone when we got to the pay phone in Arlington. We couldn't get that lucky so soon," she said. She offered the hint of a smile, and I noticed that several of the men in the room smiled back at her.

"Why do you think he made the call?" the U.S. marshal asked from the back of the room. He was balding and paunchy, and smoking a pipe.

Flanagan sighed. "Please, let me go on. Unfortunately, there's more to it than the phone call. Soneji murdered FBI agent Roger Graham last night. It happened right outside Graham's house in Virginia, in the driveway."

It's difficult to shake up an experienced group like the one gathered at the Dunnes'. The news of Roger Graham's murder did it. I know that it buckled my knees. Roger and I had shared some tight spaces together over the past few years. Whenever I worked with him, I'd always known my back would be covered. Not that I needed another reason to want to get Gary Soneji, but he'd given me a good one.

I wondered if Soneji had known that. And what it meant if he did. As a psychologist, the murder filled me with a sense of dread. It told me that Soneji was organized, confident enough to play with us, and willing to kill. It did not bode well for Maggie Rose Dunne and Michael Goldberg.

"He left a very explicit message for us," Flanagan went on. "The message was typed on an index card, or what looked like a little library card. The message was for all of us. It said, '*Roger Grahamcracker thought he was a big deal. Well, he obviously wasn't. If you work on this case, you're in grave danger!*' . . . The message was signed. He calls himself the Son of Lindbergh."

CHAPTER 15

THE PRESS COVERAGE of the kidnapping case got down and very dirty right away. A front-page headline in one of the morning papers said: SECRET SERVICE BODYGUARDS OUT FOR COFFEE. The press hadn't gotten the news about FBI agent Roger Graham yet. We were trying to sit on it.

The news gossip that morning was about how Secret Service agents Charles Chakely and Michael Devine had left their posts at the private school. Actually, they had gone out for breakfast during classes. It was pretty standard for this kind of duty. The coffee break, however, would be expensive. It would probably cost Chakely and Devine their jobs, possibly their careers.

On another front, Pittman wasn't making much use of Sampson and me so far. This went on for two days. Left on our own, Sampson and I concentrated on the thin trail left by Gary Soneji. I followed up at area stores where someone might buy makeup and special effects. Sampson went to the Georgetown library, but no one there had seen Soneji. They weren't even aware of the book thefts from their stacks.

Soneji *had* successfully disappeared. More disturbing, he

seemed to *have never existed* before taking the job at Washington Day School.

Not surprisingly, he had falsified his employment records and faked several recommendations. He'd completed each step as expertly as any of us had seen in fraud or bunco cases. He'd left no trail.

Soneji had been brazen and supremely confident about getting his job at the school. A supposed previous employer (fictitious) had contacted Washington Day School and highly recommended Soneji, who was moving into the Washington area. More recommendations came via faxes from the University of Pennsylvania, both the undergraduate and graduate school programs. After two impressive interviews, the school wanted the personable and eager teacher so badly (and had been led to believe they were in competition with other D.C. private schools), they had simply hired him.

"And we never regretted hiring him — until now, of course," the assistant headmaster admitted to me. "He was even better than advertised. If he wasn't really a math teacher before he came here, I'd be totally amazed. That would make him a superb actor indeed."

Late afternoon on the third day, I got an assignment from Don Manning, one of Pittman's lieutenants. I was asked to size up and do an evaluation of Katherine Rose Dunne and her husband. I had tried to get some time with the Dunnes on my own, but had been denied.

I met with Katherine and Thomas Dunne in the backyard of their house. A ten-foot-high graystone wall effectively kept out the outside world. So did a row of huge linden trees. Actually, the backyard consisted of several gardens separated by stone walls and a wandering stream. The gardens had their own plantsmen, a young couple from Potomac who apparently made a very nice living tending gardens around town. The plantsmen definitely made more money than I did.

Katherine Rose had thrown an old camel's hair steamer over jeans and a V-necked sweater. She could probably get away with wearing anything she wanted, I thought as we all walked outside.

I'd read somewhere, recently, that Katherine Rose was still considered among the most beautiful women in the world. She had made only a handful of movies since she'd had Maggie Rose, but she'd lost none of her beauty, not so far as I could see. Not even in her time of terrible anxiety.

Her husband, Thomas Dunne, had been a prominent entertainment lawyer in Los Angeles when they met. He'd been involved with Greenpeace and Save the Earth out there. The family had moved to Washington after he became director of the American Red Cross.

"Have you been involved with other kidnappings, Detective?" Thomas Dunne wanted to know. He was trying to figure out where I fit in. Was I important? Could I help their little girl in any way? He was a little rude, but I guess I couldn't blame him under the circumstances.

"About a dozen," I told him. "Can you tell me a little about Maggie? It could help. The more we know, the better will be our chances of finding Maggie."

Katherine Rose nodded. "Of course we will, Detective Cross. We've tried to bring Maggie up to be as normal as possible," she said. "That's one of the reasons we finally decided to move East."

"I don't know if I'd call Washington a normal place to grow up. This isn't exactly Mayberry R.F.D." I smiled at the two of them. For some reason, that statement started to break the ice between us.

"Compared to Beverly Hills it's pretty normal," Tom Dunne said. "Believe me, it is."

"I'm not even sure what 'normal' means anymore," Katherine said. Her eyes gave the appearance of being grayish blue. They penetrated when you got up close to her. "I guess 'normal' corresponds to some old-fashioned image in the rear of our minds, Tom's and mine. Maggie isn't spoiled. She's not one for 'Suze got this' or 'Casey's parents bought her that.' She doesn't have a big head about herself. That kind of 'normal.' She's just a little girl, Detective."

As Katherine Rose lovingly talked about her daughter, I found myself thinking of my own children, but especially Janelle. Jannie was "normal," too. By that, I mean that she was in balance, definitely not spoiled, lovable in every way. Finding parallels between our daughters, I listened even more carefully as they spoke of Maggie Rose.

"She's a lot like Katherine." Thomas Dunne offered a point he felt was important for me to hear. "Katherine is the most egoless person I've ever met. Believe me, to live through the adulation a star can get in Hollywood, and the nasty abuse, and to be the person she is, is very hard."

"How did she come to be called Maggie Rose?" I asked Katherine Rose.

"That's all my doing." Thomas Dunne's eyes rolled back. He liked to talk for his wife, I could see. "It was a nickname that just caught on. It started the first time I saw the two of them in the hospital."

"Tom calls us 'The Rose Girls,' 'The Rose Sisters.' We work out here in 'The Rose Garden.' When Maggie and I argue, it's 'The War of the Roses.' It goes like that."

They loved their little girl very much. I sensed it in every word they said about Maggie.

Soneji, whatever his real name was, had chosen wisely in their case. It was another perfect move on his part. He'd done his homework. Big-name movie star and a respected lawyer. Very loving parents. Money. Prestige. Maybe he liked her movies. I tried to remember if Katherine Rose had played any part that might have set him off. I didn't remember seeing her picture up in his apartment.

"You said you want to know how Maggie might react under these terrible circumstances," Katherine continued. "Why is that, Detective Cross?"

"We know from talking to her teachers that she's well behaved. That may have been a reason for Soneji choosing her." I was candid with them. "What else can you think of? Free-associate all that you can."

"Maggie's mind seems to shift between being serious — very strict and rule abiding — to having a lot of fantasies," Katherine said. "Do you have children?" she asked me.

I flinched. I'd been thinking of Jannie and Damon again. Parallels. "Two children. I also do some work with kids in the projects," I said. "Does Maggie have many friends at school?"

"Tons of them," her father said. "She likes kids who have a lot of ideas, but aren't too self-centered. All except Michael, who's intensely self-absorbed."

"Tell me about the two of them, Maggie and Michael."

Katherine Rose smiled for the first time since we'd been talking. It was so strange, this smile that I had seen many times in movies. Now I was seeing it in person. I was mesmerized. I felt a little shy, and embarrassed that I was having that kind of reaction.

"They've been best friends ever since we moved here. They're the oddest couple, but inseparable," she said. "We call them Felix and Oscar sometimes."

"How do you think Michael would react under these circumstances?" I asked.

"Difficult to judge." Thomas Dunne shook his head. He seemed to be a very impatient man. Probably used to getting what he wanted, when he wanted it. "Michael always has to have a 'plan.' His life's very orderly, very structured."

"What about his physical problems?" Michael had been a "blue baby," I knew. He still had a slight problem with a heart murmur.

Katherine Rose shrugged her shoulders. Apparently it wasn't much of an issue. "He tires sometimes. He's a little small for his age. Maggie's bigger than Michael."

"They all call him Shrimpie, which I think he likes. It makes him a little more of the gang," said Tom Dunne. "Basically, he's a whiz-kid type. Maggie calls him a brainiac. That's fairly descriptive of Michael."

"Michael is definitely a brainiac."

"How is he when he gets tired?" I went back to something Katherine had said, maybe something important. "Is he ever short-tempered?"

Katherine thought about my question before answering. "He just gets pooped. Occasionally, he'll take a nap. One time — I remember the two of them asleep near the pool. This little odd couple sprawled out on the grass. Just two little kids."

She stared at me with those gray eyes of hers and she started to cry. She had been trying hard to control herself, but finally had to let go.

However reluctant I may have been at first, I was becoming a flesh-and-blood part of the terrible case. I felt for the Dunnes and the Goldbergs. I'd made connections between Maggie Rose and my own kids. I was involved in a way that isn't always useful. The anger I had felt about the killer in the projects was being transferred to the kidnapper of these two innocent kids . . . Mr. Soneji . . . Mr. Chips.

I wanted to reach out, to tell both of them everything would be okay, to convince myself everything would be okay. I wasn't sure it would be.

CHAPTER 16

MAGGIE ROSE still *believed* she was in her own grave. It was beyond being creepy and horrible. It was a million times worse than any nightmare she'd ever imagined. And Maggie knew her imagination was a good one. She could gross out or amaze her friends, pretty much at will.

Was it nighttime now? Or was it daytime?

"Michael?" she moaned weakly. Her whole mouth, her tongue especially, felt like a lot of cotton swabs. Her mouth was unbelievably dried out. She was so thirsty. Sometimes she would gag on her tongue. She kept imagining that she was swallowing her tongue. Nobody had ever been this thirsty before. Not even in the deserts of Iraq and Kuwait.

Maggie Rose kept drifting in and out of sleep. Dreams came to her constantly. Another one had just started.

Someone was pounding on a heavy wooden door nearby.

Whoever it was called out her name. "Maggie Rose . . . Maggie Rose, *talk* to me!"

Then Maggie wasn't sure that it was a dream at all.

Someone was really there.

Was someone breaking into her grave? Was it her mom and dad? Or the police, finally?

Suddenly light from above blinded her! Maggie Rose was sure it was really light.

It was as if she were looking straight into a hundred flashbulbs, all of them going off at once.

Her heart beat so fast and so hard that Maggie Rose knew she must be alive. In some terrible, terrible place. Someone had put her there.

Maggie Rose whispered up into the light, "Who is it? Who's there? Who's up there right now? *I see a face!*"

The light was so very bright that Maggie Rose couldn't really see anything.

For the second — or third — time, it had gone from pitchblack to blinding, blinding white.

Then someone's silhouette blocked out most of the light. Maggie still couldn't see who was there. Light radiated behind the person.

Maggie clamped shut her eyes, tightly. Then opened them. She did this over and over again.

She couldn't really see anything. Couldn't focus on whoever or whatever it was. She had to keep blinking. Whoever was up there had to see the blinking, had to know she was alive.

"Mr. Soneji? Please help me," she tried to call out. Her throat was so dry. Her voice came out raspy and unrecognizable.

"*Shaddup! Shaddup!*" a voice from above shouted.

Someone was up there now! Someone was really up there and could get her out.

It sounded like . . . a very old woman's voice.

"Please help me. Please," Maggie begged.

A hand came flying down and slapped her face hard.

Maggie cried out. She was more frightened than hurt, but the blow hurt, too. She'd never been slapped before. It set off a loud roar inside her head.

"Stopyercrying!" The eerie voice was closer.

Then the person climbed down into the grave and was right over her. Maggie could smell strong body odor and someone's bad breath. She was being pinned down now, and she was too weak to fight back.

"Don't fight me, yer little bastard! Don't *ever* fight *me!* Who do yer think yer are, yer little bastard!

"Don't yer ever raise yer hand to me! Yer hear me? Don't yer ever!"

Please, God, what was happening?

"Yer that famous Maggie Rose, aren't yer? The rich, spoiled brat! Well, let me tell yer a secret. *Our secret.* Yer gonna die, little rich girl. Yer gonna die!"

CHAPTER 17

THE NEXT DAY was Christmas Eve. It didn't feel like the season to be merry. And it was going to get a whole lot worse before Christmas Day.

None of us had been able to make any of the usual, festive holiday preparations with our families. It added to the tension the Hostage Rescue Team was feeling. It magnified the misery of the depressing task. If Soneji had chosen the holiday season for this reason, he'd chosen well. He had turned everyone's Christmas to shit.

Around ten o'clock in the morning, I walked down Sorrell Avenue to the Goldberg house. Sampson, meanwhile, had sneaked off to do a little work on the murders in Southeast. We planned to get back together around noon to compare horror stories.

I talked with the Goldbergs for over an hour. They weren't holding up well. In a lot of ways, they were even more forthcoming than Katherine and Thomas Dunne. They were stricter parents than the Dunnes, but Jerrold and Laurie Goldberg loved their son dearly. Eleven years earlier, Laurie Goldberg had been told by doctors that she couldn't have children. Her uterus had been scarred. When she found herself pregnant with Michael, it had seemed a miracle. Had Soneji known about that? I wondered. How carefully had he picked out his victims? Why Maggie Rose and Michael Goldberg?

The Goldbergs allowed me to see Michael's bedroom, and to spend some time there by myself. I shut the door to the room and sat quietly for several moments. I had done the same thing in Maggie's room at the Dunnes'.

The boy's room was amazing. It was a treasure chest of state-of-the-art computer hardware and software — Macintosh, Nintendo, Prodigy, Windows. The AT&T labs had less equipment than Michael Goldberg.

Posters of Katherine Rose from her films *Taboo* and *Honeymoon* were taped up on the walls. A poster of Skid Row's lead singer, Sebastian Bach, was centered over the bed. A picture of Albert Einstein with a mauve punk haircut stared out from Michael's private bathroom. Also, a *Rolling Stone* magazine cover that asked "*Who Killed Pee-wee Herman?*"

A framed photograph of Michael and Maggie Rose was propped up on the boy's work desk. Posed arm in arm, the two kids looked like the greatest friends. What had inspired Soneji? Was it something about their special friendship?

Neither of the Goldbergs had ever met Mr. Soneji, although Michael had talked a lot about him. Soneji was the only person, child or adult, who had ever beaten Michael at Nintendo games like "Ultima" and "Super Mario Brothers." It suggested that Soneji might be a brainiac himself, another whiz kid, but not willing to let a nine-year-old beat him at video games for the sake of the cause. Not willing to lose at any game.

I was back in the library with the Goldbergs, looking out a window, when everything went completely and forever crazy on the kidnapping case.

I saw Sampson running down the street from the Dunnes'.

Each of his strides covered about a third of a block. I raced out the Goldbergs' front door at the same time that Sampson made it to the lawn. He broke stride like the San Francisco 49ers' Jerry Rice in the end zone.

"He called again?"

Sampson shook his head. "No! There's been a break, though. Something happened, Alex. The FBI's keeping it under wraps," Sampson said. "They've got something. C'mon."

A police roadblock had been set up just off Sorrell Avenue at the end of nearby Plately Bridge Lane. The roadblock of half-a-dozen wooden horses effectively stopped the press from following the cars that had left the Dunnes' just past two that afternoon. Sampson and I rode in the third car.

Seventy minutes later, the three sedans were speeding through the low hills surrounding Salisbury, Maryland. The cars circled down a winding road, to an industrial park nestled in thick pine woods.

The contemporary-looking complex was deserted on Christmas Eve. It was eerily quiet. Snow-blanketed lawns led the way to three separate whitestone office buildings. Half-a-dozen local police cars and ambulances had already arrived at the mysterious scene.

Some minor tributary that had to empty into Chesapeake Bay flowed behind the cluster of office buildings. The water was brownish red, and looked polluted. Royal blue signs on the buildings read: J. Cad Manufacturing, The Raser/Becton Group, Techno-Sphere.

Not a clue so far, not a word had been uttered about what had happened in the industrial park.

Sampson and I joined the group that headed down toward the river. Four more FBI agents were at the site, and they looked worried.

There was a patch of winter-thin, pale yellow weeds between the industrial park and the water. Then came a thirty- or forty-yard barren strip to the river itself. The sky overhead was cardboard gray, threatening more snow.

Down one muddy bank, sheriff's deputies were pouring casting compound, trying to get some footprints. Had Gary Soneji been here?

"Have they told you anything?" I asked Jezzie Flanagan as we sidestepped down the steep, muddy embankment together. Her work shoes were getting ruined. She didn't seem to notice.

"No. Not yet. Not a thing!" She was as frustrated as Sampson and I were. This was the first opportunity for the "Team" not to act like one. The Federal Bureau had their chance to cooperate. They blew it. Not a good sign. Not a promising beginning.

"Please don't let this be those kids," Jezzie Flanagan muttered as we reached flatter ground.

Two Bureau agents, Reilly and Gerry Scorse, were at the riverside. Snow flurries drifted down. A bracing cold wind blew over the slate gray water, which smelled like burning linoleum.

My heart was in my throat the whole time. I couldn't see anything down along the shoreline.

Agent Scorse made a short speech, which I think was meant to mollify the rest of us. "Listen, this 'close to the vest' approach has nothing to do with any of you. Because of the wide press coverage this case has received, we were asked — ordered, actually — not to say anything until we all got out here. Until we could see for ourselves."

"See what?" Sampson asked the FBI special agent. "You going to tell us what the hell is going on? Let's cut down on the verbal diarrhea."

Scorse signaled to one of the FBI agents, and spoke to him briefly. His name was McGoey, and he was from the director's office in D.C. He'd been in and out of the Dunne house. We all thought that he was the replacement for Roger Graham, but that was never verified.

McGoey nodded at whatever Scorse had told him, then stepped forward. He was a solemn-looking fat man with big teeth and a short white crewcut. He looked like an old military man who was close to retirement.

"The local police out here found a child floating in the river around one o'clock today," McGoey announced. "They have no way of knowing if it's one of the two kidnapped children or not."

Agent McGoey then walked all of us about seventy yards farther down the muddy riverbank. We stopped past a hump covered with moss and cattails. There wasn't a sound from anyone, just the bitter wind whistling over the water.

We finally knew why we had been brought here. A small body had been covered over with gray wool blankets from one of the EMS wagons. It was the tiniest, loneliest bundle in the universe.

One of the local policemen was asked to give us the necessary details. When he began to speak, his voice was thick and unsteady.

"I'm Lieutenant Edward Mahoney. I'm with the force here in Salisbury. About an hour and twenty minutes ago, a security guard with Raser/Becton discovered the body of a child down here."

We walked closer to the spread of blankets. The body was laid on a mound of grass that sloped into the brackish water. Beyond the grass, and to the left, was a black-looking tamarack swamp.

Lieutenant Mahoney knelt down beside the tiny body. His gray uniformed knee sank into the wet mud. Flecks of snow floated around his face, sticking to his hair and cheeks.

Almost reverently, he pulled back the wool blankets. It seemed as if he were a father, gently waking a child for some early-morning fishing trip.

Just a few hours ago, I had been looking at a photo of the two kidnapped children. I was the first to speak over the murdered child's body.

"It's Michael Goldberg," I said in a soft but clear voice. "I'm sorry to say that it's Michael. It's poor little Shrimpie."

CHAPTER 18

JEZZIE FLANAGAN didn't get home until early Christmas morning. Her head was spinning, bursting with too many ideas about the kidnapping.

She had to stop the obsessive images for a while. She had to shut down her engines, or the plant would explode. She had to stop being a cop. The difference between her and some other cops, she knew, was that she could stop.

Jezzie was living in Arlington with her mother. They shared a small, cramped condo apartment near the Crystal City Underground. Jezzie thought of it as the "suicide flat." The living arrangement was supposed to be temporary, except that she had been there close to a year now, ever since her divorce from Dennis Kelleher.

Dennis the Menace was up in northern Jersey these days, still trying to make it to the *New York Times*. He was never going to accomplish that feat, Jezzie knew in her heart. The only thing Dennis had ever been good at was trying to make Jezzie doubt herself. Dennis had been a real standout in that department. But in the end, she wouldn't let him beat her down.

She had been working too hard at the Service to find time to move out of her mother's condo. At least that was what she kept telling herself. There'd been no time to have a life. She was saving up — for something big, some kind of significant life change. She'd been calculating her net worth at least a couple of times a week, every week. She had all of twenty-four thousand dollars. That was everything. She was thirty-two now. She knew she was good-looking, almost beautiful — the way Dennis Kelleher was almost a good writer.

Jezzie *could* have been a contender, she often thought to herself. She almost had it made. All she needed was one decent break, and she'd finally realized she had to make that break for herself. She was committed to it.

She drank a Smithwich, really fine ale from the Old Sod. Smitty's had been her father's favorite brand of poison in the world. She nibbled a slice of fresh cheddar. Then she had a second ale in the shower, down dreary Hallway Number One at her mother's. Michael Goldberg's little face flashed at her again.

She *wouldn't allow* any more flash images of the Goldberg boy to come. She wouldn't feel any guilt, even if she was bursting at the seams with it. . . .

The two children had been abducted during her watch. That was how everything had started. . . . Stop the images! Stop everything for now.

Irene Flanagan was coughing in her sleep. Her mother had worked thirty-nine years for C&P Telephone. She owned the condo in Crystal City. She was a killer bridge player. That was it for Irene.

Jezzie's father had been a cop in D.C. for twenty-seven years. The end game came for Terry Flanagan, on his beloved job — a heart attack in crowded Union Station — with hundreds of complete strangers watching him die, nobody really caring. Anyway, that was the way Jezzie always told the story.

Jezzie decided, again, for the thousandth time, that she had to move out of her mother's place. No matter what. No more lame excuses. Move it or lose it, girl. Move on, move on, move on with your life.

She had completely lost track of how long she'd been drowning in the shower, holding the empty beer bottle at her side, rubbing the cool glass against her thigh. "Despair junkie," she muttered to herself. "That's really pitiful." She'd been in the shower long enough to finish the Smithwich, anyway, and get thirsty for another one. Thirsty for something.

She'd successfully avoided thinking about the Goldberg boy for a while. But not really. How could she? Little Michael Goldberg.

Jezzie Flanagan had gotten good at forgetting over the past few years, though — avoiding pain at all costs. It was dumb to be in pain, *if* you could avoid it.

Of course, that also meant avoiding close relationships, avoiding even the proximity of love, avoiding most of the natural range of human emotions. Fair enough. It might be an acceptable trade-off. She'd found that she could survive without love in her life. It sounded terrible, but it was the truth.

Yes, for the moment, especially the present moment, the trade-off was well worth it, Jezzie thought. It helped get her through each day and night of the crisis. It got her through until the cocktail hour, anyway.

She coped okay. She had all the right tools for survival. If she could make it as a woman cop, she could make it at anything. The other agents in the Service said she had *cojones*. It was their idea of a compliment, so Jezzie took it as one. Besides, they were spot on — she did have *brass cojones*. And the times that she didn't, she was smart enough to fake it.

At one o'clock in the morning, Jezzie Flanagan had to take the BMW bike for a ride; she had to get out of the suffocating, tiny apartment in Arlington.

Had to, had to, had to.

Her mother must have heard the door opening out to the hallway. She called to Jezzie from her bedroom, maybe right out of her sleep.

"Jezzie, where are you going so late? Jezzie? Jezzie, is that you?"

"Just out, Mother." *Christmas shopping at the mall*, a cynical line bounced against the walls of her head. As usual, she kept it inside. She wished Christmas would go away. She dreaded the next day.

Then she was gone into the night on the BMW K-1 — either escaping from, or chasing after, her personal nightmares, her devils.

It was Christmas. Had Michael Goldberg died for our sins? Was that what this was about? she thought.

She refused to let herself feel all the guilt. It was Christmas, and Christ had already died for everyone's sins. Even Jezzie Flanagan's sins. She was feeling a little crazy. No, she was feeling a lot crazy, but she could take control. Always take control. That's what she would do now.

She sang "Winter Wonderland" — at a hundred and ten miles an hour on the open highway heading out of Washington. She wasn't afraid of very much, but this time she was afraid.

CHAPTER 19

IN SOME PARTS of Washington and the nearby suburbs of Maryland and Virginia, house-by-house searches were conducted on Christmas morning. Police blue-and-whites toured the streets downtown. They loudly broadcasted over their PA systems:

"We are looking for Maggie Rose Dunne. Maggie is nine years old. Maggie has long blond hair. Maggie is four feet three inches tall and weighs seventy-two pounds. A substantial reward is offered for any information leading to Maggie's safe return."

Inside the house, a half-dozen FBI agents worked more closely than ever with the Dunnes. Both Katherine Rose and Tom Dunne were terribly shaken by Michael's death. Katherine suddenly looked ten years older. We all waited for the next call from Soneji.

It had occurred to me that Gary Soneji was going to call the Dunnes on Christmas Day. I was beginning to feel as if I knew him a little. I wanted him to call, wanted him to start moving, to make the first big mistake. I wanted to get him.

At around eleven on Christmas morning, the Hostage Rescue Team was hurriedly called together in the Dunnes' formal sitting room. There were close to twenty of us now, all at the mercy of the FBI for vital information. The house was buzzing. *What had the Son of Lindbergh done?*

We hadn't been given much information yet. We did know that a telegram had been delivered to the Dunne house. It wasn't being treated like any of the previous crank messages. It had to be Soneji.

FBI agents had monopolized the house phones for the past fifteen minutes or so. Special Agent Scorse arrived back at the house just before eleven-thirty, probably coming from his own family's Christmas. Chief Pittman swept in five minutes later. The police commissioner had been called.

"This is getting to be a real bad deal. Being left in the dark all the time." Sampson slouched against the room's mantel. When Sampson slouches, he's only around six feet seven. "The Fibbers don't trust us. We trust them even less than we did at the get-go."

"We didn't trust the FBI in the beginning," I reminded him.

"You're right about that." Sampson grinned. I could see myself reflected in his Wayfarers and I looked small. I wondered if the whole world looked tiny from Sampson's vantage point. "Our boy send the Western Union?" he asked me.

"That's what the FBI thinks. It's probably just his way of saying Merry Christmas. Maybe he wants to be part of a family."

Sampson peered at me over the tops of his dark glasses. "Thank you, Dr. Freud."

Agent Scorse was working his way to the front of the room. Along the way, he picked up Chief Pittman. They shook hands. Good community relations at work.

"We received another message that appears to be from Gary Soneji," Scorse announced as soon as he was in front of us. He had an odd way of stretching his neck and twisting his head from side to side when he was nervous. He did that a few times as he began to speak.

"I'll read it to you. It's addressed to the Dunnes. . . . 'Dear Katherine and Tom . . . How about ten million dollars? Two in cash. Rest in negotiable securities and diamonds. IN MIAMI BEACH! . . . M.R. doing fine so far. Trust me. TOMORROW'S big day . . . Have a merry . . . Son of L.'"

Within fifteen minutes of its arrival, the telegram had been traced to a Western Union office on Collins Avenue in Miami Beach. FBI agents immediately descended on the office to interview the manager and clerks. They didn't learn a thing — exactly the way the rest of the investigation had been going so far.

We had no choice but to leave for Miami immediately.

CHAPTER 20

THE HOSTAGE RESCUE TEAM arrived at Tamiami Airport in Florida at four-thirty on Christmas afternoon. Secretary Jerrold Goldberg had arranged for us to fly down in a private jet supplied by the Air Force.

A Miami police escort rushed us to the FBI office on Collins Avenue, near the Fountainbleu and other Gold Coast hotels. The Bureau office was only six blocks from the Western Union office where Soneji had sent the telegram.

Had he known that? Probably he had. That was how his mind seemed to work. Soneji was a control freak. I kept jotting down observations on him. There were already twenty pages in a notepad I kept in my jacket. I wasn't ready to write a profile of Soneji since I had no information about his past yet. My notes were filled with all the right buzzwords, though: *organized, sadistic, methodical, controlling, perhaps hypomanic.*

Was he watching us scurry around Miami now? Quite possibly he was. Maybe in another disguise. Was he remorseful about Michael Goldberg's death? Or was he entering a state of rage?

Private lines of emergency switchboard operators had already been set up at the FBI office. We didn't know how Soneji would communicate from here on. Several Miami police officers were added to the team now. So were another two hundred agents from the Bureau's large force in southern Florida. Suddenly, everything was rush, rush, rush. Hurry up and wait.

I wondered if Gary Soneji had any real idea about the state of chaos he was creating as his deadline approached. Was that part of his plan, too? Was Maggie Rose Dunne really okay? Was she still alive?

We would need some proof before the final exchange would be approved. At least we would *ask* Soneji for physical proof. *M.R. fine so far. Trust me*, he'd said. Sure thing, Gary.

Bad news followed us down to Miami Beach.

The preliminary autopsy report on Michael Goldberg had been faxed to the Miami Bureau office. A briefing was held immediately after we arrived, in the FBI's crisis room. We sat in a crescent arrangement of desks, each desk with its own video monitor and word processor. The room was unusually quiet. None of us really wanted to hear details about the little boy's death.

A Bureau technical officer named Harold Friedman was chosen to explain the medical findings to the group. Friedman was unusual for the Bureau, to say the least. He was an Orthodox Jew, but with the build and look of a Miami beachboy. He wore a multicolored yarmulke to the autopsy briefing.

"We're reasonably certain the Goldberg boy's death was *accidental*," he began in a deep, articulate voice. "It appears that he was knocked out with a chloroform spray first. There were traces of chloroform in his nasal passages and throat. Then he was injected with secobarbital sodium, probably about two hours later. Secobarbital is a strong anesthetic. It also has properties which can inhibit breathing.

"That seems to be what happened in this case. The boy's breathing probably became irregular, then his heart and breathing stopped altogether. It wasn't painful if he remained asleep. I suspect that he did, and that he died in his sleep.

"There were also several broken bones," Harold Friedman went on. In spite of the beachboy appearance, he was somber and seemed intelligent in his reporting. "We believe that the little boy was kicked and punched, probably dozens of times. This had nothing to do with his death, though. The broken bones and 'dents' on the skin were inflicted *after* the boy was dead. You should know that he was also sexually abused after the time of death. He was sodomized, and ripped during the act. This Soneji character is a very sick puppy," Friedman offered as his first bit of editorializing.

This was also one of the few real specifics we had about Gary Soneji's pathology. Evidently, he had flown into an angry rage when he discovered that Michael Goldberg was dead. Or that something about his perfect plan wasn't so perfect after all.

Agents and policemen shifted from buttock to buttock in their seats. I wondered if the frenzy with Michael Goldberg had a calming or inciteful effect on Soneji. More than ever, I worried about the chances Maggie Rose had to survive.

The hotel we were staying at was directly across the street from the Bureau branch office. It wasn't much by Miami Beach gold standards, but it did have a large terraced pool on the ocean side.

Around eleven, most of us had knocked off for the night. The temperature was still in the eighties. The sky was full of bright stars, and an occasional jetliner arriving from the North.

Sampson and I strolled across Collins Avenue. People must have thought the Lakers were in town to play the Miami Heat.

"Want to eat first? Or just drink ourselves numb?" he asked me midway across the avenue.

"I'm already pretty numb," I told Sampson. "I was thinking about a swim. When in Miami Beach?"

"You can't get a Miami Beach tan tonight." He was rolling an unlit cigarette between his lips.

"That's another reason for a night swim."

"I'll be operating in the lounge," Sampson said as we branched off in the lobby. "I'll be the one drawing the pretty women."

"Good luck," I called to him. "It's Christmas. I hope you get a present."

I got into a bathing suit, and wandered out to the hotel pool. I've come to believe that the key to health is exercising, so I exercise every day, no matter where I am. I also do a lot of stretching, which can be done anytime, anywhere.

The big swimming pool on the ocean side was closed, but that didn't stop me. Policemen are notorious for jaywalking, double-parking, rule-breaking in general. It's our only perk.

Someone else had the same idea. Somebody was swimming laps so smoothly and quietly that I hadn't noticed until I was walking among the deck chairs, feeling the cool wetness under my feet.

The swimmer was a woman, in a black or dark blue swim-suit. She was slender and athletic, with long arms and longer legs. She was a pretty sight on a not-so-pretty day. Her stroke looked effortless, and it was strong and rhythmic. It seemed her private place, and I didn't want to disturb it.

When she made her turn, I saw that it was Jezzie Flanagan. That surprised me. It seemed out of character for the Secret Service supervisor.

I finally climbed down very quietly into the opposite end of the pool and started my own laps. It was nothing beautiful or rhythmic, but my stroke gets the job done, and I can usually swim for a long time.

I did thirty-five laps easily. I felt as if I was loosened up for the first time in a few days. The cobwebs were beginning to go away. Maybe I'd do another twenty, then call it a night. Or maybe have a Christmas beer with Sampson.

When I stopped for a quick blow, Jezzie Flanagan was sitting right there on the edge of a lounger.

A fluffy white hotel towel was thrown casually over her bare shoulders. She was pretty in the moonlight over Miami. Willowy, very blond, bright blue eyes staring at me.

"Fifty laps, Detective Cross?"

She smiled, in a way that revealed a different person from the one I'd seen at work over the past few days. She seemed much more relaxed.

"Thirty-five. I'm not exactly in your league," I said to her. "Not even close. I learned my stroke at the downtown Y."

"You persevere." She kept her smile turned on nicely. "You're in good shape."

"Whatever my stroke is called, it sure feels good tonight. After all those hours cooped up in that room. Those boxy little windows that don't open."

"If they had big windows, all anybody would think about is escaping to the beach. They'd never get any work done anywhere in the state of Florida."

"Are we getting any work done?" I asked Jezzie.

She laughed. "I had a friend who believed in the 'doing the best you can' theory of police work. I'm doing the best I can. Under impossible circumstances. How about you?"

"I'm doing the best I can, too," I said.

"Praise the Lord." Jezzie Flanagan raised both her arms joyously. Her exuberance surprised me. It was funny, and it felt good to laugh for a change. Real good. Real necessary.

"*Under the circumstances*, I'm doing the best I can," I added.

"Under the circumstances, praise the Lord!" Jezzie raised her voice again. She was funny, or it was late, or both of the above.

"You going to catch a bite?" I asked her. I wanted to hear her thoughts about the case. I hadn't really talked to her before.

"I'd like to eat something," she answered. "I've skipped two meals already today."

We agreed to meet up in the hotel's dining room, which was one of those slow-spinning affairs on the top floor.

She changed in about five minutes, which I found impressive. Baggy tan trousers, a V-necked T-shirt, black Chinese slippers. Her blond hair was still wet. She'd combed it back, and it looked good that way. She didn't wear makeup, and didn't need to. She seemed so different from the way she acted on the job — much looser and at ease.

"In all honesty and fairness, I have to tell you one thing." She was laughing.

"What's the one thing?"

"Well, you're a strong but really clunky swimmer. On the other hand, you do look good in a bathing suit."

Both of us laughed. Some of the long day's tension began to drain away.

We were good at drawing each other out over beers and a snack. A lot of that was due to the peculiar circumstances, the stress and pressure of the past few days. It's also part of my job to draw people out, and I like the challenge.

I got Jezzie Flanagan to admit that she'd once been Miss Washington, D.C., back when she was eighteen. She'd been in a sorority at the University of Virginia, but got kicked out for "inappropriate behavior," a phrase that I loved.

As we talked, though, I was surprised that *I* was telling her much more than I'd expected to. She was easy to talk to.

Jezzie asked about my early days as a psychologist in Washington. "It was mostly a bad mistake," I told her, without getting into how angry it had made me, still made me. "A whole lot of people didn't want any part of a black shrink. Too many black people couldn't afford one. There are no liberals on the psychiatrist's couch." She got me to talk about Maria, but only a little bit. She told me how it was to be a woman in the ninety-percent macho-male Secret Service. "They like to test me, oh, about once a day. They call me 'the Man.'" She also had some entertaining war stories about the White House. She knew the Bushes and the Reagans. All in all, it was a comfortable hour that went by too quickly.

Actually, more than an hour had passed. More like two hours. Jezzie finally noticed our waitress hovering all by her lonesome near the bar. "Shoot. We are the last ones in this restaurant."

We paid our bill and got on the local elevator down from the spinning-top restaurant. Jezzie's room was on the higher floor. She probably had a view of the ocean, too. From her suite.

"That was real nice," I said at her stop. I think that's a snappy line out of a Noël Coward play. "Thanks for the company. Merry Christmas."

"Merry Christmas, Alex." Jezzie smiled. She tucked her blond hair behind her ear, which was a tic of hers I'd noticed before. "That *was* nice. Unfortunately, tomorrow probably won't be."

Jezzie pecked my cheek, and went off to her room. "I'm going to dream about you in swimsuits," she said as the elevator doors closed.

I went down four more floors, where I took my Christmas cold shower, alone in my Christmas hotel room. I thought about Jezzie Flanagan. Dumb fantasies in a lonely Miami Beach hotel room. We sure weren't going anywhere together, but I liked her. I kind of felt that I could talk to her about anything. I read some more about Styron's bout with depression, until I could sleep. I had some dreams of my own.

CHAPTER 21

CAREFUL, be oh so careful now, Gary boy.

Gary Soneji watched the fat woman out of the extreme corner of his left eye. He watched the blubbery blob the way a lizard watches an insect — just before mealtime. She had no idea that he was studying her.

She was a policewoman, so to speak, as well as a toll collector, at exit 12 on the turnpike. She slowly counted out his change. She was enormous, black as the night, completely out of it. Asleep at the switch. Soneji thought she looked like Aretha Franklin would have, if Aretha couldn't sing a note and she had to make it in the real, workaday world.

She didn't have a clue as to who was riding by in the monotonous stream of holiday traffic. Even though she and all her cohorts were supposed to be desperately searching for him. So much for "massive police dragnets" and your basic "nationwide manhunt." What a fucking letdown and disappointment. How could they possibly expect to catch him with people like this in the hunt. At least they could *try* to keep it interesting for him.

Sometimes, especially at times like this, Gary Soneji wanted to proclaim the inescapable truth of the universe.

Proclaim. Listen, you slovenly bimbo bitch cop! Don't you know who I am? Some paltry nothing disguise have you buffaloed? I'm the one you've been seeing in every news story for the past three days. You and half the world, Aretha, baby.

Proclaim. I planned and executed the Crime of the Century so perfectly. I'm already bigger than John Wayne Gacy, Jeffrey Dahmer, Juan Corona. Everything went right until the rich little blue boy got sick on me.

Proclaim. Look real close. Take a good look at me. Be a goddamn hero for once in your life. Be something besides a fat black zero on the Freeway of Love. Look at me, will you! *Look at me!*

She handed back his change. "Merry Christmas, sir."

Gary Soneji shrugged. "Merry Christmas back at you," he said.

As he pulled away from the blinking lights of the tollbooth, he imagined the policewoman with one of those smiling, have-a-nice-day heads on her. He mind-pictured a whole country full of those smiley balloon faces. It was happening, too.

It was getting worse than *The Invasion of the Body Snatchers,* actually. Drove him cra-azy if he thought about it, which he tried not to do. Country of smiling Balloonheads. He loved Stephen King, identified with His Weirdness, and wished The King would write about all the smiley fools in America. He could see the dust jacket for King's masterpiece — *Balloonheads.*

Forty minutes later, Soneji pulled the trusty Saab off Route 413, in Crisfield, Maryland. He accelerated down the rutted dirt road to the old farmhouse. He had to smile, had to laugh at this point. He had them so completely fooled and bamboozled. Completely turned inside out.

So far, they didn't know which way was up, down, or sideways. He already had the Lindbergh thing topped, didn't he? Now it was time to pull the mat out from under all the Balloonheads again.

CHAPTER 22

IT WAS DEFINITELY SHOWTIME! A Federal Express courier had arrived at the FBI offices just before ten-thirty on the morning of the twenty-sixth of December. He'd delivered the new message from the Son of Lindbergh.

We were called back to the crisis room on the second floor. The whole FBI staff seemed to be in there. This was it, and everybody knew it.

Moments later, Special Agent Bill Thompson, from Miami, rushed in. He brandished one of those familiar-looking delivery-service envelopes. Thompson carefully opened the orange-and-blue envelope in front of the entire group.

"He's going to let us see the message. Only he's not going to read it to us," Jeb Klepner from the Secret Service cracked under his breath. Sampson and I were standing there with Klepner and Jezzie Flanagan.

"Oh, he doesn't want all the heat on this one," Jezzie predicted. "He'll share with us this time."

Thompson was ready, up at the front.

"I have a message from Gary Soneji. It goes as follows.

"There's the number *one*," Thompson read the message.

"Then, spelled out in letters, *ten million*. On the next line, the number *two*. Then the words *Disney World, Orlando — The Magic Kingdom*. Next line. The number *three*. Then, *Park at Pluto 24. Go across Seven Seas Lagoon on the ferry, not the monorail. 12:50 P.M. today. This will be finished by 1:15.* Last line. *Detective Alex Cross will deliver the ransom. Alone.* It's signed *Son of Lindbergh.*"

Bill Thompson looked up immediately. His eyes searched the crisis room. He had no trouble finding me in the audience. I can absolutely guarantee that his shock and surprise were nothing compared to mine. A hit of adrenaline had already mainlined its way into my system. What the hell did Soneji want with me? How did he know about me? Did he know how badly I wanted his ass now?

"There's no attempt at any negotiation!" Special Agent Scorse began to make a fuss. "Soneji just assumes we're going to deliver the ten million."

"He does," I spoke up. "And he's right. It's ultimately the family's call how and when a kidnap ransom gets paid." The Dunnes had instructed us to pay Soneji — unconditionally. Soneji had probably guessed as much. That was undoubtedly the main reason why he'd chosen Maggie Rose. But why had he chosen me?

Standing at my side, Sampson shook his head and muttered, "The Lord, He sure does work in mysterious ways."

A half-dozen cars were waiting for us in the sunbaked parking lot behind the Bureau building. Bill Thompson, Jezzie Flanagan, Klepner, myself, and Sampson traveled in one of the FBI sedans. The securities and money went with us. *Detective Alex Cross will deliver the ransom.*

The money had been put together late the previous night. It was a tremendously complex deal to get it accomplished so quickly, but Citibank and Morgan Stanley had cooperated. The Dunnes and Jerrold Goldberg had the power to get what they wanted, and had obviously exerted great pressure. As Soneji had requested, two million of the ransom was in cash. The rest was in small diamonds and securities. The ransom was negotiable, and also very portable. It fit into an American Tourister suitcase.

The trip from downtown Miami Beach to the Opa Locka West Airport took about twenty-five minutes. The flight would take another forty. That would get us into Orlando at approximately 11:45 A.M. It would be tight.

"We can try to put a device on Cross." We listened as Agent Scorse talked over the radio to Thompson. "Portable radio transmitter. We've got one on board the plane."

"I don't like that very much, Gerry," Thompson said.

"I don't like it, either," I said from the backseat. An understatement. "No bugs. That's out." I was still trying to understand how and why Soneji had picked me. It didn't make sense. I thought that he might have read about me in the news coverage back in Washington. He had some good reason, I knew. There could be little or no doubt about that.

"There'll be unbelievable crowds at that park," Thompson said once we were on board a Cessna 310 to Orlando. "That's the obvious reason he's chosen the Disney Park. Lots of parents and kids at the Magic Kingdom, too. He just might be able to blend in with Maggie Dunne. He may have disguised her as well."

"The Disney Park fits into his pattern for big, important icons," I said. One theory in my notebooks was that Soneji might have been an abused child himself. If so, he'd have nothing but rage and disdain for a place like Disney World — where "good" little kids get to go with their "good" mommies and daddies.

"We've already got ground and aerial surveillance on the park," Scorse contributed. "Pictures are being piped into the crisis room in Washington right now. We're also filming Epcot and Pleasure Island. Just in case he pulls a last-minute switch."

I could just imagine the scene at the FBI crisis room on 10th Street. As many as a couple of dozen VIPs would be crowded in there. Each of them would have his own desk and a closed-circuit TV monitor. The aerial photography of Walt Disney World would be playing on all the monitors at once. The room's Big Board would be filled with facts . . . exactly how many agents and other personnel were converging on the park at that moment. The number of exits. Every roadway in or out. Weather conditions. Size of the day's crowd. Number of Disney security people. But probably nothing about Gary Soneji or Maggie Rose, or we would have heard about it.

"I'm going to Disney World!" One of the agents on board the plane cracked a joke. The pretty typical cop talk got some nervous laughter. Breaking the tension was good, and hard to achieve under the difficult circumstances.

The whole notion of meeting up with a madman and a kidnapped little girl wasn't a nice one. Neither was the cold reality of the holiday crowds waiting for us at Disney World. We were told that more than seventy thousand people were already inside the theme park and its parking areas. Still, this would be our best chance to get Soneji. This might be our only chance.

We rode to the Magic Kingdom in a special caravan, a police escort with flashing lights and sirens. We took the breakdown lane on I-4, passing all the regular traffic coming in from the airport.

People packed into station wagons and minivans jeered or cheered our speedy progress. None of them had any idea who we were, or why we were rushing to Disney World. Just VIPs going to see Mickey and Minnie.

We got off at exit 26-A, then proceeded along World Drive to the auto plaza. We arrived inside the parking area at a little past 12:15 P.M. That was cutting it extremely close, but Soneji hadn't given us time to organize.

Why Disney World? I kept trying to understand. Because Gary Soneji had always wanted to go there as a kid, and had never been allowed? Because he appreciated the almost neurotic efficiency of the well-run amusement park?

It would have been relatively easy for Gary Soneji to get into Disney World. But how was he going to get out? That was the most intriguing question of all.

CHAPTER 23

SENIOR DISNEY attendants parked our cars in the Pluto section, row 24. A fiberglass tram was waiting there to pick us up and take us to the ferry.

"Why do you think Soneji asked for you?" Bill Thompson said as we were getting out of the car. "Any idea at all, Alex?"

"Maybe he heard about me in the news stories back in Washington," I said. "Maybe he knows I'm a psychologist and that caught his attention. I'll be sure to ask him about that. When I see him."

"Just take it easy with him," Thompson offered some advice. "All we want is the girl back."

"That's all I want," I told him. We were both exaggerating. We wanted Maggie Rose safe, but we also wanted to capture Soneji. We wanted to burn him here at Disney World.

Thompson put his arm around my shoulder as we stood in the parking area. There was some nice camaraderie for a change. Sampson, and also Jezzie Flanagan, wished me good luck. The FBI agents were being supportive, for the time being at least.

"How're you feeling?" Sampson pulled me aside for a

moment. "You all right with all this shit? He asked for you, but you don't have to go."

"I'm fine. He's not going to hurt me. I'm used to psychos, remember?"

"You *are* a psycho, my man."

I took the single suitcase with the ransom inside. I climbed onto the bright orange tram alone. Holding tightly to an overhead metal stirrup, I headed toward the Magic Kingdom, where I was to make the exchange for Maggie Rose Dunne.

It was 12:44 P.M. I was six minutes early.

No one paid much attention to me as I moved with the congealed flow of people toward rows of ticket booths and turnstiles at the Magic Kingdom Ticket Center. Why should they?

That had to be Soneji's idea for choosing the crowded location. I clutched the suitcase tighter. I felt that as long as I had the ransom, I had a safety line to Maggie Rose.

Had he dared to bring the little girl with him? Was he here himself? Or was all this a test for us? Anything was possible now.

The mood of the Disney World crowd was lighthearted and relaxed. These were mostly family vacationers, having fun under the bright, cornflower-blue skies. A pleasant announcer's voice was chanting: "Take small children by the hand, do not forget your personal belongings, and enjoy your stay at the Magic Kingdom."

No matter how jaded you might be, the fantasyland was captivating. Everything was incredibly clean and *safe*. You couldn't help feeling completely protected, which was so goddamned weird for me.

Mickey Mouse, Goofy, and Snow White greeted everybody at the front gates. The park was immaculate. "Yankee Doodle Dandy" played from loudspeakers cleverly hidden somewhere in the manicured shrubbery.

I could feel my heart pounding under a loose-fitting sport-shirt. I was out of touch with all my backup for the moment. It would be that way until I was physically in the Magic Kingdom.

The palms of my hands were clammy, and I wiped them against my trousers. Mickey Mouse was shaking hands right in front of me. This was nuts.

I had just entered an area of deep shadows cast from the Transportation and Ticket Center. The ferry was visible, a miniature Mississippi riverboat, without the paddle wheel.

A man wearing a sport jacket and brimmed hat slid alongside me. I didn't know if it was Soneji. The sense of Disney World's safety and protection was broken immediately.

"Change of plans, Alex. I'll take you to see Maggie Rose now. Keep looking straight ahead, please. You're doing super so far. Just keep it up and we're home safe."

A six-foot-tall Cinderella walked past us, heading in the opposite direction. Children and adults oohed and aahed at her.

"Just turn around now, Alex. We're going to walk back the same way you came in. This can be a day at the beach. It's up to you, my friend."

He was perfectly calm and in control, the way Soneji had been throughout the kidnapping. There was an aura of invincibility around everything so far. He had called me Alex. We began to walk back against the flow of the crowd.

Cinderella's coiffed head of blond curls bobbed along ahead of us. Children laughed with delight as they saw the movie and cartoon heroine come to life.

"I have to see Maggie Rose first" was the only thing I said to the man in the brimmed hat. Could he be Soneji in disguise? I couldn't tell. I needed to get a better look at him.

"That's fine. But if anyone stops us, I'll tell you right now, the girl is dead." Brimmed Hat said it offhandedly, as if he was giving a stranger the time of day.

"No one's going to stop us," I assured him. "Our only concern is the girl's safety."

I hoped that was true for all the parties involved. I'd seen Katherine and Tom Dunne briefly that morning. I knew that all they cared about was getting their little girl back tonight.

Perspiration had begun to stream down my entire body. I had no control over that. The temperature was only in the mid-eighties, but the humidity was high.

I had started to worry about an inadvertent screw-up. Anything could go wrong here. It wasn't as if we'd practiced this maneuver, right in the heart of Disney World and its unpredictable crowds.

"Listen. If the FBI sees me coming outside, somebody might approach us," I decided to tell the man.

"I hope not," he said and made a *tsking* sound. He shook his head back and forth. "That would be a serious breach of etiquette."

Whoever he was, he was unnaturally cool under fire. Had he done this before? I wondered. It seemed to me that we were headed back in the direction of the rows of orange trams. One of the trams would take us back out to the parking area again. Was that the plan?

The man was too heavyset to be Soneji, I thought. Unless he had on some kind of brilliant disguise and lots of padding. The actor angle came to mind again. I hoped to God he wasn't an impostor. Someone who'd found out what was going on in Florida, then contacted us to go for the ransom. It wouldn't be the first time that had happened in a kidnapping case.

"Federal Bureau! Hands high!" I heard suddenly. It all happened gunshot-quick. My heart went up into my throat. What the hell were they doing? What were they thinking?

"Federal Bureau!"

Half-a-dozen agents had us surrounded in the parking lot.

They had their revolvers out. At least one rifle was aimed at the contact man, and therefore at me.

Agent Bill Thompson was there with the others. *We only want to get the girl back,* he'd said to me just moments ago.

"Back away! Back off!" I lost it and yelled at them. "Get the hell away from us! Get out of here!"

I looked directly at Brimmed Hat now. It couldn't be Gary Soneji. I was almost certain of that. Whoever it was didn't care if he was recognized or even photographed in Orlando.

Why was that? How could this guy be so cool?

"If you take me, the girl's dead," he said to the FBI agents surrounding us. He was stone-cold. His eyes looked dead. "There's nothing that'll stop it from happening. I can't do a thing. Neither can you. She's dead meat."

"Is she alive now?" Thompson took a step toward the man. He looked as if he might hit him, which was what we all wanted to do.

"She's alive. I saw her about two hours ago. She was home free unless you fucked this up. Which you're doing big time. Now back off, just like the detective said. Back the fuck off, man."

"How do we know you're partners with Soneji?" Thompson asked.

"One. Ten million. Two. Disney World, Orlando — The Magic Kingdom. Three. Park at Pluto 24." He reeled off the exact wording from the ransom message.

Thompson stood his ground. "We'll negotiate for the girl's release. Negotiate. You do it our way."

"What? *And kill the girl?*" Jezzie Flanagan had come up directly behind Thompson and the rest of the FBI posse.

"Put your guns down," she said firmly. "Let Detective Cross make the exchange. If you do it your way and the girl dies, I'll tell every reporter in the country. I swear I will, Thompson. I swear to God I will."

"So will I," I said to the FBI special agent. "You have my word on it."

"This isn't him. It isn't Soneji," Thompson finally said. He looked at Agent Scorse and shook his head in disgust. "Let them go," he ordered. "Cross and the ransom go to Soneji. That's the decision."

The icy contact man and I started to walk again — I was shaking. People were staring at us as we continued our trip toward the orange motor-trams. I felt completely unreal. Moments later we were inside one of the trams. We both sat down.

"Assholes," the contact man muttered. It was his first sign of any emotion. "They almost blew everything."

We stopped at a new Nissan Z in Section Donald, row 6. The car was dark blue, with tinted gray glass. No one was inside the sports car.

Brimmed Hat started the car, and we made our way out toward I-4 again. Traffic leaving the park at noon was almost nonexistent. A day at the beach, he'd said.

We headed back in the direction of Orlando International. Due east. I tried to get him to talk, but he had nothing to say to me.

Maybe he wasn't so cool and collected. Maybe he'd been scared shitless back there, too. The Bureau had almost blown everything; it wouldn't be the first time. Actually, the move at the park was probably no more than a bluff. As I thought about it, I realized it was their last chance to negotiate for the release of Maggie Rose Dunne.

A little more than half an hour had passed before we entered a private-plane annex a few miles beyond Orlando's main terminal. It was past one-thirty now. The exchange wasn't going to be in Disney World.

"The note promised this would be over by one-fifteen," I said as we climbed out of the Nissan. A warm tropical breeze blew at us across the airfield. The smells of diesel fuel and baking macadam were thick.

"The note lied," he said. He was as cold as ice again. "That's our plane. It's just you and me now. Try to be smarter than the FBI, Alex. It shouldn't be too hard."

CHAPTER 24

"SIT BACK, relax, enjoy the ride," he said once we were on board. "Seems like I'm your friendly pilot, too. Well, maybe not so friendly."

He handcuffed me to an armrest of one of the plane's four passenger seats. Another hostage taken, I thought. Maybe I could jerk the armrest out. It was metal and plastic. Flimsy enough.

The contact man was definitely the plane's pilot. He got clearance, and then the Cessna bumped on down the runway, gathering speed slowly. Finally it lifted off and was airborne, banking to the southeast, drifting out over the eastern section of Orlando and St. Petersburg. I was sure we were under surveillance thus far. From here on, though, everything depended on the contact man. And on Soneji's master plan.

The two of us were silent for the first minutes of flight. I settled back and watched him work, trying to remember every detail of the flight so far. He was efficient and relaxed at the controls. There were still no signs of stress. A professional all the way.

A strange possible connection entered my mind. We were in Florida now, heading farther south. A Colombian drug cartel had originally threatened Secretary Goldberg's family. Was that a coincidence? I didn't believe in coincidences anymore.

A rule of police work, especially police work in my experience, was passing back and forth through my mind. An important rule. Fully ninety-five percent of crimes were solved because somebody made a mistake. Soneji hadn't made any mistakes so far. He hadn't left us any openings. Now was the time for mistakes. The exchange would be the dangerous time for him.

"This has all been planned with a lot of precision," I said to Brimmed Hat. The plane was gliding farther and farther out over the Atlantic now. Toward what destination? To make the final exchange for Maggie Rose?

"You're so right. Everything's tight-assed as can be. You wouldn't believe how buttoned-up things are."

"Is the little girl really all right?" I asked him again.

"I told you, I saw her this morning. She hasn't been harmed," he said. "Not a hair on her chinny-chin-chin."

"That's real hard for me to believe," I said. I remembered the way we'd found Michael Goldberg.

The pilot shrugged his broad shoulders. "Believe what the hell you want." He didn't really care what I thought.

"Michael Goldberg was sexually abused. Why should we believe the girl's unharmed?" I said.

He looked at me. I had a gut feeling he hadn't known about the Goldberg boy's condition. It seemed to me that he wasn't a partner of Soneji's, that Gary Soneji wouldn't have any real partners. The pilot had to be hired help, which meant we had a chance of getting Maggie Rose.

"Michael Goldberg was beaten *after* he was dead," I told him. "He was sodomized. Just so you know what you're involved in. Who your partner is."

For some reason, that caused the contact man to grin. "Okay. No more helpful hints or annoying questions. Much as I appreciate your concern. Enjoy the ride. The girl hasn't been beaten, or sexually abused. You have my word as a gentleman."

"Is that what you are? Anyway, you can't know that," I said. "You haven't seen her since this morning. You don't know what Soneji's been up to, off by himself. Whatever his real name is."

"Yeah, well, we all have to trust our partners. You just sit back now and button up. Trust me. Due to a shortage of crew, there will be no complimentary beverage or snack on this flight."

Why was he so goddamn calm? He was *too* sure of himself.

Could there have been other kidnappings before this one? Maybe there had been a trial run somewhere? At least it was something to check. If I was going to be able to check anything after this was over.

I leaned back for a moment and let my eyes wander down below. We were way out over the ocean. I looked at my watch — a little more than thirty minutes from Orlando so far. The sea looked choppy, even with the bright, sunny weather. An occasional cloud cast its shadow down on the stony-looking water surface. The wavering outline of the plane appeared and disappeared. The Bureau had to be tracking us on radar, but the pilot would know that, too. He didn't seem concerned. It was a terrifying game of cat and mouse. How would the contact man react? Where were Soneji and Maggie Rose? Where were we going to make the exchange?

"Where'd you learn to fly?" I asked. "In Vietnam?" I'd been wondering about that. He seemed the right age, mid- to late-forties, though badly gone to seed. I'd treated some Viet vets who would be cynical enough to get involved in a kidnapping.

He wasn't bothered by the question, but he didn't answer me, either.

It was peculiar. He still didn't seem nervous or concerned. One of the kidnapped children was already dead. Why was he so smug and relaxed? What did he know that I didn't? Who was Gary Soneji? Who *was* he? What was their connection?

About half an hour later, the Cessna started to descend toward a small island that was ringed by white sand beaches. I had no idea where we were. Somewhere in the Bahamas, maybe? Was the FBI still with us? Tracking us from the sky? Or had he lost them somehow?

"What's the name of the island down there? Where are we? Nothing I can do about it at this point."

"This is Little Abaco," he finally answered. "Is anyone tracking us? The Fibbers? Electronic tracking? Bug on you somewhere?"

"No," I said. "No bugs. Nothing up my sleeve."

"Something they put on the money, maybe?" He seemed to know all the possibilities. "Fluorescent dust?"

"Not that I know of," I said. That much was true. I couldn't be certain, though. The FBI might not have told me everything.

"I sure hope not. Hard to really trust you people after what went on at Disney World. Place was crawling with cops and FBI. After we told you not to. Can't trust anybody nowadays."

He was trying to be humorous. He didn't care whether I reacted or not. He seemed like a man who'd been desperately down and out, but had been given a last chance at some money. The dirtiest money in the world.

There was a narrow landing strip on the beach. The hard-packed sand ran on for several hundred yards. The plane was set down easily and expertly. The pilot made a quick U-turn, then taxied straight for a stand of palm trees. It seemed like part of a plan. Every detail in its place. Perfect so far.

There was no quaint island shack here. No small reception area that I could make out. The hills beyond the beach were lush and thick with tropical vegetation.

There was no sign of anybody, anywhere. No Maggie Rose Dunne. No Soneji.

"Is the girl here?" I asked him.

"Good question," he answered. "Let's wait and see. I'll take first lookout."

He shut off the engine, and we waited in silence and suffocating heat. No more answers to my questions, anyway. I wanted to rip out the armrest and beat him with it. I'd been gritting my teeth so hard that I had a headache.

He kept his eyes pinned on the cloudless sky over the landing strip. He watched through the windshield for several minutes. I was having trouble breathing in the heat.

Is the little girl here? Is Maggie Rose alive? Damn you!

Bugs landed continually on the tinted glass. A pelican swooped by a couple of times. It was a lonely-looking place. Nothing else was happening.

It got hotter, unbearably so. Hot the way a car gets when it's left in the sun. The pilot didn't seem to feel it. He was evidently used to this kind of weather.

The minutes stretched on to an hour. Then two hours. I was drenched with sweat and dying of thirst. I tried not to think about the heat, but that wasn't possible. I kept thinking that the FBI must be watching us from the air. Mexican standoff. What was going to break it?

"Is Maggie Rose Dunne here?" I asked him a few more times. The longer this went on, the more I was afraid for her.

No answer. No indication that he had even heard me. He never checked his watch. He didn't move around, didn't fidget. Was he in some kind of trance? What was with this guy?

I stared for long stretches at the armrest he'd cuffed me to. I thought it was as close to a mistake as they'd made yet. It was old, and rattled when I tested it. I might be able to rip it out of its socket. If it came to that, I knew I was in trouble. But I had to try. It was the only solution.

Then, as abruptly and unexpectedly as we had landed, the Cessna rolled back out toward the beach runway. We took off again.

We were flying low, under a thousand feet. Cool air came into the plane. The roar of the propeller was growing hypnotic for me.

It was getting dark. I watched the sun do its nightly disappearing act, slipping completely off the horizon that lay before us. The view was beautiful, and eerie, under the circumstances. I knew what he'd been waiting for now. Nightfall. He wanted to work by night. Soneji liked the night.

About half an hour after dark, the plane began to descend again. There were twinkling specks and spots of light below us — what looked like a small town from the air. This was it. This was showdown time. The exchange for Maggie Rose was about to happen.

"Don't ask. Because I'm not telling you," he said without turning from the controls.

"Now why doesn't that surprise me?" I said. Trying to make it look like I was shifting positions in the seat, I gave the armrest a yank and felt something give. I was afraid to do more damage.

The landing strip and airfield were small, but at least there was one. I could see two other small planes near an unpainted shack. The pilot never attempted radio contact with anyone on the ground. My heart was racing.

An old-fashioned Flying A sign balanced precariously on the building's roof. No sign of anyone as we bumped to a stop. No Gary Soneji. No Maggie Rose. Not yet, anyway.

Someone left a light out, I thought to myself. Now, where the hell are they?

"Is this where we're making the exchange for Maggie Rose?" I went at the armrest again. Another yank with most of my strength behind it.

The contact man got up from his seat. He squeezed past me.

He started to climb out of the plane. He was holding the suitcase with the ten million.

"Good-bye, Detective Cross," he turned and said. "Sorry, but I have to run. Don't bother searching the area later. The girl isn't here. Not even close to here. We're back in the States, by the way. You're in South Carolina now."

"*Where is the girl?*" I yelled after him, straining at the handcuffs attached to the armrest. Where was the FBI? How far behind us were they?

I had to do something. I had to act now. I stood up to get some leverage, then pulled with all my weight and strength at the small plane's armrest. I yanked the armrest again and again. The plastic and metal piece ripped halfway out of the seat. I kept at it. The other half of the armrest broke off with a ripping noise like a deep and painful tooth extraction.

Two running strides and I was at the plane's open doorway. The contact man was already down on the ground, getting away with the suitcase. I dived at him. I needed to slow him until the Bureau got there. I also wanted to flatten the bastard, show him who was doing the controlling now.

I hit the contact man like a hawk striking a field rat. We both struck the tarmac hard, woofing out air. The armrest still dangled from my handcuffs. Metal raked across his face and drew blood. I belted him once with my free arm.

"Where is Maggie Rose? Where is she?" I shouted at the top of my lungs.

To my left, over the shiny darkness of the sea, I could see lights floating toward us, approaching fast. It had to be the Bureau. Their surveillance planes were coming to the rescue. They had managed to follow us.

Just then I was hit on the back of my neck. It felt like a lead pipe. I didn't go out immediately. *Soneji?* a voice inside me screamed. A second hard blow cracked the back of my skull, the tender part. This time, I went down for the count. I never saw who was doing the swinging, or what he had used.

When I came to, the small airfield in South Carolina was a raft of dazzling lights and activity. The FBI was there in full force. So were the local Carolina police. EMS ambulances and fire engines were everywhere.

The contact man was gone, though. So was the ten-million-dollar ransom. He'd made a clean getaway. Perfect planning on Soneji's part. Another perfect move.

"The little girl? Maggie Rose?" I asked a balding emergency doctor tending the wounds on my head.

"No sir," he said in a slow drawl. "The little girl is still missing. Maggie Rose Dunne was never seen around here."

CHAPTER 25

CRISFIELD, MARYLAND, lay under gloomy, elephant gray skies. It had been raining on and off for most of the day. A lone police car raced along rain-slicked country roads with its siren screaming.

Inside the car were Artie Marshall and Chester Dils. Dils was twenty-six, which made him exactly twenty years younger than Marshall. Like many young, rural policemen, he had dreams of getting out of the area — the same kind of hopes and dreams he'd had while attending Wilde Lake High School in Columbia.

But here he was, still in Crisfield. *Twin Peaks II*, he liked to call the town of under three thousand.

Dils almost physically ached to become a Maryland state trooper. It was tricky sledding because of the demanding trooper exams, especially the math. But becoming a trooper would get him the hell out of Somerset County. Maybe as far away as Salisbury or Chestertown.

Neither Dils nor especially mild-mannered Artie Marshall was ready for the exposure and the quicksilver reputations they were about to get. Just like that on the afternoon of the thirtieth of December. A telephone call had come into their station house on Old Hurley Road. A couple of hunters had spotted something that looked suspicious over in West Crisfield, on the way to the camping ground on Tangier Island. The hunters had found an abandoned vehicle. A blue Chevy minivan.

For the past several days, anything and everything vaguely suspicious immediately got associated with the big Washington kidnapping. That pattern had gotten old real fast. Dils and Marshall were ordered to check it out, anyway. A blue minivan had been used to take the kids from the school.

The afternoon was dying when they arrived at the farm out on Route 413. It was even a little spooky heading down the badly rutted dirt road onto the property.

"Old farm or something back here?" Dils asked his partner. Dils was behind the wheel. Doing about fifteen on the muddy, rutted road. Artie Marshall preferred to ride shotgun, *sans* the shotgun.

"Yeah. Nobody lives here now, though. I doubt this'll amount to anything monumental, Chesty."

"That's the beauty of The Job," Chester Dils said. "You never know. Monumental is always out there somewhere." He had a short-standing habit of making everything a little more glamorous than it actually was. He had his dream and all his big ideas, but Artie Marshall thought of them more as the immaturity of a younger man.

They arrived at the dilapidated barn that the hunters had mentioned in their call to the station. "Let's go for a look-see," Marshall said, trying to match the younger officer's enthusiasm.

Chester Dils hopped out of the squad car. Artie Marshall followed, though not at the same sprightly pace. They approached a badly faded red barn, a low building that looked as if it had sunk a couple of feet into the ground since its heyday. The hunters had stopped at the barn to get out of the rainstorm earlier that afternoon. Then they had called the police.

The barn was fairly dark and gloomy inside. The windows

had been covered over with cheesecloth. Artie Marshall turned on his flashlight.

"Let's have a little light on the subject," he muttered. Then, he bellowed, *"Bingo fucking Jesus!"*

There it was, all right. A big sinkhole in the middle of the dirt floor. A dark blue van parked next to the hole.

"Son-of-a-B, Artie!"

Chester Dils pulled out his service revolver. Suddenly, he was having trouble getting his breath. He was having trouble just standing there. In all honesty, he did not want to go up to the big hole in the ground. He did not want to be inside the old barn anymore. Maybe he wasn't ready for the troopers after all.

"Who's here?" Artie Marshall called out in a loud, clear voice. "Come out, right now. We're the police! This is the Crisfield police."

Christ, Artie was doing better than he was, Dils thought. The man was rising to the occasion. That got Chester Dils's feet and legs moving, anyway. He was heading farther inside the barn — to see if this was what he prayed to Almighty God it wasn't.

"Point that lamp right down in there," he said to his partner in crime-solving. They had come up right alongside the hole in the ground. He could barely breathe now. His chest felt as if it were constricted by a tourniquet. His knees were knocking against each other.

"You okay, Artie?" he asked his partner.

Marshall beamed the flashlight down into the dark, deep hole. They saw what the hunters had already seen.

There was a small box . . . almost a *casket*, in the sinkhole. The wooden case, or casket, was wide open. And it was empty.

"What the hell is that thing?" Dils heard himself asking.

Artie Marshall bent down closer. He aimed the flashlight beam directly into the hole. Instinctively, he looked around. He checked his back. Then his attention went to the black hole again.

Something was down at the bottom of the hole. Something that looked bright pink, or red.

Marshall's mind was racing. *It's a shoe . . . Christ, it must be the little girl's. This must be where they kept Maggie Rose Dunne.*

"This is where they kept those two kids," he finally spoke to his partner. "We found it, Chesty."

And they had.

Along with one of Maggie Rose's pretty-in-pink sneakers. The old trusty-dusty Reebok sneakers that were supposed to help her blend in with the other kids at Washington Day School. The really weird part was that the sneaker looked as if it had been left there to be found.

Part Two
The Son
of Lindbergh

CHAPTER 26

WHEN GARY WAS VERY UPSET, he retreated into his beloved boyhood stories and powerful fantasies. He was very upset now. His master plan seemed to be racing out of control. He didn't even want to think about it.

Speaking in a whisper, he repeated the magical words from memory: *"The Lindbergh farmhouse glowed with bright orangish lights. It looked like a fiery castle. . . . But now, the taking of Maggie Rose is the Crime of the Century. It simply is!"*

He'd had a fantasy about committing the Lindbergh kidnapping as a boy. Gary had even committed it to memory.

That was the beginning of everything: a story he had made up when he was twelve years old. A story he told himself over and over to keep from going insane. A daydream about a crime committed twenty-five years before he was born.

It was pitch-black in the basement of his house now. He had gotten used to the dark. It was livable. It could even be great.

It was 6:15 P.M., a Wednesday, January 6, in Wilmington, Delaware.

Gary was letting his mind wander now, letting his mind fly. He was able to visualize every intimate detail of Lucky Lindy and Anne Morrow Lindbergh's farmhouse in Hopewell. He'd been obsessed with the world-famous kidnapping for so long. Ever since his stepmother had arrived with her two spoiled bastard kids. Ever since he was first sent down to the cellar. *"Where bad boys go to think about what they did wrong."*

He knew more than anyone alive about the thirties kidnapping. Baby Lindbergh had eventually been dredged up from a shallow grave only four miles from the New Jersey estate. *Ah, but was it really Baby Lindbergh?* The corpse they'd found had been too tall — thirty-three inches, to only twenty-nine for Charles Jr.

No one understood the sensational, unsolved kidnapping. To this day. And that was the way it would be with Maggie Rose Dunne and Michael Goldberg.

No one was ever going to figure it out. That was a definite promise.

No one had figured out *any* of the other murders he'd done, had they? They got John Wayne Gacy, Jr., after over thirty murders in Chitown. Jeffrey Dahmer went down after seventeen in Milwaukee. Gary had murdered more than both of them put together. But no one knew who he was, or where he was, or what he planned to do next.

It was dark down in his cellar, but Gary was used to it. "The cellar is an acquired taste," he'd once told his stepmother to make her angry. The cellar was like your mind would be after you died. It could be exquisite, if you had a really great mind. Which he certainly did.

Gary was thinking about his plan of action, and the thought was simple: they hadn't really seen anything yet.

They better not blink.

Upstairs in the house, Missy Murphy was trying her best not to be too angry at Gary. She was making cookies for their daughter,

Roni, and the other neighborhood kids. Missy was really trying to be understanding and supportive. *One more time.*

She had been trying *not* to think of Gary. Usually when she baked, it worked. This time it didn't. Gary was incorrigible. He was also lovable, sweet, and bright as a thousand-watt bulb. That was why she had been attracted to him in the first place.

She'd met him at a University of Delaware mixer. Gary had been slumming at Delaware. He'd come down there from Princeton. She'd never talked to anyone so smart in her life; not even her professors at school were as smart as Gary.

The really endearing part of him was why she had married him in 1982. Against the advice of everybody. Her best friend, Michelle Lowe, believed in tarot cards, reincarnation, all that stuff. She'd done their horoscopes, Gary's and hers. "Call it off, Missy," she'd said. "Don't you ever look in his eyes?" But Missy had gone ahead with the wedding, gone against everybody's advice. Maybe that was why she'd stuck with him through thin, and thinner. Thinner than anyone had a right to expect her to put up with. Sometimes, it was as if there were a couple of Garys to put up with. Gary and his unbelievable mind games.

Something real bad was coming now, she was thinking as she spilled in a full bag of morsels. Any day now he was going to tell her he'd been fired from his job. The old, awful pattern had started up again.

Gary had already told her he was "smarter than anybody" at work. (Undoubtedly, this was true.) He'd told her he was "zooming ahead" of everybody. He'd told her his bosses loved him. (This had probably been true in the beginning.) He'd told her they were going to make him a district sales manager soon. (This was definitely one of Gary's "stories.") Then, trouble. Gary said his boss was starting to get jealous of him. The hours were impossible. (That was true enough. He was away all week and some weekends.) The danger *pattern* was in full gear. The sad part was that if he couldn't make it at *this* job, with *this* boss, how could he possibly make it anywhere?

Missy Murphy was certain that Gary would come home any day now and tell her he'd been asked to leave again. His days as a traveling sales rep for the Atlantic Heating Company were definitely numbered. Where would he find work after that? Who could possibly be more sympathetic than his current boss — her own brother, Marty.

Why did it have to be so hard all the time? Why was she such an all-day sucker for the Gary Murphys of this world?

Missy Murphy wondered if tonight was the night. Had Gary already been fired again? Would he tell her that when he got home from work tonight? How could such a smart man be such an unbelievable loser? she wondered. The first tear fell into the cookie mix, then Missy let the rest of Niagara Falls come. Her whole body began to tremble and heave.

CHAPTER 27

I'D NEVER HAD MUCH TROUBLE laughing at my frustrations as a cop or a psychologist. This time it was a lot tougher to take in stride. Soneji had beaten us down South, in Florida and Carolina. We hadn't gotten Maggie Rose back. We didn't know if she was alive or dead.

After I was debriefed for five hours by the Federal Bureau, I was flown up to Washington where I got to answer all the same questions from my own department. One of the last inquisitors was Chief of Detectives Pittman. The Jefe appeared at midnight. He was all showered and shaved for the occasion of our special meeting.

"You look like absolute hell," he said to me. Those were the first words out of his mouth.

"I've been up since yesterday morning," I explained. "I know how I look. Tell me something I don't already know."

I knew that was a mistake before the words got out. I don't usually lead with my chin, but I was groggy and tired and generally fucked up by that time.

The Jefe leaned forward on one of the little metal chairs in his conference room. I could see his gold fillings as he spoke to me. "Sure thing, Cross. I have to blow you off the kidnapping case. Right or wrong, the press is pinning a lot of what went haywire on you, *and us*. The FBI isn't taking any of the heat. Thomas Dunne's making a lot of noise, too. Seems fair to me. The ransom's gone; we don't have his daughter."

"Most of that is pure bullshit," I told Chief Pittman. "Soneji asked for me to be the contact. Nobody knows why yet. Maybe I shouldn't have gone, but I did. The FBI blew the surveillance, not me."

"Now tell me something *I* don't already know," Pittman came back. "Anyway, you and Sampson can go back on the Sanders and Turner murders. Just the way you wanted it in the first place. I don't mind if you stay in the background on the kidnapping. That's all there is to talk about." The Jefe said his piece, and then he left. Over and out. No discussion of the matter.

Sampson and I had been put back in our place: Washington Southeast. Everybody had their priorities straight now. The murders of six black people mattered again.

CHAPTER 28

TWO DAYS after I returned from South Carolina, I woke to the noise of a crowd gathered outside our house in Southeast.

From a seemingly safe place, the hollow of my pillow, I heard a buzz of voices. A line was sounding in my head: "Oh no, it's tomorrow again."

I finally opened my eyes. I saw other eyes. Damon and Janelle were staring down at me. They seemed amused that I could be sleeping at a time like this.

"Is that the TV, kids? All that awful racket I hear?"

"No, Daddy," said Damon. "TV's not on."

"No, Daddy," repeated Janelle. "It's better than TV."

I propped my head up on an elbow. "Well, are you two having a loud *party* with your friends outside? That it? Is that what I hear out my bedroom window?"

Serious headshaking came from the two of them. Damon finally smiled, but my little girl remained serious and a little afraid.

"No, Daddy. We aren't havin' a party," Damon said.

"Hmmm. Don't tell me the newspeople and the TV reporters

are here again. They were here just a few hours ago. Just last night."

Damon stood there with his hands on top of his head. He does that when he's excited or nervous.

"Yes, Daddy, it's the 'porters again."

"Piss me off," I muttered to myself.

"Piss me off, too," Damon said with a scowl. He partially understood what was going on.

A very public lynching! Mine.

The damn reporters again, the newsies. I rolled over and looked up at the ceiling. I needed to paint again, I saw. It never stops when you own.

It was now a media "fact" that I had blown the exchange for Maggie Rose Dunne. Someone, maybe the Federal Bureau, maybe George Pittman, had hung me out to dry. Somebody had also leaked the false insider information that my psychological evaluations of Soneji had dictated actions in Miami.

A national magazine ran the headline *D.C. Cop Lost Maggie Rose!* Thomas Dunne had said in a TV interview that he held me personally responsible for failing to carry out the release of his daughter in Florida.

Since then, I'd been the subject of several stories and editorials. Not one of them was particularly positive — or close to being factual.

If I had screwed up the ransom exchange in any way, I would have taken the criticism. I can take heat okay. But I hadn't screwed up. I'd put my life on the line in Florida.

More than ever, I needed to know why Gary Soneji had picked me for the exchange in Florida. Why had I been a part of his plans? Why had I been chosen? Until I found that out, there was no way I was coming off the kidnapping. It didn't matter what The Jefe said, thought, or did to me.

"Damon, you march right outside to the front porch," I told

my little boy. "Tell the reporters to beat it. Tell them to take a hike. Tell them to *hit the road, Jack.* Okay?"

"Yeah. Take a hike, Ike!" Damon said.

I grinned at Damon, who understood I was making the best of the situation. He smiled back. Janelle finally grinned, and she took Damon's hand. I was getting up. They sensed that ACTION was coming. It sure was.

I moseyed outside to the front porch. I was going to speak to the newspeople.

I didn't bother to put on my shoes. Or shirt. I thought of the immortal words of Tarzan — *Aaeeyaayaayaa!*

"How are you folks this fine winter morning?" I asked, standing there in some baggy chinos. "Anybody need more coffee or sweet rolls?"

"Detective Cross, Katherine Rose and Thomas Dunne are blaming you for the mistakes made in Florida. Mr. Dunne released another statement last night." Someone gave me the morning news — free of charge, too. Yes, I was still the scapegoat of the week.

"I can understand the Dunnes' disappointment at the results in Florida," I said in an even tone. "Just drop your coffee containers anywhere on the lawn, like you've been doing. I'll pick up later."

"Then you agree you made a mistake," someone said. "Handing over the ransom money without seeing Maggie Rose first?"

"No. I don't agree at all. I had no choice down in Florida and South Carolina. The only choice I had was not to go with the contact man at all. See, when you're handcuffed, and the other guy has the gun, you're at a serious disadvantage. When your backup gets there late, that's another problem."

It was as if they didn't hear a word I'd said. "Detective, our sources say it was your decision to pay the ransom in the first place," someone suggested.

"Why do you come here and camp out on my lawn?" I said to that bullshit. "Why do you come here and scare my family? Disrupt this neighborhood? I don't care what you print about me, but I will tell you this: you don't have a clue as to what the hell is going on. You could be endangering the Dunne girl."

"Is Maggie Rose Dunne alive?" someone shouted.

I turned away and went back inside the house. That would teach them, right. Now they understood all about respecting people's privacy.

"Hey, Peanut Butter Man. Wuz up?"

A crowd of a different sort recognized me a little later that morning. Men and women were lined up three deep on 12th Street in front of St. Anthony's Church. They were hungry and cold, and none of them had Nikons or Leicas hung around their necks.

"Hey, Peanut Butter Man, I seen you on the TV. You a movie star now?" I heard someone call out.

"Hell, yeah. Can't you tell?"

For the past few years, Sampson and I have been working the soup kitchen at St. A's. We do it two or three days a week. I started there because of Maria, who had done some of her casework through the parish. I kept on after her death for the most selfish of reasons: the work made me feel good. Sampson welcomes folks for lunch at the front door. He takes the numbered ticket they're given when they get on line. He's also a deterrent to people acting up.

I'm the physical deterrent inside the dinner hall. I'm called the Peanut Butter Man. Jimmy Moore, who runs the kitchen, believes in the nutritional power of peanut butter. Along with a full meal that usually consists of rolls, two vegetables, a meat or fish stew, and dessert, anyone who wants it gets a cup of peanut butter. Every day.

"Hey, Peanut Butter Man. You got some good peanut butter for us today? You got Skippy or that Peter Pan shit?"

I grinned at familiar, hangdog faces in the crowd. My nose filled with the familiar smells of body odor, bad breath, stale liquor. "Don't know exactly what's on the menu today."

The regulars know Sampson and me. Most of them also know we're police. Some of them know I'm a shrink, since I do counseling outside the kitchen, in a prefab trailer that says, "The Lord helps them what helps themselves. Come on the hell in."

Jimmy Moore runs an efficient, beautiful place. He claims it's the largest soup kitchen in the East, and we'll do an average of over eleven hundred meals a day. The kitchen starts serving at ten-fifteen, and lunch is over by twelve-thirty. That means if you get there at exactly one minute past twelve-thirty, you go hungry that day. Discipline, be it ever so humble, is a big part of St. A's program.

No one is admitted drunk or too obviously high. You're expected to behave during your meal. You get about ten minutes to eat — other people are cold and hungry waiting on the long line outside. Everyone is treated with dignity and respect. No questions are asked of any of the guests. If you wait on line, you get fed. You're addressed as either Sir or Ms., and the mostly volunteer staff is trained to be upbeat. "Smile checks" are actually done on the new volunteers working the serving line or the dining room.

Around noon there was a major disturbance outside. I could hear Sampson shouting. Something was going down.

People on the soup line were shouting and cursing loudly. Then I heard Sampson call for help. "Alex! Come on out here!"

I ran outside and immediately saw what was going down. My fists were clenched into tight, hard anvils. The press had found us again. They had found me.

A couple of squirrelly news cameramen were filming folks on

the soup-kitchen line, and that's very unpopular — understandably. These people were trying to keep the last of their self-respect, and they didn't want to be seen on TV standing on a soup line for a handout.

Jimmy Moore is a tough, rude Irishman who used to work on the D.C. police force with us. He was already outside, and it was Jimmy, actually, who was making most of the noise.

"You cocksucking, motherfucking sons-of-bitches!" I suddenly found myself yelling. "You're not invited here! You're not fucking welcome! Leave these people alone. Let us serve our lunch in peace." ·

The photographers stopped shooting their pictures. They stared at me. So did Sampson. And Jimmy Moore. And most everybody on the soup line. The press didn't leave, but they backed away. Most of them crossed 12th Street, and I knew they would wait for me to come out.

We were serving people their lunch, I thought to myself as I watched the reporters and photographers waiting for me in a park across the street. Who the hell did the press serve these days other than the wealthy business conglomerates and families they all worked for?

Angry rumblings were starting up around us. "People are hungry and cold. Let's eat. People got a right to eat," someone yelled from the line.

I went back inside to my post. We started to serve lunch. I was the Peanut Butter Man.

CHAPTER 29

In THE CITY OF WILMINGTON, DELAWARE, Gary Murphy was shoveling away four inches of snow. It was Wednesday afternoon, the sixth of January. He was thinking about the kidnapping. He was trying to keep under control. He was thinking about the little rich bitch Maggie Rose Dunne, when a shiny blue Cadillac pulled up alongside his small colonial-style house on Central Avenue. Gary cursed under the breath streaming from his mouth.

Six-year-old Roni, Gary's daughter, was making snowballs, setting them out on the icy crust that topped the snow. She squealed when she saw her uncle Marty climbing out of his car.

"Who's that boot-i-ful little girl?" Uncle Marty called across the yard to Roni. "Is that a movie star? It is! I think so. Is that Ron-eee? I think it is!"

"Uncle Marty! Uncle Marty!" Roni screamed as she ran toward the car.

Every time Gary saw Marty Kasajian, he thought of the really putrid movie *Uncle Buck*. In *Uncle Buck*, John Candy was an unlikable, unwelcome, unlikely relative who kept showing up to torture a whitebread Midwestern family. It was an obnoxious flick. Uncle Marty Kasajian was rich and successful; and louder than John Candy; and he was here. Gary despised Missy's big brother for all of those reasons, but most of all because Marty was his boss.

Missy must have heard Marty's commotion. How could anyone on Central Avenue or nearby North Street miss it? She came out of the back door with a dish towel still wrapped around one hand.

"Look who's here!" Missy squealed. She and Roni sounded like identical piglets to Gary.

Quel fucking surprise, Gary felt like yelling. He held it all in — the way he held in all of his true feelings at home. He imagined beating Marty to death with his snow shovel, actually murdering Kasajian in front of Missy and Roni. Show them who the man of the house really was.

"The Divine Miss M!" Marty Kasajian continued to motor-mouth a mile a minute. He finally acknowledged Gary. "Hiya doin', Gar, old buddy. How 'bout those Eagles? Randall the C's on fire. Got your Super Bowl tickets lined up?"

"Sure thing, Marty. Two tickets on the fifty-yard line."

Gary Murphy tossed his aluminum shovel into a low bank of snow. He trudged over to where Missy and Roni were standing with Uncle Marty.

Then they all went inside the house together. Missy brought out expensive eggnog, and pieces of fresh apple-raisin pie with hunks of cheddar on the side. Marty's piece was bigger than all the others. He was The Man, right?

Marty handed an envelope to Missy. It was Missy's "allowance" from her big brother, which he wanted Gary to see. Really rub salt in the wounds that way.

"Mommy, Uncle Marty, and Daddy have to talk for a coupla minutes, sweetheart," Marty Kasajian said to Roni as soon as he finished his piece of pie. "I *think* I forgot something for you out in my car. I dunno. Could be on the backseat. You better go look."

"Put your coat on first, honey," Missy said to her daughter. "Don't catch cold."

Roni laughed-squeaked as she hugged her uncle. Then she hurried away.

"Now what did you get her?" Missy whispered conspiratorially to her brother. "You're too much."

Marty shrugged as if he couldn't remember. With everybody else, Missy was okay. She reminded Gary of his real mom. She even looked like his real mom. It was only with her brother, Gary had noticed, that she changed for the worse. She even started picking up Marty's obnoxious habits and speech cadences.

"Listen, kids." Marty hunched in closer to the two of them. "We have a little problema. Treatable, because we're catching it early, but something we have to deal with. Pretend like we're all adults, y'know."

Missy was instantly on guard. "What is it, Marty? What's the problem?"

Marty Kasajian looked genuinely concerned and uncomfortable now. Gary had seen him use this hangdog look a thousand times with his customers. Especially when he had to confront somebody on an overdue bill, or fire somebody in the office.

"Gar?" He looked at Gary for help with this. "You want to say something here?"

Gary shrugged. As if he didn't have clue one, right. *Fuck you, asshole,* he was thinking to himself. *You're on your own this time.*

Gary could feel a smile spreading, coming all the way up from his stomach. He didn't want it to show, but it finally broke across his lips. This was kind of a delectable moment. Getting caught had its own subtle rewards. Might be a lesson here; something to go to school on.

"Sorry. I don't think this is funny." Marty Kasajian shook his head and said, "I really don't, Gary."

"Well, I don't, either," Gary said in a funny voice. It was high-pitched and boyish. Not really his voice.

Missy gave him a strange look. "What is going on?" she demanded. "Will you two please let me in on this?"

Gary looked at his wife. He was really angry at her, too. She was part of the trap and she knew it.

"My sales record with Atlantic really stinks this quarter," Gary finally said, and shrugged. "Is that it, Marty?"

Marty frowned and looked down at his new Timberland boots. "Oh, it's more than that, Gar. Your sales record is almost nonexistent. What's worse, what's a lot worse, is that you have over thirty-three hundred dollars in advances outstanding. You're in the red, Gary. You're minus. I don't want to say much more, or I know I'll regret it. I honestly don't know how to address this situation. This is very difficult for me. Embarrassing. I'm so sorry, Missy. I hate this."

Missy covered her face with both hands, and she began to cry. She cried quietly at first, not wanting to cry. Then the sobs became louder. Tears came into her brother's eyes.

"That's what I didn't want. I'm sorry, Sis." Marty was the one to reach out and comfort her.

"I'm all right." Missy pulled away from her brother. She stared across the breakfast table at Gary. Her eyes seemed small and darker.

"Where have you been all of these months on the road, Gary? What have you been doing? Oh, Gary, Gary, sometimes I feel like I don't even know you. Say something to make this a little better. Please say something, Gary."

Gary thought about it carefully before he said a word. Then he said, "I love you so much, Missy. I love you and Roni more than I love my life itself."

Gary lied, and he knew it was a pretty good one. Extremely well told, well acted.

What he wanted to do was to laugh in their goddamn faces. What he wanted to do most was to kill all of them. That was the ticket to punch. *Boom. Boom. Boom.* Multiple-homicide time in Wilmington. Get his master plan rolling again.

Just then, Roni came running back inside the house. A new movie cassette was clutched in her hands, and she was smiling like a *Balloonhead.*

"Look what Uncle Marty brought me."

Gary held his head in both hands. He couldn't stop the screaming inside his brain. *I want to be somebody!*

CHAPTER 30

LIFE AND DEATH went on in Southeast. Sampson and I were back on the Sanders and Turner murder cases. Not surprisingly, little progress had been made in solving the six homicides. Not surprisingly, nobody cared.

On Sunday, January 10, I knew it was time for a day of rest, my first day off-duty since the kidnapping had occurred.

I started off the morning feeling a touch sorry for myself, hanging in bed until around ten and nursing a bad head, the result of carousing with Sampson the night before. Most everything running through my head was nonproductive.

I was missing Maria like the plague for one thing, remembering how fine it had been when the two of us slept in late on a Sunday morning. I was still angry about how I'd been made a scapegoat down South. More important, I felt like shit that none of us had been able to help Maggie Rose Dunne. Early in the case, I'd drawn a parallel between the Dunne girl and my own kids. Every time I thought of her, probably dead now, my stomach involuntarily clenched up — which is not a good thing, especially on the morning after a night on the town.

I was mulling over staying in the sack until about six. Lose a whole day. I deserved it. I didn't want to see Nana and hear her guff about where I was the night before. I didn't even want to see my kids that particular morning.

I kept going back to Maria. Once upon a time, in another lifetime, she and I, and usually the kids, used to spend all of our Sundays together. Sometimes, we'd hang out in bed until noon, then we'd get dressed up and maybe go splurge for brunch. There wasn't much that Maria and I didn't do together. Every night I came home from work as early as I could manage. Maria did the same. There was nothing either one of us wanted to do more. She had gotten me over my wounds after I wasn't widely accepted in private practice as a psychologist. She had nursed me back to some kind of balance after a couple of years of too much cutting up and catting around with Sampson and a few other single friends, including the fast crowd that played basketball with the Washington Bullets.

Maria pulled me back to some kind of sanity, and I treasured her for it. Maybe it would have gone on like that forever. Or maybe we would have split up by now. Who knows for certain? We never got the chance to find out.

One night she was late coming home from her social-work job. I finally got the call, and rushed to Misericordia Hospital. Maria had been shot. She was in very bad shape was all they would tell me over the phone.

I arrived there a little past eight. A friend, a patrolman I knew, sat me down and told me that Maria was dead by the time they got her to the hospital. It had been a ride-by shooting outside the projects. No one knew why, or who could have done the shooting. We never got to say good-bye. There was no preparation, no warning at all, no explanation.

The pain inside was like a steel column that extended from the center of my chest all the way up into my forehead. I thought about Maria constantly, day and night. After three years, I was finally beginning to forget. I was learning how.

I was lying in bed, in a peaceful and resigned state, when Damon came in to the room as if his hair were on fire.

"Hey, Daddy. Hey, Daddy, you awake?"

"What's wrong?" I asked, absolutely hating the sound of those words lately. "You look like you just saw Vanilla Ice on our front porch."

"Somebody to see you, Daddy," Damon announced with breathless excitement. "Somebody's here!"

"'The Count' from *Sesame Street*?" I asked. "*Who's here?* Be a touch more specific. Not another news reporter? If it's a news reporter —"

"She says her name Jezme. It's a la-dy, Daddy."

I believe I sat up in bed, but I didn't like the view from there too much, and lay down quickly again. "Tell her I'll be right down. *Do not* volunteer that I'm in bed. Tell her I'll be down directly." Damon left the bedroom, and I wondered how I was going to deliver on the promise I'd just made.

Janelle and Damon and Jezzie Flanagan were still standing in the foyer of our house when I made it downstairs. Janelle looked a little uncomfortable, but she was getting better at her job of answering our front door. Janelle used to be painfully shy with all strangers. To help her with this, Nana and I have gently encouraged her and Damon to answer the front door during the daytime hours.

It had to be something important to have Jezzie Flanagan come to the house. I knew that half the FBI was searching for the pilot who'd collected the ransom. So far, there had been nothing on any front. Whatever had been solved about the case, I had solved myself.

Jezzie Flanagan was dressed in loose black trousers, with a simple white blouse, and scuffed tennis sneakers. I remembered her casual look from Miami. It almost made me forget what a big deal she was over at the Secret Service.

"Something's happened," I said, wincing. Pain shot across my skull, then down across my face. The sound of my own voice was too much to bear.

"No, Alex. We haven't heard any more about Maggie Rose," she said. "A few more sightings. That's all."

"Sightings" were what the Federal Bureau called eyewitness accounts from people "claiming" to have seen Maggie Rose or Gary Soneji. So far, the sightings ranged from an empty lot a few streets from Washington Day School, to California, to the children's unit at Bellevue Hospital in New York City, to South Africa, not to mention a space-probe landing near Sedona, Arizona. No day went by without more sightings being reported somewhere. Big country, lot of kooks on the loose.

"I didn't mean to intrude on you guys," she finally said and smiled. "It's just that I've been feeling bad about what's happened, Alex. The stories about you are crap. They're also untrue. I wanted to tell you how I felt. So here I am."

"Well, thanks for saying it," I said to Jezzie. It was one of the only nice things that had happened to me in the past week. It touched me in an odd way.

"You did everything you could in Florida. I'm not just saying that to make you feel better."

I tried to focus my eyes. Things were still a bit blurry. "I wouldn't call it one of my better work experiences. On the other hand, I didn't think I deserved front-page coverage for my performance."

"You didn't. Somebody nailed you. Somebody set you up with the press. It's a lot of bull."

"It's bullshit," Damon blurted. "Right, Big Daddy?"

"This is Jezzie," I said to the kids. "We work together sometimes." The kids were getting used to Jezzie, but they were still a little shy. Jannie was trying to hide behind her brother. Damon had both hands stuffed in his back pockets, just like his dad.

Jezzie went down on her haunches; she got down to their size. She shook hands with Damon, then with Janelle. It was a good instinctive move on her part.

"Your daddy is the best policeman I ever saw," she told Damon.

"I know that." He accepted the compliment graciously.

"I'm Janelle." Janelle surprised me by offering her name to Jezzie.

I could tell she wanted a hug. Janelle loves hugs more than anyone ever put on this earth. That's where she got one of her many nicknames, "Velcro."

Jezzie sensed it, too. She reached out and hugged Jannie. It was a neat little scene to watch. Damon immediately decided to join in. It was the thing to do. It was as if their long-lost best friend had suddenly returned from the wars.

After a minute or so, Jezzie stood up again. At that moment it struck me that she was a real nice person, and that I hadn't met too many of those during the investigation. Her house visit was thoughtful, but also a little brave. Southeast is not a great neighborhood for white women to travel in, even one who was probably carrying a gun.

"Well, I just stopped by for a few hugs." She winked to me. "Actually, I have a case not too far from here. Now I'm off to be a workaholic again."

"How about some hot coffee?" I asked her. I thought I could manage the coffee. Nana probably had some in the kitchen that was only five or six hours old.

She squinted a look at me and she started to smile again.

"Two nice kids, nice Sunday morning at home with them. You're not such a tough guy after all."

"No, I'm a tough guy, too," I said. "I just happen to be a tough guy who finds his way home by Sunday morning."

"Okay, Alex." She kept her smile turned on. "Just don't let this newspaper nonsense get you down. Nobody believes the funny pages, anyway. I've got to go. I'll take a rain check on the coffee."

Jezzie Flanagan opened the front door and started to leave. She waved to the kids as the door was closing behind her.

"So long, Big Daddy," she said to me and grinned.

CHAPTER 31

AFTER JEZZIE FLANAGAN had finished her business in Southeast, she drove out to the farm where Gary Soneji had buried the two children. She had been there twice before, but a lot of things still bothered her about the farm in Maryland. She was obsessive as hell, anyway. She figured that nobody wanted to catch Soneji any more than she did.

Jezzie ignored the *crime scene* signage and sped down the rutted dirt road to a cluster of buildings in disrepair. She distinctly remembered everything about the place. There was the main farmhouse, a garage for machinery, and the barn where the kids had been kept.

Why this place? she asked herself. *Why here, Soneji?* What should it tell her about who he really is?

Jezzie Flanagan had been a whiz-kid investigator since the day she'd first entered the Secret Service. She'd come there with an honors law degree from the University of Virginia, and Treasury had tried to steer her toward the FBI, where nearly half the agents had law degrees. But Jezzie had surveyed the situation and chosen the Service, anyway, where the law degree would make her stand out more. She'd worked eighty- and hundred-hour weeks from the beginning, right up to the present. She'd been a shooting star for one reason: she was smarter *and* tougher than any of the men she worked with, or the ones she worked for. She was more driven. But Jezzie had known from the beginning that, if she ever made a big mistake, her starship would crash. She'd known it. There was only one solution. She had to find Gary Soneji, somehow. She had to be the one.

She walked the farmhouse grounds until darkness fell. Then she walked them again with a flashlight. Jezzie scribbled down notes, trying to find some missing connection. Maybe it did have something to do with the old Lindbergh case, the so-called crime of the century from the 1930s.

Son of Lindbergh?

The Lindbergh place in Hopewell, New Jersey, had been a farmhouse, too.

Baby Lindbergh had been buried not far from the kidnap site.

Bruno Hauptmann, the Lindbergh kidnapper, had been from New York City. Could the kidnapper in Washington be some kind of distant relative? Could he be from somewhere near Hopewell? Maybe Princeton? How could nothing have turned up on Soneji so far?

Before she left the farm, Jezzie sat in her town car. She turned on the engine, the heat, and just sat there. Obsessing. Lost in her thoughts.

Where was Gary Soneji? How had he disappeared? Nobody can just disappear nowadays. No one is that smart.

Then she thought about Maggie Rose Dunne and "Shrimpie" Goldberg, and tears began to roll down her cheeks. She couldn't stop sobbing. That was the real reason she'd come out to the farmhouse, she knew. Jezzie Flanagan had to let herself cry.

CHAPTER 32

MAGGIE ROSE was in complete darkness.

She didn't know how long she had been there. A long, long time, though. She couldn't remember when she'd eaten last. Or when she'd seen or talked to anybody, except the voices inside her head.

She wished somebody would come right now. She held that thought in her head — for hours.

She even wished the old woman would come back and scream at her. She'd begun to wonder why she was being punished; what she'd done that was so wrong. Had she been bad, and deserved all this to happen to her? She was starting to think that she must have been a bad person for all these terrible things to be happening.

She couldn't cry again. Not even if she wanted to. She couldn't cry anymore.

A lot of the time, she thought she must be dead. Maggie Rose almost didn't feel things now. Then she would pinch herself really hard. Even bite herself. One time she bit her finger until it bled. She tasted her own warm blood and it was weirdly wonderful. Her time in the dark seemed to go on forever. The darkness was a tiny room like a closet. She —

Suddenly, Maggie Rose heard voices outside. She couldn't hear well enough to understand what was being said, but there were definitely voices. The old woman? Must be. Maggie Rose wanted to call out, but she was frightened of the old woman. Her awful screaming, her threats, her scratchy voice that was worse than horror movies her mother didn't even like her to watch. Worse than Freddy Krueger by miles.

The voices stopped. She couldn't hear anything, not even when she pressed her ear against the closet door. They had gone away. They were leaving her in there forever.

She tried to cry, but no tears would come.

Then Maggie Rose started to scream. The door suddenly burst open and she was blinded by the most beautiful light.

CHAPTER 33

ON THE NIGHT OF JANUARY 11, Gary Murphy was cozy and safe in his basement. Nobody knew that he was down there, but if snoopy Missy happened to open the basement door, he'd just flick on the lamp at his workbench. He was thinking everything through. One more time for good measure.

He was becoming nicely obsessed with murdering Missy and Roni, but he thought that he wouldn't do it just yet. Still, the fantasy was rich. To murder your own family had a certain homespun style to it. It wasn't very imaginative, but the effect would be neat: the icy chill racing through the serene, dippity-doo suburban community. All the other families doing the most ironic thing — locking their doors, *locking themselves in together*.

Around midnight he realized that his little family had gone to bed without him. No one had even bothered to call down to him. They didn't care. A hollow roar was starting inside his head. He needed about a half-dozen Nuprins to stop the white noise for a while.

Maybe he would torch the perfect little house on Central Avenue. Torching houses was good for the soul. He'd done it before; he'd do it again. God, his whole skull ached as if somebody'd been hitting it with a ball peen hammer. Was something physically the matter with him? Was it possible he was going mad this time?

He tried to think about the Lone Eagle — Charles Lindbergh. That didn't work, either. In his mind, he revisited the farmhouse in Hopewell Junction. No good. That mind-trip was getting old, too.

He was world famous himself, for Chrissakes. *He was famous now.* Everybody in the world knew about him. He was a media star all over Planet Dearth.

He finally left the cellar, and then the house in Wilmington. It was just past five-thirty in the morning. As he walked outside to the car, he felt like an animal, suddenly on the loose.

He drove back to D.C. There was more work to do there. He didn't want his public to be disappointed, did he?

He thought he had a treat for everyone now. *Don't get comfortable with me!*

Around eleven that morning, Tuesday, Gary Murphy lightly tapped the front doorbell of a well-kept brick townhouse on the edge of Capitol Hill. *Bing-bong* went a polite door chime inside.

The sheer danger of the situation, of his being in Washington again, gave him a nice chill. This was a lot better than being in hiding. He felt alive again, he could breathe, he had his own space.

Vivian Kim kept the lock chain on, but she opened the door about a foot. She'd seen the familiar uniform of Washington's PEPCO public utilities service through the peephole.

Pretty lady, Gary remembered from the Washington Day School. Long black braids. Cute little upturned nose. She clearly didn't recognize him as a blond. No mustache. Little flesh off the cheeks and chin.

"Yes? What is it? Can I help you?" she asked the man standing on her porch. Inside the house, jazzy music was playing. Thelonious.

"I hope it's the other way around." He smiled pleasantly. "Somebody called about an overcharge on the electric."

Vivian Kim frowned and shook her head. She had a tiny map of Korea hanging from rawhide around her neck. "I didn't call anybody. I know I didn't call PEPCO."

"Well, somebody called us, miss."

"Come back some other time," Vivian Kim told him. "Maybe my boyfriend called. You'll have to come back. I'm sorry."

Gary shrugged his shoulders. This was so delicious. He didn't want it to end. "I guess. You can call us again if you like," he said. "Get on the schedule again. It's an overcharge, though. You paid too much."

"Okay. I hear you. I understand."

Vivian Kim slowly stripped away the chain and opened the door. Gary stepped into the apartment. He pulled a long hunting knife from under his work jacket. He pointed it at the teacher's face. "Don't scream. *Do not scream*, Vivian."

"How do you know my name?" she asked. "Who are you?"

"Don't raise your voice, Vivian. There's no reason to be afraid. . . . I've done this before. I'm just your garden-variety robber."

"What do you want?" The teacher had begun to tremble.

Gary thought for a second before he answered her scared-rabbit question. "I want to send out another message over the TV, I guess. I want the fame I so richly deserve," he finally said. "I want to be the scariest man in America. That's why I work in the capital. I'm *Gary*. Don't you remember me, Viv?"

CHAPTER 34

SAMPSON AND I raced down C Street in the heart of Capitol Hill. I could hear the breath inside my nose as I ran. My arms and legs felt disjointed.

Squad cars from the department and EMS ambulances had the street completely blocked off. We'd had to park on F Street and sprint the last couple of blocks. WJLA-TV was already there. So was CNN. Sirens screamed everywhere.

I spotted a clique of reporters up ahead. They saw Sampson and me coming. We're about as hard to miss as the Harlem Globetrotters in Tokyo.

"Detective Cross? Dr. Cross?" the reporters called out, trying to slow us down.

"No comment," I waved them off. "From either of us. Get the fuck out of the way."

Inside Vivian Kim's apartment, Sampson and I passed all the familiar faces — techies, forensics, the DOA gang in their ghoulish element.

"I don't want to do this anymore," Sampson said. "Whole world's flowing down the piss-tubes. It's too much, even for me."

"We burn out," I mumbled to him, "we burn out together."

Sampson grabbed my hand and held it. That told me he was as fucked up about this as he got. We went inside the first bedroom on the right side of the hallway. I tried to be still inside. I couldn't do it.

Vivian Kim's bedroom was beautifully laid out. Lots of exquisite, black-and-white family photographs and art posters covered most of the wall space. An antique violin was hung on one wall. I didn't want to look at the reason I was there. Finally, I had to.

Vivian Kim was pinned to the bed with a long hunting knife. It was driven through her stomach. *Both her breasts had been removed. Her pubic hair had been shaved.* Her eyes had rolled back in her head, as if she had seen something unfathomable during her last moments.

I let my eyes wander around the bedroom. I couldn't look at Vivian Kim's mutilated body. I stared at a splash of bright color on the floor. I caught my breath. Nobody had said anything about it on the way up. Nobody had noticed the most important clue. Fortunately, nobody had moved the evidence.

"Look at this here." I showed Sampson.

Maggie Rose Dunne's second sneaker was lying on Vivian Kim's bedroom floor. The killer was leaving what the pathologists call "artistic touches." He'd left an overt message this time — the signature of signatures. I was shaking as I bent down over the little girl's sneaker. Here was the most sadistic humor at work. The pink sneaker, in shocking contrast to the bloody crime scene.

Gary Soneji had been in the bedroom. Soneji was the project killer, too. He was The Thing. And he was back in town.

CHAPTER 35

GARY SONEJI was still in Washington, indeed. He was sending out special-delivery messages to his fans. There was a difference now. He was baiting us, too. Sampson and I got a dispensation from The Jefe: we could work on the kidnapping as long as it was linked to the other murder investigations. It definitely was.

"This is our day off, so we must be having fun," Sampson said to me as we walked the streets of Southeast. It was the thirteenth of January. Bitter cold. Folks had fires blazing in the garbage cans on almost every street corner. One of the brothers had FUC U 2 razor-cut on the back of his head. My sentiments exactly.

"Mayor Monroe doesn't call anymore. Doesn't write," I said to Sampson. I watched my breath launch clouds in the freezing air.

"See, there is a silver lining," he said into the wind. "He'll come around when we catch The Thing. He'll be there to take all the bows for us."

We walked along, goofing on the situation and on each other. Sampson rapped lyrics from pop songs, something he does a lot.

That morning, it was "Now That We've Found Love." Heavy D & The Boyz. "Rev me up, rev me up, you're my little buttercup," Sampson kept saying, as if the lyrics made sense out of everything.

We were canvassing Vivian Kim's neighborhood, which was on the edge of Southeast. Canvassing a neighborhood is mind-numbing work, even for the young and uninitiated. "Did you see anyone or anything unusual yesterday?" we asked anybody dumb enough to open their doors for us. "Did you notice any strangers, strange cars, anything that sticks out in your mind? Let us decide whether it's important."

As usual, nobody had seen a thing. *Nada de nada.* Nobody was happy to see us, either, especially as we moved into Southeast on our canvass.

To top it off, the temperature was about three degrees with the windchill. It was sleeting. The streets and sidewalks were covered with icy slush. A couple of times we joined the street people warming themselves over their garbage-can fires.

"You motherfuckin' cops always cold, even in the summer," one of the young fucks said to us. Both Sampson and I laughed.

We finally trudged back toward our car around six. We were beaten up. We'd blown a long day. Nothing good had come of it. Gary Soneji had disappeared into thin air again. I felt as if I were in a horror movie.

"Want to go out a few extra blocks?" I asked Sampson. I was feeling desperate enough to try the slot machines in Atlantic City. Soneji was playing with us. Maybe he was watching us. Maybe the fucker *was* invisible.

Sampson shook his head. "*No mas,* sugar. I want to drink at least a case of brew. Then I just might do some serious drinking."

He wiped slush off his sunglasses, then put them on again. It's weird how well I know his every move. He's been dusting his glasses like that since he was twelve. Through rain or sleet or snow.

"Let's do the extra blocks," I said. "For Ms. Vivian. Least we can do."

"I knew you were going to say that."

We filed into the apartment of a Mrs. Quillie McBride at around six-twenty that night. Quillie and her friend Mrs. Scott were seated at the kitchen table. Mrs. Scott had something to tell us that she thought might help. We were there to listen to anything she had to say.

If you ever go through D.C.'s Southeast, or the north section of Philadelphia, or Harlem in New York, on a Sunday morning, you'll still see ladies like Mrs. McBride and her friend Willie Mae Randall Scott. These ladies wear blousy shirts and faded gabardine skirts. Their usual accoutrements include feathered hats and thick-heeled, lace-up shoes that bunch their feet like sausage links. They are coming or going from various churches. In the case of Willie Mae, who is a Jehovah's Witness, they distribute the *Watchtower* magazine.

"I believe I can he'p y'all," Mrs. Scott said to us in a soft, sincere voice. She was probably eighty years old, but very focused and clear in her delivery.

"We'd appreciate that," I said. The four of us sat around the kitchen table. A plate of oatmeal cookies had been set out for the occasion of anyone's visit. A triptych with photos of the two murdered Kennedys and Martin Luther King was prominent on a kitchen wall.

"I heard about the murder of the teacher," Mrs. Scott said for Sampson's and my benefit, "and, well, I saw a man driving around the neighborhood a month or so before the Turner murders. He was a white man. I am fortunate to still have a very good memory. I try to keep it that way by concentrating on whatever passes before these eyes. Ten years from today, I will be able to recall this interview on a moment-to-moment basis, detectives."

Her friend Mrs. McBride had pulled her chair beside Mrs. Scott. She didn't speak at first, though she did take Mrs. Scott's bulging arm in her hand.

"It's true. She will," Quillie McBride said.

"One week before the Turner murders, the same white man came through the neighborhood again," Mrs. Scott continued. "This second time, he was going door to door. He was a *salesman*."

Sampson and I looked at each other. "What kind of salesman?" Sampson asked her.

Mrs. Scott allowed her eyes to drift over Sampson's face before she answered the question. I figured she was concentrating, making sure she remembered everything about him. "He was selling heating systems for the winter. I went over by his car and looked inside. A sales book of some sort was on the front seat. His company is called Atlantic Heating, out of Wilmington, Delaware."

Mrs. Scott looked from face to face, either to make sure that she was being clear, or that we were getting all of what she had just said.

"Yesterday, I saw the same car drive through the neighborhood. I saw the car the morning the woman on C Street was killed. I said to my friend here, 'This can't all be a coincidence, can it?' Now, I don't know if he's the one you're looking for, but I think you should talk to him."

Sampson looked at me. Then the two of us did a rare thing of late. We broke into smiles. Even the ladies decided to join in. We had something. We had a break, finally, the first of the case.

"We're going to talk to the traveling salesman," I said to Mrs. Scott and Quillie McBride. "We're going to Wilmington, Delaware."

CHAPTER 36

GARY MURPHY got home at a little past five on the following afternoon, January 14. He'd gone into the office, just outside Wilmington. Only a few people had been there, and he'd planned to get some useless paperwork done. He had to make things look good for a little while longer.

He'd ended up thinking about larger subjects. The master plan. Gary just couldn't get serious about the paper blizzard of bills and invoices littering his desk. He kept picking up crumpled customer bills, glancing at names, amounts, addresses.

Who in their right fucking mind could care about all the invoices? he was thinking to himself. It was all so brutally small-time, so dumb and petty. Which was why the job, and Delaware, were such a good hiding spot for him.

So he accomplished absolutely nothing at the office, except blowing off a few hours. At least he'd picked up a present for Roni on the way home. He bought Roni a pink bike with training wheels and streamers. He added a Barbie Dream House. Her birthday party was set for six o'clock.

Missy met him at the front door with a hug and a kiss. Positive reinforcement was her strong suit. The party gave her something to think about. She'd been off his back for days.

"Great day, honey. I kid you not. Three home visits set up for next week. Count them, three," Gary told her. What the hell. He could be charming when he wanted to be. *Mr. Chips goes to Delaware.*

He followed Missy into the dining room, where she was setting out brightly colored plastic and paper for the party of parties. Missy had already hung a painted sheet on one wall — the kind they held up for football games at U.D., University Dumb. This one said: GO RONI — SEVEN OR BUST!

"This is pure genius, hon. You can make something out of nothing. This all looks fantastic," Gary said. "Things are sure looking up now."

Actually, he was starting to get a little depressed. He felt out of it and wanted to take a nap. The idea of Roni's birthday party seemed exhausting suddenly. There sure hadn't been any parties when he was a kid.

The neighbors started to arrive right at six o'clock. That was good, he thought. It meant the kids really wanted to come. They liked Roni. He could see it on all of their little Balloonhead faces.

Several of the parents stayed for the party. They were friends of his and Missy's. He dutifully played bartender while Missy started the kids on an assortment of games: Duck-Duck-Goose, Musical Chairs, Pin the Tail.

Everybody was having a good time. He looked at Roni, and she was like a spinning top.

Gary had a recurring fantasy — he murdered everyone attending a child's birthday party. A birthday party — or maybe a children's Easter egg hunt. That made him feel a little better.

CHAPTER 37

THE HOUSE was two-story, white-painted brick, on a wooded half-lot. It was already surrounded by cars: station wagons, Jeeps, the family vehicles of suburbia.

"This *can't* be his house," Sampson said as we parked on a side street. "The Thing doesn't live here. Jimmy Stewart does."

We had found Gary Soneji — but it didn't feel right. The monster's house was a perfect suburban beauty, a gingerbread house on a well-maintained street in Wilmington, Delaware. It was a little less than twenty-four hours since we'd spoken to Mrs. Scott in D.C. In that time, we had tracked down Atlantic Heating in Wilmington. We had gathered the original Hostage Rescue Team together.

Lights were shining through most of the house windows. A Domino's delivery truck arrived at almost the same time that we did. A lanky blond kid ran to the door with four big pizza boxes in his outstretched arms. The delivery kid got paid, then the truck was gone as quickly as it had come.

The fact that it was a nice house in a nice neighborhood made me nervous, even more leery about the next few minutes. Soneji had always been two steps ahead of us — *somehow*.

"Let's move," I said to Special Agent Scorse. "This is it, folks. The front gates of hell."

Nine of us rushed the house — Scorse, Reilly, Craig, and two others from the Bureau, Sampson, myself, Jeb Klepner, Jezzie Flanagan. We were heavily armed and wore bulletproof vests. We wanted to end this. Right here. Right now.

I entered through the kitchen. Scorse and I came in together. Sampson was a step behind. He didn't look like a neighborhood dad arriving late for the party, either.

"Who are you men? What's going on?" a woman at the kitchen counter screamed as we burst inside.

"Where is Gary Murphy?" I asked in a loud voice. I flashed my I.D. at the same time. "I'm Alex Cross. Police. We're here in connection with the Maggie Rose Dunne kidnapping."

"Gary's in the dining room," a second woman, standing over a blender, said in a trembling voice. "Through here." She pointed.

We ran down the connecting hallway. Family pictures were up on the walls. A pile of unopened presents lay on the floor. We had our revolvers drawn.

It was a terrifying moment. The children we saw were afraid. So were their mothers and fathers. There were so many innocent people here — *just like Disney World*, I was thinking. *Just like the Washington Day School*.

Gary Soneji wasn't anywhere in the dining room. Just more police, kids in birthday hats, pets, mothers and dads with their mouths open in disbelief.

"I think Gary went upstairs," one of the fathers finally said. "What's going on here? What the hell is going on?"

Craig and Reilly were already crashing back down the stairs into the front hallway.

"Not up there," Reilly yelled.

One of the kids said, "I think Mr. Murphy went down to the cellar. What'd he do?"

We ran back to the kitchen and down to the cellar — Scorse, Reilly, and myself. Sampson went back upstairs to double-check.

No one was anywhere in the two small cellar rooms. There was a storm door to the outside. It was closed and locked from the outside.

Sampson came down a moment later, two stairs at a clip. "I checked over the whole upstairs. He's not there!"

Gary Soneji had disappeared again.

CHAPTER 38

*O*KAY, *let's dial it up a notch! Let's do some serious rock and roll. Let's play for keeps now,* Gary thought as he ran for it.

He'd had escape plans in mind since he'd been fifteen or sixteen years old. He'd known the so-called authorities would come for him someday, somehow, somewhere. He'd *seen* it all in his mind, in his elaborate daydreams. The only question was when. And maybe, for what? For which of his crimes?

Then they were *there* on Central Avenue in Wilmington! The end of the celebrated manhunt. Or was it the beginning?

Gary was like a programmed machine from the moment he spotted the police. He almost couldn't believe that what he'd fantasized so many times was actually happening. They were there, though. Special dreams do come true. If you're young at heart.

He had calmly paid the pizza delivery boy. Then he went down the stairs and out through the cellar. He used a special half-hidden door and went into the garage. He relocked the door from the outside. Another side door led to a tiny alley into the Dwyers' yard. He relocked that door, also. Jimmy Dwyer's snow boots were sitting on the porch steps. Snow was on the ground. He took his neighbor's boots.

He paused between his house and the Dwyers'. He thought about letting them catch him then and there — getting caught — just like Bruno Hauptmann in the Lindbergh case. He loved that idea. But not yet. Not here.

Then he was running away, down a tight row of alleys between the houses. Nobody but kids used the little alleyway, which was overgrown with high weeds and littered with soda cans.

He felt as if he had tunnel vision. Must have something to do with the fear he felt in every inch of his body. Gary *was* afraid. He had to admit that he was. Face the adrenaline facts, pal.

He ran through backyard after backyard, down good old Central Avenue. Then into the deep woods of Downing Park. He didn't see a soul on the way.

Only when he glanced back once could he see them moving toward his house. Saw the big black Kaffirs Cross and Sampson. The vastly overrated Manhunt. The Federal Bureau in all its glory.

He was sprinting now, full out toward the Metro train station, which was four blocks from the house. This was his link to Philly, Washington, New York, the outside world.

He must have made it in ten flat — something like that. He kept himself in good shape. Powerful legs and arms, a washboard-flat stomach.

An old VW was parked at the station. It was always parked there — the trusty Bug from his unholy youth. The "scene of past crimes," to put it mildly. Driven just enough to keep the battery alive. It was time for more fun, more games. The Son of Lindbergh was on the move again.

CHAPTER 39

SAMPSON AND I were still at the Murphy house at well past eleven o'clock. The press was gathered behind bright yellow ropes outside. So were a couple of hundred close friends and neighbors from around the community of Wilmington. The town had never had a bigger night.

Another massive manhunt had already been set in motion along the Eastern Seaboard, but also west into Pennsylvania and Ohio. It seemed impossible that Gary Soneji/Murphy could get away a second time. We didn't believe he could have planned this escape the way he'd planned the one out of Washington.

One of the kids at the party had spotted a local police cruiser doing a ride-by minutes before we arrived in the neighborhood. The boy had innocently mentioned the police car to Mr. Murphy. He had escaped through sheer luck! We'd missed catching him by a few minutes at most.

Sampson and I questioned Missy Murphy for more than an hour. We were finally going to learn something about the real Soneji/Murphy.

Missy Murphy would have fit in with the mothers of the children at Washington Day School. She wore her blond hair in a no-frills flip. She had on a navy skirt, white blouse, boaters. She was a few pounds overweight, but pretty.

"None of you seem to believe this, but I know Gary. I know who he is," she told us. "He is not a kidnapper."

She chain-smoked Marlboro Lights as she spoke. That was the only gesture that betrayed anxiety and pain. We talked with Mrs. Murphy in the kitchen. It was orderly and neat, even on party day. I noted Betty Crocker cookbooks stacked beside Silver Palate cookbooks and a copy of *Meditations for Women Who Do Too Much*. A snapshot of Gary Soneji/Murphy in a bathing suit was stuck up on the fridge. He looked like the all-American father.

"Gary is not a violent person. He can't even bear to discipline Roni," Missy Murphy was saying to us.

That interested me. It fit a pattern of bell curves I had been studying for years: *reports on sociopaths and their children.* Sociopaths often had difficulty disciplining their children.

"Has he told you *why* he has difficulty disciplining your daughter?" I asked her.

"Gary didn't have a happy childhood himself. He wants only the best for Roni. He knows that he's compensating. He's a very bright man. He could easily have his Ph.D. in math."

"Did Gary grow up right here in Wilmington?" Sampson asked Missy. He was soft spoken and down to earth with the woman.

"No, he grew up in Princeton, New Jersey. Gary lived there until he was nineteen."

Sampson jotted a note, then he glanced my way. Princeton was near Hopewell, where the Lindbergh kidnapping had taken place in the 1930s. *The Son of Lindbergh*, Soneji had signed the ransom notes. We still didn't know why.

"His family is still in Princeton?" I asked Mrs. Murphy. "Can we contact them there?"

"There's no family left now. There was a fire while Gary was at school. Gary's stepmom and dad, his stepbrother and step-sister all died in the tragedy."

I wanted to probe deeply into everything Missy Murphy was saying. I resisted for the moment. A fire in the house of a disturbed young man, though? Another family dead; another family destroyed. Was that Gary Soneji/Murphy's real target? Families? If so, what about Vivian Kim? Did he kill her just to show off?

"Did you know any of the family?" I asked Missy.

"No. They died before Gary and I got together. The two of us met our senior year in college. I was at Delaware."

"What did your husband tell you about his years around Princeton?"

"Not very much. He keeps a lot inside. The Murphys lived several miles from town, I know. Their closest neighbor was two or three miles. Gary didn't have friends until he went to school. Even then he was often the odd man out. He can be very shy."

"What about the brother and sister you mentioned?" Sampson asked.

"Actually, they were his stepbrother and stepsister. That was part of Gary's problem. He wasn't close to them."

"Did he ever mention the Lindbergh kidnapping? Does he have any books on Lindbergh?" Sampson continued. His technique is to go for the jugular in Q & A.

Missy Murphy shook her head back and forth. "No. Not that I know of. There's a room filled with his books down in the cellar. You can look."

"Oh, we will," Sampson said to her.

This was rich material, and I was relieved to hear it. Before this, there had been nothing, or very little, for us to go on.

"Is his real mother alive?" I asked her.

"I don't know. Gary just won't talk about her. He won't discuss her at all."

"What about the stepmother?"

"Gary didn't like his stepmother. Apparently she was very attached to her own children. He called her 'The Whore of Babylon.' I believe she was originally from West Babylon in New York. I think it's out on Long Island somewhere."

After months without any information, I couldn't get the questions out fast enough. Everything I'd heard so far was tracking. An important question loomed: Had Gary Soneji/Murphy been telling the truth to his wife? Was he *capable* of telling the truth to another person?

"Mrs. Murphy, do you have any idea where he might have gone?" I asked now.

"Something really frightened Gary," she said. "I think maybe it relates to his job somehow. And to my brother, who's his employer. I can't imagine that he went home to New Jersey, but maybe he did. Maybe Gary went back home. He is impulsive."

One of the FBI agents, Marcus Connor, peeked into the kitchen where we were talking. "Can I see both of you for a minute? . . . I'm sorry, this will just be one minute," he said to Mrs. Murphy.

Connor escorted us down into the basement of the house. Gerry Scorse, Reilly, and Kyle Craig from the FBI were already down there, waiting.

Scorse held up a pair of Fido Dido socklets. I recognized them from descriptions of what Maggie Rose Dunne had been wearing the day of the kidnapping. Also from visits to the little girl's room, where I'd seen her collection of clothes and trinkets.

"So, what do you think, Alex?" Scorse asked me. I had noticed that whenever things got really weird, he asked for my opinion.

"Exactly what I said about the sneaker in Washington. He left it for us. He's playing a game now. He wants us to play with him."

CHAPTER 40

THE OLD DU PONT HOTEL in downtown Wilmington was a convenient place to get some sleep. It had a nice quiet bar, and Sampson and I planned on doing some quiet drinking there. We didn't think we'd have company, but we were surprised when Jezzie Flanagan, Klepner, and some of the FBI agents joined us for nightcaps.

We were tired and frustrated after the near-miss with Gary Soneji/Murphy. We drank a lot of hard liquor in a short time. Actually, we got along well. "The team." We got loud, played liar's poker, raised some hell in the tony Delaware Room that night. Sampson talked to Jezzie Flanagan for a while. He thought she was a good cop, too.

The drinking finally tailed down, and we wandered off to find our rooms, which were scattered throughout the spacious Du Pont.

Jeb Klepner, Jezzie, and I climbed the thickly carpeted stairs to our rooms on two and three. The Du Pont was a mausoleum at quarter to three in the morning. There wasn't any traffic outside on the main drag through Wilmington.

Klepner's room was on the second floor. "I'm going to go watch some soft-core pornography," he said as he split off from us. "That usually helps me get right to sleep."

"Sweet dreams," Jezzie said. "Lobby at seven."

Klepner groaned as he trudged down the hallway to his room. Jezzie and I climbed the winding flight to the next floor. It was so quiet you could hear the stoplight outside, making clicking noises as it changed from green to yellow to red.

"I'm still wound tight," I said to her. "I can see Soneji/Murphy. Two faces. They're both very distinct in my head."

"I'm wired, too. It's my nature. What would you do if you were home instead of here?" Jezzie asked.

"I'd probably go play the piano out on our porch. Wake the neighborhood with a little blues."

Jezzie laughed out loud. "We could go back down to the Delaware Room. There was an old upright in there. Probably belonged to one of the Du Ponts. You play, I'll have one more drink."

"That bartender left about ten seconds after we did. He's home in his bed already."

We'd reached the Du Pont's third floor. There was a gentle bend in the hallway. Ornate signs on the wall listed room numbers and their direction. A few guests had their shoes out to be shined overnight.

"I'm three eleven." Jezzie pulled a white card-key from the pocket of her jacket.

"I'm in three thirty-four. Time to call it a night. Start fresh in the morning."

Jezzie smiled and she looked into my eyes. For the first time that I could remember, neither of us had anything to say.

I took her into my arms, and held her gently. We kissed in the hallway. I hadn't kissed anyone like that in a while. I wasn't sure who had started the kiss, actually.

"You're very beautiful," I whispered as our lips drew apart. The words just came out. Not my best effort, but the truth.

Jezzie smiled and shook her head. "My lips are too puffy and big. I look like I was dropped face-first as a kid. You're the good-looking one. You look like Muhammad Ali."

"Sure I do. After he took too many punches."

"A few punches, maybe. To add character. Just the right number of hard knocks. Your smile's nice, too. Smile for me, Alex."

I kissed those puffy lips again. They were perfect as far as I could tell.

There's a lot of myth about black men desiring white women; about some white women wanting to experiment with black men. Jezzie Flanagan was a smart, extremely desirable woman. She was somebody I could talk to, somebody I wanted to be around.

And there we were, snuggled in each other's arms at around three in the morning. We'd both had a little too much to drink, but not a lot too much. No myths involved. Just two people alone, in a strange town, on a very strange night in both of our lives.

I wanted to be held by somebody right then. I think Jezzie did, too. The look in her eyes was sweet and comfortable. But there was also a brittleness that night. There was a network of tiny red veins in the corners of her eyes. Maybe she could still *see* Soneji/Murphy, too. We'd been so close to getting him. Only a half step behind this time.

I studied Jezzie's face in a way I couldn't have before, and never thought that I would. I ran a finger lightly over her cheeks. Her skin was soft and smooth. Her blond hair was like silk between my fingers. Her perfume was subtle, like wild-flowers.

A phrase drifted through my head. *Don't start anything you can't finish.*

"Well, Alex?" Jezzie said, and she raised an eyebrow. "This is a knotty problem, isn't it?"

"Not for two smart cops like us," I said to her.

We took the soft left turn down the hotel hallway — and headed toward room 311.

"Maybe we should think twice about this," I said as we walked.

"Maybe I already have," Jezzie whispered back.

CHAPTER 41

At ONE-THIRTY in the morning, Gary Soneji/Murphy walked out of a Motel 6 in Reston, Virginia. He caught his reflection in a glass door.

The new Gary — the Gary *du jour* — looked back at him. Black pompadour and a grungy beard; dusty shitkicker's clothes. He knew he could play this part. Put on an Old Dixie drawl. For as long as he needed to, anyway. Not too long. Don't anybody blink.

Gary got into the battered VW and started to drive. He was completely wired. He loved this part of the plan more than he loved his life. He couldn't separate the two anymore. This was the most daring part of the entire adventure. Real high-wire stuff.

Why was he so revved? he wondered as his mind drifted. Just because half the police and FBI bastards in the continental U.S.A. were out looking for him?

Because he'd kidnapped two rich brats and one had died? And the other — Maggie Rose? He didn't even want to think about that — what had really happened to her.

Darkness slowly changed to a soft gray velvet. He fought the urge to step on the gas and keep it floored. An orangish tinge of morning finally arrived as he drove through Johnstown, Pennsylvania.

He stopped at a 7-Eleven in Johnstown. He got out and stretched his legs. Checked how he looked in the VW Bug's dangling sideview mirror.

A scraggly country laborer looked back at him from the mirror. Another Gary, completely. He had all the country-hick mannerisms down cold: modified cowboy walk as if he'd been kicked by a horse; hands in pockets, or thumbs in belt loops. Finger-comb your hair all the time. Spit whenever you get the chance.

He took a jolt of high-octane coffee in the convenience store, which was a questionable move. Hard poppy-seed roll with extra butter. No morning newspapers were out yet.

A dumb-shit, stuck-up female clerk in the store waited on him. He wanted to punch her lights out. He spent five minutes fantasizing about taking her out right in the middle of the podunk 7-Eleven.

Take off the little schoolgirl white blouse, honey. Roll it down to your waist. Okay, now I'm probably going to have to kill you. But maybe not. Talk to me nice and beg me not to. What are you — twenty-one, twenty? Use that as your emotional argument. You're too young to die, unfulfilled, in a 7-Eleven.

Gary finally decided to let her live. The amazing thing was that she had no idea how close she'd come to being killed.

"You have a nice day. Come back soon," she said.

"You pray I don't."

As Soneji/Murphy drove along Route 22, he let himself get angrier than he had been in a long time. Enough of this sentimentality crap. No one was paying attention to him — not the attention he deserved.

Did the major fools and incompetents out there think they

had any chance of stopping him? Of capturing him on their own? Of trying him on national TV? It was time to teach them a lesson; it was time for true greatness. Zig when the world expects you to zag.

Gary Soneji/Murphy pulled into a McDonald's in Wilkinsburg, Pennsylvania. Children of all ages loved McDonald's, right? Food, folks, and fun. He was still pretty much on schedule. The "Bad Boy" was dependable in that regard — you could set your watch by him.

There was the usual meandering lunchtime crowd of dopes and mopes moving in and out of Mickey D's. All of them were stuck in their daily ruts and daily rutting. Shoveling down those Quarter Pounders and greasy string fries.

What was that old Hooters song — about all the zombies out there in Amerika? *All you zombies? Walk like a zombie?* Something about the millions of zombies out there. Gross understatement.

Was he the only one living near his potential? Soneji/Murphy wondered. It sure as hell seemed that way. Nobody else was special the way he was. At least he hadn't met any of the special ones.

He turned into the McDonald's dining room. A hundred trillion McBurgers served, and still counting. Women were there in droves. Women and all of their precious children. The nestbuilders; the trivializers; the silly gooses with their silly, floppy breasties.

Ronald McDonald was there, too, in the form of a six-foot cutout shilling stale cookies to the kiddies. What a day! Ronald McDonald meets Mr. Chips.

Gary paid for two black coffees and turned to walk back through the crowd. He thought the top of his head was going to blow off. His face and neck were flushed. He was hyperventilating. His throat was dry, and he was perspiring too much.

"You all right, sir?" the girl behind the register asked.

He didn't even consider answering her. *You talkin' to me?* Robert De Niro, right? He was another De Niro — no doubt about that — only he was an even better actor. More range. De Niro never took chances the way he did. De Niro, Hoffman, Pacino — none of them took chances and really stretched themselves. Not in his opinion.

So many thoughts and perceptions were crashing on him, deflecting off his brain. He had the impression that he was floating through a sea of light particles, photons, and neutrons. If these people could spend only ten seconds inside his brain, they wouldn't believe it.

He purposely bumped into people as he walked away from the McDonald's counter.

"Well, ex-*cuse* me," he said after a jarring hip-check.

"Hey! Watch it! C'mon, mister," somebody said to him.

"Watch it yourself, you jerkoff." Soneji/Murphy stopped and addressed the balding shitkicker he'd bumped. "What do I have to do to get a little respect? Shoot you in the right eyeball?"

He downed both hot coffees as he continued on through the restaurant. *Through* the restaurant. *Through* any people in his way. *Through* the cheesy Formica tables. *Through* the walls, if he really wanted to.

Gary Soneji/Murphy pulled a snub-nosed revolver from under his Windbreaker. This was it: the beginning of America's wake-up call. A special performance for all the kiddies and mommies.

They were all watching him now. Guns, they understood.

"Wake the fuck up!" he shouted inside the McDonald's dining room. "*Hot* coffee! Comin' through, you all! Wake up, and smell it!"

"That man has a gun!" said one of the rocket scientists eating a dripping Big Mac. Amazing that he could see through the greasy fog rising from his food.

Gary faced the room with the revolver drawn. "No one leaves this room!" he bellowed.

"You awake now? *Are you people awake?*" Gary Soneji/Murphy called out. "I think so. I think you're all with the program now.

"I'm in charge! So everybody stop. Look. And listen."

Gary fired a round into the face of a burger-chomping patron. The man clutched his forehead and wheeled heavily off his chair onto the floor. Now *that* got everybody's attention. Real gun, real bullets, real life.

A black woman screamed, and she tried to run by Soneji. He leveled her with a gun butt to the head. It was a really cool move, he thought. Good Steven Seagal shit.

"*I am Gary Soneji!* I am Himself. Is that a mindblower or what? You're in the presence of the world-famous kidnapper. This is like a free-for-nothing demonstration. So watch closely. You might learn something. Gary Soneji has been places, he's seen things you'll never see in your life. Trust me on that one."

He sipped the last of his McCoffee, and over the rim of his cup watched the fast-food fans quiver.

"This," he finally said in a thoughtful manner, "is what they call a dangerous hostage situation. Ronald McDonald's been kidnapped, folks. You're now officially part of history."

CHAPTER 42

STATE TROOPERS Mick Fescoe and Bobby Hatfield were about to enter the McDonald's when gunshots sounded from the dining room. Gunshots? At lunchtime in McDonald's? What the hell was going on!

Fescoe was tall, a hulk, forty-four years old. Hatfield was nearly twenty years younger. He'd been a state trooper for only about a year. The two troopers shared a similar sense of black humor, in spite of their age difference. They had already become tight friends.

"Holy shit," Hatfield whispered when the fireworks started inside McDonald's. He went into a firing crouch he hadn't learned that long ago, and had never used off the target range.

"Listen to me, Bobby," Fescoe said to him.

"Don't worry, I'm listening."

"You head toward that exit over there." Fescoe pointed to an exit up near the cash registers. "I'll go around the left side. You wait for me to make a move.

"Do nothing until I go at him. Then, if you have a clear shot, go for it. Don't think about it. Just pull the trigger, Bobby."

Bobby Hatfield nodded. "I got you." Then the two split up.

Officer Mick Fescoe couldn't get his breath as he ran around the far side of the McDonald's. He stayed close to the brick wall, brushing his back against it. He'd been telling himself for months to get his ass back in shape. He was puffing already. He felt a little dizzy. That he didn't need. Dizziness, and playing *High Noon* with a creep, was a real bad combination.

Mick Fescoe got up close to the door. He could hear the nut case shouting inside.

There was something funny, though, as if the creep were operating by remote. His movements were very staccato. His voice was high-pitched, like a young boy's.

"I'm *Gary Soneji*. You all got that? I'm The Man himself. You folks have *found me*, so to speak. You're all big heroes."

Was it possible? Fescoe wondered as he listened near the door. The kidnapper Soneji, here in Wilkinsburg? Whoever it was, he definitely had a gun. One person had been shot. A man was spread-eagled on the floor. He wasn't moving.

Fescoe heard another shot. Piercing screams of terror echoed from inside the packed McDonald's restaurant.

"You have to do something!" a man in a light green Dolphins parka yelled at the state trooper.

You're telling me, Officer Mick Fescoe muttered to himself. People were always real brave with cops' lives. You first, officer. You're the one getting twenty-five hundred a month for this.

Mick Fescoe tried to control his breathing. When he succeeded, he moved up to the glass doorway. He said a silent prayer and spun through the glass door.

He saw the gunman immediately. A white guy, already turned toward him. *As if he'd been expecting him. As if he'd planned on this.*

"Boom!" Gary Soneji yelled. At the same time, he pulled the trigger.

CHAPTER 43

NONE OF US had more than a couple of hours of sleep, some less than that. We were groggy and out of it as we cruised down U.S. Highway 22.

Gary Soneji/Murphy had been "sighted" several times in the area south of us. He had become the bogeyman for half the people in America. I knew that he relished the role.

Jezzie Flanagan, Jeb Klepner, Sampson, and I traveled in a blue Lincoln sedan. Sampson tried to sleep. I was the designated driver for the first shift.

We were passing through Murrysville, Pennsylvania, when an emergency call came over the radio at ten past noon.

"All units, we have a multiple shooting!" the dispatcher said with a flurry of radio static. "A man claiming to be Gary Soneji has shot at least two people inside a McDonald's in Wilkinsburg. He has at least sixty hostages trapped inside the restaurant at this time."

Less than thirty minutes later we arrived at the scene in Wilkinsburg, Pennsylvania. Sampson shook his head in disgust and amazement. "Does this asshole know how to throw a party or what?"

"Is he trying to kill himself? Is this suicide time?" Jezzie Flanagan wanted to know.

"I'm not surprised by anything he does, but McDonald's fits. Look at all the children. It's like the school, like Disney World," I said to them.

Across the street from the restaurant, on the roof of a Kmart, I could see police or army snipers. They had high-powered rifles aimed in the direction of the golden arches on the front window.

"It seems just like the McDonald's massacre a few years back. The one in southern California," I said to Sampson and Jezzie.

"Don't say that," Jezzie whispered, "not even as a joke."

"I'm saying it, and it isn't any joke."

We started to hurry toward the McDonald's. After all this, we didn't want Soneji shot dead.

We were being filmed. Television vans were double-parked everywhere, affiliates from all three networks. They were shooting film of everything that moved or talked. The whole mess was as bad a deal as I'd seen. It certainly reminded me of the McDonald's shootings in California; a man named James Huberty had killed twenty-one people there. Was that what Soneji/Murphy wanted us to think?

An FBI section chief came running up to us. It was Kyle Craig, who'd been at the Murphy house in Wilmington.

"We don't know if it's him for sure," he said. "This guy's dressed like a farmer. Dark hair, beard. Claims to be Soneji. But it could be some other nut."

"Let me get a look," I said to Craig. "He asked for me down in Florida. He knows I'm a psychologist. Maybe I can talk to him now."

Before Craig could answer, I had moved past him toward the restaurant. I inched my way up beside a trooper and a couple of local cops crouched near the side entrance. I flashed my badge case at them. Said I was from Washington. No sound was com-

ing from inside the McDonald's. I had to talk him back to earth.
No suicide. No big flame-out at Mickey D's.

"Is he making any sense?" I asked the trooper. "Is he coherent?"

The trooper was young and his eyes were glazed. "He shot
my partner. I think my partner's dead," the trooper said. "Dear
God in this world."

"We'll get in there and help your partner," I told the trooper.
"Is the man with the gun making sense when he talks? Is he
coherent?"

"He's talking about being the kidnapper from D.C. You can
follow what he says. He's bragging about it. Says he wants to be
somebody important."

The gunman had control of the sixty or more people inside
the McDonald's. It was silent in there. Was it Soneji/Murphy? It
sure fit. The kids and their mothers. The hostage situation. I
remembered all the pictures on his bathroom wall. He wanted
to be *the picture* other lonely boys hung up.

"Soneji!" I called out. "Are you Gary Soneji?"

"Who the hell are you?" a shout came right back from inside.
"Who wants to know?"

"I'm Detective Alex Cross. From Washington. I have a feeling
you know all about the latest hostage-rescue decision. We won't
negotiate with you. So you know what happens from here on."

"I know *all* the rules, Detective Cross. It's all public information, isn't it. The rules don't always apply," Gary Soneji
shouted back. "Not to me, they don't. Never have."

"They do here," I said firmly. "You can bet your life on it."

"Are you willing to bet all these lives, Detective? I know
another rule. Women and children go first! You follow me?
Women and children have a special place with me."

I didn't like the sound of his voice. I didn't like what he was
saying.

I needed Soneji to understand that under no circumstances was he getting away. There would be no negotiations. If he started shooting again, we would take him down. I remembered other siege situations like this that I'd been involved in. Soneji was more complicated, smarter. He sounded as if he had nothing to lose.

"I don't want anyone else hurt! I don't want you hurt," I told him in a clear, strong voice. I was beginning to sweat. I could feel it inside my jacket, all over my body.

"That's very touching. I am moved by what you just said. My heart just skipped a beat. Really," he said.

Our talk had sure become conversational in a hurry.

"You know what I mean, Gary." I softened my voice. I spoke as if he were a frightened, anxious patient.

"Certainly I do, Alex."

"There are a lot of people out here with guns. No one can control them if this escalates. I can't. Even you can't. There could be an accident. That, we don't want."

It was silent inside again. The thought pounding in my head was that if Soneji was suicidal, he'd end it here. He'd have his final shoot-out right now, his final blaze of celebrity. We'd never know what had set him off. We would never know what had happened to Maggie Rose Dunne.

"Hello, Detective Cross."

Suddenly, he was in the doorway, about five feet away from me. *He was right there*. A gunshot rang from one of the rooftops. Soneji spun and grabbed his shoulder. He'd been hit by one of the snipers.

I leaped forward and grabbed Soneji in both arms. My right shoulder crunched into his chest. Lawrence Taylor never made a surer tackle.

We fell hard to the concrete. I didn't want anyone shooting him dead now. I had to talk to him. We had to find out about Maggie Rose.

As I held him on the ground, he twisted around and stared into my face. Blood from his shoulder was smeared over both of us.

"Thank you for saving my life," he said. "Someday, I'll kill you for it, Detective Cross."

Part Three

The Last Southern Gentleman

CHAPTER 44

"MY NAME IS BOBBI," she had been taught to say. Always her new name. Never the old one.

Never, ever, Maggie Rose.

She was locked inside a dark van, or a covered truck. She wasn't sure which. She had no idea where she was now. How far or how close to her home. She didn't know how long it had been since she'd been taken away from her school.

Her thinking was clearer now. Almost back to normal. Someone had brought her clothes, which had to mean she wasn't going to be hurt right away. Otherwise, why would they bother with the clothes?

The van or truck was filthy dirty. It had no rug or covering on the floor. It smelled like onions. Food must have been kept there. Where did they grow onions? Maggie Rose tried to remember. New Jersey and upstate New York. She thought there was also the smell of potatoes. Maybe turnips or sweet potatoes.

When she put it all together, when she focused her mind, Maggie Rose thought she was probably being held somewhere down South.

What else did she know? What else could she figure out?

She wasn't being drugged anymore, not since the beginning. She didn't think Mr. Soneji had been around for a few days. The scary old lady hadn't been there, either.

They seldom talked to her. When she was spoken to, they called her Bobbi. Why Bobbi?

She was being so good about everything, but sometimes she needed to cry. Like now. She was choking on her own sobs. Not wanting anybody to hear her.

There was only one thing that gave her strength. It was so simple, but it was powerful.

She was alive.

She wanted to stay alive more than anything.

Maggie Rose hadn't noticed that the truck was slowing down. It was bumpy going for a while. Then the vehicle came to a full stop.

She heard someone getting out of the cab up front. Muffled words were spoken. She'd been told not to talk in the truck, or she'd be gagged again.

Someone pushed open the sliding door. Sunlight burst in on her. She couldn't see anything at first.

When she finally could make something out, Maggie Rose couldn't believe her eyes.

"Hello," she said in the softest whisper, almost as if she had no voice. "My name is Bobbi."

CHAPTER 45

IT TURNED OUT to be another very long day in Wilkinsburg, Pennsylvania. We interviewed each person who had been
kept hostage inside the McDonald's. The FBI, meanwhile, had
taken custody of Soneji/Murphy.

I stayed over that night. So did Jezzie Flanagan. We were
together for a second night in a row. Nothing I wanted more.

As soon as we got inside a room at the Cheshire Inn, in
nearby Millvale, Jezzie said, "Will you just hold me for a minute
or two, Alex. I probably look a little more stable than I really
feel."

I liked holding her, and being held back. I liked the way she
smelled. I liked the way she fit into my arms. Everything still
felt electric between us.

I was excited by the thought of being with her again. There
have been only a couple of people I can open up to. No woman
since Maria. I had a feeling Jezzie could be one of those people,
and I needed to be connected with someone again. It had taken
me a while to figure that one out.

"Isn't this weird?" she whispered. "Two cops in hot pursuit."

Her body was trembling as I held her. Her hand softly stroked my arm.

I had never been a committed one-night-stand type, and I thought that I probably wouldn't start now. That raised some problems and theoretical questions that I wasn't ready to deal with yet.

Jezzie closed her eyes. "Hold me for one more minute," she whispered. "You know what's really nice? Being with someone who understands what you've been through. My husband never understood The Job."

"Me neither. In fact, I understand it less every day," I joked. But I was partly telling the truth.

I held Jezzie for a lot longer than a couple of minutes. She had a startling, ageless beauty. I liked looking at her.

"This is *so strange*, Alex. *Nice* strange, but strange," she said. "Is this whole thing a dream?"

"Can't be a dream. My middle name is Isaiah. You didn't know that."

Jezzie shook her head. "I knew your middle name was Isaiah. I saw it on a report from the Bureau. Alexander Isaiah Cross."

"I see how you got to the top," I said to her. "What else do you know about me?"

"All in good time," Jezzie said. She touched a finger to my lips.

The Cheshire was a picturesque country inn about ten miles north of Wilkinsburg. Jezzie had run in to get us a room. So far, no one had seen us together at the inn, which was fine by both of us.

Our room was in a whitewashed carriage house that was detached from the main building. It was filled with authentic-looking antiques, including a hand loom and several quilts.

There was a woodburning fireplace, and we started a fire. Jezzie ordered champagne from room service.

"Let's celebrate. Let's do up the town," she said as she put down the phone receiver. "We deserve something special. We got the bad guy."

The inn, the corner room, everything was just about perfect. A bay window looked down over a snow-covered lawn, to a lake slicked with ice. A steep mountain range loomed behind the lake.

We sipped champagne in front of the blazing fire. I'd been worried about the aftereffects of our night in Wilmington, but there were none. We talked easily, and when it got quiet, that was all right, too.

We ordered a late dinner.

The room-service guy was clearly uncomfortable as he set up our dinner trays in front of the fire. He couldn't get the warming oven open; and he nearly dropped an entire tray of food. Guess he'd never seen a living, breathing taboo before.

"It's okay," Jezzie said to the man. "We're both cops and this is perfectly legal. Trust me on it."

We talked for the next hour and a half. It reminded me of being a kid, having a friend over for the night. We both let our hair down a little, then a lot. There wasn't much self-consciousness between us. She got me talking about Damon and Jannie and wouldn't let me stop.

Supper was roast beef with something masquerading as Yorkshire pudding. It didn't matter. When Jezzie finished the last bite, she started to laugh. We were both doing that a lot.

"Why did I finish all that food? I don't even like good Yorkshire pudding. God, we're having fun for a change!"

"What do we do now?" I asked her. "In the spirit of fun and celebration."

"I don't know. What are you up for? I'll bet they have really neat board games back at the main building. I'm one of a hundred living people who knows how to play Parcheesi."

Jezzie craned her neck so she could see out the window. "Or, we could hike down by the lake. Sing 'Winter Wonderland.'"

"Yeah. We could do some ice-skating. I ice-skate. I'm a wizard on skates. Was that in my FBI report?"

Jezzie grinned and slapped her knees. "That I'd like to see. I'd pay real good money to see you skate."

"Forgot my skates, though."

"Oh, well. What else? I mean, I like you too much, I respect you too much, to let you think I might be interested in your body."

"To be absolutely truthful and frank, I'm a little interested in *your* body," I said. The two of us kissed, and it still felt pretty good to me. The fire crackled. The champagne was ice-cold. Fire and ice. Yin and yang. All kinds of opposites attracting. Wildfire in the wilds.

We didn't get to sleep until seven the following morning. We even walked down to the lake, where we skated on our shoes in the moonlight.

Jezzie leaned in and she kissed me in the middle of the lake. Very serious kiss. Big-girl kiss.

"Oh, Alex," she whispered against my cheek, "I think this is going to be real trouble."

CHAPTER 46

GARY SONEJI/MURPHY was remanded to Lorton Federal Prison in the northern part of Virginia. We began hearing rumors that something had happened to him there, but no one from the Washington Police Department was allowed to see him. Justice and the FBI had him, and they weren't letting go of their prize.

From the moment it was revealed that he was being kept at Lorton, the prison was picketed. The same thing had occurred when Ted Bundy was imprisoned in Florida. Men, women, and schoolchildren assembled outside the prison parking area. They chanted emotional slogans throughout the day and night. They marched and carried lighted candles and placards.

Where Is Maggie Rose? Maggie Rose Lives! The Beast of the East Must Die! Give the Beast the Chair or Life!

A week and a half after the capture, I went in to see Soneji/Murphy. I had to call in every chip I had in Washington, but I got in to see him. Dr. Marion Campbell, the warden at Lorton, met me at a row of gunmetal elevators on the prison's sixth floor, the hospital floor. Campbell was in his sixties. He was well preserved, with a flowing mane of black hair. He looked very Reaganesque.

"You're Detective Cross?" He extended his hand and smiled politely.

"Yes. I'm also a forensic psychologist," I explained.

Dr. Campbell seemed genuinely surprised by that information. Evidently, no one had told him. "Well, you certainly have some pull to get in to talk with him. It's gotten rather complicated. Visiting rights with him are a precious commodity."

"I've been involved with this since he took the two kids in Washington. I was there when he was caught."

"Well, I'm not sure if we're talking about the same man now," Dr. Campbell said. He didn't explain. "Is it Dr. Cross?" he asked.

"Doctor Cross, Detective Cross, Alex. You pick."

"Please come with me, Doctor. You're going to find this most interesting."

Because of the gunshot wound Soneji got at McDonald's, he was being kept in a private room in the prison hospital. Dr. Campbell led me down a wide corridor inside the hospital. Prisoners occupied every available room. Lorton's a very popular place, long lines at the door. Most of the men were black. They ranged in age from as young as nineteen to their mid-fifties. They all tried to look defiant and tough, but that is a pose that doesn't work well in a federal prison.

"I'm afraid I've become a little protective of him," Campbell said as we walked. "You'll see why in a moment. Everybody wants to, needs to, see him. I've received calls from all over the world. An author from Japan had to see him. A doctor from Frankfurt. Another from London. That sort of thing."

"I get the feeling there's something you're not telling me about him, Doctor," I finally said to Campbell. "What is it?"

"I want you to draw your own conclusions, Dr. Cross. He's right here in this section near the main ward. I would very much like your opinion."

We stopped at a bolted steel door in the hospital corridor. A guard let us through. Beyond the door were a few more hospital rooms, but rooms for maximum security.

A light burned brightly inside the first room. It wasn't Soneji's. He was in a darker room on the left. The regular prison visiting area had been ruled out because it offered too much exposure. Two guards with shotguns sat outside the room.

"Has there been any violence?" I asked.

"No, not at all. I'll leave you two to talk. I don't think you have to be concerned about any violence. You'll see for yourself."

Gary Soneji/Murphy watched us from his cot. His arm was in a sling. Otherwise, he looked the same as the last time I'd seen him. I stood inside the hospital room. When Dr. Campbell walked away, Soneji studied me. There was no sign of recognition from this man who'd threatened to kill me when we'd last met.

My first professional impression was that he seemed afraid to be left alone with me. His body language was tentative, very different from the man I'd wrestled to the ground at the McDonald's in Wilkinsburg.

"Who are you? What do you want with me?" he finally said. His voice quivered slightly.

"I'm Alex Cross. We've met."

He looked confused. The expression on his face was very believable, too. He shook his head and closed his eyes. It was an incredibly baffling and disconcerting moment for me.

"I'm sorry, I don't remember you," he said then. It seemed an apology. "There have been so many people in this nightmare. I forget some of you. Hello, Detective Cross. Please, pull up a chair. As you can see, I've had plenty of visitors."

"You asked for me during the negotiations in Florida. I'm with the Washington police."

As soon as I said that, he started to smile. He looked off to the side, and shook his head. I wasn't in on the joke yet. I told him I wasn't.

"I've never been to Florida in my life," he said. "Not once."

Gary Soneji/Murphy stood up from his cot. He was wearing loose-fitting hospital whites. His arm seemed to be giving him some pain.

He looked lonely, and vulnerable. Something *was* very wrong here. What in hell was going on? Why hadn't I been told before I came? Evidently, Dr. Campbell wanted me to draw my own conclusions.

Soneji/Murphy sat down in the other chair. He stared at me with a baleful look.

He didn't *look* like a killer. He didn't *look* like a kidnapper. A teacher? A Mr. Chips? A lost little boy? All of those seemed closer to the mark.

"I've never spoken to you in my life," he said to me. "I've never heard of Alex Cross. I didn't kidnap any children. Do you know Kafka?" he asked.

"Some. What's your point?"

"I feel like Gregor Samsa in *Metamorphosis*. I'm trapped in a nightmare. None of this makes any sense to me. I didn't kidnap anyone's children. Someone has to believe me. Someone has to. I'm Gary Murphy, and I never harmed anyone in my entire life."

If I followed him, what he was telling me was that he was a multiple personality . . . truly *Gary Soneji/Murphy*.

"But do you believe him, Alex? Jesus Christ, man. That's the sixty-four-dollar question."

Scorse, Craig, and Reilly from the Bureau, Klepner and Jezzie Flanagan from the Secret Service, and Sampson and I were in a cramped conference room at FBI headquarters downtown. It was old home week for the Hostage Rescue Team.

The question had come from Gerry Scorse. Not surprisingly,

he didn't believe Soneji/Murphy. He didn't buy the multiple-personality bit.

"What does he really gain from telling a lot of outrageous lies?" I asked everyone to consider. "He says he didn't kidnap the children. He says he didn't shoot anyone at the McDonald's." I looked from face to face around the conference table. "He claims to be this pleasant enough nobody from Delaware named Gary Murphy."

"Temp insanity plea." Reilly offered the obvious. "He goes to some cushy asylum in Maryland or Virginia. Out in seven to ten years, maybe. You can bet he knows that, Alex. Is he clever enough, a good enough actor, to pull it off?"

"So far, I've spoken to him only once. Less than an hour with him. I'll say this: he's very convincing as Gary Murphy. I think he's legitimately VFC."

"What the hell is VFC?" Scorse asked. "I don't know VFC. You've lost me."

"It's a common enough psych term," I told him. "All of us shrinks talk about VFC when we get together. *Very fucking crazy*, Gerry."

Everybody around the table laughed except Scorse. Sampson had nicknamed him the Funeral Director — Digger Scorse. He was dedicated and professional, but usually not a lot of laughs.

"Very fucking funny, Alex," Scorse finally said. "That's VFF."

"Can you get in to see him again?" Jezzie asked me. She was as professional as Scorse, but a lot nicer to be around.

"Yeah, I can. He wants to see me. Maybe I'll even find out why in hell he asked for me down in Florida. Why I'm the chosen one in his nightmare."

CHAPTER 47

TWO DAYS LATER, I wangled another hour with Gary Soneji/Murphy. I'd been up the previous two nights rereading multiple-personality cases. My dining room looked like a carrel at a psych library. There are tomes written about multiples, but few of us really agree on the material. There is even serious disagreement about whether there are any real multiple-personality cases at all.

Gary was sitting on his hospital cot, staring into space, when I arrived. His shoulder sling was gone. It was hard to come and talk to this kidnapper, child-killer, serial killer. I remembered something the philosopher Spinoza once wrote: "I have striven not to laugh at human actions, not to weep at them, nor to hate them, but to understand them." So far, I didn't understand.

"Hello Gary," I said softly, not wanting to startle him. "Are you ready to talk?"

He turned around and seemed glad to see me. He pulled a chair over for me by his cot.

"I was afraid they wouldn't let you come," he said. "I'm glad they did."

"What made you think they wouldn't let me come?" I wanted to know.

"Oh, I don't know. It's just . . . I felt you were someone I might be able to talk to. The way my luck's been going, I thought they would shut you right off."

There was a naïveté about him that was troubling to me. He was almost charming. He was the man his neighbors in Wilmington had described.

"What were you just thinking about? A minute ago?" I asked. "Before I interrupted."

He smiled and shook his head. "I don't even know. What was I thinking about? Oh, I know what it was. I was remembering it's my birthday this month. I keep thinking that I'm suddenly going to wake up out of this. That's one recurring thought, a leitmotif through all my thinking."

"Go back a little for me. Tell me how you were arrested again," I said, changing the subject.

"I woke up, I came to in a police car outside a McDonald's." He was consistent on that point. He'd told me the same thing two days before. "My arms were handcuffed behind my back. Later on, they used leg-irons, too."

"You don't know how you got into the police car?" I asked. Boy, was he good at this. Soft-spoken, very nice, believable.

"No, and I don't know how I got to a McDonald's in Wilkinsburg, either. That is the most freakish thing that's ever happened to me."

"I can see how it would be."

A theory had occurred to me on the ride down from Washington. It was a long shot, but it might explain a few things that didn't make any sense so far.

"Has anything like this ever happened to you before?" I asked. "Anything vaguely like it, Gary?"

"No. I've never been in any trouble. Never been arrested. You can check that, can't you? Of course you can."

"I mean have you ever woken up in a strange place before? No idea how you got there?"

Gary gave me a strange look, his head cocked slightly. "Why would you ask that?"

"Did you, Gary?"

"Well . . . yes."

"Tell me about it. Tell me about those times when you woke up in a strange place."

He had a habit of pulling on his shirt, between the second and third buttons. He would pull the fabric away from his chest. I wondered if he had a fear of not being able to breathe, and where it might have come from if he did.

Maybe he'd been sick as a child. Or trapped with a limited air supply. Or locked up somewhere — the way Maggie Rose and Michael Goldberg had been locked away.

"For the past year or so, maybe more than that, I've suffered from insomnia. I told that to one of the doctors who came to see me," he said.

There was nothing about insomnia in any of the prison work-ups. I wondered if he'd told any of the doctors, or simply imagined that he had. There was stuff about an uneven Wechsler profile, indicative of impulsivity. There was a verbal I.Q. and a performance I.Q., both through the roof. There was a Rorschach profile that reflected severe emotional stress. There was a positive response to T.A.T. card #14, the so-called suicide card. But not a word about insomnia.

"Tell me about it, please. It could help me to understand." We'd already talked about the fact that I was a psychologist, besides being a really crackerjack detective. He was comfortable with my credentials. So far, anyway. Did that have anything to do with his asking for me down in Florida?

He looked into my eyes. "Will you really try to help me? Not trap me, Doctor, help me?"

I told him that I'd try. I'd listen to what he had to say. I'd keep an open mind. He said that was all he could ask for.

"I haven't been able to sleep for a while. This goes back for as long as I can remember," he went on. "It was becoming a jumble. Being awake, dreams. I had trouble sorting one out from the other. I woke up in that police car in Pennsylvania. I have no idea how I got there. That's really how it happened. Do you believe me? *Somebody has to believe me.*"

"I'm listening to you, Gary. When you've finished, I'll tell you what I think. I promise. For the moment, I have to hear everything you remember."

That seemed to satisfy him.

"You asked if it's happened to me before. It has. A few times. Waking in strange places. Sometimes in my car, pulled over along some road. Sometimes a road I've never seen, or even heard of before. A couple of times it's happened in motels. Or wandering the streets. Philadelphia, New York, Atlantic City one time. I had casino chips and a complimentary parking ticket in my pocket. No idea how they got there."

"Did it ever happen to you in Washington?" I asked.

"No. Not in Washington. I haven't been in Washington since I was a kid, actually. Lately, I've found I can 'come to' in a conscious state. Completely conscious. I might be eating a meal, for example. But I have no idea how I got in the restaurant."

"Did you see anybody about this? Did you try to get help? A doctor?"

He shut his eyes, which were clear chestnut brown — his most striking feature. A smile came across his face as he opened his eyes again.

"We don't have money to spend on psychiatrists. We're barely scraping by. That's why I've been so depressed. We're in the hole over thirty grand. My family is thirty thousand in debt, and I'm here in prison."

He stopped talking, and looked at me again. He wasn't embarrassed about staring, trying to read my face. I was finding him cooperative, stable, and generally lucid.

I also knew that anybody who worked with him might be the victim of manipulation by an extremely clever and gifted sociopath. He'd fooled a lot of people before me; he was obviously good at it.

"So far, I believe you," I finally said to him. "What you're saying makes sense to me, Gary. I'd like to help you if I can."

Tears suddenly welled in his eyes, and rolled down his cheeks. He put his hands out to me.

I reached out, and I held Gary Soneji/Murphy's hands. They were very cold. He seemed to be afraid.

"I'm innocent," he said to me. "I know it sounds crazy, but I'm innocent."

I didn't get home until late that night. A motorcycle eased up alongside the car as I was about to pull into my driveway. What the hell was this?

"Please follow me, sir," said the person atop the bike. The line was delivered in nearly perfect highway-patrol style. "Just fall in behind."

It was Jezzie. She started to laugh and so did I. I knew she was trying to lure me back to the land of the living again. She'd told me I was working too hard on the case. She reminded me that it was solved.

I continued into the driveway and got out of the old Porsche. I went around to where she had curbed her motorcycle.

"Quitting time, Alex," Jezzie said. "Can you do it? Is it okay for you to quit work at eleven o'clock?"

I went inside to check on the kids. They were sleeping, so I had no reason to resist Jezzie's offer. I came back out and climbed on the bike.

"This is either the worst or the best thing I've done in recent memory," I told her.

"Don't worry, it's the best. You're in good hands. Nothing to fear except instant death."

Within seconds, 9th Street was being eaten up under the glare of the single motorcycle headlamp. The bike sped down Independence, then onto the Parkway, which can be ridiculously curvy in spots. Jezzie leaned into every curve, buzzing by passenger cars as if they were standing still.

She definitely knew how to drive the bike. She wasn't a dilettante. As the landscape slashed past us, the electric wires overhead, and the roadway's dotted line just to the left of the bike's front wheel, I thought that she was doing at least a hundred, but I felt extraordinarily calm on the bike.

I didn't know where we were going, and I didn't care. The kids were asleep. Nana was there. This was all part of the night's therapy. I could feel the cold air forcing itself back through every socket and aperture in my body. It cleared my head nicely, and my head sure needed clearing.

N Street was empty of traffic. It was a long, narrow straightaway with hundred-year-old town houses on either side. It was pretty, especially in winter. Gabled roofs crusted with snow. Winking porch lights.

Jezzie opened the bike up again on the deserted street. Seventy, ninety, a hundred. I couldn't tell how fast for sure, only that we were really flying. The trees and houses were a blur. The pavement below was a blur. It was kind of nice, actually. If we lived to tell about it.

Jezzie braked the BMW smoothly. She wasn't showing off, just knew how it's done.

"We're home. I just got the place. I'm getting my home act together," she said as she dismounted. "You were pretty good. You only yelped that one time on the George Washington."

"I keep my yelps to myself."

Exhilarated by the ride, we went inside. The apartment wasn't at all what I had expected. Jezzie said she hadn't found time to fix the place up, but it was beautiful and tasteful. The overall style was sleek and modern, but not at all stark. There were lots of striking art photographs, mostly black and white. Jezzie said she'd taken them all. Fresh flowers were in the living room and kitchen. Books with bookmarks sticking out — *The Prince of Tides, Burn Marks, Women in Power, Zen and the Art of Motorcycle Maintenance.* A wine rack — Beringer, Rutherford. A hook on the wall for her cycle helmet.

"So you're a homebody after all."

"I am like hell. Take it back, Alex. I'm a tough-as-they-come Secret Service woman."

I took Jezzie in my arms and we kissed very gently in her living room. I was finding tenderness where I hadn't expected it; I was discovering sensuality that surprised me. It was the whole package I'd been searching for, only with one little catch.

"I'm glad you brought me to your house," I said. "I mean that, Jezzie. I really am touched."

"Even if I practically had to kidnap you to get you over here?"

"Fast motorcycle rides in the night. Beautiful, homey apartment. Annie Leibovitz–quality photographs. What other secrets do you have?"

Jezzie moved a finger gently down and around my jawline, exploring my face. "I don't want to have any secrets. That's what I'd like. Okay?"

I said yes. That was exactly the way I wanted it, too. It was time to open up to someone again. It was way past time, probably for both of us. Maybe we hadn't looked it to the outside world, but we'd been lonely and inner-driven for too long. That was the simple truth we were helping each other to get in touch with.

*　　　*　　　*

Early the next morning, we rode the bike back to my house in Washington. The wind was cold and rough on our faces. I held on to her chest as we floated through the dim, gray light of early dawn. The few people who were up, driving or walking to work, stared at us. I probably would have stared, too. What a damn fine and handsome couple we were.

Jezzie dropped me exactly where she'd picked me up. I leaned close against her and the warm, vibrating bike. I kissed her again. Her cheeks, her throat, finally her lips. I thought I could stay there all morning. Just like that, on the mean streets of Southeast. I had the passing thought that it should always be like this. Why not?

"I have to get inside," I finally said.

"Yep. I know you do. Go home, Alex," Jezzie said. "Give your babies a kiss for me." She looked a little sad as I turned away and headed in, though.

Don't start something you can't finish, I remembered.

CHAPTER 48

THE REST OF THAT DAY, I burned the candle at the other end. It felt a little irresponsible, but that was good for me. It's all right to put the weight of the world on your shoulders sometimes, if you know how to take it off.

As I drove out to Lorton Prison, the temperature was below freezing, but the sun was out. The sky was bright, almost blinding blue. Beautiful and hopeful. The pathetic fallacy lives in the nineties.

I thought about Maggie Rose Dunne that morning on my drive. I had to conclude that she was dead by now. Her father was raising all kinds of hell through the media. I couldn't blame him very much. I'd spoken to Katherine Rose a couple of times on the phone. She hadn't given up hope. She told me she could "feel" that her little girl was still alive. It was the saddest thing to hear.

I tried to prepare myself for Soneji/Murphy, but I was distracted. Images from the night before kept flashing by my eyes. I had to remind myself that I was driving a car in midday Metro D.C. traffic, and I was working.

That was when a bright idea hit me: a testable theory about Gary Soneji/Murphy that *seemed* to make some sense in psych terms.

Having an interesting theory *du jour* helped my concentration at the prison. I was taken up to the sixth floor to see Soneji. He was waiting for me. He looked as if he hadn't slept all night, either. It was my turn to make something happen.

I went at him for a full hour that afternoon, maybe even a little longer. I pushed hard. Probably harder than with any of my patients.

"Gary, have you ever found receipts in your pockets — hotels, restaurants, store purchases — but you have no memory of spending the money?"

"How did you know that?" His eyes lit up at my question. Something like relief washed over his face. "I *told* them I wanted you to be my doctor. I don't want to see Dr. Walsh anymore. All he's good for is scrip for chloral hydrate."

"I'm not sure that's a good idea. I'm a psychologist, not a psychiatrist like Dr. Walsh. I'm also part of the team that helped arrest you."

He shook his head. "I know all that. You're also the only one who's listened before making final judgments. I know you hate me — the idea that I took those two children, the other things I'm supposed to have done. But you listen, at least. Walsh only pretends to listen."

"You need to continue seeing Dr. Walsh," I told him.

"That's fine. I guess I understand the politics here by now. Just please, don't leave me in this hellhole by myself."

"I won't. I'm with you all the way from here on. We'll continue to talk just like this."

I asked Soneji/Murphy to tell me about his childhood.

"I don't remember a whole lot about growing up. Is that very strange?" He wanted to talk. It was in my hands, my judgment, to determine whether I was hearing the truth, or a set of elaborately constructed lies.

"That's normal for some people. Not remembering. Sometimes, things come back when you talk about them, when you verbalize."

"I know the facts and statistics. Okay. Birthdate, February twenty-fourth, nineteen fifty-seven. Birthplace, Princeton, New Jersey. Things like that. Sometimes I feel like I *learned* all that while I was growing up, though. I've had experiences where I can't separate dreams from reality. I'm not sure which is which. I'm really not sure."

"Try to give me your first impressions," I told him.

"Not a lot of fun and laughs," he said. "I've always had insomnia. I could never sleep more than an hour or two at a time. I can't remember *not* being tired. And, depressed — like I've been trying to dig myself out of a hole my entire life. Not to try to do your job, but I don't think very highly of myself."

Everything we knew about Gary *Soneji* depicted the *opposite* persona: high energy, positive attitude, an extremely high opinion of himself.

Gary went on to sketch a terrifying childhood, which included physical abuse from his stepmother as a small child; sexual abuse from his father as he got older. Over and over, he described how he was forced to split himself off from the anxiety and conflict that surrounded him. His stepmother had come with her two children in 1961. Gary was four years old, and already moody. It got worse from that point on. How much worse, he wasn't willing to tell me yet.

As part of his workup under Dr. Walsh, Soneji/Murphy had taken Wechsler Adult, Minnesota Multiphasic Personality Inventory, and Rorschach tests. Where he sailed completely off the scales was in the area of creativity. This was measured by single-sentence completion. He scored equally high in both verbal and written responses.

"What else, Gary? Try to go as far back as you can. I can only help if I understand you better."

"There were always these 'lost hours.' Time I couldn't account for," he said. His face had been drawing tighter and tighter as he spoke. The veins in his neck protruded. Light sweat rolled over his face.

"They punished me because I couldn't remember . . . ," he said.

"Who did? Who punished you?"

"My stepmother mostly."

That probably meant most of the damage had happened when he was very young, while his stepmother did the disciplining.

"A dark room," he said.

"What happened in the dark room? What kind of room was it?"

"She put me there, down in the basement. It was our cellar, and she put me down there almost every day."

He was beginning to hyperventilate. This was extremely difficult for him, a condition I'd seen many times with child-abuse victims. He shut his eyes. Remembering. Seeing a past he never really wanted to encounter again.

"What would happen down in the basement?"

"Nothing . . . nothing happened. I was just punished all the time. Left by myself."

"How long were you kept down there?"

"I don't know . . . I can't remember everything!"

His eyes opened halfway. He watched me through narrow slits.

I wasn't sure how much more he could take. I had to be careful. I needed to ease him into the tougher parts of his history, with the feeling that I cared, that he could trust me, that I was listening.

"Was it for a whole day sometimes? Overnight?"

"Oh, no. No. It was for a long, long time. So I wouldn't forget anymore. So I'd be a good boy. Not the Bad Boy."

He looked at me, but said nothing more. I sensed that he was waiting to hear something from me.

I tried praise, which seemed the appropriate response. "That was good, Gary, a good start. I know how hard this is for you."

As I looked at the grown man, I imagined a small boy kept in a darkened cellar. Every day. For weeks that must have seemed even longer than that. Then I thought about Maggie Rose Dunne. Was it possible that he was keeping her somewhere and that she was still alive? I needed to get the darkest secrets out of his head, and needed to do it faster than it's ever done in therapy. Katherine Rose and Thomas Dunne deserved to know what had happened to their little girl.

What happened to Maggie Rose, Gary? Remember Maggie Rose?

This was a very risky time in our session. He could become frightened and refuse to see me again if he sensed that I was no longer a "friend." He might withdraw. There was even a chance of a complete psychotic break. He could become catatonic. Then everything would be lost.

I needed to keep praising Gary for his efforts. It was important that he look forward to my visits. "What you've told me so far should be extremely helpful," I said to him. "You really did a great job. I'm impressed by how much you've forced yourself to remember."

"Alex," he said as I started to leave, "honest to God, I didn't do anything horrible or bad. Please help me."

A polygraph test had been scheduled for him that afternoon. Just the thought of the lie detector made Gary nervous, but he swore he was glad to take it.

He told me I could stay and wait for the results if I wanted to. I wanted to very much.

The polygraph operator was a particularly good one who had been brought from D.C. for the testing. Eighteen questions were to be asked. Fifteen of those were "controls." The other three were to be used for scoring the lie detector test.

Dr. Campbell met with me about forty minutes after Soneji/Murphy had been taken down for his polygraph. Campbell was flushed with excitement. He looked as if he might have jogged from wherever they had staged the test. Something big had happened.

"He got the highest score possible," Campbell told me. "He passed with flying colors. Plus tens. Gary Murphy could be telling the truth!"

CHAPTER 49

GARY MURPHY could be telling the truth!

I held a command performance in the boardroom inside Lorton Prison the following afternoon. The important audience included Dr. Campbell from the prison, federal District Attorney James Dowd, a representative from the governor of Maryland's office, two more attorneys from the attorney general's office in Washington, and Dr. James Walsh, from the state's health board, as well as the prison's advisory staff.

It had been an ordeal to get them together. Now that I had succeeded, I couldn't lose them. I wouldn't get another chance to ask for what I needed.

I felt as if I were back taking my orals at Johns Hopkins. I was dancing fast on the high wire. I believed the entire Soneji/Murphy investigation was at stake, right here in this room.

"I want to try regressive hypnosis on him. There's no risk, but there's a chance for high reward," I announced to the group. "I'm certain Soneji/Murphy will be a good subject, that we'll find out something we can use. Maybe we'll learn what happened to the missing girl. Certainly something about Gary Murphy."

Several complex jurisdictional questions had already been

raised by the case. One lawyer had told me the issues would make for an excellent bar-exam question. Since state lines had been crossed, the kidnapping and murder of Michael Goldberg had fallen under federal jurisdiction and would be tried in federal court. The killings in McDonald's would be tried in a Westmoreland court. Soneji/Murphy could also be tried in Washington for one or more of the killings he had apparently committed in Southeast.

"What would you ultimately hope to accomplish?" Dr. Campbell wanted to know. He'd been supportive, and was continuing to be so. Like me, he read skepticism on several faces, especially Walsh's. I could see why Gary didn't care for Walsh. He seemed mean-spirited, petty, and proud of it.

"A lot of what he's told us so far suggests a severe dissociative reaction. He appears to have suffered a pretty horrible childhood. There was physical abuse, maybe sexual abuse as well. He may have begun to split off his psyche to avoid pain and fear back then. I'm not saying that he's a multiple, but it's a possibility. He had the kind of childhood that could produce such a rare psychosis."

Dr. Campbell picked up. "Dr. Cross and I have talked about the possibility that Soneji/Murphy undergoes 'fugue states.' Psychotic episodes that relate to both amnesia and hysteria. He talks about 'lost days,' 'lost weekends,' even 'lost weeks.' In such a fugue state, a patient can wake in a strange place and have no idea how he got there, or what he had been doing for a prolonged period. In some cases, the patients have two separate personalities, often antithetical personalities. This can also happen in temporal lobe epilepsy."

"What are you guys, a tag team?" Walsh grumped from his seat. "Lobe epilepsy. Give me a break, Marion. The more you fool around like this, the better his chance of getting off in a courtroom," Walsh warned.

"I'm not fooling around," I said to Walsh. "Not my style."

222 / James Patterson

The D.A. spoke up, intervening between Walsh and me. James Dowd was a serious man in his late thirties or early forties. If Dowd got to try the case of Soneji/Murphy, he would soon be an extremely famous attorney.

"Isn't there a possibility that he's created this apparently psychotic condition for our benefit?" Dowd asked. "That he's a psychopath, and nothing more than that?"

I glanced around the table before answering his questions. Dowd clearly wanted to hear our answers; he wanted to learn the truth. The representative from the governor's office seemed skeptical and unconvinced, but open-minded. The attorney general's group was neutral so far. Dr. Walsh had already heard enough from me and Campbell.

"That's a definite possibility," I said. "It's one of the reasons I'd like to try the regressive hypnosis. For one thing, we can see if his stories remain consistent."

"*If* he's susceptible to hypnosis," Walsh interjected. "And if you can tell whether or not he'd been hypnotized."

"I suspect that he is susceptible," I answered quickly.

"And I have my doubts that he is. Frankly, I have my doubts about you, Cross. I don't care that he likes to talk to you. Psychiatry isn't about liking your doctor."

"What he likes is that I *listen*." I glared across the table at Walsh. It took a lot of self-control not to jump on the officious bastard.

"What are the other reasons for hypnotizing the prisoner?" the governor's representative spoke up.

"Frankly, we don't know enough about what he's done during these fugue states," Dr. Campbell said. "Neither does he. Neither do his wife and family, whom I've interviewed several times now."

I added, "We're also not sure how many personalities might be operating. . . . The other reason for hypnosis" — I paused to let what I was about to say sink in — "is that I do want to ask him about Maggie Rose Dunne. I want to try and find out what he did with Maggie Rose."

"Well, we've heard your arguments, Dr. Cross. Thank you for your time and efforts here," James Dowd said at the end of the presentation. "We'll have to let you know."

I decided to take things into my own hands that evening.

I called a reporter I knew and trusted at the *Post*. I asked him to meet me at Pappy's Diner on the edge of Southeast. Pappy's was one place where we would never be spotted, and I didn't want anyone to know we'd met. For both our sakes.

Lee Kovel was a graying yuppie, and kind of an asshole, but I liked him. Lee wore his emotions on his sleeve: his petty jealousies, his bitterness about the sad state of journalism, his bleeding-heart tendencies, his occasional arch-conservative traits. It was all out there for the world to see and react to.

Lee plopped down next to me at the counter. He was wearing a gray suit and light blue running shoes. Pappy's draws a real nice cross-section: black, Hispanic, Korean, working-class whites who service Southeast in some way or other. But no one anything like Lee.

"I stick out like a sore thumb in here," he complained. "I'm way too cool for this place."

"Now who's going to see you here? Bob Woodward? Evans and Novak?"

"Very funny, Alex. What's on your mind? Why didn't you call me when this story was hot? *Before* this sucker got caught?"

"Would you give this man some hot, very black coffee," I said to the counterman. "I need to wake him up." I turned back to Lee. "I'm going to hypnotize Soneji inside the prison. I'm going looking for Maggie Rose Dunne *in his subconscious*. You can have the exclusive. But you owe me one," I told Lee.

Lee Kovel almost spit out his reaction. "Bullshit! Let's hear it all, Alex. I think you left out some parts."

"Right. I'm *working* to get permission to hypnotize Soneji. There are a lot of petty politics involved. If you leak the story in the *Post*, I think it will happen. The theory of self-fulfilling prophecies. I'll get permission. *Then* you get an exclusive."

The coffee came in a beautiful old diner cup. Light brown with a thin blue line under the rim. Lee slurped the java, thoughtful as hell. He seemed amused that I was trying to manipulate the established order in D.C. It appealed to his bleeding heart.

"And if you do hear something from Gary Soneji, I'll be the second to know. After yourself, Alex."

"You drive a hard bargain, but yeah. That'll be our deal. Think about it, Lee. It's for a worthy cause. Finding out about Maggie Rose, not to mention your career."

I left Kovel to finish his Pappy's coffee and begin to shape his story. Apparently, that's what he did. It appeared in the morning edition of the *Post*.

Nana Mama is the first one up at our house every day. Probably, she's the first one up in the entire universe. That's what Sampson and I used to believe when we were ten or eleven, and she was the assistant principal of the Garfield North Junior High School.

Whether I wake up at seven, or six, or five, I always come down to the kitchen to find a light blazing and Nana already eating breakfast, or firing it up over her stove. Most mornings, it is the very same breakfast. A single poached egg; one corn muffin, buttered; weak tea with cream and double sugar.

She will also have begun to make breakfast for the rest of us, and she recognizes the variety of our palates. The house menu might include pancakes and either pork sausage or bacon; melon in season; grits, or oatmeal, or farina, with a thick pat of butter and a generous mound of sugar on top; eggs in every shape and form.

Occasionally a grape jelly omelet appears, the only dish of hers that I don't care for. Nana does the omelet too brown on the outside, and, as I've told her, eggs and jelly make about as much sense to me as pancakes and ketchup. Nana disagrees, though she never eats the jelly omelets herself. The kids love them.

Nana sat at the kitchen table on that morning in March. She was reading the *Washington Post*, which happens to be delivered by a man named Washington. Mr. Washington eats breakfast with Nana every Monday morning. This was a Wednesday, and an important day for the investigation.

Everything about the breakfast scene was so familiar, and yet I was startled as I entered the kitchen. One more time, I was made aware of how much the kidnapping had entered into our private lives, the lives of my family members.

The headline of the *Washington Post* read:

SONEJI/MURPHY
TO BE HYPNOTIZED

Attached to the story I could see photographs of both Soneji/Murphy and me. I'd heard the news late the night before. I had called Lee Kovel to give him his exclusive because of our deal.

I read Lee's story while eating two morning prunes. It said that certain unnamed "sources were skeptical about the opinions of psychologists assigned to the kidnapper"; that "medical findings may have an effect on the trial"; that "if proven insane, Soneji/Murphy could get a sentence as lenient as three years in an institution." Obviously, Lee had spoken to other sources after he talked to me.

"Why don't they just come out and say what they mean," Nana mumbled over her toast and cup of tea. I guess she didn't care for Lee's writing style.

"Why don't they say what?" I asked.

"The obvious thing here. Somebody doesn't want you messing with his neat little case. They want Tide-clean justice. Not necessarily the truth. Nobody seems to want the truth here, anyway. They just want to feel better right away. They want *the pain to be over*. People have a low tolerance for pain, especially lately. Ever since Dr. Spock began rearing our children for us."

"Is that what you've been plotting down here over your breakfast? Sounds a little like *Murder, She Wrote*."

I poured myself some of her tea. No sugar or cream. I took a muffin and put a couple of link sausages between the halves.

"No plots. Reality as plain as the nose on your face, Alex."

I nodded at Nana. She might be right, but it was too deflating to deal with before six in the morning. "Nothing like prunes this early in the morning," I said. "Mmm, mmm good."

"Hmmm." Nana Mama frowned. "I might go easy on those prunes for a while if I were you. I suspect you're going to need an extra supply of bull from here on, Alex. If I may be so blunt with you."

"Thank you, Nana. Your directness is appreciated."

"You're very welcome. For your breakfast, and this splendid advice: Don't trust white people."

"Very good breakfast," I said to her.

"How is your new girlfriend?" asked my grandmother.

She never misses a trick.

CHAPTER 50

THERE WAS A HIGH-PITCHED HUMMING in the air as I climbed out of my car at the prison. The noise was a physical thing. Reporters from newspapers and TV stations were loitering everywhere outside Lorton. They were waiting for me. So was Soneji/Murphy. He had been moved to a regular cell in the prison.

As I walked from the parking lot in a light drizzle, TV cameras and microphones jabbed at me from a dozen different angles. I was there to hypnotize Gary Soneji/Murphy, and the press knew it. I was today's big bite of news.

"Thomas Dunne says you're trying to get Soneji hospitalized, that you'll have him set free in a couple of years. Any comment, Detective Cross?"

"I have nothing to say right now." I couldn't talk to any of the reporters, which didn't make me real popular. I'd made a deal with the attorney general's office before they finally agreed to the sessions.

Hypnosis is commonly used in psychiatry these days. It's often administered by the treating psychiatrist, or a psychologist. What I hoped to discover over several interviews was what had happened to Gary Soneji/Murphy during his "lost days," his escapes from the real world. I didn't know whether this would happen quickly or, indeed, happen at all.

Once I was inside Gary's prison cell, the process was simple and straightforward. I suggested that he relax and close his eyes. Next, I asked Gary to breathe in, then out, very evenly and slowly. I told him to try to clear his mind of every thought. Finally, to count down slowly from one hundred.

He appeared to be a good subject for hypnosis. He didn't resist, and he slipped deeply into a suggestible state. As far as I could tell, he was under. I proceeded as if he were, anyway. I watched him for signs to the contrary, but I saw none.

His breathing had slowed noticeably. In the beginning of the session, he was more relaxed than I had seen him before. We chatted about casual, nonthreatening subjects for the first few moments.

Since he had actually *"come to"* or become *"himself"* in the parking lot of the McDonald's, I asked Gary about that once he was fully relaxed.

"Do you remember being arrested at a McDonald's in Wilkinsburg?"

There was a brief pause — then he said, "Oh, yes, of course I do."

"I'm glad you remember, because I have a couple of questions about the circumstances at McDonald's. I'm a little unclear about the sequence of events. Do you remember anything you might have eaten inside the restaurant?"

I could see his eyes rolling behind the closed lids. He was thinking about it before answering. Gary had on thongs and his left foot was tapping rapidly.

"No . . . no . . . can't say that I do. Did I actually eat there? I don't remember. I'm not sure if I ate or not."

At least he didn't deny he'd been inside the McDonald's.

"Did you notice any people at the McDonald's?" I asked. "Do you remember any customers? A counter girl you might have spoken to?"

"Mmmm . . . It was crowded. No one in particular comes to mind. I recall thinking that some people dress so badly it's comical. You see it in any mall. All the time at places like HoJo's and McDonald's."

In his mind, he was still inside the McDonald's. He'd come that far with me. *Stay with me, Gary.*

"Did you use the rest room?" I already knew that he had gone to the bathroom. Most of his actions were covered in the reports of the arrest.

"Yes, I used the rest room," he answered.

"How about a beverage? Something to drink? Bring me along with you. Put yourself right there as much as you can."

He smiled. "Please. Don't condescend."

He had cocked his head a little oddly. Then, Gary started to laugh. A peculiar laugh, deeper than usual. Strange, though not completely alarming. His voice patterns were becoming more rapid, and very clipped. His foot was tapping faster and faster.

"You're not smart enough to do this," he said.

I was a little surprised by the change in his tone of voice. "To do what? Tell me what you're saying, Gary. I don't follow you."

"To try and trick *him*. That's what I'm saying. You're bright, but not that bright."

"Who am I trying to trick?"

"*Soneji*, of course. He's right there in the McDonald's. He's *pretending* to get coffee, but he's really pissed off. He's about to go nuclear. He *needs* attention now."

I sat forward in my chair. I hadn't expected this.

"Why is he angry? Do *you* know why?" I asked.

"He's pissed because they got lucky. That's why."

"*Who* got lucky?"

"The police. He's pissed because stupid people could luck out and ruin everything, screw up the master plan."

"I'd like to talk to *him* about it," I said. I was trying to stay as matter-of-fact as he was. If Soneji were *here* now, maybe we could talk.

"No! No. You're not on a level with him. You wouldn't understand anything he has to say. You don't have a clue about Soneji."

"Is he still angry? Is he angry now? Being here in prison? What does Soneji think about being in this cell?"

"He says — *fuck you. FUCK YOU!*"

He lunged at me. He grabbed my shirt and tie, the front of my sport jacket.

He was physically strong, but so am I. I let him hold, and I held on to him. We were in a powerful bear hug. Our heads came together and cracked. I could have broken free, but I didn't try. He wasn't really hurting me. It was more as if he were issuing a threat, drawing a line between us.

Campbell and his guards came rushing down the corridor. Soneji/Murphy let go of me and began throwing himself at the cell door. Spit ran from the side of his mouth. He began screaming. Cursing at the top of his voice.

The guards wrestled him onto the floor. They restrained him with difficulty. Soneji was much more powerful than his slender body would have suggested. I already knew that from experience.

The R.N. followed them in, and gave him a shot of Ativan. Within minutes, he was asleep on the floor of the cell.

The guards lifted him onto his cot and wrapped him in a restraining jacket. I waited until they locked him in the cell.

Who was in the cell?

Gary Soneji?

Gary Murphy?

Or both of them?

CHAPTER 51

THAT NIGHT, Chief Pittman called me at home. I didn't think he wanted to congratulate me on my work with Soneji/Murphy. I was right. The Jefe did ask me to stop by his office the next morning.

"What's up?" I asked him.

He wouldn't tell me over the phone. I guess he didn't want to spoil the surprise.

In the morning, I made sure I was clean-shaven, and I put on my leather car coat for the occasion. I played a little Lady Day on the porch before I left the house. Think darkness and light. Be darkness and light. I played "The Man I Love," "For All We Know," "That's Life, I Guess." Then off to see The Jefe.

When I arrived at Pittman's office, there was too much activity for quarter to eight in the morning. Even The Jefe's assistant seemed fully employed for a change.

Old Fred Cook is a failed vice detective, now posing as an administrative assistant. He looks like one of the artifacts they trot out for old-timer baseball games. Fred is mean-spirited, petty, and supremely political. Dealing through him is like giving messages to a wax-museum doll.

"Chief's ready for you." He served up one of his thin-lipped smiles. Fred Cook relishes knowing things before the rest of us. Even when he doesn't know, he acts as if he does.

"What's going on this morning, Fred?" I asked him straight out. "You can tell me."

I saw that all-knowing glint in his eyes. "Why don't you just go in there and see. I'm sure the chief will explain his intentions."

"I'm proud of you, Fred. You sure can be trusted with a secret. You know, you should be on the National Security Council."

I went inside expecting the worst. But I underestimated the chief of detectives a little.

Mayor Carl Monroe was in the office with Pittman. So was our police captain, Christopher Clouser, and, of all people, John Sampson. It appeared that one of Washington's ever-so-popular morning events, a working breakfast, had been set up in the chief's inner sanctum.

"It's not *all* bad," Sampson said in a low voice. In sharp contrast to his words, Sampson looked like a large animal caught in one of those double-clawed spring-traps hunters use. I got the feeling he would happily have chewed his foot off to escape from the room.

"It's not bad at all." Carl Monroe smiled jovially when he saw the chiseled look on my face. "We have some good news for you both. Very good news. Shall I? Yeah, I think so. . . . You and Sampson are being promoted today. Right here. Congratulations to our newest senior detective and our newest divisional chief."

They clapped approvingly. Sampson and I exchanged quizzical looks. What the hell was going on?

If I'd known, I would have brought Nana and the kids along. It was like those affairs where the president gives medals and thanks to war widows. Only this time, *the dead* had been invited to the ceremony. Sampson and I were dead in the eyes of Chief Pittman.

"Maybe you'd like to tell Sampson and me what's going on here?" I smiled conspiratorially at Monroe. "You know, the sub-text."

Carl Monroe had his magnificent smile blazing away. It was so warm, and personal, and "genuine." "I was asked to come here," he said, "because you and Detective Sampson were being promoted. That's about it. I was very happy to come, Alex" — he made a comic face — "at quarter to eight this morning."

Actually, it's hard not to like Carl sometimes. He's totally aware of who and what he's become as a politician. He reminds me of the prostitutes on 14th Street who will tell you a raunchy joke or two when you have to pull them in for soliciting.

"There are a couple of other things to discuss," Pittman said, but then waved off the idea of any real substance entering the ceremonial conversation. "They can wait until after. There's coffee and sweetcakes first."

"I think we ought to discuss everything now," I said. I shifted my eyes to Monroe. "Put it out on the table with the sweet-cakes."

Monroe shook his head. "Why don't you go slow for a change?"

"I'm not going to be able to run for public office, am I?" I said to the mayor. "Not much of a politician."

Monroe shrugged, but he continued to smile. "I don't know about that, Alex. Sometimes a man changes to a more effective style as he gains experience. Sees what works, what doesn't. It's definitely more satisfying to be confrontational. Doesn't always serve the greater good, though."

"Is that what this is about? The greater good? That's the topic for this morning's breakfast?" Sampson asked the group.

"I think so. Yes, I believe it is." Monroe nodded and bit into one of the sweetcakes.

Chief Pittman poured coffee into an expensive china cup that was too small and delicate for his hand. It made me think of little watercress sandwiches. Rich people's lunches.

"We're bumping into the FBI, Justice, the Secret Service, on this kidnapping case. It's no good for anybody. We've decided to pull back completely. To take you off the case again," Pittman finally said.

Bingo. The other shoe had dropped. The truth was out at our little working breakfast.

All of a sudden, everybody in the office was talking at once. At least two of us were shouting. Neat party.

"This is total bullshit," Sampson told the mayor to his face. "And you know it. You do know it, don't you?"

"I've begun sessions with Soneji/Murphy," I said to Pittman and Monroe and Captain Clouser. "I hypnotized him yesterday. Jesus fucking Christ, no. Don't do this. Not now."

"We're aware of your progress with Gary Soneji. We had to make a decision, and we've made it."

"You want the truth, Alex?" Carl Monroe's voice suddenly rang out in the room. "You want to hear the truth about this?"

I looked at him. "Always."

Monroe stared right into my eyes. "A great deal of pressure has been used by the attorney general on a lot of people in Washington. A huge trial *will begin,* I believe, within six weeks at the most. The Orient Express has already left the station, Alex. You're not on it. I'm not on it. It's gotten much bigger than either of us. Soneji/Murphy is on it. . . .

"The prosecutor, the *Justice Department,* has decided to stop your sessions with Soneji/Murphy. A team of psychiatrists has been formally assigned to him. That's the way it will work from here on. That's the way it's going to be. This case has moved into a new phase, and our involvement won't be needed."

Sampson and I walked out on our own party. Our involvement was no longer needed.

CHAPTER 52

FOR THE NEXT WEEK, I got home from work at a sane hour, usually between six and six-thirty. No more eighty- and hundred-hour work weeks. Damon and Janelle couldn't have been happier if I'd been fired from the job outright.

We rented Walt Disney and Teenage Mutant Ninja Turtles videos, listened to the three-disc set *Billie Holiday: The Legacy 1933–1958*, fell asleep on the couch together. All sorts of amazing good stuff.

One afternoon, the kids and I visited Maria's grave site. Neither Jannie nor Damon had completely gotten over losing their mom. On the way out of the cemetery, I stopped at another grave, Mustaf Sanders's final place. I could still see his sad little eyes staring at me. The eyes were asking me, *Why?* No answer yet, Mustaf. But I wasn't ready to give up.

On a Saturday toward the end of summer, Sampson and I made the long drive to Princeton, New Jersey. Maggie Rose Dunne still hadn't been found. Neither had the ten-million-dollar ransom. We were rechecking everything on our own time.

We talked to several neighbors of the Murphys'. The Murphy family *had* all perished in a fire, but no one had suspected Gary.

Gary Murphy had been a model student as far as everyone around Princeton knew. He'd graduated fourth in his class at the local high school, though he never seemed to study or compete. Nor did he get into any kind of trouble, at least none that his neighbors in Princeton knew about. The young man they described was similar to the Gary Murphy I'd interviewed at Lorton Prison.

Everyone agreed — except for a single boyhood friend whom we located with some difficulty. The friend, Simon Conklin, now worked at one of the local produce markets as a greengrocer. He lived alone, about fifteen miles outside Princeton Village. The reason we went looking for him was that Missy Murphy had mentioned Conklin to me. The FBI had interviewed him, and gotten little for their efforts.

At first Simon Conklin refused to talk to us, to any more cops. When we threatened to haul him down to Washington, he finally opened up a little.

"Gary always had everybody fooled," Conklin told us in the disheveled living room of his small house. He was a tall unkempt man. He seemed frazzled and his clothes were hopelessly mismatched. He was very smart, though. He'd been a National Merit student, just like his friend Gary Murphy. "Gary said the great ones always fooled everybody. Great Ones in caps, you understand. Thus spake Gary!"

"What did he mean, the 'great ones'?" I asked Conklin. I thought I could keep him talking, as long as I played to his ego. I could get what I needed out of Conklin.

"He called them the Ninety-ninth Percentile," Conklin confided to me. "The *crème de la crème*. The best of the best. The World-beaters, man."

"The best of *what*?" Sampson wanted to know. I could tell he wasn't too fond of Simon Conklin. His shades were steaming up. But he was playing along, being the good listener so far.

"The best of the *real* psychos," Conklin said, and he smiled smugly. "The ones who have always been out there, and will *never ever* get caught. The ones who're too smart to get caught. They look down on everybody else. They show no pity, no mercy. They completely rule their own destinies."

"Gary Murphy was one of them?" I asked. I knew that he wanted to talk now. About Gary, but also about himself. I sensed that Conklin considered himself in the Ninety-ninth Percentile.

"No. Not according to Gary." He shook his head and kept the disturbing half smile. "According to Gary, he was a lot smarter than the Ninety-ninth Percentile. He always believed he was an original. The original. Called himself a 'freak of nature.'"

Simon Conklin told us how he and Gary had lived on the same country road about six miles outside of town. They'd taken the school bus together. They'd been friends since they were nine or ten. The road was the same one that led to the Lindbergh farmhouse in Hopewell.

Simon Conklin told us that Gary Murphy had definitely paid his family back with the fire. He knew all about Gary's child-abuse sufferings. He could never prove it, but he knew Gary had set the blaze.

"I'll tell you exactly how I know his plan. He told me — when we were twelve years old. Gary said he was going to get them for his twenty-first birthday. He said he'd do it so it looked like he was away at school. That he'd never be a suspect. And that's what the boy did, didn't he? He waited for nine long years. He had a nine-year plan for that one."

We talked to Simon Conklin for three hours one day, then five more hours the following day. He told a series of sad and gruesome stories. Gary locked away in the Murphy basement for days and weeks at a time. Gary's obsessive plans: *ten-year plans, fifteen-year plans, life plans*. Gary's secret war against small animals, especially pretty birds that flew into his stepmother's garden. How he would pluck off a robin's leg, then a wing, then a second leg, for as long as the bird had the will to live. Gary's vision to see himself way up in the Ninety-ninth Percentile, right at the top. Finally, Gary's ability to mimic, to act, to play parts.

I would have liked to have known about it while I was still meeting with Gary Murphy at Lorton Prison. I would have wanted to spend several sessions with Gary, prowling around his old Princeton haunts. Talking to Gary about his friend Simon Conklin.

Unfortunately, I had been taken off that part of the case now. The kidnapping case had moved way beyond me and Sampson, and Simon Conklin.

I gave our leads in Princeton over to the FBI. I wrote a twelve-page report on Simon Conklin. The Bureau never followed up on it. I wrote a second report and sent copies to everyone on the original search team. In my report was something Simon Conklin had said about his boyhood friend, Gary Murphy: "Gary always said he was going to do *important things.*"

Not a thing happened. Simon Conklin wasn't interviewed again by the FBI. They didn't want to open up new leads. They wanted the kidnapping case of Maggie Rose Dunne closed.

CHAPTER 53

IN LATE SEPTEMBER, Jezzie Flanagan and I went away to the islands. We escaped for a long weekend. Just the two of us. It was Jezzie's idea. I thought it was a good one. R & R. We were curious. Apprehensive. Excited about four uninterrupted days together. Maybe we wouldn't be able to stand each other for that long. That's what we needed to find out.

On Front Street on Virgin Gorda, hardly a head turned to look at us. That was nice for a change, different from D.C., where people usually stared.

We took scuba and snorkeling lessons from a seventeen-year-old black woman. We rode horses along a beach that ran uninterrupted for over three miles. We drove a Range Rover up into the jungle and got lost for a half day. The most unforgettable experience was a visit to an unlikely place that we named Jezzie and Alex's Private Island in Paradise. It was a spot the hotel found for us. They dropped us off in a boat, and left us all alone.

"This is the most awe-inspiring place that I've ever been in my life," Jezzie said. "Look at all this water and sand. Overhanging cliffs, the reef out there."

"It's not Fifth Street. But it's okay." I smiled and looked around. I did a few three-sixties at the edge of the water.

Our private island was mostly a long shelf of white sand that felt like sugar under our feet. Beyond the beach was the lushest green jungle we had ever seen. It was dotted with white roses and bougainvillea. The blue-green sea there was as clear as spring water.

The kitchen at the inn had packed a lunch — fine wines, exotic cheeses, lobster, crabmeat, and various salads. Not another person was anywhere in sight. We did the natural thing. We took off our clothes. No shame. No taboos. We were alone in paradise, right?

I started to laugh out loud as I lay on the beach with Jezzie. That was something else I was doing more than I had in a long, long time — smiling, feeling at peace with the surroundings. *Feeling,* period. I was incredibly thankful to be feeling. Three and a half years was too long a time for mourning.

"Do you have any idea how beautiful you really are?" I said to her as we lay together.

"I don't know if you've noticed, but I carry a compact in my purse. Little mirror." She looked into my eyes. She was studying something in them I would never see. "Actually, I've tried to avoid the issue of being attractive since I joined the Service. That's how screwed up things are in macho-man Washington."

Jezzie gave me a wink. "You can be so serious, Alex. But you're also full of fun. I'll bet only your kids get to see this side of you. Damon and Jannie know you. *Booga, booga.*" She tickled me.

"Don't switch subjects on me. We were talking about you."

"*You* were. Occasionally, I want to be pretty, but most times I just want to be Plain Jane. Wear big pink curlers to bed and watch old movies."

"You've been beautiful all weekend. No pink curlers. Ribbons and fresh flowers in your hair. Strapless bathing suits. Occasionally, no bathing suits."

"I want to be pretty right now. In Washington, it's different. It's one more problem to solve. Imagine going to see your boss. Important report you've been working on for months. The first thing he says is, 'You look terrific in a dress, babe.' You just want to say, 'Fuck you, asshole.'"

I reached out and we held hands. "Thank you, for the way you look," I said. "You look so beautiful."

"I did it just for you." Jezzie smiled. "And I'd like to do something else for you. I'd like you to do something *for me,* too."

And so we did one another.

So far, Jezzie and I weren't getting tired of each other. Quite the opposite was happening down here in paradise.

That night, we sat at an outdoor raw bar in town. We watched the carefree island world go by, and wondered why we didn't just drop out and become part of it. We ate shrimp and oysters and talked for a couple of hours straight. We let our hair down, especially Jezzie.

"I've been a really driven person, Alex," Jezzie said to me. "I don't mean just on the kidnapping case, butting my way into every briefing, every wild goose chase. I've been that way ever since I can remember. Once I start on an idea, I can't turn it off."

I didn't say anything. I wanted to listen to her. I wanted to know all there was to know.

 She raised her mug. "I'm sitting here with a beer in my hand, right. Well, both my parents were alcoholics. They were dysfunctional before it was fashionable. Nobody outside our house knew how bad it was. They would have screaming fights constantly. My dad usually passed out. Slept in 'his chair.' My mother would stay awake half the night at the dining-room table. She loved her Jameson's. She'd say, 'Get me another of my Jameson's, Little Jezzie.' I was their little cocktail waitress. That's how I earned my allowance until I was eleven."

Jezzie stopped talking and looked into my eyes. I hadn't seen her so vulnerable and unsure of herself. She projected such confidence most of the time. That was her reputation in the Secret Service. "Do you want to leave now? Want me to lighten up?"

I shook my head. "No, Jezzie. I want to listen to whatever you have to say. I want to know all about you."

"Are we still on vacation?"

"Yes, and I really want to hear about this. Just talk to me. Trust me. If I get bored, I'll just get up and leave you with the bar tab."

She smiled and went on. "I loved both my parents in a strange way. I believe that they loved me. Their 'Little Jezzie.' I told you once how I didn't want to be a smart failure like my parents."

"Maybe you understated things just a little." I smiled.

"Yeah. Well, anyway, I worked long nights and weekends when I got into the Service. I set impossible goals for myself — supervisor at twenty-eight — and I beat every goal. That's part of what happened with my husband. I put my job ahead of our marriage. Want to know why I started riding the motorcycle?"

"Yep. Also why you make me ride your motorcycle."

"Well, see," Jezzie said, "I could never make work stop. Couldn't turn it off when I went home at night. Not until I got the bike. When you're doing a hundred and twenty, you have to concentrate on the road. Everything else goes away. The Job finally goes away."

"That's partly why I play the piano," I said to her. "I'm sorry about your parents, Jezzie."

"I'm glad I finally told you about them," Jezzie said. "I've never told anyone before you. Not one other person knows the whole true story."

Jezzie and I held each other at the little island raw bar. I'd never felt so close to her. Sweet little Jezzie. Of all the times we were together, it was one I'd never forget. Our visit to paradise.

Suddenly, and way too quickly, our busman's holiday was over.

We found ourselves trapped on board an American Airlines flight back to Washington, back to dreary, rainy weather, according to reports. Back to The Job.

We were a little distant from each other during the flight. We started sentences at the same time, then had to play "you go first" games. For the first time during the entire trip, we talked shop, the dreaded shoptalk.

"Do you really think he has a multiple personality, Alex? Does he know what happened to Maggie Rose? Soneji knows. Does Murphy know?"

"On some level, he knows. He was scary that one time he talked about Soneji. Whether Soneji is a separate personality or his real persona, he's frightening. *Soneji* knows what happened to Maggie Rose."

"Too bad we never will now. It seems that way, anyhow."

"Yeah. Because I think I could get it out of him. It just takes some time."

National Airport in D.C. was a natural disaster that several thousand of us got to experience together. Traffic just barely crept along. The line for cabs curled back into the terminal. Everybody looked soaked to the skin.

Neither Jezzie nor I had raincoats and we were getting soaked through. Life was suddenly depressing, and all too real again. The stalled investigation was here in D.C. The trial was coming. I probably had a message from Chief Pittman on my desk.

"Let's go back. Let's turn around." Jezzie took my hand, and she pulled me close in front of the glass doorway to the Delta Shuttle.

The warmth and familiar smells of her body were still nice. The last scents of cocoa butter and aloe still lingered.

People turned to stare at us as they passed. They looked. They judged. Almost every person who passed us looked.

"Let's get out of here," I said.

CHAPTER 54

*P*OW. At 2:30 on Tuesday afternoon (I got back to Washington at eleven o'clock), I got a call from Sampson. He wanted to meet me at the Sanders house. He thought we'd made a new connection between the kidnapping and the project murders. He was pumped as hell with his news. Hard work was paying off on one of our early leads.

I hadn't been back to the Sanders crime scene in several months, but it was all sadly familiar. The windows were dark from the outside. I wondered if the house would ever be sold, or even rented again.

I sat in my car in the Sanders driveway, and read through the original detectives' report. There was nothing in the reports I didn't already know and hadn't gone over a dozen times.

I kept staring at the house. The yellowing shades were drawn, so I couldn't see inside. Where was Sampson, and what did he want with me here?

He pulled up behind me at three o'clock sharp. He climbed out of his battered Nissan and joined me in the front seat of the Porsche.

"Oh, you *are* brown sugar now. You look sweet enough to eat."

"You're still big and ugly. Nothing changes. What do you have here?"

"Police work at its very best," Sampson said. He lit up a Corona. "By the way, you were right to keep after this thing."

Outside the car, the wind was howling and heavy with rain. There had been tornadoes down through Kentucky and Ohio. The weather had been bizarre the whole weekend that we were away.

"Did you snorkel, and sail, play tennis in your club whites?" Sampson asked.

"We didn't have time for that kind of stuff. We did a lot of spiritual bonding you wouldn't understand."

"My, my." Sampson talked like a black girlfriend, played the part well. "I love to talk the trash, don't you, sister?"

"Are we going inside?" I asked him.

Selective scenes from the past had been flashing into my head for several minutes, none of them pleasant. I remembered the face of the fourteen-year-old Sanders girl. And three-year-old Mustaf. I remembered what beautiful children they had been. I remembered how nobody cared when they died here in Southeast.

"Actually, we're here to visit the next-door neighbors," he finally said. "Let's go to work. Something happened here that I don't understand yet. It's important, though, Alex. I need your head on it."

We went to visit the Sanderses' next-door neighbors, the Cerisiers. It *was* important. It got my full attention, immediately.

I already knew that Nina Cerisier had been Suzette Sanders's best friend since they were little girls. The families had been living next door to each other since 1979. Nina, as well as her mother and father, hadn't gotten over the murders. If they could have afforded to, they would have moved away.

We were invited in by Mrs. Cerisier, who shouted upstairs

for her daughter Nina. We were seated around the Cerisiers' kitchen table. A picture of a smiling Magic Johnson was on the wall. Cigarette smoke and bacon grease were in the air.

Nina Cerisier was very cool and distant when she finally appeared in the kitchen. She was a plain-looking girl, about fifteen or sixteen. I could tell that she didn't want to be there.

"Last week," Sampson said for my benefit, "Nina came forward and told a teacher's aide at Southeast that she might have seen the killer a couple of nights before the murders. She'd been afraid to talk about it."

"I understand," I said. It is almost impossible to get eyewitnesses to talk to police in Condon or Langley, or any of D.C.'s black neighborhoods.

"I saw he been caught," Nina said in an offhand manner. Beautiful rust-colored eyes stared at me from her plain face. "I wasn't so scared no more. I'm still some scared, though."

"How did you recognize him?" I asked Nina.

"Saw him on the TV. He did that big kidnapping thing, too," she said. "He all over TV."

"She recognized Gary Murphy," I said to Sampson. That meant she'd seen him without his schoolteacher disguise.

"You sure it was the same man as on TV?" Sampson asked Nina.

"Yes. He watch my girlfriend Suzette's house. I thought it real strange. Not many whites 'round here."

"Did you see him in the daytime, or at night?" I asked the girl.

"Night. But I know it him. Sanderses' porch light on bright. Missus Sanders afraid of everything, everybody. Poo 'fraid you say boo. That's what Suzette, me, used to say she like."

I turned to Sampson. "Puts him at the murder scene."

Sampson nodded and looked back at Nina. Her pouty mouth was open in a small "o." Her hands constantly twirled her braided hair.

"Would you tell Detective Cross what else you saw?" he asked.

"Another white man with him," Nina Cerisier said. "Man wait in his car while the other, he looking at Suzette's house. Other white man here all the time. Two men."

Sampson turned the kitchen chair around to face me. "They're busy rushing him to trial," he said. "They don't have *a clue* what's really going on. They're going to finish it, anyway. Bury it. Maybe *we* have the answer, Alex."

"So far, we're the only ones who have a few of the answers," I said.

Sampson and I left the Cerisier house and drove downtown in separate cars. My mind was racing through everything we knew so far, half-a-dozen possible scenarios culled from thousands. Police work. An inch at a time.

I was thinking about Bruno Hauptmann and the Lindbergh kidnapping. After he'd been caught, and possibly framed, Bruno Hauptmann had been rushed to trial, too. Hauptmann had been convicted, maybe wrongly.

Gary Soneji/Murphy knew all about that. Was it all part of one of his complex game plans? A ten- or twelve-year plan? Who was the other white man? The pilot down in Florida? Or someone like Simon Conklin, Gary's friend from Princeton?

Could there have been *an accomplice* right from the beginning?

Later that night, I was with Jezzie. She insisted that I quit work at eight. For over a month, she'd had tickets for a Georgetown basketball game I wanted to see in the worst way. On our ride over there, we did something we rarely do: we talked about nothing but The Job. I dropped the latest bomb, the "accomplice theory," on her.

"I don't understand one beguiling aspect of all this," Jezzie said after she had listened to me tell Nina Cerisier's story. She was still nearly as hooked on the kidnapping case as I was. She was more subtle about it, but I could tell she was hooked.

"Ask the Shell Answer Man. I understand everything beguiling. I know beguiling up the wazoo."

"Okay. This girl was friends with Suzette Sanders, right? She was close to the family. And still, she didn't talk. Because relations with the police are that bad in the neighborhood? I don't know if I buy it. All of a sudden, *now,* she comes forward."

"I buy it," I told Jezzie. "The Metro police are like rat poison with lots of folks in these neighborhoods. I live there, they know me, and I'm just barely accepted."

"It's still strange to me, Alex. It's just too odd. The girls were supposed to be friends."

"It sure is strange. The PLO would talk to the Israeli Army before some of the people in Southeast would talk to the police."

"So what do you think now that you've heard the Cerisier girl and her supposed revelation? What do you make of this . . . *accomplice*?"

"It doesn't quite track for me yet," I admitted. "Which means that it tracks perfectly with everything that's happened so far. I believe the Cerisier girl saw *someone.* The question is, who?"

"Well, I have to say it, Alex, this lead sounds like a wild goose chase. I hope you don't become the Jim Garrison of this kidnapping."

Just before eight, we arrived at the Capital Centre in Landover, Maryland. Georgetown was playing St. John's from New York City. Jezzie had choice tickets. That proved she knew everyone in town. It's easier to get into an inauguration ball than certain Big East games.

We held hands as we strolled across the parking lot toward the glittery Cap Centre. I like Georgetown basketball, and I admire their coach, a black man named John Thompson. Sampson and I catch two or three home games a season.

"I'm psyched to see the Beast of the East," Jezzie supplied

some basketball lingo, with a wink, as we got close to the stadium.

"Versus the Hoyas," I said to her.

"The Hoyas are the Beast of the East." She popped her gum and made a face at me. "Don't get cute with me."

"You're so smart about every goddamn thing." I grinned. She was, too. It was difficult to bring up a subject she hadn't read about, or experienced. "What's the nickname for St. John's?"

"The St. John's Redmen. Chris Mullin came from there. They're also called the Johnnies. Chris Mullin plays for Golden State in the pros now. They're called the Warriors."

We both stopped talking at the same time. Whatever I was about to say caught in my throat.

"*Hey . . . hey, nigger-lover!*" someone had shouted across the parking lot. "Say hey, salt and pepper."

Jezzie's hand tightened around mine.

"Alex? Be cool. Just keep going," Jezzie said to me.

"I'm right here," I told her. "I'm as cool as can be."

"Let it go. Just walk into the Cap Centre with me. They're assholes. It doesn't deserve a response."

I let go of her hand. I walked in the direction of three men who were standing at the rear of a silver and blue four-by-four. Not Georgetown students, or St. John's Redmen, either. The men were wearing parkas, and peaked hats with company or team logos. They were free, white, and over twenty-one. Old enough to know better.

"Who said that?" I asked them. My body felt wooden, unreal. "Who said, 'Hey, nigger-lover'? Is that supposed to be funny? Am I missing a good joke here?"

One of them stepped forward to accept the credit. He spoke up from under a peaked Day-Glo Redskins hat. "What's it to you? You wanna go three on one, Magic? That's the way it's gonna be."

"I know it's a little unfair, me against the three of you, but I might just do that," I told him. "Maybe you can find a fourth real quick."

"Alex?" I heard Jezzie coming up behind. "Alex, please don't. Just walk away from them."

"Fuck you, Alex," one of the men said. "You need your lady's help on this one?"

"You like Alex, honey? Alex your main man?" I heard. "Your very own jungle bunny?"

I heard a sharp snap behind my eyes. The sound of the snap seemed very real. I felt myself snap.

I hit Redskins Hat with my first punch. I pivoted smoothly, and smacked a second one of the trio on the side of his temple.

The first man went down hard, his ball hat flying like a Frisbee. The second guy was staggered. Out on his feet. He went down on one knee and stayed there, indefinitely. All the fight was out of him.

"I am so tired of shit like this happening. I'm sick of it." I was shaking as I spoke.

"He had too much to drink, mister. We all did," the guy who was still standing said. "He's been all fucked up. Lot of pressure these days. Hell, we work with black guys. We got black friends. What can I say? We're sorry."

So was I. More than I cared to say to these assholes. I turned away from them, and Jezzie and I walked back to the car. My arms and legs felt as if they were made of stone. My heart was pounding like an oil derrick.

"I'm sorry," I said to her. I felt a little sick. "I can't take shit like that. I can't walk away anymore."

"I understand," Jezzie said softly. "You did what you had to." She was at my side. In this thing for the good and the bad.

We held one another inside my car for a long moment. Then we went home to be together.

CHAPTER 55

I GOT TO SEE Gary Murphy again on the first of October. "New evidence" was the stated reason. By that time, half the world had talked to Nina Cerisier. The "accomplice theory" had a life of its own.

We were using S.I.T. to scour the neighborhood around the Cerisier house. I'd tried everything from mug shot books to Identikit drawings with Nina Cerisier. So far, it hadn't helped her find a likeness of the "accomplice."

We knew it was a male, white, and Nina thought he had a stocky frame. The FBI claimed to be intensifying their search for the pilot in Florida. We'd see about that. I was back in the game again.

Dr. Campbell walked me down the maximum-security corridor inside Lorton Prison. Inmates glared out at us as we passed by. I glared back. I'm a good glarer, too.

Finally, we arrived at the cell block where Gary Soneji/ Murphy was still being kept.

Soneji/Murphy's cell, the entire corridor, was well-lighted, but he squinted up from his cot. It was as if he were peering out from a darkened cave.

It took a moment for him to recognize me.

When he finally did, he smiled. He still looked like this nice, small-town young man. Gary Murphy. A character out of a nineties remake of *It's a Wonderful Life.* I remembered his friend Simon Conklin telling me how Gary Murphy could play any role he needed to. It was all part of his being in the Ninety-ninth Percentile.

"Why did you stop coming to see me, Alex?" he asked. His eyes had an almost mournful look now. "I had nobody I could talk to. Those other doctors don't ever listen. Not really, they don't."

"They wouldn't let me see you for a while," I told him. "But it's worked out, so here I am."

He looked hurt. He was nibbling on his lower lip and staring down at his canvas prison shoes.

Suddenly, his face contorted and he laughed loudly. The sound echoed through the small cell.

Soneji/Murphy leaned closer to me. "You know, you're really just another dumb bastard," he said. "So fucking easy to manipulate. Just like all the others before you. Smart, but not smart enough."

I stared at him. Surprised. Maybe a little shocked.

"The lights are on, but there's nobody home," he commented on the expression that must have been on my face.

"No. I'm here," I said. "I just underestimated you more than I should have. My mistake."

"Caught up with reality, have we?" The terrible smirk remained across his face. "You sure you understand? You sure, Doctor-Detective?"

Of course I understood. I had just met Gary *Soneji* for the very first time. We had just been introduced by Gary Murphy. The process is called rapid cycling.

The kidnapper was staring out at me. He was gloating, showing off, being himself for the first time with me.

The child-murderer sat before me. The brilliant mimic and actor. The Ninety-ninth Percentile. The Son of Lindbergh. All of those things and probably more.

"You okay?" he asked. He was mimicking my earlier concern for him. "You feeling all right, Doctor?"

"I'm just great. No problem at all," I said.

"Really? You don't seem okay to me. Something's wrong, isn't it? Alex?" Now, he seemed deeply concerned.

"Hey, listen!" I finally raised my voice. "Fuck off, *Soneji*. How's that for reality testing?"

"Wait a minute." He shook his head back and forth. The wolfish grin had disappeared just as suddenly as it had appeared a moment before. "Why are you calling me Soneji? What is this, Doctor? What's going on?"

I watched his face, and I *could not believe* what I was seeing. He'd changed again. Snap. Gary Soneji was gone. He'd changed personas two, maybe three times in a matter of minutes.

"Gary Murphy?" I tested.

He nodded. "Who else? Seriously, Doctor, what's the matter? What is going on? You go away for weeks. Now you're back."

"Tell me what just happened," I said. I continued to stare at him. "Just now. Tell me what *you* think just happened."

He looked confused. Totally baffled by my question. If all of this was an act, it was the most brilliantly awesome and convincing performance I had ever seen in my years as a shrink.

"I don't understand. You come here to my cell. You seem a little tense. Maybe you were embarrassed because you haven't been around lately. Then you call me Soneji. Completely out of the blue. That's not supposed to be funny, is it?"

Was he serious now? Was it possible he didn't know what had happened less than sixty seconds ago?

Or was this Gary Soneji, still play-acting with me? Could he be slipping in and out of his fugue state so easily, and so seamlessly? It *could* be, but it was rare. In this case, it could create an unbelievable mockery of a courtroom trial.

It could even get Soneji/Murphy off.

Was that his plan? Had it been his escape valve right from the beginning?

CHAPTER 56

WHEN SHE WORKED with the others, picking fruits and vegetables on the side of the mountain, Maggie Rose tried to remember how it had been back home. At first, her "list," the things she remembered, was basic and very general.

Most of all, she missed her mother and father so much. She missed them every minute of every day.

She also missed her friends at school, especially Shrimpie.

She missed Dukado, her "fresh" little boy kitten.

And Angel, her "sweet" little boy kitten.

And Nintendo games and her clothes closet.

Having parties after school was so great.

So was taking a bath in the third-floor room over the gardens.

The more she thought about home, though, the more she remembered, the more Maggie Rose improved her memory list.

She missed the way she sometimes would get between her mother and father when they hugged or kissed. "We three," she called it.

She missed characters her father had enacted for her, mostly when she was little. There was Hank, a big Southern-drawling father, who loved to exclaim "Whooooo's talkin' to you?" There was "Susie Wooderman." Susie was the star of anything Maggie wanted to be in her father's stories.

There was the primal ritual whenever they had to get into the car in cold weather. They would all holler at the top of their voices, "Yuck chuck-chuck, chuck-a, chuck-a, yuck chuck-chuck."

Her mother would make up songs and sing them to her. Her mother had sung to her ever since she could remember.

She sang, "I love you so much, Maggie, there's nothing I wouldn't do for you. Nothing in the whole wide world." Maggie would sing, "Will you take me to Disneyland?" Her mom would answer, "I would do that, Maggie Rose." "Would you give Dukado a big kiss on the mouth?" "I'd do it for you, Maggie Rose. There's nothing I wouldn't do."

Maggie could remember whole days she had spent in school, going from class to class. She remembered Ms. Kim's "special winks" for her. She remembered when Angel would curl up in a chair and sweetly make a sound like *"wow."*

"I'd do anything for you, dear, anything, 'cause you mean everything to me." Maggie could still hear her mom singing the words to her.

"Would you please, please come and take me home?" Maggie sang inside her head. "Would you please, please come?"

But no one sang anything. Not anymore. No one ever sang to Maggie Rose. No one remembered her anymore. Or so she believed in her broken heart.

CHAPTER 57

I MET WITH SONEJI/MURPHY half-a-dozen times over the next two weeks. He wouldn't let me get close to him again, though he claimed this wasn't so. Something had changed. I'd lost him. *Both of him.*

On the fifteenth of October, a federal judge ordered a stay, temporarily halting the commencement of the kidnapping trial. This was to be the final of several delaying tactics by Soneji/Murphy's defense lawyer, Anthony Nathan.

Within one week, lightning speed for this kind of complex legal maneuvering, Judge Linda Kaplan had denied the defense requests. Requests for injunctions and restraining orders to the Supreme Court were also denied. Nathan called the Supreme Court "a very organized lynch mob" on all three TV networks. The fireworks were just beginning, he said to the press. He'd established a tone for the trial.

On the twenty-seventh of October, the trial of the *State* v. *Murphy* began. At five minutes to nine that morning, Sampson and I headed for a back entrance into the Federal Building on Indiana Avenue. As best we could, we were traveling incognito.

"You want to lose some money?" Sampson said as we turned the corner onto Indiana.

"I hope you're not talking about wagering money on the outcome of this kidnapping and murder trial?"

"Sure am, sweet pie. Make the time pass faster."

"What's the bet?"

Sampson lit a Corona and took a victory puff. "I'll take . . . I say he goes to St. Elizabeths, some hospital for the criminally insane. That's the bet."

"You're saying that our judicial system doesn't work."

"I believe it in every bone of my body. Specially this time around."

"All right — I'll take guilty, two counts kidnapping. Guilty, murder one."

Sampson took another victory puff. "You want to pay me now? Fifty be an acceptable amount for you to lose?"

"Fifty's fine with me. You got a bet."

"Get it on. I love to take what little money you have."

Out front on 3rd Street, a crowd of a couple of thousand surrounded the main courthouse entrance. Another two hundred people, including seven rows of reporters, were already inside. The prosecutor had tried to bar the press, but it had been denied.

Somebody had printed up signs and they were everywhere: *Maggie Rose Is Alive!*

People were handing out roses at the trial site. Up and down Indiana Avenue, volunteers circulated with the free roses. Others sold commemorative pennants. Most popular of all were the small candles that people burned in the windows of their homes as remembrances of Maggie Rose.

A handful of reporters were waiting at the back entrance, which is reserved for deliveries, as well as for a few shy judges and lawyers. Most veteran cops who come to the courthouse, and don't appreciate the crowds, also choose the back gate.

Microphones were immediately pushed at me and Sampson. TV camera lenses gawked. Neither instrument fazed us anymore.

"Detective Cross, is it true that you were cut out of the case by the FBI?"

"No. I have an okay relationship with the FBI."

"Are you still seeing Gary Murphy at Lorton, Detective?"

"That makes it sound as if we're dating. It's not that serious yet. I'm part of a team of doctors who see him."

"Are there racial overtones to this case, as it relates to you?"

"There are racial overtones to a lot of things, I guess. There's nothing special here."

"The other detective? Detective Sampson. You agree, sir?" a young dude in a bow tie asked.

"Well, sir yourself, we're going in the back door, aren't we? We're the back-door men." Sampson grinned for the camera. He didn't take off his shades.

We finally made it to a service elevator, and tried to keep the reporters out of the same car, which wasn't easy.

"We have a confirmed rumor that Anthony Nathan is going for a temporary-insanity plea. Any comment on that?"

"None at all. Ask Anthony Nathan."

"Detective Cross, will you take the stand to say Gary Murphy isn't insane?"

The ancient doors finally shut. The elevator started to rumble up toward the seventh floor, "Seventh Heaven," as it's known in the trade.

The seventh had never been quieter, or more under control. The usual train-station scene of policemen, young thugs and their families, hardened crooks, lawyers and judges, had been stemmed by an order restricting the floor to the single case. This was the big one. "Trial of the Century." Wasn't that the way Gary Soneji wanted it?

In the absence of chaos, the Fed Building was like an elderly person rising from bed in the morning. All the wrinkles and bruises were visible in the early-morning light that streamed from cathedral windows on the east side of the floor.

We arrived just in time to see the prosecutor enter the courtroom. Mary Warner was a diminutive thirty-six-year-old U.S. attorney from the Sixth Circuit. She was supposed to be the courtroom equal of defense lawyer Anthony Nathan. Like Nathan, she had never tasted defeat, at least not in any significant case. Mary Warner had a glowing reputation for tireless preparation, and faultless, highly persuasive courtroom demeanor. A losing opponent had said, "It's like playing tennis with somebody who always hits it back. Your best spin shot — back it comes. Your gamer — it comes back. Sooner or later, she beats you into the ground."

Supposedly, Ms. Warner had been handpicked by Jerrold Goldberg, and Goldberg could have had any prosecutor he chose. He had chosen her over James Dowd and other early favorites for the job.

Carl Monroe was there, too. Mayor Monroe couldn't stay away from the crowds. He saw me, but didn't come over, just flashed a patented smile across the broad concourse.

If I hadn't known exactly where I stood with him, I did now. My appointment to divisional chief would be my last upgrade. They'd done that to prove I had been a good choice for the Hostage Rescue Team, to validate their decision, and to cover up any possible questions about my conduct in Miami.

Leading up to the trial day, the big news around Washington had been that Secretary of the Treasury Goldberg was working on the prosecution case himself. That, and Anthony Nathan being the defense attorney.

Nathan had been described in the Post as a "ninja warrior in court." He had regularly been making front-page news since the day he'd been retained by Soneji/Murphy. Nathan was a subject that Gary wouldn't talk to me about. On one occasion, he'd said, "I need a good lawyer, don't I? Mr. Nathan convinced me. He'll do the same for the jury. He's extremely cunning, Alex." *Cunning?*

I asked Gary if Nathan was as smart as he was. Gary smiled and said, "Why do you always say I'm smart when I'm not? If I were so smart, would I be here?"

He hadn't strayed once from the Gary Murphy persona in weeks. He'd also declined to be hypnotized again.

I watched Gary's super-lawyer, Anthony Nathan, as he obnoxiously swaggered around the front of the courtroom. He was certainly manic, widely known for infuriating witnesses during cross-examination. Did Gary have the presence of mind to select Nathan? What had drawn the two of them together?

In one way, though, it seemed a natural pairing — a borderline madman defending another madman. Anthony Nathan had already publicly proclaimed: "This will be an absolute zoo. A zoo, or a Wild West frontier justice show! I promise you. They could sell tickets for a thousand dollars a seat."

My pulse was racing as the bailiff finally stood before the assemblage and called the room to order.

I saw Jezzie across the room. She was dressed like the important person that she is in the Service. Pin-striped suit, heels, shiny black attaché case. She saw me, and rolled her eyes.

On the right side of the courtroom, I saw Katherine Rose and Thomas Dunne. Their presence brought even more of an aura of unreality. I couldn't help thinking of Charles and Anne Morrow Lindbergh and of the world-famous kidnapping trial that had taken place sixty years before.

Judge Linda Kaplan was known as an eloquent and energetic woman who never let lawyers get the best of her. She had been on the bench for less than five years, but had already handled some of the biggest trials in Washington. Often, she stood during entire proceedings. She was known to rule her courtroom with complete authority.

Gary Soneji/Murphy had been quietly, almost surreptitiously, escorted to his place. He was already seated, looking well behaved, as Gary *Murphy* always did.

Several well-known journalists were present, at least a couple of them writing books about the kidnapping.

The opposing lawyer teams looked supremely confident and well prepared on the first day, as though their cases were invincible.

The trial began with a small flourish, opening-bell theatrics. At the front of the courtroom, Missy Murphy began to sob. "Gary didn't hurt anybody," she said in an audible voice. "Gary would never hurt another person."

Someone in the courtroom audience called out, "Oh, give us a break, lady!"

Judge Kaplan smacked her gavel and commanded, "Silence in this courtroom! Silence! That will be enough of that." Sure it will.

We were off and running. Gary Soneji/Murphy's Trial of the Century.

CHAPTER 58

EVERYTHING SEEMED to be in perpetual motion and chaos, but especially my relationship to the original investigation and the trial. After court that day, I did the one thing that made total sense to me: I played flag-football with the kids.

Damon and Janelle were whirlwinds of activity, competing for my attention throughout the afternoon, smothering me with their need. They distracted me from unpleasant prospects that would stretch on for the next few weeks.

After dinner that night, Nana and I stayed at the table over a second cup of chicory coffee. I wanted to hear her thoughts. I knew they were coming, anyway. All during the meal, her arms and hands had been twirling like Satchel Paige about to deliver a screwball.

"Alex, I believe we need to talk," she finally said. When Nana Mama has something to say, she gets quiet first. Then she talks a lot, sometimes for hours.

The kids were busy watching *Wheel of Fortune* in the other room. The game-show cheers and chants made for good domestic background noise.

"What shall we talk about?" I asked her. "Hey, did you hear that one in four kids in the U.S. now lives in poverty? We're going to be the moral majority soon."

Nana was real composed and thoughtful about whatever was coming. She had been preparing this speech. I could tell that much. The pupils in her eyes had become brown pinpoints.

"Alex," she said now, "you know that I'm always on your side when something is important."

"Ever since I arrived in Washington with a duffel bag and, I think, seventy-five cents," I said to her. I could still vividly remember being sent "up North" to live with my grandmother; the very day I'd arrived in Union Station on the train from Winston-Salem. My mother had just died of lung cancer; my father had died the year before. Nana bought me lunch at Morrison's cafeteria. It was the first time I ever ate in a restaurant.

Regina Hope took me in when I was nine. Nana Mama was called "The Queen of Hope," back then. She was a schoolteacher here in Washington. She was already in her late forties, and my grandfather was dead. My three brothers came to the Washington area at the same time that I did. They stayed with one relative or another until they were around eighteen. I stayed with Nana the whole time.

I was the lucky one. At times Nana Mama was a super queen bitch because she knew what was good for me. She had seen my type before. She knew my father, for good and bad. She had loved my mother. Nana Mama was, and is, a talented psychologist. I named her Nana Mama when I was ten. By then, she was both my nana and my mama.

Her arms were folded across her chest now. Iron will. "Alex, I believe I have some bad feelings about this relationship you're involved in," she said.

"Can you tell me why?" I asked her.

"Yes, I can. First, because Jezzie is a white woman, and I do not trust most white people. I would like to, but I can't. Most of them have no respect for us. They lie to our faces. That's their way, at least with people they don't believe are their equals."

"You sound like a street revolutionary. Farrakhan or Sonny Carson," I said to her. I started to clear the table, carting plates and silverware to stack in our old porcelain sink.

"I'm not proud of these feelings I have, but I can't help them, either." Nana Mama's eyes followed me.

"Is that Jezzie's crime, then? That she's a white woman?"

Nana fidgeted in her chair. She adjusted her eyeglasses, which were hung around her neck by twine. "Her crime is that she goes with you. She seems willing to let you throw away your police career, everything you do here in Southeast. All the good that's been in your life. Damon and Jannie."

"Damon and Janelle don't seem hurt or concerned," I told Nana Mama. My voice was rising some. I stood there with a stack of dirty dishes in my arms.

Nana's palm slammed down on the wooden armrest of her chair. "Well dammit, that's because you have blinders on, Alex. You are the sun and the sky for them. Damon is afraid you'll just leave him."

"Those kids are upset only if you get them upset." I said what I was feeling, what I believed to be the truth.

Nana Mama sat all the way back in her chair. The tiniest sound escaped from her mouth. It was pure hurt.

"That is so wrong for you to say. I protect those two children just like I protected you. I've spent my life caring for other people, looking out for others. I don't hurt anyone, Alex."

"You just hurt me," I said to her. "And you know you did. You know what those two kids mean to me."

There were tears in Nana's eyes, but she held her ground. She kept her eyes locked tightly onto mine. Our love is a tough, uncompromising love. It's always been that way.

"I don't want you to apologize to me later on, Alex. It doesn't matter to me that you'll feel guilty about what you just said to me. What matters is that you are guilty. You are giving up everything for a relationship that just can't work."

Nana Mama left the kitchen table, and she went upstairs. End of conversation. Just like that. She'd made up her mind.

Was I giving up everything to be with Jezzie? Was it a relationship that could never work? I had no way of knowing yet. I had to find that out for myself.

CHAPTER 59

A PARADE of medical experts now began to testify at the Soneji/Murphy trial. Assistant medical examiners took the stand, some of them strangely quirky and flamboyant for scientists. Experts came from Walter Reed, from Lorton Prison, from the army, from the FBI.

Photos and four-by-six-foot schematic drawings were displayed and overexplained; crime-scene locations were visited and revisited on the eerie charts that dominated the trial's first week.

Eight different psychiatrists and psychologists were brought to the stand to build the case that Gary Soneji/Murphy was in control of his actions; that he was a deviate sociopath; that he was rational, cold-blooded, and very sane.

He was described as a "criminal genius," without any conscience or remorse; as a brilliant actor, "worthy of Hollywood," which was how he'd manipulated and fooled so many people along the way.

But Gary Soneji/Murphy *had* consciously and deliberately kidnapped two children; he had killed one or both of them; he had killed others — at least five, and possibly more. He was the human monster we all have nightmares about. . . . So said all the prosecution experts.

The chief of psychiatry from Walter Reed was on the stand for most of one afternoon. She had interviewed Gary Murphy on a dozen occasions. After a long description of a disturbed childhood in Princeton, New Jersey, and teenage years marked by violent outbursts against both human beings and animals, Dr. Maria Ruocco was asked to give her psychiatric evaluation of Gary Murphy.

"I see someone who is an extremely dangerous sociopath. I believe Gary Murphy is fully aware of all his actions. *I absolutely do not believe he is a multiple personality.*"

So it was that Mary Warner artfully laid out her case every day. I admired her thoroughness, and her understanding of the psychiatric process. She was assembling a terribly complex jigsaw puzzle for the judge and jury. I'd met with her several times and she was good.

When she was finished, the jurors would have an exquisitely detailed picture in their minds . . . of the mind of Gary Soneji/Murphy.

Each day of the trial she would concentrate on one new puzzle piece. She would show them the piece. She would explain it thoroughly. She would then insert the piece into the puzzle.

She showed the jury exactly how the new piece related to everything else that had gone before. Once or twice, spectators in the courtroom audience were moved to applaud the soft-spoken prosecutor and her impressive performance.

She accomplished all of this while Anthony Nathan was objecting to virtually every point she attempted to make.

Nathan's defense was simple enough, and he never wavered from it: Gary Murphy was innocent because he had committed no crime.

Gary Soneji had.

*   *   *

Anthony Nathan paced the front of the courtroom with his usual swagger. He wore a fifteen-hundred-dollar tailored suit, but didn't look at all comfortable in it. The suit was cut well, but Nathan's posture was impossible — it was like trying to dress a jungle gym.

"I am not a nice person." Anthony Nathan stood before the jury of seven women and five men on the Monday of the second week. "At least not in the courtroom. People say that I have a perpetual sneer. That I'm a pompous man. That I'm an insufferable egomaniac. That I'm impossible to be around for more than sixty seconds. It's *all true,*" Nathan said to his captive audience. "It's all true.

"And that's what gets me into trouble sometimes. I do tell the truth. I'm obsessed with telling the truth. I have no patience, none at all, with half truths. And I have *never* taken a case where I cannot tell The Truth.

"My defense of Gary Murphy is simple, perhaps the least complex and controversial I've ever delivered to any jury. It is about Truth. It is all black and white, ladies and gentlemen. Please, listen to me.

"Ms. Warner and her team understand how strong the defense is, and that's precisely why she has just laid before you more facts than the Warren Commission used to prove exactly the same thing — ABSOLUTELY NOTHING. If you could cross-examine Ms. Warner, and she would answer honestly, she would tell you that. Then we could all go home. Wouldn't that be nice? Yes, that would be very nice."

There were snickers from around the courtroom. At the same time, some members of the jury were leaning in closer to listen and watch. Each time that Nathan passed by, he got a half step closer to them.

"Someone, several someones, asked me why I took this case. I told them, as simply as I'll tell you now, that the evidence makes this a certain winner for the defense. The Truth is over-whelming for the defense. I know you don't believe that now. You will. You will.

"Here's a stunning statement of *fact*. Ms. Warner did not want to bring this trial to jury at this time. Her boss, the secretary of the treasury, forced this case to trial. He forced the trial to take place in record time. Never have the wheels of Justice moved so fast. Those same wheels never would have moved this fast for you or your family. That is the truth.

"But in this particular instance, because of the suffering of Mr. Goldberg and his family, the wheels have moved very fast. And because of Katherine Rose Dunne and her family, who are famous and rich and very powerful, and who also want their suffering to end. Who can blame them for that? I certainly don't.

"But NOT AT THE EXPENSE OF THE LIFE OF AN INNO-CENT MAN! This man, Gary Murphy, does not deserve to suffer as they have suffered."

Nathan now walked over to where Gary sat. Blond, athletic-looking Gary Murphy, who looked like a grown-up Boy Scout. "This man is as good a man as you will find anywhere in this courtroom. I'll prove it to you, too.

"*Gary Murphy is a good man*. Remember that. There's another fact for you.

"It is one of *two* facts, just two, that I want you to remember. The other fact is that Gary *Soneji* is *insane*.

"Now, I must tell you, I am a little insane, too. Just a little. You've seen that already. Ms. Warner has drawn your attention to it. Well, Gary *Soneji* IS A HUNDRED TIMES MORE INSANE THAN I AM. Gary *Soneji* is the most insane person I've ever met. And I've met Soneji. *You will, too*.

"I promise you this. You will all meet Soneji, and once you have, you will not be able to convict Gary *Murphy*. You will end up liking Gary *Murphy*, and *rooting* for him in his personal battle with Soneji. Gary *Murphy* cannot be convicted of murders and a kidnapping . . . that were committed by Gary *Soneji.* . . ."

Anthony Nathan now proceeded to call character witness after character witness. Surprisingly, they included staff members at Washington Day, as well as some students. They included neighbors of the Murphys from Delaware.

Nathan was always gentle with the witnesses, always articulate. They seemed to like Nathan and to trust him.

"Would you please state your name for everyone?"

"Dr. Nancy Temkin."

"And your occupation, please."

"I teach art at Washington Day School."

"You knew Gary Soneji at the Day School?"

"Yes I did."

"Was Mr. Soneji a good teacher during his time at Washington Day School? Did you ever observe anything that would make you think he wasn't a good teacher?"

"No, I did not. He was a very good teacher."

"Why would you say that, Dr. Temkin?"

"Because he had a passion both for his subject matter and for communicating it to the students. He was a favorite teacher at school. His nickname was 'Chips,' as in 'Mr. Chips.'"

"You've heard some medical experts say that he is insane, a severe split personality? How does that strike you?"

"Frankly, it is the *only* way I can comprehend what happened."

"Dr. Temkin, I know this is a hard question under the circumstances, but was the defendant a friend of yours?"

"Yes. He was a friend of mine."

"Is he still a friend of yours?"

"I want to see Gary get the help he needs."

"And so do I," said Nathan. "So do I."

*   *   *

Anthony Nathan fired his first real salvo late on Friday of the trial's second week. It was as dramatic as it was unexpected. It started with a side-bench conference Nathan and Mary Warner had with Judge Kaplan.

During the conference, Mary Warner raised her voice for one of the few times during the trial. "Your Honor, *I object!* I must object to this . . . *stunt.* This is a stunt!"

The courtroom was already buzzing. The press, in front-row seats, was alert. Judge Kaplan had apparently ruled in favor of the defense.

Mary Warner returned to her seat, but she had lost some of her composure. "Why weren't we informed of this beforehand?" she called out. "Why wasn't this revealed in pretrial?"

Nathan held up his hands and actually quieted the room. He gave everyone the news. "I call Dr. Alex Cross as a defense witness. I am calling him as a hostile and uncooperative witness, but a witness for the defense nonetheless."

I was the "stunt."

Part Four

Remember Maggie Rose

CHAPTER 60

"LET'S WATCH the movie again, Daddy," Damon said to me. "I'm serious about this now."

"Shush up. We're going to watch the news," I told him. "Maybe you'll learn something about life beyond *Batman*."

"The movie's funny." Damon tried to talk some sense into me.

I let my son in on a little secret. "So is the news."

What I didn't tell Damon was that I was unbelievably tense about testifying in court on Monday, *testifying for the defense*.

On television that night, I had seen a news piece reporting that Thomas Dunne was expected to run for the Senate in California. Was Thomas Dunne trying to piece together his life again? Or could Thomas Dunne somehow be involved in the kidnapping himself? By now I was ruling nothing out. I'd become paranoid about too many things related to the kidnapping case. Was there more to the report from California than what it seemed? Twice, I had requested permission to go to California to investigate. Both times the request was denied. Jezzie was helping me out. She had a contact in California, but so far nothing had come of it.

We watched the news from the living-room floor. Janelle and

Damon were snuggled up beside me. Before the news, we had reviewed our tape of *Kindergarten Cop* for the tenth, or twelfth, or maybe it was the twentieth time.

The kids thought I should be in the movie instead of Arnold Schwarzenegger. I thought Arnold was turning into a pretty good comic actor myself. Or maybe I just preferred Schwarzenegger to another turn with *Benji* or *The Lady and the Tramp*.

Nana was out in the kitchen, playing pinochle with Aunt Tia. I could see the phone on the kitchen wall. The receiver was dangling off the hook to stop calls from coming in from reporters and other cranks *du jour*.

The phone calls I had taken from the press that night all eventually got around to the same questions. Could I hypnotize Soneji/Murphy in a crowded courtroom? Would Soneji ever tell us what had happened to Maggie Rose Dunne? Did I think he was psychotic, or a sociopath? No I wouldn't comment.

Around one in the morning, the front doorbell sounded. Nana had gone upstairs long before that. I'd put Janelle and Damon to bed around nine, after we'd shared some more of David Macaulay's magical book *Black and White*.

I went into the darkened dining room and pulled back the chintz curtains. It was Jezzie. She was right on time.

I went out to the porch and gave her a hug. "Let's go, Alex," she whispered. She had a plan. She said her plan was "no plan," but that was seldom the case with Jezzie.

Jezzie's motorcycle truly ate up the road that night. We moved past other traffic as if it were standing still, frozen in time and space. We passed darkened houses, lawns, and everything else in the known world. In third gear. Cruising.

I waited for her to slip it up into fourth, then fifth. The BMW roared steadily and smoothly beneath us, its single headlamp piercing the road with its beckoning light.

Jezzie switched lanes easily and frequently as we hit fourth, then rose to the pure speed of fifth gear. We were doing a hundred and twenty miles an hour on the George Washington Parkway, then a hundred and thirty on 95. Jezzie had once told me that she'd never taken the bike out without getting it up to at least a hundred. I believed her.

We didn't stop hurtling through time and space until we came down, until we landed at a run-down Mobil gas station in Lumberton, North Carolina.

It was almost six in the morning. We must have looked as crazed as the local gas jockey ever got to see. Black man; blond white woman. Big-assed motorcycle. Hot time in the old town tonight.

The attendant at the station looked kind of out of sorts himself. He had skateboard pads over his farmer-gray blue jeans. He was in his early twenties, with one of those spiked or "skater" haircuts you're more likely to see on the beaches of California than in this part of the country. How had the hairdo gotten to Lumberton, North Carolina, so quickly? Was it just more madness in the air? Free flow of ideas?

"Morning, Rory." Jezzie smiled at the boy.

She peeked between two of the gas pumps and winked at me.

"Rory's the eleven-to-seven shift here. Only station open for fifty miles either way. Don't tell anybody you're not sure about." She lowered her voice. "Rory sells ups and downs around these parts. Anything necessary to get you through the night. Bumblebees, black beauties, diazepam?"

She had slipped into a slight drawl, which sounded pretty to the ear. Her blond hair was all blown out, which I liked, too. "Ecstasy, methamphetamine hydrochloride?" she went on with the menu.

Rory shook his head at her, as if she were crazy. I could tell that he liked her. He brushed imaginary hair away from his eyes. "Man oh man," he said. A very articulate young man.

"Don't worry about Alex." She smiled again at the gas jockey. His spiked hair made him three inches taller. "He's okay. He's just another cop from Washington."

"Oh, man! Jezzie, goddamn you! Jee-zus! You and your cop friends." Rory spun on his engineer's boot heels as if he'd been burned by a torch. He'd seen plenty of crazy out here, working the emergency-room shift off the interstate. The two of us were crazy for sure. Tell me about it. What other cop friends?

Less than fifteen minutes later, we were at Jezzie's lake house. It was a small A-frame cottage sitting right on the water, surrounded by fir and birch trees. The weather was near perfect. Indian summer, later than it ever ought to come. Global warming marches on.

"You didn't tell me you were landed gentry," I said as we sped down a picturesque winding road toward the cottage.

"Hardly, Alex. My grandfather left this place to my mother. Grandpop was a local scoundrel and thief. He made a little money in his day. The only one in our family who ever did. Crime seems to pay."

"So they say."

I hopped off the bike, and immediately stretched out my back muscles, then my legs. We went inside the house. The door had been left unlocked, which stretched my imagination some.

Jezzie checked out the fridge, which was generously stocked. She put on a Bruce Springsteen tape, then she wandered outside. I followed her down toward the shimmering, blue-black water. A new dock had been built on the water. A narrow walkway went out to a broader deck set up with bolted-down chairs and a table. I could hear music from the *Nebraska* album playing.

Jezzie pulled off her boots, then her striped-blue knee socks. She dipped one foot in the perfectly still water.

Her long legs were wonderfully athletic. Her feet were long, too, nicely shaped, as beautiful as feet get. For the moment, she reminded me of ladies who went to the University of Florida, Miami, South Carolina, Vanderbilt. I hadn't found a part of her that wasn't special to look at.

"Believe it or not, this water's seventy-five degrees," she said with a big slow-motion smile.

"On the dot?" I asked.

"I'd have to say so. On the button. Are you game, or are you lame?"

"What will the neighbors say? I didn't pack my bathing suit. Or anything else."

"That was the basic plan, *no plan*. Imagine. A whole Saturday with no plan. No trial. No press interviews. No missiles from the Dunnes. Like Thomas Dunne on Larry King this week. Complaining about the investigation leading up to the trial, peppering my name everywhere again. No earthshaking kidnapping case to weigh down on you. Just the two of us out here in the middle of nowhere."

"I like the sound of that," I told Jezzie. "In the middle of nowhere." I looked around, following the line where the fir trees met clear blue sky.

"That's our name for this place, then. In the Middle of Nowhere, North Carolina."

"Seriously, Jez. What about the neighbors? We're in the Tarheel State, right? I don't want any tar on my heels."

She smiled. "There's nobody around for a couple of miles at least, Alex. No other houses, believe it or not. It's too early for anybody but the bass fishermen."

"I don't want to meet a couple of backwoods Tarheel bass fishermen, either," I said. "In their eyes, I might be a black bass. I've read James Dickey's *Deliverance*."

"Fishermen all go to the south end of the lake. Trust me, Alex. Let me undress you. Make you a little more comfortable."

"We'll undress each other." I surrendered and gave myself over to her, to the slow-down pace of the perfect morning.

On the dock of the bay we undressed each other. The morning sun was toasty warm and I was aware of the lake breeze fanning our bare skin.

I tested the water with my foot, my own well-turned ankle. Jezzie wasn't exaggerating about the temperature.

"I wouldn't lie to you. I never have yet," she said with another smile.

She dived in perfectly, then, making almost no splash on the water surface.

I followed in the light trail of her bubbles. As I penetrated the underwater, I was thinking: a black man and a beautiful white woman swimming together.

In the middle South. In this Year of Our Lord, nineteen hundred and ninety-three.

We were being reckless, and maybe just a little crazy.

Were we wrong? Some people would say so, or at least think it. But why was that? Were we hurting anyone by being together?

The water was warm on top. But it was much colder five or six feet down. It looked blue-green. It was probably spring-fed. Near the bottom, I could feel strong undercurrents striking my chest and genitals.

A thought struck me hard: *Could we be falling deeply in love? Was that what I was feeling now?* I came up for air.

"Did you touch bottom? You have to touch bottom on the day's first dive."

"Or what?" I asked Jezzie.

"Or you're a lily-livered chicken, and you'll drown or be lost forever in the deep woods before day's end. That's a true tale. I've seen it happen many, many times here in the Middle of Nowhere."

We played like children in the lake. We'd both been working hard. Too hard — for almost a year of our lives.

There was a cedar ladder, the easy way back up onto the dock. The ladder was newly built. I could smell the freshness of the wood. There weren't any splinters yet. I wondered if Jezzie had built it herself — on her vacation — just before the kidnapping.

We held on to the ladder, and on to each other. Somewhere distant on the lake, ducks honked. It was a funny sound. There was little more than a ripple on the water table that stretched out before us. Tiny waves tickled under Jezzie's chin.

"I love you when you're like this. You get so vulnerable," she said. "The real you starts to show up."

"I feel like everything's been unreal for such a long time," I said to Jezzie. "The kidnapping. The search for Soneji. The trial in Washington."

"This is the only thing that's real for the moment. Okay? I like being with you *so*." Jezzie put her head on my chest.

"You like it *so?*"

"Yes. I like it *so*. See how uncomplicated it can be?" She gestured around at the picturesque lake, the deep ring of fir trees. "Don't you see? It's all so natural. It will be fine. I promise. No bass fishermen will ever come between us."

Jezzie was right. For the first time in a very long time, I felt as if everything could work out — everything that might happen from now on. Things were as slow and uncomplicated and good as could be. Neither of us wanted the weekend to end.

CHAPTER 61

"I'M A HOMICIDE DETECTIVE with the Washington Police Department. My official rank is divisional chief. Sometimes, I get assigned to violent crimes where there are psychological considerations that might mean something to the case."

I stated this under oath inside a crowded, hushed, very electric Washington courtroom. It was Monday morning. The weekend seemed a million miles away. Beads of perspiration started to roll across my scalp.

"Can you tell us why you are assigned cases with psychological implications?" Anthony Nathan asked me.

"I'm a psychologist as well as a detective. I had a private practice before I joined the D.C. police force," I said. "Prior to that, I worked in agriculture. I was a migrant farmworker for a year."

"Your degree is from?" Nathan refused to be distracted from establishing me as an impressive-as-hell person.

"As you already know, Mr. Nathan, my doctorate is from Johns Hopkins."

"One of the finest schools in the country, certainly this part of the country," he said.

"Objection. That's Mr. Nathan's opinion." Mary Warner made a fair legal point.

Judge Kaplan upheld the objection.

"You've also published articles in *Psychiatric Archives*, in the *American Journal of Psychiatry*." Nathan continued as if Ms. Warner and Judge Kaplan were inconsequential.

"I've written a few papers. It's really not such a big deal, Mr. Nathan. A lot of psychologists publish."

"But not in the *Journal* and *Archives*, Dr. Cross. What was the subject of these learned articles?"

"I write about the criminal mind. I know enough three- and four-syllable words to qualify for the so-called learned journals."

"I admire your modesty, I honestly do. Tell me something, Dr. Cross. You've observed me these past few weeks. How would you describe my personality?"

"I'd need some private sessions for that, Mr. Nathan. I'm not sure if you could pay me enough for the therapy."

There was laughter throughout the courtroom. Even Judge Kaplan enjoyed a rare moment of mirth.

"Hazard a guess," Nathan continued. "I can take it."

He had a quick and very inventive mind. Anthony Nathan was highly creative. He had first established that I was my own witness, not an "expert" in his pocket.

"You're neurotic." I smiled. "And probably devious."

Nathan faced the jury and turned his palms up. "At least he's honest. And if nothing else, I get a free shrink session this morning."

More laughter came from the jury box. This time, I got the feeling that some of the jurors were beginning to change their minds about Anthony Nathan, and maybe about his client as well.

They had intensely disliked him at first. Now they saw that he was engaging, and very, very bright. He was doing a professional, maybe even a brilliant, job for his client.

"How many sessions have you had with Gary Murphy?" he asked me now. Gary *Murphy*, not Soneji.

"We had fifteen sessions over a period of three and a half months."

"Enough to form some opinions, I trust?"

"Psychiatry isn't that exact a science. I would like to have had more sessions. I do have some preliminary opinions."

"Which are?" Nathan asked me.

"Objection!" Mary Warner rose once again. She was a busy lady. "Detective Cross has just said he would need more sessions to form a final medical opinion."

"Overruled," Judge Kaplan said. "Detective Cross has also stated he has some preliminary opinions. I'd like to hear what those are."

"Dr. Cross," Nathan continued as if none of the interruptions had occurred, "unlike the other psychiatrists and psychologists who have seen Gary Murphy, you've been intimately involved in this case right from the start — both as a police officer and as a psychologist."

The prosecutor interrupted Nathan again. She was losing her patience. "Your Honor, does Mr. Nathan have a question to ask?"

"Do you, Mr. Nathan?"

Anthony Nathan turned to Mary Warner and snapped his fingers at her. "A question? — no sweat." He turned back to me.

"As a police officer involved from the very beginning of this case, and as a trained psychologist, can you give us your professional opinion of Gary Murphy?"

I looked at Murphy/Soneji. He appeared to be Gary Murphy. At this moment, he looked like a sympathetic and decent man who was trapped in the worst possible nightmare that anyone could possibly imagine.

"My first feelings and honest impressions were very basic and human. The kidnapping by a teacher shocked and disturbed me," I began my answer. "It was a profound breach of trust. It got much worse than that. I personally saw the tortured body of Michael Goldberg. It's something I will never forget. I have talked with Mr. and Mrs. Dunne about their little girl. I feel as if I know Maggie Rose Dunne. I also saw the murder victims at the Turner and Sanders houses."

"Objection!" Mary Warner was on her feet again. "Objection!"

"You know better than that." Judge Kaplan froze me with a very cold look. "Strike it from the record. The jury is instructed to disregard. There is no proof that the defendant is involved in any way with the events just mentioned."

"You asked for an honest answer," I said to Nathan. "You wanted to hear what I believe. That's what you're getting."

Nathan was nodding his head as he walked to the jury box. He turned back toward me.

"Fair enough, fair enough. I am sure we'll get absolute honesty from you, Dr. Cross. Whether I like that honesty or not. Whether or not Gary Murphy likes it. You are an extremely honest man. I won't interrupt your honest opinion, so long as the prosecution doesn't. Please go on."

"I wanted to catch the kidnapper so badly that it hurt. All of us on the Hostage Rescue Team did. It got very personal with most of us."

"You actually hated the kidnapper. You wanted to see *whoever* it was punished to the maximum allowable by law?"

"I did. I still do," I answered Nathan.

"When Gary Murphy was apprehended, you were there. He was charged with the crime. You then had several sessions with him. What do you believe right now about Gary Murphy?"

"I honestly don't know what to believe right now."

Anthony Nathan didn't miss a beat. "Then there is *reasonable doubt in your mind?*"

Mary Warner was wearing a spot into the ancient floorboards of the courtroom. "Suggestive. Leading the witness."

"The jury will disregard," said Judge Kaplan.

"Tell us what your feelings are at this moment about Gary Murphy. Give us a professional opinion, Dr. Cross," said Nathan.

"There's no way yet for me to know if he *is* Gary Murphy — or Gary Soneji. I'm not sure if two personalities do exist in this man. I believe there is a chance he *could* be a split personality."

"And if he were a split personality?"

"If that were true, Gary Murphy could have little or no conscious idea about the actions of Gary Soneji. He could also be a brilliant sociopath who's manipulating every one of us. You, too."

"Okay. I can accept those perimeters. So far, so good," Nathan said. He had his hands in front of his chest as if he were holding a small ball. He was obviously working to get a tighter definition out of me.

"This concept of doubt seems pivotal, doesn't it?" he continued. "This is the whole ball game. I would therefore like you to help the jury make their important decision. Dr. Cross, *I want you to hypnotize Gary Murphy!*" he announced.

"Here, in this courtroom. Let the jurors decide for themselves. And I have the fullest confidence in this jury and their decision. I have all the confidence in the world that when these people see all the evidence, they'll arrive at the right decision. Don't you, Dr. Cross?"

CHAPTER 62

THE FOLLOWING MORNING two simple red-leather armchairs were brought in for the session between Gary and me. To help him get relaxed, more oblivious to his surroundings, the room's overhead lighting was dimmed. Both of us were miked. Those were the only extra touches allowed by Judge Kaplan.

An alternative to this would have been a videotape of our session, but Gary said he believed he could be hypnotized inside the courtroom. He wanted to try. His lawyer wanted him to try.

I had decided to conduct the hypnosis as if Soneji/Murphy were in his cell. It was important to block out some of the obvious distractions inside the courtroom. I had no idea if this would work, or what the outcome might be. My stomach was in knots as I sat in one of the armchairs. I tried not to look out into the courtroom audience. I didn't appreciate being on stage, but especially now.

In the past, I'd used a simple verbally suggestive technique with Gary. We began the courtroom hypnosis in that same way. Hypnosis isn't nearly as complex as most people think.

"Gary," I said, "I want you to sit back and try and relax and we'll see what happens."

"I'll do the best I can," he said, sounding as sincere as he looked. He was wearing a navy blue suit, crisp white shirt, striped rep tie. He looked more like a lawyer than his own lawyer.

"I'm going to hypnotize you again because your lawyer feels it may help your case. You've told me that you want that help. Is that correct?"

"Yes, it is," Gary said. "I want to tell the truth . . . I want to *know* the truth myself."

"All right, then, I'd like you to count backwards from one hundred. We've done this before. Feel yourself relaxing with each number. You can begin to count."

Gary Murphy began to count backwards.

"Your eyes are starting to close. You feel much more relaxed now . . . in a sleeping state . . . breathing deeply," I said in a voice that got quieter and quieter, almost a monotone.

The courtroom was very nearly silent. The only sound was a thick, vibrating hum from the room's air conditioner.

Gary finally stopped counting.

"Are you comfortable? Is everything okay?" I asked him.

His brown eyes were glassy and moist. He appeared to have slipped fairly easily into the trance. There was no way to be certain.

"Yes. I'm fine. I feel good."

"If you want to stop the session, for any reason, you know the way back out of this."

He nodded softly as he spoke. "I do. I'm okay, though." He seemed to be only half listening.

Under all the pressure and the circumstances of the trial, it didn't seem likely that he could be faking this.

I said, "At another time, in a past session, we talked about your waking up at the McDonald's. You told me that you 'woke as if you'd been dreaming.' Do you remember that?"

"That's right. Sure I remember," he said. "I woke up in a police car outside McDonald's. I came to, and the police were there. They were arresting me."

"How did you feel when the police arrested you?"

"I felt like it couldn't be happening. No way. It had to be a bad dream. I told them I was a salesman, told them where I lived in Delaware. Anything I could think of to show they had the wrong person. Not a criminal. I don't have any record with the police."

I said, "We talked about the time just before you were arrested. That day. When you went into the fast-food restaurant."

"I don't . . . I'm not sure if I can remember. Let me try and think about it. . . ." Gary appeared to be struggling a little. Was it an act? Or was he uncomfortable with the truth as he remembered it now?

Originally, I'd been surprised that he had revealed the Soneji persona in our prison session. I wondered if he would do it again. Especially under these difficult circumstances.

"You stopped to go to the bathroom inside the McDonald's restaurant. You also wanted some coffee, to keep you alert on your drive."

"I remember . . . I remember a little of that. I can see myself at the McDonald's for sure. I remember being there. . . ."

"Take your time. We have plenty of time, Gary."

"Very crowded with people. The restaurant area was crowded, I mean. I went up to the bathroom door. Then I *didn't* go inside for some reason. I don't know why not. That's funny, but I don't remember."

"What were you feeling then? When you remained outside the rest room. Do you remember how you felt?"

"Agitated. Getting worse. I could feel the blood pumping inside my head. I didn't understand why. I was upset, and I didn't know why."

Soneji/Murphy was staring straight ahead. He was looking to the left of where I sat. I was a little surprised at how easy it was for me to forget the courtroom audience that was watching both of us.

"Was *Soneji* there in the restaurant?" I asked him.

He tilted his head slightly. The gesture was oddly touching.

"*Soneji's* in there. Yes, he's in the McDonald's." He became excited. "Pretending to get coffee, but he looks angry. He's, I think he's *really mad*. Soneji's a nut case, a bad seed."

"Why is he mad? Do you know? What is it that gets Soneji angry?"

"I think it's because . . . things got ruined on him. The police were unbelievably lucky. His plan to be famous got screwed up. Totally messed up. Now he feels like Bruno Richard Hauptmann. Just another loser."

This was news. He hadn't talked about the actual kidnapping before. I was oblivious to everything in the courtroom. My eyes stayed on Gary Soneji/Murphy.

I tried to sound as casual and nonthreatening as I could. Easy does it. Nice and slow. This was like walking on the edge of a chasm. I could help him, or we could both fall in. "What went wrong with Soneji's plan?"

"Everything that could go wrong," he said. He was still Gary Murphy. I could see that. He had not transferred into the Soneji personality. But Gary Murphy knew about Gary Soneji's activities; under hypnosis, *Gary Murphy knew Soneji's thoughts*.

The courtroom remained silent and very still. There wasn't a flicker of motion anywhere in my peripheral vision.

More details about the kidnapping came from Gary. "He checked on the Goldberg boy, and the boy was dead. His face was all blue. Must have been too much of the barbiturate. . . . Soneji couldn't believe that *he'd* made a mistake. He'd been so thorough and careful. He'd talked to anesthesiologists beforehand."

I asked a key question: "How did the boy's body get so bruised and beaten? What exactly happened to the Goldberg boy?"

"Soneji went a little crazy. He couldn't believe his bad luck. He hit the Goldberg boy's body over and over with a heavy shovel."

The way he was talking about Soneji was extremely credible so far. It was possible that he was a multiple-personality victim after all. That would change everything about the trial, and possibly the verdict.

"What shovel was that?" I asked.

He was talking faster and faster now. "The shovel he used to dig them up. They were buried in the barn. They had an air supply for a couple of days. It was like a fallout shelter, you see. The air system worked beautifully; everything did. Soneji invented it himself. He built it himself."

My pulse was hammering. My throat was very, very dry. "What about the little girl? What about Maggie Rose?" I asked him.

"She was fine. Soneji gave her Valium the second time. To put her back to sleep. She was terrified, screaming — because it was so dark under the ground. Pitch-black. But it wasn't *that* bad. Soneji had seen worse himself. The *basement*."

I proceeded very cautiously at this point. I didn't want to lose him here. What about the basement? I'd try to get back to the basement later.

"Where is Maggie Rose now?" I asked Gary Murphy.

"Don't know," he said without hesitation.

Not, *she's dead*. Not, she's alive. . . . *Don't know*. Why would he block that information? Because he knew I wanted it? Because everyone in that courtroom wanted to know the fate of Maggie Rose Dunne?

"Soneji went back to get her," he said next. "The FBI had agreed to the ten-million ransom. Everything was all set. But she was *gone!* Maggie Rose wasn't there when Soneji came back again. *She was gone! Somebody else had taken the girl out of there!*"

The spectators in the courtroom were no longer quiet. But I still kept my concentration on Gary.

Judge Kaplan was reluctant to bang her gavel and ask for order. She did stand up. She motioned for quiet, but it was a useless gesture. *Somebody else had taken the girl out of there. Somebody else had the girl now.*

I rushed in a few more questions before the room went completely out of control, and maybe Soneji/Murphy with it. My voice remained soft, surprisingly calm under the circumstances.

"Did *you* dig her up, Gary? Did *you* rescue the little girl from Soneji? Do *you* know where Maggie Rose is now?" I asked him.

He didn't like that line of questioning. He was perspiring heavily. His eyelids flickered. "Of course not. No, I had nothing to do with any of it. It was Soneji all the way. I can't control him. Nobody can. Don't you understand that?"

I leaned way forward in my chair. "Is Soneji here right now? Is he here with us this morning?"

Under any other circumstances, I wouldn't have tried to push him this far. "Can I ask *Soneji* what happened to Maggie Rose?"

Gary Murphy shook his head repeatedly from side to side. He knew something else was happening to him now.

"It's too scary now," he said. His face was dripping with perspiration and his hair was wet. "It's scary. Soneji's real bad news! I can't talk about him anymore. I won't. Please, help me, Dr. Cross! Please, help me."

"All right, Gary, that's enough." I brought Gary out of hypnosis immediately. It was the only humane thing to do under the circumstances. I had no choice.

Suddenly, Gary Murphy was back in the courtroom with me. His eyes focused on mine. I saw nothing but fear in them.

The courtroom crowd was out of control. TV and print reporters rushed to make calls to their newsrooms. Judge Kaplan slammed her gavel over and over again.

Somebody else had Maggie Rose Dunne. . . . Was that possible?

"It's all right, Gary," I said. "I understand why you were afraid."

He stared at me, then his eyes very slowly trailed around the loudly buzzing courtroom. "What happened?" he asked. "What just happened in here?"

CHAPTER 63

I STILL REMEMBERED some Kafka. In particular, the chilling opening of Kafka's *The Trial*: "Someone must have been telling lies about Joseph K., for without having done anything wrong he was arrested one fine morning." That was what Gary Murphy wanted us to believe: that he was trapped in a nightmare. That he was as innocent as Joseph K.

I had my picture taken a couple of dozen times as I left the courthouse. Everybody had a question to ask. I had no comments to make. I never miss a good chance to shut up.

Was Maggie Rose still alive? the press wanted to know. I wouldn't say what I thought, which was that she probably *wasn't*.

As I was leaving the courthouse, I saw Katherine and Thomas Dunne walking toward me. They were flanked by TV and print newspeople. I wanted to talk to Katherine, but not to Thomas.

"Why are you helping him?" Thomas Dunne raised his voice. *"Don't you know he's lying?* What's wrong with you, Cross?"

Thomas Dunne was extremely tense and red-faced. Out of control. The veins in his forehead couldn't have been more prominent. Katherine Rose looked miserable, completely desolate.

"I've been called as a hostile witness," I said to the Dunnes. "I'm doing my job, that's all."

"Well, you're doing your job badly." Thomas Dunne continued to attack me. "You lost our daughter in Florida. Now you're trying to free her kidnapper."

I'd had enough from Thomas Dunne finally. He'd made personal attacks on me in the press and on TV. As much as I wanted to get his daughter back, I wasn't about to take any more abuse from him.

"The hell I am!" I shouted back as cameras shushed and whirred around us. "I've had my hands tied. I've been taken off the case, on a whim, then put back on. And I'm the only one who's gotten any results."

I whirled away from both of the Dunnes and headed down a steep flight of stairs. I understood their anguish, but Thomas Dunne had been badgering me for months. He'd gotten personal, and he was wrong. Nobody seemed to get one simple fact: I was the one still trying to get at the truth about Maggie Rose. I was the only one.

As I reached the bottom of the stairs, Katherine Rose came up from behind. She had run after me. Photographers had followed her. They were everywhere, their automatic film-wasters clicking like crazy. The press was elbowing in.

"I'm sorry about all that," she said before I could manage a word. "Losing Maggie is destroying Tom, destroying our marriage. I know you've done your best. I know what you've gone through. I'm sorry, Alex. I'm sorry for everything."

It was a strange, strange moment. I finally reached out and took Katherine Rose Dunne's hand. I thanked her, and promised her I wouldn't stop trying. The photographers continued to snap pictures. Then I quickly left the scene, refusing to answer another question, absolutely refusing to tell them what had just passed between Katherine Rose and myself. Silence is the best revenge with the press jackals.

I headed home. I was still searching for Maggie Rose Dunne — but *inside Soneji/Murphy's mind now.* Could she have been taken from the kidnapping site by somebody else? Why would Gary Murphy tell us that she had? As I drove into Southeast, I wondered about what Gary Murphy had said under hypnosis. Was Gary Soneji setting us all up beautifully in the courtroom? That was a scary possibility, and a very real one. Was all this part of one of his terrifying plans?

The next morning, I tried to put Soneji/Murphy under hypnosis a second time. The Amazing Detective/Doctor Cross was back on center stage! That's how it sounded in the morning news, anyway.

The hypnosis didn't work this time. Gary Murphy was too frightened, or so his lawyer claimed. There was too much hubbub in the crowded courtroom. The room was cleared once by Judge Kaplan, but that didn't help, either.

I was cross-examined by the prosecution that day, but Mary Warner was more interested in getting me off the stand than in questioning my credentials. My part in the trial was over. Which was just fine by me.

Neither Sampson nor I came to court for the rest of that week, a time of more expert testimony. We went back on the street. We had new cases. We also tried to rework a couple of troubling angles concerning the actual day of the kidnapping. We reanalyzed everything, spending hours in a conference room filled with files. If Maggie Rose had been taken from the site in Maryland, she could still be alive. There was still a slim chance.

Sampson and I returned to Washington Day School one more time to interview some of the school's teachers. To put it mildly, most of them weren't overjoyed to see us again. We were still testing the "accomplice" theory. It was definitely a possibility that Gary Soneji had been working with someone from the start. Could it be Simon Conklin, his friend from around Princeton?

If not Conklin, then who? No one at the school had seen anyone to support the notion of an "accomplice" for Gary Soneji.

We left the private school before noon and had lunch at a Roy Rogers in Georgetown. Roy's chicken is better than the Colonel's, and Roy has those swell "hot wings." Lots of zing in those babies. Sampson and I settled on five orders of wings and two thirty-two-ounce Cokes. We sat at a tiny picnic table by Roy's kiddie playground. After lunch maybe we'd go on the see-saw.

We finished our lunch and decided to drive out to Potomac, Maryland. For the rest of the afternoon, we canvassed Sorrell Avenue and the surrounding streets. We visited a couple of dozen houses, and were about as welcome as Woodward and Bernstein would be. Not that the cold reception stopped us.

No one had noticed any strange cars or people in the neighborhood. Not in the days before or after the kidnapping. No one could remember seeing an unusual delivery truck. Not even the usual kind — utility repairs, flower, and grocery deliveries.

Late that afternoon, I went for a drive by myself. I headed out toward Crisfield, Maryland, where Maggie Rose and Michael Goldberg had been kept underground during the first days of the kidnapping. *In a crypt? In a cellar?* Gary Soneji/Murphy had mentioned "the basement" under hypnosis. He'd been kept in a dark cellar as a child. He'd been friendless for long stretches of his life.

I wanted to see the farm all by myself this time. All the "disconnects" in the case were bothering the hell out of me. Loose fragments were flying around inside my head as disconcerting as shrapnel. Could someone else have taken Maggie Rose from Soneji/Murphy? I couldn't have cared less if Einstein was investigating the case — the possibilities would have made his head spin and maybe straightened his hair.

As I wandered around the grounds of the eerie, deserted

farm, I let the facts of the case run freely through my mind. I kept coming back to the Son of Lindbergh and the fact that the Lindbergh baby had been abducted from a "farmhouse."

Soneji's so-called accomplice. That was one unresolved problem.

Soneji had also been "spotted" near the Sanders murder house — if we could believe Nina Cerisier. That was a second loose end.

Was this really a case of split personality? The psychology community remained divided over whether there was such a phenomenon. Multiple-personality cases are rare. Was all of this a Byzantine scheme by Gary Murphy? Could he be acting out both personas?

What had happened to Maggie Rose Dunne? It always came back to her. What had happened to Maggie Rose?

On the battered dashboard of the Porsche, I still kept one of the tiny candles that had been handed out around the courthouse in Washington. I lit it. I drove back to Washington with it burning against the gathering night. *Remember Maggie Rose.*

CHAPTER 64

I HAD A DATE to see Jezzie that night, and it had kept me going with anticipation through most of the day. We met at an Embassy Suites motel in Arlington. Because of all the press in town for the trial, we were being especially cautious about being seen together.

Jezzie arrived at the room after I did. She looked absolutely alluring and sexy in a low-cut black tunic. She had on black seamed stockings and high-heeled pumps. She wore red lipstick and a scarlet blush. A silver comb was set in her hair. Be still my heart.

"I had a power lunch," she said by way of explanation. She kicked off her high heels. "Do I make the social register or not?"

"Well, you're definitely having a positive effect on my social register."

"I'll just be a minute, Alex. One minute." Jezzie disappeared into the bathroom.

She peeked out of the bathroom after a few minutes. I was on the bed. The tension in my body was draining into the mattress. Life was good again.

302 / James Patterson

"Let's take a bath. Okay? Wash away the road dust," Jezzie said.

"That's not dust," I said to her. "That's just me."

I got up and went into the bathroom. The tub was square and unusually large. There was a lot of gleaming white and blue tile, all mounted a foot or so higher than the rest of the bathroom. Jezzie's fancy clothes were strewn on the floor.

"You in a hurry?" I asked her.

"Yep."

Jezzie had filled the tub to the brim. A few independent-minded soap bubbles floated up and popped against the ceiling. Wisps of steam rose steadily. The room smelled like a country garden.

She stirred the bathwater with her fingertips. Then she came over to me. She still had the silver comb in her hair.

"I'm a little wired," she said.

"I could tell. I can tell about these things."

"I think it might be time for a little healing."

We went for it. Jezzie's hands played with the buttons on my trousers, then the zipper. Our mouths came together, lightly at first, then hard.

Suddenly, Jezzie took me inside her as we stood beside the steamy tub. Just two or three quick strokes — then she moved away from me again. Her face, neck, and chest were flushed. For a moment, I thought something was wrong.

I was caught by surprise — shock — pleasure — entering her, then parting so quickly. She *was* wired. Almost violent.

"What was that all about?" I asked.

"I'm going to have a heart attack," Jezzie whispered. "Better figure out a story for the police. *Whew*, Alex."

She took my hand and pulled me into the tub. The water was warm, just right. So was everything else.

We started to laugh. I still had my underwear on, but Pete was poking and peeking around. I pulled off the shorts.

We maneuvered in the tub until we were facing each other. Jezzie got on top of me somehow. We were unwilling to give up any contact. Jezzie leaned way back. She braced her hands behind her head. She watched my face with curious fascination. The red on her neck and chest was getting deeper.

Her long legs suddenly lifted straight out of the water and hooked around my head. Jezzie jerked forward a couple of times, then both of us exploded. Her body went stiff. We thrashed and moaned a lot. Waves of water splashed from the tub.

Somehow Jezzie got her arms around me — her arms and her legs. I settled back in water just under my nose.

Then I went under. Jezzie was on top of me. The feeling of being close to climax rushed through my body. We were both coming. I was also going to drown. I heard Jezzie yell again, a strange water-muffled sound above the surface.

I climaxed as I was about to run out of air. I swallowed water and coughed.

Jezzie rescued me. She pulled me up, and took my face in both her hands.

Release. Blessed release.

We stayed there holding each other. Spent, as they used to say in gentler times. There was more water on the floor than in the bathtub.

All I knew right then was that I was falling deeper and deeper in love. That much I was sure about. The rest of my life was mystery and chaos, but at least there was a lifeline. There was Jezzie.

Around one o'clock in the morning, I had to leave to go home. That way, I would be there when the kids got up. Jezzie understood. After the trial, we were going to sort everything out a lot better. Jezzie wanted to get to know Jannie and Damon; it had to be done just right, we agreed.

"I miss you already," she said as I got ready to go. "Damn. *Don't* go . . . I *know* you have to go."

She took the silver comb out of her hair and pressed it into my hand.

I went out into the night, with her voice still in my head. At first, there was nothing but the pitch-darkness of the parking lot.

Suddenly, two men stepped out in front of me. I automatically reached for my shoulder holster. One of them switched on a glaring light. The other had a camera aimed at my face.

The press had found me and Jezzie. *Oh, shit!* The kidnapping was so big that everything around it was a story. It had been like that from the start.

A young woman trailed along behind the two men. She had long, frizzy black hair. She looked like part of a movie crew from New York or L.A.

"Detective Alex Cross?" one of the men asked. Meanwhile, his partner took several rapid shots with the camera. The flashes lit up the dark parking lot.

"We're from the *National Star*. We want to talk to you, Detective Cross." I picked up a British accent. The *National Star* was an American tabloid based in Miami.

"What does this have to do with anything that's happened?" I said to the Brit. I was fingering Jezzie's silver comb in my pocket. "This is private. This isn't news. This isn't anybody else's business."

"That's our job to decide," he said. "I don't know, though, mate. Major communications breakthrough between the D.C. police and the Secret Service. Secret talks, and *whatever*."

The woman was already knocking at the motel door. Her voice was as loud as the metallic rapping. "This is the *National Star!*" she announced.

"Don't come out," I shouted to Jezzie.

The door opened, and Jezzie stood there fully dressed. She stared at the frizzy-haired woman and didn't bother to conceal her contempt.

"This must be a really proud moment," she said to the reporter. "This is probably as close as you'll ever get to a Pulitzer."

"Nah." The reporter had a comeback. "I know Roxanne Pulitzer. And now I know you two."

CHAPTER 65

I PLAYED A MEDLEY of Keith Sweat, Bell Biv Devoe, Hammer, and Public Enemy pop songs on the piano. I stayed out on the porch entertaining Damon and Janelle until about eight that morning. It was Wednesday of the week Jezzie and I had gotten our little lurid surprise in Arlington.

Nana was in the kitchen reading a hot copy of the *National Star*, which I'd bought for her at Acme. I waited for her to call me inside.

When she didn't, I got up from my pumping piano and went to face her music. I told Damon and Janelle to stay put. "Stay just the way you are. Don't ever change."

Just like on any other morning, Nana was sipping tea. The remains of her poached egg and toast were still in evidence. The tabloid was casually folded over on the kitchen table. Read? Unread? I couldn't tell from her face, or the condition of the newspaper.

"You read the story?" I had to ask.

"Well, I read enough to get the gist of it. Saw your picture on the front page, too," she said to me. "I believe that's how people read that kind of paper. I always used to be surprised, people buying a paper like that on Sunday morning after church."

I sat down across from her at the breakfast table. A wave of powerful old feelings and memories came rushing over me. I recalled so many talks like this one in our collective past.

Nana took up a little crust of toast. She dipped it in marmalade. If birds could eat like humans, they would eat like Nana Mama. She is quite a piece of work.

"She's a beautiful and I'm sure a very interesting white woman. You're a very handsome black man, sometimes with a good head on your shoulders. A lot of people don't like that idea, that picture. You're not too surprised, are you?"

"How about *you*, Nana? Do you like it?" I asked her.

Nana Mama sighed very softly. She put down her teacup with a clink. "Tell you what, now. I don't know the clinical terms for these things, Alex, but you never seemed to get over losing your mother. I saw that when you were a little boy. I think I still see it sometimes."

"It's called post-traumatic stress syndrome," I said to Nana. "If you're interested in the name."

Nana smiled at my retreat into jargon. She'd seen that act before. "I would never make any judgments about what happened to you, but it's affected you since you arrived here in Washington. I also noticed that you didn't always fit in with the crowd. Not the way some kids do. You played sports, and you shoplifted with your friend Sampson, and you were always tough. But you read books, and you were moderately sensitive. You follow me? Maybe you got tough on the outside, but not on the inside."

I didn't always buy into Nana's conclusions anymore, but her raw observations were still pretty good. I hadn't exactly fit in as a boy in Southeast D.C., but I knew I'd gotten a lot better at it. I was accepted okay now. Detective/Doctor Cross.

"I didn't want to hurt you, or disappoint you with *this*." I returned to the subject of the tabloid story.

"I'm not disappointed in you," my grandmother said to me. "You are my pride, Alex. You bring me tremendous happiness almost every day of my life. When I see you with the kids, and see the work you do here in this neighborhood, and know that you still care enough to humor an old woman —"

"That last one *is* a chore," I told her. "About the so-called news story, though. It's going to be impossible for a week or so. Then nobody will care very much."

Nana shook her head. Her little white helmet of hair turned neatly in place. "No. People *will* care. Some people will remember this for the rest of your life. What's that saying? 'If you can't do the time, don't do the crime.'"

I asked her, "What was the crime?"

Nana used the back of her knife to clear away toast crumbs. "You'll have to tell me that yourself. Why are you and Jezzie Flanagan sneaking around if everything is aboveboard? If you love her, you love her. Do you love her, Alex?"

I didn't answer Nana right away. Of course I loved Jezzie. But how much? And where was it going? Did it have to be going somewhere?

"I don't know for sure, at least not in the way I think you're asking the question," I finally said. "That's what we're trying to find out now. We both know the consequences of what we're doing."

"If you love her for sure, Alex," my grandmother said to me, "then I love her. I love you, Alex. You just paint on a very large canvas. Sometimes you're too bright for your own good. And you can be very peculiar — by the ways of the white world."

"And that's why you like me so much," I said to her.

She said, "It's just one of the reasons, sonny boy."

My grandmother and I held each other for a long moment at

the breakfast table that morning. I am big and strong; Nana is tiny, frail, but just as strong. It seemed like old times, in the sense that you never really grow up completely, not around your parents or grandparents. Not around Nana Mama, certainly.

"Thank you, *old woman*," I said to her.

"And *proud* of it." As usual, she had the last word.

I called Jezzie a few times that morning, but she wasn't home, or she wasn't answering her phone. Her answering machine wasn't on, either. I thought about our night in Arlington. She'd been so wired. Even before the *National Star* had arrived on the scene.

I thought about driving over to her apartment, but I changed my mind. We didn't need any more tabloid photographs or news stories while the trial was winding down.

Nobody said much to me at work that day. If I'd had any doubts before, that showed me how serious the damage was. I'd taken a hit, all right.

I went to my office and sat there all alone with a container of black coffee and stared at the four walls. They were covered with "clues" from the kidnapping. I was starting to feel guilty, and rebellious, and angry. I wanted to punch glass, which I'd actually done once or twice after Maria was shot.

I was at my government-issue, gunmetal desk, facing away from the door. I'd been staring at my work schedule for the week, but I wasn't really seeing anything written on the sheet.

"You're in this one all alone, motherfucker," I heard Sampson say at my back. "You're all by your lonesome this time. You are meat cooked on a barbecue spit."

"Don't you think you're understating things a little?" I said without turning to him.

"I figured you'd talk when you wanted to talk about it," Sampson said. "You knew that *I knew* about the two of you."

A couple of coffee-cup rings on the work schedules held my eye. The Browning effect? What the hell was that? My memory and everything else were deserting me lately.

I finally turned around and faced him. He was decked out in leather pants, an old Kangol hat, a black nylon vest. His dark glasses were an effective mask. Actually, he was trying to be charming and softhearted.

"What do you figure is going on now?" I asked him. "What are they saying?"

"Nobody's real happy about the way the holy-shit kidnapping case has gone down. Not enough 'attaboys' coming down from upstairs. I guess they're lining up potential sacrificial lambs. You're one of them for sure."

"And Jezzie?" I asked. But I already knew the answer.

"She's one, too. Associating with known Negroes," Sampson said. "I take it you haven't heard the news?"

"Heard what news?"

Sampson let out a short burst of breath, then he gave me the latest hot-breaking story.

"She took a leave of absence, or maybe she left the Service altogether. Happened about an hour ago, Alex. Nobody knows for sure if she jumped or was pushed."

I called Jezzie's office immediately. The secretary said that she was "gone for the day." I called Jezzie's apartment. No answer there.

I drove to her apartment, breaking a couple of speeding laws on the way. Derek McGinty was talking over WAMU radio. I like the sound of Derek's voice even if I'm not listening to the words.

Nobody was home at Jezzie's. At least no photographers were lurking around. I thought about driving down to her lake cottage. I called North Carolina from a pay phone down the street. The local operator told me the number had been disconnected.

"How recently was that?" I asked with surprise in my voice. "I called that number last night."

"Just this morning," the operator told me. "The local number was disconnected this very morning."

Jezzie had disappeared.

CHAPTER 66

THE VERDICT in the Soneji/Murphy trial was coming down soon.

The jury went out on the eleventh of November. They returned after three days, amid nonstop rumors that they had been unable to decide either the guilt, or the innocence, of the defendant. The whole world seemed to be waiting.

Sampson picked me up that morning and we rode to the courthouse together. The weather had turned warm, after a brief cool spell that foreshadowed winter.

As we approached Indiana Avenue, I thought about Jezzie. I hadn't seen her in over a week. I wondered if she would show up in court for the verdict. She'd called me. She told me she was down in North Carolina. That was all she'd really said. I was a loner again, and I didn't like it.

I didn't see Jezzie outside the courthouse, but Anthony Nathan was climbing out of a silver Mercedes stretch. This was his big moment. Reporters climbed all over Nathan. They were like city birds on stale bread crumbs.

The TV and print people tried to grab a little piece of me and

Sampson before we could escape up the courthouse steps. Neither of us was too excited about being interviewed again.

"Dr. Cross! Dr. Cross, please," one of them called out. I recognized the shrill voice. It belonged to a local TV news anchorwoman.

We had to stop. They were behind us, and up ahead. Sampson hummed a little Martha and the Vandellas, "Nowhere to Run."

"Dr. Cross, do you feel that your testimony might actually help to get Gary Murphy off the hook for murder one? That you may have inadvertently helped him to get away with murder?"

Something finally snapped inside me. "We're just happy to be in the Super Bowl," I said straight-faced into the glare of several minicam lenses. "Alex Cross is going to concentrate on his game. The rest will take care of itself. Alex Cross just thanks Almighty God for the opportunity to play at this level." I leaned in toward the reporter who'd asked the question. "You understand what I'm saying? You're clear now?"

Sampson smiled and said, "As for me, I'm still open for lucrative endorsements in the sneaker and the soft-drink categories."

Then we continued up the steep stone steps and into the federal courthouse.

As Sampson and I entered the cavernous federal courthouse lobby, the noise level might have done real damage to our eardrums. Everyone was pushing and milling about, but in a sort of civilized manner, the way folks in evening wear push into your back at the Kennedy Center.

Soneji/Murphy wasn't the first criminal trial where multiple personality was the center of the defense. It was by far the most celebrated case, though. It had raised emotional questions about guilt and innocence, and those questions genuinely left the verdict in doubt. . . . *If Gary* Murphy *was innocent, how could he be convicted of kidnapping and murder?* His lawyer had planted that question in all of our minds.

I saw Nathan again upstairs. He had accomplished everything he'd hoped for with his courtroom session. "*Clearly*, there are two personalities battling each other inside the defendant's mind," he'd told the jurors during his summation. "One of them is as *innocent* as you are. You *cannot* convict Gary Murphy of kidnapping or murder. Gary *Murphy* is a good man. Gary *Murphy* is a husband and a father. *Gary* Murphy *is innocent!*"

It was a difficult problem and dilemma for the jurors. Was Gary Soneji/Murphy a brilliant and evil sociopath? Was he aware, and in control, of his actions? Had there been an "accomplice" to the kidnapping and at least one child-murder? Or had he acted alone from the beginning?

No one knew the truth except maybe Gary himself. Not the psychology experts. Not the police. Not the press. And not me.

Now how would the jury of Gary's "peers" decide?

The first real event of the morning occurred when Gary was escorted into the packed, noisy courtroom. He looked his usual clean-cut and characteristically boyish self in a plain blue suit. He looked as if he worked in some small-town bank, not like someone on trial for kidnapping and murder.

There was a smattering of applause. It proved that even kidnappers can have a cult following these days. The trial had definitely attracted its share of weirdos and sick creeps.

"Who says America doesn't have any more heroes?" Sampson said to me. "They like his crazy ass. You can see it in their shiny, beady little eyes. He's the new and improved Charlie Manson. Instead of a berserk hippie, a berserk yuppie."

"The Son of Lindbergh," I reminded Sampson. "I wonder if this is how he wanted it to turn out. All part of his master plan for fame?"

The jury filed into the courtroom. The men and women

looked dazed and unbearably tense. What had they decided —
probably very late the night before?

One of the jurors stumbled as they moved one by one into
the dark mahogany jury box. The man went down on one knee
and the procession behind him stopped. That one brief moment
seemed to underscore the frailty and humanity of the whole trial
process.

I glanced at Soneji/Murphy and thought I saw a faint smile
cross his lips. Had I witnessed a tiny slipup? What thoughts
were racing through his head now? What verdict did he expect?

In any event, the persona known as Gary Soneji, the "Bad
Boy," would have appreciated the irony of the moment. Everything was ready now. An incredible extravaganza. With him at
center stage. No matter what, this was the biggest day of his life.

I want to be somebody!

"Has the jury reached a verdict?" Judge Kaplan asked once
they were seated.

A small, folded slip of paper was passed to the judge. Judge
Kaplan's face was expressionless as she read the verdict. Then it
went back to the jury foreman. The process of due process.

The foreman, who had remained standing, began to speak in
a clear but shaky voice. He was a postal worker named James
Heekin. He was fifty-five, and had ruddy, almost crimson, col-
oring that suggested high blood pressure, or maybe just the
stress of the trial.

James Heekin proclaimed, "On two charges of kidnapping,
we find the defendant *guilty*. On the charge of the murder of
Michael Goldberg, we find the defendant *guilty*." James Heekin
never used the name *Murphy*, just *the defendant*.

Chaos broke out all over the courtroom. The noise was deaf-
ening as it echoed off the stone pillars and marble walls. Reporters raced for the telephones in the hallway. Mary Warner was
emotionally congratulated by all the young associates on her

staff. Anthony Nathan and his defense team quickly left the room, avoiding questions.

There was a strangely poignant moment in the front of the courtroom.

As court officers were leading Gary away, his wife, Missy, and his little girl, Roni, ran up to him. The three of them fiercely hugged. They sobbed openly.

I had never seen Gary cry before. If it was a performance, it was another brilliant one. If he was acting in front of the courtroom, the scene was entirely believable.

I couldn't take my eyes off him. Not until a pair of court officers finally pried Gary away and led him out of the courtroom.

If he was acting, there hadn't been a single false move. He was completely absorbed with his wife and little girl. He never once looked around the courtroom to see if he had an audience.

He played it perfectly.

Or was Gary Murphy an innocent man who had just been convicted of kidnapping and murder?

CHAPTER 67

"**P**RESSURE, pressure," Jezzie sang along with the tune playing loudly inside her head.

The skin was tight against her forehead as Jezzie maneuvered down the winding mountain road without caution or fear. She leaned into every curve, keeping the powerful bike in fourth gear. The fir trees, jutting boulders, and ancient telephone wires were a blur as she sped along. Everything was fuzzy. She felt as if she'd been in free-fall for over a year, maybe for her whole life. She was going to explode soon.

Nobody understood what it was like to be under so much pressure for so long. Even when she was a kid, she had always been afraid of making a single mistake, afraid that if she wasn't perfect little Jezzie, she would never be loved by her mother and father.

Perfect Little Jezzie.

"Good is not good enough," and "Good is the enemy of great," her father used to tell her almost every day. And so she was a calculating, straight-A student; she was Miss Popular; she was on every fast track she could find. Billy Joel had recorded a song a few years back, "Pressure." That was an approximation for the way she felt every day of her life. She had to make it stop somehow, and now maybe she had a way.

Jezzie downshifted into third as she approached the lake cottage. All the lights were on. Otherwise, everything around the lake seemed at peace. The water was a sleek black table that seemed to merge with the mountains. *But the lights were on.* She hadn't left them on.

Jezzie got off the bike and quickly went inside. The front door was unlocked. No one was in the living room.

"Hello?" she called out.

Jezzie checked the kitchen, then both bedrooms. No one there. There was no sign that anyone had been in either room. Except for the lights.

"Hey, who's here?"

The kitchen screen door was unlatched. She walked outside and down toward the dock.

Nothing.

Nobody.

The sudden burr of a wing beat sounded off to the left. Blurred wings flapped just over the surface of the water.

Jezzie stood at the edge of the dock and let out a long sigh. The Billy Joel song still played in her head. Self-mocking and taunting. "Pressure. Pressure." She could feel it in every inch of her body.

Someone *grabbed* her. Extremely strong arms like a vise were around Jezzie. She held back a scream.

Then something was being put into her mouth.

Jezzie inhaled. She recognized Colombian Gold. Very good dope. She inhaled a second time. Relaxed a little in the strong arms that held her.

"I've missed you," she heard a voice say.

Billy Joel screamed inside her head.

"What are you doing here?" she finally asked.

Part Five

The Second
Investigation

CHAPTER 68

MAGGIE ROSE DUNNE was in darkness again.

She could see shapes all around her. She knew what they were, and where she was, even why she was there.

She was thinking about escaping again. But the *warning* jumped into her head. Always the warning.

If you try to escape, you won't be killed, Maggie. That would be too easy. You'll be put under the ground again. You'll go back in your little grave. So don't ever try to escape, Maggie Rose. Don't even think about it.

She was starting to forget so much now. Sometimes she couldn't even remember who she was. It all seemed like a bad dream, like lots of nightmares, one after the other.

Maggie Rose wondered if her mother and father were still looking for her. Why would they be? It was so long ago that she'd been kidnapped. Maggie understood that. Mr. Soneji had taken her from the Day School. But then she never saw him again. There was only the *warning*.

Sometimes, she felt as if she were only a story character she'd made up.

Tears filled her eyes. It wasn't so dark now. Morning was coming. She wouldn't try to escape again. She hated this, but she never wanted to go under the ground again.

Maggie Rose knew what all the shapes were.

They were *children*.

All in just one room of the house.

From which there was no escape.

CHAPTER 69

JEZZIE CAME BACK to Washington the week after the trial ended. It seemed like a good time for beginnings. I was ready. God Almighty, was I ready to move on with life.

We'd talked over the phone some, but not too much, about her state of mind. Jezzie did tell me one thing. She said it was really bizarre that she had invested so much in her career, and now she didn't care about it at all.

I had missed Jezzie even more than I thought I could. My mind was on her while I investigated the murder of two thirteen-year-olds over a pair of Pump sneakers. Sampson and I caught the killer, a fifteen-year-old from "Black Hole." That same week, I was offered a job in Washington as VICAP coordinator between the D.C. police department and the FBI. It was a bigger, higher-paying job than the one I had, but I turned it down flat. It was my buyout from Carl Monroe. No thanks.

I couldn't sleep at night. The storm that had begun inside my head the very first day of the kidnapping was still there. I couldn't get Maggie Rose Dunne completely out of my head. I couldn't give up on the case. I wouldn't let myself. I watched anything and everything on ESPN, sometimes at three and four in the morning. I played Alex the Shrink in the old prefab trailer over at St. A's. Sampson and I drank a few cases of beer together. Then we tried to work it off at the gym. In between, we spent long hours at work.

I drove to Jezzie's apartment the day she came back. On the way over there, I listened to Derek McGinty on WAMU again. My talk-show brother. His voice calmed my nervous stomach. One time, I'd actually called in to his night show. Disguised my voice. Talked about Maria, the kids, being on the edge for too long.

When Jezzie opened the door, I was startled by the way she looked. She'd let her hair grow and fan out so that it looked like a sunburst. She was tan, and looked as healthy as a California lifeguard in August. She looked as if nothing could ever be wrong in her life.

"You look rested and all," I told her. I was feeling a little resentful, actually. She had taken off before the trial had ended. No good-byes. No explanations. What did that tell me about who she was?

Jezzie had always been trim, but she was leaner and tighter now. The circles that had been under her eyes so many times during the kidnapping investigation were gone. She had on denim shorts and an old T-shirt that said IF YOU CAN'T DAZZLE THEM WITH BRILLIANCE, BAFFLE THEM WITH BULLSHIT. She was dazzling in all ways.

She smiled gently. "I'm a lot better, Alex. I think I'm almost healed."

She came out on the porch and into my arms, and I felt a little healed myself. I held her and thought that I had been on this strange planet, all alone for a while. I could see myself on this barren moonscape. It had been up to me to find someone new to be with, someone to love again.

"Tell me everything that's been happening. What's it like to fall off the earth?" I asked. Her hair smelled so fresh and clean. Everything about her seemed new and refreshed.

"It's pretty good, actually, falling off the earth. I haven't *not* worked since I was sixteen years old. It was scary the first few days. Then it was fine," she said with her head still buried in my chest. "There was only one thing I missed," she whispered. "I wanted you there with me. If that sounds corny, too bad."

That was one of the things I wanted to hear. "I would have come," I said.

"I needed to do it the way I did. I had to think everything through one time. I didn't call anybody else, Alex. Not one other person. I found out a lot about myself. Maybe I even found out who Jezzie Flanagan really is."

I raised her chin up, and looked into her eyes. "Tell me what you found out. Tell me who Jezzie is."

Arm in arm, we went inside the house.

But Jezzie didn't talk very much about who she was, or what she'd found out about herself down at her lake cottage. We fell into old habits, and ones that, I must admit, I had missed. I wondered if she still cared for me, and just how much she'd wanted to come back to D.C. I needed a sign from her.

Jezzie began to unbutton my shirt, and there was no way I was going to stop her. "I did miss you so much," she whispered against my chest. "Did you miss me, Alex?"

I had to smile. My physical condition at that moment was the obvious answer to her question. "Now what do you think? Take a guess."

Jezzie and I got a little wild that afternoon. I couldn't help remembering the night the *National Star* showed up outside our motel room. She was definitely leaner and tighter, and she'd been in playing shape before she'd gone away. Jezzie was also tan all over.

"Who's darker?" I asked her and grinned.

"I definitely am. Brown as a berry, as they say around the lake."

"You're just dazzling me with your brilliance," I told her.

"Uh huh. How long can we keep this up? Talking and looking, not touching. Will you unbutton the rest of your shirt buttons? Please."

"Does that excite you?" I asked. My voice caught in my throat a little.

"Uh huh. Actually, you can take the shirt off."

"You were going to tell me something about who you are, what you learned on your retreat," I reminded her. Confessor and lover. A sexy concept in itself.

"You can kiss me now. If you want to, Alex. Can you kiss me without anything but our lips touching?"

"Uhm, I'm not sure about that. Let me turn a little this way. And that way. Are you trying to shut me up, by the way?"

"Why would I want to do that? Doctor Detective?"

CHAPTER 70

I THREW MYSELF into work again. I had promised myself that I'd solve the kidnapping case somehow. The Black Knight would not be vanquished.

One miserable, cold, rainy night I trudged out by myself to see Nina Cerisier again. The Cerisier girl was still the only person who'd actually seen Gary Soneji's "accomplice." I was in the neighborhood, anyway. Right.

Why was I in the Langley Terrace projects, at night, in a cold, drizzling rain? Because I had become a nut case who couldn't get enough information about an eighteen-month-old kidnapping. Because I was a perfectionist who had been that way for at least thirty years of my life. Because I needed to know what had really happened to Maggie Rose Dunne. Because I couldn't escape the gaze of Mustaf Sanders. Because I wanted the truth about Soneji/Murphy. Or so I kept telling myself.

Glory Cerisier wasn't real happy to see me camped on her front doorstep. I'd been standing on the porch for ten minutes before she finally opened the door. I'd knocked on the dented aluminum door a half-dozen times.

"Detective Cross, it's late, you know. Can't we be allowed to move on with our lives?" she asked as she finally swung open the door. "It's hard for us to forget the Sanderses. We don't need you to remind us over and over."

"I know you don't," I agreed with the tall, late-fortyish woman eyeballing me. Almond-shaped eyes. Pretty eyes on a not-very-pretty face. "These are murder cases, though, Mrs. Cerisier, terrible murders."

"The killer has been *caught*," she said to me. "Do you know that, Detective Cross? Have you heard? Do you read newspapers?"

I felt like crap being out there again. I believe she suspected I was crazy. She was a smart lady.

"Oh, Jesus Christ." I shook my head and laughed out loud. "You know, you're absolutely right. I'm just fucked up. I'm sorry, I really am."

That caught her off guard, and Glory Cerisier smiled back at me. It was a kindly, crooked-toothed grin that you see sometimes in the projects.

"Invite this poor nigger in for some coffee," I said. "I'm crazy, but at least I know it. Open the door for me."

"All right, all right. Why don't you come in then, Detective. We can talk one more time. That's it, though."

"That's it," I agreed with her. I had broken through by simply telling her the truth about myself.

We drank bad instant coffee in her tiny kitchen. Actually, she loved to talk. Glory Cerisier asked me all sorts of questions about the trial.

She wanted to know what it was like being on TV. Like many people, she was curious about the actress Katherine Rose. Glory Cerisier even had her own private theory about the kidnapping.

"That man didn't do it. That Gary Soneji, or Murphy, or whoever he is. Somebody set him up, you see," she said and laughed. I suppose she thought it funny that she was sharing her crazy ideas with a crazy D.C. policeman.

"Humor me one last time," I said, finally getting around to what I really wanted to talk to her about. "Run me through what Nina said she saw that night. Tell me what Nina told you. As close as you remember it."

"Why you doin' this to yourself?" Glory wanted to know from me first. "Why you here, ten o'clock at night?"

"I don't know why, Glory." I shrugged and sipped the truly bad-tasting coffee. "Maybe it's because I need to know why I was chosen down in Miami. I don't know for sure, but here I am."

"It made you crazy, hasn't it? The kidnapping of those children."

"Yes. It's made me crazy. Tell me again what Nina saw. Tell me about the man in the car with Gary Soneji."

"Nina, ever since she been little, she love the window seat on our stairway," Glory began the story again. "That's Nina's window on the world, always has been. She curl up there and read a book or just pet one of her cats. Sometimes, she just stare out at nothing. She was at the window seat when she saw that white man, Gary Soneji. We get few white men in the neighborhood. Black, some Hispanic, sometimes. So he caught her eye. The more she watched, the stranger it seemed to her. Like she told you. He was *watching* the Sanderses' house. Like he was spying on the house or something. And the other man, the one in the car, he was watching him watch the house."

Bingo. My tired, overloaded mind somehow managed to catch the key phrase in what she'd just said.

Glory Cerisier was all set to go on, but I stopped her. "You just said the man in the car was *watching* Gary Soneji. You said he was *watching him.*"

"I did say that, didn't I? I forgot all about it. Nina been saying the men was together. Like a salesman team or something. You know, the way they come stake out a street, sometimes. But way back, she told me the man in the car was *watching* the other one. I believe that what she said. I'm almost sure. Let me get Nina. I'm not so sure anymore."

Soon, the three of us were sitting together and talking. Mrs. Cerisier helped me with Nina, and Nina finally cooperated. Yes, she was sure the man in the car *had been watching Gary Soneji.* The man wasn't there *with* Soneji. Nina Cerisier definitely remembered the man in the car *watching* the other man.

She didn't know whether it had been a white or a black man watching. She hadn't mentioned it before because it didn't seem important, and the police would have asked even more questions. Like most kids in Southeast, Nina hated the police and was afraid of them.

The man in the car had been *watching* Gary Soneji.

Maybe there hadn't been an "accomplice" after all, but someone *watching* Gary Soneji/Murphy as he staked out potential murder victims? Who could it have been?

CHAPTER 71

I WAS ALLOWED to visit Soneji/Murphy, but only in connection with the Sanders and Turner murder investigations. I could see him about crimes that would probably never go to trial, but not about one that could possibly remain unsolved. So goes the tale of the red tape.

I had a friend out at Fallston, where Gary was imprisoned. I'd known Wallace Hart, the chief of psychiatry at Fallston, since I'd joined the D.C. police force. Wallace was waiting for me in the lobby of the ancient facility.

"I like this kind of personal attention," I said as I shook his hand. "First time I've ever got any, of course."

"You're a celebrity now, Alex. I saw you on the tube."

Wallace is a small scholarly-looking black man who wears round bottle glasses and baggy blue business suits. He reminds people of George Washington Carver, maybe crossed with Woody Allen. He looks as if he were black *and* Jewish.

"What do you think about Gary so far?" I asked Wallace as we took a prison elevator up to the maximum-security floor. "Model prisoner?"

"I've always had a soft spot for psychopaths, Alex. They keep shit interesting. Imagine life without the real bad guys. Very boring."

"You're not buying the possibility of multiple personalities, I take it?"

"I think it's a possibility, but very slim. Either way, the bad boy in him is really bad. I'm surprised he got his ass in a sling, though. I'm surprised he got caught."

I said, "Want to hear one off-the-wall theory? Gary *Murphy* caught Soneji. Gary Murphy couldn't handle Soneji, so he turned him in."

Wallace grinned at me. He had a big toothy smile for such a little face. "Alex, I do like your crazy mind. But do you really buy that? One side turning in the other?"

"Nope. I just wanted to see if you would. I'm beginning to think he's a psycho all the way. I just need to know how far all the way is. I observed a definite paranoid personality disorder when I was seeing him."

"I agree with that. He's mistrustful, demanding, arrogant, driven. Like I say, I love the guy."

I was a little shocked when I finally saw Gary this time. His eyes appeared to be sunken into his skull. The orbs were red-rimmed, as if he were suffering from conjunctivitis. The skin was pulled tight all around his face. He'd lost a lot of weight, maybe thirty pounds, and he'd been fit and trim to begin with.

"So I'm a little depressed. Hello, Doctor." He looked up from his cot and spoke to me. He was Gary *Murphy* again. At least he seemed to be.

"Hello, Gary," I said. "I couldn't stay away."

"Long time no visits. You must want something. Let me guess — you're doing a book about me. You want to be the next Anne Rule?"

I shook my head. "I wanted to come and see you long before

this. I had to get a court order first. I'm here to talk about the Sanders and Turner murders, actually."

"Really?" He seemed resigned and his affect was indifferent and passive. I didn't like the way he looked. It struck me that his personality could be on the verge of complete disintegration.

"I'm only *allowed* to talk to you about the Sanders and Turner murders, in fact. That's my purview. But we could talk about Vivian Kim, if you like."

"Then we don't have a lot to talk about. I don't know anything about those killings. I haven't even read the newspapers. I swear on my daughter's life I haven't. Maybe our friend Soneji knows. Not me, Alex." He seemed real comfortable calling me Alex by now. Nice to know you can make friends, anywhere.

"Your lawyer must have explained the murder cases to you. There could be another trial this year."

"I won't see any more lawyers. It's got nothing to do with me. Besides, those cases won't get to trial. Too expensive."

"Gary." I talked to him as if he were a patient of mine. "I'd like to put you under hypnosis again. Will you sign the papers if I can get all the bullshit arranged? It's important for me to talk *to Soneji*. Let me try to talk *to him*."

Gary Murphy smiled and he shook his head. Finally he nodded. "Actually, I'd like to talk with him myself," he said. "If I could, I'd kill him. I would kill Soneji. Like I'm supposed to have killed all those other people."

That evening I went to see former Secret Service Agent Mike Devine. Devine was one of the two agents who had been assigned to Secretary Goldberg and his family. I wanted to ask him about the "accomplice" theory.

Mike Devine had taken voluntary retirement about a month after the kidnapping. Because he was still in his mid-forties, I

334 / James Patterson

assumed he'd been pushed out of his job. We talked for a couple
of hours out on his stone terrace overlooking the Potomac.

It was a tasteful, well-appointed apartment for a now-single
man. Devine was tan and looked rested. He was one of the better
advertisements I'd seen for getting out of police work while you
can.

He reminded me a little of Travis McGee in the John Mac-
Donald novels. He was well built, with lots of character in his
face. He'd do well in early-retirement-land, I thought: movie-
hero good looks, lots of curly brown hair, an easy smile, stories
galore.

"My partner and I were pushed out, you know," Devine con-
fessed over a couple of Corona beers. "One fuck-up that happened to turn into World War Three, and we were both history
at the Service. We didn't get a lot of support from our boss,
either."

"It was a public case. I guess there had to be heroes and
villains." I could be as philosophical as the next guy over a cold
beer.

"Maybe it's all for the best," Mike Devine mused. "You ever
think about starting over, doing something else while you still
have the energy? Before the Alzheimer's sets in?"

"I've thought about private practice," I said to Devine. "I'm a
psychologist. I still do some pro bono work in the projects."

"But you love The Job too much to leave it?" Mike Devine
grinned and squinted into late afternoon sunlight coming off the
water. Gray seabirds with white chests flew right by the terrace.
Nice. Everything about the layout was nice.

"Listen, Mike, I wanted to go over, once more, those last
couple of days before the kidnapping," I said to him.

"You *are* goddamn hooked, Alex. I've been over every square
inch of that territory myself. Believe me, there's nothing there.
It's fallow ground. Nothing grows. I've tried and tried, and finally
I gave up the ghost."

"I believe you. But I'm still curious about a late-model sedan that might have been seen out in Potomac. Possibly a Dodge," I said. It was the car that Nina Cerisier remembered parked on Langley Terrace. "You ever notice a blue or black sedan parked on Sorrell Avenue? Or anywhere around the Day School?"

"Like I said, I've been over and over all of our daily logs. There wasn't any mystery car. You can look at the logs yourself."

"I have," I told him and laughed at the seeming hopelessness of my case.

Mike Devine and I talked for a while more. He couldn't come up with anything new. In the end, I listened to him praise the beach life, bonefishing on the Keys, "hitting the little white ball." His new life was just starting. He'd gotten over the Dunne-Goldberg kidnapping a lot better than I had.

Something still bothered me, though. The whole "accomplice" thing. Or "the watcher" thing. More than that, I had a gut feeling about Devine and his partner. A bad feeling. Something told me they knew more than they were willing to tell anybody.

While I was still as hot as a ten-dollar pistol, I decided to contact Devine's ex-partner, Charles Chakely, later that same night. After his dismissal, Chakely and his family had settled in Tempe, Arizona.

It was midnight my time; ten o'clock in Tempe. Not too late, I figured. "Charles Chakely? This is Detective Alex Cross calling from Washington," I said when he got on the phone.

There was a pause, an uncomfortable silence, before he answered. Then Chakely got hostile — real strange, it seemed to me. His reaction only served to fuel my instincts about him and his partner.

"What the hell do you want?" he bristled. "Why are you calling me here? I'm retired from the Service now. I'm trying to put what happened behind me. Leave me the hell alone. Stay away from me and my family."

"Listen, I'm sorry to bother you —" I started to apologize.

He cut me off. "Then *don't*. That's an easy fix, Cross. Butt out of my life."

I could just about picture Charles Chakely as I spoke to him. I remembered him from the days right after the kidnapping. He was only fifty-one, but he looked over sixty. Beer belly. Most of his hair gone. Sad, kind of withdrawn eyes. Chakely was physical evidence of the harm The Job could do to you, if you let it.

"Unfortunately, I'm still assigned to a couple of murders," I said to him, hoping he'd understand. "They involved Gary Soneji/Murphy, too. He came back to kill one of the teachers at the school. Vivian Kim?"

"I thought you didn't want to bother me. Why don't you pretend you never called, huh? Then I'll pretend I never picked up the phone. I'm getting good at playing 'let's pretend' out here on the painted desert."

"Listen, I could get a subpoena. You know I can do that. We could have this conversation in Washington. Or I could fly out there and come over to your house in Tempe. Show up for a barbecue some night."

"Hey, what the fuck's the matter with you? What's with you, Cross? The goddamn case is over. Leave it alone, and leave me the fuck alone."

There was something very strange in Chakely's tone. He sounded ready to explode.

"I talked to your partner tonight," I said. *That* kept him on the line.

"So. You talked to Mickey Devine. I talk to him myself now and then."

"I'm happy for both of you. I'll even get out of your hair in a minute. Just answer a question or two."

"One question. That's it," Chakely finally said.

"Do you ever remember seeing a dark late-model sedan parked on Sorrell Avenue? Anywhere around the Goldberg or Dunne house? Maybe a week or so prior to the kidnapping?"

"Hell, no; Christ, no. Anything out of the ordinary would have gone in our log. The kidnapping case is closed. It's over in my book. So are you, Detective Cross."

Chakely hung up on me.

The tone of the conversation had been too weird. The unsolved "watcher" angle was driving me a little crazy. It was a big loose end. Too important to ignore if you were any kind of detective. I had to talk to Jezzie about Mike Devine and Charlie Chakely, and the logs they had kept. Something wasn't checking out about the two of them. They were definitely holding back.

CHAPTER 72

JEZZIE AND I spent the day at her lake cottage. She needed to talk. She needed to tell me how she had changed, what she'd found out about herself on her sabbatical. Two very, very strange things happened down there In the Middle of Nowhere, North Carolina.

We left Washington at five in the morning and got to the lake just before eight-thirty. It was the third of December, but it could have been the first of October. The temperature was in the seventies all afternoon, and there was a sweet mountain breeze. The chirp and warble of dozens of different birds filled the air.

The summer people were gone for the season, so we had the lake to ourselves. A single speedboat swooped around the lake for an hour or so, its big engine sounding like a race car from Nascar. Otherwise, it was just the two of us.

By mutual agreement, we didn't push into any heavy subjects too quickly. Not about Jezzie, or Devine and Chakely, or my latest theories on the kidnapping.

Late in the afternoon, Jezzie and I went for a long trek into the surrounding pine forests. We followed the spoor of a perfectly crystalline stream that climbed into the surrounding mountain range. Jezzie wore no makeup and her hair was loose and wild. She was in jean cutoffs, and a University of Virginia sweatshirt missing the sleeves. Her eyes were a beautiful blue that rivaled the color of the sky.

"I told you that I found out a lot about myself down here, Alex," Jezzie said as we hiked deeper and deeper into the forest. She was talking softly. She seemed almost childlike. I listened carefully to every word. I wanted to know all about Jezzie.

"I want to tell you about me. I'm ready to talk now," she said. "I need to tell you why, and how, and everything else."

I nodded, and let her go on.

"My father . . . my father was a failure. In his eyes. He was street-smart. He could get along so beautifully socially — when he wanted to. But he came from the shanty side, and he let it put a huge chip on his shoulder. My father's negative attitude got him in trouble all the time. He didn't care how it affected my mother or me. He got to be a heavy drinker in his forties and fifties. At the end of his life, he didn't have one friend. Or really any family. I imagine that's why he killed himself. . . . *My father killed himself*, Alex. He did it in his unmarked car. There wasn't any heart attack in Union Station. That's a lie I've been telling ever since my college days."

We were both silent as we walked on. Jezzie had only talked about her mother and father once or twice. I'd known about their drinking problem, but I wouldn't push her — especially because I couldn't be Jezzie's doctor. When she was ready, I'd thought that she would talk about it.

"I didn't want to be a failure like my father or my mother. That's the way they saw themselves, Alex. That's how they talked all the time. Not low esteem — no esteem. I couldn't let myself be like that."

"How do you see them?"

"As failures, I guess." A tiny smile came with the admission. A painfully honest smile.

"They were both so unbelievably smart, Alex. They knew everything about everything. They read every book in the universe. They could talk to you about any subject. Have you ever been to Ireland?"

"I've been to England once, on police business. That's the one and only time I've been to Europe. Never had the money to spare."

"Some villages you go to in Ireland — the people are so articulate, but they live in such poverty. You see these 'white ghettos.' Every third storefront seems to be a pub. There are so many educated failures in that country. I didn't want to be another smart failure. I've told you about that fear of mine. That would be hell on earth to me. . . . I pushed myself so hard in school. I needed to be number one, no matter what the cost. Then in the Treasury Department. I got ahead, comfortably ahead. Alex, for whatever reasons, I was becoming happy with my career, with my life in general."

"But it disintegrated after the Goldberg-Dunne kidnapping. You were the scapegoat. You weren't the golden girl anymore."

"Just like that, I was finished. Agents were talking behind my back. Eventually, I quit, left the Service. I didn't have a choice. It was total bullshit and unfair. I came down here. To figure out who the hell I was. I needed to do it all by myself."

Jezzie reached out, and she put her arms around me in the heart of the woods. She began to sob very quietly. I had never seen her cry before. I held Jezzie tightly in my arms. I'd never felt so close to her before. I knew she was telling me some hard truths. I owed her some hard truth in return.

We were down in a secluded knoll, talking quietly, when I became aware of someone watching us in the woods. I kept my head rock-steady, but my eyes darted to the right. Somebody else was in the woods.

Someone was *watching* us.

Another *watcher*.

"Somebody's up there, Jezzie. Just beyond that hill to our right," I whispered to her. She didn't look in that direction. She was still a cop.

"Are you sure, Alex?" she asked.

"I'm sure. Trust me on this one. Let's split up," I said. "If whoever it is starts to take off, we run them down."

We separated, and walked so that we'd flank the hill where I'd seen the watcher. That probably confused whoever it was.

He took off!

The *watcher* was a man. He had on sneakers and a dark, hooded jumpsuit that blended in with the woods. I couldn't tell about his height or build. Not yet, anyway.

Jezzie and I raced behind him for a good quarter of a mile. Both of us were barefoot, so we didn't gain any distance on the watcher. We probably lost a few yards during our all-out sprint. Branches and thorns tore at our faces and arms. We finally burst out of the pine woods, and found ourselves at a blacktop country road. We were just in time to hear a car accelerating around a nearby curve. We never saw the car, not even a glimpse of the license plate.

"Now that's really goddamn weird!" Jezzie said as we stood by the roadside, trying to catch our breath. Sweat was rolling down our faces, and our hearts pounded in synch.

"Who knows you're down here? Anyone?" I asked her.

"No one. That's why it's so weird. Who the hell was that? This is scary, Alex. You got any ideas?"

I had jotted down at least a dozen theories on the *watcher* whom Nina Cerisier had seen. The most promising theory I had was the simplest. The police had been watching Gary Soneji. But which police? Could it have been anyone in my own department? Or Jezzie's?

It certainly was scary.

We made it back to Jezzie's cabin just before it turned dark. A wintry chill was entering the air.

We built a big fire inside and cooked a fine meal that would have fed four.

There was sweet white corn, a huge salad, a twenty-ounce steak for each of us, a dry white wine with *Chassagne-Montrachet, Premier Cru, Marquis de Laguiche* etched on the label.

After we ate we got around to talking about Mike Devine and Charlie Chakely, and the *watcher*. Jezzie couldn't help too much. She told me I was probably looking in the wrong place with the Secret Service agents. She said that Chakely was an excitable type who just might blow up over a call to Arizona. She told me he was bitter on the job, so he'd probably be bitter off it. In her opinion, Mike Devine and Chakely were both good, but not great, agents. If something was worth noting during the Goldberg family surveillance, they would have seen it. Their logs would have been accurate. Neither of them was clever enough to pull off a cover-up. Jezzie was sure of that.

She didn't doubt that Nina Cerisier had seen a car parked on her street the night before the Sanders murder, but she didn't believe that somebody had been *watching* Soneji/Murphy. Or even that Soneji had been down near the projects himself.

"I'm not on the case anymore," Jezzie finally said to me. "I don't represent the interests of Treasury or anybody else. Here's my honest opinion, Alex. Why don't *you* just give it up? It's over. Let it go."

"I can't do that," I told Jezzie. "That isn't how we do things at King Arthur's Round Table. I can't give up on this case. Every time I try, something pops up and changes my mind."

That night we went to bed fairly early. Nine, nine-fifteen. The Chassagne-Montrachet, Premier Cru did its job. There was still passion, but there was also warmth and tenderness between us.

We cuddled, and we laughed, and we didn't go to *sleep* early. Jezzie dubbed me "Sir Alex, the Black Knight of the Round

Table." I called her "Lady of the Lake." We finally fell asleep whispering like that, peaceful in each other's arms.

I don't know what time it was when I woke up. I was on top of ruffled bed covers and comforter, and it was very cold.

There was still an orangish glow from the fire, a quiet crackling noise. I wondered how it could be so *cold* in the bedroom with the fire still going.

What my eyes saw, what my body was feeling, didn't add up. I mulled on that for a few seconds.

I crawled under the covers and pulled them up to my chin. The glow reflected against the windowpane looked strange.

I thought about how odd it was to be there with Jezzie again. In the Middle of Nowhere. I couldn't imagine ever *not* being with her now.

I was tempted to wake her. Tell her that. Talk to her about anything and everything. The Lady of the Lake. And the Black Knight. Sounded like Geoffrey Chaucer for the 1990s.

Suddenly I realized it *wasn't* a glow from the fireplace that was flickering against the window.

I jumped out of bed and ran to take a look. I was witnessing something I had heard about all of my life, but had never expected to see.

A cross was burning very brightly on Jezzie's lawn.

CHAPTER 73

A MISSING LITTLE GIRL *named Maggie Rose.*
Murders in the projects. The thrill-killing of Vivian Kim.
A psychopath. Gary Soneji/Murphy.
An "accomplice." A mystery watcher.
A fiery cross in North Carolina.

When would the pieces finally fit together? Would the pieces ever fit? From that moment in Jezzie's cottage until the end of everything, my head was filled with powerful, disturbing images. I couldn't give up the case, as Jezzie had suggested. Events the following week added to my paranoia.

I came home late from work on Monday. Damon and Janelle swarmed all over me as I stomped the dozen paces from the front door to the kitchen.

"Phone! Phone! Phone!" Damon chanted as he romped along at my side.

Nana was holding the phone out to me from the kitchen. She said it was Wallace Hart calling from Fallston Prison.

"Alex, I'm sorry to bother you at home," Wallace said. "Could you swing by here? It might be important."

I was trying to peel my jacket off. I stopped — one arm in, one out. The kids were helping me. Sort of helping me; sort of trying to get me to throw out my back.

"What is it, Wallace? I've kind of got my hands full tonight." I stuck my tongue out at Damon and Jannie. "Couple of little problems around the house. Nothing I can't handle, though."

"He's asking for you. He wants to talk to you, and only you. Says it's very important."

"Can't it hold until morning?" I asked Wallace. I'd already put in a long day. Besides, I couldn't imagine anything new Gary Murphy could tell me.

"He's *Soneji*," Wallace Hart said over the phone. "*Soneji* wants to talk to you now."

I was speechless. Then I managed, "I'm on my way, Wallace."

I arrived at Fallston in under an hour. Gary was being housed on the prison building's top floor. High-profile patients like Squeaky Fromme and John Hinckley had spent time up there. It was the high-rent district, just the way Gary wanted it.

When I arrived at his cell, Gary was lying face up on a narrow cot without sheets or a blanket. A guard watched him continuously. He was on "specials," as one-to-one surveillance is called.

Wallace Hart said, "I was thinking of putting him in a quiet room for the night. Keep him on specials and seclusion for a while. Until we know what's up with him. He's flying, Alex."

"One of these times he'll fly apart," I said, and Wallace nodded agreement.

I entered Gary's cell and sat without being asked. I was tired of asking for permission from people. Gary's eyes were pinned to the ceiling. They seemed pushed back into his skull. I was certain he knew that I was there. Heeere's Alex!

"Welcome to my *psikhushka*, Doctor," he finally said in an eerie, gravelly monotone. "Do you know *psikhushka*?" It was Soneji all right.

"The prison hospitals in Russia. It's where they put political prisoners in the Soviet Union," I said.

"Exactly so. Very good." He looked over at me. "I want to make a new deal with you. Clean slate."

"I'm not aware of any deal," I told him.

"I don't want to waste any more of my time here. I can't keep playing Murphy. Wouldn't you rather find out what makes Soneji tick? Sure you would, Dr. Cross. You could be famous yourself. You could be very important in whatever circle you choose to participate in."

I didn't believe this could be a fugue state, one of his "escapes." He appeared to be very much in control of what he was saying.

Had he been Gary Soneji all along? The "Bad Boy"? Right from the first time we'd met? That had been my diagnosis. I held to it.

"Are you with me so far?" he asked from his cot. He stretched his long legs out in a leisurely manner and wriggled his bare toes.

"You're telling me now that you were fully conscious of everything you did. There was never a split personality. No fugues. You played both parts. Now you're tired of playing Gary Murphy."

Soneji's eyes were focused and extremely intense. His gaze was colder and more penetrating than usual. Sometimes, with severe schizophrenics, the fantasy life becomes more important than the real one.

"That's right. That's the ticket, Alex. You're so much brighter than the others. I'm very proud of you. You're the one who keeps things interesting for me. The only one who can hold my attention for long stretches at a time."

"And what do you want from us?" I tried to keep him on track. "What can I do you, Gary?"

"I need a few little things. But mainly, I just want to be myself. So to speak. I want to be recognized for all my achievements."

"Do we get anything in return?"

Soneji smiled at me. "I'll tell you what happened. From the beginning. I'll help you solve your precious case. I'll tell *you*, Alex."

I waited for Soneji to go on. I kept going back to the pronouncement over Gary Soneji's bathroom mirror: *I want to be somebody!* He had probably wanted to take credit from the very beginning.

"I had always planned to murder *both* children. I couldn't wait. I have this love-hate thing with childhood, you know. Cut-off breasts and shaved genitals, so my adult victims are more like kiddies. Anyway, killing the little bunions would be the logical and safe conclusion of the whole affair." Soneji smiled again. It was such a weird, inappropriate smile, as if he were confessing a white lie. "You're still interested in why I really decided on the kidnapping, aren't you? Why I chose Maggie Rosebud and her friend Shrimpie Goldberg?"

He was using the nicknames to be provocative — and flip. He loved the "Bad Boy" act. He had revealed a very dark sense of humor over the months.

"I'm interested in everything you have to say, Gary. Go right on."

"You know," he said, "one time I figured out that I've killed over two hundred people. A lot of children, too. I do what I feel like. Whatever hits me at the moment."

The greasy, automatic little smile appeared again. He was no longer Gary Murphy. No longer the all-American-looking yuppie husband and father from Wilmington, Delaware. Had he been killing since he was a boy?

"Is that true? Are you still trying to shock me?"

He shrugged. "Why should I? . . . When I was a boy, I read volumes about the Lindbergh kidnapping case. Then, all the big crimes! I made copies of all the clippings I could find in the Princeton library. I've told you some of this, haven't I? How I was fascinated, absolutely enthralled, obsessed with kidnapping children. Having them completely under my control. . . . I wanted to torture them like helpless little birds. I practiced with a *friend*. You met him, I believe. *Simon Conklin*. Just a small-time psycho, Doctor. Not worth your time . . . *not* a partner. *Not* an accomplice. I especially like the idea that kidnapping gets *the parents* so upset. They will destroy other adults, but God forbid if someone takes one little child. *Unthinkable! Unspeakable crimes!* they shriek. What rubbish. What utter hypocrisy. Think about it. A million dark-skinned children die in Bangladesh, Dr. Cross. Nobody cares. Nobody rushes to save them."

"Why did you murder the black families in the projects?" I asked him. "What's the connection?"

"Who says there has to be a connection? Is that what you learned at Johns Hopkins? Maybe those were my good deeds. Who says I can't have a social conscience, hmmm? There must be *balance* in every life. I believe that. *I Ching*. Think about those victims I chose. Hopeless drug users. A teenage girl who was already a prostitute. A small boy who was already doomed."

I didn't know whether to believe him or not. He was flying. "Do you have a warm spot for us?" I asked him. "I find that real moving."

He chose to ignore my irony. "Actually, I had a black friend once, yes. A maid. Woman who took care of me, if you must know, while my father was divorcing my real mother. Laura Douglas was her nameo-nameo. She went back to Detroit, though, deserted me. Big fat lady, with a howling laugh I *adored*. After she left for Motown was when Mommy Terror started locking troublesome, hyperkinetic me in the basement.

"You're looking at the original latch-key kid. Meantime, my

stepbrother and stepsister were upstairs in my *father's house!* They were playing with *my* toys. They used to taunt me down through the floorboards. I was locked in the basement for weeks at a time. That's the way I recall it. Are little light bulbs and warning bells going off in your head, Dr. Cross? Tortured boy in the cellar. Pampered children buried in a barn. Such nice, neat parallels. All the pieces starting to fit? Is our boy Gary telling the truth now?"

"*Are* you telling the truth?" I asked him again. I thought that he was. It all fit.

"Oh, yes. Scout's honor. . . . The murders in Southeast D.C. Actually, I rather liked the concept of being the first celebrated serial killer of blacks. I don't count the clod in Atlanta, if indeed they have the right man down there. Wayne Williams was an amateur all the way. What's with all these serial killer *Waynes,* anyway? Wayne Williams. John Wayne Gacy, Jr. Patrick Wayne Hearney, who dismembered thirty-two human beans on the West Coast."

"You *didn't* murder Michael Goldberg?" I went back to something he'd said earlier.

"No. It wasn't intentional at the time. I *would* have — everything in good time. He was a spoiled little bunion. Reminded me of my 'brother,' Donnie."

"How did the bruises get on Michael Goldberg's body? Tell me what happened."

"You love this, don't you, Doctor. What does that tell us about you, hmmm? Well, when I saw that he'd died on me, I was so angry. I flew into a rage. Kicked the fucking body all over the lot. Hit it with my digging shovel. I don't remember what else I did. I was so pissed. Then I threw his dead ass in that river out in the sticks. The River Sticks?"

"But you didn't harm the girl? You didn't hurt Maggie Rose Dunne?"

"No, *I didn't hurt the girl.*"

He mimicked my concern. It was a pretty fair approximation of my voice. He definitely could act, play different parts. It was frightening to watch and to be in the same room with him. Could he have killed hundreds of times? I thought so.

"Tell me about her. What really happened to Maggie Rose Dunne?"

"All right, all right, all right. The Maggie Rose Dunne story. Light a candle, sing a hymn to Jesus for sweet mercy. After the abduction, she was groggy. The first time I looked in on her, anyway. She was coming off the secobarbital. I played Mommy Terror for little Maggie. I sounded the way Mommy T. used to sound at the basement door in our house. '*Stopyercryin'* . . . *Shaddup. Shaddup, you spoiled little bunion!*' That scared her pretty good, I'll tell you. Then I put her out again. I carefully checked both of their pulses because I was certain the Fibbers would require some evidence that the children were alive."

"Their pulses were both all right?"

"Yes. Just fine, Alex. I put my ear to each little chest. I controlled my natural urge to *stop* heartbeats rather than preserve them."

"Why the national kidnapping? Why all the publicity? Why take such a big chance?"

"Because *I was ready*. I'd been practicing for a long, long time. I wasn't taking any chances. I also needed the money. I deserved to be a millionaire. Everybody else is."

"You came back to check the children again the following day?" I asked him.

"The next day she was fine, too. But the day after Michael Goldberg died, Maggie Rose was *gone!* I drove into the barn, and there was the hole in the ground where I'd buried the box. Big hole in the ground. Empty! I didn't harm her. I didn't get the ransom money down in Florida, either. Somebody else has it. Now, *you* have to figure out what happened, Detective. *I think I have!* I think I know the big secret."

CHAPTER 74

I WAS UP at three in the morning. Flying! Playing Mozart and Debussy and Billie Holiday on the porch. Junkies were probably calling the police to complain about the noise.

I visited with Soneji again in the morning. The "Bad Boy." I sat in his small windowless room. All of a sudden he wanted to talk. I thought I knew where he was going with all of this; what he was going to tell me soon. Still, I needed to have my opinion confirmed by him.

"You have to understand something that is extremely foreign to your nature," he said to me. "I was in heat when I was scouting the fucking famous girl and her actress mother. I am a 'cheap thrill' artist and junkie. I needed a fix." I couldn't help thinking of my own child-abuse patients as I listened to him relate his bizarre, grisly experiences. It was pathetic to hear a *victim* talking about his many *victims*.

"I understood the 'rill state' perfectly, Doctor. My theme song is 'Sympathy for the Devil.' The Rolling Stones? I always tried to take proper precautions — without breaking *the spell*. I had figured out escape routes, and backup escape routes, ways in and out of every neighborhood that I entered. One of these involved a sewer-system tunnel that goes from the edge of the ghetto out to Capitol Hill. I had a change of clothing inside the tunnel, including a wig. I'd thought of everything. I wouldn't get caught. I was very confident about my abilities. I believed in my own omnipotence."

"Do you still believe in your omnipotence?" It was a serious question. I didn't think he'd tell me the truth, but I wanted to hear what he had to say, anyway.

He said, "What happened back then, my one mistake, was I permitted my successes, the applause of millions of admirers, to rush to my head. The applause can be a drug. Katherine Rose suffers from the same disease, you know. Most of the movie people, the sports icons, they do, too. Millions are cheering for them, you understand. They're telling these people how 'special' and how 'brilliant' they are. And some of the stars forget any limitations they might have, forget the hard work that got them to the plateau originally. I did. At the time. That is precisely why I was caught. *I believed I could escape from the McDonald's!* Just as I had always escaped before. I would just dabble in a little 'spree' killing, then get away. I wanted to sample all the high-impact crimes, Alex. A little Bundy, a little Geary, a little Manson, Whitman, Gilmore."

"Do you feel omnipotent now? Since you're older and wiser?" I asked Soneji. He was being ironic. I assumed I could be, too.

"I'm the closest thing to it you'll ever see. I'm a way to understand the concept, no?"

He smiled that blank killer smile of his again. I wanted to hit him. Gary Murphy was a tragic and almost likable sort of man. Soneji was hateful, pure evil. The human monster; the human beast.

"When you scouted the Goldberg and Dunne houses, were you at the height of your powers?" *Were you omnipotent then, shithead?*

"No, no, no. As *you* know, Doctor, I was already becoming

sloppy. I'd read too many news accounts of my 'perfect' killing in Condon Terrace. 'No traces, no clues, the perfect killer!' Even I was impressed."

"What went wrong out in Potomac?" I thought I knew the answer. I needed him to confirm it.

He shrugged. "I was being followed, of course."

Here we go, I thought to myself. *The "watcher."*

"You didn't know it at the time?" I asked Soneji.

"Of course not." He frowned at the question. "I realized I was being followed much later. Then it was confirmed at the trial."

"How was that? How did you find out you were being followed?"

Soneji stared into my eyes. He seemed to be staring straight through to the back of my skull. He considered me beneath him. I was just a vessel for his outpouring. But he found me more interesting than the others to talk to. I didn't know whether to feel honored or defiled. He was also curious about what I knew, or what I didn't know.

"Let me stop to make a point," he said. "This one is important to me. I have secrets to tell you. Lots of big and little secrets. Dirty secrets, juicy secrets. I'm going to give you one secret now. Do you know why?"

"Elementary, my dear Gary," I told him. "It's hell for you to be under *the control* of others. You need to be in charge."

"That's very good, Doctor Detective. But I do have some neat things to trade. Crimes that go all the way back to when I was twelve and thirteen years old. There are major unsolved crimes that go back that far. Believe me. I have a treasure trove of goodies to share with you."

"I understand," I told him. "I can't wait to hear about them."

"You always *did* understand. All you have to do is convince the other zombies to walk and chew Juicy Fruit at the same time."

"The *other* zombies?" I smiled at his slip.

"Sorry, sorry. I didn't mean to be rude. Can you convince the zombies? You know who I mean. *You* have less respect for them than I do."

That was true enough. I'd have to convince Chief of Detectives Pittman for one. "You'll help me out? Give me something concrete? I have to find out what happened to the little girl. Let her parents have some peace at last."

"All right. I *will* do that," Soneji said. It was so simple in the end.

You wait. And you wait. That's the way it goes in almost every police investigation. You ask thousands of questions, literally thousands. You fill entire file cabinets with unnecessary paperwork. Then you ask more questions. You follow countless leads that go nowhere. Then something goes right for a change. It happens every once in a while. It was happening now. A payout for thousands of hours of work. A reward for coming to see Gary again and again.

"I didn't notice any surveillance back then," Gary Soneji continued. "And none of what I'm going to tell you about happened near the Sanders house. It occurred on Sorrell Avenue in Potomac. In front of the Goldberg house, in fact."

Suddenly I was tired of his chest-beating games. I had to know what he knew. I was getting close. *Talk to me, you little fucker.*

"Go on," I said. "What happened out in Potomac? What did you see at the Goldbergs'? *Who* did you see?"

"I drove by there one of those nights before the kidnapping. A man was walking on the sidewalk. I thought nothing of him. It never registered until I saw the same man at the trial."

Soneji stopped talking for a moment. Was he playing again? I didn't think so. He stared at me as if he were looking right into my soul. *He knows who I am. He knows me, perhaps better than I know myself.*

What did he want from me? Was I a substitute for something missing from his childhood? Why had I been chosen for this horrific job?

"Who was the man you recognized at the trial?" I asked Gary Soneji.

"It was the Secret Service agent. It was *Devine*. He and his pal Chakely must have seen me watching the Goldberg and Dunne houses. They were the ones who followed me. They took precious Maggie Rose! *They* got the ransom in Florida. You should have been looking for cops all this time. *Two cops* murdered the little girl."

CHAPTER 75

MY HUNCH about Devine and Chakely had been right after all. Soneji/Murphy was the only eyewitness, and he'd confirmed it. Now we had to move.

I had to personally reopen the Dunne-Goldberg case — and with news that no one in Washington would want to hear.

I decided to talk to the FBI first. . . . *Two cops had murdered Maggie Rose.* The investigation had to be opened up again. The kidnapping hadn't been solved the first time. Now the whole mess was going to blow up once more.

I dropped in on my old buddy of buddies, Gerry Scorse, at FBI headquarters. After I cooled my heels for forty minutes in reception, Scorse brought me coffee and invited me into his office. "Come right in, Alex. Thanks for waiting."

He listened politely, and with apparent concern, as I went over what I had previously learned, and then what Soneji had told me concerning Secret Service agents Mike Devine and Charles Chakely. He took notes, a lot of notes on yellow foolscap.

After I'd finished, Scorse said, "I have to make a phone call. Sit tight, Alex."

When he returned, he asked me to come upstairs with him. He never said it, but I assumed he was impressed by the news from Gary Soneji.

I was escorted to the deputy director's private conference room on the top floor. The deputy, Kurt Weithas, is the number-two person at the Bureau. They wanted me to understand that this was an important meeting. I got it.

Scorse went with me into the impressive, very cushy conference room. All the walls and most of the furnishings were dark blue, very sober and severe. The room reminded me of the cockpit of a foreign car. Yellow pads and pencils were laid out for us.

It was clearly Weithas's meeting from the start. "What we'd like to accomplish is twofold, Detective Cross." Weithas spoke and acted like a very successful, very cool Capitol Hill lawyer. In a manner of speaking, that's what he was. He wore a brilliant white shirt with a Hermès tie. He slipped off his wire-rimmed reading glasses when I entered the room. He appeared to be in a dark mood.

"I'd like to show you all the information we have on agents Devine and Chakely. In return, we must ask for your full cooperation in keeping this matter absolutely confidential. What I'm telling you now ... is *that we've known about them for a while, Detective.* We were running a parallel investigation to your own."

"You have my cooperation," I said, trying not to show my surprise at *his* news. "But I'm going to have to file a report back at the department."

"I've already spoken to your commanding officer about the matter." Weithas brushed that little detail aside. He'd already broken my confidence; he absolutely expected me to keep his. "You've been ahead of us a couple of times during the investigation. This time, maybe we're a little ahead of you. Half a step."

"You have a little bigger staff," I reminded him.

Scorse took over for Weithas at that point. He hadn't lost his touch for condescension. "We started our investigation of agents

Devine and Chakely at the time of the kidnapping," he said. "They were obvious suspects, though not ones we took seriously. During the course of the investigation a great deal of pressure was placed on both men. Since the Secret Service reports directly to the secretary of the treasury, you can imagine what they were subjected to."

"I watched most of it firsthand," I reminded both FBI men.

Scorse nodded, then went on.

"On the fourth of January, Agent Charles Chakely resigned from the Service. He stated that he'd been thinking about the move long before the kidnapping, anyway. He said he couldn't handle the innuendos, all the media attention. His resignation was accepted immediately. At about the same time, a small error in the daily logs kept by the agents was discovered by us. A date had been inadvertently reversed. It was nothing major, except that we were checking everything about the case at the time.

"We eventually got nine hundred of our agents directly or indirectly involved," the deputy director added. I had no idea what his point was yet.

"Other inconsistencies in the agents' logs were eventually discovered," Scorse continued. "Our technical experts concluded that two of the individual reports had been doctored, that is, rewritten. We ultimately came to believe that what was taken out were references to the teacher Gary Soneji."

"They had spotted him checking out the Goldberg house in Potomac," I said. "If Soneji can be believed."

"On this point, I think he can. What you've recently had confirmed corresponds to our findings. We believe that the two agents observed Soneji watching Michael Goldberg and Maggie Rose Dunne. We think one of the agents followed Soneji, and discovered the hiding place in Crisfield, Maryland."

"You've been watching the two agents ever since?" I asked Gerry Scorse.

He nodded once, just as efficient as ever. "For a couple of months, anyway. We also have good reason to believe they know we're watching. Two weeks after Chakely resigned, Devine also resigned from the Service. He said he and his family couldn't take the pressure associated with what had happened, either. Actually, Devine and his wife are separated."

"I assume Chakely and Devine haven't tried to spend any of the money," I said.

"To our knowledge, no. As I said before, they know we're suspicious. They aren't dumb. Not at all."

"It's come down to a rather delicate and intricate waiting game," Weithas said. "We can't prove anything yet, but we can disrupt their lives. We can sure as hell keep them from spending any of the ransom money."

"What about the pilot in Florida? There was no way I could run an investigation down there. Did you ever find out who he was?"

Scorse nodded. The FBI had been withholding a lot from me. From everybody. I wasn't surprised. "He turned out to be a drug runner named Joseph Denyeau. He was known to some of our people in Florida. It's conceivable that Devine knew Denyeau and hired him."

"What happened to this Joseph Denyeau?"

"In case we had any doubts about whether Devine and Chakely play for keeps — they do. Denyeau was murdered in Costa Rica. His throat was cut. He wasn't supposed to be found."

"You're not going to bring Devine and Chakely in at this point?"

"We don't have any proof, Alex. None. Nothing that will hold up. What you got from Soneji cements it, but won't help in court."

"What happened to the little girl? What happened to Maggie Rose Dunne?" I asked Weithas.

Weithas didn't say anything. He blew out air over his upper lip. I got the feeling he was having a long day. In a long year.

"We don't know," Scorse answered. "There's still nothing on Maggie Rose. That's the amazing thing in all this."

"There's another complication," Weithas said to me. He was seated with Scorse on a dark leather sofa. Both FBI men were leaning over a glass coffee table. An IBM computer and printer sat off to one side.

"I'm sure there are a lot of complications," I said to the deputy director. Leave it to the FBI to keep most of them to themselves. They could have helped me along the way. Maybe we would have found Maggie Rose if we'd worked together.

Weithas glanced at Agent Scorse, then he looked back at me. "Jezzie Flanagan is the complication," Weithas said.

I was stunned. I felt as if I'd been punched hard in the stomach. For the last few minutes, I knew something else was coming from them. I just sat there, feeling cold and empty inside, well on my way to feeling *nothing*.

"We believe she's deeply involved in this with the two men. Has been from the start. Jezzie Flanagan and Mike Devine have been lovers for years."

CHAPTER 76

AT EIGHT-THIRTY that night, Sampson and I walked along New York Avenue. It is in the tenderloin of D.C.'s ghettos. It's where Sampson and I hang out most nights. It's home.

He had just asked me how I was holding up. "Not too good, thanks. Yourself?" I said.

He knew about Jezzie Flanagan. I'd told him everything I knew. The plot thickened and thickened. I couldn't have felt any worse than I did that night. Scorse and Weithas had laid out a thorough case involving Jezzie. She'd done it. There was no room for doubt. One lie had led to another. She'd told me a hundred if she'd told me one. Never flinched once. She was better at it than Soneji/Murphy. Real smooth and confident.

"You want me to keep my mouth shut? Or talk at you?" Sampson asked me. "I'll do it either way."

His face was expressionless, as it usually is. Maybe it's the sunglasses that create that impression, but I doubt it. Sampson was like that when he was ten years old.

"I want to talk," I told John. "I could use a cocktail. I need to talk about psychopathic liars."

"I'll buy us a few drinks," Sampson said.

We headed toward Faces. It's a bar we've been going to since we first joined the police force. The regulars in Faces don't mind that we're tough-as-nails D.C. detectives. A few of them even admit that we do more good than harm in the neighborhood.

The crowd in Faces is mostly black, but white people come by for the jazz. And to learn how to dance, and dress.

"Jezzie was the one who assigned Devine and Chakely in the first place?" Sampson reviewed the facts as we waited for the stoplight at 5th Street.

A couple of local punks eyed us from their lookout in front of Popeye's Fried Chicken. In times past, the same kind of street trash would have been on the same corner, only without so much money, or guns, in their pockets. "Yo, brothers." Sampson winked at the thugs. He fucks with everybody's head. Nobody fucks back.

"Right, that's how it all started. Devine and Chakely were one of the teams assigned to Secretary Goldberg and his family. They worked under Jezzie."

"And nobody ever suspected them?" he asked me.

"Not at first. The FBI checked them out. They checked everybody out. Chakely's and Devine's daily logs were off. That's when they became suspicious. Some watchdog analyst at the Bureau figured out that the logs had been doctored. They had twenty people for every one we had. Besides that, the FBI removed the doctored logs so none of us could find them."

"Devine and Chakely spotted Soneji checking out one of the kids. That's how the whole circus began? The double take." Sampson had the general rhythm of the thing now.

"They followed Soneji and his van out to the farm in Maryland. They realized they were stalking a potential kidnapper. *Somebody* got the idea to kidnap the kids *after* the actual kidnapping."

"Ten-million-dollar idea." Sampson glowered. "Was Ms. Jezzie Flanagan in on it from the beginning?"

"I don't know. I think so. I'll have to ask her about that sometime."

"Uh huh." Sampson nodded with the flow of our conversation. "Your head above, or below, the water line right now?"

"I don't know that, either. You meet somebody who can lie to you the way she did, it changes your perspective on things. This is very tough to handle, man. You ever lie to me?"

Sampson showed some of his teeth. It was halfway between a smile and a growl. "Sounds like your head's a little below water to me."

"Sounds like it to me, too," I admitted. "I've had better days. But I've had worse. Let's have that beer."

Sampson gave the gunner's salute to the punks on the corner. They laughed and gave us the high sign. Cops and robbers in the 'hood. We crossed the street to Faces. A little oblivion was in order.

The bar was crowded, and would be that way until closing. People who knew Sampson and me said hello. A woman I'd gone out with was at the bar. A real pretty, real nice social worker who had worked with Maria.

I wondered why nothing had come of it. Because of some deep-down character flaw I have? No. Couldn't be that.

"You see Asahe over there?" Sampson gestured.

"I'm a detective. I see everything, right. Don't miss a trick," I said to him.

"You soundin' *a little* sorry for yourself. Little ironic, I'd say. Two beers. Nah, make it four," he told the bartender.

"I'll get over it," I said to Sampson. "You just watch. I just had never put her on our suspect list. My mistake."

"You're tough, man. Got your nasty old grandma's genes. We gonna fix you up," he said to me. "*Fix her ass*, too. Ms. Jezzie's."

"Did you like her, John? Before any of this came up?"

"Oh yeah. Nothing not to like. She lies real good, Alex. She's got talent. Best I've seen since that movie *Body Heat*," said Sampson. "And no, I never lie to you, my brother. Not even when I should."

The hard part came after Sampson and I left Faces that night. I'd had a few beers, but I was mostly coherent, and nearly dulled to the worst of the pain. And yet it was such a shock that Jezzie had been part of it all this time. I remembered how she'd led me away from Devine and Chakely as suspects. She'd pumped me for anything new the D.C. police had picked up. She'd been the ultimate insider. So confident and cool. Perfect in her part.

Nana was still up when I got back to the house. So far I hadn't told her about Jezzie. Now was about as awful a time as any. The beers helped some. Our history together helped even more. I told Nana the truth straight out. She listened without interrupting, which was an indication of how she was taking the news.

After I had finished, the two of us sat there in the living room, just looking at each other. I was on the hassock, with my long legs spread out in her general direction. Screaming silence was everywhere around us.

Nana was bunched under an old oatmeal-colored blanket in her easy chair. She was still nodding gently, biting her upper lip, thinking over what I'd told her.

"I have to start someplace," she finally said, "so let me start here. I will not say, 'I told you so,' because I had no idea it would be this bad. I *was* afraid for you, that's all. But not about anything like this. I could never have imagined this terrible thing. Now please give me a hug before I go up and say my prayers. I will pray for Jezzie Flanagan tonight. I really will. I'll pray for us all, Alex."

"You know what to say." I told her the bottom-line truth. She knew when to slap you down and when to give a needed pat on the rear end.

I gave Nana a hug, and then she trudged upstairs. I stayed downstairs and thought about what Sampson had said earlier — *we were going to fix Jezzie's ass.* Not because of anything that had happened between the two of us, though. Because of Michael Goldberg and Maggie Rose Dunne. Because of Vivian Kim, who didn't have to die. Because of Mustaf Sanders.

We were going to get Jezzie, somehow.

CHAPTER 77

ROBERT FISHENAUER was a supervisor at Fallston Prison. Today, he thought, that was a very good thing. Fishenauer believed that he just might know where the ten million dollars in kidnap money was hidden. At least a large part of the ransom. He was going to take a little peekaboo right now.

He also had a pretty good idea that Gary Soneji/Murphy was still messing with everybody's head. Big time. And nonstop.

As Fishenauer drove his Pontiac Firebird down Route 50 in Maryland, a host of questions was circulating through his head. Was Soneji/Murphy the kidnapper? Did he really know where the ransom money was? Or was Gary Soneji/Murphy full of shit? Just one more tutti-frutti nut case out at Fallston.

Fishenauer figured he would know everything pretty soon. Another few miles of state road, and he'd know more than anybody, except for Soneji/Murphy himself.

The turnoff was the seldom-used back way into the old farm. The road was almost completely gone now. Fishenauer saw this as he made the right turn off the main highway.

Cattails and sunflowers grew the length of what had obviously once been a road. There weren't even wheel ruts in the crusted-over dirt.

The vegetation was knocked down. Someone had come crashing through here in the past few months. Was it the FBI and local police? They had probably searched the farmhouse grounds a dozen times.

But had they searched the grounds of the deserted farm well enough? Robert Fishenauer wondered to himself. That was the ten-million-dollar question now, wasn't it?

Around five-thirty in the afternoon, Fishenauer pulled his dusty red Firebird up alongside a dilapidated garage just to the left of the main farmhouse. The adrenaline was really pumping now. Nothing like a treasure hunt to get the juices flowing.

Gary had raved about how Bruno Hauptmann had hidden part of the Lindbergh ransom *in his garage* in New York City. Hauptmann had been trained as a carpenter, and he'd built a secret compartment for the money into a wall in his garage.

Gary said he'd done something like that out at the old farm in Maryland. He'd sworn it was the truth, and that the FBI would never find it.

Fishenauer switched off the Firebird's rumbling engine. The sudden quiet was eerie. The old house sure looked deserted, and very creepy. It reminded him of a movie called *The Night of the Living Dead*. Except that *he* was starring in this creepy-crawler.

Weeds were growing everywhere, even springing out of the roof of the garage. Water stains ran down the sides of the garage.

"Well, Gary-boy, let's see if you're completely full of shit. I hope to hell you're not."

Robert Fishenauer took a deep breath and climbed out of his low-slung car. He'd already figured out what he would say if he got nailed here. He'd just say that Gary had told him where he'd buried Maggie Rose Dunne. But Fishenauer had figured it was only some of his crazy talk.

Still, it had gnawed at him.

So now here he was in Creepsville, Maryland, checking it out. Actually, he felt dumb. He also felt kind of bad, guilty, but he had to check this one for himself. Had to, man. This was his personal ten-million-dollar lottery. He had his ticket.

Maybe he was about to find out where little Maggie Rose Dunne was buried. Jesus, he hoped not. Or maybe it was the buried treasure that Gary had promised him.

He and Gary-boy had talked a lot, for hours at a time, back at the hole. Gary loved to talk about his exploits. His *baby,* as he called the kidnapping caper. His "perfect" crime.

Right! So "perfect" he was serving life plus in a max-security prison for the criminally insane.

And here Robert Fishenauer was, right at the moldy front door into Creepsville. The scene of the crime, as they say.

There was a badly rusted metal latch on the door. Fishenauer slipped on a pair of winter golf gloves — hard to explain *those* if he got caught snooping out here. He flipped up the door latch. He had to pull the door hard toward him through the thick overgrowth.

Flashlight time. He took out his lamp and turned it on full blast. Gary said he'd find the money on the right side of the garage, the far right corner, to be exact.

A lot of old, broken-down farm machines lay all around the garage. Cobwebs stuck against his face and neck as he walked forward. The strong smell of decay was on everything.

Halfway into the garage, Fishenauer stopped and turned around. He stared out the open door, and *listened* for what must have been a full ninety seconds.

He heard a jet plane somewhere off in the distance. There was no other sound. He sure hoped there was no one else around.

How long could the FBI afford to watch a deserted farm? Not almost two years after the kidnapping!

Satisfied that he was alone, Fishenauer continued to the back of the garage. Once he was there, he started to work.

He pulled a sturdy old workbench over — Gary had said the bench would be there. He'd seen by now that Gary had described the place in pretty amazing and accurate detail. Gary'd said where every broken piece of machinery lay. He'd told Fishenauer the exact location of just about every slat of wood in the rotting garage walls.

Standing on the old workbench, Fishenauer began to pull away old boards, up where the garage roof met the wall. *There was a space back there.* Just like Gary said there was.

Fishenauer aimed his flashlight into the hole in the wall. There it was, part of the ransom money that Gary Soneji/Murphy wasn't supposed to have. He couldn't believe his eyes. A stack of money was right there in the garage walls.

CHAPTER 78

At 3:16 the following morning, Gary Soneji/Murphy pressed his forehead against the cold metal bars that separated his cell from the prison corridor. He had another big part to act out. Hellzapoppin!

He started to throw up onto the highly polished linoleum floor — just as he had planned to. He was violently ill inside the cell. He yelled for help between wheezing gasps.

Both of the night guards came running. There had been a suicide watch on Gary since his first day there. Laurence Volpi and Phillip Halyard were veterans of many years' service at the federal prison. They weren't too keen on disturbances in the cell block, particularly after midnight.

"What the hell's the matter with you?" Volpi yelled as he watched the green and brown puddle slowly spreading on the floor. "What's your problem, asshole?"

"I think I've been poisoned," Soneji/Murphy gasped and wheezed, the sound coming from deep inside his chest. "Somebody's poisoned me. I've been poisoned! I think I'm dying. Oh my God, I'm dying!"

"Best news I've heard lately," Phillip Halyard said to his partner and grinned. "Wish I'd thought of it first. Poison the bastard."

Volpi took out his walkie-talkie, and called for the night supervisor. The suicide watch on Soneji was a big deal with the prison higher-ups. It sure wasn't going to happen on Volpi's shift.

"I'm going to be sick again," Gary Soneji/Murphy moaned. He sagged heavily against the bars and threw up a second time — violently.

Moments later, the floor's supervisor arrived. Laurence Volpi quickly told his boss what had happened. It was his standard cover-thy-ass speech.

"He says he's been poisoned, Bobby. I don't know what the hell happened. It's possible. Enough of these bastards hate his guts."

"I'll take him downstairs to the hospital myself," Robert Fishenauer said to his men. Fishenauer was a take-charge guy, anyway. Volpi had counted on it. "They'll have to pump his stomach, I guess. If there's anything left to pump. Cuff him for me good. Hands and legs. He doesn't look in shape to be much trouble tonight."

Moments later, Gary Soneji/Murphy figured he was halfway to daylight. The prison elevator was padded. The walls were covered with heavy cloth mats. Other than that, it was ancient and painfully slow. His heart was pounding like a bass drum. A little healthy fear in his life. He'd missed the adrenaline kick.

"You all right?" Fishenauer asked as he and Gary Soneji/Murphy descended, seemingly inch by inch. A single bare lightbulb protruded from a hole in the mats. It cast a dim light.

"Am I all right? What does it look like? I made myself good and sick. I *am* sick," Soneji/Murphy told him. "Why the hell doesn't this thing move faster?"

"You going to puke again?"

"It's entirely possible. A small price to pay." Soneji/Murphy managed a thin smile. "A very small price, Bobby."

Fishenauer grunted. "I guess so. Just keep it away from me if you decide to pukeski again."

The elevator bypassed the next floor, and the next. It was nonstop. It dropped all the way to the basement of the building, where it landed with a hollow thump.

"We see anybody, we're going for X-rays," Fishenauer said as the elevator door opened. "X-ray is down here in the basement."

"Yes, I'm aware of the plan. It's my plan," said Gary Soneji/Murphy.

Because it was past three in the morning, they saw no one as they started their walk down the long tunnel in the prison basement. Halfway through the tunnel, there was a side door. Fishenauer used his key to open it.

There was another short stretch of silent empty hallway. Then they were at a security door. This was where the shit would hit the fan, and Soneji/Murphy had to do his stuff. This was where Fishenauer would see if Gary Soneji/Murphy was as good as his reputation. Fishenauer didn't have a key to the security door.

"Give me your gun now, Bobby. Just think about ten million dollars. I can do this next bit, so all you have to worry about is your part of the money."

This was it. Soneji made it sound so easy. *Do this, do that. Get a piece of ten million dollars.* Fishenauer reluctantly handed over his revolver. He didn't want to think about what he was doing anymore. This was his chance to get out of Fallston, too. His only chance. Otherwise, Fishenauer knew he would be at Fallston for the rest of his life.

"There's nothing fancy here, Bobby, but this will work. You play everything to Kessler. Look real scared."

"I *am* fucking scared."

"You should be, Bobby. I have your gun."

There were two prison guards on the other side of the security door. A waist-high Plexiglas window gave them a view of the unbelievable sight coming their way.

They saw Soneji/Murphy with a gun stuck to the left temple of supervisor Bob Fishenauer. Soneji/Murphy had on arm and leg cuffs, but he also had a gun. Both guards stood up fast. They held their riot shotguns above the glass. They didn't have time to make another move.

"You're gawking at a dead guard," Gary screamed at the top of his voice, "unless you open that fucking door in about five seconds. No more than that!"

"Please!" Fishenauer suddenly screamed at his fellow guards. He was scared, all right. Soneji had the gun pressed hard against his temple. "He killed Volpi upstairs."

It took less than five seconds for an older guard — Stephen Kessler — to make his decision. He turned the key that opened the security door. Kessler was a friend of Robert Fishenauer's, and Soneji had counted on that. Soneji had thought of everything. He'd known that Robert Fishenauer was a "lifer" at the prison; that he was trapped there just like the inmates. He'd talked about Fishenauer's anger and frustrations, and he'd been spot on. He was the smartest fucker Robert Fishenauer had ever met. He was going to make Fishenauer a millionaire.

The two of them headed for Fishenauer's car. The Firebird was parked close to the front gate. Fishenauer had left the sports-car door unlocked.

They were inside the car in a flash.

"Very nice wheels, Bobby," said Gary Soneji/Murphy. "Now you'll be able to buy a Lamborghini. Two or three, if you want to make a *statement*."

Soneji lay down across the backseat. He slid under a blanket that Fishenauer's collie usually slept on. It smelled strongly of dog.

"Now let's get out of this rattrap," Soneji/Murphy said from the back. Robert Fishenauer started up the Firebird.

Less than a mile from the prison, they changed cars. A Bronco was parked on the street and they quickly jumped inside.

A few minutes later, they were on the highway. Light traffic, but more than enough for them to get lost in.

A little less than ninety minutes later, the Bronco turned onto the overgrown driveway of the old farm in rural Maryland. During the ride, Soneji/Murphy had allowed himself the small, but exquisite, pleasure of savoring his original master plan. He loved the idea that two years before, he'd actually thought to leave some cash hidden in the garage. Not the ransom money, of course. *Just for this moment in time.* How prescient of him.

"Are we there yet?" Gary Soneji/Murphy finally spoke up from under the blanket.

Fishenauer didn't answer right away, but Gary knew that they were there by the bumps in the road. He sat up in the cramped backseat of the Bronco. He was almost home free home. He *was* invincible.

"It's time to get rich," he said and laughed out loud. "Do you plan to take off these matching cuffs at some point?"

Robert Fishenauer didn't bother to turn around. As far as he was concerned, this was still a keeper/keepee relationship. "Just as soon as I have my part of the ransom money," he spoke out of the corner of his mouth. "Then, and only then, you're free!"

Soneji/Murphy talked to the back of Fishenauer's head. "You sure you have the keys to these cuffs, Robert?"

"Don't worry about it. You sure you know where the rest of the ransom money is hidden?"

"I'm sure."

Soneji/Murphy was also sure that Fishenauer had the keys on him. Gary had been extremely claustrophobic during the past hour and a half. That was one of the reasons he'd put his mind elsewhere: into his master plan. Memories of the basement back home had been flashing before him during the whole trip. He'd seen his stepmother. Seen her two spoiled bastard kids. He'd played himself as a boy again — the glorious adventure of the Bad Boy. His fantasy life had taken over for a while.

As the Bronco very slowly bumped along down memory lane, Gary Soneji/Murphy brought both his hands down over Fishenauer's head and viciously around his throat. Element of surprise in that. He forced the metal of the cuffs straight back into the prison guard's Adam's apple.

"What can I tell you, Bobby — I *am* a psychopathic liar, after all."

Fishenauer began to thrash and struggle fiercely. He couldn't breathe. It was as if he were drowning.

His knees cracked up hard under the dashboard and the steering wheel. The night was filled with the loud, animalistic growls coming from both men.

Fishenauer managed to get his legs all the way over to the passenger side of the front seat. His work boot kicked the ceiling of the Bronco. His torso was twisted sideways, as if it were hinged. He gasped, and made the strangest noise. It sounded like metal burning, crackling on a stove.

Fishenauer's struggling eased off and finally stopped, except for some twitching of his limbs.

Gary was free. Just as he had known from the very beginning he would be — Gary Soneji/Murphy was on the loose again.

CHAPTER 79

JEZZIE FLANAGAN walked down the hall to room 427 inside the Marbury Hotel in Georgetown. She was feeling compulsive again. Driven. She wasn't happy about this secretive meeting and wondered what it was about. Jezzie *thought* that she knew, and hoped she was wrong. She wasn't wrong too often.

Jezzie rapped her knuckles against the door. She peered around behind her. It wasn't paranoia on her part. She knew half the people in Washington were busy watching the other half.

"It's open. C'mon in," she heard from inside.

Jezzie opened the door and saw him lounging on the couch. He'd gotten a suite, which was a bad sign. He wanted to burn money.

"Suites for the sweet." Mike Devine smiled from the couch. He was watching the Redskins on TV. Cool as could be. In a lot of ways, he reminded Jezzie of her father. Maybe that was why she'd gotten involved with him. The perversity of it had been a turn-on.

"Michael, this is very dangerous right now." Jezzie stepped into the hotel room and shut the door. Bolted it. She made her voice seem concerned, rather than angry at him. Sweet, nice Jezzie.

"Dangerous or not, we have to talk. You know, your boyfriend came to see me recently. He was parked outside my building this morning."

"He's not my boyfriend. I've been pumping him for information that *we've* needed."

Mike Devine smiled. "You pump him, he pumps you. Is *every-body* happy? I'm not."

Jezzie sat down next to Devine on the couch. He was definitely sexy and he knew it. He had Paul Newman's looks, minus the unbearably beautiful blue eyes. He also liked women, and it showed.

"I shouldn't be here, Michael. We shouldn't be together now." Jezzie rubbed her head against his shoulder. She gently kissed his cheek, his nose. She felt like doing anything but cuddling up with him now. But she could do it if she had to. She could do whatever it took.

"Yeah, you *should* be here, Jezzie. What good is all this money if we can't spend it, and we can't be together."

"I seem to remember a few days down at the lake recently. Did I imagine that?"

"To hell with stolen moments. Come to Florida with me."

Jezzie kissed his throat. He was clean-shaven and he always smelled nice. She unbuttoned his shirt and slid her hand in. Then she let her fingers graze the lump in his trousers. She was on automatic control now. Whatever it took.

"We might have to get rid of Alex Cross. I'm serious," he said in a whisper. "You hear me, Jezzie?"

She knew he was testing her, trying to get a reaction. "It's a serious thing to say. Let me work on it a little. I'll find out what Alex knows. Be patient."

"You're fucking him, Jezzie. That's why you're patient."

"No, *I'm not.*"

She was undoing his belt, being a little clumsy with her left hand. She needed to keep him in line for a while longer.

"How do I know you haven't fallen for Alex Cross?" he persisted.

"Because, Michael, I'm in love with you." She pushed closer to Devine and held him. He was easy to fool. They all were. All she had to do now was wait out the FBI, and they were home free. Perfect. The crime of the century.

CHAPTER 80

I WAS ASLEEP when I got the call at four in the morning. A devastated Wallace Hart was on the line. He was calling from Fallston, where he had a serious problem on his hands.

An hour later I was at the prison. I was one of four privileged insiders secreted in Wallace's cramped, overheated office.

The press hadn't been told about the sensational escape yet. They had to be alerted soon — there was no getting around that. They'd have a field day with the news flash that Soneji/Murphy was back on the loose.

Wallace Hart was slumped over his paper-littered desk as if he'd been gut-shot. The others in the office were the prison warden and the prison's attorney.

"What do you know about this missing guard?" I asked Wallace at the first opportunity.

"His name's Fishenauer. Thirty-six years old. He's been at the prison eleven years with a good service record," said Hart. "Until today, he did his job."

"What's your best guess? Is this guard Gary's latest hostage?" I asked Wallace.

"I don't think so. I think the son-of-a-bitch bastard *helped* Soneji escape."

That same morning, the FBI set up round-the-clock surveillance on Michael Devine and Charles Chakely. One theory was that Soneji/Murphy might come after them. He knew that they had screwed up his master plan.

The body of prison guard Robert Fishenauer was found in a dilapidated garage on the abandoned farm in Crisfield, Maryland. A twenty-dollar bill was stuffed into his mouth. The bill was not part of the Florida ransom money.

The usual rumors of Soneji/Murphy "sightings" went on throughout the day. Nothing came of them.

Soneji/Murphy was out there somewhere, laughing at us, probably howling in some dark cellar. He was back on the front page of every newspaper in the country. Just the way Gary liked it. The number-one Bad Boy of all time.

I drove to Jezzie's apartment that night around six. I didn't want to go over there. My stomach wasn't doing too well. My head was in even worse shape. I had to warn her that Soneji/Murphy might have her on his list, especially if he'd connected Jezzie with Devine and Chakely. I had to warn Jezzie, without telling her everything else I knew.

As I climbed the familiar, red-brick porch stairs, I could hear rock music playing inside the house, making the walls tremble. It was Bonnie Raitt's *Taking My Time* album. Bonnie was wailing "I Gave My Love a Candle."

Jezzie and I had played the Bonnie Raitt tape over and over at her lake cabin. Maybe she was thinking of me that night. I'd been doing a lot of thinking about Jezzie the past few days.

I rang the bell, and Jezzie opened the screen door. She was wearing her usual attire: a wrinkled T-shirt, cutoffs, thongs. She smiled and looked glad to see me. So calm, cool, and collected.

My stomach was knotted up tight. The rest of me was very cold. I knew what I had to do now. At least I thought I did.

"And one more thing," I said, as if we'd just finished our last conversation a minute ago.

Jezzie laughed and opened the screen door. I didn't go inside. I stood my ground on the porch. Wind chimes sounded from the house next door. I watched for some false move, something that would show me she didn't have her act down perfectly. There was nothing.

"How about a ride in the country? My treat," I said to Jezzie.

"Sounds good to me, Alex. I'll put on some long pants."

A few minutes later we were on the bike, blasting away from her place. I was still humming "I Gave My Love a Candle." I was also thinking everything through one final time. *Making my plan, checking it twice. Gonna find out who's naughty and nice.*

"We can talk *and* ride the bike at the same time." Jezzie turned her head and shouted into the wind.

I held on to her back and chest tighter. That made me feel a little worse than I'd been feeling. I shouted against the side of her hair. "I was worried about you, with Soneji on the loose." That much was true. I didn't want to find Jezzie murdered. With her breasts cut off.

She turned her head. "Why's that? Why were you worried about me? My Smith and Wesson is at the house."

Because you helped ruin his perfect crime spree, and maybe he knows that, I wanted to say to her. *Because you took that little girl from the farmhouse, Jezzie. You took Maggie Rose Dunne, and then you had to kill her, didn't you?*

"He knows about the two of us from the newspapers," I said to Jezzie instead. "He might go after anybody who was involved with the case. Especially anybody he thinks helped spoil his little plan."

"Is that the way his mind works, Alex? *You'd* know if anybody would. You're the criminal shrink."

"He wants to show the world how superior he is," I said. "He needs this to be as big and as complicated as the Lindbergh thing was in its day. I believe that's his Lindbergh angle. He wants his crime to be the biggest and the best. He isn't through yet. Probably thinks he's just getting started again."

"Who's Bruno Hauptmann in our story? Who is Soneji trying to set up?" Jezzie called out over the wind.

Was Jezzie trying to give me her own alibi? Was it possible that she'd been framed by Soneji somehow? That would be the ultimate . . . But how? And why?

"Gary *Murphy* is Bruno Hauptmann," I told her, because I thought I knew the answer. "*He's* the one Gary Soneji cleverly framed. He was convicted and went to jail, and *he's* innocent."·

We talked back and forth for the first half hour of the ride. Then it got quiet for mile after mile of open highway.

We were both off in our own private worlds. I found myself just holding on to her back. I was remembering different things about us. Feeling so bad inside; wanting all the feeling to stop. I knew that she was a psychopath, just like Gary. No conscience. I believed that business, the government, Wall Street were filled with people like that. No regret for their actions. Not unless they got caught. Then the crocodile tears started.

"What if we go away again?" I finally asked Jezzie the question I'd been working up to. "Go down to the Virgin Islands again? I need it."

I wasn't sure if she'd heard me. Then Jezzie said, "All right. I'd like some time in the sun. The islands it is."

I moved in behind her on the speeding motorcycle. The deed was done. We streaked through the beautiful countryside, but all the blurred passing scenes, everything that was happening now, hurt my head and it wouldn't stop hurting.

CHAPTER 81

MAGGIE ROSE Dunne wanted to live more than anything else. She understood that now.

She wanted her life to return to the way it had been. She wanted to see her mother and father so much. To see all of her friends, her Washington and Los Angeles friends, but especially Michael. What had happened to Shrimpie Goldberg? Had they let him go? Had he been ransomed, but for some reason she hadn't?

Maggie worked picking vegetables every day, and the work was hard, but, most of all, the work was the most boring thing she could ever imagine doing. She had to put her mind somewhere else during the long days under the burning sun. She just had to get her mind off what she was doing, and where she was.

Nearly a year and a half after the kidnapping, Maggie Rose Dunne escaped from where they were hiding her.

She had disciplined herself to wake up early every morning, before any of the others. She did this for weeks before she tried anything. It was still dark outside, but she knew the sun would start to rise in almost an hour. Then it would be so hot.

She went into the kitchen in her bare feet, holding her work shoes in her hand. If they caught her now, she could say she was only going to the bathroom. Her bladder was full, a precaution she'd taken in case she was caught.

They'd told her that she would never escape, not even if she got out of that particular village. It was over fifty miles to another town, in any direction she chose. So they told her.

The mountains were full of snakes and dangerous cats. Sometimes she heard the cats growl at night. She would never make it to another town. They told her that.

And if they did catch her, they would put her under the ground for at least a year. Did she remember what it was like being buried? Never seeing the light for days at a time?

The kitchen door was locked. She had learned where the key was kept, with a lot of other rusty old keys in a tool closet. Maggie Rose took the key, and also a small hammer to use as a weapon. She slid the hammer under the elastic of her shorts.

Maggie used the key for the kitchen door. It opened, and she was outside. For the first time in so long, she was free. Her heart soared like the hawks she sometimes saw flying high over the hiding place.

Just the act of walking by herself felt so good. Maggie Rose walked for several miles. She had decided to go downhill, rather than up the mountains — even though one of the children swore there was a town not far in that direction.

She had taken two hard rolls from the kitchen and she snacked on them through the early morning. It started to get warm as the sun rose. By ten o'clock, it was quite hot. She had been following a dirt road for miles, not walking in the road, but staying close enough. She always kept the road in sight.

She walked on through the long afternoon, amazed that her strength held up in the heat. Maybe all the hard work in the fields had paid off. She was stronger now than she had ever been. She had muscles everywhere.

Late in the afternoon, Maggie Rose could see the town as she continued down the mountainside. It was bigger and more modern than where she had been kept for so many months.

Maggie Rose started to run down the final hills. The dirt road finally intersected with a concrete one. A real road. Maggie followed the road a short distance, and then there was a gas station. It was an ordinary gas station. *Shell*, the sign said. She'd never seen anything more beautiful in her life.

Maggie Rose looked up and the man was there.

He asked her if she felt all right. He always called her Bobbi, and she knew that the man cared about her a little. Maggie told him that she was fine. She had just been lost in a thought.

Maggie Rose didn't tell him that she'd been making up stories again, wonderful fantasies to help her escape from her pain.

CHAPTER 82

GARY SONEJI/MURPHY undoubtedly still had his master plan. Now, I had mine. The question was: How well could I finish mine off? How powerful was my resolve to succeed, no matter what the human cost? How far was I willing to go? How close to the edge?

The trip to Virgin Gorda began in Washington, D.C., on a bleak, rainy Friday morning. It was about fifty degrees. Under normal circumstances, I couldn't have gotten out of there fast enough.

We had to change to a three-engine Trislander in sun-drenched Puerto Rico. By three-thirty in the afternoon, Jezzie and I were gliding down toward a white sandy beach, a narrow landing strip bordered by tall palms swaying in the sea breeze.

"There it is," she said from the seat beside me. "There's our place in the sun, Alex. I could stay here for about a month."

"It does look like what the doctor ordered," I had to agree. We'd soon see about that. We'd see how long the two of us wanted to be alone together.

"This weary traveler wants to be in that water. Not looking

down at it," Jezzie said. "Exist on fish and fruit. Swim till we drop."

"That's what we came here for, isn't it? Fun in the sun? Make all the bad guys go away?"

"Everything *is* good, Alex. It can be. Just go with it a little." Jezzie always sounded so sincere. I almost wanted to believe her.

As the door of the Trislander opened, the fragrant smells of the Caribbean breezed in. Warm air rushed over the nine of us inside the small plane.

Everybody was decked out in sunglasses and brightly colored T-shirts. Smiles broke out on nearly every face. I forced a smile, too.

Jezzie took my hand. Jezzie was right there — and yet she wasn't. Everything seemed dreamlike to me. What was happening now . . . couldn't be happening.

Black men and women with British accents took us through a sort of relaxed minicustoms. Neither Jezzie's nor my bags were searched. This had actually been prearranged with the help of the U.S. State Department. Inside my bag was a small-caliber revolver — loaded and ready.

"Alex, I still love it here," Jezzie said as we approached the tiny queue for taxis. Along with the cabs were a number of scooters, bicycles, dirty minivans. I wondered if we'd ever take another motorcycle ride together again.

"Let's stay here forever," she said. "Pretend we never have to leave. No more clocks, no radios, no news."

"I like the sound of that," I told her. "We'll play 'let's pretend' for a while."

"You're on. Let's do it." She clapped her hands like a small child.

The island scene seemed unchanged since our last visit. This had probably been the case since the Rockefeller family began to buy up the island back in the 1950s.

Cruise ships and sailboats were collecting out on the sparkling sea. We passed small restaurants and shops for snorkeling gear. The brightly painted one-story homes all had TV antennas sticking from their rooftops. *Our place in the sun. Paradise.*

Jezzie and I had time to catch a swim at the hotel. We showed off a little. We stretched our bodies, racing out and back to a distant reef. I remembered our first swim together. The hotel pool in Miami Beach. The beginning of her act.

Afterward, we sprawled on the beach. We watched the sun drop down onto the horizon, bleed into it, then disappear from sight.

"Déjà vu, Alex." Jezzie smiled. "Just like before. Or did I dream that?"

"It's different now," I said, then quickly added, "We didn't know each other so well before."

What was Jezzie really thinking? I knew that she must have a plan now, too. I figured she knew I was on to Devine and Chakely. She needed to know what I planned to do about them.

A young black stud, muscular and trim in his white bathing suit and crisp hotel T-shirt, carried piña coladas down to our beach chairs.

Let's play "pretend" didn't get any better than this.

"Is this your honeymoon?" He was loose and carefree enough to joke with us.

"It's our second honeymoon," Jezzie told him.

"Well, enjoy it doubly," said the smiling beach waiter.

The slowdown pace of the island took over eventually. We had dinner at the hotel's pavilion restaurant. More eerie déjà vu for the two of us. Sitting there in the perfect Caribbean surroundings, I believe that I felt more duplicitous, and completely unreal, than I had in my entire life.

I watched the grilled pompano and grouper and turtle come and go. I listened to the reggae band get ready. And all the while,

I was thinking that this beautiful woman beside me had let Michael Goldberg die. I was also certain she had murdered Maggie Rose Dunne, or at least been an accomplice. She'd never shown a hint of remorse.

Somewhere back in the States was her share of the ten-million-dollar ransom. But Jezzie was smart enough to let me "split" the trip expenses with her. "Right down the middle, Alex. No free rides here, okay?"

She ate island lobster and an appetizer plate of shark bites. She drank two ales at dinner. Jezzie was so smooth and smart. In a way, she was even scarier than Gary Soneji/Murphy.

What do you talk about to a murderer, and someone you loved, over a perfect dinner and cocktails? I wanted to know so many things, but I couldn't ask any of the real questions pounding in my head. Instead, we talked of the coming vacation days, a "plan" for the here and now in the islands.

I stared across the dining table at Jezzie and I thought that she had never looked more physically striking. She kept tucking her blond hair behind one ear. It was such a familiar and intimate gesture, that nervous tic. What was Jezzie nervous and concerned about? How much did she know?

"All right, Alex," she finally said. "Do you want to tell me what we're really doing on Virgin Gorda? Is there another agenda working here?"

I had prepared myself for the question, but it still took me by surprise. She had fired it in beautifully. I was ready to lie. I could rationalize what I had to do. I just couldn't make myself feel particularly good about it.

"I wanted us to be able to talk, to *really* talk to each other. Maybe for the first time, Jezzie."

Tears started in the corners of Jezzie's eyes. They slowly ran down her cheeks. Shiny streams in the candlelight.

"I love you, Alex," Jezzie whispered. "It's just that — it will always be so hard for the two of us. It's been hard so far."

"Are you saying the world isn't ready for us?" I asked her. "Or aren't we ready for the world?"

"I don't know which of those is right. Does it matter that it's just so hard?"

We walked along the beach after dinner, down toward a shipwrecked galleon. The picturesque wreck was stranded about a quarter of a mile from the main pavilion and restaurant. The beach appeared to be deserted.

There was some moonlight, but it got darker as we approached the fallen ship. Shredded pieces of clouds streamed across the sky. Finally, Jezzie was little more than a dark shape beside me. Everything about the moment made me extremely uncomfortable. I had left my gun in the room.

"Alex." Jezzie had stopped walking. At first, I thought she'd heard something, and I looked over my shoulder. I knew Soneji/ Murphy couldn't be down here. Was it possible I could be wrong?

"I was wondering," Jezzie said, "thinking about something from the investigation, and I don't want to. Not down here."

"What's bothering you?" I asked her.

"You stopped talking to me about the investigation. How did you wind up with Chakely and Devine?"

"Well, since you brought the subject up," I said to her, "I'll tell you. You were right all the time about the two of them. Another stone-cold dead end. Now. Let's have a real vacation. We've both earned it."

CHAPTER 83

GARY SONEJI/MURPHY *watched*, and his mind wandered. His mind traveled all the way back to the perfect Lindbergh kidnapping.

He could still picture Lucky Lindy. The lovely Anne Morrow Lindbergh. Baby Charles Jr. in his crib, up in the second-story nursery of the farmhouse in Hopewell, New Jersey. Those were the days, my friends. Fantasy days at their best.

What was he actually watching in the much more banal here and now?

First, there was the pair of FBI goonigans in a black Buick Skylark. A male and a female goonie, to be precise, who were on stakeout duty. They were certainly harmless enough. No problem for him there. No challenge whatsoever.

Next, there was the modern high-rise building where agent Mike Devine still lived in Washington. The Hawthorne, it was called. After Nathaniel, of the dark, brooding heart? Rooftop pool and sun deck, garage parking, concierge service around the clock. Very nice digs for the ex-agent. And the FBI goons were watching the building as if it might sprout wings and fly away.

A few minutes past ten o'clock that morning, a Federal Express deliveryman entered the chichi apartment building.

Moments later, dressed in the Federal Express uniform and carrying actual packages for two tenants in the Hawthorne, Gary Soneji/Murphy pushed the buzzer for 17J. *Avon calling!*

When Mike Devine opened the door, Soneji sprayed him with the same strong chloroform potion he'd used on Michael Goldberg and Maggie Rose Dunne. Fair is fair.

Just like the two children, Devine crumpled onto the wall-to-wall carpeting in his foyer. Rock music played from inside the apartment. The inimitable Bonnie Raitt. "Let's Give Them Something to Talk About."

Agent Devine woke up after several minutes. He was woozy and had double vision. All of his clothes had been stripped off. He was totally confused and disoriented.

He was propped up in the bathtub, with cold water halfway to the rim. His ankles were handcuffed to the faucet handles.

"What the fuck is this?" His first words came out slurred and sloppy. He felt as if he'd had about a dozen highballs.

"*This* is an extremely sharp knife." Gary Soneji/Murphy bent over and showed off his Bowie hunting knife. "Watch this graphic demonstration. Focus those big blurry blue eyes of yours now. *Fo-cus, Michael.*"

Gary Soneji/Murphy barely nicked the former agent's upper arm with the knife. Devine cried out. A dangerous-looking three-inch cut opened up instantly. Blood flowed into the cold, swirling bathwater.

"Not another peep," Soneji warned. He brandished the knife, threatening Devine with another nick. "This isn't exactly the Sensor razor from Gillette or the Schick Tracer. More like *scratch and bleed.* So please, be careful."

"Who are you?" Devine attempted to speak again. He was still slurring badly. "*Whoreyou?*" he said.

"Please allow me to introduce myself, I am a man of wealth and taste," Soneji said. All right, *yes*, he *was* giddy with success. The prospects for his future were shining so bright again.

Devine was even more confused now.

"That's from 'Sympathy for the Devil.' The Stones? I'm Gary Soneji/Murphy. Excuse the tacky delivery-boy uniform, the rather crude disguise. But I'm in sort of a hurry, don't you know. It's a pity, because I've been wanting to meet you for months. You *rascal*, you."

"What the hell do you want?" Devine struggled to maintain some of his authority, in spite of the very dicey circumstances.

"Cut to the chase, hmmmm. Okay, good. Because I *am seriously rushed*. Now. You have two very clear choices. ONE — I'll have to cut off your penis here and now, put it in your mouth as a convenient gag, and then torture you with little flesh cuts, hundreds of cuts, starting with the face and neck, until you tell me what I need to know. All right so far? Am I being clear? To repeat — choice number one: painful torture leading inevitably to exsanguination."

Devine's head involuntarily leaned back away from the looming madman. His vision was clearing, unfortunately. His eyes, in fact, were wide open. Gary Soneji/Murphy? In his apartment? With a hunting knife?

"SECOND OPTION," the madman continued to rant in his face. "I am going to get the truth from you *right now*. Then I'll go get my money, *wherever* you've stashed it. I'll come back and kill you, but nicely — no theatrics. Who knows, you might even manage to escape while I'm gone. That's doubtful, but hope springs eternal. I have to tell you, Michael, that's the option I'd choose."

Mike Devine was clearheaded enough to make the correct choice, too. He told Soneji/Murphy where his share of the ransom money was. It was right there in Washington.

Gary Soneji/Murphy believed him, but then, who could really tell about these things. He was dealing with a police officer, after all.

Gary paused at the apartment door on his way out. In his best Arnold Schwarzenegger/Terminator voice, he said, "I'll be back!"

Actually, he was feeling exceptionally good about things today. He was solving the goddamned kidnapping himself. He was playing policeman, and it was kind of neat. The plan was going to work. Just like he'd always known it would.

Cool beans.

CHAPTER 84

I SLEPT RESTLESSLY, waking just about every hour on the hour. There was no piano to go pound out on the porch. No Jannie and Damon to go wake. Only the murderer peacefully sleeping at my side.

Only the plan I was there to execute.

When the sun finally rose, the hotel kitchen staff fixed us a fancy box lunch to go. They packed a wicker basket with fine wines, French bottled water, expensive gourmet goodies. There were also snorkeling gear, fluffy towels, a striped yellow-and-white beach umbrella.

Everything was already loaded onto a speedboat when we arrived on the dock, at just past eight. It took the boat about thirty minutes to get to our island — a beautiful, secluded spot. Paradise regained.

We would be out there alone all day. Other couples from the hotel had their own private islands to visit. A coral reef encircled our beach, stretching out about seventy to a hundred yards from shore.

The water was the clearest bottle-green. When I looked straight down, I could see the texture of the sand on the bottom.

I could have counted grains of sand. Angel and warrior fish darted around my legs in small spirited schools. A smiling pair of five-foot-long barracuda had followed our boat almost to the shoreline, then lost interest.

"What time would you like me to come back?" the boat driver asked. "It's your choice."

He was a muscular fisherman — a sailor in his forties. A happy-go-lucky type, he had shared big-fish and other colorful island stories on the way out. He seemed to think nothing of Jezzie and my being together.

"Oh, I think two or three o'clock?" I looked for some help from Jezzie. "What time should Mr. Richards come back for us?"

She was busy laying out beach towels and the rest of our exotic gear. "I think three is good. That sounds great, Mr. Richards."

"All right, then, have fun, you two." He smiled. "You're all alone. I can see my services are no longer required."

Mr. Richards saluted us, then hopped back into the boat. He started the engine, and soon had vanished from sight.

We were all alone on our private island. Don't worry, be happy.

There is something so strange and unreal about lying on a beach towel next to a kidnapper and murderer. I went over and over all of my feelings, plans, the things I knew I had to do.

I tried to get control of my confusion and rage. I had loved this woman who was now such a stranger. I closed my eyes and let the sun relax my muscles. I needed to untense, or this wouldn't work.

How could you have murdered the little girl, Jezzie? How could you do that? How could you tell so many lies to everybody?

Gary Soneji flew out of nowhere! He came suddenly, and with no warning.

He had a foot-long hunting knife like the one he'd used in

the D.C. ghetto killings. He was arched high overhead, his shadow covering me completely.

There was no way he could have gotten onto the island. No way.

"*Alex. Alex,* you were dreaming," Jezzie said. She put a cool hand on my shoulder. She gently touched my cheek with the tips of her fingers.

The long, mostly sleepless night . . . the warm sun and the cooling sea breeze . . . I had fallen asleep on the beach.

I looked up at Jezzie. *She* had been the shadow over my body, not Soneji. My heart was pounding loudly. Dreams are as powerful as the real world to our nervous systems.

"How long was I out?" I asked. "Whew."

"Just a couple of minutes, baby," she said. "Alex, let me hold you."

Jezzie moved against me on the beach towel. Her breasts brushed my chest. She had taken off her bathing-suit top while I slept. Her smooth skin glowed with tanning oil. A thin line of moisture beaded on her upper lip. She couldn't help looking good.

I sat up and moved away from Jezzie on the towel. I pointed to where a garden of bougainvillea grew, almost to the seawater.

"Let's walk down along the beach. Okay? Let's take a walk. I want to talk to you about a few things."

"What kind of things?" Jezzie asked me. She was clearly disappointed that I was putting her off, even for a moment. She'd wanted to make love on the beach. I didn't.

"C'mon. Let's walk and talk a little," I said. "This sun feels so good."

I pulled Jezzie up and she came along with me somewhat reluctantly. She didn't bother to put her top back on.

We walked along the shoreline with our feet in the clear, calm water. We weren't touching now, but we were only inches apart. It was so strange and unreal. It was one of the worst moments of my life, if not the worst.

"You're being so serious, Alex. We were going to have fun, remember? Are we having fun yet?"

"I know what you did, Jezzie. It's taken a while, but I finally pulled it together," I told her. "I know that you took Maggie Rose Dunne from Soneji. I know that you killed her."

CHAPTER 85

"**I** WANT TO TALK about all of it. I don't have a wire on me, Jezzie. Obviously."

She half smiled at that. Always the perfect actress. "I can see you don't," she said.

My heart was booming at a tremendous rate. "Tell me what happened. Just tell me *why*, Jezzie. Tell me what I spent almost two years trying to find out, and you knew all the time. Tell me your side of this."

Jezzie's mask, which was always her perfectly beautiful smile, had finally disappeared. She sounded resigned. "All right, Alex. I'll tell you some of what you want to know, what you just wouldn't leave alone."

We continued to walk, and Jezzie finally told me the truth.

"How did it happen? Well, in the beginning, we were just doing our job. I swear that's true. We were babysitting the secretary's family. Jerrold Goldberg wasn't used to getting threats. The Colombians made a threat against him. He acted like the civilian that he is. He overreacted. He demanded Secret Service protection for his entire family. That's how it all began. With a surveillance detail that none of us thought was necessary."

"So you assigned two lightweight agents."

"Two friends, actually. Not lightweights at all. We figured the detail would be a boondoggle. Then Mike Devine noticed that one of the teachers, a math teacher named Gary Soneji, had made a couple of passes by the Goldberg house. At first we thought he had a crush on the boy. Devine and Chakely thought he might be a pederast. Nothing much more than that. We had to check him out, anyway. It was in the original logs that Devine and Chakely kept."

"One of them followed Gary Soneji?"

"A couple of times, yes. To a couple of places. We weren't really concerned at that point, but we were following through. One night, Charlie Chakely tailed him into Southeast. We didn't connect Soneji to the murders there, especially since the story never made any splash in the papers. Just more inner-city murders, you know."

"Yeah. I do know. When did you suspect something else about Gary Soneji?"

"We didn't suspect a kidnapping until he actually picked up the two kids. Two days before that, Charlie Chakely had followed him out to the farm in Maryland. Charlie didn't suspect a kidnapping at the time. No reason to.

"But he knew where the farm was located now. Mike Devine called me from the school when it all came crashing down. They wanted to go after Soneji then. That's when it struck me about taking the ransom ourselves. I don't know for sure. Maybe I'd thought of it before. It was so easy, Alex. Three or four days and it would be over. Nobody would be hurt. Not any more than they'd already been hurt. We'd have the ransom money. Millions."

The way Jezzie spoke about the kidnapping plot so casually was scary. She downplayed it, but it had been her idea. Not Devine's or Chakely's idea, Jezzie's. She was the mastermind.

"What about the children?" I asked. "What about Maggie Rose and Michael?"

"They'd already been kidnapped. We couldn't stop what had already happened. We staked out the farm in Maryland. We were confident that nothing could happen to the kids. He was a math teacher. We didn't think he'd hurt them. We thought he was nothing but an amateur. We were completely in control."

"He buried them in a box, Jezzie. And Michael Goldberg died."

Jezzie stared out to sea. She nodded slowly. "Yes, the little boy died. That changed everything, Alex. *Forever.* I don't know if we could have prevented it. We moved in and took Maggie Rose then. We made our own kidnap demands. The whole plan changed."

The two of us continued to walk along the edge of the shimmering water. If anyone had seen us, they probably would have thought we were lovers, having a serious talk about our relationship. The second half of that was true enough.

Jezzie finally looked at me. "I want to tell you how it was between us, Alex. My side of things. It's not what you think."

I had no words for her. It felt as if I were standing on the dark side of the moon again, and about to explode. My mind was screaming. I let Jezzie go on, let her talk. It didn't really matter now.

"When it started, down in Florida, I needed to know whatever you could find out. I wanted a connection inside the D.C. police. You were supposed to be a good cop. You were also your own man."

"So you used me to watch your flanks. *You* chose me to hand over the ransom. You couldn't trust the Bureau. Always the professional, Jezzie."

"I knew you wouldn't do anything to endanger the little girl. I knew you'd deliver the ransom. The complications started after we got back from Miami. I don't know exactly when. I swear this is the truth."

I felt numb and hollow inside as I listened to her. I was dripping with perspiration, and not because of the beating sun.

I wondered if Jezzie had brought a gun to the island? *Always the professional,* I reminded myself.

"For what it's worth now, I fell in love with you, Alex. I did. You were so many of the things I'd given up looking for. Warm and decent. Loving. Understanding. Damon and Janelle touched me. When I was with you, I felt whole again."

I was a little dizzy, and nauseated. It was exactly the way I'd felt for about a year after Maria died. "For what it's worth, I fell in love with you, too, Jezzie. I tried not to, but I did. I just couldn't have imagined anybody lying to me the way you did. Lying and deceiving. I still can't believe all the lies. What about Mike Devine?" I asked.

Jezzie shrugged her shoulders. That was her only answer.

"*You* committed the perfect crime. A masterpiece," I told her then. "You created the master crime that Gary Soneji always wanted to commit."

Jezzie peered into my eyes, but she seemed to be looking right through me. There was just one more piece to the puzzle now — one last thing that I had to know.

One unthinkable detail.

"What really happened to the little girl? What did you, or Devine and Chakely, do with Maggie Rose?"

Jezzie shook her head. "No, Alex. That I can't tell you. You know that I can't."

She had folded her arms across her chest when she'd begun to reveal the truth. Her arms remained tightly folded.

"How could you kill a little girl? How could you do it, Jezzie? How could you kill Maggie Rose Dunne?"

Jezzie suddenly whirled away from me. It was too much, even for her. She headed back toward the beach umbrella and towels. I took a quick step and I caught her arm. I grabbed the crook of her elbow.

"*Get your hands off me!*" she screamed. Her face contorted.

"Maybe you can *trade* me the information about Maggie Rose," I shouted back. "Maybe we can make a trade, Jezzie!"

She turned around. "They're not going to let you open this case again. Don't kid yourself, Alex. They don't have a thing on me. Neither do you. I'm not going to trade you information."

"Yeah. Yeah, you are," I said. My voice had gone from loud to close to a whisper. "*Yes, you are, Jezzie.* You're going to trade information. . . . *You definitely are.*"

I pointed up toward the barranca and the palm trees that thickened as you got farther from the sandy beach.

Sampson stood up from his hiding spot in the deep island brush. He waved something that looked like a silver wand. What he was actually holding was a long-distance microphone.

Two FBI agents got up and waved, too. They stood beside Sampson. They'd all been out in the bush since before seven that morning. The agents were as red as lobsters around the face and arms. Sampson probably had the tan of his life, also.

"My friend Sampson up there. He's recorded everything you said since we started our walk."

Jezzie closed her eyes for several seconds. She hadn't expected I would go this far. She didn't think I had it in me.

"You'll tell us now how you murdered Maggie Rose," I demanded.

Her eyes opened and they looked small and black. "You don't get it. You just don't get it, do you?" she said.

"What don't I get, Jezzie? You tell me what I don't get."

"You keep looking for the good in people. But it's not there! Your case will get blown up. You'll look like a fool in the end, a complete and utter fool. They'll all turn on you again."

"Maybe you're right," I said, "but at least I'll have this moment."

Jezzie moved to hit me, but I blocked her fist with a forearm. Her body twisted and she went down. The hard fall was a lot less than she deserved. Jezzie's face was a brittle mask of surprise.

"That's a start, Alex," she said from her sandy seat on the beach. "You're becoming a bastard, too. Congratulations."

"Nah," I said to Jezzie. "I'm just fine. There's nothing wrong with me."

I let the FBI agents and Sampson make the formal arrest of Jezzie Flanagan. Then I took a skiff back to the hotel. I packed and was on my way back to Washington within the hour.

CHAPTER 86

TWO DAYS after we returned to D.C., Sampson and I were back on the road. We were headed for Uyuni, Bolivia. We had reason to hope and believe that we might have finally found Maggie Rose Dunne.

Jezzie had talked and talked. Jezzie had traded information. She had refused to talk to the Bureau, though. *She'd traded with me.*

Uyuni is in the Andes Mountains, one hundred and ninety-one miles south of Oruro. The way to get there is to land a small plane in Río Mulato, then go by jeep or van to Uyuni.

A Ford Explorer held eight of us for the final leg of the difficult trip. I was in the minivan with Sampson, two special agents from Treasury, the U.S. ambassador to Bolivia, our driver, and Thomas and Katherine Rose Dunne.

Charles Chakely and Jezzie had both been willing to trade information about Maggie Rose during the last grueling thirty-six hours. The butchered body of Mike Devine had been found in his Washington apartment. The manhunt for Gary Soneji/Murphy had intensified after the body was discovered. But so far, nothing. Gary was certainly watching the story of our trip to Bolivia on TV. Gary was watching his story.

Chakely and Jezzie told virtually the same tale about the kidnapping. There had been an opportunity to take the ten-million-dollar ransom and get away with it. They couldn't return the girl. They needed us to believe that Soneji/Murphy was the kidnapper. The girl could dispute that. They'd drawn the line at killing Maggie Rose, though. Or so they said back in Washington.

Sampson and I were quiet inside the minivan for the last miles of the trip through the Andes. So was everyone else.

I watched the Dunnes as we approached Uyuni. They sat together quietly, a little distant from each other. As Katherine had told me, losing Maggie Rose had nearly destroyed their marriage. I was reminded of how much I had liked them in the beginning. I still liked Katherine Rose. We had talked for a while during the trip. She thanked me with genuine emotion and I would never forget that.

I hoped their little girl was waiting safely at the end of this long and horrible ordeal. . . . I thought about Maggie Rose Dunne — a little girl I had never met, and was about to meet soon. I thought about all the prayers said for her, the placards held outside a D.C. courthouse, the candles burning in so many windows.

Sampson elbowed me as we drove through the village. "Look up the hill there, Alex. I won't say this makes it all worthwhile. But maybe it comes close."

The minivan was climbing a steep hill in the village of Uyuni. Tin and wood shacks lined both sides of what was virtually an alleyway cut into rock. Smoke spiraled from a couple of the tin rooftops. The narrow lane seemed to continue straight up into the Andes Mountains.

Maggie Rose was there waiting for us halfway up the road.

The eleven-year-old girl stood in front of one of the nearly identical shacks. She was with several other members of a family called Patino. She had been with them for nearly two years. It looked as if there were a dozen other children in the family.

From a hundred yards away, as the van strained up the rutted dirt road, we could all see her clearly.

Maggie Rose wore the same kind of loose shirt, cotton shorts, and thongs as the other Patino children, but her blond hair made her stand out. She was tan; she appeared to be in good health. She looked just like her beautiful mother.

The Patino family had no idea who she really was. They had never heard of Maggie Rose Dunne in Uyuni. Or in nearby Pulacayo, or in Ubina eleven miles over the high and mighty Andes Mountains. We knew that much from the Bolivian officials and police.

The Patino family had been paid for keeping the girl in the village, keeping her safe, but keeping her there. Maggie had been told by Mike Devine that there was *nowhere* for her to escape to. If she tried, she would be caught and she would be tortured. She would be kept under the ground for a long, long time.

I couldn't take my eyes off her now. This little girl, who had come to mean so much to so many people. I thought of all the countless pictures and posters, and I couldn't believe she was really standing there. After all this time.

Maggie Rose didn't smile, or react in any way, as she watched us coming up the hill in the U.S. embassy van.

She didn't seem happy that someone had finally come for her, that she was being rescued.

She appeared very confused, wounded, and afraid. She would take a step forward, then a step backward, then look back at her "family."

I wondered if Maggie Rose knew what was happening. She had been severely traumatized. I wondered if she could feel anything at all. I was glad I could be there to help.

I thought of Jezzie again, and I shook my head involuntarily.

The storm inside wouldn't stop. How could she have done this to the little girl? For a couple of million dollars? For all the money in the known universe?

Katherine Rose was the first one out of the minivan. At that very moment, Maggie Rose opened her arms. "Mommy!" she cried out. Then, hesitating for only a split second, she seemed to leap forward. Maggie Rose ran toward her mother. They ran into each other's arms.

For the next minute, I couldn't see much of anything through my tears. I looked at Sampson and saw a tear seeping from under his dark glasses.

"Two tough *de*-tectives," he said and grinned at me. It was that lone wolf's smile I love.

"Yeah, we sure are Washington, D.C.'s finest," I said.

Maggie Rose was finally going home. Her name was an incantation in my head — Maggie Rose, Maggie Rose. It was worth everything, just to see that moment.

"The End," Sampson pronounced.

Part Six

The Cross House

CHAPTER 87

THE CROSS HOUSE was right there across the street. There it was, in all of its humble glory.

The Bad Boy was mesmerized by the glittering orangish house lights. His eyes roamed from window to window. A couple of times, he caught sight of a black woman shuffling past one of the windows downstairs. Alex Cross's grandmother, no doubt.

He knew her name, Nana Mama. He knew Alex had named her that as a boy. In the last few weeks, he'd learned everything there was to know about the Cross family. He had a plan for them now. A neat little fantasy.

Sometimes the boy liked to be afraid like this. Afraid for himself; afraid for the people in the house. He enjoyed this feeling as long as he could control it, and turn it on and off at will.

He finally urged himself to leave his hiding place, to go even closer to the Cross house. *To be the fear.*

His senses were much sharper when the fear was with him. He could concentrate and maintain focus for very long stretches of time. As he crossed 5th Street, there was nothing in his consciousness other than the house and the people inside.

The boy disappeared into the bushes that ran alongside the front of the house. His heart was beating strongly now. His breathing was fast and shallow.

He took one deep breath, then slowly let it out through his mouth. *Slow down, enjoy this,* he thought.

He turned so that he *faced away* from the house. He could actually feel warmth from the walls on his back. He watched the inner-city street through the tangle of branches. It was always darker in Southeast. Streetlights were never replaced.

He was careful. He took his sweet time. He watched the street for ten minutes or more. No one had seen him. No one was spying on him this time.

"One last touch, and then on to other bigger and better things."

He thought the words, or spoke them under his breath. Sometimes he couldn't tell which was which anymore. A lot of things were coming together now, becoming one: his thoughts, his words, his actions, his stories to himself.

Each detail had been thought through hundreds of times before this particular night. Once they were all sound asleep, probably between two and three in the morning, he would take the two children, Damon and Janelle.

He would drug them, right there in their bedroom on the second floor. He would let Doctor/Detective Alex Cross sleep through everything.

He had to do that. The famous Dr. Cross needed to suffer a great deal now. Cross had to be part of the new search. That was the way it had to be. It was the only worthy solution. He would be the victor.

Not that Cross would need any extra motivation, but he'd get it, anyway. First, the boy would murder the old woman, Cross's grandmother. Then he would go to the children's bedroom.

None of it would ever be solved, of course. The Cross children would never ever be found. No ransom would be asked for. Then, finally, he could go on to other things.

He'd forget about Detective Cross. But Alex Cross would never, ever forget about him. Or about his own missing children.

Gary Soneji/Murphy turned toward the house.

CHAPTER 88

"ALEX, THERE'S SOMEONE inside the house. Alex, someone's in here with us," Nana whispered close to my ear.

I was up and out of bed before she finished speaking the words. Years on Washington's streets had taught me to move quickly.

I heard the softest *thump* somewhere. Yes, someone was definitely in the house. The noise hadn't been manufactured by our ancient heating system.

"Nana, you stay here. *Don't* come out until I call you," I whispered to my grandmother. "I'll yell when it's okay."

"I'll call the police, Alex."

"No, you stay right here. I *am* the police. Stay here."

"The children, Alex."

"I'll get them. You stay here. I'll bring the children. Please obey me this one time. *Please obey me.*"

There was no one in the darkened hallway upstairs. No one I could see, anyway. My heart raced uncontrollably as I hurried to the children's room.

I listened for another sound in the house. It was too still now.

I thought about the horrible violation: *someone's inside our house.* I chased the thought away.

I had to concentrate *on him.* I knew who it was. I'd kept my guard up for weeks after Sampson and I had returned with Maggie Rose. Finally, I'd let it down just a little. *And he'd come.*

I hurried to the children's room. I started to run down the upstairs hallway.

I opened the creaking door. Damon and Janelle were still asleep in their beds. I would wake them quickly, then carry them both back to Nana. I never kept my gun upstairs because of the children. It was downstairs in the den.

I switched on the lamp beside the bed. *Nothing!* The light didn't come on.

I remembered the Sanders and Turner murders. Soneji had loved darkness. The darkness had been his calling card, his signature. He had always turned the electricity off. The Thing was here.

Suddenly, I was struck very hard, with terrifying force.

Something had hit me like a speeding runaway truck. I knew it was Soneji. *He'd sprung on me!* He nearly took me out with one blow.

He was brutally strong. His body, his muscles, had been tensing and untensing for his entire life. He'd been doing isometrics since he'd been locked away in the basement of his father's house. He'd been wound tight for almost thirty years: plotting to get even with the world, plotting to get the fame he thought he deserved.

I Want to Be Somebody!

He came again. We went down with a loud crash. The air was crushed from my stomach.

The side of my head struck a sharp edge of the children's bureau. My vision was clouded. My ears rang. I saw bright dancing stars everywhere.

"Dr. Cross! Is that you? Did you forget whose show this is?"

I could barely see Gary Soneji's face when he screamed out my name. He tried to physically hurt me with the ear-splitting scream, the sheer force of his voice.

"You can't touch me!" he screamed again. "You can't touch me, Doctor! Do you get it? Do you get it yet? I'm the star. Not you!"

Blood was smeared all over his hands and arms. Blood was everywhere. I could see it now. *Who had he hurt? What had he done in our house?*

I could see shapes in the shifting darkness of the children's room. He had a knife raised high in one hand, canted in my direction.

"I'm the star here! I'm Soneji! Murphy! Whoever I want to be!"

I realized whose blood was swabbed all over his hands and arms. *My blood.* He'd stabbed me when he hit me the first time.

He raised the knife to strike a second time and growled like an animal. The children were awake now. Damon screamed, "Daddy!" and Jannie started to cry.

"Get out of here, kids!" I shouted. But they were too terrified to leave their beds.

He feinted with the knife once, then the blade slashed at me again. I moved, and the knife cut a glancing blow across my shoulder.

This time the pain was there, and I knew exactly what it was. Soneji's knife had sliced into my upper shoulder.

I yelled loudly at Soneji/Murphy. The children were crying. I wanted to kill him now. My mind was going to burst. There was nothing left in me but rage at this monster inside my house.

Soneji/Murphy raised his knife again. The lethal blade was

long, and so sharp I hadn't even felt the first wound. It had cut right through.

I heard another scream — a fierce shriek. Soneji stood frozen for the eeriest split second.

Then he whirled around with another growl.

A figure came sweeping at him from the doorway. Nana Mama had distracted him.

"This is our house!" she shouted with all her fury. "Get out of our house!"

A glint of light caught my eye on the bureau. I reached out and grabbed the scissors on top of Jannie's book of paper dolls. A pair of Nana's shearing scissors.

Soneji/Murphy slashed out with his knife again. The same knife he'd used in his murders around the projects? The knife he'd used on Vivian Kim?

I swung the scissors at him and felt tearing flesh. The shearing scissors slashed down across his cheeks. His cry echoed through the bedroom. "Motherfucker!"

"Something to remember me by," I taunted him. "Who's bleeding now? Soneji or Murphy?"

He screamed something I didn't understand. Then he rushed at me again.

The scissors caught him somewhere on the side of his neck. He jumped back, pulling them right from my hand.

"C'mon, you bastard!" I yelled.

Suddenly he reeled and staggered out of the children's bedroom. He never struck out at Nana, the mother figure. Maybe he was too badly wounded to strike back.

He held his face in both hands. His voice rose in a high, piercing scream as he ran from the room. Could he be in another fugue state? Was he lost inside one of his fantasies?

I had gone down on one knee and wanted to stay there. The noise was a loud roar in my head. I managed to get up. Blood was splattered everywhere, on my shirt, all over my shorts, my bare legs. My blood, and his.

A rush of adrenaline kept me going. I grabbed some clothes and went after Soneji. He couldn't escape this time. I wouldn't let him.

CHAPTER 89

I RAN TO THE DEN and grabbed my revolver. I knew he had a plan — in case he had to escape. Every step would have been thought through a hundred times. He lived in his fantasies, not in the real world.

I thought that he would probably leave our house. *Escape*, so he could fight again. Was I beginning to think like him? I thought that I was. Scary.

The front door was wide open. I was on track. So far. Blood was smeared all over the carpet. Had he left a trail for me?

Where would Gary Soneji/Murphy go if something went wrong at our house? He would always have a backup plan. Where was the perfect place? The completely unexpected move? I was finding it hard to think with blood dripping from my side and left shoulder.

I reeled outside and into the early morning darkness and biting cold. Our street was as silent as it ever got. It was 4 A.M. I had only one idea where he might have gone.

I wondered if he thought I'd try to follow him. Was he already expecting me? Was Soneji/Murphy still two jumps ahead of me again? So far, he always had been. I had to get ahead of him — just this once.

The Metro underground ran a block from our house on 5th Street. The tunnel was still being built, but a few neighborhood kids went down there to walk the four blocks over to Capitol Hill . . . *underground*.

I hobbled, and half ran, to the subway entrance. I was hurting, but I didn't care. *He'd come inside my house. He'd gone after my children.*

I went downstairs into the tunnel. I drew my revolver from the shoulder holster I'd slung over my shirt.

Every step I took put a ragged stitch in my side. Painfully, I began to walk the length of the tunnel in a low shooter's crouch.

He could be watching me. Had he expected me to come here? I walked forward in the tunnel. It could be a trap. There were plenty of places for him to hide.

I made it all the way to the er.d. There was no sign of blood, anywhere. Soneji/Murphy wasn't in the underground. He'd escaped some other way. He'd gotten away again.

As the adrenaline rush slowed, I felt weak and weary and disoriented. I climbed the stone stairs out of the underground.

Night people were coming and going from the Metro paper store and from Fox's all-night diner. I must have been a sorry sight. Blood was spattered all over me. No one stopped, though. Not a single person. They had all seen too much of this ghoulish stuff in the nation's capital.

I finally stepped in front of a truck driver dropping off a bundle of *Washington Posts*. I told him I was a police officer. I was feeling a little high with the loss of blood. Slightly giddy now.

"I didn't do nothin' wrong," he said to me.

"You didn't shoot me, motherfucker?"

"No, sir. What're you, crazy? You really a cop?"

I made him take me home in his paper-delivery truck. For the whole six-block ride, the man swore he'd sue the city.

"Sue Mayor Monroe," I told him. "Sue Monroe's ass bad."

"You really a cop?" he asked me again. "You ain't a cop."

"Yeah, I'm a cop."

Squad cars and EMS ambulances were already gathered at my house. This was my recurring nightmare — *this very scene.* Never before had the police and medics actually come to my house.

Sampson was already there. He had a black leather jacket over a ratty old Baltimore Orioles sweatshirt. He wore a cap from the Hoodoo Gurus tour.

He looked at me as if I were crazy. Crimson and blue emergency lights twirled behind him. "Wuz up? You don't look so good. You all right, man?"

"Been stabbed twice with a hunting knife. Not as bad as the time we got shot over in Garfield."

"Uh huh. Must look worse than it is. I want you to lie down here on the lawn. Lie down now, Alex."

I nodded, and walked away from Sampson. I had to finish this. Somehow, *it had to be over with.*

The EMS people were trying to get me down on the lawn. Our tiny lawn. Or get me on their stretcher.

I had another idea. *The front door had been left wide open. He'd left the door to the house open. Why had he done that?*

"Be right with you," I said to the medics as I walked past them. "Hold that stretcher, though."

People were yelling at me, but I pushed forward, anyway.

I moved silently and purposefully through the living room and into the kitchen. I opened the door that's catty-cornered to our back door, and hurried downstairs.

I didn't see anything in the basement. No movement. Nothing out of order. The cellar was my last good idea.

I walked over to a bin near the furnace where Nana dumps all the dirty laundry for the next washload. It's the farthest corner of the basement from the stairs. No Soneji/Murphy in the dark basement.

Sampson came running down the cellar stairs. "He's not here! Someone saw him downtown. He's down around Dupont Circle."

"He wants to make one more big play," I muttered. "Son-of-a-bitch." *Son of Lindbergh.*

Sampson didn't try to stop me from going with him. He could see in my eyes that he couldn't, anyway. The two of us hurried to his car. I figured I was all right. I'd drop if I wasn't.

A young punk from the neighborhood looked at the sticky blood down the front of my shirt. "You dying, Cross? That be good." He gave me my eulogy.

It took us ten minutes or so to get down to Dupont Circle. Police squad cars were parked everywhere — flashing eerie red and blue in the dawn's earliest light.

It was late in the night shift for most of these boys. Nobody needed a madman on the loose in downtown Washington.

One more big play.

I Want to Be Somebody.

During the next hour or so nothing happened — except that it got light out. Pedestrians began to appear around the circle. The traffic thickened as Washington opened up for business.

The early risers were curious and stopped to ask the police questions. None of us would tell them anything, except to "please keep moving along. Just keep walking, please. There's nothing to see." Thank God.

An EMS doctor treated my wounds. There was more blood than actual damage. He wanted me to go straight to the hospital, of course. That could wait. *One more big play. Dupont*

Circle? Downtown Washington, D.C.? Gary Soneji/Murphy loved
to play in the capital.

I told the EMS doc to back off, and he did. I hit him up for
a couple of Percodan. They did the trick for the moment.

Sampson stood by my side, sucking on a cigarette. "You're
gonna just fall over," he said to me. "You'll just collapse. Like
some big African elephant had a sudden heart attack."

I was savoring my Percodan buzz. "Wasn't a sudden heart
attack," I said to him. "Big African elephant got knifed a couple
of times. Wasn't an elephant, either. It was an African antelope.
Graceful, beautiful, powerful beast."

I eventually started to walk back toward Sampson's car.

"You got an idea?" he called after me. "Alex?"

"Yeah. Let's *ride*, no good standing around here at Dupont
Circle. He's not going to start shooting up rush-hour traffic."

"You sure about that, Alex?"

"I'm sure about it."

We rode around downtown Washington until just before
eight. It was getting hopeless. I was starting to get real sleepy in
the car.

This big African antelope was about ready to fall over. Beads
of sweat slipped across my eyebrows, dripping down my nose. I
was trying to think like Gary Soneji/Murphy. Was he downtown
now? Or had he already escaped from Washington?

A call came over the car radio at 7:58.

"Suspect spotted on Pennsylvania Avenue, near Lafayette
Park. Suspect has an automatic weapon in his possession. Suspect is approaching the White House. All cars move in!"

One more big play. At least I finally had him figured out a
little. He was less than two blocks from 1600 Pennsylvania Avenue when they'd found him. That was two blocks from the
White House.

I Want to Be Somebody.

*   *   *

They had him pinned down between a shoe-repair shop and a brownstone building full of law offices. He was using a parked Jeep Cherokee for cover.

There was another complication. He had hostages. He'd taken two young kids who had been on their way to school early that morning. The children looked to be eleven or twelve, about the same age Gary had been when his stepmother started locking him up. There was a boy and a girl. Shades of Maggie Rose and Michael Goldberg, almost two years before.

"I'm Divisional Chief Cross," I said and got through the police barricades that were already set up across Pennsylvania Avenue.

The White House was clearly visible down the street. I wondered if the president was watching us on TV. At least one CNN news truck was already on the scene.

A couple of news-station helicopters moved in overhead. This was restricted air space near the White House, so they couldn't get too close. Somebody said Mayor Monroe was on his way. Gary had bigger prey in mind. He had demanded to see the president. Otherwise, he'd kill the two children.

Traffic on Pennsylvania Avenue and the intersecting streets was already backed up as far as I could see. Several drivers and other passengers were deserting their vehicles, leaving them on the street. Scores of them stayed to watch the spectacle, though. Millions now watched on television.

"You think he's heading for the White House?" Sampson asked.

"I know a few states he'd probably carry," I said.

I talked to the police SWAT team leader behind the barricades. I told him I thought Gary Soneji/Murphy was ready to go down in flames. He offered to light the match.

A negotiator was already at the scene. He was more than willing to hand over the honor to me. I was finally going to negotiate a settlement with Soneji/Murphy.

"We get the chance" — Sampson grabbed me and spoke very directly — "we're going to pop him. Nothing tricky, Alex."

"Tell that to him," I said to Sampson. "But if you get the chance, hit him. Do him."

I wiped my face several times on my sleeve. I was sweating bullets. I was also nauseated and dizzy. I had an electric bullhorn and I flicked the power on.

The power was in my hands. *I want to be somebody, too.* Was that true? Was that what it had finally come to?

"This is Alex Cross," I called out. A few wiseguys in the crowd cheered. Mostly, it got very quiet on the downtown D.C. street.

A burst of wild gunfire suddenly erupted across the street. Loud noise. Car windows blew out all over Pennsylvania Avenue. He did an amazing amount of damage in just a few seconds. Nobody was hurt that I could see. The two children were unharmed. Hi back at ya, Gary.

Then a voice came from across the street. Gary's voice.

He was shouting at me. It was just the two of us. Was that what he wanted? His own High Noon in the middle of the capital. Live national TV coverage.

"Let me see you, Dr. Cross. Come on out, Alex. Show your pretty face to everybody."

"Why should I?" I spoke over the bullhorn to Soneji.

"Don't even think about it," Sampson whispered from behind me. "You do, I'll shoot you myself."

There was another explosion of gunfire from across the avenue. This one went on even longer than the first burst. Washington was starting to look like downtown Beirut. Cameras whirred and clicked everywhere.

I stood up suddenly and came out from behind a police sedan. Not too far, just enough to get killed. Some more assholes at the scene cheered me on.

"The TV stations are here, Gary," I shouted. "They're filming this now. They're filming *me* as I stand here. I'm gonna wind up as the big star. Slow start, but a hell of a finish for me."

Soneji/Murphy started to laugh. His laughter went on for a while. Was he manic? Depressive?

"You finally got me figured out?" he shouted at me. "*Have* you? Do you know who I am now? Do you know what I want?"

"I doubt it. I know that you're hurt. I know you think you're dying. Otherwise" — I stopped to make this sound as dramatic as it would be to him — "otherwise, *you wouldn't have let us catch you again.*"

Directly across Pennsylvania Avenue, Soneji/Murphy stood up behind the bright red Jeep. Both children lay on the sidewalk behind him. Neither seemed to be hurt so far.

Gary took a theatrical bow in my direction. He looked like the all-American boy, just as he did in court.

I was walking toward him now. Getting closer and closer.

"Nice touch," he called to me. "Well said. But *I'm* the star." He suddenly shifted his gun in my direction.

A shot rang out behind me.

Gary Soneji/Murphy flew back in the direction of the shoe-repair shop. He landed on the sidewalk, then rolled over. Both young hostages started to scream. They scrambled up and ran away.

I sprinted as fast as I could across Pennsylvania Avenue. "Don't shoot!" I yelled. "Hold your fire."

I turned and saw Sampson standing there. His service revolver was still aimed at Gary Murphy. He turned the revolver up toward the sky. He kept his eyes on me. He'd finished it for both of us.

Gary lay in a crumpled heap on the sidewalk. A stream of bright red blood flowed steadily from his head and mouth. He wasn't moving. The automatic rifle was still clutched in his hand.

I reached out and took the gun away first. I heard cameras clicking away behind us. I touched his shoulder. "Gary?"

Very carefully, I turned the body over. There was still no movement. No sign of life. He looked like the all-American boy again. He'd come to this party as himself, as Gary Murphy.

As I looked down, Gary's eyes suddenly opened and rolled back. He looked straight up at me. His lips parted slowly.

"Help me," he finally whispered in a soft, choked voice. "Help me, Dr. Cross. Please help me."

I knelt down close beside him. "Who are you?" I asked him.

"I'm Gary. . . . Gary Murphy," he said.

Checkmate.

Frontier Justice

(1994)

Wˢᴴᴱᴺ THE FATEFUL DAY finally arrived, I couldn't sleep, not even a couple of hours. I couldn't play the piano out on our porch. I didn't want to see anyone to talk about what was going to happen in just a few hours. I slipped in and kissed Damon and Jannie while they slept. Then I left the house around two in the morning.

I arrived at Lorton Federal Prison at three. The marchers were back, carrying their homemade placards under a moonlit sky. Some were singing protest songs from the 1960s. Many prayed. There were several nuns, priests, ministers. A majority of the protesters were women, I noticed.

The execution chamber at Lorton was a small, ordinary room with three windows. One window was reserved for the press. One was for official observers from the state. The third window was reserved for friends and family of the prisoner.

There were dark blue curtains over each of the three windows. At three-thirty in the morning, a prison official opened them one by one. The prisoner was finally revealed, strapped down on a hospital gurney. The gurney had a makeshift extension panel for the left arm.

Jezzie had been staring up at the room's ceiling, but she became alert and seemed to tense as two technicians walked to the gurney. One of them carried the needle on a stainless-steel hospital tray. The insertion of the catheter needle was the only physical pain involved if the execution by lethal injection was done correctly.

I had been coming out to Lorton to visit both Jezzie and Gary Murphy for several months. I was on leave from the D.C. police force, and although I was writing this book, I had plenty of time for visits.

Gary appeared to be coming apart. It was in all his workup reports. He spent most days lost in his complex fantasy world. It became harder and harder to coax him back to the real one.

Or so it appeared. And that saved him another trial, that saved him from the possibility of death row. I was certain that he was playing games, but nobody wanted to listen. I was sure he was making up another plan.

Jezzie had agreed to talk to me. We had always been able to talk. She wasn't surprised the state had gotten the death penalty for her and Charles Chakely. She was responsible for the death of the son of the secretary of the treasury, after all. She and the Secret Service men had kidnapped Maggie Rose Dunne. They were responsible for Michael Goldberg's death, and also Vivian Kim's. Jezzie and Devine had murdered the Florida pilot, Joseph Denyeau.

Jezzie told me that she felt remorse, and had from the very beginning. "But not enough to stop me. Something must have broken inside me along the way. I'd probably do the same thing today. I'd take that kind of chance for ten million dollars. So would a lot of people, Alex. It's the age of greed. But not for you."

"How do you know that?" I asked her.

"Somehow, I do. You are the Black Knight."

She told me that I shouldn't feel bad after it was over. She said the marchers and other protesters angered her. "If their child had died, most of them would act a lot differently about this."

I felt very bad. I didn't know how much I believed Jezzie, but I felt bad. I didn't want to be there at Lorton, but Jezzie had asked me to come.

There was no one else at the window for Jezzie. Not a single person in the world. Jezzie's mother had died not long after her arrest. Six weeks earlier, the former Secret Service agent Charles Chakely had been executed in front of his family. That had sealed Jezzie's fate.

Long plastic tubes connected the needle in Jezzie's left arm to several intravenous drips. The first drip, which had already started, dispensed a harmless saline solution.

At a signal from the warden, sodium thiopental would be added to the intravenous. This was a barbiturate used as an anesthetic and to put patients gently to sleep. Then a heavy dose of Pavulon would be added. This would induce death in about ten minutes. To speed the process, an equal dose of potassium chloride was administered. This drug relaxes the heart and stops its pumping. It would cause death in about ten seconds.

Jezzie found my face in her "friends" window. She gave a little wave with her fingertips, and she even tried to smile. She had bothered to comb her hair, which was cut short now, but still beautiful. I thought of Maria, and how we hadn't gotten to say good-bye before she died. I thought that this might be a little worse. I wanted to leave the prison so badly, but I stayed. I had promised Jezzie I would stay. I always kept my promises.

In reality, it was nothing very graphic. Jezzie finally closed her eyes. I wondered if any of the lethal drugs had been administered, but I had no way of knowing that.

She took a deep breath, and then I saw her tongue drop back

in her mouth. That was all there was to the modern execution of a human being. That was the end of the life of Jezzie Flanagan.

I left the prison and hurried to my car. I was a psychologist and a detective, I told myself. I could take this. I could take anything. I was tougher than anybody. Always had been.

My hands were jammed deeply into the pockets of my overcoat. In my right hand, so tightly clutched that it hurt, was the silver hair comb Jezzie had given me, once upon a time.

When I got to my car, an ordinary white envelope was stuck under the driver-side wiper. I stuffed it in my coat pocket, and didn't bother to open it until I was on my way back to Washington. I thought I knew what it was, and I was right. The Thing had sent me a message. Up close and personal. In my face.

Alex,

> *Did she sob, and whine, and beg for forgiveness before they pricked her? Did you shed a tear?*
>
> *Remember me to the family. I want to be remembered.*

> *Always,*
> *Son of L.*

He was still playing his terrible mind games. He always would be. I'd told that to anyone willing to listen. I'd written a diagnostic profile for the journals. Gary Soneji/Murphy was responsible for his acts. I felt that he ought to be tried for the murders he'd committed in Southeast. The families of his black victims ought to have justice and retribution, too. If anyone deserved to be on death row, it was Soneji/Murphy.

The note told me that he'd found a way to con one of the guards. He'd gotten to somebody inside Lorton. He had another plan. Another ten- or twenty-year plan? More of his fantasies and mind games.

As I drove toward D.C., I wondered who was the more skilled manipulator. Gary or Jezzie? I knew both of them were psychopaths. This country is turning out more of them than any other place on the planet. They come in all shapes and sizes, all races and creeds and genders. That's the scariest thing of all.

After I got home that morning, I played some "Rhapsody in Blue," on the porch. I played Bonnie Raitt's "Let's Give Them Something to Talk About." Janelle and Damon hung out and listened to their favorite piano player. Next to Ray Charles, that is. They sat on the piano bench with me. All three of us were content to listen to the music, and let our bodies touch for several moments.

Later, I headed down to St. A's for lunch and such. Peanut Butter Man lives.

Hide and Seek

James Patterson

THE INTERNATIONAL BESTSELLER

First, there was the No 1 bestselling, page-turning *Along Came a Spider*. Next, the electrifying No 1 bestseller *Kiss the Girls*. Now, a breathtaking new novel of terror and suspense which proves, once again, that no one makes the pages turn faster than James Patterson.

Maggie Bradford is on trial for murder – in the celebrity trial of the decade. As one of the world's best-loved singer-songwriters, she seems to have it all. So how could she have murdered not just one, but two of her husbands?

Will Shepherd was Maggie's second husband. A magnificent athlete and film star, he was just as famous. But Will had dark, dangerous secrets that none of his fans could have imagined . . . that his own wife could never have dreamed of.

'James Patterson does everything but stick our finger in a light socket.'   *New York Times Book Review*

'It's interesting to note the point at which the word-of-mouth on a thriller writer becomes urgent recommendation. In Patterson's case, it began with *Along Came a Spider*. This latest will consolidate that esteem. *Hide and Seek* barrels along with an unforced drive. This well-paced novel could be the book that clinches Patterson's position.'

Publishing News

ISBN 0 00 649852 3

Jack and Jill

James Patterson

THE SPELLBINDING NEW
ALEX CROSS THRILLER

James Patterson burst onto the thriller scene with his No 1 bestseller *Along Came a Spider*, which first introduced Washington homicide detective Alex Cross. His memorable hero returned in spectacular fashion in another No 1 bestseller, *Kiss the Girls*, which is now a major film, starring Morgan Freeman.

Now – in James Patterson's most explosive and powerful novel yet – Alex Cross is back on home territory, tangling with a pair of killers who are picking off the rich and famous one by one with chilling professional efficiency.

As the whole country awaits the identity of the next celebrity victim, only Alex Cross, with his ability to get into the minds of deranged killers, has the skills and the courage to crack the case – but will he discover the truth before 'Jack and Jill' set their sights on Washington's ultimate celebrity target?

A relentless rollercoaster of heart-pounding suspense and jolting plot twists, *Jack and Jill* proves once again that no one can write a more compelling thriller than James Patterson – the master of the non-stop nightmare.

ISBN 0 00 649312 1

Kiss the Girls

James Patterson

HIS NEW NO 1 BESTSELLER

Along Came a Spider was one of the most talked-about thrillers for years – a phenomenal international No 1 bestseller. Now its memorable hero detective Alex Cross is back – thrust into a case he will never forget.

This time there isn't just one killer, there are two. One collects beautiful, intelligent women on college campuses on the east coast of the USA. The other is terrorising Los Angeles with a series of unspeakable murders. But the truly chilling news is that the two brilliant and elusive killers are communicating, cooperating, *competing*.

'As good as a thriller can get. With *Kiss the Girls*, Patterson joins the elite company of Thomas Harris.'
San Francisco Examiner

'This novel is hard to set aside. Pattterson's complex tale chills, enthrals and entertains the reader in a dazzling and unforgettable reading experience.' *Toronto Star*

'James Patterson's *Kiss the Girls* is a ripsnorting, terrific read.' *USA Today*

'Patterson hit the ball out of the park with his last go-round, the bestselling *Along Came a Spider*; *Kiss the Girls* is even better.' *Dallas Morning News*

ISBN 0 00 649315 7

Black Market

James Patterson

From the author who would go on to create the superbly chilling international bestsellers *Along Came a Spider*, *Kiss the Girls*, *Jack and Jill*, *Hide and Seek*, *The Midnight Club* and *Cat and Mouse* comes an early work of astonishing pace and tension – a breathtaking novel of high finance, international terrorism and irresistible page-turning suspense.

The threat was absolute. At 5.05 p.m. Wall Street would be destroyed. No demands, no ransom, no negotiations. A multiple firebombing – orchestrated by a secret militia group – would wipe out the financial heart of America. Stop the world's financial system dead.

Faced with catastrophe on an unimaginable scale, Federal agent Archer Carroll and Wall Street lawyer Caitlin Dillon are pitched into a heart-stopping race against time, tracking the unknown enemy through a maze of intrigue, rumour and betrayal towards a truly shocking climax.

'The action is fast and furious.'   *Wall Street Journal*

'A tough, twisting tale.'   *New York Daily News*

'Among the best writers of crime stories ever.' *USA Today*

ISBN 0 00 649314 9

The Midnight Club

James Patterson

Time after time, in an acclaimed series of runaway international No 1 bestsellers, James Patterson has delivered breathtaking rollercoaster thrills and incomparable page-turning readability. Now comes a mesmerising tale of non-stop action and suspense.

Nobody knows the underbelly of the city like New York cop John Stefanovitch. He's out to get Alexandre St-Germain, the most powerful member of the Midnight Club – a secret international society of ruthless crime czars, all of whom are 'respectable' businessmen. And Stef's the ideal man for the job – until he's levelled by a blast from St-Germain's shotgun and left for dead.

Now, Stef is back, wheelchair-bound, yet sworn to destroy St-Germain. With the help of a beautiful journalist and a Harlem cop, Stef is determined to crack the Midnight Club. And he's up against odds that are as unknown as they are deadly . . .

'It just might be his best ever.' *USA Today*

'Guaranteed: you'll devour this yarn-burner in one sitting.'
New York Daily News

'A fast-moving narrative that never lets up. The villain is one of the most awful monsters I've encountered in recent fiction.' campbell armstrong

'Sleek, fast, skilful and larger than life.' *Los Angeles Times*

ISBN 0 00 649313 0

James Patterson is one of the best-know[n] [be]st-selling writers of all time. He is the auth[or] [...] of the most popular series of the past decade: [...] s Murder Club, the Alex Cross novels and M[...]de, and he has written many other number [...]lers including romance novels and stand-alone [...] . He has won an Edgar Award, the mystery world's hig[h]est honour. He lives in Florida with his wife and son.

Praise for James Patterson:

'The man is a master of this genre. We fans will have one wish for him: write even faster'   *USA Today*

'Unputdownable. It will sell millions'   *The Times*

'Packed with white-knuckled twists'   *Daily Mail*

'A novel which makes for sleepless nights'   *Daily Express*

'Breakneck pacing and loop-the-loop plotting'
Publishers Weekly

'Reads like a dream'   *Kirkus Reviews*

'A fast-paced, electric story that is utterly believable'
Booklist

'Ticks like a time bomb – full of threat and terror'
Los Angeles Times

'Absolutely terrific'   *Bookseller*

'Patterson's action-packed story keeps the pages flicking by'   *The Sunday Times*

'A fine writer with a good ear for dialogue and pacing. His books are always page-turners'   *Washington Times*

'Patterson is a phenomenon'   *Observer*

'Keeps the adrenaline level high'   *Publishing News*

By *James Patterson and available from Headline*

When the Wind Blows
Cradle and All
Miracle on the 17th Green *(and Peter de Jonge)*
Suzanne's Diary for Nicholas
The Beach House *(and Peter de Jonge)*
The Jester *(and Andrew Gross)*
The Lake House
Sam's Letters to Jennifer
SantaKid
Honeymoon *(and Howard Roughan)*
Lifeguard *(and Andrew Gross)*
Beach Road *(and Peter de Jonge)*
Judge and Jury *(and Andrew Gross)*
Step on a Crack *(and Michael Ledwidge)*
The Quickie *(and Michael Ledwidge)*
You've Been Warned *(and Howard Roughan)*

Alex Cross novels
Cat and Mouse
Pop Goes the Weasel
Roses are Red
Violets are Blue
Four Blind Mice
The Big Bad Wolf
London Bridges
Mary, Mary
Cross
Double Cross

The Women's Murder Club series
1st to Die
2nd Chance *(and Andrew Gross)*
3rd Degree *(and Andrew Gross)*
4th of July *(and Maxine Paetro)*
The 5th Horseman *(and Maxine Paetro)*
The 6th Target *(and Maxine Paetro)*

Maximum Ride series
Maximum Ride: The Angel Experiment
Maximum Ride: School's Out Forever
Maximum Ride: Saving the World and Other Extreme Sports

JAMES
PATTERSON

1ST
TO DIE

headline

First published in Great Britain in 2001
by HEADLINE BOOK PUBLISHING

This edition published in 2009
by HEADLINE PUBLISHING GROUP

10

Cataloguing in Publication Data is available from the British Library

ISBN 978 0 7553 4926 5

Typeset in Palatino Light by Palimpsest Book Production Limited,
Grangemouth, Stirlingshire

Printed and bound in Great Britain by
Clays Ltd, St Ives plc

Headline's policy is to use papers that are natural, renewable
and recyclable products and made from wood grown in
sustainable forests. The logging and manufacturing processes
are expected to conform to the environmental regulations of
the country of origin.

HEADLINE PUBLISHING GROUP
An Hachette UK Company
338 Euston Road
London NW1 3BH

www.headline.co.uk
www.hachette.co.uk

1ST
TO DIE

My thanks to the following people, whose hard work and expertise helped in the writing of this book:

Dr Gerg Zorman, Chief of Neurosurgery, Lakeland Hospital, Fort Lauderdale, Florida, who I'd like on my side in a crisis.

The lovely and talented Fern Galperin, Mary Jordan, Barbara Groszewski and Irene Markocki.

Prologue

Inspector
Lindsay Boxer

Chapter 1

I t is an unusually warm night in August, but I'm shivering badly as I stand on the substantial gray stone terrace outside my apartment. I'm looking out over glorious San Francisco and I have my service revolver pressed against the side of my temple.

'Goddamn You, God!' I whisper. Quite a sentiment, but appropriate and just, I think to myself.

I hear Sweet Martha whimpering. I turn and see she is watching me through the glass doors that lead to the terrace. She knows something is wrong. 'It's okay,' I call to her through the door. 'Everything's fine. Go lie down, girl.'

Martha won't leave, though, won't look away. She's a kind, loyal friend who's been nuzzling me good night every single night for the past six years. As I stare into the Border Collie's eyes, I think that maybe I should go inside and call the girls. Claire, Cindy, and Jill would be here almost before I hung up the phone. They would hold me, hug me, say all the right things. *You're special,*

Lindsay. Everybody loves you, Lindsay.

Only I'm pretty sure that I'd be back out here tomorrow night, or the night after. I just don't see a way out of
this mess. I have thought it all through a hundred times.
I can be as logical as hell but I am also highly emotional,
obviously. That was my strength as an Inspector with the
San Francisco Police Department. It is a rare combination, and I think it is why I was more successful than any
of the males in Homicide. Of course, none of them are
up here getting ready to blow their brains out with their
own guns.

I lightly brush the barrel of the revolver down my cheek
and then up to my temple again. Oh God, oh God, oh
God. I am reminded of *soft hands*, of Chris, and that starts
me crying.

Lots of images are coming way too fast for me to
handle.

The terrible, indelible honeymoon murders that have
terrified our city, mixed with close-ups of my mom and
even a few flashes of my father. My best girls – Claire,
Cindy, and Jill – our crazy club. I can even see myself – the
way I used to be, anyway. Nobody ever, *ever* thought that I
looked like an Inspector, the only woman Homicide
Inspector in the entire SFPD. My friends always said I was
more like Helen Hunt married to Paul Reiser in *Mad About
You*. I was married once. I was no Helen Hunt; he sure was
no Paul Reiser.

This is so hard, so bad, so wrong. It's so unlike me. I
keep seeing David and Melanie Brandt, the first couple

who were killed in the Mandarin Suite of the Grand Hyatt. I see that horrifying hotel room where they died senselessly and needlessly.

That was the beginning.

Book One

David and Melanie

Chapter One

Beautiful long-stemmed red roses filled the hotel suite – the perfect gifts, really. *Everything* was perfect.

There might be a luckier man somewhere on the planet, David Brandt thought, as he wrapped his arms around Melanie, his new bride. Somewhere in Yemen, maybe – some Allah-praising farmer with a second goat. But certainly not in all of San Francisco.

The couple looked out from the living room of the Grand Hyatt's Mandarin Suite. They could see the lights of Berkeley off in the distance, Alcatraz, the graceful outline of the lit-up Golden Gate Bridge.

'It's incredible,' Melanie beamed. 'I wouldn't change a single thing about today.'

'Me neither,' he whispered. 'Well, maybe I wouldn't have invited my parents.' They both laughed.

Only moments before, they had bid farewell to the last of the 300 guests in the hotel's ballroom. The wedding was finally over – the toasts, the dancing, the schmoozing, the photographed kisses over the cake. Now it was just the two of them. Both were twenty-nine years old and had the rest of their lives ahead of them.

David reached for a pair of filled champagne glasses he had set on a lacquered table. 'A toast,' he declared, 'to the second-luckiest man alive.'

'The second?' she said, and smiled in pretended shock. 'Who's the first?'

They looped arms and took a long, luxurious sip from the refreshing crystal. 'This farmer with two goats. I'll tell you later,' he said.

'I have something for you,' David suddenly remembered. He had already given her the perfect five-carat diamond on her finger, which he knew she wore only to please his folks. He went to his tuxedo jacket, which was draped over a high-backed chair in the living room, and returned with a jewelry box from Bulgari.

'No, David,' Melanie protested. '*You're* my gift.'

'Open it, anyway,' he said to her. 'This, you'll like.'

She lifted the lid. Inside a suede pouch was a pair of earrings; large silver rings around a pair of whimsical moons made from diamonds.

'They're how I think of you,' he said.

Melanie held the moons against the lobes of her ears. They were perfect, and so was she.

'It's you who pulls my tides,' David whispered.

They kissed, and he unfastened the zipper of her dress, letting the neckline fall just below her shoulders. He kissed her neck. Then the top of her breasts.

There was a knock on the door of the suite.

'Champagne,' called a voice from outside.

For a moment, David thought of just yelling, 'Leave it there!' All evening, he had longed to peel away the dress from his wife's soft white shoulders.

'Oh, go get it,' Melanie said, dangling the earrings in front of his eyes. 'I'll put these on.'

She wiggled out of his grasp, backing toward the Mandarin's master bathroom, a smile in her liquid brown eyes. *God, he loved those eyes.*

As he went to the door, David was thinking he wouldn't trade places with anybody in the world.

Not even for a second goat.

Chapter Two

Phillip Campbell had imagined this moment, this exquisite scene, so many times. He knew it would be the groom who opened the door. He stepped into the room.

'Congratulations,' Campbell muttered, handing over the champagne. He stared at the man in the open tuxedo shirt and black tie dangling around his neck.

David Brandt barely looked at him as he inspected the brightly ribboned box. Krug. Clos du Mesnil, 1989.

'What is the worst thing anyone has ever done?' Campbell murmured to himself. 'Am I capable of doing it? Do I have what it takes?'

'Any card?' the groom said, fumbling in his pants pocket for a tip.

'Only this, sir.'

Campbell stepped forward and plunged a knife deeply into the groom's chest, between the third and fourth rib, the closest route to the heart.

'For the man who has everything,' Campbell said. He

pushed his way into the room and slammed the door shut with a swift kick. He spun David Brandt around and shoved his back against the door and powered the blade in deeper.

The groom stiffened in a spasm of shock and pain. Guttural sounds escaped from his chest – tiny, gurgling, choking breaths. His eyes bulged in disbelief.

This is amazing, Campbell thought. He could actually feel the groom's strength leaking away. The man had just experienced one of the great moments of his life and now, minutes later, he was dying.

Why?

Campbell stepped back and the groom's body crumpled to the floor. The room tilted like a listing boat. Then everything began to speed up and run together. He felt as if he were watching a flickering newsreel. Awesome. Nothing like he had expected.

Campbell heard the wife's voice and had the presence of mind to pull the blade out of David Brandt's chest.

He rushed to intercept her as she came from the bedroom, still in her long, lacy gown.

'David?' she said, with an expectant smile that turned to shock at the sight of Campbell. 'Where's David? Who are you?'

Her eyes traveled over him, terror-ridden, fixing on his face, the knife blade, then moving to her husband's body on the floor.

'*Oh, my God! David!*' she screamed. '*Oh David, David!*'

Campbell wanted to remember her like this. The frozen,

wide-eyed look. The promise and hope that just moments ago had shined so brightly were now shattered.

The words poured from his mouth. 'You want to know why? Well, *so do I.*'

'What have you done?' Melanie said hoarsely. She struggled to understand. Her terrified eyes darted back and forth, sweeping the room for a way out.

She made a sudden dash for the living-room door. Campbell grabbed her wrist and brought the bloody knife up to her throat.

'Please,' she whimpered, her eyes frozen. 'Please don't kill me.'

'The truth is, Melanie, I'm here to save you.' He smiled into her quivering face as he stepped close.

Campbell lowered the blade and sliced into her. The slender body jolted up with a sudden cry. Her eyes flickered like a weak electric bulb. A deathly rattle shot through her. 'Why?' her begging eyes pleaded. 'Why?'

It took a full minute for him to regain his breath. The smell of Melanie Brandt's blood was deep in his nostrils. He almost couldn't believe what he had done.

Why?

He carried the bride's body back into the bedroom and placed her on the bed. She was beautiful, with delicate features. And so young. He remembered when he had first seen her and how he had been taken with her then. She had thought the whole world was in front of her.

He rubbed his hand against the smooth surface of her cheek and cupped one of her earrings – a smiling moon.

'What is the worst thing anyone has ever done?' Phillip Campbell asked himself again, heart pounding in his chest.

Was this it? Had he just done it?

'Not yet,' a voice inside answered. 'Not quite yet.'

Slowly, he lifted the bride's beautiful white wedding dress.

Chapter Three

I t was a little before eight-thirty on a Monday morning in June, one of those chilly, gray summer mornings for which San Francisco is famous. I was starting the week off badly, flipping through old copies of the *New Yorker* while waiting for my GP, Dr Roy Orenthaler, to free up.

I'd been seeing Dr Roy, as I still sometimes called him, ever since I was a sociology major at San Francisco State University, and I obligingly came in once a year for my check-up. That was last Tuesday. To my surprise, he called at the end of the week and asked me to stop in today before work.

I had a busy day ahead of me: two open cases and a deposition to deliver at district court. I was hoping I could be at my desk by nine.

'Ms Boxer,' the receptionist finally called to me, 'the doctor will see you now.'

I followed her into his office.

Generally, Orenthaler greeted me with some

well-intended stab at police humor, such as, 'So if you're here, who's out on the street after *them*?' I was now thirty-four, and for the past two years, lead Inspector on the Homicide detail out of the Hall of Justice.

But today, he rose stiffly and uttered a solemn, '*Good morning.*' He motioned me to the chair across from his desk. Uh-oh.

Up until then, my philosophy on doctors was simple. When one of them gave you that deep, concerned look and told you to take a seat, three things could happen. Only one of them was bad. They were either asking you out, getting ready to lay on some bad news, or they'd just spent a fortune re-upholstering the furniture.

'I want to show you something,' Orenthaler began. He held an X-ray up against a light, pointed to splotches of tiny ghostlike spheres in a current of smaller pellets. 'This is a blow-up of the blood smear we took from you. The larger globules are erythrocytes. Red blood cells.'

'They seem happy,' I joked, nervously.

'Those are, Lindsay,' the doctor said, without a trace of a smile. 'Problem is, you don't have many.'

I fixed on his eyes, hoping they would relax, and that we'd move on to something trivial like, 'You better start cutting down those long hours.'

'There's a condition,' Orenthaler went on, 'called Negli's aplastic anemia. It's rare. Basically, the body no longer manufactures red blood cells.' He held up an X-ray photo. 'This is what a normal blood work-up looks like.'

On this one, the dark background looked like the intersection of Market and Powell at 5:00 p.m. – a virtual traffic jam of compressed, energetic spheres. Speedy messengers all carrying oxygen to parts of someone else's body. In contrast, mine looked about as densely packed as a political headquarters two hours after the candidate had conceded.

'This is treatable, right?' I asked him. More like, I was telling him.

'It's treatable,' Orenthaler said, after a pause. 'But it's serious.'

A week ago, I had come in simply because my eyes were runny and blotchy and I'd discovered some blood in my panties; and every day, by three, I was suddenly feeling like some iron-deficient gnome was inside me siphoning off my energy. Me, of the regular double shifts and fourteen-hour days. Six weeks accrued vacation.

'How serious are we talking about?' I asked, my voice catching.

'Red blood cells are vital to the body's process of oxygenation,' Orenthaler began to explain. 'Hemopoiesis, the formation of blood cells in the bone marrow.'

'Dr Roy, this isn't a medical conference. Please tell me how serious it is.'

'What is it you want to hear? Diagnosis or possibility?'

'I want to hear the truth.'

Orenthaler nodded. He got up and came around the desk and took my hand. 'Then here's the truth, my dear. What you have is life-threatening.'

'Life-threatening?' My heart stopped. My throat was as dry as parchment.

'Fatal, Lindsay.'

Chapter Four

The cold, blunt sound of the word hit me like a hollow-point shell between the eyes.

Fatal.

I waited for Dr Roy to tell me this was all some kind of sick joke. That he had my X-ray mixed up with someone else's.

'But, I want to send you to a hematologist,' he went on. 'Like a lot of diseases, there are stages. Stage One is when there's a mild depletion of cells. It can be treated with monthly transfusions. Stage Two is when there's a systematic shortage of red cells. Stage Three would require hospitalization – a bone-marrow transplant. Potentially, the removal of your spleen.'

'So where am *I*?' I asked, sucking in a cramped lungful of air.

'Your erythrocytic count is barely two hundred per cc of raw blood. That puts you on the cusp.'

'The cusp?'

'The cusp,' the doctor said, 'between Stages Two and Three.'

There comes a point in everybody's life when you realize the stakes have suddenly changed. The carefree ride of your life slams into a stone wall; all those years of merely bouncing along, life taking you where you want to go, abruptly ends. In my job, I see this moment forced on people all the time.

Welcome to mine.

'So what does this mean?' I asked weakly. The room was spinning a little now.

'What it means, my dear, is that you're going to have to undergo a prolonged regimen of intensive treatment.'

I shook my head. 'What does it mean for my job?'

I'd been in Homicide for six years now, the past two as lead Homicide Inspector. With any luck, when my Lieutenant was up for promotion, I'd be in line for his job. The Department needed strong women. They could go far. Until that moment, I had thought that I would go far.

'Right now,' the doctor said, 'I don't think it means anything. As long as you feel strong while you're undergoing treatment, you can continue work. In fact, it might even be good therapy.'

Suddenly, I was suffocating.

'I want to give you the name of a hematologist, Dr Victor Medved,' Orenthaler said.

He went on about the doctor's credentials, but I was no longer hearing him. I was thinking, Who am I going to tell? Mom had died ten years before, from breast cancer. Dad had been out of the picture since I was thirteen. I had a sister, Cat, but she was living a nice, neat life down in

Newport Beach; and for her, just making a right turn on red brought on a moment of crisis.

The doctor pushed the referral toward me. 'I know you, Lindsay. You'll pretend this is something you can fix by working harder – but you can't. This is deadly serious. I want you to call him *today*.'

Suddenly my beeper sounded. I fumbled for it in my bag and looked at the number. It was the office – Jacobi.

'I need a phone,' I said.

Orenthaler shot me a reproving look.

'Like you said . . .' I forced a nervous smile. 'Therapy.'

He nodded to the phone on his desk and left the room. I went through the motions of dialing my partner.

'Fun's over, Boxer,' Jacobi's gruff voice came on the line. 'We got a double one-eight-oh. The Grand Hyatt.'

My head was spinning with what the doctor had told me. In a fog, I must not have responded.

'You hear me, Boxer?' Jacobi asked. 'Worktime. You on the way?'

'Yeah,' I finally said.

'And wear something nice,' my partner grunted. 'Like you would to a wedding.'

Chapter Five

H ow I got from Dr Orenthaler's office, out in Noe Valley, all the way to the Hyatt in Union Square, I don't remember. I kept hearing the doctor's words sounding over and over in my head. *'In severe cases, Negli's can be fatal.'*

All I know is that barely twelve minutes after Jacobi's call, my ten-year-old Bronco screeched to a halt in front of the hotel's atrium entrance.

The street was ablaze with police activity. Jesus, what the hell had happened? The entire block between Sutter and Union Square had been cordoned off by a barricade of black-and-whites. In the entrance, a cluster of uniforms checked people going in and out, waving the crowd of onlookers away.

I badged my way into the lobby. Two uniformed cops whom I recognized were standing in front: Murray, a potbellied cop in the last year of his hitch, and his younger partner, Vasquez. I asked Murray to bring me up to speed.

'What I been told is that there's two VIPs murdered on the thirtieth floor. All the brainpower's up there now.'

'Who's presiding?' I asked, feeling my energies returning.

'Right now, I guess you are, Inspector.'

'In that case, I want all exits to the hotel immediately shut down. And get a list from the manager of all guests and staff. No one goes in or out unless they're on that list.'

Seconds later, I was riding up to the thirtieth floor.

The trail of cops and official personnel led me down the hall to a set of open double doors marked *Mandarin Suite*. There I ran into Charlie Clapper, the Crime Scene Unit crew chief, lugging in his heavy cases with two techs. Clapper being here himself meant this *was* big.

Through the open double doors, I saw roses first – they were everywhere. Then I spotted Jacobi.

'Watch your heels, Inspector,' he called loudly across the room.

My partner was forty-seven, but looked ten years older. His hair was white and he was beginning to go bald. His face always seemed on the verge of a smirk over some tasteless wisecrack. He and I had worked together for two and a half years. I was senior, Inspector/Sergeant, though he had seven years on me in the Department. He reported to me.

Stepping inside, I almost tripped across the legs of Body Number One, the groom. He was lying just inside the door, crumpled up in a heap, wearing an open tuxedo shirt. Blood matted the hair on his chest. I took a deep breath.

'May I present Mr David Brandt,' Jacobi intoned, with a crooked smile. 'Mrs David Brandt's in there.' He gestured toward the bedroom. 'Guess things went downhill for them quicker than most.'

I knelt down and took a long, hard look at the dead groom. He was handsome, with short, dark, tousled hair and a soft jaw, but the wide, apoplectic eyes locked open and the rivulet of dried blood on his chin marred the features. Behind him, his tuxedo jacket lay on the floor.

'Who found them?' I asked, checking his pocket for a wallet.

'Assistant manager. They were supposed to fly to Bali this morning. The island, not the casino, Boxer. For these two, assistant managers do wake-up calls.'

I opened the wallet: a New York driver's license with the groom's smiling face. Platinum cards, several hundred-dollar bills.

I got up and looked around the suite. It opened up into a stylishly decorated museum of Oriental art: celadon dragons, chairs and couches pictured with Imperial court scenes. The roses, of course. I was more the cozy bed-and-breakfast type, but if you were into making a statement, this was about as substantial a statement as you could make.

'Let's meet the bride,' Jacobi said.

I followed through a set of open double doors into the master bedroom and stopped. The bride lay on her back on a large canopy bed.

I'd been to a hundred homicides and could radar in on

the body as quick as anyone, but this I wasn't prepared for. It sent a wave of compassion racing down my spine.

The bride was still in her wedding dress.

Chapter Six

You never see so many murder victims that it stops making you hurt, but this one was especially hard to look at.

She was so young and beautiful: calm, tranquil, and undisturbed, except for the three crimson flowers of blood spread on her white chest. She looked as if she was a sleeping princess awaiting her prince, but her prince was in the other room, his guts spilled over the floor.

'Whad'ya want for thirty-five hundred bucks a night?' Jacobi shrugged. 'The whole fairy tale?'

It was taking everything I had just to keep my grip on what I had to do. I glared, as if a single, venomous look could shut Jacobi down.

'Jeez, Boxer, what's goin' on?' His face sagged. 'It was just a joke.'

Whatever it was, his childlike, remorseful expression brought me back. The bride was wearing a large diamond on her right hand and fancy earrings on her ears. Whatever the killer's motive, it wasn't robbery.

A tech from the ME's office was about to begin his initial examination. 'Looks like three stab wounds,' he said. 'She must've showed a lot of heart. He got the groom with one.'

What flashed through my mind was that fully 90 per cent of all homicides were about money or sex. This one didn't seem to be about money.

'When's the last time anyone saw them?' I asked.

'A little after ten last night. That's when the humongous reception ended downstairs.'

'And not after that?'

'I know this isn't exactly your terrain, Boxer,' Jacobi said. He broke into a grin. 'But generally people don't see the bride and groom for a while after the party.'

I smiled thinly, stood up, looked back across the large, lavish suite. 'So surprise me, Jacobi. Who springs for a room like this?'

'The groom's father is some Wall Street big shot from back East. He and his wife are down in a room on the twelfth floor. I was told it was quite a shindig downstairs. Up here, too. Look at all these goddamn roses.'

I went back over to the groom, and spotted what looked like a gift box of champagne on a marble console near the door. There was a spray of blood all over it.

'Assistant manager noticed it,' Jacobi said. 'My guess is, whoever did this brought it in with him.'

'They see anyone around?'

'Yeah, a lot of people in tuxes. It was a wedding, right?'

I read the champagne bottle label. 'Krug. Clos du Mesnil, 1989.'

'That tell you something?' Jacobi asked.

'Only that the killer has good taste.'

I looked at the blood-smeared tuxedo jacket. There was a single slash mark on the side where the fatal knife wound had gone through.

'I figure the killer must've stripped it off after he stabbed him,' Jacobi shrugged.

'Why the hell would he do that?' I muttered out loud.

'Dunno. We'll have to ask him.'

Charlie Clapper was eyeing me to see if it was okay to get started. I nodded him in. Then I went back over to the bride. I had a bad, bad feeling about this one. If it's not about money, then it must be to do with sex.

I lifted the fancy tulle lining of her skirt. The coldest, bitterest confirmation sliced through me.

The bride's panties had been pulled down and were dangling off one foot.

A fierce anger rose in my chest. I looked into the young woman's eyes. Everything had been ahead of her, every hope and dream. Now she was a slaughtered corpse, defiled, possibly raped on her wedding night.

As I stood there, blinking, I suddenly realized that I was crying.

'Warren, I want you to speak with the groom's parents,' I said. 'I want everyone who was on this floor last night interviewed. If they've checked out, I want them traced. And a list of all hotel staff on duty last night.'

I knew if I didn't get out now, I couldn't hold back the tide any longer. 'Now, Warren. Please . . . now.'

I avoided his eyes as I skirted past him out of the suite.

'What the hell's wrong with Boxer?' Charlie Clapper asked.

'You know women,' I heard Jacobi reply. 'They always cry at weddings.'

Chapter Seven

Phillip Campbell was walking along Powell Street toward Union Square and the Hyatt. The police had actually blockaded the street and the crowd outside the hotel was growing quickly. The howling screams of police and emergency vehicles filled the air. This was so unlike civilized and respectable San Francisco. He loved it!

Campbell almost couldn't believe he was headed back to the crime scene. He just couldn't help himself. Being here again helped him to relive the night before. As he walked closer and closer on Powell, his adrenaline surged, his heart pounded, almost out of control.

He edged through the mob that populated the final block outside the Hyatt. He heard the rumors swirling through the crowd, mostly well-dressed business people, their faces creased with anguish and pain. There were rumors of a fire at the hotel, a jumper, a homicide, a suicide, but nothing came close to the horror of the actual event.

Finally, he got close enough so that he could watch the San Francisco police at work. A couple of them were surveying the crowd, *looking for him*. He wasn't worried about being discovered, not at all. It just wasn't going to happen. He was too unlikely, probably in the bottom 5 per cent of the people the police might suspect. That comforted him, thrilled him actually.

God, he had done it – caused all of this to happen, and he was only just beginning. He had never experienced anything like this feeling, and neither had the city of San Francisco.

A businessman was coming out of the Hyatt and reporters and other people were asking him questions as if he were a major celebrity. The man was in his early thirties and he smirked knowingly. He had what they all wanted, and he knew it. He was lording it over everyone, enjoying his pitiful moment of fame.

'It was a couple – murdered in the penthouse,' he could overhear the man saying. 'They were on their honeymoon. Sad, huh?'

The crowd around Phillip Campbell gasped, and his heart soared.

Chapter Eight

What a scene! Cindy Thomas pushed her way through the murmuring crowd, the looky-loos surrounding the Grand Hyatt. Then she groaned at the sight of the line of cops blocking the way.

There must've been a hundred onlookers tightly pressed around the entrance: tourists carrying cameras, business-people on their way to work; others were flashing press credentials and shouting, trying to talk their way in. Across the street, a television news van was already setting up with the backdrop of the hotel's façade.

After two years spent covering local interest on the Metro desk of the *Chronicle*, Cindy could feel a story that might jump-start her career. This one made the hairs on her neck stand up.

'Homicide down at the Grand Hyatt,' her city editor, Sid Glass, informed her, after a staffer picked up the police transmission. Suzie Fitzpatrick and Tom Stone, the *Chronicle*'s usual crime reporters, were both on assignment. 'Get right down there,' her boss barked, to her amazement. He didn't have to say it twice.

But now, outside the Hyatt, Cindy felt her brief run of luck had come to an end.

The street was barricaded. More news crews were pulling up by the second. If she didn't come up with something now, Fitzpatrick or Stone would soon be handed the story. What she needed was inside. And here she was, out on the curb.

She spotted a line of limos and went up to the first one – a big beige stretch. She rapped on the window. The driver looked up over his paper, the *Chronicle* of course, and lowered the window as she caught his eye.

'You waiting for Steadman?' Cindy asked.

'Uh-uh,' the driver replied. 'Eddleson.'

'Sorry, sorry,' she waved. But inside she was beaming. *This was her way in.*

She lingered in the crowd a few seconds longer, then elbowed her way to the front. A young patrolman blocked her path. 'Excuse me,' said Cindy, looking harried. 'I've got a meeting in the hotel.'

'Name?'

'Eddleson. He's expecting me.'

The entrance cop paged through a computer printout fastened to a clipboard. 'You have a room number?'

Cindy shook her head. 'He said to meet him in the Grill Room at eleven.' The Grill Room at the Hyatt was the scene of some of San Francisco's best power breakfasts.

The entrance cop gave her a careful once-over. In her black leather jacket, jeans, sandals from Earthsake, Cindy figured she didn't look the part of someone arriving for a power brunch.

'My meeting,' said Cindy, tapping her watch. 'Eddleson.'

Distractedly, the cop waved her through.

She was inside. The high glass atrium rose around her, gold columns reaching to the third floor. It gave her a giggle, all that high-priced talent and recognizable faces still outside on the street.

And Cindy Thomas was first in. Now she only had to figure out what to do.

The place was definitely buzzing: cops, businessmen checking out, tour groups, crimson-suited hotel staff. The chief said it was a homicide. A daring one, given the hotel's prominent reputation. But she didn't know which floor, or when it took place. She didn't even know if it involved a guest.

She may be inside, but she didn't know shit.

Cindy spotted a cluster of suitcases unattended on the far side of the lobby. They looked like they were part of some large tour. A bellhop was dragging them outside. She wandered over and knelt by one of the bags, as if she were taking something out.

A second bellhop passed by. 'Need a taxi?'

Cindy shook her head no. 'Someone's picking me up.' Then, sweeping a view of the chaos, she rolled her eyes. 'I just woke up. What did I miss?'

'You haven't heard? You must be the only one. We had some fireworks in the hotel last night.'

Cindy widened her eyes.

'Two murders. On thirty.' He lowered his voice as if he were letting her in on the secret of her life. 'You happen to run into that big wedding last night? It was the bride and groom. Someone broke in on them in the Mandarin Suite.'

'Jesus!' Cindy pulled back.

'Sure you don't need these brought out to the front?' the bellhop checked.

Cindy forced a smile. 'Thanks. I'll wait in here.'

On the far side of the lobby, she noticed another elevator opening. A bellhop came out, wheeling a cart of luggage. It must be a service elevator. From what she could see, the cops hadn't blocked it off.

She wound through the lobby traffic toward the elevator, punched the button and the shiny gold doors opened. Thank God, it was empty. Just as quickly, Cindy jumped in and the door closed. She couldn't believe it. She couldn't believe what she was doing. She pressed 30.

The Mandarin Suite.

A double homicide.

Her story.

Chapter Nine

As the elevator came to a stop, Cindy held her breath. Her heart was pumping like a turbine. She was on 30. She was in. She was really doing this.

The doors had opened to a remote corner of the floor. She thanked God there wasn't a cop waiting in front of them. A buzz of activity was coming from the other side of the hall. All she had to do was follow the noise.

As she hurried down the hallway, the voices grew louder. Two men in yellow jackets bearing CSU in large black letters walked past her. At the end of a corridor, a group of cops and investigators stood in front of an open double doorway marked *Mandarin Suite*.

She wasn't only inside; she was right in the fucking middle of it.

Squaring her shoulders resolutely, Cindy made her way toward the double doors. The cops weren't even looking in her direction; they were letting in police staff who had come from the main elevators.

She had made it all the way. The Mandarin Suite. She

could see inside. It was huge, opulent. Roses were every-where. Then her heart stopped. She thought she might be sick.

The groom, in a bloodstained tuxedo shirt, lay unmoving on the floor.

Cindy's legs buckled. She had never seen a murder victim before. She wanted to lean forward, to let her eyes memorize every detail, but her body wouldn't move.

'Who the hell are you?' a brusque voice suddenly demanded. A large, angry cop was staring directly at her face.

All of a sudden, she was grabbed and pushed hard against the wall. It hurt. In a panic, Cindy nervously pointed to her bag and her wallet, where a pictured Press credential was displayed.

The angry cop began leafing through her IDs and credit cards as if they were junk mail.

'Jesus,' the thick-necked patrolman scowled with a face like a slobbering Doberman. 'She's a reporter.'

'How in hell did you get up here?' his partner came over and demanded.

'Get her the hell out,' Doberman barked to him. 'And keep the ID. She won't get within a mile of a police briefing for the next twelve months.'

As his partner dragged her by the arm to the main elevator bank, over her shoulder Cindy got a final glimpse of the dead man's legs splayed near the door. It was awful – terrifying, and sad. She was shaking.

'Show this *reporter* the front door,' the officer instructed a third cop manning the elevator. He flicked her Press ID as if it were a playing card. 'Hope losing this was worth the ride up.'

As the doors closed, a voice yelled, '*Hold it!*'

A tall woman in a powder-blue T-shirt and brocade vest with a badge fastened to her waist stepped in. She was nice-looking, with sandy-blonde hair, but she was clearly upset. She let out a deep sigh as the doors closed.

'Rough in there, Inspector?' the cop accompanying Cindy inquired.

'Yeah,' the woman said simply, not even turning her head.

The word 'Inspector' went off like a flash in Cindy's mind. She couldn't believe it. The scene must be beyond awful for an Inspector to be that upset. As the elevator descended, she rode the entire thirty floors just blinking her eyes and looking straight ahead.

When the doors opened to the lobby, the woman in the blue T-shirt rushed off.

'You see the front door?' the cop said to Cindy. 'Go through it. Don't come back.'

As soon as the elevator doors had closed, she spun around and scanned the vast lobby for sight of the Inspector. She caught a flash of her going into the ladies' room.

Cindy hurriedly followed her in. The place was empty – there were just the two of them in there.

The detective stood in front of a mirror. She looked close to six foot tall, slender, and impressive. To Cindy's amazement, it was clear she had been crying. Jesus, Jesus. She was back on the inside again. What had the Inspector seen to get her so upset?

'You okay?' Cindy finally inquired, in a soft voice.

The woman tensed up when she realized she wasn't alone. But she had this look on her face, as if she were on the verge of letting it all out. 'You're that reporter, aren't you? You're the one who got upstairs.'

Cindy let out a breath and nodded.

'So how did you make it all the way up there?'

'I don't know. Luck, maybe.'

The detective pulled out a tissue and dabbed at her eyes. 'Well, I'm afraid your luck's over, if you're looking for something from me.'

'I didn't mean that,' Cindy said. 'You sure you're all right?'

The cop turned around. Her eyes shouted, *'I've got nothing to say to you!'* but they lied. It was as if she needed to do exactly that, talk to someone, more than anything in the world.

It was one of those strange moments when Cindy knew there was something under the surface. If the roles just shifted, and she had the chance, the two of them might even become friends.

Cindy reached into her pocket, pulled out a card, and placed it on the sink counter in front of the detective. 'If ever you want to talk . . .'

The color came back into the Inspector's pretty face. She hesitated, then gave Cindy the faintest glimmer of a smile.

Cindy smiled in return. 'As long as I'm here . . .' She went up to the sink and took out her makeup kit, catching the policewoman's eye in the mirror.

'Nice vest,' she said.

Chapter Ten

I work out of the Hall of Justice. The Hall, as we referred to the gray, ten-story granite slab that housed the city's Department of Justice, was located just west of the freeway on Sixth and Bryant. If the building itself, and its faded antiseptic halls, didn't communicate that law enforcement lacked a total sense of style, the surrounding neighborhood surely did. It consisted of handpainted bailbondsman shacks, autoparts stores, parking lots, and dingy cafés.

Whatever ailed you, you could find at the Hall: Auto Theft, Sex Crimes, Robbery. The District Attorney was on eight, with cubicles filled with bright young prosecutors. A floor of holding cells on ten. One-stop shopping, arrest to arraignment. Next door, we even had the morgue.

After a hasty, bare-bones news conference, Jacobi and I agreed to meet upstairs and go over what we had so far.

The twelve of us who covered Homicide for the entire city shared a twenty-by-thirty squad room lit by the glare of harsh fluorescent lights. My desk was choice – by the window, overlooking the entrance ramp to the freeway. It was always crammed with folders, stacks of photos, Department releases. The one really personal item on it was a Plexiglas cube my first partner had given me. It was inscribed with the words *You can't tell which way the train went by looking at the tracks*.

I made myself a cup of tea and met Jacobi in Interrogation Room One. I drew two columns on a freestanding chalkboard: one for what we knew, one for what we had to check out.

Jacobi's initial talk with the groom's parents had produced nothing. The father was a big-time Wall Street guy who ran a firm that handled international buyouts. He said that he and his wife had stayed until the last guest had left, and 'walked the kids upstairs'. They didn't have an enemy in the world. No debts, addictions, threats. Nothing to provoke such a horrible, unthinkable act.

A canvass of guests on the thirtieth floor was slightly more successful. A couple from Chicago noticed a man lingering in the hallway near the Mandarin Suite last night around ten-thirty. They described him as medium build, with short dark hair and said he wore a dark suit or maybe a tuxedo. He was carrying what may have been a box of liquor in his hands.

Later, two used tea bags and two empty push-through Pepcids on the table were the clearest signs that we'd been bouncing these questions back and forth for several hours. It was quarter past seven. Our shift had ended at five.

'No date tonight, Lindsay?' Jacobi finally asked.

'I get all the dates I want, Warren.'

'Right, like I said – no date tonight.'

Without knocking, our Lieutenant, Sam Roth, whom we called 'Cheery', stuck his head into the room. He tossed a copy of the afternoon *Chronicle* across the table. 'You see this?'

The boldface headline announced: WEDDING NIGHT MASSACRE AT HYATT. I read aloud from the front page: ' "Under a stunning view of the Bay, in a world only the rich would know, the body of the twenty-nine-year-old groom lay curled up near the door." '

He knotted his brow. 'What did we invite this reporter in for – a house tour of the crime scene? She knows the names, maps out the scene.'

The byline read *Cindy Thomas*. I thought of the card in my purse. *Cindy Goddamn Thomas.* 'Maybe I should call her up and ask *her* if we got any leads,' Roth went on sarcastically.

'You want to come on in?' I asked. 'Look at the board. We could use the help.'

Roth just stood there, chewing on his puffy lower lip. He was about to close the door behind him, but he turned back. 'Lindsay, be in my office at a quarter of nine tomorrow. We need to lay this thing out carefully. For now, it's yours.' Then he shut the door.

I sat back on the table. A heavy weight seemed to be pressing me into the floor. The whole day had passed. I hadn't found a single moment to deal with my own news.

'You okay?' Jacobi asked.

I looked at him, on the verge of letting it all out, or maybe crying again.

'That was a tough crime scene,' he said, at the door. 'You should go home, take a bath or something.'

I smiled at him, grateful for a sudden, out-of-character sensitivity.

After he left, I faced the blank columns of the board. I felt so weak and empty I could barely push myself up. Slowly, the events of the day, my visit to Orenthaler, wove their way back into my mind. My head spun with his warning: '*Fatal, Lindsay.*'

Then I was hit with the crushing realization. It was going on eight o'clock, and I had never called Orenthaler's specialist.

Chapter Eleven

That night when I got home, I did sort of take Jacobi's advice.

First, I walked my dog, Sweet Martha. Two of my neighbors take care of Martha during the day, but she's always ready for our nightly romp. After the walk, I kicked off my Aerosole pumps, tossed my gun and clothes on the bed, and took a long, hot shower, bringing in a Killian's with me.

The image of David and Melanie Brandt washed away for the night; they could sleep. But there was still Orenthaler, and Negli's. And the call to the specialist I had dreaded the whole day, and never made.

No matter how many times I lifted my face into the hot spray, I could not rinse the long day away. My life had changed. I was no longer just fighting murderers on the street. I was fighting for my life.

When I got out, I ran a brush through my hair and looked at myself for a long time in the mirror. A thought came into my mind that rarely occurred to me: I was pretty. Not a beauty, but cute. Tall, almost five-ten; decent shape for somebody who occasionally binges on beer and butterscotch praline ice cream. I had these animated, bright brown eyes. I didn't back down.

How could it be that I was going to die?

Tonight, my eyes were different, though. Scared. Everything seemed different. 'Surf the waves,' I heard a voice inside me. 'Stand tall. You always stand tall.'

As much as I tried to press it back, the question formed. *Why me?*

I threw on a pair of sweats, tied up my hair in a short ponytail and went into the kitchen to boil water for pasta and heat up a sauce I had placed in the fridge a couple of nights before. While it simmered I put on a CD, Sarah McLachlan, and sat at the kitchen counter with a glass of day-old Bianco red. I petted Sweet Martha as the music played.

Ever since my divorce became final two years ago, I've lived alone. *I hate living alone.* I love people, friends. I used to love my husband Tom more than life itself – until he left me, saying, 'Lindsay, I can't explain it. I love you, but I have to leave. I need to find somebody else. There's nothing else to say.'

I guess he was being truthful, but it was the dumbest, saddest thing I've ever heard. Broke my heart into a million pieces. It's still broken. So even though I hate living alone – except for Sweet Martha, of course – I'm afraid to be with somebody again. What if they suddenly stop loving me? I couldn't take it. So I turn down, or shoot down, just about every man who comes anywhere near me.

But God, I hate being alone.

Especially this night.

My mother had died from breast cancer when I was just out of college. I had transferred back to the city school from Berkeley to assist her, and help take care of my younger sister, Cat. Like most things in her life, even Dad walking out, Mom dealt with her illness only when it was too late to do anything about it.

I had seen my father only twice since I was thirteen. He wore a uniform for twenty years in Central. Was known as a pretty good cop. He used to go down to this bar, the Alibi, and stay for the Giants game after his shift. Sometimes he took me, 'his little mascot', for the boys to admire.

When the sauce was ready I poured it over fusilli and dragged the plate and a salad out to my terrace. Martha tagged along. She's been my shadow since I adopted her from the Border Collie Rescue Society. I live on Potrero Hill, in a renovated blue Michaelian townhouse with a view of the Bay. Not the fancy view like the one from the Mandarin Suite.

I propped my feet up on a neighboring chair and balanced the plate on my lap. Across the Bay, the lights of Oakland glimmered like a thousand unsympathetic eyes.

I looked out at the galaxy of flashing lights, felt my

eyes well up, and for the second time today, realized that I was crying. Martha nuzzled me gently, then she finished the fusilli for me.

Chapter Twelve

Quarter to nine the next morning, I was rapping at the fogged window of Lieutenant Roth's office at the Hall. Roth is fond of me – I'm like another daughter, he says. He has no idea how condescending he can be. I'm tempted to tell Roth that I'm fond of him, too – *like a grandfather*.

I was expecting a crowd – at least a couple of suits from Internal Affairs, or maybe Captain Welting, who oversaw the Bureau of Inspectors – but, as he motioned me in, there was only one other person in the room.

The stranger was a nice-looking type dressed in a chambray shirt and striped tie, with short, dark hair and strong shoulders. He had a handsome, intelligent face that seemed to come to life as I walked in, but it only meant one thing to me:

Polished brass. Someone from the Department's press corps, or City Hall.

I had the uneasy feeling they'd been talking about me.

On the way over, I had rehearsed a convincing rebuttal

about the breach in press security – how I'd arrived late on the scene myself, and the real issue was the crime. But Roth surprised me. ' "Wedding Bell Blues", they're calling it,' he said, tossing the morning's *Chronicle* in my face.

'I saw it,' I replied, relieved to focus back on the case.

He looked at Mr City Hall. 'We'll be reading about this one every step of the way. Both kids were rich, Ivy League, popular. Sort of like young Kennedy and that blonde wife of his – their tragedy.'

'Who they were doesn't matter to me,' I answered back. 'Listen, Sam, about yesterday . . .'

He stopped me with his hand. 'Forget about yesterday. Chief Mercer's already been on the line with me. This case has his full attention.' He glanced at the smartly dressed political type in the corner. 'Anyway, he wants there to be close reins on this case. What happened on other high-profile investigations can't happen here.' Then he said to me, 'We're changing the rules on this one.'

Suddenly, the air in the room got thick with the uneasy feel of a set-up.

Then Mr City Hall stepped forward. I noticed his eyes bore the experienced lines of someone who had put in his time. 'The Mayor and Chief Mercer thought we might handle this investigation as an interdepartmental alliance. That is, if you were up to working with someone new,' he said.

'New?' My eyes bounced back and forth between the two, ultimately settling on Roth.

'Meet your new partner,' Roth announced.

'I'm getting royally screwed,' the voice inside me declared. 'They wouldn't do this to a man.'

'Chris Raleigh,' Mr City Hall Hotshot said, extending his hand.

I didn't reach out to take it.

'For the past few years,' Roth went on, 'Inspector Raleigh has worked as a Community Action liaison with the Mayor's office. He specializes in managing potentially sensitive cases.'

'Managing?'

Raleigh rolled his eyes at me. He was trying to be self-effacing. 'Containing . . . controlling the damage . . . healing any wounds in the community afterwards.'

'Oh,' I shot back, 'I see. You're a marketing man.'

He smiled. Every part of him oozed a practiced, confident air I associated with the types who sat around large tables at City Hall.

'Before that,' Roth went on, 'Chris was a District Captain over in Northern.'

'That's Embassy Row,' I sniffed. Everybody joked about the blue-blooded Northern district that ranged from Nob Hill to Pacific Heights. Hot crimes there were society women who heard noises outside their townhouses and late-arriving tourists locked out of their bed and breakfasts.

'We also handled traffic around the Presidio,' Raleigh countered with another smile.

I ignored him. I turned to Roth. 'What about Warren?' He and I had shared every case for the past two years.

'Jacobi'll be reassigned. I've got a plum job for him, and his big mouth.'

I didn't like leaving my partner behind, dumb-ass wise-cracks and all. But Jacobi was his own worst enemy.

To my surprise, Raleigh asked, 'You okay with this, Inspector?'

I didn't really have a choice. I nodded yes. 'If you don't get in the way. Besides, you wear nicer ties than Jacobi.'

'Father's Day present,' he beamed. I couldn't believe I felt a tremor of disappointment shooting through me. Jesus, Lindsay. I didn't see a ring. *Lindsay!*

'I'm taking you off all other assignments,' Roth announced. 'No conflicting obligations. Jacobi can handle the back-end, if he wants to stay on the case.'

'So who's in charge?' I asked Cheery. I was senior partner to Jacobi; I was used to running my own cases.

Cheery chortled, 'He works with the Mayor. He's an ex-District Captain. Who do you think's in charge?'

'How about – in the field, you lead?' Raleigh suggested. 'What we do with what we find is mine.'

I hesitated, giving him an evaluating stare. God, he was so smooth.

Roth looked at me. 'You want me to ask Jacobi if he's got similar reservations?'

Raleigh met my eyes. 'Look, I'll let you know when we can't work it out.'

It was as good a negotiation as I was going to get. The deal had changed. But at least I kept my case. 'So what do I call you? Captain?'

With a casual ease, Raleigh wrapped a light brown sports coat over his shoulder and reached for the door. 'Try my name. I've been a civilian now for five years.'

'Okay, Raleigh,' I said, with a faint smile. 'You ever get to see a dead body while you were in Northern?'

Chapter Thirteen

The joke in Homicide about the morgue was that in spite of the lousy climate, the place was good for business. There's nothing like the sharp smell of formaldehyde or the depressing sheen of hospital-tiled halls to make the drudgery of chasing down dead leads seem like inspired work.

But as they say, that's where the bodies are.

That, and I got to see my buddy, Claire.

There wasn't much to say about Claire Washburn, except that she was brilliant, totally accomplished, and absolutely my best friend in the world. For six years, she had been the city's Chief Medical Examiner, which everyone in Homicide knew was as under-deserving a title as there was, since she virtually ran the office for Anthony Righetti. Righetti is her overbearing, power-thumping, credit-stealing boss, but Claire rarely complains.

In our book, Claire is the Office of the Coroner. Maybe the idea of a female ME still didn't cut it, even in San Francisco.

Female, and black.

When Raleigh and I arrived, we were ushered into Claire's office. She was wearing her white doctor's coat with the nickname *Butterfly* embroidered on the upper-left pocket.

The first thing you noticed about Claire was that she was carrying fifty pounds she didn't need, and had, since the day I met her. 'I'm in shape,' she always laughed. 'Round's a shape.'

The second was her bright, confident demeanor. You knew she couldn't give a damn. She had the body of a Brahman, the mind of a hawk, *and* the gentle soul of a butterfly.

As we walked in, she gave me a weary but satisfied smile, as if she'd been up working most of the night. I introduced Raleigh, and Claire flashed me an impressed wag of the eyes.

Whatever I had accumulated over the years in street smarts, she threw off in natural wisdom. How she balanced the demands of her job, and placating her credit-seeking boss, with raising two teenage kids was a marvel. And her marriage to Edmund, who played bass drum for the San Francisco Symphony Orchestra, gave me faith that the institution still had some hope.

'I've been expecting you,' she said as we hugged. 'I called you last night from here. Didn't you get the message?'

With her comforting arms around me, a flood of emotion welled up. I wanted to tell her everything. If it weren't for Raleigh, I think I would've spilled it all out –

Orenthaler, Negli's – right there.

'I was beat,' I answered back. 'And beat up. Long, tough day.'

'Don't tell me,' Raleigh chuckled, 'you guys have met.'

'Standard autopsy preparation,' grinned Claire, as we pulled apart. 'Don't they teach you that stuff down at City Hall?'

He playfully spread his arms.

'Uh-uh,' said Claire, squeezing my shoulder, 'this you gotta earn. Anyway,' she regained a tone of seriousness, 'I finished the preliminaries just this morning. You want to see the bodies?'

I nodded yes.

'Just be prepared, these two don't make much of an advertisement for *Modern Bride*.'

She led us through a series of closed compression doors towards the Vault, the large refrigerated room where the bodies were stored.

I walked ahead with Claire, who pulled me close and whispered, 'Let me guess. You gave Jacobi a kiss on the nose, and all of a sudden this charming prince appeared.'

'He works for the Mayor, Claire,' I smiled back. 'They sent him here to make sure I don't faint at the first sign of blood.'

'In that case,' she replied, pushing the heavy door to the Vault open, 'you better hold on tight to that man.'

Chapter Fourteen

I had been having very close encounters with dead bodies for six years now. But what I saw sent a shiver of revulsion racing through me.

The mutilated bodies of the bride and groom were lying side by side. They were on retractable gurneys, their faces frozen in the horrifying moment of their deaths.

David and Melanie Brandt.

In their stark, ghostly expressions was the strongest statement I have ever seen that life may not be governed by anything fair or clement. I locked on the face of Melanie. Yesterday, in her wedding dress, she had seemed somehow tragic and tranquil. Today, in her slashed, naked starkness, her body was snarled in a freeze-frame of grotesque horror. Everything I had buried deep yesterday rushed to the surface.

Six years in Homicide, and I had never turned away. But I turned away now.

I felt Claire bolstering my arm, and leaned into it. To my surprise, it turned out to be Raleigh. I righted myself with a mixture of anger and embarrassment. 'Thanks,' I exhaled. 'I'm okay.'

'I've been doing this job eight years,' Claire said quietly, 'and this one, I wanted to turn away myself.'

She picked up a folder on an examining table across from David Brandt, then pointed to the raw, gaping knife wound on the left side of his chest. 'He was stabbed once in the right ventricle. You can see here how the blade pierced the juncture between the fourth rib and the sternum on the way in. Ruptured the A-V node, which provides the heart's electrical powering. Technically, he arrested.'

'He died of a heart attack?' Raleigh asked.

She pulled a pair of tight surgical gloves over her hands and red-lacquered nails. 'Electro-mechanical dissociation. Just a fancy way of describing what happens when you get stabbed in the heart.'

'What about the weapon?' I spoke up.

'At this point, all I know is that it was a standard, straight-edged blade. No distinguishing marks or entry pattern. One thing I can tell you is that the killer was of medium height – anywhere from five-seven to five-ten – and right-handed, based on the angle of impact. You can see here the path of the incision is angled slightly upwards. Here,' she said, poking around the wound. 'The groom was six feet. On his wife, who was five-five, the angle of the first incision was slanted in a downward path.'

I checked the groom's hands and arms for abrasions. 'Any signs of a struggle?'

'Couldn't. The poor man was scared right out of his mind.'

I nodded, as my eyes fell on the groom's face.

Claire shook her head. 'That's not exactly what I meant. Charlie Clapper's boys scraped up samples of a fluid from the groom's shoes and the hardwood floor in the foyer where he was found.' She held up a small vial containing droplets of a cloudy liquid.

Raleigh and I stared at it, uncomprehending.

'Urine,' explained Claire. 'The poor man apparently went in his pants. Must have been a gusher.' She pulled the white sheet back over David Brandt's face and shook her head. 'I figure that's one secret we can keep to ourselves.

'Unfortunately,' she sighed, 'things didn't happen nearly as swiftly for the bride.' She led us over to the bride's gurney. 'Maybe she surprised him. There are marks on her hands and wrists that indicate a struggle. Here,' she pointed to a reddened abrasion on her neck. 'I tried to lift some tissue from under her nails, but we'll see what comes back. Anyway, the first wound was in the upper abdomen and tore through the lungs. With time, given the loss of blood, she might have died from that.'

She pointed to a second and third ugly incision under the left breast in a similar location as the groom's. 'Her pericardium was filled with so much blood you could've wrung it out like a wet dishrag.'

'You're getting technical again,' I said.

'The tissue-like membrane around the heart. Blood collects in this space and compresses the muscle so that the heart can no longer fill with blood from the main return. Ultimately, it ends up strangling itself.'

The image of the bride's heart choking on her own blood chilled me. 'It's almost as if he wanted to duplicate the wounds,' I said, studying the knife-entry points.

'I thought of that,' said Claire. 'Straight line to the heart.'

Raleigh furrowed his brow. 'So the killer could be professional?'

Claire shrugged. 'By the technical pattern of the wounds, perhaps. But I don't think so.'

There was a hesitancy in her voice. I looked up and fixed on her grim eyes. 'So what I need to know is, was she sexually molested?'

She swallowed. 'There are clear signs of some sort of post-mortem penetration. The vaginal mucosa was severely extended, and I found small lacerations around the introitus.'

My body stiffened in rage. 'So she was raped.'

'*If* she was raped,' Claire replied, 'it was a very bad deal. The vaginal cavity was as wide as I've ever seen it. Honestly, I don't think we're talking penile entry at all.'

'Blunt instrument?' Raleigh asked.

'Possibly . . . but there are abrasions along the vaginal walls consistent with some kind of ring.' Claire took in a breath. 'Personally, I'd go with a fist.'

The angry, shocking nature of Melanie Brandt's death made me shiver again. A fist. It had a savage finality to it. Her assailant wasn't just trying to act out his nightmare, he wanted to shame her as well. Why?

'If you can handle one more, follow me,' Claire said.

She led us out through a swinging door into an adjoining lab. On an apron of white sterile paper lay the blood-smeared tuxedo jacket we had found next to the groom.

Claire picked it up by the collar. 'Clapper loaned it to me. Of course, the obvious thing was to confirm whose blood was actually on it.'

The left front panel was slashed through with the fatal incision and sprayed with dark blotches of blood. 'This is where it starts to get really interesting,' Claire informed us. 'You see, it wasn't just David Brandt's blood that I found on the front of the jacket.'

Raleigh and I gaped in surprise.

'The killer's?' he said, wide-eyed.

She shook her head. 'No – the bride's.'

I made a fast mental recollection of the crime scene. The groom had been killed at the door; his wife, thirty feet away in the master bedroom.

'How could the bride's blood get on his jacket?' I said, confused.

'I struggled with the same thing. So I went back and lined up the jacket against the groom's torso. The slash mark didn't quite match up with his wound. Look, the groom's wound was here. Fourth rib. The slash marks on the jacket are three inches higher. Checking further, the damned jacket isn't even the same brand as the pants. This is Joseph Abboud.'

Claire winked, seeing the gears of my brain shift into place.

The jacket wasn't the groom's. It belonged to the man who killed him.

Claire rounded her eyes. 'Ain't no professional I know would leave that behind.'

'He could've been just trying to utilize the wedding as a cover,' Raleigh replied.

An even more chilling possibility had already struck me. 'He could have been a guest.'

Chapter Fifteen

At the offices of the *San Francisco Chronicle*, Cindy Thomas's frantic brain was just barely staying ahead of her fingers.

The afternoon deadline was only an hour away.

From the bellhop at the Hyatt, she had been able to obtain the names of two guests who had attended the Brandt wedding and who were still at the hotel. After running down there again last night, she was able to put together a heart-wrenching, tragic account – complete with vows, toasts, and a romantic last dance – of the bride and groom's final agonizing moments.

All the other reporters were still piecing together the sparse details released by the police. But she was ahead so far. She was winning, and it felt great. She was also certain this was the best writing she'd done since arriving at the *Chronicle*, and maybe since she'd been an undergraduate at Michigan.

At the paper, Cindy's coup at the Hyatt had turned her into an instant celebrity. People she scarcely knew were

suddenly stopping and congratulating her. Even the pub-
lisher, whom she rarely saw on the Metro floor, came
down to find out who she was.

Metro was covering some demonstration in Mill Valley
about a construction rerouting that had built up traffic near
a school zone.

She was writing the front page.

As she typed, she noticed Sidney Glass, her city editor,
coming up to her desk. Glass was known at the newspaper
as El Sid. He parked himself across from her with a stiff
sigh. 'We need to talk.'

Her fingers slowly settled to a halt as she looked up.

'I've got two very pissed-off senior crime reporters itch-
ing to get into this. Suzie's at City Hall awaiting a statement
by the Police Chief and the Mayor. Stone's put together
profiles on both families. They have twenty years and two
Pulitzers between them. And it is their beat.'

Cindy felt her heart nearly come to a stop. 'What did you
tell them?' she asked.

In El Sid's hardened eyes, she could see the greedy jaws
of the first-team crime staff, senior reporters with their
own researchers trying to elbow their way in and carve this
story up. *Her* story.

'Show me what you've got,' the city editor finally said.
He got up, peered over her shoulder, read a few lines off
the computer screen. 'A lot of it's okay. You probably know
that. "Anguished" belongs over here,' he pointed out. 'It
modifies "bride's father". Nothing pisses Ida Morris off like
misplaced modifiers and inversions.'

Cindy could feel herself blushing. 'I know, I know. I'm trying to get this in. Deadline's at—'

'I know when deadline is,' the editor glowered. 'But down here, if you can get it in, you can get it in right.'

He studied Cindy for what seemed an interminable duration, a deep, assessing stare that kept her on edge.

'Especially if you intend to stay on this thing.' Glass's generally implacable face twitched, and he *almost* smiled at her. 'I told them it was yours, Thomas.'

Cindy repressed an urge to hug the cranky, domineering editor right on the bullpen floor. 'You want me at City Hall?' she asked.

'The real story's in that hotel suite. Go back to the Hyatt.'

El Sid, his hands, as always, thrust into his trouser pockets, began to walk away.

But a moment later, he turned back. ''Course, if you intend to stay on this story, you'd better find a police source on the inside – and quick.'

Chapter Sixteen

A fter leaving the morgue, Raleigh and I walked back to the office, mostly in silence. Lots of details about the murders were bothering me. Why would the killer take away the victim's jacket? Why leave the champagne bottle? It made no sense.

'We've got a sex crime now. Bad one.' I finally turned to him on the asphalt walkway leading to the Hall. 'I want to run the autopsy results through Milt Fanning and the FBI computers. We also need to meet with the bride's parents. We'll need a history on anyone she may have been involved with before David. And a list of everyone at that wedding.'

'Why don't we wait for some confirmation on that one,' my new partner said, 'before we go all out on that angle.'

I stopped walking and stared at him. 'You want to see if anybody checked in for a bloody jacket with Lost and Found? I don't understand. What's your concern?'

'My concern,' Raleigh said, 'is that I don't want the Department intruding on the grief of the families with a lot of hypotheticals until we have more to go on. We may or may not have the killer's jacket. He may or may not have been a guest.'

'Who do you think it belonged to – the rabbi?'

He flashed me a quick smile. 'It could've been left there to set us off.'

His tone seemed suddenly different. 'You're backing off?'

'I'm not backing off,' he said. 'But until we have a lead of some sort, every old boyfriend of the bride or casualty of some corporate downsizing Gerald Brandt had a hand in could be rolled out as a possible suspect. I'd rather the spotlight wasn't aimed back at them unless we have something firm to go on.'

Here it was. The spiel. Packaging, containment. Brandt and Chancellor Weil were VIPs. Find us the bad guys, Lindsay. Just don't put the Department at any risk along the way.

I chuffed back, 'I thought the possibility that the killer could've been at that wedding *was* what we had to go on.'

'All I'm suggesting, Lindsay, is let's get some confirmation before we begin ripping into the sexlife of the best man.'

I nodded, all the while fixing in on his eyes. 'In the meantime, *Chris*, we'll just follow up on our *other* really strong leads.'

We stood there in edgy silence.

'All right, why do you think the killer changed jackets with the groom?' I asked him.

He leaned back against the edge of a stone retaining

wall. 'My guess is that he was wearing it when he killed them. It was covered with blood. He had to get out undetected. The groom's jacket was lying around. So he just switched.'

'So you figure he went to all that trouble making the slash marks and all, thinking no one would notice. Different size, different maker. That it would just slip by. Raleigh, *why did he leave it behind*? Why wouldn't he stuff the bloody jacket into a bag? Or roll it under his new jacket?'

'Okay,' Raleigh sighed. 'I don't know. Your guess is?'

I didn't know why he had left it behind, but a chilling idea was beginning to form in the back of my mind. 'Possibility one,' I answered, 'he panicked. Maybe the phone rang or someone knocked at the door.'

'On their wedding night?'

'You're starting to sound like my *ex*-partner.'

I started toward the Hall, and he caught up. He held the glass doors open for me. As I walked through, he took my arm. 'And number two?'

I stood there, staring squarely into his eyes, trying to assess just how far I could go with him. 'What's your real expertise here, anyway?' I asked.

He smiled, his look confident and secure. 'I used to be married.'

I didn't reply. Possibility two: the killer was signing his murders. He was toying with us – purposely leaving clues. One-off crime-of-passion killers didn't leave clues like the jacket. Professionals didn't, either.

Serial killers left clues.

Chapter Seventeen

The window that Phillip Campbell was staring out of had a startling view of the Bay, but he didn't really notice the sights. He was lost in his thoughts.

It's finally started. Everything is in play, he was thinking. The city on the Bay will never be the same, will it? I will never be the same. This was complicated – not what it seemed to be but beautiful in its own way.

He had closed his office door, as he always did when he was absorbed in research. Lately, he had stopped catching lunch with his co-workers. They bored him. Their lives were filled with petty concerns. The stock market. The Giants and 49ers. Where they were headed on vacation. They had such shallow, simple, middle-class dreams. His were soaring. He was like the moguls thinking up their new, new things over in Silicon Valley.

Anyway, that was all in the past. Now, he had a secret. The biggest secret in the world.

He pushed his business papers to the corner of his desk.

This is the old world, he thought. The old me. The bore. The worker bee.

He unlocked the top left drawer of his desk. Behind the usual personal clutter was a small, gray lockbox. It was barely large enough to hold a packet of three- by five-inch cards.

This is my world now.

He thought back to the Hyatt. The bride's beautiful porcelain face, the blossoms of blood on her chest. He still couldn't believe what had taken place. The sharp *crack* of the knife ripping through cartilage. The gasp of her last breath. And his, of course.

What were their names? Oh Jesus Christ, he'd forgotten. No, he hadn't! The Brandts. They were all over the newspapers and the TV news.

With a key off his chain, he opened the small box. What spilled out into the room was the intoxicating spell of his dreams.

A stack of index cards. Neat and orderly. Alphabetically arranged. One by one, he skimmed through them. New names ... *DeGeorge* ... *King* ... *Merced* ... *Passeneau* ... *Peterson*.

All the brides and grooms.

Chapter Eighteen

Several urgent messages were on my desk when I got back from the morgue. Good – urgent was appropriate.

Charlie Clapper from CSU. Preliminary report in. Some reporters – from the AP, local television stations. Even the woman from the *Chronicle* who had left me her card.

I picked at a grilled chicken and pear salad I had brought up as I dialed Clapper back. 'Only good news, please,' I joked, as his voice came on the phone.

'In that case, I can give you a nine hundred number. For two bucks a minute they'll tell you anything you want to hear.'

I could hear it in the tone of his voice. 'You got nothing?'

'Tons of partials, Lindsay,' the CSU chief sighed, meaning inconclusive prints his team had lifted from the room. 'The bride's, the groom's, the assistant manager's, housekeeping's.'

'You dusted the bodies?' I pressed. The killer had pulled

Melanie Brandt up off the floor. 'And the box of champagne?'

'Of course. Nothing. Somebody was careful.'

'What about off the floor? Fibers, shoeprints?'

'Besides the pee.' Clapper laughed. 'You think I'm holding out on you? You're cute, Lindsay, but I get off on bagging killers more. Meanwhile, I've got someone running that tux under the microscope. I'll let you know. Roger Wilco.'

'Thanks, Charlie,' I muttered disappointedly.

Flipping further through my stack of messages, Cindy Thomas's name came to the top. I wasn't normally in the habit of phoning back reporters in the middle of an ongoing investigation, but this one had been smart and cool making her way up to the crime scene, yet kind in backing off when she had me cornered in the bathroom.

I found her at her desk. 'Thanks for calling me back, Inspector,' she said, in an appreciative tone.

'I owe you, I guess. Thanks for cutting me some slack at the hotel.'

'Happens to us all. But I have to ask, do you always react so personally at a crime scene? You're a homicide detective, right?'

I didn't have the time or heart to get into a battle of wits, so I used Jacobi's line. 'It was a wedding – I always cry at them. What can I do for you, Ms Thomas?'

'Please, call me Cindy. Actually, I'm about to do you another favor. When I reach five, maybe you'll do one for me.'

'This is a homicide we have here, a very bad one. We're not going to play Let's Make a Deal. And if we meet again, you'll find I'm not at my cheeriest when I feel indebted.'

'I guess that's what I was hoping for,' she admitted. 'I wanted to hear your spin on the bride and groom.'

'Doesn't Tom Stone cover homicide for the *Chronicle*?' I asked.

I heard her take in a breath. 'I won't lie to you. I normally handle Local Interest out of Metro.'

'Well, you got yourself a real story now. MARRIAGE MADE IN HEAVEN ENDS UP IN HELL. You're quick out of the gate.'

'Truth is, Inspector,' her voice grew softer, 'I'd never seen anything like that before. Seeing David Brandt lying there, on his wedding night . . . I know what you must think, but it's not just about the story. I'd like to help any way I can.'

'I appreciate that, but since we've got all these eager people with badges walking around here, we ought to give them a shot, don't you think? Anyway, you should know that you sneaking your way up to the thirtieth floor didn't exactly get me invited to the Commissioner's for brunch. I had tactical responsibility at the crime scene.'

'I never thought I'd actually make it through.'

'So we've established we don't know who owes whom here. But since it's my dime . . .'

The reporter's voice took on a businesslike tone. 'I called to get your reaction to a story we're going to break later today. You know the groom's father runs a buyout firm. Our business editor pulled off Bloomberg that they backed out of a proposed agreement at the last minute with the third largest Russian automaker, Kolya-Novgorod. Brandt was providing up to two hundred million dollars for a significant stake. Kolya's one of those Russian conglomerates taken over by a new branch of black-market capitalists. Without the cash, I'm told it's virtually bankrupt. My source tells me the mood got very fractious.'

I laughed. 'Fractious, Ms Thomas? I might be getting a little fractious myself.'

'Apparently, some of the Russians were left hanging with their Uncle Vanyas out.'

I smiled again. 'Conspiracy to commit murder is a federal crime,' I told her. 'If there's something to it, you should make the call to Justice.'

'I just thought I'd let you know. In the meantime, you want to throw me a comment on any other possibilities you're looking into?'

'Sure. I'd feel safe in saying that they're "ongoing".'

'Thanks,' she sighed. 'Have you narrowed into any other suspects yet?'

'This is what they tell you to ask at the *Chronicle*? You know I can't divulge that.'

'Off the record. No attribution. As a friend.'

As I listened, I remembered when I was a recruit trying to elbow my way in. How the police world was barred, closed off, until someone opened up the tiniest crack to let me crawl through. 'Like I said, Ms Thomas,' my tone was less severe now, 'no promises.'

'Cindy,' the reporter said. 'At least call me Cindy. For the next time you get cornered in the bathroom with your guard down.'

'Okay, *Cindy*. I'll be sure to keep you in mind.'

Chapter Nineteen

I didn't want to go home. And I knew I couldn't stay at the Hall any longer. I grabbed my bag, rushed down to the underground garage, started up my trusty-dusty Bronco without a clear sense of where I was headed, then I just drove – Fourth, Third, on Mission, past the Moscone Center – cafés, closed-up shops. All the way down toward the Embarcadero.

I wrapped around Battery, heading away from the Bay. I had nowhere to go, but my hands seemed to act on their own, leading me somewhere. Flashes of the murdered bride and groom flickered in my head. Echoes of Orenthaler. I had finally called Dr Medved for an appointment.

I was approaching Sutter, and I turned. Suddenly, I knew where I was heading. I pulled onto Powell, close to Union Square, and within minutes I found myself in front of the brightly lit entrance of the Hyatt.

I badged the manager, and took the elevator up to the thirtieth floor.

A single uniformed guard sat in front of the Mandarin

Suite. I recognized him – it was David Hale out of Central. He stood up as he saw me approach. 'Nowhere to go, Inspector?'

A crisscrossing barrier of yellow tape blocked the entrance to the Mandarin Suite. Hale gave me the key. I peeled off a band or two and slipped under the rest. I turned the lock and I was inside.

If you've never wandered alone at the site of a freshly committed murder, you don't really know the feeling of restless unease. The room seemed to whisper with the dark ghosts of David and Melanie Brandt.

I was sure I had missed something. I was also sure it was here. *What could it be?*

The suite was pretty much as I left it two days before. The Oriental carpet in the living room was gone to Clapper's lab, but body positions and blood sites were clearly marked out with blue chalk.

I looked at the spot where David Brandt had died. In my mind, I retraced what had likely taken place.

They are toasting each other. I knew that from the half-filled champagne glasses on a table near the terrace. Maybe he just gave her the earrings. The open box was on the master bathroom counter.

There's a knock. David Brandt goes to answer. I could feel secrets buzzing in the thick air, alive with horror.

The killer comes in, carrying the wine. Maybe David knows him – maybe he just left him an hour before at the reception. The knife comes out. Only one thrust. The groom is pinned against the door, apoplectic. It happens so fast that he cannot scream. 'Poor man pees right in his pants,' Claire had said.

Where is the bride? Maybe she's in the bathroom. (The jewelry box.) Maybe she went to put on the earrings.

The killer hunts through the suite. He intercepts the bride, coming out unsuspectingly.

I envision Melanie Brandt – radiant, full of joy. He sees it, too. Was it someone she knew? Had she just left him? Did Melanie know her killer?

There's a Navajo saying, Even the still wind has a voice. In the quiet, confessing hotel room, I listen.

Tell me, Melanie. *I am here for you.* I'm listening.

My skin tingles with the chill of resurrecting each detail of the murder. She fights, tries to run away. (The bruises and small abrasions on her arms and neck.) The killer stabs her at the foot of the bed. He is horrified, yet wildly excited about what he has done. She doesn't die immediately. He has no choice. He has to stab her again. And once more.

When he is finished, he carries her to the bed. Carries, not drags. There is no sign of blood trailing behind. This is important. He is gentle with her. It makes me think he knows her.

Maybe he once loved Melanie? He folds her arms on her waist in a restful pose. A princess sleeping. Maybe he pretends what has taken place is only a bad dream.

Nowhere in the room do I feel the clinical pattern of professionals or hired killers. Or even someone who has killed before.

I'm listening.

A ferocious anger rises up in his blood. He realizes he will never see her again. His princess . . .

He's so angry. He wants to lie down with her this one time. Feel her. But he cannot – that would defile her. Yet he must have her! So he lifts her dress. Uses his fist.

It is all screaming at me, but I'm sure there is one last thing I am not seeing. What am I missing? What has everyone missed so far?

I step over to the bed. I picture Melanie, her horrifying stab wounds, but her face is calm, unaccusing. He leaves her like that. He doesn't take the earrings. He doesn't take the huge diamond ring.

Then it hit me with the power of a train exploding from a dark tunnel!

Rings.

I ran my mind over the mental image of her lying there. Her delicate, blood-smeared hands. *The diamond was still there, but . . . Jesus! Was it possible?*

I ran back to the door and brought to mind the crumpled body of the groom.

They were married just a few hours before. They had just completed their vows. But they weren't wearing gold bands.

Wedding rings.

The killer doesn't take the earrings, I realized.

He takes the rings.

Chapter Twenty

Nine the next morning, I was in the office of Dr Victor Medved, a pleasant, smallish man with a narrow, chiseled face who, with a trace of an Eastern European accent, scared the hell out of me.

'Negli's is a killer,' he stated evenly. 'It robs the body of its ability to transport oxygen. In the beginning, the symptoms are listlessness, a weakening of the immune system, and some light-headedness. Ultimately, you may experience similar brain dysfunction to a stroke and begin to lose mental capacity as well.'

He got up, walked over to me, cradled my face in his gentle hands. He stared at me through thick glasses. 'You're already looking peaked,' he said, pressing my cheeks with his thumbs.

'Always takes me a while for the blood to get hopping in the mornings,' I said with a smile, trying to mask the fear in my heart.

'Well, in three months,' Dr Medved said, 'unless we reverse it, you will look like a ghost. A pretty ghost, but a ghost all the same.' He went back to his desk and picked up my chart. 'I see you are a police detective.'

'Homicide,' I told him.

'Then there should be no reason to go forward under any delusions. I don't mean to upset you – aplastic anemia *can* be reversed. Up to thirty per cent of patients respond to a regimen of bi-weekly transfusions of packed red blood cells. Of those who do not respond, a similar percentage can be ultimately treated through a bone-marrow transfer. But this involves a painful process of chemotherapy first in order to boost up the white cells.'

I stiffened. Orenthaler's nightmarish predictions were coming true. 'Is there any way to know who responds to the treatment?'

Medved clasped his palms together and shook his head. 'The only way is to begin. Then we see.'

'I'm on an important case. Dr Orenthaler said I could continue to work.'

Medved pursed his lips skeptically. 'You may continue as long as you feel the strength.'

I had a moment of despair. How long could I hide this? Who could I tell? 'If it works, will there be a rapid improvement?' I asked with some hope.

He frowned. 'This is not like popping aspirin for a headache. I'm afraid we're in this for the long haul.'

The long haul. I thought of Roth's likely response. My chances at Lieutenant.

This is it, Lindsay. This is the greatest challenge of your life.

'And if it doesn't work, how long before things start to . . .'

'Start to get worse? Let us attack this with optimism and hope. We'll discuss that as we go along.'

Everything was thrown open now. The case, my career, all the goals of my life. The stakes had changed. I was walking around with a time bomb ticking in my chest, tightly wound, incendiary. And the fuse was disappearing slowly.

I closed my eyes briefly, then asked, 'When do we start?'

He scribbled down the details of an office in the same building. Third floor. Moffet Outpatient Services. There was no date.

'If it's all the same to you,' he said, 'I'd like to start right now.'

Chapter Twenty-One

The story about Gerald Brandt's aborted business deal with the Russian car manufacturers had broken. It was on every newsstand – bold headline reading GROOM'S FATHER MAY HAVE TRIGGERED RUSSIAN WRATH.

The *Chronicle* reported that the FBI was seriously looking into the matter. *Great.*

Two half-liter bags of hemoglobin-enriched blood were pumping through me as I finally reached my desk about ten-thirty. It took everything I had to push the image of the' thick, crimson blood slowly dripping into my veins from my mind.

When Roth called my name, the usual disgruntled glower was all over his face. '*Chronicle* says it's the Russians. The FBI seems to agree.' He leaned over my desk and thrust a copy of the morning's paper at me.

'I saw it. Don't let the FBI in on this,' I said. 'This is our case.'

I told him about last night, my going back to the crime scene. How I was pretty sure the sexual assault on the corpse, the bloody jacket, the missing rings, added up to a single, obsessed killer.

'It's not some Russian professional. He put his fist inside her,' I reminded him. 'He did this on her wedding night.'

'You want me to tell the Feds to back off,' Roth said, 'because you have strong feelings about the case?'

'This is a *murder* case. A kinky, very nasty sex crime, not some international conspiracy.'

'Maybe the Russian killer needed proof. Or maybe he *was* a sex maniac.'

'Proof of what? Every paper and TV station in the country carried the story. Anyway, don't the Russki hitters usually cut off the finger, too?'

Roth rattled a frustrated sigh. His face showed more than its usual tic of agitation.

'I've got to run,' I said. I shot my fist in the air and hoped that Roth got the joke.

Gerald Brandt was still at the Hyatt, waiting for his son's body to be released. I went to his suite and found him there alone.

'You see the papers?' I asked him as we sat at the umbrellaed table on the terrace.

'The papers, Bloomberg, some woman reporter from the *Chronicle* calling in all night. What they're suggesting is total madness,' he said.

'Your son's death was an act of madness, Mr Brandt. You want me to be straight with you when it comes to the investigation?'

'What do you mean, Inspector Boxer?'

'You were asked the other day if you knew anyone who might want to cause you harm—'

'And I told your detective, *not in this way*,' he said quietly.

'You don't think certain factions in Russia might be a little angry at you for pulling out of their deal?'

'We don't deal with factions, Ms Boxer.' His voice was stronger now. 'Kolya's shareholders include some of the most powerful men in this country. Anyway, you make me feel like I'm a suspect. It was business. Negotiations. In what we do, we deal with this sort of thing every week. David's death has nothing to do with Kolya.'

'Mr Brandt, how can you be so sure? Your son and his wife are dead.'

'Because negotiations *never broke off*, Detective. That was a ruse we used for the media. We closed on the deal last night.'

He stood up and I knew my interview was over.

My next call was to Claire. I ached to talk to her, anyway. I craved my daily Claire fix. I also needed help on the case.

When I phoned, her secretary said she was in the middle of a conference call and could I please hold.

'Forensic specialists,' Claire grumbled as she came on the line. 'Listen to this ... some guy's driving sixty in a thirty-five zone, rams into an elderly man in a Lexus, double-parked, waiting for his wife. DOA. Now the driver's tying up the guy's estate with a suit that the victim was illegally parked. All each side wants is to grab a piece of the estate, experts included. Righetti's pushing me in 'cause the case is being written up in an AAFS journal.

Some of these bastards, you give them a penny for their thoughts, you know what you get?'

'Change,' I answered with a smile. Claire *was* funny.

'You got it. I've got about thirty-one seconds. How you doing?' she inquired. 'I love you, sweetheart. I miss you. What do you *want*, Lindsay?'

I hesitated, part of me wishing I could let the whole thing burst out, but all I asked was if the Brandts were wearing any wedding bands when they were brought in.

'To my knowledge, no,' she replied. 'We inventoried earrings and a diamond as large as an eyeball. But no wedding bands. I noticed that myself. In fact, that's why I was calling you last night.'

'Great minds think alike,' I said.

'Busy minds, at least,' she countered. 'How's your grisly, godawful case coming on?'

I sighed. 'I don't know. Next thing we have to do is go through three hundred guests to see if any might've been carrying any special grudges. You saw how this is being played up in the press. Russian revenge. The FBI's creeping around and Chief Mercer's barking in Roth's ear to put a *real* detective on it. Speaking of which, I have Jacobi out trying to trace down the jacket. Other than that, the case is moving along smoothly.'

Claire laughed. 'Stick with it, sweetie. If anyone can solve these murders, it's you.'

'I wish it were only that . . .' I let my voice drop.

'Is everything all right?' Claire came back. 'You don't sound your usual chatty, irreverent self.'

'Actually, I need to talk with you. Maybe we can get together later?'

'Sure,' Claire said. 'Oh damn . . . I teach at four today. And we've got Reggie's graduation tonight. Can it keep a day? I could drive in for brunch on Sunday.'

'Of course it can,' I said, swallowing my disappointment. 'Sunday would be great. I'd like that.'

I hung up with a smile. For a moment, I actually felt better about things. Just making the date with Claire made it seem as if a weight had been lifted off my shoulders. Sunday would give me some time to prepare, about how I was going to deal with the treatment, and my job.

Raleigh wandered up. 'You want to grab a coffee?'

I thought he was needling me about what time I'd come in. He must have sensed my resentment.

He wagged a legal-sized manila envelope in my face and shrugged. 'It's the Brandts' wedding list. I thought you'd want to see who made the cut.'

Chapter Twenty-Two

We went down to Roma's, one of those stucco-on-stucco, high-ceilinged, Euro-style coffee joints across the street from the Hall. I prefer Peet's, but Roma's is closer.

I ordered a tea, while Raleigh came back with some fancy mocha latte and a slice of homemade pumpkin bread that he pushed in front of me.

'You ever wonder how these places make any money?' he asked.

'What?' I looked at him.

'There's one on every corner. They all serve the same thing and their average sale's gotta be, what . . . two dollars and thirty-five cents?'

'This isn't a *date*, Raleigh,' I snapped. 'Let's go through the list.'

'Maybe closer to three or three-fifty. Lucky if the places *gross* four hundred thousand.'

'Raleigh, please,' I said, losing patience.

He pushed the envelope toward me.

I opened it and fanned out eight or nine pages of names and addresses bearing Chancellor Weil's office crest. I recognized some of the guests on the groom's side immediately. Bert Rosen, former Secretary of the Treasury of the United States. Sumner Smith, some billionaire who had made his money in the eighties through big-time LBOs. Chip Stein, of E-flix, Spielberg's buddy. Maggie Sontero, the hot SoHo designer from New York. Lots of big names and big trouble.

From the bride's side, there were several prominent names from the San Francisco area. Mayor Fernandez for one. Arthur Abrams, the prominent local attorney. I had gone up against his firm once or twice in the witness box, testifying in homicide cases. Willie Upton, Superintendent of Public Schools.

Raleigh pulled his seat over to me. Side by side we scanned the rest of the list, which contained columns of impressive-sounding couples with the titles of 'Dr' or 'Honorable' in front of their names.

It was a long, unrevealing, seemingly impenetrable list.

I don't know what I expected – just *something* to jump out at me. Some name resonating with a culpability even the families didn't recognize.

Raleigh let out a worrisome breath. 'This list is *scary*. You take the first fifty, I'll take the second, we'll give the balance to Jacobi. We'll all meet back here in two weeks and see what we've got.'

The prospect of hammering away at these people – each one horrified and indignant at our inquiries – didn't fill me with joy or high hopes.

'You think Mayor Fernandez might be a sex killer?' I muttered.

'I do.'

What came out of me next was a complete surprise. 'So you said you were married?'

If we were going to be thrown together we might as well get it out. And the truth was, I was curious.

Raleigh nodded after a short pause. I thought I saw pain in his eyes. 'Actually, I still am. Our divorce is coming up next month. Seventeen years.'

I flashed him a sympathetic wag of my eyes. 'I'm sorry. Let's stop the Q and A.'

'It's okay. Things happen. Suddenly, it seemed we were just traveling in different circles. To be more precise, Marion fell in love with the guy who owned the real-estate office where she worked. It's an old story. I guess I never quite learned which fork to use.'

'I could've saved you some pain,' I said. 'It goes left to right. Are there kids?'

'Two great boys. Fourteen and twelve. Jason is the jock. Teddy's the brain. Set up a home page for his sixth-grade class. I get them every other weekend. Lights of my life, Lindsay.'

I could actually see Raleigh as Superdad. Kicking the ball around on Saturdays, installing the computer in the den. On top of it, the guy did have affectionate eyes. It was gradually dawning on me that he wasn't the enemy.

'I guess,' he grinned back at me, 'getting the order of forks right didn't exactly help you, either. You're divorced, right?'

'Oohh. Somebody's been checking around,' I said. 'I was just out of the Police Academy. Tom was in his second year of law school at Berkeley. At first, he was going to go criminal. We had sort of a Carville and Matalin thing going. I imagined me testifying, Tom Terrific socking it to me on the cross. Ultimately, he opted for corporate.'

'And?'

'It was his picture, not mine. I wasn't ready for the country club. It's an old story, right?' I smiled. 'The truth is, he walked out on me. Kind of broke my heart into tiny pieces.'

'Sounds like we've got some things in common,' Raleigh said gently. He did have nice eyes. *Stop it, Lindsay.*

'If you must know,' I replied, deadpan, 'for the past six months I've been having this torrid affair with Warren Jacobi.'

Raleigh laughed and pretended to look surprised. 'Jeez, Jacobi doesn't seem like your type. What's the fatal attraction?'

I thought of my ex-husband Tom, then one other man I had been sort of serious about. What always attracted me when I let someone get close. 'Soft hands. And, I guess, a soft heart.'

'So whad'ya think?' Raleigh said. 'You put a few home-made jams on the shelves, give the coffees some sexier names – Arabian Breeze, Sirocco. You think we can hike up the average sale?'

'Why are you going through this, Raleigh?'

He gave me a look that was sort of between an embarrassed grin and a sparkle in his clear, blue eyes. 'I've been doing police work for sixteen years. So you get to thinking . . . I have this favorite place. Up in Tahoe. Maybe one of these franchises . . .'

'Sorry, I don't see you behind the counter picking out the muffins.'

'Nicest thing you've said to me so far.'

I got up, tucked the envelope under my arm and headed toward the door. 'On second thought, you might make a better baker than a cop.'

'That's my girl,' he smiled. 'Wiseguy answer for everything. Keep those defenses up.'

As we left the shop, I softened and said to him, 'I have this favorite place, too.'

'Maybe you'll show me one day.'

'Maybe I will.'

I was surprised by Raleigh – live and learn – he was actually a nice guy. I wondered if he had soft hands.

Chapter Twenty-Three

When Rebecca Passeneau looked at herself in the full splendor of her wedding dress, she knew that she was no longer her mother's little girl. *You're my baby.* She had heard those words from her very first days on the planet.

With three older brothers it wasn't so hard to imagine why. Her mother had always wanted a girl – Daddy, too – but as the years went on they assumed their time had passed. The oldest – Ben, the daredevil – had been killed before she was born. Her parents were crushed. They couldn't even think of more children. Then, miraculously, Becky came.

'My baby!' she heard her mother exclaim from where she stood behind Becky.

'Oh, Mom,' her daughter sighed, but she also smiled.

She continued to look at herself. She was beautiful. In her long white strapless dress, an avalanche of tulle, she shone like the most lovely and beautiful thing in the world. Michael would be so happy. With all the arrangements – the hotel in Napa, the flowers, the last-minute alterations to the dress – she had never thought this day would actually come. But now it was almost here. *Saturday.*

Ms Perkins, the department manager at Saks, could only stand and admire. 'You're gonna knock 'em dead, sweetheart.'

Becky spun around, catching herself in every view of the three-paneled mirror. She grinned. 'I will, won't I?'

'Your father and I want you to have something,' her mother said.

She reached into her purse and pulled out a small suede jewelry pouch. In it was her diamond brooch, a four-carat oval on a string of pearls, passed on from her own mother. She stepped closer to Becky, clasped the strand around her neck.

'It's gorgeous,' the girl gasped. 'Oh, *Mom.*'

'It was given to me on my wedding day,' her mother said. 'It has brought me a beautiful life. Now it's for you.'

Becky Passeneau stood there in the spell of the mirror. The glorious dress, the diamond in the hollow of her throat.

She finally stepped off the alteration platform and hugged her mother. 'I love you, Mom. You're the best.'

'Now it's complete,' her mother said, with a tear in her eye.

'No, not quite,' said Ms Perkins. She ran into the back and hurriedly returned with a bouquet of flowers. Imitations, sales accessories, but at the moment they looked like the most resplendent blossoms in the world.

She gave them to Becky, who hopped back up on the platform, hugging them to her. She saw her beaming smile reflected three times. They all stood there and admired.

'Now you are complete,' Ms Perkins approved.

Standing nearby in Saks, watching Becky model her stunning dress, Phillip Campbell couldn't have agreed more.

'Your big day is almost here,' he whispered softly. 'You look beautiful.'

Chapter Twenty-Four

The following morning, Milt Fanning from the FBI Sex Crime Unit reported in. His computer had popped up a handful of related crimes, but he was letting me know that none of them was a strong lead.

They had started by plugging in fists used in the act of sexual assault and that produced several cases, mostly gay crimes. One was in connection with a couple of murdered prostitutes in Compton that dated back to 1992, but Nicholas Chito was serving twenty-five years to life in San Quentin.

There had been several hotel murders, even one involving newlyweds in Ohio, in which the groom opened up the womb of his beloved with a 30-30 when he discovered he wasn't the first. But there was nothing local or still outstanding, nothing tangible to give us a direction.

I was disappointed, but not surprised. Everything we had uncovered so far convinced me that when David and Melanie Brandt ran into their killer at the Hyatt, it wasn't the first time they had met.

I saw Jacobi wandering in from outside. For two days, he had been avoiding me – running down his assignments – specifically the searches for the champagne and the jacket. After two years, I knew that when Jacobi wasn't needling me, it meant he wasn't happy.

'How's the search going?' I asked.

He flashed me a tight-lipped smirk. 'Chin and Murphy are out calling every fricking wine store in a forty-mile radius. You think any of these guys keep track of this sort of thing? They all tell me that bottle could've been ordered from anywhere in the country. Then there's mail order to consider. The Internet. Cripes!'

I knew it was a long shot. How many people pay two hundred bucks for a bottle of champagne?

'Still,' he finally faced me, 'we came up with some names.'

As if to torture me, Jacobi leafed through his notepad to what must've been page thirty. Then he squinted, cleared his throat, saying, 'Yeah, here we go . . . Golden State Wine Shop, on Crescent. *Krug. Clos du Mesnil*,' he pronounced, bludgeoning the French. 'Nineteen eighty-nine. Someone ordered a case of the stuff last March. Name of Roy C. Shoen.'

'You check him out?'

He nodded. 'Never heard of any Brandt. He's a dentist. I guess rich dentists like fancy wine, too.' He flipped over the page. 'Then there's Vineyard Wines in Mill Valley. Murphy handled it.' For the first time in a couple of days he really smiled at me. 'The guy who bought the wine was named Murphy, too. Regular customer there. Threw a dinner party for his wife's birthday. You want to give me a morning off I'll check him out, but I thought I'd send Murphy himself. Just for the laugh.'

'Any luck with the tuxedo jacket?'

'We called the manufacturer. Fifteen stores in the area sell this brand – if it even came from around here. We're bringing in their local rep. Tracking down the owner of this thing . . . it ain't gonna be easy.'

'While you're out there,' I teased him, 'see if you can pick yourself up a decent tie.'

'Ho, ho. So how you getting along without me?' Jacobi inquired, but I could see the disappointment all over his face. Made me feel bad.

'I'm coping.' Then, seriously, 'I'm sorry, Warren. You know that I didn't ask for this guy.'

He nodded self-consciously. 'You want me to check out everyone we dig up who's into fancy champagne?'

I shook my head. I got up, dropped a copy of the Brandt wedding list on his desk. 'What I want you to do is check and see if they match against this list.'

He leafed through the pages, whistling at a few of the more prominent names. 'Too bad, Boxer. No Shoen or Murphy. Maybe we'll just have to wait and take a shot at Couple Number Two.'

A chill ran through me. 'What makes you say that?' I asked. Jacobi was a pain in the ass, but he was a good cop with a good nose for sniffing out a pattern.

'We're looking for a spiffy dresser who likes to get dirty with dead brides, right?'

I nodded. I remembered something my first partner had told me. *'Never wrestle with a pig, Lindsay. You both get dirty. And the pig likes it.'*

'I figure it's gotta be hard for a guy like that to find a date,' said Jacobi.

Chapter Twenty-Five

The first week of the Bride and Groom investigation was gone. Unbelievable.

Jacobi's team pounded the jacket-and-champagne search, but so far they had come up empty. Raleigh and I had spoken to twenty guests, from the Mayor to the groom's best friend. All of them were numb and sickened, but unable to put their finger on any one thing that might move us along.

All I could focus on was that we needed something firm – fast – before this guy who took the rings would kill again.

I underwent my second transfusion. As I watched the thick red blood drip into my veins, I prayed it was making me stronger, but was it? It had the slow, steady beat of a ticking clock.

And the clock *was* ticking. Mine, Chief Mercer's.

Saturday at six, Jacobi folded his pad, put on his sports jacket, and tucked his gun into his belt. 'See ya, Boxer,' he said.

Raleigh stopped by before heading out. 'I owe you a beer. You want to collect?'

A beer would be nice, I thought. I was even growing used to Raleigh's company. But something told me if I went with him now, I'd let everything out: Negli's, my treatments, the fear in my heart.

I shook my head. 'Think I'll stick around,' I said politely.

'You got plans tomorrow?'

'Yeah. I'm meeting Claire, then I'll come in here. What about you?'

'Jason's in a soccer tournament in Palo Alto. I'm taking both boys down.'

'Sounds nice.' It did sound nice. It had the truth of something I might miss out on in life.

'I'll be back tomorrow evening.' He had given me his beeper the first day we hooked up. 'I'm an hour away. Call if anything comes up.'

With Raleigh gone, my corner of the squad room became shrouded in silence. The investigation was shut down for the night. One or two of the night staff were chatting in the outside hall.

I had never felt so lonely. Yet somehow I knew that if I went home now, I'd be leaving behind some vital nexus to the case, to Melanie. Failing some unsaid promise I had made. One more look, I told myself. One more pass.

Why would the killer take the rings?

A wave of exhaustion washed its way through my veins. My new fighting cells were stealing my strength even as they defended me, and multiplied. The cavalry, charging into the rescue. Hope attacking doubt. It seemed crazy.

I had to let David and Melanie sleep for the night. I

bound the thick crime file up in its elastic cord and placed it in the gray bin marked *Open Cases*. Next to similar files, with similar names.

Then I sat at my desk in the dark squad room for a couple of minutes more. I started to cry.

Book Two

The Women's Murder Club

Chapter Twenty-Six

B ecky DeGeorge, in the bloom of her first full day as Michael's wife, walked out of the hotel lobby, holding her husband's hand. She breathed in the cool night air, the first fresh air she had inhaled all day.

In the brief span of their marriage, she and Michael had made love several times and taken two steamy showers together. They poked their heads out for an obligatory, but at last, final brunch with the families. They begged off the trip to Opus One, scurried back upstairs, and popped a last bottle of champagne. Michael put on a sex video and they both played out some unusual and exciting roles as they watched the film. He seemed to have several fantasies about wearing women's clothes.

Tomorrow, they'd be off to Mazatlan, for another heavenly week exploring all those sexy spots on his body she had yet to find. Who knows, maybe they'd even come out once or twice to see the dolphins.

So far, she decided, things were going very well.

They were headed to the French Laundry, the finest

restaurant in Napa. Everyone said it was *the* place to eat, and they had booked the reservation almost six months in advance. Becky's mouth watered as she dreamed of some fabulous sequence of tastes: foie gras, wild berry duck, all washed down with an expensive champagne.

On the short walk to the car, a black limo pulled up alongside them. The passenger window opened and a uniformed driver stuck his head out. 'Mr and Mrs DeGeorge?'

They looked at each other, puzzled, then smiled. 'That's us.'

'I'm at your service,' the driver announced. 'Compliments of the hotel.'

Becky was ecstatic. 'You mean for us?' Once, in her job as a legal secretary, at a big closing, she had ridden in a fabulous stretch; but she was jammed in the back seat with four preoccupied lawyers.

'Booked and paid for the night,' the driver said, and winked.

The newlyweds exchanged a bright, exclamatory look.

'No one mentioned anything about this,' said Michael, who seemed pleased with the notion that he was thought of as a VIP.

Becky peeked inside. 'Oh, Michael!' There were lush leather back seats and a polished mahogany bar with crystal glasses, and the lights were dimmed to a romantic glow. There was even a bottle of Chardonnay on ice. She thought of pulling up to the most fashionable restaurant in Napa in this wonderful car.

'C'mon, honey,' she laughed, almost pulling him in. 'It'll be a trip.'

'I can be waiting at the restaurant when you come out,' the driver said, 'and as it happens, you're talking to someone who knows the most scenic routes through Napa.'

She saw Michael's mild hesitation begin to crack. 'Don't you want to take your princess in style?'

Just as it was when she had first smiled his way in the office, just as it was in bed last night, she saw him slowly come around. He was a little cautious sometimes. Accountants often were. But she'd always found ways of loosening him up.

'Whatever Mrs DeGeorge wants,' Michael finally said.

Chapter Twenty-Seven

'Just married?' Phillip Campbell asked, his heart jumping. The bright lights of oncoming cars shot through him like X-rays, exposing his innermost desires.

'Twenty-six hours, eleven minutes and . . . forty-five seconds,' Becky chirped.

Campbell's heart pounded loudly. She was perfect. They were perfect together. *Even better than he had hoped.*

The road was blank and seemed directionless, but he knew where he was going. 'Help yourself to a drink,' he invited them. 'That's a Palmeyer in the bucket. Some people think it's the best in the valley.'

As he drove, the killer's nerves were taut and excited. *What is the worst thing anyone has ever done? Can I do it again? More to the point, can I ever* stop *doing it?*

He glanced back and saw Becky and Michael pouring the Palmeyer wine. He heard the clink of raised glasses, then something about years of good luck. With a chill in his heart, he watched them kiss. He hated every smug, deluded pore in their bodies. 'Don't you want to take your princess in style?' Huh! He fingered the gun resting in his lap. He was changing murder weapons.

After a while, Campbell turned the limo up a steep hill off the main road.

'Where're we heading, driver?' The husband's voice came from the back.

He glanced in the mirror and smiled confidently at the DeGeorges. 'I thought I'd take you the scenic way. Best views in the valley. And I'll still have you to the restaurant by eight.'

'We don't want to be late,' the groom warned sheepishly. 'These reservations were harder to get than the damn hotel.'

'Oh, c'mon, honey,' Becky chimed in with perfect timing.

'Things start to open up just ahead,' he told them. 'It's real pretty. In the meantime, relax. Put on some music. I'll show you the best views . . . very romantic.'

He pushed a button, and a thin band of pulsing lights began to shoot around the roof of the back compartment, a soft, seductive light show.

'Oooh,' Becky said, as the lights came on. 'This is *so* great.'

'I'll put up the privacy screen for the rest of the trip. You're only newlyweds once. Feel free to do whatever. Just look at it as your night.'

He left the screen slightly open, so he could still see and hear them as he drove deeper into the hills. They were nuzzling now, sharing kisses. The groom's hand was moving up Becky's thigh. She pushed her pelvis into him.

The road became bumpy and, at intermittent points, the rough split concrete gave way to gravelly dirt. They were climbing. On both sides, the slopes were patterned with grids of darkened vines.

Becky's teasing laughter gave way to a steady rhythm of deep-throated sighs. Phillip Campbell's breath began to race. Only inches away, he could hear her panting. A warm, velvety sensation began to burn in his thighs, as it had a week ago at the Grand Hyatt. Michael was entering Becky and she moaned.

What is the worst thing?

At a clearing, he pulled the car to a stop, turned the headlights off. He took the gun and pulled back the double-clicking action.

Then he lowered the privacy screen.

In the ambient light, there was Becky, her black cocktail dress pulled up around her waist.

'Bravo!' he exclaimed.

They looked up, startled.

He saw a flicker of fear in the bride's eyes. She tried to cover herself.

Only then did the killer recognize that the warm flood burning his thighs and his knees was his own urine.

He emptied the gun into Becky and Michael DeGeorge.

Chapter Twenty-Eight

That Sunday morning, I woke for the first time all week with a sense of hopefulness. It's the way I am ... or *was*.

It was clear and beautiful outside; the Bay was shimmering as if it were thrilled, too. And it was the day of my brunch with Claire. My confession to her.

Sunday mornings I had this place I always went to. My favorite place, I had told Raleigh.

First I drove downtown, to the Marina Green, in my tights, and jogged in the shadow of the bridge. Mornings like this, I felt infused with everything that was beautiful about living in San Francisco. The brown coast of Marin, the noises of the Bay, even Alcatraz, standing guard.

I ran my usual three-plus miles south of the harbor, then up the 212 stone stairs, into Fort Mason Park. Even with Negli's I could still do it. This morning it seemed to be letting me free.

I jogged past yelping dogs running loose, lovers on a morning walk, gray-clad, bald-headed Chinese men bickering over mah-jongg. I always went to the same spot, high on the cliff, looking east over the Bay. It was 7:45.

No one knew I came here. Or why. Like every Sunday, I came upon a small group practicing their t'ai chi. They were mostly Chinese, led, as every week, by the same old man in a gray knit cap and sweater vest. I huffed to a stop and joined in as I had every Sunday for the past ten years, since my mother died.

They didn't know me. What I did. Who I was. I didn't know them. The old man gave me the same quick, welcoming nod he always did.

There's a passage in Thoreau: 'Time is but the stream I go a-fishing in. I drink at it, but while I drink, I see the sandy bottom and detect how shallow it is. Its current slides away, but eternity remains. I would drink deeper, fish in the sky, whose bottom is pebbly with stars.'

I guess I've read that a hundred times. It's the way I feel up here. Part of the stream.

No Negli's.

No crimes, no faces twisted in death.

No Bride and Groom murders.

I did my Morning Swan, my Dragon, and I felt as light and free as I did before Orenthaler first dropped the news on me.

The leader nodded. No one asked me if I was well. Or how the week was. I just welcomed the day, and knew that I was lucky to have it.

My favorite place.

I got home just before eleven, a half-finished coffee and the Sunday *Chronicle* in my arms. I figured I'd poke through the Metro section, see if there was anything on the case from my new best friend Cindy Thomas. Then I'd take a shower, and be ready by noon to go meet Claire.

It was 11:25 when the phone rang. To my surprise, the voice on the line was Raleigh's.

'You dressed?' he asked.

'Sort of. Why? I have plans.'

'Cancel them. I'm picking you up. We're going to Napa.'

'Napa?' There was no trace of anything light or playful in his voice. 'What's up?'

'I went in this morning just to check. While I was there, someone named Hartwig got transferred from Central Dispatch. He's a Lieutenant in Napa. He's got some couple out there who are missing. They're newlyweds on their honeymoon.'

Chapter Twenty-Nine

B y the time I called Claire to cancel, showered, put my wet hair under a turned-back Giants cap, and threw on some clothes, Raleigh's white Explorer was beeping me from below.

When I got downstairs, I couldn't help but notice him looking me over – wet hair, jeans, black leather jacket.'You look nice, Boxer.' He smiled as he put the car in gear.

He was casually dressed in crumpled khakis and a faded blue polo shirt. He looked nice, too, but I wasn't going to say it.

'This isn't a date, Raleigh,' I told him.

'You keep saying that,' he shrugged, then stepped down on the gas.

An hour and fifteen minutes later, we pulled up to the Napa Highlands Inn, the exact time, I noted, I was supposed to be pouring my heart out to Claire.

The inn turned out to be one of those fancy, high-end spas I always dreamed about going to. It was tucked into the mountains on Stag's Leap Road. With its main lodge built of stacked giant redwoods and arcing windows of tempered glass, the guests here were not exactly into self-denial.

Two green-and-white police units were parked in the rotary outside the hotel's entrance. In the lobby, we were directed to the manager's office where a nervous, red-haired management type, who seemed just a few days out of the training program, was standing with a couple of local cops.

'I'm Hartwig,' said a tall, lanky man in street clothes. He was holding a paper cup from Starbucks. 'Sorry to bust up your weekend,' he apologized in a friendly drawl.

He passed us a wedding photo of the missing couple. It was enclosed in one of those Plexiglas 'shaky toys' with the Golden Gate Bridge in the foreground. 'Party favor,' he sighed. 'Mr and Mrs Michael DeGeorge. From down your way. They both worked in the city at a large accounting firm. Married on Friday night.'

Actually, it was a sweet photo. She, bright-eyed, with thick brown hair; he, ruddy and serious-looking, wire-rimmed glasses.

'So when were they last seen?' I asked.

'Seven-forty-five last night. Hotel staff saw them come down on their way to dinner at the French Laundry,' Hartwig said. 'The concierge wrote them out directions, but they never showed.'

'They drove off to go to dinner and were never heard from again?'

Hartwig kept rubbing the side of his face. 'The manager

said they checked in the day before in a gold Lexus. Door staff confirm they drove it briefly that afternoon.'

'Yeah?' I nodded, fast-forwarding him.

'Car's still in the lot.'

I asked, 'Any messages from the outside we should know about?'

Hartwig went back to a desk and handed me a small stack of slips. I skipped through them. *Mom. Dad. Julie and Sam. Vicki and Don. Bon voyage.*

'We thoroughly searched the grounds around the property. Then we widened the search. It's sort of like your murder down there. Big wedding, celebration. Then *poof,* they're gone.'

'Sort of like our thing,' I agreed, 'except we had *bodies.*'

The Napa cop's face tightened. 'Believe me, I didn't call you guys all the way out here just to help us with the missing-persons forms.'

'What makes you so sure?' Raleigh asked.

' 'Cause the concierge did receive one call last night. It was from the restaurant, confirming their reservations.'

'So?'

Hartwig took a sip of his coffee before he met our eyes. 'No one at the French Laundry made that call.'

Chapter Thirty

The honeymoon couple had received no unusual visitors, scheduled no other conflicting side trips. The reservation at the French Laundry had been just for two.

What made this all the more grave was that they had missed their scheduled flight to Mexico.

While Raleigh poked around outside, I made a quick check of their room. There was this enormous redwood bed neatly turned down, a suitcase laid out, clothes stacked, toiletries. Lots of flowers – mostly roses. Maybe Becky DeGeorge had brought them from the reception.

There was nothing to indicate that the DeGeorges weren't set to board their plane the next morning.

I caught up with Raleigh outside. He was talking with a bellhop who was apparently the last person who saw the DeGeorges leave.

When it was just the two of us, Raleigh said, 'A couple of the local guys and I swept a hundred yards into the woods.' He shook his head in exasperation. 'Not even a footprint. I looked around the car, too. It's locked. No blood, no sign of a struggle. But *something* happens to them out here. Someone accosts them. Twenty, thirty yards from the hotel.'

I took a frustrated 360-degree scan of the driveway and the nearby parking lot. A local police cruiser was set up outside the property gate. 'Not accosts them. Too risky – it's in plain view. Maybe someone picked them up.'

'The reservations are only for two,' he countered. 'And the guy at the front door insists they were headed to their car.'

'Then they *vanish*?'

Our attention was diverted by the swoosh of a long black limousine turning into the resort's pebbly driveway. It pulled up under the redwood overhang in front of the entrance.

Raleigh and I watched the hotel door open and the doorman emerge rolling a trolley of bags. The driver of the limo hopped out to open the trunk.

It hit us both at the same time.

'It's a long shot,' said Raleigh, meeting my eyes.

'Maybe,' I agreed, 'but it would explain how someone gained access without diverting anyone's attention. I think we should check if any limos have been reported stolen lately in the Bay area.'

Another car turned into the driveway, a silver Mazda, and parked near the far end of the circle. To my dismay, a woman in cargo pants and a University of Michigan sweatshirt jumped out.

'Raleigh, you said one of your particular skills was containment, didn't you?'

He looked at me as if I had asked Dr Kevorkian, 'You're sort of good at mixing chemicals, aren't you?'

'Okay,' I said, eyeing the approaching figure, 'contain this.'

Walking up to us was Cindy Thomas.

Chapter Thirty-One

'**E**ither you've got the sharpest nose for a story I've ever seen,' I said to her angrily, 'or I may start to think of you as a murder suspect.'

This was the second time Cindy Thomas had intruded into the middle of a possible crime scene.

'Don't tell me I'm stepping on some inter-office romance?' she quipped.

That made me steaming mad. We had a developing situation here. If it got out prematurely, it would hurt any chance the Department had to control this case. I could just imagine the nightmare headlines I'd be seeing: BRIDE AND GROOM KILLER STRIKES AGAIN. And Roth would be livid. This would be the second time I had failed to control the crime scene with the same reporter.

'Who's your friend?' Raleigh asked.

'Cindy Thomas,' she announced, extending her hand. 'And you?'

'Cindy's with the *Chronicle*,' I alerted him.

Raleigh did a startled double-take, left in midshake like

a fired worker holding the hand of his replacement.

'Listen very clearly, Ms Thomas,' I said firmly. 'I don't know if you've been around long enough to develop a sense for how this is supposed to work, but if you're planning on doing anything except telling me why you're here, then pack up your little reporter's kit and drive away. You're definitely gonna make the Department's shit list in a hurry.'

'*Cindy*,' she reminded me, 'but first, the much more interesting question is, why am I out here bumping into you?'

Raleigh and I both glared at her with deepening impatience. 'Why are you here?' I pressed.

'All right.' She took a breath and pursed her lips. 'You two shooting down here on a Sunday; Captain Raleigh kicking around the woods and the parking lot; your grilling the hotel staff; both of you looking stumped. I have to figure it all starts to add up. Like the fact that the place hasn't been cordoned off, so no crime's been committed yet. That someone could be missing. Since we all know what you two are working on, it's not a far reach to assume it might be a couple who just got married. Possibly, that our Bride and Groom killer found himself Number Two.'

My eyes were wide, worried.

'Either that,' she smiled, 'or I've grossly misjudged things and you guys are just here zin-tasting for the Department's wine club.'

'You picked up all that from watching us?' I asked her.

'Honestly? No.' She nodded toward the hotel gate. 'Most

of it was from the big-mouth local cop I was yapping with out there.'

Without meaning to, I started to smile.

'Seriously, you realize you can't run with anything here,' Raleigh said.

'Another dead bride and groom? Same MO,' she snorted with resolve. 'Damn right I'm going to run with it.'

I was starting to see the situation going straight downhill. 'One thing I'd *strongly* consider would be to get in your car and just drive back into town.'

'Would you say that to Fitzpatrick or Stone?'

'If you went back to town, then I really *would* owe you one.'

She smiled thinly. 'You're kidding, aren't you? You want me to just walk away?'

'Yeah, just walk away.'

Cindy shook her head. 'Sorry. One, I'd probably get fired and two, there's just no way I could let this pass.'

'What if I drove back with you?' I said, spur of the moment. 'What if you can have pretty much what you're looking for, be on the inside, and give me some consideration at the same time.'

Raleigh's eyes almost bulged out of his head, but I gave him my best let-me-handle-this expression.

'When this story does break,' Cindy insisted, 'it's gonna be larger than any of us can control.'

'And when it does, it'll be *yours*.'

Her eyes narrowed. She was rolling around in her head whether she could trust me. 'You mean from you, exclusive?'

I waited for Raleigh to object. To my amazement, he went along.

'You said Chief Mercer was handling all the releases,' Cindy pressed.

'He is. All the *public* ones.'

I looked at Raleigh with my nerves leaping around like a Mexican jumping bean. If I couldn't trust him, then when we got back to town, I could be facing maximum rebuke. I would have Roth at my desk, or worse, Mercer. But I already felt I could trust him.

'So *I'm* gonna catch a ride back to town with Ms Thomas,' I said, waiting for his response.

'*Cindy*,' the reporter repeated, with renewed determination.

Raleigh began to nod in a gradual, acquiescent way. 'I'll finish up with Hartwig. I'll talk to you soon, Lindsay. Ms Thomas, an unexpected pleasure.'

I shot him a grateful smile. Then I took the reporter by the arm and said, 'C'mon, *Cindy*, I'm gonna explain the rules along the way.'

Chapter Thirty-Two

I don't know why I did it.

It was risky and rash, precisely the opposite of whatever had gotten me as far as I was. Maybe I just wanted to say *Screw it*, in the face of authority. To Roth, Mercer. To play things my own way. Maybe the case was widening, and I just wanted to keep the illusion that it was in my control.

Or maybe all I wanted to do was let someone else in.

'Before we go anywhere,' I said, grasping Cindy's wrist as she started up the car, 'I need to know something. How did you find out about what was going on down here?'

She took a deep breath. 'So far, all that's happened is you've pushed me away from the story of my career. Now I have to give up my sources, too?'

'Anything we do from here on is dependent on it.'

'I'd kind of prefer it if I can keep you guessing,' Cindy said.

'If this is gonna work, it's gotta be based on trust.'

'Then trust goes two ways, doesn't it, Detective?'

We sat there, baking in the hot Mazda littered with empty fast-food drink cups, sort of squaring off.

'Okay,' I finally relented. I gave her what little we knew about why we were in Napa that afternoon. The DeGeorges missing in action. That they had been married Friday night. The possibility that they were Couple Number Two. 'None of this goes to print,' I insisted, 'until we have confirmation. Then I'll give you the okay.'

Her eyes beamed with her suppositions suddenly confirmed.

'Now it's your turn. There was no press down here, even local. How did you get onto this?'

Cindy put the Mazda in gear. 'I told you I was from Metro,' she said, as the car putted out onto the main road, 'and that I've been fighting to stay on this story. My boss gave me the weekend to come up with something solid on this biggie. You had already brushed me off, so I parked myself down your street since yesterday and waited for something to turn up.'

'You followed me?'

'Pretty desperate, huh? But effective.'

I scrolled back over the past two days. 'To the movies. To the marina this morning?'

She blushed slightly. 'I was about to call it quits when your partner came by. I just tagged along for the ride.'

I pressed myself back in my seat and started to laugh. 'Not so desperate,' I muttered. 'Bad guys've been falling for it for years.' I was both embarrassed and relieved.

On the drive back to town, I explained the rules of our

agreement. I had done this before, when a reporter got too close on a story and threatened an investigation. Cindy couldn't go out with this story until we had confirmation. When we did, I'd make sure she had it first. I'd keep her ahead of the story, but just slightly ahead.

'There's a catch,' I said firmly. 'What we have now is what you would call a prioritized relationship. It goes past anything you already have – with your boyfriend or someone at work. Even your boss. Anything I give you is totally between us, and it stays with us, until I give you the okay to run with it.'

Cindy nodded, but I wanted to make sure she understood.

'Your boss asks you where any of this comes from, you just shrug. Some big shot in the Department . . . I don't care if it's Chief Mercer himself . . . parks his limo outside your door and calls you in about some leak, you say, "Thanks for the ride." The District Attorney's office calls you down to a grand jury, asks you to give up your sources, and a judge slaps you into a cell. You just make sure you bring enough reading material to fill the time.'

'I understand,' Cindy said. I could see in her eyes that she did.

The rest of the trip we talked about ourselves, our jobs, hobbies, and an unexpected development began to take shape. I started to like Cindy.

She asked me how long I'd been a cop, and I took her through more of the story than I had planned to. How my father was a police officer, and how he'd left when I was thirteen. How I was sociology at SF State. How I wanted to prove I could make a difference in a man's world. How a lot of who I was and what I did was simply trying to prove I belonged.

She came back that she was sociology, too, at Michigan. And before we even hit Marin, we had discovered a few other startling things we had in common.

Her younger brother was born on my birthday, 5 October. She was also into yoga, and the woman who had first taught me, years before in South San Francisco, was now instructing her in Corte Madera. We both liked to read travel books, and mysteries – Sue Grafton, Patricia Cornwell, Elizabeth George. We *loved* Gordon's *House of Fine Eats.*

Cindy's father had died early – some seventeen years ago – eerily, when she was only thirteen, too.

But the most chilling coincidence, the one that went right through me, was that he died of leukemia, cousin of the same degenerating disease that was coursing through me.

I thought of telling her my secret, but I stopped short. That was Claire's to hear. But as we drew close to the Golden Gate, I had a premonition I was riding with someone I was meant to be with, and definitely someone I liked to be with.

Approaching the city, I called Claire. It was hours after we were supposed to meet, but she still seemed eager to get together – and I had a lot to share. We agreed to keep our date at Susie's, this time for an early dinner instead of a brunch. When she pressed me for what I had found during the day, I told her, 'I'll fill you in when I get there.'

Then I did the second thing that surprised me that day. I asked, 'Do you mind if I bring a friend?'

Chapter Thirty-Three

Cindy and I were already into our second margarita by the time Claire walked in. From ten feet away, her smile seemed to brighten the entire room. I stood up and gave her a big hug.

'Couldn't wait for the old mom?' she said, eyeing the array of empty glasses.

'It's been a long day,' I sighed. 'Say hey to Cindy.'

'Pleasure,' said Claire brightly, grasping Cindy's hand. Though the date was planned for just her and me, Claire was one of those people who rolled easily with whatever came up.

'Lindsay's been telling me all about you,' Cindy said, over the din.

'Most of it's true, unless she's been saying I'm some kind of crackerjack forensic pathologist,' Claire said, grinning.

'Actually, all she's been saying is that you're a real good friend.'

Susie's was a bright, festive café with faux-painted walls and pretty good Caribbean food. They played a little reggae, a little jazz. It was a place where you could kick back, talk, shout, even shoot a rack of pool.

Our regular waitress, Loretta, came up, and we swayed Claire into a margarita for herself and another round of spicy, jerked wings for us.

'Tell me about Reggie's graduation,' I said.

Claire stole a wing from our bowl and wistfully shook her head. 'It's nice to know after all those years of school, they can actually say a few words that aren't "phat" or "it's the bomb". They looked like a bunch of street-struttin' kids auditioning for the Grammys, but the Principal swears they'll come out of it in time for their college interviews.'

'If they don't, there's always the Academy,' I grinned, feeling light-headed.

Claire smiled. 'I'm glad to see *you* looking up. When we spoke the other day, it sounded like Cheery was treading those big, ugly shoes of his all over your toes.'

'Cheery?' asked Cindy.

'My boss. We call him Cheery 'cause he inspires us with his humanistic concern for those entrusted to his command.'

'Oh, I thought you were talking about my city editor,' snickered Cindy. 'The guy's only truly happy when he can threaten someone with their benefits. He has *no clue* how demeaning and condescending he is.'

'Cindy's with the *Chronicle*,' I said to Claire, seeing her react with surprise. There was an undeclared no-fly zone between the force and the press. To cross it, as a reporter, you had to earn your place.

'Writing your memoirs, child?' Claire asked me, with a guarded smile.

'Maybe.' The short version. But with lots to tell.

Claire's margarita arrived, and we raised our glasses.

'To the powers that be,' I toasted.

Cindy laughed. 'Powers that be full of shit, powers that be pompous jerks, powers that be trying to keep you down.'

Claire yelped in approval, and we clinked glasses as if we were old friends.

'Y'know, when I first came to the paper,' Cindy said, nibbling a wing, 'one of the senior guys told me it was this particular editor's birthday. So I e-mail him this Happy Birthday message. I figure, him being my boss and all, it's a way to break the ice, maybe get a smile out of him. Later that day, the jerk calls me in. He's all polite and smiley. He's got bushy eyebrows as big as squirrels' tails. He nods me into the seat across from him. I'm thinking, Hey . . . the guy's human like everybody else.'

Claire smiled. Enthusiastically, I drained the last of my second drink.

'So, then the bastard narrows his eyes and says, "Thomas, in the next hour and a half, I have sixty reporters trying to take everything that doesn't make sense in this fucking world and somehow cram it into forty pages. But it's reassuring to know that while everyone else is madly rushing against the clock, you've got the time to paste a happy little smiley face on my day." He ended up assigning me a week of picking a winner from a fifth grade *Why I Want to Be an Editor for a Day* contest.'

I laughed, and coughed up a little of my drink. 'Goes under the heading of, No Good Deed Goes Unpunished. What did you do?'

Cindy had a great smile. 'E-mail it was the boss's birthday to every guy in the Department. Jerks were slumping out of his office with their faces white all day.'

Loretta came around again, and we ordered meals: chicken in a fiery sauce, fajitas, and a large salad to share. Three Dos Equis to go with them. We poured this lethal Jamaican hot sauce, Toasty Lady, on our wings and watched Cindy's eyes glaze over from the first fiery blast.

'Rite of initiation,' I grinned. 'Now you're one of the girls.'

'It's either the hot sauce, or a tattoo,' Claire announced, straight-faced.

Cindy scrunched up her eyes, in an evaluating sort of way, then turned around and rolled up the sleeve of her T-shirt. She exposed two small G clefs etched on the back of her shoulder. 'The downside of a classical education,' she said, with a crooked smile.

My eyes met Claire's – and both of us hooted with approval.

Then Claire yanked up her own shirt with a blush. Just below her ample brown waist, she revealed the outline of a tiny butterfly.

'Lindsay dared me one day,' she told Cindy. 'After you broke up with that prosecutor from San Jose, remember, honey? We went down to Big Sur overnight, just the girls, to let off some steam. Ended up coming back with these.'

'So where's yours?' Cindy turned to me.

'Can't show you.' I shook my head.

'C'mon,' she protested. 'Let's see it.'

With a sigh, I rolled onto my left buttock and patted my right. 'It's a one-inch gecko, with this really cute little tail. When I push some suspect up against a wall, if he's giving me a hard time, I tell him I'll stick it in his face so tight it's gonna seem as large as Godzilla.'

A warm silence fell over us. For a moment, the faces of David and Melanie Brandt, even Negli's, seemed a million miles away. We were just having fun.

I felt something happening, something that hadn't happened in a long time, that I desperately needed.

I felt connected.

Chapter Thirty-Four

'So now that we're all friends,' said Claire, after we had gone through another plateful of ribs, 'how'd the two of you meet up, anyway? Last I heard, you were going out to Napa to check on some missing newlyweds.'

Michael and Becky DeGeorge, who a moment ago had seemed so far away, came hurtling back with a crash.

I had so much to tell her, but the day had changed so subtly from what I had planned. I almost felt deceitful, withholding, filling her in on what had taken place in Napa, yet leaving out the important development that was going on inside of me.

Claire took it in, digesting it all with that sharp mind of hers. She had consulted on several serial-homicide cases, both as a lead examiner and an expert witness.

An idea was rolling through my head. In my weakened condition, I didn't relish the responsibility of running a media-intensive investigation into multiple homicides. What I came back with surprised even me.

'How'd you like to lend me some help?'

'Help?' Claire blinked with surprise. 'How?'

'This thing is about to explode, Claire,' I said. 'If there's a Bride and Groom killer out there, the attention will be national. We all have an interest in this case. Maybe we could meet like this. The three of us . . . off the record.'

Claire looked at me warily. 'You're suggesting we do this on our own?'

'We've got the top guns of the ME's office, Homicide, even the press, eye-deep in margaritas at this table.' The more I thought it out, the more I knew it could work.

We could reassemble whatever clues came out of the official investigation, share what we had, cut through the political cover-your-ass and the bureaucracy. Three women, who would get a kick from showing up the male orthodoxy. More important, we shared a heartfelt empathy for the victims.

Suddenly, the idea seemed lit with brilliance.

Claire shook her head in an incredulous way.

'C'mon,' I encouraged her, 'you don't think it would work? You don't think we'd be good at this?'

'That's not it at all,' she replied. 'It's just that I've known you for ten years, and never once, on anything, have I heard you ask for help.'

'Then feel very surprised,' I said, looking her straight in the eye,' 'cause I'm asking for it now.'

I tried to let her see that something was troubling me, something maybe larger than the case. That I wasn't sure I could handle it. That I could use the help. That there was more to it.

Claire gradually broke into the slimmest, acquiescent grin. 'In margaritas veritas. I'm in.'

I beamed back, grateful, then turned to Cindy. 'How about you? You in?'

She stammered, 'I have no idea what Sid Glass would say – but fuck him. I'm in.'

We clinked glasses.

The Women's Murder Club was born.

Chapter Thirty-Five

The next morning, I arrived at the office straight from an eight o'clock transfusion, feeling light-headed, slightly woozy. First thing I did was scan the morning *Chronicle*. To my relief, there was nothing on the front page about anything relating to the disappearance in Napa. Cindy had kept her word.

I noticed Raleigh coming out of Roth's office. His sleeves were rolled up, exposing his thick forearms. He gave me a guarded smile – one that told me that behind it was his discomfort at my cutting a deal yesterday with Cindy. With a flick of his brown eyes, he motioned me outside to the corridor.

'We have to talk,' he said, as we huddled near the staircase.

'Listen, Raleigh,' I exhaled, 'I'm really sorry about yesterday. I thought it would buy us some time.'

His dark eyes smoldered. 'Maybe you should tell me why she was worth compromising control of this case.'

I shrugged. 'You see anything about Napa in the papers this morning?'

'You contramanded a direct order from the Chief of Police. If that doesn't leave you in a hole, it sure digs one for me.'

'So you'd rather be digging out of a story in the *Chronicle* about a serial killer?'

He backed against the wall. 'That's Mercer's call.'

A policeman I knew skipped up the stairs past us, grunting hello. I barely nodded back.

'Okay,' I said, 'so how do you want to play it? You want me to go in and spill my guts to Sam Roth? If so, I will.'

He hesitated. I could see he was torn, clicking through the consequences. After what seemed like a minute, he shook his head. 'What's the point now?'

I felt a wave of relief. I touched his arm and smiled at him for a couple of long beats. 'Thanks.'

'Lindsay,' he added, 'I checked with the State Highway Patrol. There's no record of any limos reported stolen in the past week.'

That news, the dead end that it represented, discouraged me.

A voice shouted out from the squad room. 'Boxer out there?'

'I'm here,' I hollered back.

It was Paul Chin, one of the bright efficient junior grades assigned to our team. 'There's a Lieutenant Frank Hartwig on the line. Says you know him.'

I ran back in, grabbed the phone on our civilian clerk's desk. 'This is Lindsay Boxer.'

'We found them, Inspector,' Hartwig said.

Chapter Thirty-Six

'**C**aretaker discovered them,' Hartwig muttered, with a grim shake of his head. He was guiding us up a dirt path leading to a small Napa winery. 'I hope you're ready for this. It's the worst thing I've ever seen. They were killed making love.'

Raleigh and I had rushed up to St Helena, turning east off 29, 'the wine road', onto Hawk Crest Road until it wound high into the mountains, no longer paved. We finally came upon an obscure wooden sign: *Sparrow Ridge*.

'Caretaker comes up here twice a week. Found them at seven this morning. The place is no longer in regular use,' Hartwig continued. I could tell he was nervous, shook up.

The winery was barely more than a large corrugated shed filled with shiny, state-of-the-art equipment: crushers, fermenting tanks, staggered rows of stacked, aging barrels.

'You're probably used to this sort of homicide,' Hartwig said, as we walked in. The sharp, rancid smell hit our nostrils. My stomach rolled. No, I felt like telling him, you never get used to homicide scenes.

They were killed making love.

Several members of the local SCU team were huddled over the open bay of a large, stainless steel grape presser. They were inspecting two splattered mounds. The mounds were the bodies of Michael and Becky DeGeorge.

'Awhh, shit, Lindsay,' Raleigh muttered.

The husband, in a blazer and khakis, stared up at us. A dime-sized penetration cut the center of his forehead. His wife, whose black dress was pushed up to her neck, was thrown on top of him. White-eyed fear was frozen on her face. Her bra was pulled down to her waist, and I could see blood-spattered breasts. Her panties were down to her knees.

It was an ugly, nauseating sight. 'You have an approximate time?' I asked Hartwig. He looked close to being sick.

'From the degeneration of the wounds, the ME thinks they've been dead twenty-four to thirty-six hours. They were killed the same night they disappeared. Jesus, they were just kids.'

I stared at the sad, bloodied body of the wife, and my eyes fell to her hands.

Nothing there. No wedding band.

'You said they were killed in the act?' I muttered. 'You're sure about that?'

Hartwig nodded to the assistant medical examiner. He gently rolled Becky DeGeorge's body off her husband.

Sticking out of Michael DeGeorge's unfastened khakis was a perfectly preserved remainder of his final erection.

A smoldering rage ripped through me. The DeGeorges were just kids. Both were in their twenties, like the Brandts. Who would do such a terrible thing?

'You can see over here how they were dragged,' Hartwig said, pointing to smears of dried blood visible on the pitched, concrete floor. The smears led to car tracks that were clearly delineated in the sparsely traveled soil. A couple of sheriff's men were marking off the tracks in yellow tape.

Raleigh bent down and studied them. 'Wide wheel base, but fourteen-inch tires. The tread is good, kept up. An SUV would have sixteen-inch wheels. I would guess it was some kind of large, luxury sedan.'

'I thought you were just a desk cop?' I said to him.

He grinned. 'I spent a summer in college working in the pit crew on the NASCAR circuit. I can change a tire faster than a beer man at 3Com can change a twenty. My guess would be, a Caddy. Or a Lincoln.' Limo, his eyes were saying.

My own mind was racing through what Claire had said last night. *Link the crimes.*

It was uncommon for a pattern killer to switch methods. Sexual killers liked closeness to their victims: strangulation, bludgeoning, knives. They wanted to feel their victims struggle, expire. They liked to invade a victim's home. Shooting was detached, clinical. It provided no thrill.

For a moment, I wondered if there were two crimes going on. Copycat killers. It couldn't be.

No one else knew about the rings.

I went over to Becky DeGeorge as the doctor was zipping her up in the body bag. I gazed down into her eyes. They were making love. Did he force them? Did he surprise them?

A sexual psycho who changes his methods. A killer who leaves clues.

What did he leave here?

What were we missing?

Chapter Thirty-Seven

Fresh air filled my lungs as soon as we stepped outside. Chris Raleigh, Hartwig, and I walked down the barren dirt road. The grid of the valley floor stretched out below us. Rows of fallow grapes hugged each side. We were silent. Shell-shocked.

A scary idea shot through me. We were a thousand feet up, totally isolated. Something didn't sit right. 'Why here, Hartwig?'

'How about it's remote and no one ever comes up here?'

'What I meant,' I said, 'is why *here* – this particular spot. Who knows about this place?'

'There's isolated property all up and down these slopes. The consortiums have eaten up the valley floor. These properties take more work than capital. They represent labors of love. Check the listings. Dozens of them dry up every season. Anyone around here knows places like this.'

'The first killings were in the city. Yet he knew exactly where to come. Who owns this plot?'

Hartwig shook his head. 'Dunno.'

'I'd find out. And I would also make another pass through their room. Someone had them targeted, knew all their plans. We'll take a look at their travel brochures, business cards – see if there's anything from any limousine services.'

From below I heard the sound of a large vehicle climbing up the gravel road and caught sight of a white San Francisco Medical Examiner's Bronco pulling to a stop.

Claire Washburn was behind the wheel. I had asked her down – in the hope of matching evidence to both crime scenes.

I opened her door and said gratefully, 'Thanks for coming, sweetie.'

Claire solemnly shook her head. 'I only wish they had turned up differently. It's a call I never like to receive.' She pulled her heavy frame out of the car with surprising ease. 'I have a meeting later back in town, but I thought I'd look over the crime scene, introduce myself to the presiding on-site.'

I introduced Claire to Frank Hartwig. 'Your ME is Bill Toll, isn't he?' she asked with authority.

He blinked warily, clearly nervous. First, he had Raleigh and me down here as consults. But he had asked us in. Now, the San Francisco ME pulls up.

'Relax, I already patched through to his cell phone,' Claire said. 'He's expecting me.' She spotted the medical team standing over the yellow bags. 'Why don't I go take a look.'

Trying to hold on to some sense of order, Hartwig followed closely behind.

Raleigh came and stood next to me. He looked pale and stressed.

'You okay?' I asked.

He shook his head. He kept his eyes fixed on the shed where the bodies had been dumped.

I remembered how he had steadied me at the morgue. 'Been a while since you took in a really bad one?'

'That's not it,' he said, with the same unsettled look. 'I just want you to know that wherever this leads, it's not about interfacing with City Hall. Or containment. Lindsay, I want this guy.'

I was already there in my head. This wasn't about the big collar. Or my shot at Lieutenant. Or even fighting Negli's.

We stood there side by side for a while.

'Not that either of us,' he finally said, breaking the silence, 'is in much of a position to be the last line of defense for the institution of marriage.'

Chapter Thirty-Eight

P hillip Campbell had driven since the first light of dawn, setting out in the bulky, rented stretch limo. He was nervous, wired – and he absolutely loved it.

Chewing up the miles in a steady, purposeful daze, crossing the Bay Bridge and continuing east on 80, he finally broke free of the morning traffic near Vallejo, and maintained a vigilant sixty on the speedometer as he headed east.

He didn't want to be stopped.

The papers called him a monster. Psychotic, sociopathic. Expert witnesses on TV analyzed his motives, his past, his future possible murders.

They knew nothing. They were all wrong. They'll only find what I want them to find, he thought. They'll only see what I want them to see.

From the Nevada border, it was a short drive down into Reno, which he considered a vulgar, aging cowboy town. He stayed on the highway, avoiding the Strip with its wide, stucco-lined boulevards of gas stations, gun dealerships, pawnshops. You could get anything here without a lot of questions. It was the place to come to buy a gun, or unload a car, or both.

Out by the Convention Center, he turned into Lumpy's. He pulled the car up to an open area in the lot, recovered the folded paperwork from the glove compartment and breathed a sigh of relief.

The limo was spotless. All day yesterday, he had cleaned and polished it, scrubbing out the bloodstains until the last trace of evidence was gone. It was as if Michael and Becky DeGeorge had never existed.

In minutes he had paid for the car and called a cab to take him to the airport.

At the airport, he checked in, looked through a San Francisco paper at a newsstand. There was nothing about Becky and Michael. He made his way to the gate, buying on the way a bottle of Fruitopia apricot drink and a vegetarian wrap at a fast-food counter.

He checked in at Gate 31, Reno Air to San Francisco, took a seat, and started eating his lunch.

An attractive young woman sat next to him. Blonde hair, tight ass, just tawdry-looking enough to attract his eye. She wore a gold chain around her neck with her name on it in script – *Brandee* – and a tiny diamond ring.

He smiled a quick, inadvertent greeting.

She pulled out a Kipling knapsack, took a swig from a plastic water bottle, and produced a paperback, *Memoirs of a Geisha*. It interested him that, of all things, she was reading about a woman in bondage. These were promising signs.

'Good book?' He smiled her way.

'That's what everyone says,' she replied. 'I'm just starting.'

He leaned over and breathed in the cheap, citrusy scent of her perfume.

'Hard to believe,' he went on, 'it was written by a man.'

'I'll let you know.' She flipped a few pages, then added, 'My fiancé gave it to me.'

Phillip Campbell felt the short thin hairs on his arms stand up on edge.

His heart began to throb. He ran a tremulous finger along the edge of his goatee.

'Oh – when's the big day?'

Chapter Thirty-Nine

R aleigh drove back to town in our car. I hung around and caught a ride with Claire. I needed to tell her what was going on with me. Claire and I have been best friends for years. We talk at least once every day. I *knew* why I was having trouble telling her about my illness – I didn't want to hurt her. Or to burden Claire with my problems. I loved her so much.

As the ME's van bumped down the mountain road, I asked if she had been able to pick anything up at the murder scene.

'There was definitely sexual activity going on before they were killed,' she replied confidently. 'I could see labial distending around the vagina. Secretions on her thighs. This is guesswork – I only had a few minutes – but I think the husband was shot first, Lindsay. The one clean wound to the head suggests he was dispatched without resistance, head on. The wounds on Rebecca indicate something else. She was shot from the rear – through the shoulder-blades, the neck. From a distance, I would estimate, of no more than three-to-five feet. If the semen matches up, and they were in the act when it took place, it suggests that she was on top. That would mean someone had to get in fairly close, unobserved, while they were at it. Come up at them from behind. Since you said they didn't use their own car that night, they were obviously on their way somewhere. I think it's consistent with your theory that they were in some kind of vehicle when this took place, the killer in the front seat. So why not a limousine?'

'That's all?' I shook my head and smiled at Claire.

'Like I said, I only had a few minutes. Anyway, it was your theory. If it ends up proving out, all I did was connect the dots.'

We drove on a bit. I was still fumbling for the right words. Claire asked, 'So how's the new partner?'

I flashed her an affirming nod. 'Turns out he's okay. He's backed me up with Roth and Mercer.'

'And you were so sure he was only a watchdog from the Mayor's office.'

'So I was wrong.'

'Wouldn't be the first time you ended up wrong about a guy,' Claire said.

I wrinkled my face in pretended offense and ignored her grin.

'Anyway, watchdog or not,' Claire continued, 'he's a damn sight better to look at than Jacobi.'

'Smarter, too. When we drove up to Napa yesterday, I flipped on the stereo in his Explorer. A tape of *The Shipping News* came on.'

'So,' Claire went on, with a look of inquisitiveness, 'anything going down?'

'You mean other than four innocent people being killed?'

'I mean with Chris Raleigh, Lindsay! He's working out of the Mayor's office, he's a hunk, and your social calendar isn't exactly Gwyneth Paltrow's. You can't tell me he's not your type.'

'We've been wrapped up in the case, Claire.'

'Yeah,' she chortled. 'He's not married, right?'

'C'mon,' I pleaded. 'I'm just not ready.'

As she winked at me, I found myself imagining something going on with Raleigh. If I had driven back with *him* the other day from Napa, instead of Cindy. If I had asked him up, it being nothing but a lonely Sunday, thrown together something out of the fridge. Shared a beer on the terrace as the sun melted into the Bay. In my mind, I caught him checking me over again. *You look good, Boxer.* He had noticed. Truth was, I had noticed things about him, too. Like his patient, sensitive eyes.

Even as I sat there pretending I could fall in love with someone, the daydream crashed. Life was slowly leaking out of me.

Something with Raleigh, or anyone, just wasn't a possibility now.

I flashed a glance at Claire, who was pulling the car onto 101, and I took a deep breath.

'You ever hear of something called Negli's aplastic anemia?' I asked.

Chapter Forty

It came out of the blue, so unexpectedly that it didn't even dawn on Claire what I had just said.

She answered as if she were fielding a medical question in her lab. 'Blood disorder. Pretty rare, serious. The body stops producing erythrocytes.'

'Red blood cells,' I said.

Claire glanced at me. 'Why? It's not Cat?' referring to my sister.

I shook my head. I sat rigid and stared straight ahead. My eyes were glassy. It was probably the long pause that caused it to slowly sink in.

Claire whispered, 'Not you?'

An awful stillness took hold in the car.

'Oh, Lindsay.' Claire's jaw dropped. She pulled the Bronco onto the shoulder of road and immediately reached out and hugged me. 'What has your doctor told you?'

'That it's serious. That it can be fatal.'

I saw the gravity of that wash over her face. The hurt, the

pain. Claire was a doctor, a pathologist. She had taken in what was at stake before I even met her eyes.

I told her that I was already undergoing packed red cell transfusions twice a week.

'That's why you wanted to get together the other day?' she declared. 'Oh, Lindsay. Why couldn't you just tell me?'

None of my past reasoning seemed clear now. 'I wanted to so much, but I was afraid. Maybe even more to admit it to myself. Then I allowed myself to get wrapped up in the case.'

'Does anyone know? Jacobi? Roth?'

I shook my head.

'Raleigh?'

I took a breath. 'Still think I'm ready for Mr Right?'

'You poor baby,' Claire said softly. 'Oh Lindsay, Lindsay, Lindsay.'

Her body was shaking. I could feel it. I *had* hurt her.

Suddenly, I let it all go – fear and shame and uncertainty rushing through me. I held onto Claire, and I realized she was all that kept me from hurtling out of control. I started to cry, and then we both did. It felt good, though. I wasn't alone anymore.

'I'm here for you, sweetheart,' Claire whispered. 'I love you, girl.'

Chapter Forty-One

The murder in Napa changed everything.

There were blistering attacks on the way the SFPD was trying to solve the case. We took heat from everywhere.

Sensational headlines announced the handiwork of a sadistic, deranged, completely new kind of killer. Out-of-town news crews buzzed around the Hall. Tragic wedding pictures and wrenching family scenes were the lead on every TV newscast.

The task force that I was heading was meeting twice a day. Two other Inspectors from SCU and a forensic psychologist were added on. We had to provide our files for the FBI. The investigation was no longer confined to some embittered figure lurking in David or Melanie Brandt's past. It had grown larger, deeper, more tragic and foreboding.

Canvassing area wine shops, Jacobi's team had unearthed a few names, nothing more.

The bloody jacket was coming up empty, too. The problem was, the tux style was from four to five years ago. Of the fifteen Bay Area stores, not one maintained records of manufacturers' styles, so it was virtually impossible to trace. We had to go over their records invoice by invoice.

Mercer tripled our investigators.

The killer was choosing his victims with careful precision. Both murders took place within a day of their marriage; both reflected specific knowledge of the victims, their lodgings, their itineraries. Both couples still had all of their valuables: watches, wallets, jewelry. The only things missing were the wedding rings.

He had dumped the DeGeorges in a seemingly isolated place, but one where they were sure to be found. He had left other blockbuster clues for us to follow up. It didn't make sense.

The killer knows exactly what he's doing, I thought. He knows what you're doing, too. *Link the crimes.*

I had to find the common denominator. How he knew his victims. How he knew so much about them.

Raleigh and I divided up the possibilities. He took whoever booked the Brandts' and the DeGeorges' itineraries: travel agencies, limo services, hotels. I took guests at both weddings. Ultimately, we would find some link between the crimes.

'If we don't make progress soon,' Raleigh grumbled, 'there'll be a lot of priests and rabbis in this town with a shitload of dead time. What's this maniac after?'

I didn't say, but I thought I knew. He was after happiness, dreams, expectations. He was trying to destroy the one thing that kept all of us going – hope.

Chapter Forty-Two

That night, Claire Washburn took a cup of tea into her bedroom, quietly closed the door, and started to cry again. 'Goddamn it, Lindsay,' she muttered. 'You could have trusted me.'

She needed to be alone. All that evening, she had been moody and distracted. And it wasn't like her. On Mondays, an off-night for the symphony, Edmund always cooked. It was one of their rituals, a family night – Dad in the kitchen, the boys clean up afterwards. Tonight he cooked their favorite meal, chicken in capers and vinegar. But nothing went right, and it was her fault.

One thought was pounding in her. She was a doctor, a doctor who dealt only in death. Never once had she saved a life. She was a doctor who did not heal.

Claire opened her closet, put on flannel pajamas, went into the bathroom and carefully cleansed her smooth brown face. She looked at herself.

She was not beautiful, at least not in the shape society taught us to admire. She was large and soft and round, her shapeless waist merging with her hips. Even her hands – her well-trained, efficient hands that controlled delicate instruments all day – were pudgy and full.

The only thing light about her, her husband always said, was when she was on the dance floor.

Yet, in her own eyes, she had always felt blessed and radiant. Because she had made it up from a tough, mostly black neighborhood in San Francisco to become a doctor. Because she was loved. Because she was taught to give love. Because she had everything in her life that she ever wanted.

It didn't seem fair. Lindsay was the one who attacked life, and now it was seeping out of her. She couldn't even think of it in a professional way, as a doctor, where she viewed the inevitability of disease with a clinical detachment. It pained her as a friend.

The doctor who could not heal.

After he finished helping the boys with the dishes, Edmund came in. He sat on the bed beside her.

'You're sick, kitty kat,' he said, with a hand that kneaded her shoulder. 'Whenever you curl up before nine o'clock, I know you're getting sick.'

She shook her head. 'I'm not sick, Edmund.'

'Then what is it? This grotesque case?'

Claire raised a hand. 'It's Lindsay. I rode back from Napa with her yesterday. She told me the most awful news. She's got a rare blood disorder, a form of anemia. It's called Negli's aplastic.'

'It's severe, this Negli's anemia?'

Claire nodded, her eyes dim. 'Damned severe.'

'Oh, God,' Edmund muttered. 'Poor Lindsay.' He took her hand and they sat there for a moment in stunned silence.

Claire finally spoke. 'I'm a doctor. I see death every day. I know the causes and symptoms, the science inside out. But *I can't heal.*'

'You heal us all the time,' Edmund said quietly. 'You heal me every day of my life. But there are times when even all your love and even your amazing intelligence can't change things.'

She nestled her body in his strong arms and smiled. 'You're pretty smart for a guy who plays the drums. So then what the hell *can* we do?'

'Just this,' he said, wrapping his arms around her.

He held Claire tightly for a long time, and she knew he thought she was the most beautiful woman in the whole world. That helped.

Chapter Forty-Three

The following afternoon, I got my first glimpse of the killer's face.

Chris Raleigh was talking to the people who had handled the travel arrangements of both sets of victims while I was checking into who had planned their weddings.

There were two different companies. For the DeGeorges, White Lace. For the Brandts, a fancy consultant, Miriam Campbell. That wasn't the link.

I was at my desk when the duty clerk patched through a call. It was Claire, phoning from her lab. She had just returned from examining the bodies of the victims with the County Coroner in Napa. She sounded excited.

'Get down here,' she said. 'And hurry.'

'You found a link,' I said immediately. 'Rebecca DeGeorge was sexually disturbed?'

'Lindsay, we're dealing with one sick dude.'

Minutes later, when I met her in the lab, Claire told me, 'They were *definitely* in the act when they were killed. Semen traces found in Rebecca DeGeorge matched those I scraped off her husband. And the angle of the wounds confirmed what I suspected. She was shot from behind. Rebecca's blood was all over her husband's clothes. She was straddling him . . . but that's not why I asked you down.'

She fixed her large wide eyes on me, and I could tell it was something more important.

'I thought it best to keep this quiet,' she said. 'Only the local ME and I know.'

'Know what? Tell me, for God's sake!' In the lab, I spotted a microscope on a counter and one of those airtight Petri dishes I remembered from high-school chemistry.

'As with the first victims,' she said excitedly, 'there was additional sexual disturbance of the corpse. Only this time, it wasn't so obvious. The labia was normal, what you would expect, post-intercourse, and there were no internal abrasions like with the first bride. Bill Toll missed it . . . but I was *looking* for signs of additional abuse. And there it was, and inside the vagina, sort of shouting, "Come and get me, Claire!" '

She picked up the Petri dish and a tweezer, and gently removed the top. From out of the clear dish she lifted a single, half-inch reddish-gray hair.

'It's not the husband's?'

Claire shook her head. 'Look for yourself.'

She flicked on the microscope. I leaned in, and against the brilliant white background of the lens, I saw two hairs: one thin, shiny, black-brown; the other, short, curly, sickle-shaped.

'You're looking at two sections from Michael DeGeorge,' she explained. 'The long one's from his head. The other is genital.'

Then she placed the hair from the Petri dish on another slide and inserted it in the microscope lens bay, side by side with the others. My pulse was starting to race. I thought I knew where she was going with this.

The new hair was reddish-gray in hue and twice the size in thickness. It had tiny filaments twisted around the cortex. It clearly belonged to someone else.

'It's neither cranial nor pubic. *It's from a beard.*' Claire announced, leaning over me.

I pulled back from the scope and looked at her, shocked.

The killer's facial hair had turned up in Becky DeGeorge's vagina.

'Post-mortem,' she said, to drive it home.

Chapter Forty-Four

A s Claire said, we were piecing our killer together, step by step. His height, his face, his fetishes. The way he murdered.

Now I had to figure out how he was tracking his victims.

Raleigh and I were going full force on the travel and wedding-planner thing. We had fifteen detectives out there following up leads. Now that we had a facial characteristic, we went back to the guests, combing them for a guy with a beard who might have been seen strolling around.

I felt confident some aspect of this widening search would yield results. One of the guests would have noticed someone. Or there'd be a travel agent in common, a link somewhere. Or one of Jacobi's searches would come up with a match.

The following morning, Hartwig called in. 'Sparrow Ridge Vineyards . . . it's owned by a group here known as Black Hawk Partners. A local guy, Ed Lester, an attorney, puts together real-estate partnerships.'

'You know where he was over the weekend?'

'Yeah, I checked. Portland. He ran in a marathon there. I caught him when he got back to the office. He was definitely in Portland.'

I still felt certain whoever had dumped the bodies there hadn't stumbled on the remote vineyard by accident. It meant something to the killer. 'He owns this place outright?'

'Nope. Black Hawk put together deals. They bring in outside money from well-heeled guys down your way – people who want to break into the wine game. Lester acts as the managing partner.'

'So who's he partnered with on this one?'

'I don't know. Investors.'

I sucked in my breath, trying to remain patient. '*Which* investors?'

'Generally, investors who want to remain private. Listen, Inspector, I know where you're heading, but this guy only deals with pretty established people. Believe me, anyone could've found that dump site. Real-estate agents, someone who'd checked it out, anyone local. I have to deal with these people long after you're gone.'

I cradled the phone in my neck and spun around in my seat toward the window. 'This is a multiple-murder investigation, Lieutenant, the worst I've ever seen. The dump site is three miles up a deserted dirt road. Anyone riding around in the dark with two bodies could've safely dumped them anytime before. Whoever did this had to know the vineyard was there. And I don't think it's a local. I don't think he would draw attention so close to where he lives.'

I paused to let my words sink in. 'Come back to me when you know who Lester's partners were.' I hung up on Hartwig.

Some of my optimism began to unravel.

Raleigh turned up nothing on the travel agents. The Brandts had booked through Travel Ventures, a society agent that catered to a high-end crowd. The DeGeorges used Journeytime, out of Los Altos, where Michael DeGeorge worked.

We had people scour through the personnel records. There was no connection between the two firms: no cooperative arrangements, not a single travel agent who had worked for both of them. It was possible someone had tapped into their systems, said the manager of Journeytime. But finding that was next to impossible.

My end was equally disappointing. I had the files from both wedding planners. Engravers, bands, photographers, caterers, florists. Nothing matched up. The Brandts and the DeGeorges lived in two separate worlds. How the killer was identifying the victims remained a mystery. I hadn't found a single clue.

Chapter Forty-Five

I called Claire and Cindy together for a second meeting of the girls. This time, the mood was decidedly different. There was no laughter or high fives. No festive margaritas. Two more people were dead. We had no suspects, only a widening case. Clues that were rapidly leading nowhere. Intense pressure coming down on all of us.

Claire was first to arrive. She hugged me and asked how I was feeling.

'I don't know,' I admitted. I had gone through three treatments. Sometimes I felt strong. At other times, especially in the afternoon, I felt like a ghost of myself. 'Medved said he'd review my red cell count next week.'

Cindy arrived next. She was wearing a halter under a man's plaid shirt, a pair of embroidered jeans. She was very pretty, and city-cool. I hadn't spoken to her since Monday, when I let her run with the story of the second killings. Even holding her story back that one day, she still scooped the city.

'I guess I'm buying,' she announced. She tossed us a new business card with the bright red logo of the *Chronicle* on it. I read the card: *Cindy Thomas, Reporter, Metro Crime Desk.*

We toasted her with warm congratulations, then we roasted her a little, just to keep her ego in balance. What else are friends for?

I told them that the travel agents and wedding planners had led nowhere. 'A couple of things really bother me,' I said. 'The gun, for instance. Sexual killers don't usually change their methods. The methods are part of the sexual thrill.'

'It's a strange combination,' agreed Claire. 'He's so in control when he plans his strikes. He seems to know everything. Where they're married, their hotel room numbers, what their honeymoon itinerary is. How to get away. Yet, when he kills, he's close to rage. It's not enough to merely kill them. He has to *defile.*'

I nodded. 'That's the key. He's striking at weddings; something about them is intolerable to him. But I think his obsession's with the brides. Both of the grooms were dispatched quickly. It's as if they didn't even matter to him. But the brides . . . that's his real fascination.'

I pondered on this for a moment. 'So where would this guy go,' I asked aloud, 'to scout potential victims? If you wanted to kill brides, where would you check them out?'

'They had to choose a ring,' suggested Claire. 'A jeweler.'

'Or City Hall,' volunteered Cindy. 'They'd need a license.'

I looked at her and chuckled. 'It sure would fit if a government employee was the one behind this.'

'Postal employee.' Claire and Cindy spoke simultaneously.

'Photographers,' said Claire.

I could see a twisted bastard hiding behind the lens. They were all good possibilities. It only required legs and manpower to check them before the killer struck again.

'This bride business isn't exactly my expertise,' I said to Claire. 'That's why you're here.'

'What happened to all that three sharp cookies crap?' she laughed. 'And the part about my being a top-notch ME?'

There was a ripple of frustrated laughter around the table. We took another sip of beer. The Women's Murder Club. This was good. No men allowed.

'Where's the goddamn link?' I fretted. 'He *wants* us to find it. That's why he's leaving clues. He wants us to uncover the link.'

Everyone was silent, lost in thought.

'I can feel it,' I went on. 'In the ceremony, the celebration, he finds something that drives him into psychopathic rage. Something he needs to stamp out. Is it hope, innocence? The husbands he kills right away, as I've said. But the brides? How does he find the brides?'

'If he's living in this twisted dreamworld,' said Cindy, thinking aloud, 'he would go to where the fantasy was the strongest, the most vivid. He might want to build up his anger by observing them in an unsuspecting state.'

Then Claire looked at us with a spark in her eye. 'I was thinking, I'd go where they bought their wedding dresses. That's where I would pick the victims out.'

Chapter Forty-Six

When I got to work the following morning, there was a fax from Hartwig listing the partners at Sparrow Ridge. I gave them to Jacobi to check. Then I called my contacts at both wedding planners, White Lace and Miriam Campbell.

I wasn't expecting much. So far, everything had come back empty. Then, to my shock, both planners confirmed it.

Melanie Brandt and Becky DeGeorge *had* bought their dresses at the same place.

The Bridal Boutique at Saks.

It was the first tangible link between the two cases. It could lead to nothing, but I felt in my bones it had the real, promising sensation of something good.

I was at Saks by the time the store opened at ten. The Bridal Boutique was on the third floor, tucked away in a corner next to Gifts and Fine China.

I caught Maryanne Perkins as she was arriving for the day, a cup of steaming coffee in her hand. The Department

Manager was a stylish, affable woman of about fifty, just the type who would work with brides for twenty years. She had someone cover for her and sat down with me in a cluttered back room filled with magazine photos of brides.

'I was devastated when I heard about it.' She shook her head, ashen-faced. 'Melanie was just here, two weeks ago.' She stared at me, glassily. 'She was so beautiful . . . my brides are like my children, Inspector. I feel as if I've lost one of my own.'

'One?' I fixed on her eyes. 'You haven't heard?'

'Heard what?'

I told Maryanne Perkins about Rebecca Passeneau, the late Mrs DeGeorge.

Shock and horror swept over her face. Her green eyes bulged, welled with a rush of tears. She stared through me as if she were looking into the wall. 'Oh, my God . . .' She took in a heart-jolting breath. 'My husband and I were at our cabin in Modesto for a few days. Young Becky was just in here with her Mom. Oh, my God. What's going on here, Inspector?'

An immediate flood of questions tumbled out. Who would know about their customers? Other salespersons? Managers? The killer had been sighted as a male. Did any men work in the department?

Each of them elicited a disbelieving, negative response from Maryanne Perkins. The staff had all been together for a minimum of eight years. No males. *Just like our murder club.*

She leaned back in her chair, scrolling her memory for

any details that she could recall. 'We were admiring her. Becky . . . she was stunning. It was as if she had never thought of herself in quite that way, but seeing herself in her dress, it suddenly became clear. Her mother had given her this brooch – pearls, diamonds – and I ran back to the office for flowers. That's when I noticed someone. Standing over there,' she pointed. 'He was staring in Becky's direction. I remember thinking, See, even he thinks you're beautiful. I remember now.'

Frantically, I took down a description: late forties, maybe younger. 'I didn't get a really good look,' the bridal manager said. 'He had a beard.'

I was sure it was him! It confirmed that Claire was right. Saks had to be where he found his victims, where he tracked them.

I pressed her hard. 'How would anyone find out details about someone's wedding? Dates, locations – where they would honeymoon?'

'We collect that information,' Maryanne Perkins said, 'when the girls choose a gown. Some of it we need to know to help us, like dates, deadlines. And, it just helps us get a feel for the bride. Most of them register with us as well.'

A feel for the bride.

'Who has access to this information?'

She shook her head. 'Just us . . . me and my assistants. It's a small department. Sometimes we share it with Fine China and Gifts.'

I felt I was finally close. My heart was slamming inside

my chest. 'I need to see a copy of anything you have on Melanie Brandt and Becky DeGeorge, and every customer you're currently working with.' *He was spotting his potential victims here, wasn't he?* There was a good chance he would come back. Someone on the store's list could be next in line.

I saw Ms Perkins's jaw drop again. She appeared to be focusing on a horrible sight. 'There's something else you'll want to know.'

'What?'

'About a month ago, after inventory, we noticed that our folder on the brides was missing.'

Chapter Forty-Seven

As soon as I got back to the Hall, I did two things: I called Claire and Cindy and told them what I'd found out at Saks, then I went to find Raleigh.

I shared everything with Chris, and we decided to put a woman detective from the Sex Crime Unit inside the department store. I sent a sketch artist over to see Maryanne Perkins at Saks.

Then Chris shared something important with me. Roth and Mercer had handed over our case files to the FBI.

I felt a knifing pain deep in my chest. I rushed into the bathroom, closed the door behind me, pressed my back against the cold, chipped tile. *Goddamn, son-of-a-bitch,* controlling men. *Goddamn Roth and Mercer!*

I stared at my face in the mirror. My cheeks were flushed. My skin was burning.

The FBI! This was my case – and Claire's, Cindy's, and Raleigh's. It meant more to me than any other I'd ever worked on.

Suddenly, my legs felt wobbly. Negli's? The doctor said

I'd be feeling fits of nausea or light-headedness. I had my fourth transfusion scheduled at the hematology clinic at five-thirty.

An overwhelming emptiness tugged at me, alternating between anger and fear. I was just starting to crack this thing. I didn't need outsiders in dark suits and tie pins buzzing around with a clumsy, alternative investigation.

I blinked into the mirror. My skin, apart from the burning cheeks, looked pallid and lifeless. My eyes were watery and gray. My whole body seemed drained of color.

I stared at myself until a familiar voice came alive inside me. *'Come on. Get yourself together, Lindsay. You win – you always win.'*

I splashed cold water on my face. The flashing sweat on my neck began to subside.

You're allowed *one* of these, I told myself with a thin smile. *Just don't do that again.*

I looked at my watch. It was four-twenty. I had to be at the clinic soon. I'd start on the names tomorrow. After applying a few dabs of makeup, I made my way back to my desk. To my chagrin, Raleigh wandered up.

'Now you can manage *their* fall-out,' I snapped unnec-essarily, referring to the FBI.

'I didn't know,' he said mildly. 'As soon as I did, I told you.'

'Yeah,' I nodded. 'Right.'

Raleigh got up, came around and sat on the edge of my desk, facing me. 'Something's wrong, isn't it? Tell me. Please.' How did he know? Maybe he was a lot better detective than I gave him credit for.

For a moment, I really wanted to tell him. God, I wanted it to come out. Then Raleigh did something totally unexpected. He flashed one of those trusting smiles that I couldn't help but give myself over to. Then he pulled me out of my chair and gave me a hug.

I was so surprised I didn't even resist. I was quivering jelly in his arms. It wasn't quite sexual, but no burst of passion had ever rippled through me more powerfully.

Raleigh held me until the anxiety had slowly melted away. Right there, in the fucking squad room. I didn't know what to do, but I didn't want to pull back. Or have him let me go.

'I could write you up for this,' I finally mumbled into his shoulder.

He didn't move. 'You want a pen?'

Slowly, I pulled myself away. Every nerve in my body felt as if it had retreated from a tense state of alert. 'Thanks,' I muttered, with appreciation.

'You didn't seem yourself,' he said gently. 'Shift's almost done. Want to talk about it over coffee? Just coffee, Lindsay, *not a date.*'

I looked at my watch again and suddenly saw that it was almost five o'clock. I was late for my appointment.

I gave him a look that I hoped reflected, *Ask me again*, but said, 'I can't. Gotta go.'

Chapter Forty-Eight

The pretty smiling reservation clerk politely nodded for the next person in line. 'Welcome to the Lakefront Hilton, sir.'

Phillip Campbell stepped up to the counter. He noticed her name, Kaylin. Bright-eyed, bushy-bushed Kaylin. He smiled back, flirted subtly. He handed her a confirmation slip.

'First time with us, Mr Campbell?' the desk clerk asked in a high-pitched chirp.

He beamed, let her know that it was.

As she punched in his reservation, he followed her movements, thoughtfully stroking the rough hairs of his beard. He wanted her to notice. To remember his face – maybe something he had said. One day, when some diligent FBI agent came by with a drawing or photograph, he wanted this chirpy little squirrel to think back and recall this moment in a close and chilling way. He wanted her to remember everything.

As had the saleswoman in the Bridal Boutique at Saks.

'Here for a visit to the museum, Mr Campbell?' Kaylin asked, as she typed.

'For the Voskuhl wedding,' he volunteered.

'Everyone's saying that,' she smiled.

He followed the click of her peach-colored nails against the keys as she typed in his reservation. 'I've got you a deluxe room with a beautiful view,' she said, handing him a key, then added: 'Enjoy the wedding. And have a nice stay.'

'I will,' Campbell said pleasantly. Before he turned away, he caught her eye and said, 'Speaking of weddings – I like your ring.'

Upstairs, he pulled the curtains aside and, as promised, before him was a sweeping view.

Of Cleveland, Ohio.

Chapter Forty-Nine

I *saw him, that bastard. What was he doing here?*
In a large, fast-moving crowd, on Lower Market. Just a quick movement in the throng fighting its way toward the Ferry.

My blood froze with the sight of him.

He was wearing an open blue shirt, a brown corduroy jacket. He looked like some college professor. On any other day, I could have passed him by, never noticed. He was thin, gaunt, totally unremarkable in every way but one.

It was the reddish-brown beard.

His head bobbed in and out of the rushing crowd. I followed, unable to narrow the distance.

'Police!' I shouted, over the din. My cry dissolved into the hurrying, unheeding crowd. At any moment I might lose him.

I didn't know his name – I only knew his victims. *Melanie Brandt. Rebecca DeGeorge.*

Suddenly, he stopped. He bucked against the flow,

turned right toward me. His face seemed illuminated, shining against a dark background like one of those medieval Russian icons. Amid the commotion, our eyes met.

There was a moment of captured, enlightened recognition, frozen apart from the chaos of the crowd. He knew that it was me. That I was the one after him.

Then, to my horror, he fled; the crowd engulfed him, swept him away.

'*Stop!*' I shouted. 'I'll shoot!' A cold sweat broke out on my neck. I drew my gun. '*Get down!*' I cried, but the rush-hour crowd pushed on, shielding him. I was going to lose him. The killer was getting away.

I raised the gun, focused on the image of his red beard. He turned – with the sneer of someone who had totally out-witted me. I drew a breath, steadied my aim. As if in slow motion, every face in the crowd turned toward me, too.

I stepped back. In horror, I lowered the gun.

Every face in the crowd had the same red beard.

I must have been dreaming. I found myself at my kitchen counter, blinking into swirling circles in my Chardonnay. There was a familiar calm in my apartment. No rushing crowds, no fleeing faces. Only Sweet Martha lounging on her futon.

A pot of boiling water was steaming on the stove. I had my favorite sauce ready to go – ricotta, zucchini, basil. A CD was on, Tori Amos.

Only an hour ago, I had tubes and IV lines sticking out of me. My heart kept pace to the metronome-like rhythm of a monitor's steady beep.

Damn it, I wanted my old life back. My old, favorite dreams. I wanted Jacobi's sarcasm, Sam Roth's scorn, jogging on the Marina Green. I wanted kids, too – even if it meant I had to get married again.

Suddenly, the downstairs buzzer rang. Who would be here now? I shuffled over and said, 'Who is it?'

'I thought you had somewhere to go?' a static voice replied.

It was Raleigh.

Chapter Fifty

'What're you doing here?' I called back in surprise. I was pleased, but suddenly tingling with nerves. My hair was pulled up, I was in an old Berkeley T-shirt that I sometimes slept in, and I felt drained and anxious from my transfusion. My little place was a mess.

'Can I come up?' Raleigh said.

'This business or personal?' I asked. 'We don't have to go back to Napa, do we?'

'Not tonight.' I heard him laugh. 'This time I brought my own.'

I didn't quite understand that, but I buzzed him up. Then I ran back to the kitchen, turned the heat down on the pasta and, in the same breath, threw a couple of pillows from the floor onto the couch and transferred a pile of magazines to a chair in the kitchen.

I put some lip gloss on and shook out my hair as the doorbell rang.

Raleigh was in an open shirt and baggy khakis. He was carrying a bottle of wine – Kunde. Very nice. He tossed me an apologetic smile. 'I hope you don't mind me barging in.'

'Nobody barges in here. I let you in,' I said. 'What're you doing here anyway?'

He laughed. 'I was in the neighborhood.'

'The neighborhood, huh? You live across the Bay.'

He nodded, abandoning his alibi without much resistance. 'I just wanted to make sure you were okay. You didn't seem yourself back at the station.'

'That's nice, Raleigh,' I said, looking into his eyes.

'So? Are you?'

'So. I was just feeling a little overwhelmed. Roth. This FBI thing. I'm fine now. Really.'

'Glad to hear it,' he said. 'Hey – something smells good.'

'I was just throwing some pasta together.' I paused, thinking about what I wanted to say next. 'You had dinner?'

He shook his head. 'No, no. I don't want to intrude.'

'That why you came with the wine?'

He gave me one of those irresistible smiles. 'If you weren't home, I have a corner of Second and Brannan I always head to.'

I smiled back and finally held open the door.

When Raleigh came into my apartment, he looked around with sort of an impressed nod, gazing at some of the pottery, a black-and-gold satin baseball jacket from Willie Mays, my terrace with its view of the Bay. He held out the bottle.

'There's one already open on the counter,' I said. 'Pour yourself a glass. I'll check on the food.'

I went into the kitchen, reminding myself that I had just

come from the outpatient clinic for a serious disease, and we were partners, anyway. With an irrepressible flicker of excitement, I took out an extra setting.

'Number twenty-four, Giants?' he called to me. 'This warm-up jacket is the real thing?'

'Willie Mays. My father gave it to me for my tenth birthday. He wanted a boy. I kept it all these years.'

He came into the kitchen, spun a stool around at the counter. While I stirred the penne he poured himself a glass of wine. 'You always cook for yourself like this?'

'Old habit,' I said. 'Growing up, my mother worked late. I had a sister six years younger. Sometimes my mother didn't get home till eight. From the time I can remember, I had to make dinner.'

'Where was your dad?'

'Left us,' I said, whipping together some mustard, grape-seed oil, balsamic, and lemon into a vinaigrette for the salad. 'When I was thirteen.'

'So your mother brought you up?'

'You could say. Sometimes I feel like I brought myself up.'

'Until you got married.'

'Yeah, then I sort of brought him up, too.' I smiled. 'You're pretty nosy, Raleigh.'

'Cops generally are. Didn't you know that?'

'Yeah. Real cops.'

Raleigh feigned being hurt. 'What can I help you with?' he offered.

'You can grate,' I said and grinned. I pushed a block of

Parmesan and a metal grater his way.

We sat there, he grating, me waiting for the pasta to cook. Sweet Martha padded into the kitchen and let Raleigh pet her.

'You didn't seem yourself this afternoon,' he said, as he stroked Martha's head. 'Usually, you handle Roth's bullshit without even blinking. Seemed like there was something wrong.'

'Nothing's wrong,' I lied. 'At least not now. If you were asking.'

I leaned against the counter and looked at him. He was my partner, but even more than that, he was a person I thought I could trust. It had been a long, hard time since I had put my trust in anybody whose gender started with an *m*. Maybe, in a different time . . . I was thinking.

Tori Amos's haunting voice hung in the air.

'You like to dance?' Raleigh suddenly asked.

I looked at him, really surprised. 'I don't dance, I cook.' I stammered a little.

'You don't dance . . . you cook?' Raleigh repeated, scrunching up his brow.

'Yeah. You know what they say about cooking.'

He looked around. 'What *I'd* say is that it doesn't seem to be working. Maybe you should try dancing.'

The music was soft and languorous, and as much as I tried to deny it, part of me just yearned to be held.

Without my even saying yes, my goddamn partner took my hand and pulled me from around the counter. I wanted to hold back, but a soft, surrendering voice inside me said,

'Just go with it, Lindsay. He's okay. You know you trust him.'

So I gave in, and let Chris Raleigh hold me. I liked being in his arms.

At first we sort of stood there, swaying stiffly. Then I found myself letting my head fall on his shoulder, and feeling like nothing could ail me there, at least not for a while.

'This isn't a date,' I muttered, and let myself drift to a real nice place where I felt love and hope and dreams were still there to reach for.

'To tell the truth,' I told Raleigh. 'I'm glad you stopped by.'

'Me too.'

Then I felt him put his arms around me, hold me close. A tingle raced down my spine, one that I almost didn't recognize anymore.

'You've got it, don't you, Raleigh?' I said dreamily.

'What's that, Lindsay?'

Soft hands.

Chapter Fifty-One

K athy and James Voskuhl were having their first dance – and to break with tradition it was a rocker.

The loud, driving beat of 'La Bamba' jolted through the brightly lit atrium of the Rock and Roll Hall of Fame in Cleveland.

'Everybody!' the groom shouted. 'Rock and roll! Join us!'

Hip young girls in dyed hair and wearing shiny green and red prom dresses – sixties style – swung around on the dance floor, their partners in retro silk shirts, Travolta-like. The bride and groom, having changed into party garb, joined in, butting thighs, whooping, arms in the air.

It almost ruined everything, Phillip Campbell thought. He had wanted her in white. And here she was, sweaty red-streaked hair, cat's-eye-shaped glasses, a tight green dress.

This time, Kathy, you've gone too far.

Forty tables, each with the likeness of some rock-and-roll icon as a centerpiece, filled out the Great Hall of the museum. A glittery banner that hung from the glass roof proclaimed: *James and Kathy.*

After a loud crescendo the music stopped. A throng of sweaty wedding guests milled back toward their tables, fanning themselves. Waiters in black waistcoats scurried about the room, filling wine glasses.

The bride went over and embraced a happy tuxedoed couple. Mom and Dad. Phillip Campbell couldn't take his eyes off her. He saw her father give her a loving look, as if to say: 'We've come through a lot, honey, but now everything will be all right. Now you're part of the club, trust funds, and Country Day, little peach-haired grandkids.'

The groom wandered over and whispered something in Kathy's ear. She squeezed his arm, flashing him a smile that was both affectionate and coy. As he walked away, the tips of her fingers lingered, as if she were saying, 'I'll be right along.'

With a hitch of his belt, the groom drifted out of the main hall. He glanced back once or twice, and Kathy waved.

Campbell decided to follow, hanging back at a safe distance. He went down a wide, well-lit corridor off the atrium. Halfway down, James Voskuhl opened a door and went in. The men's room.

The killer moved forward. No one else was in the hall. He felt an irrepressible urge building with force. His fingers made their way into his jacket pocket, touched the cold heel of the gun. He flicked the safety off. He could no longer control what was going on inside his head.

Go in, a voice dared him. *Do it.*

He entered in a filmy, sallow light. No one was at the

urinals or sinks. The groom was in a closed stall. A pungent smell filled his nostrils, marijuana.

'That you, love?' the groom's affectionate voice called out.

Every wicklike nerve in Campbell's body stood at attention. He mumbled something barely audible.

'Better get in here, hon,' James Voskuhl gulped, 'If you want the end of this bone.'

Phillip Campbell pushed open the door.

The groom looked up, bewildered, the tip of a joint on his lip. 'Hey, man, who the hell are you?'

'I'm the one who kills useless worms like you.' With that, he fired. Just once.

James Voskuhl's head snapped back. A splatter of red sprayed against the tile. The groom rocked once, then crumpled forward in a heap.

The echo of the gun blast seemed to concuss the entire room. It left an effluvium of cordite that mingled with the pot.

A strange calm took over Phillip Campbell, a fearlessness. He pulled the groom's head back and set him upright.

Then he waited.

The sound of the outer door opening and echoes of the distant party rushing in went right through him.

'That you, Vosk?' a woman's voice called out.

It was her. The bride.

'What're you smoking in there – tar?' Kathy giggled. She went over to the sinks, and he heard the sound of running water coming on.

Campbell could see her through a crack in the stall. She was at the sink, wide, cat-shaped glasses, thrashing a comb through her hair. A vision came to him. How he would set this up. *What the police would find.*

It took everything he had to control himself – to let her come to him.

'You better save me a hit or two, mister,' the bride called out.

He watched her dance over to the stall. *So close now. So unbelievably delicious. What a moment.*

When she opened the door, it was her *look* that meant everything to him.

The sight of James, red drool leaking from his mouth. The startled recognition of the killer's face suddenly clicking in; the gun aimed right at her eyes.

'I like you better in white, Kathy,' was all the killer said.

Then he squeezed the trigger – and a blinding white flash exploded through the green cat's-eye-shaped lens.

Chapter Fifty-Two

I was in early Monday morning, feeling a little nervous about my first contact with Raleigh after our dancing-and-dining experience, wondering where all this was going to go – when one of the task force Inspectors, Paul Chin, rushed up to me. 'Lindsay, there's a woman in Interrogation Room Four I think you should check out.'

Ever since a physical description of the assailant had hit the airwaves, people were calling in with fake sightings and dead-end leads. One of Chin's jobs was to follow them up, no matter how unlikely.

'This one a psychic or a police buff?' I asked with a skeptical smile.

'I think this one's the genuine article,' said Chin. 'She was at the first wedding.'

I almost leaped out of my chair after him. At the front of the squad room, I spotted Raleigh coming in. *Chris.*

For a moment, a tingle of pleasure rushed through me. He'd left about eleven, after we ended up polishing off both bottles of wine. We ate, chewed over our separate stints on the force, and the ups and downs of being married or single.

It had been a sweet evening. Took the heat off from the case. It even got my mind off Negli's. What scared me a little was the tremor inside that it could be something more. I caught myself staring at him Friday night, while he helped out with the dishes, thinking, If times were different . . .

Raleigh ran into me, carrying coffee and a paper. 'Hey,' he smiled. 'Nice vest.'

'Chin's got a live one in four,' I said, grabbing his arm. 'Claims to have a physical sighting. You want to come along?'

In my haste, I was already by him, not even giving him a second of recognition. He put down his paper on our civilian-clerk's desk and caught up on the stairs.

In the cramped interrogation room sat a nicely dressed, attractive woman of about fifty. Chin introduced her to me as Laurie Birnbaum. She seemed tight, nervous.

Chin sat down next to her. 'Ms Birnbaum, why don't you tell Detective Boxer what you just told me.'

She was frightened. 'It was the beard that made me remember. I didn't even think of it all week. It was so horrible.'

'You were at the Brandts' wedding?' I asked her.

'We were guests of the Weils,' she replied. 'My husband works with Chancellor Weil at the university.' She took a nervous sip from a cup of coffee. 'It was just a brief thing. But he gave me the chills.'

Chin pushed down the record button of a portable recorder.

'Please, go ahead,' I told her, soothingly. Once again, I felt close to *him* – the bastard in the red beard.

'I stood next to him. He had this graying red beard, like a goatee – the kind they wear in Los Angeles. He looked older, maybe forty-five, fifty, but there was something about him. I'm not saying this right, am I?'

'You spoke to him?' I asked, trying to communicate that even though she didn't do this every day, I did. Even the male detectives admitted that I was the best at Q and A on the floor. They joked that it was 'a girl thing'.

'I had just come in from the dance floor,' she said. 'I looked up, and there he was. I said something like, "Nice affair . . . bride or groom?" For a moment, I thought he looked kind of appealing. Then he just sort of glared at me. I took him for one of those arrogant investment-banker types from the Brandt side.'

'What did he say to you?' I said.

She massaged her brow, straining to recall. 'He said, in the weirdest way, that they were *lucky*.'

'Who was lucky?'

'Melanie and David. I may have said, "Aren't they lucky?" meaning the two of them. They were so stunning, and he replied, "Oh, they're *lucky*." ' She looked up with a confused expression on her face. 'He called them something else . . . *chosen*.'

'Chosen?'

'Yes. He said, "Oh, they're lucky . . . you could even say they were chosen." '

'You say he had a goatee?'

'That's what was so strange. The beard made him seem older, but the rest of him was young.'

'The rest of him? What do you mean?'

'His face. His voice. I know this must sound strange, but it was only for a moment, as I came off the dance floor.'

We got as much as we could from her. Height, hair color. What he was wearing. Everything confirmed the sparse details that we already had. The killer was a man with a short, reddish-gray beard. He was in a tux. The tux jacket he had left behind in the Mandarin Suite.

A fire was building inside me. I felt sure that Laurie Birnbaum was credible. *The beard. The tux.* We were piecing together his face. 'Is there anything more, anything at all that stands out to you? Some physical characteristic – a mannerism, perhaps.'

She shook her head. 'It happened so quickly. It was only when I saw the drawing of him in the *Chronicle*.'

I looked at Chin, conveying it was time to call down an artist to firm up the details. I thanked her, made my way back to my desk. We'd get a sketch from her, and one from Maryanne Perkins at Saks.

The murder investigation had entered a new phase. It was very hot. We had a stakeout operational outside the Bridal Boutique at Saks. One by one, we were contacting the names on the list, anyone who had ordered a wedding dress in the past several months.

My heart was pounding. The face I had imagined, my dream of the red-bearded man, was starting to fill in. I felt we had him contained.

My phone rang. 'Boxer,' I answered, still shuffling through the names in the Saks wedding folder.

'My name's McBride,' a deep, urgent voice said. 'I'm a homicide detective. In Cleveland.'

Chapter Fifty-Three

'I got a homicide here that fits the pattern of what you've been dealing with,' McBride explained. 'Gun shot wounds, both of them, right between the eyes.' He described the quick, but grotesque deaths of Kathy and James Voskuhl, killed at their wedding at the Rock and Roll Hall of Fame in Cleveland. This time, the killer didn't even wait for the wedding to end.

'What kind of weapon your guy use in Napa?' McBride asked.

'Nine millimeter,' I told him.

'Same.'

I was reeling a little bit. *Cleveland?* What the hell was Red Beard doing in Ohio? We had just made the breakthrough, found out where he was casing his victims. Did he know that? If so – *how?*

Cleveland was either a copycat killing, which was entirely possible, or this case had just broken wide open and could lead anywhere.

'Did your victims end up in sexually explicit positions, McBride?' I asked.

The officer grunted. 'Yeah. Got the crime-scene photos here in front of me. Nasty. They're sexually explicit all right.'

'Can you get me a close-up of their hands?'

'Okay, but why the hands?'

'What were they wearing, McBride?'

I heard him shuffling through photos. 'You mean rings?'

'Good guess, Detective. Yeah.' I was praying that it wasn't our guy. Cleveland . . . it would shatter everything that made me feel we were getting close to him. Was Red Beard taking his killing act across the country?

A minute later, McBride confirmed exactly the thing I didn't want to hear. 'There are no wedding bands.'

The bastard was on the move. We had a stakeout going where we thought he might show up and meanwhile he was 2,000 miles away. He'd just murdered a couple at their reception in Ohio. Shit, shit, shit.

'You said the bodies were found in a sexually explicit position?' I prompted McBride.

The Cleveland cop hesitated. He finally said, 'The groom was shot sitting on the john. We found him there. Sitting up, legs open. The bride was shot in the stall, too, as she was coming in. There was enough of her brains on the inside of the door to confirm it. But when we found her, she was kneeling down. Uh, her face was stuffed between his legs.'

I was silent, forming the image in my mind, hating this

cruel, inhuman bastard more every day.

'You know . . . fellatio-style,' McBride managed. 'There's a few things my investigators want to ask you.'

'Ask me yourself. I'm gonna be there tomorrow.'

Chapter Fifty-Four

Six-thirty the next morning, Raleigh and I were on our way to Cleveland, of all places. McBride met us at the plane. He wasn't how I had imagined him. He wasn't flabby, middle-aged, Irish-Catholic. He was intense, sharp-boned, maybe thirty-eight, and black.

'You're younger than I thought.' He smiled at me.

I smiled back. 'And you're definitely less Irish.'

On the way into town, he brought us up to speed. 'Groom's from Seattle. Had something to do with the music business. Worked with rock bands. Producer . . . marketing guy. Bride grew up here in Ohio – Shaker Heights. Father's a corporate attorney. Girl was cute, a redhead, with freckles and glasses.'

He pulled a manila envelope off the dashboard and tossed it over to me in the passenger's seat. Inside were a series of glossy eight-by-elevens of the crime scene: stark, graphic, somewhat resembling old photos of gangland rubouts. The groom was sitting on the stall with a surprised expression and the top of his head blown off. The bride was slumped over his lap, curled in a pool of blood, hers and his.

The sight of the couple filled me with a cold dread. As long as the killer was in northern California, I felt we had him contained. Now he was on the loose.

We grilled McBride about the venue – how the victims might have ended up in the men's room and what security was like at the Hall of Fame.

Each answer I heard convinced me even more that it was our guy. But what the hell was he doing *here*?

We pulled off the highway at Lake Shore Boulevard. A modern skyline rose all around us. 'There she is,' McBride announced.

From a distance, I saw the Rock and Roll Hall of Fame glinting up ahead like a jaggedly cut jewel. A twisted killer had struck in the city's most celebrated venue. By now, he might already be back in San Francisco. Or Chicago, New York, Topeka . . . Planning another gruesome double murder. Or maybe he was in a hotel room across the square, watching us arrive.

Red Beard could be anywhere.

Chapter Fifty-Five

I t was the third time in two weeks I had to go over a harrowing double-murder scene.

McBride walked us up to the second floor and through an eerie, empty atrium devoid of pedestrian traffic to a men's room blocked off by crisscrossing yellow crime tape and cops.

'Public bathroom,' Raleigh said to me. 'He's getting nastier each time.'

This time there were no bodies, no horrifying discoveries. The victims had long been transferred to the morgue. In their place were grim outlines of tape and chalk; gut-wrenching black-and-white crime photos taped to the walls.

I could see what had happened. How the groom had been killed first, his blood smeared on the wall behind the toilet. How Red Beard had waited, surprised the bride as she came in, then moved Kathy Voskuhl into the provocative position between her husband's legs. *Defiled her.*

'How did they both end up here in the middle of their wedding?' Raleigh asked.

McBride pointed to a crime-scene photo on the wall. 'We found a smoked-down joint next to James Voskuhl. Figured he came here to cop a buzz. My guess is the bride went up to join him.'

'No one saw anything, though? They didn't leave the reception with anyone?'

McBride shook his head.

I felt the same smoldering anger I had felt twice before. I hated this killer, this savager of dreams. With each act I hated him more. The bastard was taunting us. Each murder scene was a statement. Each one more degrading.

'What was security like that night?' I asked.

McBride shrugged. 'All exits except the main one were closed down. There was a guard at the front desk. Everyone from the wedding arrived at the same time. A couple of half-assed guards were floating around, but generally at these affairs, they like to keep a low profile.'

'I saw cameras all around,' Raleigh pressed. 'They must have some film?'

'That's what I'm hoping,' said McBride. 'I'll introduce you to Sharp, Head of Security. We can go over that now.'

Andrew Sharp was a trim, wiry man with a square chin and narrow, colorless lips. He looked scared. A day ago he had a fairly cushy job, but now the police and the FBI were all over him. Having to explain things to two outside cops from San Francisco didn't help matters. He brought us into his office, popped a Marlboro Light out of a pack, and looked at Raleigh.

'I got a meeting with the Executive Director in about eight minutes.'

We didn't even bother to sit down. I asked, 'Did your guards notice anyone unusual?'

'Three hundred guests, Madam Detective. Everyone congregated in the entrance atrium. My staff doesn't usually get involved a whole lot except to make sure no one with too much to drink gets too close to the exhibits.'

'What about how he got out then?'

Sharp wheeled in his chair, pointing to a blowup of the museum layout. 'Either the main entrance, here, where you came in, or one we left open off the back verandah. It leads down to the Lake Walk. There's a café there during the summer. Mostly it's blocked off, but the families wanted it open.'

'Two shots fired,' I said. 'No one heard anything?'

'It was supposed to be a high-class crowd. You think they want my guards milling around? We keep two, three guys, to make sure overzealous guests don't wander into restricted areas. I should have guards patrolling the corridors down by the rest rooms? What ya gonna take, toilet paper?'

'Security cameras?' Raleigh asked.

Sharp sighed. 'We've got the exhibition halls covered, of course. The main exits . . . a remote sweep of the Main Hall. But nothing on the corridor where the shooting took place. Nothing in the crapper. Anyway, the police are scanning tape with members of each family as we speak. It would make it a helluva lot easier if we knew who on earth we're looking for.'

I reached into my briefcase and took out a copy of a bare-bones artist's sketch of a red-bearded man. It showed a thin face with a jutting chin, hair combed back and a lightly shaded goatee.

'Why don't we start with him.'

Chapter Fifty-Six

M cBride had to be back in the office for a press briefing on the investigation. I needed to figure out why the killer had come to Cleveland, and what, if any, connections there were to our murders back in San Francisco. The next step was to talk to the parents of the bride.

Shaker Heights was a posh, upper-end suburb in the height of midsummer bloom. On every street, green lawns led up to graceful, tree-sheltered homes. One of McBride's men drove me out, while Raleigh went back to the Lakefront Hilton to meet with the family of the groom.

The Koguts' home was a warm, redbrick Normandy under a canopy of tall oaks. I was met at the door by an older sister of the bride, who introduced herself as Hillary Bloom. She sat me down in a comfy, picture-filled den: books, large-screen TV, photos of the two of them as kids, weddings. 'Kathy was always the rebellious one,' Hillary explained. 'A free spirit. It took her a while to find herself, but she was just settling down. She had a good job – a publicist for a firm in Seattle, where she met James. She was just coming around.'

'Coming around from what?' I asked.

'Like I said – she was a free spirit. That was Kathy.'

Her parents, Hugh and Christine Kogut, came into the room. For the third time, I witnessed the glazed, bewildered shock of people whose lives had been shattered.

'She was always in and out of relationships,' her mother eventually admitted. 'But she also had a passion for life.'

'She was just young,' her father said brokenly. 'Maybe we spoiled her too much. She always had an urge to experience things.'

From her pictures – the wispy red hair and dare-me eyes – I could see the same joy for life the killer had obviously seen in his first two victims. It made me feel sad, weary.

'Do you know why I'm here?' I asked.

The father nodded. 'To determine if there was any connection to those other horrible crimes out West.'

'So, can you tell me, did Kathy have any connection to San Francisco?'

I could see a cast of grim recognition creep its way onto their faces.

'After college, for a while, she did live there,' Christine Kogut said carefully.

'She went to UCLA,' Hugh told me. 'For a year or so after, she stayed in Los Angeles. Tried to catch on with one of the studios. She started out with a temp job at Fox, then she got this publicity job in San Francisco, covering music. It was a very fast life. Parties, promotions, no doubt a lot worse. We weren't happy, but for Kathy, she thought it was her big break.'

She lived in San Francisco. I asked if they had ever heard of Melanie Weil or Rebecca Passeneau.

They shook their heads.

'What about any relationships that might've ended badly? Someone, who out of jealousy or obsession, might've wanted to do her harm?'

'Recklessness always seemed like a basis for Kathy's relationships,' Hillary said with an edge.

'I did warn her.' Her mother shook her head. 'She always wanted to do things on her terms.'

'Did she ever mention anyone special from the time she lived in San Francisco?'

Everyone looked at Hillary. 'No. No one special.'

'No one stands out? She lived there for quite a while. She didn't keep up with anyone after she left?'

'I seem to remember her saying she still went down there every once in a while,' her father said. 'On business.'

'Old habits are hard to crack,' smirked Hillary, with a tightening of her lips.

There had to be some connection. Some contact from the year she had spent there. *Someone* came all the way here to see her dead.

'What about anyone from San Francisco invited to the wedding?' I asked.

'There was one girlfriend,' her father said.

'Merrill,' said her mother. 'Merrill Cole. Shortley now. I think she's at the Hilton, if she's still here.'

I pulled out the artist's sketch we had of the killer's possible appearance. 'It's only a rough likeness, but do you know this man? Is it someone who knew Kathy? Did you see anyone like this at the wedding?'

One by one, the Koguts shook their heads.

As I got up to go, I told them if anything came to mind, regardless how small or insignificant, to get in touch with me. Hillary walked me to the door.

'There is one more thing,' I said. I knew it was a long shot. 'By any chance, did Kathy buy her wedding dress in San Francisco?'

Hillary looked at me blankly and shook her head. 'No, from a vintage shop. In Seattle.'

At first, the answer deflated me. But then, in a flash, I saw that this was really a connection I was looking for. The first two murders had been committed by someone stalking his victims from afar. That's why he found them in the way he did. Tracked them.

But with this one, Kathy, she had been chosen in a different way.

I was certain that whoever had done this had known her.

Chapter Fifty-Seven

I drove straight to the Hilton on Lake Shore Boulevard and was able to catch Merrill Shortley just as she was packing her things, about to depart to the airport. She turned out to be stylish, maybe twenty-seven, with shoulder-length, chestnut brown hair tied back in a bun.

'A group of us were up all night,' she said, apologizing for the swollen lines around her face. 'I'd like to stay on, but who knows when they'll finally release the body. I have a one-year-old at home.'

'The Koguts told me you live in San Francisco.'

She sat on the edge of the bed across from me. 'Los Altos. I moved down two years ago when I got married.'

'I need to know about Kathy Kogut in San Francisco,' I explained. 'Lovers. Breakups. Someone who might have a cause to do this.'

'You think she *knew* this madman?' Her face was clenched.

'Maybe, Merrill. You can help us decide. *Will* you help us?'

'Kathy hooked up with guys,' Merrill said after a pause. 'She was always free about things in that way.'

'Are you saying she was promiscuous?'

'If you want to see it that way. Men liked her. There was a lot of energy going on back then. Music, film. Alternative stuff. Whatever made her feel alive.'

I was getting the picture. 'Does that include drugs?'

'Like I said, whatever made her feel alive. Yes, Kathy did recreational drugs.'

Merrill had the pretty, but hard-edged face of a street survivor who had now remade herself as a soccer-mom.

'Anyone come to mind who might've wanted to hurt her? Someone who was overly fascinated? Maybe jealous when she moved on?'

Merrill thought a bit, shook her head. 'I don't think so.'

'You two were close?'

She nodded. At the same time, her eyes hooded.

'Why did she move away?'

'She landed a great job. Must've seemed like she was finally climbing the ladder. Her father and mother always wanted that. It's the Shaker Heights thing. Look, I really have to catch a plane.'

'What are the chances Kathy was running away from something?'

'You live the way we lived, you're always running from something.' Merrill Shortley shrugged and looked bored.

There was an attitude, a coldness about Merrill I didn't like. She still surrounded herself with the cynical aura of a dissolute past. And I had the suspicion she was withholding. 'So what'd *you* do, Merrill? Marry the dime-bag mambo king of Silicon Valley?'

She shook her head. Finally, she smiled thinly. 'Fund manager.'

I leaned forward. 'So you don't remember anyone special? Someone she might've kept up with? Been scared of?'

'Those years,' Merrill Shortley said, 'I have a hard time remembering anyone special at all.'

'This was *your friend*,' I said, my voice rising. 'You want me to show you what she looks like now?'

Merrill stood up, stepped over to the dresser, and began to pack a leather bag with toiletries and makeup. At some point, she stopped and caught a glimpse of herself in the mirror. Then she looked over her shoulder and caught my eye. 'Maybe there was this one guy Kathy was into. Big shot. Older. She said I'd know who he was – but she wouldn't give me a name. I think she met him through the job. As I remember, he was married. I don't know how it ended. Or who ended it. *Or if it ever did.*'

My adrenaline began to flow. 'Who is he, Merrill? He might have killed your friend.'

She shook her head.

'You ever see this man?'

She shook her head again.

I pushed on. 'You're the one friend from back then she invites to her wedding and you never met him once? You don't even know a name?'

She gave me a cool smile. 'She was protective. She didn't

tell me everything. Scout's honor, Detective. I assume he was a public figure.'

'You see her much in the past couple of years?'

Merrill shook her head again. She was being a real bitch. New money in Silicon Valley.

'Her father told me she still used to come to town. On business.'

Merrill shrugged. 'I don't know. Look – I have to go.'

I yanked open my bag and removed one of the crime-scene photos McBride had given me, the one of Kathy, wide-eyed, slumped in a bloody heap in front of her husband.

'Someone she *knew* did this. You want to be met at the plane and thrown in a holding cell as a material witness? You can call in your husband's lawyer, but it'll still take him two days to get you out. How would the tech-fund crowd react to that news? I'm sure I could get it in the *Chronicle*.'

Merrill turned away from me, her jaw quivering. 'I don't know who it was. Just that he was older, married, some big-time SOB. Kinky, and not nice about it. Kathy said he played sex games on her. But whoever he was, she was always quiet about it, protective. The rest you'll have to do on your own.'

'She still continued to see this guy, didn't she?' I was starting to put it together. 'Even after she moved to Seattle. Even after she met her husband.'

She gave me the slightest smile. 'Good answer, Inspector. Right up to the end.'

'How close to the end?'

Merrill Shortley picked up the phone. 'This is four-oh-two. Checking out. I'm in a rush.'

She stood up, slung a Prada bag over her shoulder, an expensive-looking raincoat over her arm. Then she looked at me and said dryly, 'To the very end.'

Chapter Fifty-Eight

'**N**o wonder the bride didn't wear white,' Raleigh frowned and said, as I told him about my interview with Merrill Shortley.

McBride had set us up for dinner at Nonni's, an Italian place on the lake, a short walk from our hotel.

Raleigh's interview with the groom's parents had yielded nothing eventful. James Voskuhl had been an aspiring musician who had floated on the edge of the music scene in Seattle, finally hooking his way into representing a couple of upcoming bands. He had no known connection to San Francisco.

'The killer knew Kathy,' I said. 'How else would he find her here? They had a relationship.'

'*Right up to the end*,' he mused.

'To the *very* end,' I answered. 'Meaning, maybe here, in Cleveland. These weren't choirgirls. Merrill said this guy was older, married, kinky, predatory. It fits the pattern of the murders. Someone she knew in San Francisco must have seen Red Beard. *Somebody knows.* Merrill claims that

Kathy was protecting her lover, possibly because he was a celebrity.'

'You think this Merrill Shortley has more to add?'

'Maybe. Or the family. I got the feeling they were holding something back.'

He had ordered a '97 Chianti and when it came he tilted his glass. 'Here's to David and Melanie, Michael and Becky, James and Kathy.'

'Let's toast them when we catch this pathetic bastard,' I said.

It was the first time we'd been alone in Cleveland, and suddenly I was nervous. We had an entire evening to fill, and no matter how we kept steering back to the case, or joked how 'this wasn't a date', there was this pull, this bass chord twanging inside me, telling me that this was no time to start anything with anyone, not even handsome and charming Chris Raleigh.

Then why had I changed into a baby-blue sweater and nice slacks instead of staying with the chambray shirt and khakis I'd worn all day?

We ordered. I had osso bucco, spinach, a salad; Raleigh, a veal paillard.

'Maybe it was someone on her job?' Raleigh said. 'Or connected with her job?'

'I told Jacobi to check out her firm in Seattle. Her father said she still came down to San Francisco on business. I want to see if that's the case.'

'And if it isn't?'

'Then either she was hiding something, or they are.'

He took a sip of wine. 'Why would she go through with a wedding if she was still involved with this guy?'

I shrugged. 'They all said Kathy was finally settling down. I'd like to see what she was like back then, if this is what they meant by settling down.' I was thinking that I wanted another talk with the sister, Hillary. I remembered something she had said. *Old habits are hard to crack.* I had thought she was talking about drugs, parties. Did she mean Red Beard?

'McBride tells me tomorrow morning we should be able to review some film at the museum.'

'The guy was *there*, Raleigh,' I said with certainty. 'He was there that night. Kathy knew her killer. We just have to find out who he is.'

Raleigh poured a little more wine into my glass. 'We're partners now, aren't we, Lindsay?'

'Sure,' I said, a little surprised by the question. 'Can't you tell I trust you?'

'I mean, we've been through three double murders, which we're committed to solving; I backed you up with Mercer – I even helped clean up after dinner at your place.'

'Yeah, so?' I grinned. But his face had a cast of seriousness to it. I was trying to figure out where he was going.

'What do you say, maybe it's about time you started calling me Chris.'

Chapter Fifty-Nine

After dinner, Chris and I walked down by the tree-lined lakefront toward our hotel. A cool, misty breeze lapped at my face.

We didn't say much. That same nervous apprehension was tingling on the surface of my skin.

Occasionally, our arms brushed. He had his jacket off, and there was a solid outline to his shoulders and arms. Not that I was noticing superficial things like that.

'It's still early,' he said.

'Five-thirty, our time,' I replied. 'I could still catch Roth. Maybe I should bring him up to date.'

Raleigh grinned. 'You already called Jacobi. I bet he was probably in Roth's office before he hung up the phone.'

As we walked, it was as if this unbearable force were pulling me close, then pushing me away. 'Anyway,' I said, 'for once I don't feel like calling in.'

'What do you feel like?' Raleigh asked.

'Why don't we just walk.'

'The Indians are playing. You want to sneak our way in . . . in the fifth inning?'

'We're cops, Raleigh.'

'Yeah, that would be bad. You want to dance, then?'

'*No*,' I said, even firmer. 'I don't want to dance.' Every word seemed charged with a hidden, electric message. 'What I'm starting to feel like . . .' I turned to him, 'is that I'm having a hard time remembering to call you *Chris*.'

'And what I'm starting to feel like,' he answered, facing me, 'is I'm having a hard time trying to pretend that nothing's going on.'

'I know,' I muttered breathlessly, 'but I just can't.'

It sounded really stupid, but as much as I wanted him, there was a greater hesitation inside holding me back.

' "I know . . . but I just can't." What does that mean?'

'It means, I'm feeling things, too. And that part of me wants to go with those feelings. But right now, I just don't know if I can. It's complicated, Chris.' Every nerve in my body was on alert.

We found ourselves walking again, the breeze from the lake suddenly cooling the sweat that had broken out on my neck.

'You mean it's complicated because we're working together?'

'*That*,' I lied. I'd dated guys on the force once or twice.

'*That* . . . and what else?' Raleigh said.

A thousand desires inside me were screaming to give in. What was going through my mind was crazy. I wanted him to touch me; and I didn't. We were alone on the waterfront. At that moment, if he held me, if he bent and kissed me, I don't know what I would've done.

'I *do* want to,' I said, my fingers reaching for his hand, staring into his deep blue eyes.

'You're not telling me the whole story,' he said.

It took everything I had to hold off confessing. I don't know why I didn't. A deep part of me wanted him to want me, and to keep thinking I was strong. I could feel the heat from his body, and I thought he could feel the wavering resolve in mine. 'I just can't right now,' I said softly.

'You know, I won't always be your partner, Lindsay.'

'I know that. And maybe I won't always be able to say no.'

I don't know if I was disappointed or relieved to see our hotel up ahead. I was sort of happy I wouldn't have to make a decision – when Raleigh took me by surprise. He leaned over without warning and pressed his lips on mine. The kiss was so soft, as if he were gently asking, 'Is this okay?'

I let the kiss linger, warmly. *Soft hands . . . soft lips.*

It wasn't as if I hadn't imagined this happening. Now here it was, out of the blue, and I was giving in. But just as I was starting to give him myself, the fear caught up to me – the fear of the inescapable truth.

I dropped my head, slowly pulled away.

'That was nice. For me, anyway,' Raleigh said, our foreheads coming to rest against each other.

I nodded, but said, 'I can't, Chris.'

'Why are you always holding back, Lindsay?' he asked.

I wanted to say, *'Because I am deceiving you.'* Tell him everything that was going on. But I continued to deceive, though I did it with the greatest yearning I had felt in years. 'I just want to nail Red Beard,' I answered.

Chapter Sixty

T he next morning, Detective McBride left a message for
us to meet him in Sharp's office at the Hall of Fame.
Something had come back on the film.

In a sparsely decorated conference room, the museum's
Security Chief, McBride, and several members of the CPD
Homicide staff sat facing a wide-screen video monitor on a
walnut cabinet.

'At first,' Sharp began self-importantly, 'we were just
randomly going through the tape with members of the
families, stopping on anyone who didn't look familiar. Your
sketch,' he turned to me, 'helped narrow it down.'

He flicked a handheld controller toward the screen. 'The
first clips you're gonna see are the main entrance.'

The screen lit up, standard black-and-white surveillance
footage. It was so weird and strange. Several gaudily
dressed guests seemed to be arriving at once, many of them
outfitted as famous rockers. One was Elton John. His date
had teased his hair dyed in various light and dark shades,
Cyndi Lauper-style. I recognized a Chuck Berry, a Michael

Jackson, a couple of Madonnas, Elvis, Elvis Costello.

Sharp fast-forwarded, the film advancing like individual, edited stills. An older couple arrived dressed in traditional evening wear. Behind them, almost tucked into their backs, came a man who was clearly shying away from the camera, averting his face.

'*There!*' Sharp said.

I saw him! My heart pumped madly in my chest. Goddamn Red Beard!

It was a horrible, grainy likeness. The man, sensing the direction of the camera, quickly hurried by. Maybe he came there earlier, scouting for security cameras. Maybe he was just smart enough to avoid a direct shot. Whatever it was, he sneaked into the crowd and disappeared.

A ball of anger knotted in my chest. 'Can you back up, home in?' I said to Sharp. 'I need to see his face.'

He leveled his remote and the image channeled into a higher magnification.

I stood up. I was staring at a partially obscured shot of the killer's face. No eyes, no clear feature. Only a shadowy profile. A jutting chin. And the outline of a goatee.

There was no doubt in my mind that this was the killer. I didn't know his name; I could barely see his face. But the fuzzy image I had first sketched together in my mind with Claire was now clear in front of me.

'Is that the best you can do?' Raleigh pressed.

A member of the museum tech staff replied, 'Might be able to get it technologically enhanced. On this rough footage, this is what we have.'

'We pick him up again later on,' Sharp said.

He quickly fast-forwarded and stopped at a wide-angle view of the Main Hall, the wedding reception. They were able to home in on the same tuxedoed man standing at the edge of the crowd, observing. When the image was magnified, though, it became grainy and lost its resolution.

'He's purposely avoiding looking at the camera,' I whispered to Raleigh. 'He knows where they are.'

'We ran these shots by both families,' Sharp said. 'No one places him. No one can identify who he is. I mean, there's a chance it's not him. But considering your sketch . . .'

'It's him all right,' I said firmly. My eyes burned on the grainy screen. I was also sure we were looking at Kathy Voskuhl's mysterious lover.

Chapter Sixty-One

H illary knew. I was almost sure of it. But why she would conceal such a thing related to her sister's death, I couldn't imagine. *Old habits are hard to crack*, she had said.

I wanted another shot at her, and I reached her by phone at the family house in Shaker Heights.

'I had a chance to speak to Merrill Shortley,' I told her. 'Now I just need a few details cleared up.'

'You realize this is a very stressful time for my family, Detective,' Hillary replied. 'We told you what we knew.'

I didn't want to come on too strong. She had lost her sister in a horrible way. Her parents' home was filled with mourners and grief. And she was under no obligation to talk to me at all.

'Merrill told me a few things about Kathy. Her lifestyle . . .'

'*We* told you all that,' she replied defensively. 'But we also told you that after meeting James she had begun to settle down.'

'That's what I want to talk to you about. Merrill recalled

there *was* someone she was seeing in San Francisco.'

'I thought we told you, Kathy dated lots of men.'

'This one went on for a long time. He was older. Married. Some kind of big shot. Possibly famous.'

'I wasn't my sister's keeper,' Hillary complained.

'I need a name, Ms Bloom. This man could be her killer.'

'I'm afraid I don't understand. I already told you what I know. My sister didn't exactly confide in me. We lived very different lives. I'm sure you've put two and two together already – there was a lot I didn't approve of.'

'You said something to me the first time we talked. *Old habits are hard to crack.* What sort of habits were you referring to?'

'I'm afraid I don't know what you mean. The Cleveland police are handling this, Inspector. Can't we just let them do their job?'

'I'm trying to help you, Ms Bloom. Why did Kathy move away from San Francisco? I think you know. Was someone abusing her? Was Kathy in trouble?'

Hillary sounded frightened. 'I appreciate what you're trying to do, but I'm going to hang up now, Inspector.'

'It's going to come out, Hillary. It always does. An address book, her phone bill. It's not just Kathy. There are four others, back in California. They were just as hopeful about the rest of their lives as your sister. Just as deserving.'

There was a tiny sob in her voice. 'I have no idea what you're talking about.'

I felt I had one last chance. 'Here's the really ugly truth about murder. If I've learned one thing as a homicide detective, it's that the lines don't stay fixed. Yesterday you were an innocent victim, but now you're in this, too. This killer will strike again, and when he does, you will regret you didn't tell me for the rest of your life.'

There was a heavy silence on the line. I knew what it meant. It was the struggle inside Hillary Bloom's conscience.

Then I heard a click. She had hung up the phone.

Chapter Sixty-Two

Our flight back to San Francisco left at 4:00 p.m. I hated, *hated* to leave without a name. Especially when I felt we were so close.

Somebody famous.

Kinky.

Why were they protecting him?

Anyway, we had accomplished a lot in just two days. It was clear to me that all three murders were committed by the same person. We had a strong lead tying him to San Francisco, a possible identity, a confirmed ID. The trail was warm here, and would grow ever hotter when we got home.

Both investigations would proceed locally. Cleveland would contact the Seattle police force to do a search and seizure on the bride's home. Maybe something in her personal effects, an address book, an e-mail in her computer, would divulge who her San Francisco lover was.

Waiting to board our plane out of Cleveland, I called my voice mail for messages. There was one each from Cindy and Claire inquiring about my trip, *our case*. Reporters pushing for my comments on the Cleveland crime. Then I heard the throaty voice of Merrill Shortley. She had left her California number.

I punched the number as fast as I could. A housekeeper answered, and I could hear the wail of a baby crying.

When Merrill got on, I could tell that some of her cool veneer had cracked. 'I was thinking,' she began, 'there was something I didn't mention yesterday.'

'Yes? That's good to hear.'

'This guy I told you about – the one Kathy was hooked up with in San Francisco? I was telling you the truth. I never knew his name.'

'Okay, I hear you.'

'But there were some things . . . I said he didn't treat her well. He was into intense sex games. Props, scenarios. Maybe even a little filming. Problem was, Kathy liked the games.'

There was a long pause before Merrill went on. 'Well . . . I think he pushed her, forced her to do more than she was comfortable with. I remember marks on her face, bruises on her legs. Mostly it was her spirit that was broken. None of us were exactly bringing home Tom Cruise then, but there was a time when Kathy was real scared. She was in his control.'

I began to see where this was heading. 'It's why she moved away, wasn't it?' I said.

I could hear Merrill Shortley sigh on the other end. 'Yes, it was.'

'Then why did she continue to see him from Seattle? You said she was involved with him. Right up to the end.'

'I never said,' Merrill Shortley sounded sad, 'that Kathy knew what was good for her.'

Now I saw Kathy Kogut's life take on the shape of tragic inevitability. I was sure she had fled San Francisco, tried to escape from the grip of this man. But she couldn't break free.

Was that true of the other murdered brides?

'I need a name, Ms Shortley. Whoever this was, he might've killed your friend. There are four others. The longer he's out there, the greater the chance he'll do it again.'

'I told you, I didn't know his name, Detective.'

I raised my voice above the din in the terminal. 'Merrill, *someone* must know. You were with her for four years, you partied together.'

Merrill hesitated. 'In her own way, Kathy was loyal. She said his name was well-known. He was some kind of celebrity – someone I would know. She was protecting him. Or maybe protecting herself.'

My mind raced to the film and music businesses. She was into a bad scene. She was over her head, and like people who feel trapped, she ran. She just couldn't get far enough away.

'She must've told you something,' I pressed. 'What he did, where he lived – where they would meet. You guys were like sisters?' *Wicked sisters?*

'I swear, Inspector. I've been racking my brain.'

'Then someone else must know. Who? Tell me!'

I heard Merrill Shortley let out a mirthless laugh. 'Ask her sister.'

Before we boarded, I beeped McBride and left a detailed message on his voice mail. Kathy's lover was probably someone famous. It was why she had moved away. The profile fit the pattern of our killer. Her sister, Hillary, might know the killer's name.

On board, all I could think about was that we were getting close. Raleigh was there beside me. As the plane rose, I leaned into his arm, surrendering to total exhaustion.

All my physical troubles seemed a million miles away. I remembered what I'd said to Claire. I told her that finding this bastard gave me the resolve to go on. The red-bearded man in my dream who had gotten away would not be free for much longer.

'We're going to get him,' I said to Raleigh. 'We can't let him kill another bride and groom.'

Chapter Sixty-Three

E ight the next morning, I was at my desk and calling
Cleveland.

There were several ways I could go with this investigation. Hillary Bloom was the most direct, assuming, as
Merrill implied, she was able to give us a name. It was clear
that, in a twisted way, she was trying to save her family the
added pain of having Kathy publicly branded as some kind
of pathetic sexual victim, cheating on her husband-to-be
right up until their vows.

Sooner or later a name would emerge. From her, or from
Seattle.

Before I did anything else, I called Medved's office and
rescheduled the blood treatment I had canceled. I would
see him at five o'clock today. After a brief wait, the
receptionist said the doctor would meet me there himself.

Maybe it was good news. Truth was, I *was* feeling a little
stronger. Maybe the treatments were beginning to do their
work.

It was hard picking up where I left off in San Francisco.

The best leads were now in Cleveland. I read some reports on the evidence Jacobi was tracking down; held a meeting of the Task Force at ten.

Actually, the most promising leads – the hair and the Bridal Boutique at Saks – had come from my meetings with Claire and Cindy. I couldn't resist calling Claire a little before noon.

'Bring me up to date,' she said excitedly. 'I thought we were partners.'

'I will,' I replied. 'Get Cindy. Meet me for lunch.'

Chapter Sixty-Four

The three of us leaned against the side of a stone wall in City Hall Park, picking at salad sandwiches we had bought at a nearby grocer's. *The Women's Murder Club meets again.*

'You were right,' I said to Claire. I passed her a copy of the security photo showing Red Beard sneaking into the Cleveland wedding.

She stared at it, her eyes focusing intensely. Claire looked up only when the confirmation of her physical supposition brought out a curious half-smile. 'I only read whatever that bastard left behind.'

'Maybe,' I said, tossing her a wink. 'But I bet Righetti would've missed it.'

'This is true,' she allowed with a satisfied beam.

It was a bright, breezy June day; the air was fragrant from a crisp Pacific breeze. Office folk worked on their tans, secretaries gabbed in groups. I recounted what I had found in Cleveland. I never mentioned what took place by the lake between Chris Raleigh and me.

When I finished with Merrill's shocking revelation, Cindy said, 'Maybe you should've stayed out there, Lindsay.'

I shook my head. 'It's not my case,' I explained. 'I was only there on a consult. Now I'm running point between three jurisdictions.'

'You think Merrill Shortley has more to tell?' asked Claire.

'I don't think so. If she knew, I think she would have told me.'

'The bride must have had other friends here,' said Cindy. 'She was in publicity. If this guy was famous, maybe she met him through her job.'

I nodded. 'I have someone checking that out. We also have the Seattle PD combing through her apartment.'

'Where'd she work when she lived here?' Claire asked.

'An outfit called Bright Star Media. Apparently, she was connected into the local music scene.'

Cindy took a sip of iced tea. 'Why not let me have a go at it.'

'You mean like you did at the Hyatt?' I said.

She grinned. 'No, more like Napa. C'mon . . . I'm a reporter. I sit all day with people trained to find the dirt on anybody.'

I bit into my sandwich. 'Okay,' I mumbled. 'Be my guest.'

'In the meantime,' Cindy inquired, 'can I run with what we have so far?'

Much of it was classified. If it came out, it would point back to me. 'You can run with the similar pattern of murder in Cleveland. How we found the bodies. The bride's background here. Absolutely *no mention* of Merrill Shortley.' In that way, I hoped the killer would sense that we were closing in on him. It might cause him to think twice about killing again.

When Cindy went over to a nearby ice-cream cart to buy a gelato, Claire took the moment to ask, 'So how are you feeling? You okay?'

I shrugged. 'Queasy. Light-headed. I was told to expect it. I'm having a blood treatment this afternoon. Medved said he'd be there.' I shut up when I saw Cindy on her way back.

'Here,' our young friend announced brightly. She was carrying three ices.

Claire clutched her chest and pretended she was going into cardiac arrest. 'I need gelato about as much as Texas needs a warm breeze in August.'

'Me too,' I laughed. But it was mango, and with the infection attacking me inside, it seemed like wasted caution to refuse.

Claire ended up taking hers, too. 'So what you specifically haven't told us,' she said, with a slow roll of her tongue, 'is what went on between you and Mr Chris Raleigh in Oh-hi-oh.'

' 'Cause there was nothing to tell,' I said.

'One thing about cops,' Cindy laughed, 'is you would think they would learn how to lie.'

'You writing for the gossip page now?' I asked. Against my will, I felt my face blush. Claire and Cindy's greedy eyes bore down on me, driving home that it was pointless to resist.

I pulled a knee up on the edge of the wall and sat yoga-style. Then I took them through where things stood: the long, slow dance in my apartment; the anticipation of sitting next to him on the plane; the nervous walk down by the lake; my own doubts, hesitation; the inner conflicts holding me back.

'Basically, it took every bit of self-control not to rip his clothes off right there on Lakefront Walk,' I concluded – and laughed at how it must have sounded.

'Girl, why didn't you?' Claire said, wide-eyed. 'Might've done you some good.'

'I don't know,' I said, shaking my head.

But I did know. And though she tried to smile through it, Claire knew, too. She squeezed my hand. Cindy looked on, not knowing what was going on.

Claire joked, 'I'd give up losing twenty pounds to see Cheery's expression if the two of you got picked up for going at it in the woods.'

'Two San Francisco cops,' announced Cindy in a newscaster tone, 'in pursuit of the Bride and Groom killer, were discovered *au naturel* in the bushes by the Cleveland waterfront.'

The three of us choked with laughter and it felt *so good*.

Cindy wagged a finger at me. 'That, Lindsay, I would've *had* to print.'

'From now on,' Claire giggled, 'I can see things growing pretty humid in that squad car.'

'I don't think that's Chris's style,' I defended him. 'You forget, the man's into *The Shipping News*.'

'Oh . . . it's Chris now, huh?' mooned Claire. 'And don't be so sure about that. Edmund plays three instruments, knows everything from Bartok to Keith Jarret, but he's risen to the occasion in some very unexpected places.'

'Like where?' I laughed, the surprise caught in my throat.

She coyly shook her head. 'I just don't want you thinking that 'cause a man keeps himself with a certain dignity, there's any dignity when it comes to that.'

'C'mon,' I exhorted, 'you put it in play. Let's hear.'

'Let's just say that a few John Does aren't the only things that have been stiff on our examining tables.'

I almost fumbled my gelato onto the ground. 'You've got to be kidding. You? And Edmund?'

Claire's shoulders jiggled in delight. 'As long as I've gone this far . . . once we did it in a parterre box at the Symphony. After a rehearsal, of course.'

'Whatta you guys do? Just go around leaving your mark like poodles?' I exclaimed.

Claire's round face broadened with delight. 'You know, it was a long time ago. But as I think of it, that time in my office at the coroner's Christmas party . . . that wasn't so long ago.'

'As long as we're baring our souls,' injected Cindy, 'when I first got to the *Chronicle* I had this fling with one of the senior guys from Datebook. We used to meet down in the library, in the far reaches of the Real Estate section. Nobody ever went there.'

Cindy scrunched her face, abashed, but Claire cackled with approval. I was amazed. I was learning the hidden, suppressed side of a person I had known for ten years. But there was a little shame building in me as well. *I didn't have a list.*

'So,' Claire said, looking at me. 'What's Inspector Boxer got to share from her closet?'

I tried to recall a single moment when I'd done something totally crazy. I mean, when it came to sex, I didn't think of myself as someone who held back. But somehow, no matter how hard I searched my memory, my passion always ended up between the sheets.

I shrugged, empty-handed.

'Well, you better get started,' Claire remonstrated. 'When I'm drawing my last breath, I won't be thinking about all those fancy degrees or conferences I spoke at. You only have a few times in your life to really cut loose, so you might as well take 'em when they come.'

A little tremor of remorse knifed through me. At that moment, I didn't know what I wanted more: my place on the list – or a goddamn name for Red Beard. I suppose I wanted both.

Chapter Sixty-Five

A couple of hours later, I sat in my hospital smock in the hematology clinic.

'Dr Medved would like a word with you before we start,' said Sara, my transfusion nurse.

I felt a stab of apprehension as she unpacked an IV setup for my treatment. Truth was, I had been feeling okay. Not much pain or nausea other than the incident in the ladies' room last week.

When Dr Medved walked in with a manila folder under his arm, his face was friendly but unconfiding.

I smiled weakly. 'Only good news?'

He sat across from me on the ledge of a counter. 'How are you feeling, Lindsay?'

'I wasn't feeling so bad when I saw you before.'

'Fatigued?'

'Only a little. End-of-day kind of thing.'

'Sudden nausea? Queasiness?'

I admitted I *had* vomited suddenly once or twice. He made a quick notation on a chart, paged through some other medical charts in the folder. 'I see we've undergone four packed red cell transfusions so far . . .'

My heart was racing, the longer he took. Finally, he put down the folder and looked squarely into my face.

'I'm afraid your erythrocyte count has continued to decline, Lindsay. You can see the trend line here.'

Medved passed me a sheet. Leaning forward, he took a pen out of his breast pocket. The paper had a computer graph on it. He traced the pattern with his pen. The line went steadily down. *Shit.*

'I'm getting worse,' I said hoarsely.

'To be frank,' the doctor acknowledged, 'it's not the trend we were hoping for.'

I had ignored that this might happen, burying myself in the case, sure that the numbers would improve. I had built this view on a natural trust that I was too young and energetic to be truly sick. I had work to do, important work, a life to live.

I was dying, wasn't I? Oh, God.

'What happens now?' I managed to say. My voice came out as a whisper.

'I want to continue with the treatments,' Medved replied. 'In fact, increase them. Sometimes these things take a while to kick in.'

'Super hi-test,' I chuckled glumly.

He nodded. 'From this point on, I'd like you to come in three times a week. And I'm going to increase the dosage by thirty per cent.' He shifted his weight off the counter. 'In and of itself, there's no immediate cause for alarm,' he declared, in a marginally uplifting tone. 'You can continue to work – that is if you feel up to it.'

'I *have* to work,' I told Medved.

Chapter Sixty-Six

I drove home in a daze. One moment I was battling to unravel this damned case, and the next I was fighting for my life.

I wanted a name. I wanted it now more than ever. And I wanted my life back. I wanted a shot at the whole deal – happiness, success, someone to share it with, a child. And now that I had met Raleigh, I knew there was a chance that I could have these things. If I could hold out. If I could will the good cells into my body.

I went into my apartment. Sweet Martha was all over me so I took her for a short walk. But then I moped around, alternating between a resolve to fight through this mess, and sadness that I couldn't. I even contemplated making a meal. I thought it would calm me.

I took out an onion, and cut two desultory slices. Then I realized how crazy it all was. I needed to talk to someone. I wanted to shout, 'I don't fucking deserve this!' and this time I wanted someone to hear it.

I thought of Chris, his comforting arms around me. His

eyes, his smile. I wished I could tell him. He would come in an instant. I could rest my head on his shoulder.

I called Claire. She could tell from my first tremulous sound that something was terribly wrong.

'I'm scared,' was all I said.

We talked for an hour on the phone. At least – *I* talked.

I went back and forth with Claire in a numbed state – panicked by the impending nearness of Negli's next stage. Then Claire reminded me of what I had said when I first told her about the disease. That nailing this bastard gave me the will to fight on. It separated me from being just another person who was sick. I had a special purpose.

'Has that changed for you, Lindsay?' she asked softly.

'No. I want to get him more than ever.'

'Then that's what we're going to do. You, me, little Cindy. We're here to help you fight. We're your support, darlin'. Just this one time, don't try to do it all yourself.'

In an hour, she had calmed me enough, so we could say goodnight.

I curled up on the couch. Martha and I snuggled under a blanket and watched the movie *Dave* – one of my favorites. When Sigourney Weaver visits Kevin Kline in his new campaign office at the end, it always makes me cry.

I fell asleep, hoping for a happy ending in my own life.

Chapter Sixty-Seven

T he next morning I went at it stronger than ever. I still believed we were close, maybe just hours from a name for Red Beard.

I checked in with Roth's contact, a Jim Heekin on the Seattle police force. Heekin said they were sorting through the bride's possessions as we spoke. If something came up he would let me know immediately.

We got a reply back from Infortech, where Kathy Voskuhl had worked in Seattle. In the three years she held her job as a junior account manager, there was no record of any reimbursements for business trips to San Francisco. Her job was to work with developing clients in Seattle. If she repeatedly went down there, she was on her own.

Finally, I called McBride. The Koguts were still claiming that they knew nothing more. But yesterday he'd met with the father, who seemed ready to give in. It was wrenching that some desperate attempts to hold together their daughter's virtue was clouding their judgment.

Since I was a woman, maybe one more try from me

would push them over the edge. I placed a call to Christine Kogut, the bride's mother.

When she came on, her voice was different – remote, but freer, as if she were in a less tormented state. Maybe I just hoped she was.

'Your daughter's killer is running free,' I said immediately. I could no longer hold back. 'Two other couples' families are suffering as well. I think you *know* who was hurting Kathy. Please, Mrs Kogut, help me put him away.'

I heard her take in a long breath. When she spoke, grief and the release of shame trembled in her voice. 'You raise a child, Detective, she is always part of you. You love her so much and you think there is always that part that will never go away.'

'I know,' I said. I could feel she was teetering. *She knew his name, didn't she?*

'She was this beautiful thing . . . she could make anyone love her. A free spirit. One day, we thought that some other free spirit would shape her into the kind of person she was meant to be. We cultivated that freedom in our children. My husband insists we always favored Kathy. Maybe we helped bring it all on.'

I didn't say a word. I knew what it was like to finally give up what you were holding inside you. I wanted to let her reach that point on her own.

'Do you have children, Detective?'

'Not yet,' I told her.

'It's so hard to believe, that your baby can be the cause of so much pain. We begged her to break free. We even got her the new job. Moved her ourselves. We thought, if she could only get away from him . . .'

I was silent, letting her go at her own pace.

'She was sick, like an addict is sick, Detective. She couldn't stop herself. But what I don't understand is *why* he would hurt her so badly. He took away all that was pure about her. Why did he need to hurt our Kathy?'

Give me the name. Who is he?

'She was mesmerized by who he was. It was as if she had no self-control when it came to this man. She shamed us right up until the end. But even now . . .' her voice lowered '. . . I still wonder how someone who loved my daughter could possibly kill her. I'm afraid that I don't believe it. That's partly why I wouldn't tell you.'

'Tell me now,' I said.

'I think she met him at the opening of one of his films. He told her he had a face like hers in mind when he dreamed up one of his characters. His *heroine.*'

It was then that Mrs Kogut told me.

My body went numb.

I knew the name. Recognized it. He was famous – Red Beard.

Chapter Sixty-Eight

I sat there, ratcheting the possible connection through my mind. Things were starting to piece together. He was one of the minority partners at Sparrow Ridge Vineyards, where the *second* couple had been dumped. He had known Kathy Kogut for years in San Francisco. Preyed on her. He was older. Married.

Famous.

By itself, the suspect's name proved nothing. He had merely known the last bride. He had a circumstantial connection to the crime scene of the second killings. But based on the descriptions of Merrill Shortley and the grieving Christine Kogut, he had the brutal temperament, and maybe the motive, to commit these vicious murders. The conviction built up inside me that this *was* Red Beard. I grabbed Raleigh.

'What's going on?' he asked, startled. 'Where's the fire?'

'I'm going to start one in here. Watch.' I dragged him into Roth's office. 'I have a name,' I announced.

They looked at me in wide-eyed surprise.

'*Nicholas Jenks.*'

'The writer?' Raleigh gaped.

I nodded. 'He was Kathy Kogut's lover here in San Francisco. Her mother finally gave it up.' I walked them through the not-so-random connections he had with at least two of the victims.

'This guy's . . . *famous*,' blurted Roth. 'He made those movies, blockbusters.'

'That's exactly the point. Merrill Shortley said it was someone Kathy was trying to conceal. The guy's got two connections, Sam.'

'He's got connections, all right,' Roth cried. 'Jenks and his wife are invited to all the big affairs. I've seen his picture with the Mayor. Wasn't he part of the bid to keep the Giants here?'

The air in Cheery's office became heavy with the weight of dangerous possibilities and risk.

'You should have heard how the Koguts described him, Sam,' I said. 'Like some kind of animal. A predator. I think we're going to find he had something going with *all three girls*.'

'I think Lindsay's right, Sam,' Chris said.

We watched Roth slowly clicking the facts into his head. Nicholas Jenks was famous. A national figure. Untouchable. The Lieutenant's face twisted as if he had swallowed a bad clam.

'You've got nothing right now,' he came back. 'All of it. It's beyond circumstantial.'

'His name has popped up in connection with four dead

people. We could get face to face, like I would with anyone else. We could talk to the District Attorney.'

Roth held up a hand. Nicholas Jenks was one of San Francisco's most prominent citizens. Implicating him on a murder charge was dangerous. *We'd better be right.* I didn't know what Cheery was thinking. Finally, there was the slightest relaxation in his neck, only a tight swallow, but in Roth-speak, it was a go-ahead.

'You could talk to the DA,' he agreed. 'Call Jill Bernhardt.' He turned to Raleigh. 'This *can't* get out until we have something really firm.'

Unfortunately, Assistant District Attorney Jill Bernhardt was stuck in court. Her secretary said she wouldn't be out until the end of the day. Too bad. I knew Jill a little, liked her. She was tough, with dazzling smarts. She even had a conscience.

Raleigh and I got a cup of coffee, going over what we should do next. Roth was right. As far as a warrant was concerned, we had nothing. A direct confrontation could be dangerous. A guy like this, you had to be sure. He would fight back.

Warren Jacobi shuffled in, a self-satisfied smirk puffing up his face. 'Must be raining champagne today,' he muttered.

I took it as another sardonic zinger aimed at Raleigh and me.

'For weeks I can't even get a bite on this shit.' He sat down and cocked his head toward Raleigh. '*Bite . . . champagne . . .* that works, Counselor, doesn't it?'

'Works for me,' Raleigh said.

Jacobi continued, 'So yesterday Jennings comes back with three places that had sold a few cases of the bubbly in question. One of them's this accountant in San Mateo. Funny thing is, his name's on file. Ends up he did two years up in Lampoc for securities fraud. Kind of a reach, isn't it? Serial killing, securities fraud . . .'

'Maybe the guy's got a thing against people who file joint returns,' I said, and smiled at Jacobi.

He puckered up his face. 'The other's some woman manager at 3Com who's stocking up for a fortieth birthday bash. This Clos du Mesnil is a real collectible. It's French, I'm told.'

I glanced up, waiting for him to get to the point.

'Now the third one, that's what I mean by *raining* . . . big auction house, Butterfield and Butterfield. Three years back, sold two cases of the eighty-nine. Went for twenty-five hundred per case, plus commish. Private collector. At first they wouldn't give out the name. But we squeezed. Turns out he's a big shot. My wife, she happens to be a fan. Read every one of his books.'

Raleigh and I froze. 'Whose, Warren?' I pressed.

'I figure, I check it out I can be a hero, bring home a signed copy. You ever read *Lion's Share* by Nicholas Jenks?'

Chapter Sixty-Nine

Jacobi's statement felt like an elbow to my solar plexus. At the same time it removed all doubt for me.

Kathy Kogut, Sparrow Ridge, the Clos du Mesnil champagne. Jenks was now tied into all three murders.

He was Red Beard.

I wanted to run and confront Jenks, but I knew I couldn't. I wanted to get up close, glare in his smug eyes, let him know I knew. At the same time, a suffocating tightness swept up in my chest. I didn't know if it was a flash of nausea, Negli's, or the release of my bottled-up rage. Whatever it was, I knew I had to get out.

'Let's go,' I said to Raleigh in a pleading voice.

He looked stunned and confused, as I rushed out.

'Hey, I say something wrong?' I heard Jacobi say.

I grabbed my jacket and purse and ran down the steps to the street. My blood was rioting inside me – angry, accusing, scared. A cold sweat had broken out all over me.

I ran out into the cool day, started to walk fast. I had no idea where I was going. I felt like a foreign tourist wandering in the city for the first time. Soon, there were crowds, stores, people rushing by who knew nothing about me. I wanted to lose myself for a few minutes. Starbucks, Kinko's, Empress Travel. Familiar names flashed by.

I felt drawn by a single, irrepressible urge. *I wanted to look in his eyes.*

On Post, I found myself standing in front of a Borders bookshop. I went inside. It was large and open, bright with merchandised stands and shelves of all the current books. I didn't ask, I just looked. On a table in front of me, I spotted what I was searching for.

Lion's Share. Maybe fifty copies – thick, bright blue, some stacked, some propped up.

Lion's Share by Nicholas Jenks.

My chest was exploding. I felt in the grip of unspeakable, but undeniable right. A mission, a purpose. This was why I was an investigator. *For this very moment.*

I took a copy of Jenks's book and looked at the back cover. I was staring at the killer of the brides and grooms. I was sure of it. It was the cut of Nicholas Jenks's face, sharp as a stone's edge, that told me. The blue eyes, cold and sterile, controlling.

And one more thing.

The red beard was flecked with gray.

Book Three

Red Beard

Chapter Seventy

Jill Bernhardt, the tough, savvy Assistant District Attorney assigned to the Bride and Groom case, kicked off her Ferragamos, and curled her legs up on the leather chair behind her desk. She fixed her sharp blue eyes directly at my face.

'Let me get this straight. You think the Bride and Groom killer is Nick Jenks?' she asked.

'I'm sure of it,' I said.

Jill was dark, disarmingly attractive. Curly jet-black hair framed a narrow, oval face. She was an achiever, thirty-four, a rising star in Bennett Sinclair's office.

All you needed to know about Jill was that as a third-year prosecutor, it was she who had tried the La Frade case, when the Mayor's old law partner was indicted on a RICO charge for influence peddling. No one, including the DA himself, wanted to submarine his or her career by taking on the powerful fundraiser. Jill nailed him, sent him away for twenty years. Got herself promoted to the office next to Big Ben himself.

One by one, Raleigh and I laid out Nicholas Jenks's connections to the three double murders: the champagne found at the first scene; his involvement in Sparrow Ridge Vineyards; his volatile relationship with the third bride, Kathy Voskuhl.

Jill threw back her head and laughed. 'You want to bust this guy for messing up someone's life, be my guest. Go try the *Examiner*. Here, I'm afraid, they make us do it with facts.'

I said, 'We have him tied to three double murders, Jill.'

Her lips parted into a skeptical smile that read, *Sorry, some other time.* 'The champagne connection might fly, *if* you had him nailed down. Which you don't. The real-estate partnership's a non-starter. None of it pins him directly to any of the crimes. A guy like Nicholas Jenks – public, connected – you don't go around making unsubstantiated accusations.'

With a sigh, she shifted a tower of briefs aside. 'You want to take on the big fish, guys? Go back, get yourself a stronger rod.'

My mouth dropped at her hard-edged reaction to our case. 'This isn't exactly my first homicide, Jill.'

Her strong chin was set.

'And this isn't exactly my first Page One case.' Then she smiled, softened. 'Sorry,' she said. 'It's one of Bennett's favorite expressions. I must be spending too much time around the sharks.'

'We're talking about a multiple killer,' Raleigh said, the frustration mounting in his eyes.

Jill had that implacable, prove-it-to-me resistance. I had worked with her on murder cases twice before, knew how tireless and prepared she was when she got to court. Once, she had invited me to go 'spinning' with her during a trial at which I was a witness. I gave up in a sweat after thirty grueling minutes but Jill, pumping without pause, went on at a mad pace for the full forty-five. Two years out of Stanford Law, she married a rising young partner at one of the city's top venture firms. Leapfrogged a squadron of career prosecutors to the DA's right hand. In a city of high achievers, Jill was the kind of girl for whom everything clicked.

I passed her the security photo from the Hall of Fame, then Nicholas Jenks's photograph.

She studied them, shrugged. 'You know what an adversarial expert witness would do with these? It's pupshit. If the cops in Cleveland feel they can convict with this, be my guest.'

'I don't want to lose him to Cleveland,' I said.

'So come back to me with something I can take to Big Ben.'

'How about a Search and Seizure,' Raleigh suggested. 'Maybe we can match up the champagne bottle from the first crime scene to the lot he purchased.'

'I could run it by a judge,' Jill mused. 'There must be someone out there on the bench who thinks Jenks has done enough to bring down the structure of literary form to the point where they'd go for it. But I think you'd be making a mistake.'

'Why?'

'Some two-time crack whore, *her* you can bring in on suspicion. You bring in Nicholas Jenks, you better arraign. You alert him that you're on to him – you'll spend more time fending off his lawyers and the press than making your case. If he's it, you're gonna have one shot and one shot only to dig up what you need to convict. Right now, you need more.'

'Claire has a hair in her lab from the second killing – the DeGeorges,' I said. 'We can make Jenks give us a sample of his beard.'

She shook her head. 'With what you have, his compliance would be totally voluntary. Not to mention, if you're wrong, what you might lose.'

'You mean by narrowing the search?'

'I was talking politically. You know the game rules, Lindsay.'

She riveted those intense blue eyes directly at me. I could envision the headlines, turning the case back against us. Like the screw-ups with O.J. Simpson, or Jon Benet Ramsey. In both cases, it seemed the cops were as much on trial as any possible defendants.

'Look, if the guy's guilty, I'd like to tear him apart as much as you,' Jill told us. 'But all you're bringing me is an unlucky preference in champagne and an eyewitness on her third vodka and tonic. Cleveland's at least got a prior relationship with one of the victims, bringing up a possible motive, but right now, none of the jurisdictions have enough to go on.'

Jill got up, smoothed her navy skirt, then leaned on her desk. 'Look,' she finally admitted, 'I've got two of the biggest headline grabbers in the city looking over my every move. You think the District Attorney and the Mayor want to pass this thing on?' Then she fixed unflappably on me. 'What's the litmus test here? You're sure it's him, Lindsay?'

He was linked to all three cases. The desperate voice of Christine Kogut was clear in my mind. I gave Jill my most convincing nod. 'He's the killer.'

She got up and made her way around the desk. With a half-smile, she said, 'I'm gonna make you pay if this blows off any chance of getting my memoirs in print by forty.'

Through the sarcasm, I saw a look flare up in Jill Bernhardt's eyes, the same resolute look I had seen when she was spinning. It hit me like a spray of Mace. 'Okay, Lindsay, let's make this case.'

I didn't know what made Jill tick. Power? An urge to do right? Some manic drive to outperform? Whatever it was, I didn't think it was far from what had always burned through me.

But, listening to her cogently mapping out what we needed to indict, a tantalizing thought took hold of me.

I thought about getting her together with Claire and Cindy.

Chapter Seventy-One

A t an old-fashioned steel desk in the dingy halls of the *Chronicle*'s basement library, Cindy Thomas scrolled through four-year-old articles on microfiche. It was late. After eight. Working alone, in the underbelly of the building, she felt as if she were some isolated Egyptologist scraping the dust off of long-buried hieroglyphic tablets. She now knew why it was referred to as 'the Tombs'.

But she felt she was onto something. The dust was coming off secrets and something worthwhile would soon be clear to her.

February . . . March, 1996. The film shot by with indistinguishable speed.

Someone famous, the Cleveland bride's friend had said. Cindy pushed the film onward. This was how stories were earned. Late nights and elbow grease.

Earlier, she had called the public relations firm Kathy Kogut had worked for in San Francisco, Bright Star Media. News of their former staffer's death had reached them only that day. Cindy inquired about any feature films

Bright Star might've had an association with. She was disappointed when she was told the firm didn't handle films. The Capitol, she was told. The concert palace. That was Kathy's account.

Undeterred, Cindy plugged Bright Star's name into the *Chronicle*'s data bank. Any subjects of articles, names, companies, reviews written in the past ten years were recorded there. To her mild delight, the search came back with several live responses.

It was assiduous work, and discouraging. The articles covered a period of more than five years. That would tie in with the time Kathy was in San Francisco. Each article was on a different microfiche cassette.

It required going back into the files. Requisitioning. Three items at a time. After four sets, the night librarian handed her the clipboard, saying, 'Here, Thomas, it's all yours. Knock yourself out.'

It was quarter past ten – she hadn't heard a peep from anyone in over two hours – when she finally came upon something interesting. It was dated February 10, 1995. *Arts Today* section. FOR LOCAL BAND, SIERRA, NEW FILM TAPS INTO A HIT.

Cindy's eyes shot down the text, fast-forwarding to anything that stuck out: plans for their album, an eight-city tour. Quotes from the lead singer.

'*Sierra will perform the song at tomorrow night's bash at the Capitol to kick off release of the film* Crossed Wire.'

Her heart stood still. She zoomed ahead to the following day's *Arts* section.

She consumed the article almost in a single suspended breath: ... *took over the Capitol. Chris Wilcox, the star, was there.* A photo, with a dishy actress. *Bright Star ... other recording stars in attendance.*

Her eyes traveled over the three accompanying new photos. In tiny print, underneath each shot, she noticed the photographer's name: *Photography by Sal Esposito. Property of the* Chronicle.

Photography! Cindy jumped out of her seat at the microfiche desk and hurried back through the musty, ten-foot-high stacks of bundled, yellowing editions. On the other side of the Tombs was the *Chronicle's* photography morgue. Rows and rows of unused shots.

She had never even been in here – didn't know how it was laid out.

Creepy, creepy place, especially this late at night.

She recognized the aisles were chronological. She followed the signs at the end of each aisle until she found February 1995. She ran her eyes along the outside of the stacked plastic bins dated the tenth.

When she spotted it, it was on the highest shelf. Where else? She stepped up on the lower shelf, on her tiptoes, and wiggled the bin down.

On the dusty floor, Cindy frantically leafed through folders bunched up in elastic. As if in a dream, she came upon one marked in large black letters: *'Crossed Wire' Opening – Esposito.* This was it.

Inside were four contact sheets, several black-and-white glossies. Someone, probably the reporter, had written the names of each person, in pen, at the bottom of each shot.

Her eyes froze as she came upon the photo she was hoping for. Four people were toasting the camera, with arms locked. She recognized Kathy Kogut's face from the photos Lindsay had come back with. Red hair, curly. Trendy, in-laid glasses.

And next to her, smiling into the camera, was another face she knew. It took her breath away. Her fingers trembled with the realization that she had the hieroglyphics at last.

It was the trimmed, reddish-colored beard. The narrow, complicit smile – as if he knew where all this might one day lead.

Next to Kathy Kogut was the novelist Nicholas Jenks.

Chapter Seventy-Two

I was totally surprised when Cindy appeared at my door at half-past eleven. With a look of wide-eyed elation and pride, she blurted, 'I know who Kathy Kogut's lover was.'

'Nicholas Jenks,' I replied. 'C'mon in, Cindy. *Down*, Martha.' She was tugging at my Giants nightshirt.

'Oh God,' she wailed loudly. 'I was so pumped up. I thought *I* had found it.'

She *had* found it. She had beaten McBride and Seattle, two squads of trained investigators as well as the FBI. I looked at her with genuine admiration. 'How?' I asked.

Too restless to sit, Cindy stalked around my living room, as she took me through the steps of her amazing discovery. She unfolded a copy of the news photo showing Jenks and Kathy Kogut at the movie opening. I watched her circle the couch, trying to keep up with herself: Bright Star . . . Sierra . . . *Crossed Wire* . . . She was hyper. 'I'm a good reporter, Lindsay,' she said.

'I know you are.' I smiled at her. 'You just can't *write* about it.'

Cindy stopped, the sudden realization of what she had overlooked hitting her like a pie in the face.

'Oh God,' she moaned. 'That's like being in a shower with Brad Pitt, but you can't touch.' She looked at me, half-smiling, half like nails were being driven into her heart.

'Cindy,' I reached out and held her, 'you wouldn't have even known to look for him if I hadn't clued you in on Cleveland.' I went to the kitchen. 'You want some tea?' I called out.

She collapsed on the couch and let out another wail. 'I want a beer. No, not beer. Bourbon.'

I pointed to my small bar near the terrace. In a few moments, we sat down. Me, with my Nocturnal Seasonings, Cindy, with a stiff glass of Wild Turkey, Martha comfortable at our feet.

'I'm proud of you, Cindy,' I told her. 'You did crack the name. You scooped two police forces. When this is over, I'm gonna make sure you get a special mention in the press.'

'I *am* the press!' Cindy exclaimed, forcing herself to smile. 'And what do you mean, "When this is over." You have him.'

'Not quite.' I shook my head. I explained that everything we had, even stuff she didn't know – the vineyard, the champagne – was circumstantial. We couldn't even force him to submit a hair.

'So what do we need to do?'

'Tie Nicholas Jenks solidly into the first crime.'

Suddenly, she began pleading. 'I have to run with it, Lindsay.'

'No,' I insisted. 'No one knows. Only Roth and Raleigh. And one more . . .'

'Who?' Cindy blinked.

'Jill Bernhardt.'

'The Assistant District Attorney? That office is like a colander trying to sail across the Pacific. It's nothing but leaks.'

'Not Jill,' I promised. 'She won't leak this.'

'How can you be so sure?'

'Because Jill Bernhardt wants to nail this guy as much as we do,' I said, with conviction.

'That's all?' groaned Cindy.

I sipped a soothing mouthful of tea, met her eyes. 'And because I invited her to join our group.'

Chapter Seventy-Three

The following day we met after work for a drink at Susie's; it was Jill's first introduction to our group.

All day, I couldn't fix on anything other than the thought of confronting Jenks with what we knew and bringing him in. I wanted to accelerate everything – bring about a face-to-face confrontation. I wanted to let him know we had him. *Goddamn Red Beard.*

As we waited for drinks, I threw out a couple of new developments. A search of Kathy Kogut's home in Seattle had uncovered Jenks's name and phone number in the dead bride's phonebook. A trace by Northwest Bell had turned up three calls to him in the past month – including one three days before the Cleveland wedding. It confirmed what Merrill Shortley had told us.

' "Right up to the very end", ' Claire quoted. 'Creepy. Both of them, actually.'

We ran Jenks's photo by Maryanne Perkins of Saks as part of a photospread with five others. We desperately needed something that pinned him to the first crime. She paused over his likeness for a few seconds. 'It's him,' she declared. Then she paused. 'But then it's hard to tell. It was so quick. And far away.'

The thought of a defense attorney cross-examining her didn't sit well. It was no surprise to me that Jill agreed.

It took no longer than a single margarita for her to make a seamless introduction into our group.

Claire had met Jill a few times when she testified at trials. They had developed a mutual respect for each other's rise through their male-dominated departments.

We asked Jill about herself and she told us she was Stanford Law, and her father was a corporate attorney back in Dallas. No interest in the corporate thing. That was for her husband, Steve, who was running a venture fund for Bank America. They lived in Burlingame – affluent, exclusive – took rock-climbing treks in the desert at Moab. No kids. 'It just doesn't fit, right now,' she said.

Jill seemed to live the epitome of the fast, successful life. At the same time, there seemed to be something missing. Maybe she was tired from the grind, the pace of her accomplishments.

When our drinks arrived, Claire and I toasted Cindy's ingenuity in coming up with Jenks's name in such a short time. And beating two Police Departments to the punch.

Claire raised a glass to her. 'You're pretty good for a rookie, honey. But you're still not the king.' She smiled at me.

'So I'm thinking,' Jill said, looking around the table, 'I know I can hold my own at dinner parties and all . . . but that's not why you asked me in, is it? Seems like we have all the angles covered here: the press, the force, Medical Examiner. Just what kind of a group is this?'

I answered, since it was I who had invited her in. 'Women. Climbing the ladder in their careers. Law enforcement.'

'Yeah, with soft, pushover types for bosses,' grinned Cindy.

'Well, I qualify there,' said Jill. 'And it doesn't hurt that each of you seems to have some connection with the Bride and Groom cases.'

I held my breath. Jill could blow this whole thing if she wanted to but she was here. 'We have been sort of working together,' I admitted. 'Outside the investigation.'

Over margaritas, I explained how we had originally gotten together. And how we had come upon this case, trying to solve it, sharing what we knew, freelance. How it had become a sort of bond. How things had just gotten a bit deeper.

Jill arched her eyebrows. 'I assume you're sharing all this with the investigation?'

'Of course,' I insisted. 'Well, sort of.' I told her how we were giving Cindy only what the Department was about to release to the press-at-large. How there was a thrill in cutting through the Department, advancing the case.

'I know it's a different game when everything starts to get legal,' I said. 'If any of this makes you uncomfortable . . .'

We were all sort of hanging there, awaiting her response. Loretta came and we ordered another round. We were still hanging – waiting on Jill.

'How about I let you know when things start to get uncomfortable,' she said eventually, opening her blue eyes wide. 'In the meantime, you're gonna need a lot stronger corroboration if we want to take this thing to court.'

The three of us breathed a sigh of relief. We tilted our near-empty glasses toward our new member.

'So, this outfit have a name?' Jill inquired.

We looked around, shrugged, shook our heads. 'We're sort of a women's murder club,' I said.

'Lindsay's deputized us,' grinned Claire.

'The Margarita Posse,' Jill threw out. 'That has possibilities.'

'Bad-ass bitches,' giggled Claire.

'One day, we're all gonna be running things,' Cindy said. 'Homicide Chicks,' she came back, with a satisfied grin. 'That's who we are. That's what we do.'

'Just shut me up if I start to roar,' laughed Jill.

We looked around the table. We were bright, attractive, take-no-shit women. We were going to run things – some day.

The waitress brought our drinks. We raised four glasses toward one another. 'To us.'

Chapter Seventy-Four

I was driving home, really pleased at having brought Jill into the group, but it didn't take long for the thought to worm its way in that I was still *withholding* from my friends.

My beeper sounded.

'What're you doin'?' Raleigh asked, when I buzzed him back.

'I was headed home. *Beat.*'

'You up for talking just a little? I'm at Mahoney's.' Mahoney's was a dark, crowded bar near the Hall that was usually thick with off-duty cops.

'Already ate,' I told him.

'Meet me, anyway,' Raleigh said. 'It's about the case.'

I was only a few minutes away. Mahoney's was on Brannan. To get to Potrero, I had to go right by it.

I found myself a little nervous again. I was scared we were no longer playing things by the book. The book was, partners didn't get involved. Nor people with their lives ebbing away. I knew that if I let things go, anything could happen. This wasn't some casual fling we could go at for a night and try to rationalize away the next day. As much as I wanted him, I was holding back. Scared to let it all come out. Of letting myself go. Of dragging him in.

I was relieved when I saw Raleigh waiting for me outside the bar. He came up to my car. I couldn't help noticing that he looked good, as usual.

'Thanks for not making me go in,' I said.

He leaned on the edge of my open window. 'I looked into Nicholas Jenks,' he said.

'And?'

'The guy's forty-eight. Went to law school, but never finished. Started writing novels his first year. Wrote two books that didn't go anywhere. Then this twisted thriller, *Crossed Wire*, hit. So he bagged the law for good.'

'Sounds like a good career move,' I said, pushing the hair out of my eyes.

'There's something you should know. More than five years ago, cops were called out to his home in a domestic dispute.'

'Who made the call?'

'His wife. His first wife.' Raleigh leaned in closer. 'I pulled up the report. First-on-the-scene described her as pretty beat-up. Bruises up and down her arms. Large bruise on her face.'

A thought flashed in my head. Merrill Shortley, on Kathy's boyfriend: '*He was into intense sex games.*'

'Did the wife file?' I asked.

Chris shook his head. 'That's as far as it went. Never

pressed charges. Since then, he's cashed in, big-time. Six huge bestsellers. Movies, screenplays. New wife, too.'

'That means there's an old one out there who might be willing to talk.'

He had a satisfied expression on his face. 'So, can I buy you a meal, Lindsay?'

A hot bead of sweat burned a slow path down my neck. I didn't know whether to get out or stay in. 'Chris, I already ate. Had a commitment.'

'Jacobi,' he grinned. He could always get me with that smile of his.

'Sort of a woman's thing, a group of us. We meet once a month. Go over our lives. You know, nanny problems, personal trainers, country homes. Affairs, things like that.'

'Anyone I know?' Raleigh smiled.

'Maybe one day I'll introduce you.'

We sort of hung there, my blood slowly throbbing in my chest. The hair on Raleigh's forearm gently grazed against mine. This was driving me insane. I had to say something. 'Why'd you call me out here, Chris?'

'Jenks,' he replied. 'I didn't tell you everything. We ran a firearms check on him with Sacramento.' He looked back with a glint in his eye. 'He's got several registered. A Browning twenty-two caliber hunting rifle, a Renfield thirty-thirty. A Remington forty-point-five.'

He was leading me on. I knew he had struck pay dirt.

'There's also a Glock Special, Lindsay. Nineteen-ninety issue. *Nine millimeter.*'

A rush of validation shot through my veins.

Chris frowned. 'He has the weapon of choice, Lindsay. We've got to find that gun.'

I made a fist and brought it down against Raleigh's in triumph. My mind was racing. Sparrow Ridge, the phone calls, now a Glock Special. It was all still circumstantial, but it was falling into place.

'What're you doing tomorrow, Raleigh?' I asked with a smile.

'Wide open. Why?'

'I think it's time we talked to this guy face to face.'

Chapter Seventy-Five

High on the cliffs above the Golden Gate Bridge, 20 El Camino del Mar was a stucco, Spanish-style home with an iron gate guarding the terracotta driveway.

Red Beard lived here – Nicholas Jenks.

Jenks's home was low, stately, surrounded by decorously trimmed hedges and bright, blossoming azaleas. In the driveway's circle, there was a large iron sculpture, Botero's *Madonna and Child*.

'Fiction must be good,' whistled Raleigh, as we stepped up to the front door. We had made an appointment through Jenks's personal assistant to meet him at noon. I had been warned by Sam Roth not to come on too hard.

A pleasant housekeeper greeted us at the door and took us back to a spacious sunroom, informing us Mr Jenks would be down in a short while. The lavish room seemed straight out of some designer magazine – with rich Jacquard wallpaper, Oriental chairs, a mahogany coffee-table, shelves of mementos and photographs. It opened onto a fieldstone patio overlooking the Pacific.

I had lived in San Francisco all my life, but never knew you could come home every night to this kind of spectacular view.

While we waited, I examined photos arranged on a side table. Jenks with a series of well-known faces: Michael Douglas, the top guy from Disney, Bill Walsh from the 49ers. Others were with an attractive woman I took to be his new wife – sunny, smiling, with strawberry-blonde hair – in various, exotic locations, on beaches, skiing, a Mediterranean isle.

In a silver frame, there was a four-by-six of the two of them in the center of an enormous, lit-up rotunda. The dome of the Palace of Fine Arts. It was a wedding photo.

It was then that Nicholas Jenks walked in. I recognized him immediately from his photographs.

He was slighter than I had imagined. Trim, well-built, no more than five-ten, wearing an open white dress-shirt over well-worn jeans. My eyes were drawn immediately to the reddish, gray-flecked beard.

Red Beard, it's good to meet you, finally.

'Sorry to put you off, Inspectors,' he said with an easy smile, 'but I'm afraid I get cranky if I can't get my morning pages in.' He held out his hand, noticing the photograph I was still holding on to. 'A bit like the set of *Marriage of Figaro*, wasn't it? Myself, I would've gone for a small civil ceremony, but Chessy said if she could snare me in a tux, she'd never ever doubt my commitment to her.'

I wasn't interested in being charmed by this man, but he was handsome and immediately in control. I could see what some women found attractive about him. He motioned us to the couch.

'We were hoping,' I said, 'to ask you a few questions.'

'About the Bride and Groom killings – my assistant advised me. Crazy . . . terrible. But these acts, so incredibly desperate, cry out for at least a small measure of sympathy.'

'For the victims,' I said, placing his wedding photograph back on the table.

'Everyone always goes to the plight of the victims,' Jenks said, 'but it's what's inside the killer's head that puts cash in the account. Most people figure these acts are simply about revenge. The *sickest* kind of revenge. Or even subjugation, like most rapes. But I'm not so sure.'

'What's your theory, Mr Jenks?' Chris asked. He made it sound as if he were a fan.

Jenks held out a pitcher of iced tea. 'Something to drink? I know it's a hot one, though I've been holed up in the study since eight.'

We shook our heads. I took a manila folder out of my bag and placed it on my lap. I remembered Cheery's admonition: 'Keep it light. Jenks is a VIP. You're not.'

Nicholas Jenks poured himself a tall glass of tea and went on. 'From what I've read, these killings appear to be a form of rape, the rape of innocence. The killer is acting in a way that *no one can forgive*, in the most sacred setting of our society. To me, these killings are the ultimate act of purification.'

'Unfortunately, Mr Jenks,' I said, ignoring his bullshit, 'we didn't come up here seeking your professional advice. I have some questions related to these killings we'd like to run by you.'

Jenks sat back in his chair. He looked surprised. 'You make that sound awfully official.'

'That's entirely up to you,' I said. I took out a portable cassette tape-player from my bag. 'You mind if I turn this on?'

He stared at me, his eyes shifting suspiciously, then he waved his hand, as if it were of no concern.

'So where I'd like to start, Mr Jenks, is with these killings. Do you have any specific knowledge of any of the crimes other than what you've read in the papers?'

'Knowledge?' Jenks paused, nominally reflecting. Then he shook his head. 'No. None at all.'

'You read there was a third killing? Last week. In Cleveland.'

'I did see that. I read five or six papers every day.'

'And did you also read who the victims were?'

'From Seattle, weren't they? One of them, I remember, was some kind of concert promoter.'

'The groom,' I nodded. 'James Voskuhl. The bride actually lived for a while in town, here. Her maiden name was Kathy Kogut. Do either of those names mean anything to you?'

'No. Should they?'

'So you never met either of them? Any interest you had in this case was just like anyone else's . . . morbid curiosity.'

He fixed his eyes on me. 'That's right. Morbid curiosity's my business.'

I opened my manila folder and took out the top photo. He was playing us, just as he had been playing us by leaving dead-ending clues along the way.

I slid the photo across the table. 'This might sharpen your memory,' I said. 'That's Kathy Kogut, the bride who was murdered the other night. The man next to her, I believe, is *you*.'

Chapter Seventy-Six

Slowly, Red Beard picked up the photo and stared at it. 'It is me,' he declared. 'But the lady, though quite beautiful, I don't recognize. If I can ask, where's this picture from?'

'The San Francisco opening of *Crossed Wire*.'

'Ah,' he sighed, as if that classified something for him.

I watched the gears in his brain start to shift for the right response. He was definitely smart, and a pretty good actor.

'I meet a lot of people at these events. It's why I try to avoid them. You say this was that girl who was killed in Cleveland?'

'We were hoping this was someone you might've remembered,' I replied.

Jenks shook his head. 'Too many fans, not much appetite to meet them, even the really pretty ones, Detective.'

'The price of fame, I imagine.' I took the photo back, thumbed it for a moment, then slid it back in front of him.

'Nevertheless, I have to come back to this particular fan. I'm curious why she doesn't stick out for you. From *all those other fans.'* I withdrew a copy of a Northwest Bell phone bill from my folder and handed it to him. On it were several highlighted calls. 'This is your private number?'

Jenks held the copy of the bill. His eyes dimmed. 'It is.'

'She called you, Mr Jenks. Three times in just the past few weeks. Once . . . *here,* I circled it for you . . . for a whole twelve minutes only last week. Three days before she was married, then killed.'

Jenks blinked. Then he picked up the photo again. This time he was different: somber, apologetic. 'Truth is, Inspector,' he said, 'I was *so, so* sorry to hear what had taken place. She seemed, in the last month, so full of anticipation, of hope. I was wrong to mislead you. It was foolish. I *did* know Kathy. I met her the night of the photo there. Sometimes, my fans are rather impressionable. And attractive. At times I, too, to my detriment, can be an impressionable man.'

I wanted to lunge across the table and rip Nicholas Jenks's impressionable face off. I was certain he was responsible for six vicious murders. Now he was mocking us, and the victims. Goddamn him.

'So you're admitting,' Raleigh interjected, 'that you *did* have a relationship with this woman.'

'Not in the way you're insinuating,' Jenks sighed. 'Kathy was a woman who hoped to satisfy her own vague artistic aspirations through an association with someone engaged in the act of creating. She wanted to write herself. It's not exactly brain surgery, but I guess if it was so damn easy we'd all have a book on the bestseller list?'

Neither of us responded.

'We spoke, maybe met, a few times over a couple of years. It never went beyond that. That's the truth.'

'Sort of mentoring?' Raleigh suggested.

'Yes, that's right. Good choice of words.'

'By any chance,' I leaned forward, no longer able to control my tone, 'were you *mentoring* Kathy in Cleveland last Saturday, the night she was killed?'

Jenks's face turned granitelike. 'That's ridiculous. What an inappropriate thing to say.'

I reached into the folder one more time, this time taking out a copy of the security photo of the killer arriving at the Hall of Fame. 'This is a security photo from the night she was killed. Is that you, Mr Jenks?'

Jenks didn't even blink. 'It might be, Detective, *if* I had been there. Which I categorically was not.'

'Where were you last Saturday night?'

'Just so I understand,' he said stonily, 'are you suggesting *I'm* a suspect in these crimes?'

'Kathy Kogut talked, Mr Jenks.' I glared at him. 'To her sister. To her friends. We know how you treated her. We know she left the Bay Area to try to get away from your domination. We know things were going on between you right up to the wedding night.'

I wouldn't take my eyes off Jenks. There was nothing in the room but him and me.

'I *wasn't* in Cleveland,' he said. 'I was right here that night.'

I ran the whole body of evidence by him. From the bottle of Clos du Mesnil left behind at the Hyatt to his involvement in the real-estate trust that owned Sparrow Crest Vineyards to the fact that two of the murders had been committed with nine-millimeter guns, and according to the state, he owned one.

He laughed at me. 'This is not what you're basing your assumptions on, I hope. I got that champagne ages ago.' He shrugged. 'I don't even recall where it is. It's probably at our country home, in Montana.'

'You *can* locate it, I assume?' Raleigh asked, then explained that it was a sign of respect that we were asking him to turn it over voluntarily.

'Would you mind supplying us with a hair sample from your beard,' I asked.

'*What!*' His eyes met mine with a churlish defiance. I imagined the look Melanie Brandt might have seen as he attacked her. What Kathy Kogut saw as he raised his gun to her head.

'I think,' Nicholas Jenks finally answered, 'that this fascinating interview has come to an end.' He held out his wrists. 'Unless you're intent on taking me away, my lunch is waiting.'

I nodded. 'We'll need to follow up. On your whereabouts. And on the gun.'

'Of course,' Jenks said, standing up. 'And should you need any further cooperation – feel free to request it through my attorney.'

I assembled the photographs back into the folder. Raleigh and I got up. At that moment, the attractive strawberry blonde from the photographs walked into the room.

She was undeniably pretty, with gentle, aquamarine eyes, a pale complexion, long, free-flowing hair. She had a tall dancer's body, and was dressed in thigh-length tights and a Nike T-shirt.

'Chessy!' Jenks exclaimed. 'These are officers from the San Francisco Police Department. My wife, Inspectors.'

'Sorry, Nicky,' Chessy Jenks apologized. 'Susan's coming over. I didn't know you had guests.'

'They were just leaving.'

We nodded stiffly, moved toward the door. 'If you could locate what we talked about,' I said to him, 'we'll send someone by to pick it up.'

He gazed right through me.

I hated to leave without taking him in, and to have treated him with kid gloves. But we were still a few steps away from an arrest.

'So,' Chessy Jenks smiled and said, 'has my husband finally gone homicidal?' She went up to Jenks, clasped his arm in a teasing way. 'I always told him, with those creepy-crawly characters he writes about, it was inevitable.'

Could she know? I wondered. She lived with him, slept with him. How could she not be aware of what was going on inside his head?

'I truly hope not, Ms Jenks,' was all I said.

Chapter Seventy-Seven

'What did she mean by that?' Chessy Jenks went up to her husband, confused, after the Police Inspectors left the house.

Jenks brushed her away. He paced over to the large French doors leading out to the Pacific.

'Idiots,' he muttered. 'Amateurs. Who the hell do they think they're dealing with?'

He felt a prickly, stabbing heat racing over his shoulders and back. They were stupid, tiny-minded. Beetles. That's why they were cops. If they had any brains, they'd be doing what he was doing. Living high over the Pacific.

'That's why they dig landfills,' he replied distractedly. 'A place for cops to feel at home.'

Chessy picked up the wedding photo from the coffee-table and set it back in its rightful spot. 'What did you do now, Nick?'

Why did she always drive him to this? Why did she always need to know?

She came over, looked at him with those lucid, patient eyes.

As always, his anger leaped up in a flash.

He didn't even realize he had hit her.

It was just that suddenly his hand hurt and Chessy was sprawled on the floor – and the bamboo table on which the wedding pictures were had toppled over – and she was holding her mouth.

He shouted. 'Don't you know when to keep away from me? What do you need, a road map?'

'Uh-uh, Nick,' Chessy said. 'Not here . . . not now.'

'Not here, what?' he was shouting. He knew he was shouting, losing control. That the staff might hear.

'Please, Nick,' Chessy said, pulling herself off the floor. 'Susan will be here soon. We're going to lunch.'

It was the notion that Chessy thought she could just sit there and judge him that really set him off. Didn't she see who she really was? Just some blonde with freckles he had picked out of a cattle call and turned into God's gift to Martha Stewart.

He grabbed her by the arm and put his face inches from her beautiful terrified eyes. 'Say it!'

The arm he held was trembling. A tiny stream of mucus ran out of her nose. 'Jesus, Nick . . .'

That's what he liked, her fear of him, even though she never showed it in public.

'I said, say it, Chessy.' He twisted her arm behind her back.

She was breathing heavily now, sweat forming under

her T-shirt. Her little tits poked through. When she glared back at him, with her paltry defiance, he twisted harder, digging his fingers into her arm. He shoved her toward the bedroom, her bare feet stumbling along.

In the bedroom he kicked the door shut.

Who did the lead cop think she was? Coming in here . . . accusing him like that. In her cheap Gap ensemble. What a fucking insolent bitch.

He dragged Chessy into the clothes closet. *Hers.* It was dark in there. Only the dark and her sobs and the pervasive smell of her perfume. He pushed her forward against the wall, rubbed himself against her buttocks.

He pulled Chessy's gym shorts down, her panties along with them. 'Please!' she cried. 'Nicky?'

He found the familiar place where her small cheeks parted. He was very hard and he pushed himself in deep.

He was driving himself inside Chessy. 'Say it,' he gasped. 'You know how to make it stop. Say it.'

'Ruff,' she finally murmured in a tiny whisper.

Now she was loving it, as she always did. It wasn't bad – it was good. They all ended up wanting and loving it. He always picked them so well.

'Ruff,' she whimpered. 'Ruff, ruff. Is that what you want, Nick?'

Yes, that was part of what he needed. It was all he expected from Chessy.

'You love it, Chessy,' he whispered back. 'That's why you're here.'

Chapter Seventy-Eight

We kept a close watch on Jenks's movements with a surveillance team of three cars. If he made a move to dump the gun, we'd know. If he moved to kill again, we hoped we could stop him. No matter how clever he was, I didn't see how he could plan and execute another murder right now.

I wanted to speak with someone who knew him, who might be willing to talk. Raleigh had mentioned an ex-wife, a history of violence between them. I needed to talk with her.

It wasn't hard to track Joanna Jenks down, now Joanna Wade. A search through the police files had her maiden name listed as part of the domestic complaint she had filed against her husband years before. A Joanna Wade was currently residing at 1115 Filbert Street on Russian Hill.

It was an attractive, limestone townhouse on the steepest part of the Hill. I buzzed, identified myself to the house-keeper who opened the door. She informed me Ms Wade was not at home.'*Ehersizing*,'she said.'*Gold's Gym. On Union.*'

I found the gym around the corner between a Starbucks and an Alfredson's market. At reception, a buffed, pony-tailed staffer informed me Joanna was in Exercise Room C. When I asked what Joanna Wade looked like, the staffer laughed. 'Think blonde. And kiss-ass fit.'

I wandered in, and through a large observation window, spotted a tai-bo class in Exercise Room C. About eight women sweating in Lycra and jog bras were kicking their legs out, karate-style, to loud music. I knew that tai bo was the latest exercise craze, the biggest burn. Any one of these women looked as if they could take a resisting suspect up against a wall, then beat the patrol car back to the precinct with breath to spare.

The only blonde was in front. Trim, sculpted, pushing herself hard and barely breaking a sweat. It was her class.

I hung around until she finished up, and most of the class had rushed out. She toweled off the sweat on her face.

'Great workout,' I said, as she headed my way.

'The best in the Bay Area. Looking to sign up?'

'Maybe. First, I thought I could ask you a couple of questions.'

'Try Diane up front. She can tell you the whole deal.'

'I wasn't talking tai bo.' I flashed her my badge. 'I'm talking Nicholas Jenks.'

Joanna stared at me, flapping her blonde ponytail off her shoulders to cool her neck. She smirked. 'What'd he do, get caught shoplifting one of his books out of Stacey's downtown?'

'Can we talk?' I asked.

She shrugged and led me over to a changing area that was unoccupied. 'So what could I tell you about Nick that you couldn't find out from one of his own jacket flaps?'

'I know it was several years ago,' I said, 'but you once filed a domestic complaint against him.'

'Listen, in case the paperwork didn't catch up, I dropped the charge back then.'

I could see the terror of the moment exploding all over again for her. 'Look,' I said genuinely, 'no one's trying to dig up old wounds, Ms Wade. I'd just like a read on your ex-husband.'

'Up to his old tricks again?'

I could see her sizing me up. Was I an ally or a foe? Then she let out a capitulating breath and looked right at me.

'If you're here about Chessy, I could've warned her – if he hadn't been such a creep about how he dumped me. How did he put it: "*I write through her, Jo. She inspires me.*" You ever read his books, Detective? She didn't have to inspire him by holding a job down while he went off and found himself, did she? She didn't have to read his drafts, deal with his rages when he got rejected, tell him every night how much she believed in him. You know where he met her, Detective? In the makeup room at *Entertainment Tonight.*'

'What I'm asking, Ms Wade,' I said, 'is how violent is Nicholas Jenks?'

There was a pause while she looked away. When she turned back, her eyes had filled up as if she were about to cry.

'You come in here after all these years and make me go through this again. What do you want me to say? That his mother didn't love him? That he's a screwed-up, dangerous man? Life with Nick . . . it's so hard. He's holding something in and God only knows when it's going to come out. I used to ask myself why? What had I done? I was just a kid.' Her eyes glistened.

'I'm sorry.' I truly felt for her. For both Mrs Jenkses. I couldn't even imagine what it was like to wake up and find myself married to someone like him.

'I need to ask,' I said, 'what are the chances things with your ex-husband have intensified? Become more serious?'

She looked stunned. 'Is Chessy all right, Detective?'

'*Chessy*'s all right,' I nodded, making it clear I felt there were others who might not be.

She waited for me to blink. When I didn't, she gave me a mirthless laugh. 'So I guess we're talking a lot deeper than pilfering a book from Stacey's bookstore?'

I nodded again. Woman to woman now, I said, 'I need to ask you a crucial question, Ms Wade.'

Chapter Seventy-Nine

What I asked Joanna Wade was this: 'Is Nicholas Jenks capable of murder?'

I couldn't tell her the reason, but it didn't matter. Joanna was a quick study. I saw the shock in her eyes. After she calmed, I watched her go through a thoughtful evaluation.

Finally, she looked at me and asked again: 'Have you read his books, Detective?'

'One, *Fatal Charm*. Tough book.'

'He lives with those characters, you see. Sometimes I think he forgets it's only what he does for a living.'

I saw the self-judging look in her eyes. I leaned in closer. 'I don't mean to hurt you, but I have to know.'

'Could he kill? Is he capable of murder? I know he's capable of completely debasing another human being. That's murder, isn't it? He's what they call a sexual sadist. His father used to beat his mother in their bedroom closet as an aphrodisiac. He preys on weakness. Yes, the famous Nicholas Jenks humiliated me. But let me tell you the worst thing, the very worst. He left me, Detective. I didn't leave him.'

Joanna leaned back and gave me sort of a compassionate smile. 'I've seen Chessy around a few times. Luncheons, benefits. We've even spoken a bit. He hasn't changed. She knows I know exactly what she's going through, but it's something we can't share. I see the fear; I know how it is. When she looks in the mirror, she no longer recognizes the person she once was.'

My blood was at boiling point. Through the tough veneer, I saw a glimpse of the woman Joanna Wade had been – young, needful, confused. I reached out and touched her hand. I had my answer. I closed my pad, ready to get up, when the other woman surprised me.

'I thought it was him. I immediately thought of Nick when I heard about those terrible crimes. I remembered his book, and I said, "It could be him." '

I stopped Joanna. 'What book?'

'That first thing he wrote – *Always A Bridesmaid*. I figured that's what brought you here, what connected him to the murders.'

I stared at her, confused. 'Just what are you talking about?'

'He wrote it before we met. I was lucky enough to come in for the second unpublished one which, I'm told, he recently sold for two million. But this book, I'd totally forgotten about. It was about a student in law school who discovers his wife with his best friend. He kills them both. Ends up going on a rampage.'

'What kind of rampage?' I asked. What she said next took my breath away.

'He goes around killing brides and grooms. A lot like what happened.'

Chapter Eighty

That was a piece of the puzzle I needed. If Jenks had premeditated these crimes, mapped them out in some early book, it would constitute unimpeachable knowledge. No longer circumstantial. With everything else we had, I could definitely bring him in.

'Where can I find this book?' I asked.

'It wasn't very good,' Joanna Wade replied. 'Never published.'

Every nerve in my body was standing on end. 'Do you have a copy?'

'Trust me, if I did I would have burned it years ago. Nick had this agent in town, Greg Marks. He dumped him when he got successful. If anyone would have it, it might be him.'

I called Greg Marks from the car. I was really humming now. I loved this.

The operator connected me and after four rings, an answering tape came on: *You've reached Greg Marks Associates* . . . I cringed with disappointment. Damn, damn, damn!

Reluctantly, I left him my pager number. 'It's a matter of great urgency,' I said. I was about to tell him why I was calling, when a voice cut in on tape: 'This is Greg Marks.'

I explained I needed to see him immediately. The marina wasn't too far; I could be there in ten minutes. 'I have an engagement at One Market at six-fifteen,' the agent replied curtly. 'But if you can get here . . .'

'You just stay right there,' I told him. 'This is police business, and it's important. If you leave, I'll arrest you!'

Greg Marks worked out of his brownstone, a third-floor loft with a partial view of the bridge. He answered the door, a short, balding man, smartly dressed, in a Jacquard shirt buttoned to the top. He looked at me suspiciously.

'I'm afraid you haven't picked a popular topic with me, Detective. Nicholas Jenks hasn't been a client for over six years. He left me the day *Crossed Wire* hit the *Chronicle*'s bestseller list.'

'Are you still in touch?' I wanted to make sure anything I asked him wouldn't get back to Jenks.

'Why? To remind him how I babysat him through the years when he could barely use a noun with an adjective; how I took his obsessed midnight calls, stroked that gigantic ego?'

'I'm here about something Jenks wrote early on,' I interrupted. 'Before any big deals. I spoke to his ex-wife.'

'Joanna?' Marks exclaimed, with surprise.

'She said he had written a book that never got published. She thought it was called *Always A Bridesmaid*.'

The agent nodded. 'It was an uneven first effort. No real

narrative power. Truth is, I never even sent it out.'

'Do you have a copy?'

'Packed it back to him as soon as I turned the final page. I would think Jenks must, though. He thought the book was a suspense masterpiece.'

'I was hoping I wouldn't have to go through him,' I said, without conveying the basis of my interest. I leaned forward. 'How do I get my hands on a copy of that novel, without going to Jenks directly?'

'Joanna didn't save it?' Marks rubbed a finger across his temple. 'Jenks was always paranoid about people ripping him off. Maybe he had it copyrighted. Why don't you check into that?'

I needed to run this by someone. I needed to run it by the girls.

'Do you want to hear something really scary about Jenks?' the agent said, then.

'Not really, but please go ahead.'

'Here's the idea for a book he always wanted to write. It's about a novelist who is obsessed – the kind of thing Stephen King does so well. In order to write a better book, a *great* book, he actually murders people to see what it's like. Welcome to the horrible mind of Nicholas Jenks.'

Chapter Eighty-One

This was why I had become a homicide detective. I rushed back to the office, my head whirling with how to get my hands on this lost book, when the next bombshell hit.

It was McBride.

'Are you sitting down?' he asked, as if he were about to deliver the coup de grâce. 'Nicholas Jenks was here in Cleveland the night of the Hall of Fame murders. The son-of-a-bitch was here.'

Jenks had lied right to my face. He didn't even blink.

It was now clear, the unidentifiable man at the Hall of Fame had been him after all. He *had* no alibi.

McBride explained how his men had scoured the local hotels. Finally, they uncovered that Jenks had been at the Westin, and amazingly, he registered under his own name. A desk clerk working there that night remembered him. She knew it the minute she saw Jenks – she was a fan.

My mind raced with the ramifications. This was all McBride needed. They had a prior relationship with the victim, a possible sighting at the scene. Now, Jenks was placed in his town. He had even lied under questioning.

'Tomorrow, I'm going to the District Attorney for an indictment,' McBride announced. 'As soon as we have it, I want you to pick Nicholas Jenks up.'

The truth hit me like a sledgehammer. We could lose him to Cleveland. All the evidence, all those right hunches, wouldn't help us. Now, we might only be able to tag on a concurrent life sentence at a second trial. The victims' families would be crushed. *Mercer would go ballistic.*

I was left with an absolutely demoralizing choice: either pick Jenks up and hold him for McBride, or make our move now with less than an airtight case.

I should run this up the ladder, the voice sounded in my head.

But the voice in my heart said, *Run it by the girls.*

Chapter Eighty-Two

I got the three of them together on an hour's notice.

'Cleveland's ready to indict,' I told them. Then I dropped the bombshell about the book *Always A Bridesmaid*.

'You've got to find it,' Jill declared. 'It's the one link we can tie in to all three crimes. Given that it was unpublished, it's as good as exclusive knowledge of the killings. It might even parallel the actual crimes. You find that book, Lindsay, we put Jenks behind bars. For ever!'

'How? Joanna Wade mentioned a prior agent and I went to see him. *Nada*. He said to check out the office of copyrights. Where is that?'

Cindy shook her head. 'Washington, I think.'

'That'll take days, or more. We don't have days.' I turned to Jill. 'Maybe it's time for a Search and Seizure. Blow in on Jenks. We need the gun. Now, this book. And we need them now.'

'We do that,' Jill said nervously, 'we might bungle this whole investigation.'

'Jill, you want to lose him?'

'Anyone know about this yet?' she asked.

I shook my head. 'Just the first team – you guys. But when Mercer finds out, he'll want to jump in with everything he has. Cameras, microphones, the FBI waiting in the wings.'

'If we're wrong, Jenks'll sue our ass,' Jill said. 'I don't even want to think about it.'

'And Cleveland'll be waiting,' said Claire. 'Make us look like a bunch of fools.'

Finally, Jill sighed, 'All right . . . I'm with you, Lindsay. If you can't think of another way.'

I looked at all three of them to make certain we were unanimous. Suddenly, Cindy blurted: 'Can you give me another twenty-four hours?'

I was puzzled. 'Why?'

'Just until tomorrow. And I need Jenks's Social Security number.'

I shook my head. 'You heard what I said about McBride. Anyway, for what?'

She had that same look as the other night, when she burst into my apartment – holding the photo of Jenks and Kathy Kogut, the third bride. 'Just give me until tomorrow morning. Please.'

Then she got up and left.

Chapter Eighty-Three

The following morning, Cindy sheepishly pushed open the glass doors leading to the office of the San Francisco Writers Guild. This felt a lot like the day at the Grand Hyatt. At the reception desk, a middle-aged woman with the punctilious air of a librarian looked up at her. 'May I help you?' she asked.

Cindy sucked in a deep breath. 'I need to find a manuscript. It was written quite a while ago.'

The word copyright had set her off. She had written short stories in college. They were barely good enough to get into the school's literary journal, but her mother had insisted, 'Get them copyrighted.' When she investigated, it turned out it took months, and was way too costly. But a friend who had published told her about another way she could register documents locally. He told her that all the writers did it. If Nicholas Jenks had wanted to protect himself in his salad days, he might've gone the same route.

'It's sort of a family thing,' Cindy told the woman. 'My

brother wrote this history, going back three generations. We don't have a copy.'

The woman shook her head. 'This isn't the library. I'm afraid that whatever we have here is restricted. If you want to find it, you'll have to have your brother come in.'

'I can't,' Cindy said solemnly. 'Nick is dead.'

The woman softened, looked at her slightly less officiously. 'I'm sorry.'

'His wife said she can't locate a copy. I'd like to give it to our dad, a sixtieth birthday present.' She felt guilty, foolish, lying through her teeth like this, but everything was riding on getting this book.

'There's a process for all of this,' the woman replied sanctimoniously. 'Death certificate. Proof of next-of-kin. The family lawyer should be able to help you. I can't just go letting you in here.'

Cindy thought swiftly. This wasn't exactly Microsoft here. If she had found her way to the crime scene in the Grand Hyatt, tracked Lindsay to the second crime, she ought to be able to handle this. Everyone was counting on her.

'There must be a way you can let me take a look – please?'

'I'm afraid not, dear. Not without some documentation. What makes you even think it's registered with us?'

'My sister-in-law is sure it is.'

'Well, I can't just go giving out registered documents on someone's hunch,' she said, with finality.

'Maybe you can at least look it up,' Cindy proposed. 'To see if it's even here.'

The dachshund-nosed defender of the free press finally relaxed. 'I guess I can do that. Do you have any idea when?'

Cindy felt an adrenaline surge. 'Yes, about ten years.'

'And the name?'

'I think it was called *Always A Bridesmaid*.' She felt a chill just saying the words.

'I meant the name of the author, please.'

'Jenks,' Cindy said, holding her breath. 'Nicholas Jenks.'

The woman peered at her. 'The mystery writer?'

Cindy shook her head, faked a smile. 'The insurance salesman,' she said, as calmly as she could.

The woman gave her a strange look, but continued to punch in the name. 'You have proof of relationship?'

Cindy handed her a piece of paper with Jenks's Social Security number on it. 'This should be on his registration.'

'That won't do,' the woman said.

Cindy fumbled through a zipper in her knapsack. She felt the moment slipping away. 'At least tell me if it's here. I'll come back later with whatever you want.'

'Jenks,' the woman muttered skeptically. 'Looks like your brother was a bit more prolific than you thought. He's got *three* manuscripts registered here.'

Cindy wanted to let out a shout. 'The only one I'm looking for is called *Always A Bridesmaid*.'

It took what seemed like several minutes, but the stony resistance of the woman finally weakened. 'I don't know why I'm doing this, but if you can verify your story, there seems to be a record of that manuscript's being here.'

Cindy felt a surge of validation. The manuscript was the final piece they needed to crack a murder case and put away Jenks.

Now, she just had to get it out.

Chapter Eighty-Four

'**I** found it,' exclaimed Cindy, her voice breathless on the phone. '*Always A Bridesmaid!*'

I pounded my desk in elation. This meant we could definitely make our move. 'So what does it say, Cindy?'

'I *found* it,' Cindy went on. 'I just don't actually *have* it.' She told me about the Writers' Guild. The book was there, but it would take a little coaxing to actually get it in our hands.

In fact, it took barely two hours, starting with a frantic call to Jill. She had a judge pulled out of chambers, who signed our court order mandating the release of Jenks's manuscript *Always A Bridesmaid*.

Then Jill and I ran down to meet Cindy. On the way, I made one more call, to Claire. It seemed fitting that all of us should be there.

Twenty minutes later, Jill and I met Cindy and Claire in front of a drab building on Geary, where the Writers Guild maintained its offices. Together, we rode to the eighth floor.

'I'm back,' announced Cindy, to a surprised woman

behind the reception desk. 'And I brought my documentation.'

She eyed us suspiciously. 'Who are these – cousins?'

I flashed the clerk my badge and also presented the officially stamped search warrant.

'What's going on with this book?' the woman gasped. Clearly feeling that matters were now out of her authority, she went inside and came back with a supervisor who read over the court order.

'We only hold them for up to eight years,' he said with some uncertainty. Then he disappeared for what seemed like ages.

We all sat there, in the stark reception area, waiting like pacing relatives for a baby to be born. What if it had been thrown out? Ten years was a long time.

Finally, the supervisor came out with a dusty bundle wrapped in brown paper. 'In the back of the bins,' he sighed, with a self-satisfied smile.

There was a coffee shop right down the street. We took a table in the back and crowded around with anticipation. I plopped the manuscript down on the table, peeled off the brown-paper wrapping.

I read the cover. *Always A Bridesmaid – A novel by Nicholas Jenks.*

Nervously, I opened it and read the first page. The narrator was reflecting on his crimes from jail. His name was Phillip Campbell.

What is the worst thing, the novel began, *anyone has ever done?*

Chapter Eighty-Five

We split up the book into four sections. We each paged silently through our section, searching for some scene or detail that would parallel the real-life crimes.

Mine was about this guy's life, Phillip Campbell. His picture-perfect wife, catching her with another man. He killed them both – and his life changed for ever.

'Bingo!' Jill spoke up suddenly. She read out loud, bending back the sheaf of paper like a deck of cards.

She described a scene with Phillip Campbell – *'breath pounding inside, voices ringing in his head'* – stealing through the corridors of a hotel. It's the Grand Hyatt. A bride and groom are in a suite. Campbell breaks in on them – and kills them without having a second thought.

'In a single act,' Jill read from the manuscript, *'he had washed away the stench of betrayal, and replaced it with a fresh, heretofore unimagined desire. He liked to kill.'*

Our eyes locked. This was beyond creepy. Jenks was crazy – but was he also crafty?

Claire was next. It was another wedding. This time, the scene is outside a church. The bride and groom are coming down the steps, rice is being thrown to shouts of congratulations, applause. The same man, Phillip Campbell, is waiting at the wheel of the limo that will take them away.

We looked at one another, stunned. It was how the second murders were committed.

Jill murmured, 'Holy shit.'

Claire just shook her head. She looked sad and shocked. I guess we all were.

A long-suppressed cry of satisfaction built up in my chest. We had done it! We had solved the Bride and Groom murders!

'I wonder how it ends?' Cindy mused, fanning to the end of the book.

'How else?' said Jill grimly. 'With an arrest.'

Chapter Eighty-Six

I rode up to Jenks's house with Chris Raleigh. We barely spoke, both of us brimming with anticipation. Outside, we were met by Charlie Clapper and his CSU team. They would grid-search the house and grounds as soon as we took Jenks in.

We rang the bell. Each second I waited, my heart pounded harder. Every reason I became a cop was grinding in my chest. This was it.

The door opened and the same housekeeper answered. This time, her eyes went wide as she took in the convergence of police cars.

I flashed my badge and hurried past her. 'We need to see Mr Jenks.'

We found our way back to the sitting room where we had met only two days before. A startled Chessy Jenks met us in the hall. 'Inspector,' she gasped, recognizing me. 'What's going on? What are all those cops doing out front?'

'I'm sorry,' I said, meeting her eyes. I *was* sorry for her. 'Is your husband at home?'

'Nick!' she cried, realizing in a panic why we had come. Then she ran along with us, trying to block me, shouting. 'You can't just come in here like this. This is our home.'

'Please, Mrs Jenks,' Raleigh implored.

I was too wound up to stop. I wanted Nicholas Jenks so bad it hurt. A second later, he appeared, coming in from the back lawn overlooking the Pacific. He was holding a golf club.

'I thought I told you,' he said icily, looking perfectly unruffled in his white shirt and linen shorts, 'the next time you need something from me you should contact my lawyer.'

'You can tell him yourself,' I said. My heart was racing. 'Nicholas Jenks, you are under arrest for the murders of David and Melanie Brandt, Michael and Rebecca DeGeorge, James and Kathleen Voskuhl.'

I wanted him to hear every name, to bring to mind every one of them he'd killed. I wanted to see the callous indifference disintegrate in his eyes.

'This is insane.' Jenks glared at me. His gray eyes burned with intensity.

'Nick!' cried his wife. 'What are they talking about? Why are they here in our house?'

'Do you know what you're doing?' he hissed, the veins bulging on his neck. 'I asked you, *do you have any idea what you're doing?*'

I didn't answer, just recited the Miranda.

'What you're doing,' he raged, 'is engaging in the biggest mistake of your little life.'

'What are they saying?' His wife was pale. 'Nick, please tell me. What is going on?'

'Shut up,' Jenks spat out at her. Suddenly, he spun back toward me with a vicious fire in his eyes. He lunged forward with his fist and swung at me.

I cut his feet out from under him. Jenks fell across an end table to the floor, photos falling everywhere, glass shattering. The writer moaned loudly in pain.

Chessy Jenks screamed, stood there in a paralyzed state. Chris Raleigh cuffed her husband and dragged him to his feet.

'Call Sherman,' Jenks shouted at his wife. 'Tell him where I am, what's happened.'

Raleigh and I pushed Jenks out to our car. He continued to struggle and I saw no reason to be gentle.

'What's your theory on the murders now?' I asked him.

Chapter Eighty-Seven

After the last news conference had ended, after the last flashbulb had dimmed, after I had rehashed, for what seemed the hundredth time, how we had narrowed in on Jenks, after a beaming Chief Mercer had been chauffeured away, I hugged Claire, Cindy, and Jill. I then passed on a celebratory beer, and wandered back to the Hall of Justice.

It was well past eight and only the prattle of the night-shift interrupted my being alone.

I sat at my desk, in the well-earned silence of the squad room, and tried to remember the last time I felt this *good*.

Tomorrow, we would begin meticulously compiling the case against Nicholas Jenks: interrogating him, accumulating more evidence, filling out report after report. But we had done it. We had caught him just as I hoped we eventually would. I had fulfilled the promise I made to Melanie Brandt that horrible night in the Mandarin Suite at the Grand Hyatt.

I felt proud of myself. Whatever happened with the

Negli's, even if I never made Lieutenant, no one could take this away.

I got up, stepped over to the freestanding blackboard that listed the cases we were working on. Under *Open Cases*, somewhere near the top was her name: *Melanie Brandt*. I took the brush and rubbed her name, then her husband's, until they disappeared, until the blue smear of chalk was no more.

'I bet that feels good.' Raleigh's voice sounded behind me.

I turned. He was there, looking smug.

'What are you doing here?' I asked. 'So late.'

'Thought I'd straighten up Roth's desk, steal a few brownie points,' he said. 'What do you think, Lindsay? I came to find you.'

We were in a corner of the squad room and there was no one around. He never had to move. I went to him. Nothing in the way. No reason to deny this.

I kissed him. Not like before, not just to let Chris know I was interested. I kissed him the way I had wanted him to kiss me that night on the tree-lined lakefront in Cleveland. I wanted to steal the breath right out of him. To say, '*I wanted to do this from the first time I saw you.*'

When we finally pulled apart, he repeated with a smile, 'Like I said, I bet that feels good.'

It did feel good. Right now, it all felt good. It also felt unavoidable.

'What are your plans?' I smiled at him.

'How loosely are we talking?'

'Specifically, right now. Tonight. The next several hours, at least.'

'I thought I would come back, straighten Cheery's desk, and see if you wanted me to take you home.'

'Let me get my purse.'

Chapter Eighty-Eight

I don't know how we got all the way to my apartment in the Potrero. I don't know how Chris and I talked and drove and ignored what was tearing at us inside.

Once we got through my doors, there was no stopping it. I was all over Chris; he was all over me. We only got as far as the rug in the foyer, kissing, touching, fumbling for the buttons, the zippers, breathing loudly.

I had forgotten how good it was to be touched like this, to be held, to be desired by somebody I wanted, too. Once we touched, we knew enough to take our time. We both wanted it to last. Chris had what I needed more than anything else – *soft hands.*

I loved kissing him, loved his gentleness, then his roughness, the simple fact that he was concerned about my pleasure as much as his own. You never know until you try it out – but I loved being with Chris. I absolutely loved it.

I know it's a cliché, but that night I made love as if it might never happen again. I felt Chris's current, warming me, electrifying – from my womb to my thighs to the tips of my fingers and my toes. His grasp was all that held me together, kept me from breaking apart. I felt a trust for him that was unquestioning.

I held nothing back. I gave myself to Chris in a way I never had to anyone before. Not only with my body and my heart; these were things I could pull back. I gave him my hope that I could still live.

When I cried out, tremors exploding inside me, my fingers and toes stiff with joy, a voice inside me whispered what I knew was true.

I gave him everything. He gave it back.

Finally, Chris pulled off me. We were both tingling, still on fire.

'What?' I gasped for breath. 'Now what?'

He looked at me and smiled. 'I want to see the bedroom.'

Chapter Eighty-Nine

A cool breeze was blowing in my face. Oh God, what a night. What a day. What a rollercoaster!

I sat wrapped in a quilt out on my terrace, overlooking the south end of the Bay. Nothing was moving, only the lights of San Leandro in the distance. It was quarter of two.

In the bedroom, Chris lay asleep. He'd earned some rest.

I couldn't sleep. My body was too alive, tingling, like a distant shore with a thousand flickering lights.

I couldn't help but smile at the thought: It *had* been a great day. 'June seventh,' I said aloud. 'I'm gonna remember you.' First, we found the book. Then we arrested Jenks. I never imagined it could go any further.

But it had. It went *way* further. Chris and I made love that night twice more, the last three hours a sweet dance of touching, panting, loving. I didn't want his hands to ever leave me. I didn't ever want to miss the heat of his body. It was a new sensation. For once, I had held nothing back, and that was very, very good.

But here, in the dark of the night, an accusing voice

needled me. I was lying. I hadn't given it all. There was the one, inescapable truth that I was concealing.

I hadn't told him about Negli's. I didn't know how to. Just as we had felt such life, how could I tell him I was dying? That my body, which a moment ago was so alive with passion, was infected. In a single day, it seemed that everything in my life was transformed. I wanted to soar. I deserved it. I deserved to be happy.

But he deserved to know.

I heard a rustling behind me. It was Chris.

'What are you doing out here?' he asked. He came up behind me, placed his hands on my neck and shoulders.

I was hugging my knees, the quilt barely covering my breasts. 'It's gonna be hard,' I said, leaning my head on him, 'to go back to the way things were.'

'Who said anything about going back?'

'I mean, like partners. Watching you across the room. Tomorrow we have to interrogate Jenks. Big day for both of us.'

His fingers teased my breasts, then the back of my neck. He was driving me crazy. 'You don't have to worry,' he said. 'Once the case is made, I'm going back. I'll stick around for the interrogation.'

'Chris,' I said, as a chill shot through me. I had gotten used to him.

'I told you, we weren't going to be partners for ever.' He bent down, inhaling the smell of my hair. 'At least, not *those* kind of partners.'

'What kind does that leave?' I murmured. My neck was

on fire where his hands caressed me. Oh, let this go somewhere, I begged inside. Let this go all the way to the moon.

Could I just tell him? It was no longer that I couldn't find a way. It was just, now that we were here, I didn't want it to end.

I let him take me into the bedroom.

'This keeps getting better and better,' I whispered.

'Doesn't it? I can't wait to see what happens next.'

Chapter Ninety

I had just gotten to my desk the following morning and was flipping through the *Chronicle* to get to the continuation of Cindy's article on Jenks's arrest when my phone rang.

It was Charlie Clapper. His Crime Scene team had spent most of the night going through everything in Jenks's house.

'You make a case for me, Charlie?' I was hoping for a murder weapon, maybe even the missing rings. Something solid that would melt Jenks's sneering defiance.

The CSU leader let out a weary breath. 'I think you should come down here and see.'

I grabbed my purse and the keys to our work car. In the hallway, I ran into Jacobi. 'Rumors say,' he grunted, 'I'm no longer the man of your dreams.'

'You know you should never believe what you read in the *Star*,' I quipped.

'Right, or hear from the night-shift.'

I pulled myself to a stop. Someone had spotted Chris

and me last night. My mind flashed through the red-hot copy that was probably running through the office-rumor mill. Behind my anger, I knew that I was blushing.

'Relax,' Jacobi said. 'You know what can happen when you get caught up in a good collar. And it *was* a good collar.'

'Thank you, Warren,' I said. It was one of those rare moments when neither of us had anything to hide. I winked and hit the stairs.

'Just remember,' he called after me, 'it was the champagne match that got you on your way.'

'I remember. I'm grateful. Thank you, Warren.'

I drove down Sixth to Taylor and California to Jenks's home in Sea Cliff. When I arrived, two police cars were blocking the street, keeping a circle of media vans at bay. I found Clapper – looking tired and unshaven – catching a few minutes' rest at the dining-room table.

'You find me a murder gun?' I asked.

'Just these.' He pointed to a pile of guns in plastic bags on the floor.

There were hunting rifles, a showcase Minelli shotgun, a Colt automatic .45 pistol. No nine millimeter. I didn't make a move to examine them.

'We went through his office,' Clapper wheezed. 'Nothing on any of the victims. No clippings, no trophies.'

'I was hoping you might've come across the missing rings.'

'You want rings?' Clapper said. He wearily pushed himself up. 'His wife's got rings. Plenty of them. I'll let you go through them. But what we did find was this. Follow me.'

On the floor of the kitchen, with a yellow *Evidence* marker on it, was a crate of champagne. Krug. Clos du Mesnil.

'That we already knew,' I said.

He kept looking at me, as if I had somehow insulted him with the obvious. Then he lifted a bottle out of the open case.

'Check the numbers, Lindsay. Each bottle's registered with its own number. Look here, four-two-three-five-five-nine. Must make it go down all the more smoothly.' He took out a folded-up green copy of a *Police Property* voucher from his chest pocket. 'The one from the Hyatt was from the same lot. Same number.' The CSU man smiled.

The bottles *were* the same. It was solid evidence that tied Jenks to where David and Melanie Brandt were killed. It wasn't a weapon, but it was damning, no longer circumstantial. A rush of excitement shot through me. I high-fived the pale, heavy-set CSU man.

'Anyway,' Charlie said, almost apologetically, 'I wouldn't have brought you all the way out here for just that.'

Clapper led me through the finely furnished interior of the house to the master bedroom. It had a vast picture window looking out on the Golden Gate Bridge. He took me into a spacious closet. Jenks's.

'You remember the bloody jacket we found at the hotel?' In the rear of the closet, Charlie squatted over a large shoe-rack. 'Well, now it's a set.'

Clapper reached behind the shoe-rack and pulled out a crumpled Nordstrom's shopping bag. 'I wanted you to see how we found it.'

Out of the bag, he pulled balled-up black tuxedo trousers.

'I already checked. It's the other half of the jacket at the Hyatt. Same maker. Look inside, same style number.'

I might as well have been staring at a million dollars in cash, or a ton of stolen cocaine. I couldn't take my eyes off the pants, imagining how Nicholas Jenks would squirm now. Claire had been right. She'd been right from the start. The jacket hadn't come off the victim. It had always belonged to Jenks.

'So whad'ya think, Detective?' Charlie Clapper grinned. 'Can you close your case or what? Oh yeah,' the CSU man exclaimed, almost absent-mindedly. 'Where'd I put it?'

He patted his pockets, searched around his jacket. He finally found a small plastic bag.

'Straight out of the sucker's electric razor,' Charlie announced.

In the bag were several short red hairs.

Chapter Ninety-One

C laire said, 'I've been expecting you, honey.' She took my arm and led me back into the lab to a small room lined with chemicals. Two microscopes were set up side by side on a granite-block counter.

'Charlie told me what he came up with,' she said. 'The champagne. Matching pantalones. You got him, Lindsay.'

'Match these,' I held out the plastic bag, 'we put him in the gas chamber.'

'Okay, let's see,' she said, smiling. She opened a yellow envelope marked *Priority Evidence*, and took a Petri dish identical to the one I had seen after the second murders. It had *Subject: Rebecca DeGeorge, #62340* in bold marker written on the front.

With a tweezer, she placed the single hair that had come from the second bride onto a clear slide. Then she inserted it under the scope. She leaned over it, adjusting the focus, then caught me by surprise, asking, 'So how're you feeling, woman?'

'You mean Negli's?'

'What else would I mean?' she said, peering into the scope.

In the rush of apprehending Jenks, it was the first time in the past few days that I had really thought about it. 'I saw Medved late last week. My blood count's still down.'

Claire finally looked up. 'I'm sorry, Lindsay.'

Trying to sound upbeat, I walked her through my regimen. The increased dosage. The higher frequency. I mentioned the possibility of a bone-marrow transplant.

She gave me a broad smile. 'We're gonna have to find a way to get those red cells of yours shaken up.'

Even in the laboratory, I must've started to blush.

'What?' asked Claire. 'What're you hiding? Trying unsuccessfully to hide?'

'Nothing.'

'*Something's* going on – between you and Mr Chris Raleigh, I bet. C'mon, this is *me* you're talking to. You can't pull that blue-wall-of-silence stuff.'

I told her. From the first kiss at the precinct to the slow, torturous ride home to the burst of heat right there on the foyer floor.

Claire grasped me by my shoulders. Her eyes were as bright and excited as mine. 'So?'

'So?' I laughed. 'So . . . it was awesome. It was . . . *right*.' I felt a chill of doubt come over me. 'I just don't know if I'm doing the right thing. Considering what's going on.' I hesitated. 'I could love him, Claire. Maybe I already do.'

We stared at each other. There wasn't much more to say.

'Well,' Claire's eyes returned to her microscope, 'let's see what we have here. Hairs from his chinny-chin-chin.'

The three hairs from Jenks's razor were set on a cellular slide. She loaded it into a scope. The two scopes were side by side.

Claire looked first, leaned over, as she focused the new one in. Then she went back and forth. 'Mm-hmm,' she uttered.

I held my breath. 'What do you think?' I asked.

'You tell me.'

I leaned in. Immediately, I remembered the first hair, the one from inside Rebecca DeGeorge's vagina. Thick, reddish-gray, a white filament twisted around its base like the coil of a snake.

Then I looked at the hairs from Jenks's razor. There were three of them, shorter, clipped, but each had that same reddish hue, that same coil of filament around them.

I was no expert. But there was no doubt in my mind.

The hairs were a perfect match.

Chapter Ninety-Two

Nicholas Jenks was in a holding cell on the tenth floor of the Hall of Justice. He was headed to arraignment later today.

His lawyer, Sherman Leff, was with him, looking as if this were all just a formality, and the scales of justice were resting on the shoulders of his English-tailored suit.

Jill Bernhardt accompanied Raleigh and me. Jenks had no idea what was coming his way. We had the champagne, the tuxedo pants, matching hairs from his beard. We had him in the suite with David and Melanie Brandt. I couldn't wait to tell him all the good news.

I sat down across from Jenks and looked him in the eye. 'This is Assistant District Attorney Jill Bernhardt,' I said. 'She's going to be handling your case. She's going to convict you, too.'

He smiled – the same gracious, confident and condescending glint as if he were receiving us in his own home. *Why* does he look so confident? I wondered.

'If it's all right,' Jill said, 'I'd like to begin.'

'Your meeting,' Sherman Leff said. 'I've no objection.'

Jill took a breath. 'Mr Jenks, in an hour you are going to be arraigned for the first-degree murder of David and Melanie Brandt at the Grand Hyatt Hotel on June fifth. Shortly after, I believe a Cleveland court will do the same for the murders of James and Katherine Voskuhl. Based on what the Medical Examiner has just uncovered, I believe you can expect a Napa Valley court to follow through as well. We have overwhelming evidence linking you to all three of these crimes. We're sharing this with you, and with your counsel, in the hope that your response to this evidence might spare the city, the families of the deceased, and your family, the further humiliation of a trial.'

Sherman Leff finally cut in. 'Thank you, Ms Bernhardt. As long as consideration is the spirit of the day, we'd like to begin by expressing my client's deep regret for his emotional outburst toward Inspector Boxer at the time of his arrest. As you might imagine, the shock and the suddenness of such an accusation, so totally preposterous after he had fully complied with your questioning, in his own home . . . I'm certain you can understand how the wrong emotions might take hold.'

'I do deeply regret that, Inspector,' Jenks spoke up. 'I realize how this must look. My being less than forthcoming about my relationship with one of the deceased. And now you seem to have stumbled upon that unfortunate book.'

'Which,' Leff interjected, 'I must advise you, we will be

making a motion to suppress. Obtaining it was an unjustified intrusion into my client's private domain.'

'The warrant was totally justified,' Jill said calmly.

'On what grounds?'

'On the grounds that its existence was revealed during follow-up questioning necessitated by your client's false testimony concerning his whereabouts when Kathy Voskuhl was killed.'

Leff hung in midmotion, stunned.

'Your client *was* in Cleveland, Counselor,' I sprang on him. Then I said to Jenks, 'You were registered under your own name at the Westin Hotel. You stayed two nights, coinciding with the Voskuhl murders. You said you were at home, Mr Jenks. But you were *there*. And you were at the Hall of Fame.'

Jenks's smile disappeared and his eyes flicked around the room. He swallowed, and I could see the knot sliding down his throat. He was retracing his alibis and lies. He looked at Leff, somewhat apologetically.

'I *was* there,' he admitted. 'I *did* conceal it. As it happens, I was in town to address a local readers' group. You can check – the Argosy Bookstore. I didn't know how to explain it. Coupled with knowing Kathy, it seemed so incriminating. But let me make this clear. You're wrong about the wedding. I was nowhere near it.'

My blood rose. I couldn't believe this guy. 'You had a reading? When, Mr Jenks?'

'Saturday afternoon. At four. A small group of very loyal fans. The Argosy was very kind to me when I first started out.'

'And after that?'

'After that I do what I always do. I went back to the hotel and wrote. I took a swim, had an early dinner. You can ask my wife. I always spend the evenings alone when I'm on the road. It's been written up in *People* magazine.'

I leaned across the table. 'So this was all some bizarre coincidence, right? A woman with whom you've denied having a sexual relationship for years is brutally murdered. You just happen to be in town. You just happen to lie about being there. Your likeness just happens to be caught by a security camera at the scene. Is that how it goes, Mr Jenks?'

Leff placed a cautionary hand on Jenks's arm.

'*No!*' his client snapped, his self-control clearly chipping away.

Then he became calmer and wiped the sweat off his brow. 'I lied for Chessy – to preserve my marriage.' He straightened himself up in the wooden chair. His alibi was collapsing. 'I'm not a perfect man, Detective. I slip. I deceived you about Kathy. It was wrong. The answer is yes, what you assume to be true is. We *were* lovers on and off for three years. It continued well into her relationship with James. It was folly. It was the desperate thrill of a fool. But it was *not* murder. I did not kill Kathy. And I did not kill the others!'

Jenks stood up. For the first time, he looked scared. The panic of what was happening was clearly sinking in.

I leaned forward and said, 'A bottle of champagne was left in the suite at the Hyatt where the Brandts were killed.

It matched the same lot you purchased at an auction at Butterfield and Butterfield in November nineteen-ninety-six.'

Leff objected, 'We know that. Surely the unfortunate coincidence of my client's taste in champagne doesn't implicate him in this act. He didn't even know the Brandts. That wine could have been purchased anywhere.'

'It could have, yes – however, the registration numbers on the bottle from the Hyatt matched those from the rest of the lot we uncovered at your home last night.'

'This is getting absurd,' Jenks said angrily. 'This sort of bullshit wouldn't even make one of my books.'

'Hopefully, this will be better then.' From under the table, I pulled out the Nordstrom's shopping bag holding the balled-up tuxedo pants. I tossed them on the table in front of everybody's eyes. 'You recognize these?'

'Pants . . . what kinds of games are we playing now?'

'These were found last night. In this bag. In the back of your bedroom closet.'

'So? What're you saying – they're mine? Joseph Abboud. They could be. I don't understand where you're going.'

'Where I'm going is that these pants match the tuxedo jacket that was found in the Brandts' suite. They're a suit, Mr Jenks.'

'A suit?'

'It's the pants to the jacket you left in their hotel room. Same brand. Same style number. Same size.'

A deepening panic began to sweep over his face.

'And if all that still falls short of your usual material,' I said, fixing on his eyes, 'then how's this? *The hair matched.* The hair you left inside poor Becky DeGeorge matches hairs taken from your house. It belonged to you, you animal. You convicted yourself.'

Jill leaned forward. 'You're going away, Jenks. You're going away until the appeals finally run out and they come to stick a loaded needle in your arm.'

'This is insane,' he cried. He was leaning over me, veins in his neck swelling, shouting in my face. 'You bitch! You're setting me up! You fucking ice-bitch! I didn't kill anyone.'

Suddenly, I found that I couldn't move. Seeing Jenks unwind was one thing. But there was something else going on. I felt pinned to my chair. I *knew*, but I couldn't fight it – it was the Negli's.

I finally got up and went to the door, but my head swirled and the room tilted. My legs began to buckle. Not here, I begged.

Then I felt Raleigh supporting me. 'Lindsay . . . you all right?' He was looking at me, worried, unsuspecting. I saw Jill there, too.

I leaned against the wall. I begged my legs to work. 'I'm okay,' I whispered, holding onto Raleigh's arm.

'I just hate that bastard,' I said, and walked out of the interrogation room. I was white, very weak, swaying. I barely made it to the ladies' room.

Inside, I felt faint, then nauseated, as if some angry spirit were trying to claw its way out of my lungs. I closed my eyes, leaned over the sink. I coughed, a raw burning stinging in my chest, then I shook and coughed some more.

Gradually, I felt the spell recede. I took a breath, opened my eyes and shuddered.

There was blood all over the sink.

Chapter Ninety-Three

Four hours later, in District Criminal Court, I felt well enough to watch Nicholas Jenks be arraigned for murder.

A buzzing crowd filled the halls outside the courtroom of Judge Stephen Bowen. Photographers flashed cameras blindly, reporters surged for a glimpse of the sullen, shaken, bestselling writer.

Raleigh and I squeezed through, took a seat behind Jill in the front row. My strength having returned, the riot in my chest subsided. *I wanted Jenks to see me there.*

I saw Cindy, sitting in the press section. And in the back of the courtroom, I spotted Chancellor Weil and his wife.

It was over before it began. Jenks was led in, his eyes as dead and hollow as a crater on the moon. The clerk read the docket, the suspect rose. The bastard pleaded Not Guilty. What were they going to argue – that all the evidence was inadmissible?

Leff, the consummate showman, was unusually respectful, even demure before Judge Bowen. He made a pleading case for release on recognizance based on Jenks's stature in the community. For a moment, the killer's accomplishments even swayed me.

Jill fought him head-on. She graphically detailed the savagery of the murders. She argued that the suspect had the means and the lack of roots to flee.

I felt a surge of triumph rippling through me when the Judge struck his gavel and intoned, 'Bail Denied.'

Chapter Ninety-Four

N ow, we were celebrating.
It was the end of the day, a day for which I had
long waited, and I met the girls for a drink at Susie's.

We had earned this. Nicholas Jenks had been arraigned.
No bail. No consideration of the court. The four of us had
pulled it off.

'Here's to the Women's Murder Club,' Cindy cheered,
with her beer mug in the air.

'Not bad for a collection of gender-impaired public
servants,' Claire agreed.

'What did Jenks call me?' I shook my head and smiled. 'A
fucking ice-bitch?'

'I can do ice-bitch,' Jill said, grinning.

'To the ice-bitches of the world,' Cindy toasted, 'and the
men who cannot thaw us out.'

'Speak for yourself,' said Claire. 'Edmund thaws me just
fine.' We all laughed and clinked beers.

'Still,' I said, letting out a deep breath, 'I'd like to turn up a
murder weapon. And I want to nail him to the second crime.'

'When I'm through with him,' Jill tugged at her beer and said, 'you won't have to worry about him serving time for the second crime.'

'You see Jill chop down his lawyer's bail request?' Cindy said, with admiration. 'You see the look on his face?' She made her fingers into scissors. 'Snip, snip, snip, snip, snip. Straight for the testicles. That man was left standing there in his suit with a two-inch dick.' Cindy's cherubic nose twisted as she said, *Snip, snip, snip.*

'And yet,' I said, 'without a weapon, his motive still needs work.'

'Damn his motive, child,' Claire exclaimed. 'Let well enough alone.'

Jill agreed. 'Why can't his motive simply be that he's a sick bastard? He's had a history of sexual sadism for years. He's brutalized three women that we know of. I'm sure more will come out as the trial moves on.'

'You saw him, Lindsay,' Jill went on. 'He's crazed. His little perfect world gets rocked, he goes insane. This morning, he was about to plant a death grip on your throat.' She grinned toward the group. 'Lindsay just sort of glares up at him like, *Get the fuck out of my face.*'

They were about to raise a glass to me – the tough hero cop who would always carry the tag that she was the one who nailed Jenks – when the realization shot through me that I could never have done it without them. It wasn't my steel nerves that had taken over in the interrogation room, but the grip of my disease squeezing the life out of me. I had kept it concealed – not shared it even with the ones who had become my closest friends.

'That wasn't about Jenks,' I said.

'Sure seemed like it.'

'I don't mean the confrontation. I mean what happened after.' I bit my lower lip. 'When I almost collapsed, that wasn't about Jenks.'

They were still smiling, except Claire, but one by one the gravity in my eyes alerted them.

I looked around the table and told them about the Pac Man-like disease that was eating my red blood cells. I'd been fighting it for three weeks now, I said, with transfusions. And yet my blood count was deteriorating. I was getting worse.

I started strong, my voice firm, because it'd been part of my life for a while now, but when I finished, I was speaking in a hushed, scared tone. I was blinking back tears.

Jill and Cindy just sat there, rocked in disbelieving silence. Then, there were three hands reaching out for me – Cindy's, Jill's, then last and warmest, Claire's. For a long time, no one said anything. They didn't have to.

Finally, I smiled, choking back tears. 'Isn't it just like a cop to go and shut down a party just when it's going good.'

It broke the tension, cut through the sudden pall.

They never said, *We're with you*. They never told me, *You're gonna be all right*. They didn't have to.

'We're supposed to be celebrating,' I said.

Then I heard Jill's voice, out of the blue, solemn, confessing. 'When I was a little girl, I was real sick. I was in a brace and hospitals between the ages of four and seven. It broke my parents, their marriage. They split up as soon as I got better. I guess that's why I always felt I had to be stronger and better than anyone else. Why I always had to win. 'It started in high school,' she went on.

I wasn't sure what she was referring to.

'I didn't know if I would be good enough. I used to . . .' She unbuttoned the cuffs of her blouse, rolled the sleeves up over her elbows. 'I've never showed these to anybody except Steve.'

Her arms were marked with scars. I knew what they were – self-inflicted slashes. Jill had been a cutter.

'What I meant to say was, you just have to fight it. You fight it, and fight it, and fight it . . . and every time you feel it getting stronger, you fight it some more.'

'I'm trying,' I whispered, my voice choking. 'I really am trying.' Now I knew what propelled her, what was behind that steely gaze. 'But how?'

Jill's hands were holding mine. There were tears in our eyes.

'It's like with Jenks, Lindsay,' she said. 'You just don't let it win.'

Chapter Ninety-Five

I n the cold, cramped cell, Nicholas Jenks paced anxiously. He felt as if dynamite were about to explode at the center of his chest. How could they destroy his name, attack him with those wild allegations, disgrace him all over the news? He wasn't guilty. He was innocent!

It was dark and he was freezing. The cot in his jail cell wasn't fit for a monk. He was still in the damp clothes he'd been wearing when they had brought him in. Sweat began to break out on his palms.

He'd make the little Inspector-bitch pay. One way or another, he'd get her in the end. That was a promise.

What was his fucking poodle of a lawyer doing? When would Leff get him out of there?

It was as if all reason had been sucked out of his world.

What the hell was going on?

Or, at least, Phillip Campbell thought to himself, That's what Jenks *ought* to be feeling. What he thought the bastard would be saying in his mind.

Campbell sat in front of the mirror. *Time for you to go away. Your work is finally done. The last chapter's been written.*

He dabbed a wet cloth in a bowl of warm water. It was the last time he would ever have to play the part.

So how does it feel, Nicholas?

He pulled out the pins that held in his hair and let his locks shake out.

How does it feel to be a victim, a prisoner? To feel the same degradation and shame you cast on others?

Slowly, he wiped the dark makeup off his eyes, dabbing with the cloth, feeling a smooth sheen begin to return to his face.

How does it feel to be helpless and alone? To be kept in a dark space? To feel betrayed?

One by one, Phillip Campbell tugged at the hairs of the reddish beard on his chin, until the fake hairs came out and a new person was revealed.

Not able to recognize in the mirror the person you once were?

Scrubbing the face until it came clean and smooth. Unbuttoning the shirt, Nicholas's shirt, and soon, from underneath a bodysuit, a well-defined woman's body came to life: the outline of breasts, shapely, smooth legs, arms rippling with lean strength.

She sat there, newly revealed, a bright glow in her eyes.

This is rich.

How does it feel, Nicholas, to be royally fucked? The tables turned for once.

She couldn't restrain the thought that it was fitting and funny, that in the end he had been trapped by his own twisted mind. It was more than funny. It was absolutely brilliant.

Who's laughing now, Nick?

Book Four

The Whole Truth

Chapter Ninety-Six

The night following Jenks's arraignment, Chief Mercer had gotten the skybox at PacBell from one of his wealthy buddies. He invited several of us, including me, Raleigh and Cheery, to a Giants game. It was a warm summer evening. They were playing the Cards. My father would have loved it.

I didn't really want to go, didn't want to feel on display as the cop who'd caught Jenks, but Mercer insisted.

And it was Mark McGwire and all, so I put on a windbreaker and we went along for the ride.

All evening long, Chris and I kept sneaking looks at each other. There was a special energy in the box, a glowing ring around just him and me.

The game was background noise. In the third, Mighty Mac hit one off Ortiz that went out of sight and almost landed in the Bay. The stadium cheered wildly, even for a Card. In the fourth, Barry Bonds tied it with a shot of his own.

Chris and I couldn't stop watching each other. We had

our legs up on the same chair, like school kids, and every once in a while, our calves brushed together. *Jesus, this was better than the ball game.*

Finally, he winked at me. 'Want something to drink?' he said.

He went over to the bowl of drinks, which was elevated from the seats, and I followed. The others didn't look back. As soon as we were out of sight, he placed his hands on my thighs and kissed me. 'You want to hang around?'

'Still beer left,' I joked.

His hand brushed against the side of my breast, and I felt a tremor. *Soft hands.* My breath quickened. A flicker of sweat broke through my neck.

Chris kissed me again. He drew me in close, and I felt the cadence of a heart, pounding between us. I didn't know if it was his or mine.

'Can't wait,' he said.

'Okay, let's get out of here.'

'No,' he shook his head. 'I meant I *can't* wait.'

'Oh Jesus,' I gasped. I couldn't hold back. My whole body was heating up to the boiling point. I glanced down at Cheery and the two Mill Valley types. *This is crazy, Lindsay.*

But everything lately was crazy, everything speeding out of control.

It seemed as if every natural force in the universe was driving Chris and me to find a secluded spot. There was a bathroom in the skybox, barely large enough to put on makeup in. We didn't care.

Chris led me inside while the baseball crowd roared at something. We could barely squeeze in. I could not believe I was doing this here. He unbuttoned my blouse, I unfastened his belt. Our thighs were pressed tightly onto each other's.

Gently, Chris lifted me onto him. I felt as if a shooting star had exploded in my veins. Chris was up against the counter; I was in the palms of his hands, squeezed into this tiny space, but we were in a perfect rhythm.

A crowd roar echoed in from outside – maybe McGwire had hit another, maybe Bonds had robbed him – who cared. We kept rocking. Chris and I. We were both breathing hard. My body was slick with sweat. I couldn't stop. Chris kept it going, I gripped on tight, and in a moment, we both gasped.

Two hero cops, I thought.

It was the best – the freest, the most excited I had ever felt. Chris rested his forehead on my shoulder. I kissed his cheek, his neck.

Then the strangest thought took hold of me. I began to laugh, a mixture of laughter and exhausted sighs. We were pinned there, spent, a few feet from my boss. I was giggling like a damn fool. I was going to get us caught!

'What's so funny?' Chris whispered.

I was thinking of Claire and Cindy. And what we had just done.

'I think I just made the list,' I said.

Chapter Ninety-Seven

The next day, Jenks asked to meet again. Jill and I went to see him on the tenth floor. We wondered what was up.

This time, there was no cat and mouse, no bullshit at all. Leff was there, but he rose – humbly – as soon as we came in.

Jenks looked far less threatening in his gray prison outfit. The worried look on his face was a clear message.

'My client wants to make a statement,' Leff said, as soon as we sat down.

I was thinking, This is it. He wants to make a deal. He's seen how ridiculous it is to play this game.

But he came out with something unexpected.

'I'm being framed,' Jenks announced.

It took about a half-second for Jill's eyes to bump into mine.

'I have to hear this again,' she said. 'What's going on?' She looked at Jenks, then at Leff.

'We've got your client tied to all three crime scenes;

we've got him in Cleveland at the time of the last murder; we've got his lying about a prior relationship with Kathy Kogut, one of the last victims; we've got his book detailing an astonishingly similar criminal pattern; we've got his facial hairs matched to one found in another victim's vagina. And you're claiming *he's being framed*?'

'What I'm claiming,' Jenks said, ashen-faced, 'is that I'm being set up.'

'Listen, Mr Jenks,' Jill said, still looking at Leff, 'I've been doing this eight years. I've built cases on hundreds of criminals, put over fifty murderers behind bars myself. I've never seen such a preponderance of evidence implicating a suspect. Our case is so airtight it can't breathe.'

'I realize that,' sighed Jenks. 'And that I've given you every reason to find my plea implausible. I've lied about being in Cleveland, my relationship with Kathy. On the others, I can't even account for my whereabouts. But I also know set-ups. I've mapped out more of them than anybody. I'm a master at this. And I can assure you, someone is setting me up.'

I shook my head with disbelief. 'Who, Mr Jenks?'

Jenks actually looked scared. 'I don't know.'

'Someone hates you enough to set all this up?' Jill couldn't hold back a snicker. 'The little I know of you, I might buy that.' She turned to Leff. 'You looking forward to presenting this case?'

'Just hear him out, Ms Bernhardt,' the lawyer pleaded.

'Look,' Jenks said, 'I know what you think of me. I'm guilty of many things. Selfishness, cruelty, adultery. I have a temper, sometimes I can't hold it in. And with women . . . you can probably line up a dozen of them who would help put me away for these murders. But clear as that is, I did not kill these people. Any of them. Someone is trying to set me up. That's the truth. Someone has done a brilliant job.'

Chapter Ninety-Eight

'**Y**ou buy any of that shit?' Jill smirked at me, as we waited for the elevator outside Jenks's holding cell.

'I might buy that he somehow believes it,' I told her.

'Give me a break. He'd be better off going for insanity. If Nicholas Jenks wants to narrow down a list of people who might want to set him up, he might as well start with anyone he ever fucked.'

I laughed, agreeing that the list would be long. Then the elevator door opened and, to my surprise, out walked Chessy Jenks. She was dressed in a long, taupe summer dress. I immediately noticed how pretty she was.

Our eyes met in an awkward, silent moment. I had just arrested her husband. My Crime Scene team had ripped apart her house. She would have every reason to look at me with complete disdain – but she didn't.

'I'm here to see my husband,' she said in a shaky voice.

I stiffly introduced her to Jill, then I pointed her to the visiting area. At that moment, she seemed about as alone and confused as anyone I had ever seen.

'Sherman tells me there's a lot of evidence,' she said.

I nodded politely. I don't know why I felt something for her, other than she seemed a young, vulnerable woman whose fate was to fall in love with a monster.

'Nick didn't do this, Detective,' Chessy Jenks said.

Her outburst surprised me. 'It's only natural for a wife to want to defend her husband,' I acknowledged. 'If you have some concrete alibi . . .'

She shook her head. 'No alibi. Only that I know my husband.'

The elevator door had closed, and Jill and I stood there waiting again. As in hospitals, it would take minutes for it to go down and come back up. Chessy Jenks made no move to walk away.

'My husband's not a simple man. He can be very tough. I know he's made enemies. I know how he came at you. From the outside, it must be very hard to believe this, but there are times when he's also capable of tenderness, incredible generosity, and love.'

'I don't mean to sound unsympathetic, Ms Jenks,' Jill stepped in, 'but under the circumstances you really shouldn't be talking with us.'

'I have nothing to hide,' she came back. Then she looked downcast. 'I already know what you know.'

I was dumbfounded. *I already know what you know?*

'I spoke with Joanna,' Chessy Jenks continued. 'She told me you'd been by. I know what she told you about him. She's bitter. She's got every right to be. But she doesn't know Nick like I do.'

'You should review the evidence, Ms Jenks,' I told her.

She shook her head. 'Guns . . . maybe, Detective – if that's all there was. But a knife? That first murder – slicing that poor couple to bits. Nick can't even fillet a fish.'

My first thought was that she was young and deluded. How had Jenks described it? *Impressionable* . . . but something struck me as curious. 'You said that you and Joanna talk?'

'We have, Detective. A lot more in the past year. I've even had her over – when Nick was away, of course. I know she was bitter after the divorce. I know he hurt her. But it's sort of our own support group.'

'Your husband knew about this?' I asked.

She forced a smile. 'He didn't even mind. He still likes Joanna. And, Detective, she's still in love with him.'

The elevator came and we said goodbye. As the door closed, I looked at Jill. Her eyes were wide and her tongue was puffing out her cheek.

'Whole fucking family gives me the creeps,' she shuddered.

Chapter Ninety-Nine

I knew it the minute Medved walked in the office. I saw it in his face. He didn't have to say a word.

'I'm afraid I can't be very positive, Lindsay,' he said quietly, meeting my eyes. 'Your red count continues to decline. The fainting spells, the fatigue, blood in your chest. The disease is progressing.'

'Progressing?' I whispered.

Medved nodded, soberly. 'Stage Three.'

The words thundered in my head, bringing with them the fears of the increased treatments I dreaded. 'What's the next step?' I asked weakly.

'We can give it one more month,' Medved said. 'Your count's twenty-four hundred. If it continues to decline, your strength will start to go. You'll have to be hospitalized.'

I could hardly comprehend what he was saying. A month. That was too close. Too fast. Things were just starting to work out now that Jenks was arrested. Everything else, everything I wanted to hold onto, was resolving, too.

A month – four lousy weeks.

When I got back to the office, a few of the guys were standing around, grinning at me. There was a beautiful bouquet of flowers on my desk. Wildflowers.

I smelled them, taking in the sweet, natural scent, and read the card. *There's a hill of these where I have a cabin up at Heavenly. Tomorrow's Friday. Take the day off. Let's go there.*

It was signed *Chris*.

It sounded like what I needed. The mountains. Chris. I would have to tell him now that the truth would come clear soon.

My phone rang. It was Chris. 'So?' No doubt someone in the office, playing Cupid, had alerted him that I was back.

'Haven't opened your card yet.' I bit my lip. 'Too many others to sort through.'

I heard a disappointed sigh, let it linger just a moment. 'But on the chance you were asking me away, the answer is I'd love to. It sounds great. Let's be on the road by eight.'

'Late riser,' he said. 'I was hoping we'd beat the morning rush.'

'I was talking tonight.'

I had a month, I was thinking. Mountain air, running streams and wildflowers is a good way to begin.

Chapter One Hundred

We spent the next two days as if we were in a beautiful dream.

Chris's cabin was funky and charming, a redwood A-frame ski chalet on Mason Ridge overlooking Heavenly. We hiked in the woods with Sweet Martha, took the tram to the top of the mountain, and walked all the way down. We grilled swordfish on the deck.

In between, we made love in the comfort of his large, four-poster bed; on the sheepskin rug in front of the wood-burning stove; in the chilly thrill of the outdoor shower. We laughed and played and touched each other like teenagers, discovering love again.

But I was no starry-eyed adolescent. I knew exactly what was taking place. I felt the steady, undeniable current rising inside me like a river spilling over its banks. I felt helpless.

Saturday, Chris promised me a day I would never forget.

We drove down to Lake Tahoe, to a quaint marina on the California side. He had rented a platform boat, an old puttering wooden barge. We bought sandwiches and a bottle of Chardonnay, and went out to the middle of the lake. The water calm and turquoise, the sky cloudless and bright. All around, the rocky tips of snow-capped mountains ringed the lake like a crown.

We moored, and for a while, it was our own private world. Chris and I stripped down to our suits. I figured we'd kick back, enjoy the wine and the sun, look at the view, but Chris had sort of an expectant dare-you look in his eye. He ran his hands through the frigid water.

'No way,' I said, shaking my head. 'It's got to be fifty degrees.'

'Yeah, but it's a dry cold,' he teased.

'Right,' I chortled. 'You go, then. Catch me a coho if you see one swim by.'

He came toward me with playful menace in his eyes. 'You can catch one yourself.'

'Not a chance.' I shook my head in defiance. But I was laughing, too. As he stepped forward, I backed to the rear of the craft until I had run out of room.

He put his arms around me. I felt the tingle of his skin on mine. 'It's sort of an initiation,' he said.

'An initiation for what?'

'Exclusive club. Anyone who wants to be in it has to jump in.'

'Then leave me out,' I laughed, squirming in his strong arms. With only weak resistance, he yanked me up on the cushion seat in the stern of the boat.

'Shit, Chris,' I cried as he took hold of my hand.

'Geronimo works better,' he said, pulling at me. I screamed, '*You bastard!*' and we toppled in.

The water was freezing, a total, invigorating rush. We hit the surface together and I screamed in his face, '*Goddamn you!*' Then he kissed me in the water, and all at once I felt no chill. I held onto him, at first for warmth, but also because I never wanted to let him go. I felt a trust for him that was so complete, it was almost scary. The water was fifty degrees, but I was burning up.

'Check this out,' I dared him, kicking free of his grasp. There was an orange boat marker bobbing fifty yards away. 'Race you to that buoy.' Then I cut out, surprising him with my speed.

Chris tried to keep up with steady, muscular strokes, but I blew him away.

Near the buoy I slowed, waited for him to catch up.

Chris looked totally confounded. 'Where'd you learn to swim?'

'South San Francisco YMCA fourteen-, fifteen-, sixteen-year-old Division Champ,' I boasted. 'No one else could keep up. Looks like I still have it.'

Moments later, we had guided the boat to a private, shady cove near the shore. Chris cut the engine, and put up a canvas shade around the cabin that was supposed to protect us from the sun. With bated breath, we crept inside, blocked off from anyone's view.

I let him slowly unfasten my bathing suit, and he licked beads of water off my arms and breasts. Then I kneeled down and unbuttoned his shorts. We didn't have to speak.

Our bodies were saying everything. I lay back, pulling Chris onto me.

I had never felt so connected to another person, or a place. I arched against him, silently, the lake lapping gently at our sides. I thought, If I speak, it will change everything.

Afterward, I just lay there, tremors of warmth radiating through my body. I never wanted this to end, but I knew that it had to. Reality always gets in the way, doesn't it?

Chapter One Hundred
and One

Sometime that evening, I found myself starting to cry.

I had made spaghetti carbonara, and we ate in the moonlight on the deck with a bottle of Pinot Noir. Chris put a cello concerto by Dvořák on the stereo, but eventually we switched to the Dixie Chicks.

As we ate, Chris asked about where and how I had grown up.

I enlarged on what I had already told him about my mom, and how my dad had left when I was just a kid; how Mom had worked as a bookkeeper at the Emporium for twenty years. How I had practically raised my sister.

'Mom died of breast cancer when she was only fifty.' The irony of this certainly wasn't lost on me.

'What about your father? I want to know everything about you.'

I took a sip of wine, then told him how I'd only seen him twice since I was thirteen. At my mother's funeral. And the day I became a cop. 'He sat in the back, apart from everybody else.' Suddenly, my blood became hot with long-buried feelings. 'What was he doing there?' I looked up, my eyes moist. 'Why did he spoil it?'

'You ever want to see him?'

I didn't answer. Something was starting to take shape in my head. My mind drifted, struck by the fact that here I was, maybe the happiest I had ever been, but it was all built on a lie. I was blinking back the impact of what was going through my mind. Not doing real well.

Chris reached over and grasped my hand. 'I'm sorry, Lindsay. I had no right to . . .'

'That's not it,' I whispered and squeezed his hand. I knew it was time to really trust him, time to finally give myself over to Chris. But I was scared, my cheeks trembling, my eyes holding back tears.

'I have something to tell you,' I said. 'This is a little heavy, Chris.'

I looked at him with all the earnestness and trust my worried eyes could manage. 'Remember when I almost fainted in the room with Jenks?'

Chris nodded. Now he looked anxious. His forehead was furrowed with deep lines.

'Everyone thought I was just freaked out, but it wasn't that. I'm sick, Chris. I may have to go into the hospital soon.'

I saw the light in his eyes suddenly dim. He started to speak, but I put my finger to his lips.

'Just listen to me for a minute. Okay?'

'Okay. I'm sorry.'

I poured out everything about Negli's. I was not

responding to treatments. Hope was fading. What Medved had warned only days before. I was in Stage Three, serious. A bone-marrow transplant might be next.

I didn't cry. I told him straight-out, like a cop. I wanted to give him hope, to show him I was fighting, to show him I was the strong person I thought he loved. When I was done, I clasped his hands and took a monumental breath. 'The truth is, I could die soon, Chris.'

Our hands were tightly entwined. Our eyes locked. We couldn't have been more in touch.

Then he placed his hand gently on my cheek and rubbed it. He didn't say a word, just took me and held me in the power and softness of his hands and drew me to him.

And that's what made me cry. He was a good person. I might lose him. And I cried for all the things we might never do.

I cried and cried, and with each sob he pressed me harder. He kept whispering, 'It's all right, Lindsay. It's all right. It's all right.'

'I should've told you,' I said.

'I understand why you didn't. How long have you known?'

I told him. 'Since the day we met. I feel so ashamed.'

'Don't be ashamed,' he said. 'How could you know you could trust me?'

'I trusted you pretty quickly. I didn't trust myself.'

'Well, now you do,' Chris whispered.

Chapter One Hundred and Two

I think we rocked all night. We laughed some, cried some. I don't even remember how I woke up in bed.

The following day, I barely left his touch. With all that was threatening, all that seemed so uncertain, I felt so safe and sure in his arms. I never wanted to leave.

But something else happened during that weekend – apart from Negli's, apart from Chris and me. Something gripping, invading my sense of comfort and security.

It was something Jacobi had said that planted the thought.

One of those thrown-out remarks you pay no attention to, but which somehow get filed away in your mind. Then it comes back at the oddest time, with more force and logic than before.

It was Sunday night. The weekend was over. Chris had driven me home. Hard as it was to leave him, I needed to be alone for a while, to take inventory of the weekend, to figure out what I would do next.

I unpacked, made some tea, curled up on my couch

with Her Sweetness. My mind wandered to the murder case.

Nicholas Jenks was behind me now. Only the countless reports to fill out remained. Even though he was still ranting about being set up. It was just more insanity, more lies.

It was then that Jacobi's words snaked into my brain.

'Good collar,' he'd said, early Tuesday morning. He had that annoying, persistent look in his eyes. 'Just remember,' he'd called after me, 'it was the champagne match that got you on your way. Why do you think Jenks left that champagne?'

I was barely paying attention. Jenks was locked away; the case was a slam dunk. I was thinking about the night before, and Chris. 'I don't know, Warren. We've been over this. Heat of the moment, maybe.'

'You're right,' he nodded. 'That must be why he didn't ball up the jacket and take it with him, too.'

I looked at him, like, 'Why are we going through this now? Jenks needed a clean tux jacket to get out of the hotel undetected.' The DNA match on the hair made it all academic, anyway.

Then he said it. 'You ever read the whole book?' he asked.

'Which book?'

'Jenks's book. *Always A Bridesmaid.*'

'The parts that matter,' I replied. 'Why?'

He said, 'I don't know, it just sort of stuck with me. Like I said, my wife happens to be a fan. There were some copies of the manuscript around, so I took one home. It was interesting how it all came out in the end.'

I looked at him, trying to figure out where all this was heading.

'It was a set-up,' Jacobi said. 'This Phillip Campbell guy, he gets off. He pins the whole thing on someone else.'

Days later, Warren's words came creeping back into my mind. *A set-up. He pins the whole thing on someone else.*

It was ridiculous, I told myself, that I was even dignifying this scenario by running through it in my mind. Everything was solid, airtight.

'I must be an idiot,' I said aloud. 'Jenks is clinging to any story he can to wiggle his way out of this.'

I got up, brought my tea into the bathroom, began to wash my face.

In the morning I would tell Cheery about my disease. I had some free time coming. I would face this thing head-on. Now that the case was complete, it was the right time. *Now that the case was complete!*

I went into the bedroom, ripped the tags off a *Little Bit of Heaven* T-shirt Chris had bought me. I got into bed and Martha came around for her hug. Memories of the weekend began to drift into my head. I closed my eyes. I could hardly wait to share it with the girls.

Then a thought from out of the blue hit me. I shot up, as if I'd had a nightmare. I stiffened. 'Oh no. Oh Jesus, no,' I whispered.

When Jenks lunged at me at his house, he had swung with his left hand.

When he'd offered me a drink, he'd picked up the pitcher with his left hand.

Impossible, I thought. This can't be happening.

Claire was certain David Brandt's killer had been *right-handed*.

Chapter One Hundred
and Three

Jill, Claire and Cindy looked at me as if I were insane.

The words had barely tumbled out of my mouth. 'What if Jenks is right? What if someone *is* trying to set him up?'

'That's a crock!' snapped Jill. 'Jenks is desperate, and only moderately clever. We've got him!'

'I can't believe you're saying this!' exclaimed Cindy. 'You're the one who found him. *You're* the one who made the case.'

'I know. I know it seems crazy. Hopefully, it *is* crazy. Please – just hear me out.'

I took them through Jacobi's comment about the book; then my lightning bolt about Jenks's left-handedness.

'Proves nothing,' Jill said.

'I can't get past the science, Lindsay,' Claire said with a shake of her head. 'We've got this goddamn DNA at the scene.'

'Look,' I protested, 'I want the guy as much as anybody. But now that we have all this evidence – well, it's just so *neat.* The jacket, the champagne. Jenks has set up complicated murders in his books. Why would he leave clues behind?'

'Because he's a sick bastard, Lindsay. Because he's an arrogant prick who's connected to all three crimes.'

Jill nodded. 'He's a writer. He's an amateur at actually *doing* anything. He just fucked up.'

'You saw his reactions, Jill. They were deeper than simply desperation. I've seen killers on Death Row still in denial. This was more unsettling. Like *disbelief.*'

Jill stood up, her icy-blue eyes spearing down at me. 'Why, Lindsay? Why the sudden about-face?'

For the first time I felt alone and separated from the people I had most learned to trust. 'No one could possibly hate this man more than me,' I declared. 'I hunted him. I saw what he's done to these women.' I turned to Claire. 'You said the killer was right-handed.'

'*Probably* right-handed,' she came back.

'What if he simply held the knife in his other hand?' proposed Cindy.

'Cindy, if you were going to *kill* someone,' I said, 'someone larger and stronger, would you go at him with your opposite hand?'

'Maybe not,' injected Jill, 'but you're throwing all this up in the face of facts. Evidence and reason, Lindsay. All the things we worked to assemble. What you're giving me back is a set of hypotheticals. "Jenks holds his pitcher with his left hand. Phillip Campbell sets someone up at the end of his book." Look, we have the guy pinned to three double murders. I need you firm on this.' Her jaw was quivering. 'I need you to testify.'

I didn't know how to defend myself. I had wanted to nail Jenks as eagerly as any one of us. More. But now, after being so sure, I couldn't put it away, the sudden doubt.

Did we have the right man?

'We still haven't uncovered a weapon,' I said to Jill.

'We don't need a weapon, Lindsay. We have his hair *inside* one of the victims!'

Suddenly, we were aware that people from other tables were looking at us. Jill sat back down. Claire put her arms around my shoulders. I slumped back against the cushion of the booth.

Finally, Cindy said quietly, 'We've been behind you all the way. We're not going to abandon you now.'

Jill shook her head. 'You want me to let him go, guys, while we reopen the case? If we don't try him, Cleveland will.'

'I don't want you to let him go,' I stammered. 'I only want to be one hundred per cent sure.'

'I *am* sure,' Jill replied, her eyes ablaze.

I sought out Claire, and even she had a skeptical expression fixed firmly in my direction. 'There's an awful lot of physical evidence that makes it pretty clear.'

'If this gets out,' Jill warned us, 'you can toss my career out with the cat litter. Bennett wants this guy's blood on the Courthouse wall.'

'Look at it this way,' Cindy chuckled, 'if Lindsay's right, and you sent Jenks up, they'll be studying this case as a

"How *Not* To" for twenty years to come.'

Numbly, we looked around the table. It was as if we were staring at the pieces of some shattered, irreplaceable vase.

'Okay, so if it's not him,' Claire sighed, 'then how do we go about proving who it is?'

It was as if we were all the way back at the beginning – all the way back at the first crime. I felt awful.

'What was the thing that nailed our suspicion on Jenks?' I asked.

'The hair,' said Claire.

'Not quite. We had to get to him before we knew who it belonged to.'

'Merrill Shortley,' Jill said. 'Jenks and Merrill? You think?'

I shook my head. 'We still needed one more thing before we could take him in.'

Cindy said, '*Always A Bridesmaid*. His first wife.'

I nodded slowly.

Chapter One Hundred
and Four

O ver the next few days, I went back over everything
we had on Joanna Wade.

First, I reread the domestic complaint she had filed
against Jenks. I looked at pictures of Joanna taken at the
station, bruised, puffy-faced. I read through the officers'
account of what they found at the scene. Exchanges laced
with invectives. Jenks swinging wildly, clearly enraged. He
had to be subdued, had resisted arrest.

The report was signed by two officers from Northern,
Samuel Delgado and Anthony Fazziola.

The following day, I went back out to visit Greg Marks,
Jenks's former agent. He was even more surprised at my
visit when I told him I was here on a different aspect of
Jenks's past. 'Joanna?' he replied, with an amused smile.
'Bad judge of men, Inspector, but a worse judge of timing.'

He explained that their divorce had been finalized only
six months before *Crossed Wire* hit the stands. The book
sold nearly a million copies in hardcover alone. 'To have
put up with Nicholas through all the lean years, then come

away with barely more than a cab fare,' he shook his head. 'The settlement was a pittance compared to what it would've been if they had filed a year later.'

What he told me painted a different picture of the woman I had met in the gym. She seemed to have put it all behind her.

'She felt used, dropped like worn baggage. Joanna had put him through school, supported him when he first started writing. When Nick bagged law school, she even went back to her job.'

'And afterward,' I asked, 'did she continue to hate him?'

'I believe she continued to try and *sue* him. After they split up, she tried to sue him for a lien against future earnings. Non-performance, breach of contract. Anything she could find.'

I felt sorry for Joanna Wade. But could it drive her to *that* kind of revenge? Could it cause her to kill six people?

The following day, I obtained a copy of the divorce proceedings from County Records. Through the usual boilerplate, I got the sense it was an especially bitter case. She was seeking three million dollars judgment against future earnings. She ended up with five thousand a month, escalating to ten if Jenks's earnings substantially increased.

I couldn't believe the bizarre transformation that was starting to take over my mind.

It had been Joanna who had first alluded to the book. Who felt cheated, spurned, and carried a resentment far deeper than what she had revealed. Joanna, the tai bo instructor who was strong enough to take down a man twice her size. Who had misled me about her relationship with Chessy. Who even had access to the Jenkses home.

It seemed crazy to be thinking this way. More than preposterous . . . it was impossible.

The murders were committed by a male, by Nicholas Jenks.

Chapter One Hundred
and Five

The next day, as we shared a hot dog and a pretzel in front of City Hall, I told Chris what I had found.

He looked at me in much the same way the girls had a few days before. With shock, confusion. Disbelief. But he didn't get negative.

'She could've set the whole thing up,' I said. 'She knew about the book. She lobbed it out there for us to find. She knew Jenks's taste – in champagne, in clothes – about his involvement with Sparrow Ridge. She even had access to the house.'

'I might buy it,' he said, 'but these murders were committed by a man. Jenks, Lindsay. We even have him on film.'

'Or someone made up to look like Jenks. Every sighting of him was inconclusive.'

'Lindsay, the DNA was a match.'

'I spoke to the officers who went to the house when he beat Joanna,' I pressed on. 'They said, as enraged as Jenks was, she was dishing it right back to him, just as strong.

They had to restrain *her* as they took him away in the car.'

'She dropped the charges, Lindsay. She got tired of being abused. She may not have gotten what she deserved, but she filed and started a new life.'

'That's just it, Chris. *She* didn't file. It was Jenks who left her. His agent, Greg Marks, told me. She sacrificed everything for him. He described her as a model of co-dependency.'

I could see Chris was unconvinced. I had a man in jail with almost incontrovertible evidence against him. And here I was, unraveling everything. What was the matter with me?

Then, out of the blue, something came back to me, something I had filed away long ago. Laurie Birnbaum, a guest of the Weils at the Brandt wedding had described the man she saw in these words: 'The beard made him seem older, but the rest of him was young.'

Joanna Wade, medium-height, right-handed, the tai bo instructor, was strong enough to handle a man twice her size. And Jenks's nine millimeter – he said he hadn't seen it in years. *At the house in Montana.* The records showed he bought the gun ten years ago, when he was married to Joanna.

'You should see her,' I said, with rising conviction. 'She's tough enough to handle any of us. She's the one link who knew about everything: wine, clothes, *Always A Bridesmaid*. She had the means to pull it all together. The photos, the sightings, were all inconclusive. What if it was her, Chris?'

I held his hand – my mind racing with the possibilities – when I felt a sudden, awful tightness in my chest. I thought it was the shock of what I had just proposed, but it hit me with the speed of an express train.

Vertigo, nausea. It swept from my chest to my head.

'Lindsay?' Chris said. I felt his hand bracing my shoulder.

'I feel kind of weird,' I muttered. The sweats followed, then a rush, then a terrible light-headedness. As if armies were marching and clashing in my chest.

'Lindsay?' he said again, this time with real concern.

I leaned into him. This was the scariest sensation. I felt both momentarily robbed of strength and then back in control; lucid, then very woozy.

I saw Chris, and then I didn't.

I saw who killed the brides and grooms. And then it faded away.

I felt myself falling toward the sidewalk.

Chapter One Hundred and Six

I found myself coming to on a wooden park bench in Chris's arms. He held me tightly while my strength returned.

Orenthaler had warned me. It was Stage Three. Crunch time in my body. I didn't know which held more apprehension for me: going on chemo and gearing up for a bone-marrow transplant, or feeling my strength eaten away from the inside.

You can't let it win.

'I'm okay,' I told him, my voice getting stronger. 'I knew this would happen.'

'You're trying to do too much, Lindsay. Now you're talking about reopening a whole new investigation.'

I took a deep breath and nodded. 'I just need to be strong enough to see this through.'

We sat there for a while, the color in my face reviving, the strength in my limbs returning. Chris held me, cuddled me tenderly. We must've looked like two lovers trying to find privacy in a very public place.

Finally, he said, 'What you were describing, Lindsay, about Joanna – you really think it's true?'

It could still add up to nothing. She had not lied about her separation from Jenks, and about her current relationship with him and Chessy. Had she concealed a bitter hatred? She had the knowledge, the means.

'I think the killer is still out there,' I said.

Chapter One Hundred
and Seven

I decided to take a huge risk. If I blew it, it could knock the lid right off my case.

I decided to run what I suspected by Jenks.

I met him in the same visiting room. He was accompanied by his lawyer, Leff. He didn't want to meet, convinced there was no longer a point in talking with the police. And I didn't want to convey my true intent and end up feeding their defense arguments, if I was wrong.

Jenks was sullen, almost depressed. His cool and meticulous appearance had deteriorated into an edgy, unshaven mess.

'What do you want now?' he sneered, barely meeting my eyes.

'I want to know if you were able to come up with anyone who would like to see you in here,' I said.

'Pounding the lid on my coffin?' he said, with a mirthless smile.

'Let's just say, in the interest of doing my duty, I'm giving you one final chance to pry it back open.'

Jenks snorted skeptically. 'Sherman tells me I'm about to be charged in Napa with two more murders. Isn't that great? If this is an offer of assistance, I think I'll take my chances on proving it myself.'

'I didn't come here to trap you, Mr Jenks. I came to hear you out.'

Leff leaned over and whispered in his ear. He seemed to be encouraging Jenks to talk.

The prisoner looked up with a disgusted glare. 'Someone's running around, intent to look like me, familiar with my first novel. This person also wants to see me suffer. Is it so hard to figure out?'

'I'm willing to hear any names,' I told him.

'Greg Marks.'

'Your former agent?' I asked.

'He feels like I owe him my fucking career. I've cost him millions. Since I left, he hasn't gotten a worthwhile client. And he's violent. Marks belongs to a shooting club.'

'How would he have gotten his hands on your clothing? Or been able to get a sample of your hair?'

'You find that out. You're the police.'

'Did he know you'd be in Cleveland that night? Did he know about you and Kathy Kogut?'

'Nick is merely proposing,' Leff cut in, 'that other possibilities do exist for who could be behind these crimes.'

I shifted in my seat. 'Who else knew about the book?'

Jenks twitched. 'It wasn't something I paraded around. Couple of old friends. My first wife, Joanna.'

'Any of them have any reason to want to set you up?'

'My divorce, as you may know,' Jenks sighed uncomfortably, 'was not exactly what they call "mutually agreeable". No doubt there was a time Joanna would've been delighted to find me on a deserted road while she was cruising along at sixty. But now that she's back on her feet, with a new life, now that she's even gotten to know Chessy . . . I don't think so. No. It isn't Joanna. Trust me on that.'

I ignored the remark and looked firmly in his eyes. 'You told me your ex-wife has been to your house.'

'Maybe once or twice.'

'So she'd have access to certain things. Maybe the wine? Maybe what was in your closet?'

Jenks seemed to contemplate the possibility for a moment, then his mouth crinkled into a contemptuous smile. 'Impossible. No, it isn't Joanna.'

'How can you be so sure?'

He looked at me as if he were stating an understood fact. 'Joanna loved me. *She still does.* Why do you think she hangs around, cultivates a relationship with my new wife? Because she misses the view? It's because she cannot replace what I gave her. How I loved her. She is empty without me.

'What do you think,' he said, 'Joanna's been holding specimens of my hair in a jar ever since we were divorced?' He sat there, stroking his beard, while his face softened a little. 'Someone has it in for me, but not Joanna. She was just a little clerk when I met her. She didn't know Ralph Lauren from J.C. Penneys. I gave her self-esteem. I devoted myself to her, and she to me. She sacrificed everything for me, even worked two jobs when I decided to write.'

It was hard to think of Jenks as anything other than the ruthless bastard who was responsible for these horrible crimes, but I kept at him. 'You said the tuxedo was an old suit. You didn't even recognize it. And the gun, Mr Jenks, the nine millimeter. You said you hadn't seen it in years, that you thought it was kept somewhere at your house in Montana. Are you so sure this might not have been planned for some time?'

I could see Jenks subtly shifting his expression, as he came around to the impossible conclusion.

'You said that when you started writing, Joanna took a second job to help support you. What sort of job was it?'

Jenks stared up toward the ceiling, then he seemed to remember.

'She worked at Saks.'

Chapter One Hundred and Eight

Slowly, unavoidably, I was starting to feel as if I were on the wrong airplane, heading to the wrong city.

Against all logic, I was growing surer and surer that Nicholas Jenks might not be the killer. *Oh brother!*

I had to figure out what to do. Jenks in handcuffs was the lead picture in both *Times* and *Newsweek*. He was being arraigned in Napa for two additional murders the following day. Maybe I should just stay on the wrong plane, get out of town, never show my face in San Francisco again.

I got the girls together. I took them through the mosaic that was starting to come clear: the acrimonious contest over the divorce; Joanna's sense of being discarded; her direct access to the victims through her contacts at Saks.

'She was an assistant store manager,' I told them. 'Coincidence?'

'Get me *proof*,' Jill said. 'Because as of now, I have proof against Nick Jenks. All the proof I need.'

I could hear the worry and frustration in her voice. The whole country was watching this case, watching her every move. We had worked so hard to sell Mercer and her boss, Bennett Sinclair, that it was Jenks. And now, after all that – to propose a new theory and suspect.

'Authorize a search,' I told Jill. 'Joanna Wade's house. Something has to be there. The missing rings, a weapon, details on the victims. It's the only way we'll ever pin it down.'

'Authorize a search on what basis? Suspicion of new evidence? I can't do that without blowing this case wide open again. If we show we're not even sure, how can I convince a jury?'

'We could check where she worked,' proposed Cindy. 'See if she had specific access to information on the brides.'

'That's circumstantial. It's crap,' Jill cried. 'One of my neighbors works at Saks. Maybe she's the murderer.'

'You can't go through with this,' argued Cindy, 'if we still have doubt.'

'*You* have doubt,' said Jill. 'What I have is everything in place for a slam-dunk conviction. To you, it's a story, you follow it where it leads. My whole career is on the line.'

Cindy looked stunned. 'You think I'm here for just the story? You think I sat on every lead, agonized over not being able to go to copy, just so I could wind up with the book rights later on?'

'C'mon, girls,' said Claire, her arm on Cindy's shoulder. 'We have to be together on this.'

Slowly, Jill's intense blue eyes grew calmer. She turned to Cindy. 'I'm sorry,' she said. 'It's just that when this gets out, Leff will plant more doubt in that jury's mind.'

'But if they turned out to be right,' said Claire. 'We can't back down now just because it's bad tactics. There *could* be a murderer out there, a multiple murderer.'

I said to Jill, 'Authorize a search. C'mon, Jill.'

I had never seen her look so upset. Everything she had achieved in her career, everything she stood for, was being placed squarely on the line. She shook her head. 'Let's try it Cindy's way. We'll start with Saks, check Joanna out there.'

'Thank you, Jill,' I said. 'You're the best.'

She sighed resignedly. 'Find out if she's had any contact with anyone who had access to those names. Connect Joanna with those names, and I'll get you what you want. But if you can't, be prepared to fry Jenks.'

From across the table, I took her hand. She gripped mine. We both exchanged a nervous smile.

Jill finally joked, 'Personally, all I hope you come back with is the hot item to be featured in next year's Christmas catalog.'

Claire laughed loudly. 'Now that wouldn't be a total loss, would it?'

Chapter One Hundred and Nine

The following day, the day Nicholas Jenks was set to be arraigned for the murders of Rebecca and Michael DeGeorge, I set out to track down a new killer.

I couldn't let Jenks know we were looking that closely at Joanna. Nor did I want Joanna to know we were focusing suspicion on her, either. And I didn't want to face Mercer's or Roth's reactions.

With all this going on, it was my Medved day, too. Shit, shit, shit. After that spell in the park with Chris three days before, I had gone for a blood test. Medved called back himself, told me he wanted me to come in. Being called in again like that scared me. Like that first time with Dr Roy.

That afternoon, Medved kept me waiting. When he finally called me in, there was another doctor in his office – older, with white hair and bushy white eyebrows. He introduced himself as Dr Robert Yatto.

The sight of a new doctor sent a chill through me. He could only be there to talk about the bone-marrow procedure.

'Dr Yatto is Head of Hematology at Moffett Hospital,' Medved said. 'I asked him to look at your latest sample.'

Yatto smiled. 'How are you feeling, Lindsay?'

'Sometimes okay, sometimes incredibly weak,' I answered. My chest felt tight now. *Why did I have to go through this with someone new?*

'Tell me about the other day.'

I did my best to recount the reeling spell I'd had in City Hall Park.

'Any emissions of blood?' Yatto asked, matter-of-factly.

'No, not lately.'

'Vomiting?'

'Not since last week.'

Dr Yatto got up, came across the desk to me. 'Do you mind?' he asked, as he cradled my face in his hands. He expressionlessly squeezed my cheeks with his thumbs, pulled down my eyes and peered into my pupils, under my lids.

'I know I'm getting worse,' I said.

Yatto released my face, nodded toward Medved. Then, for the first time since I had started seeing him, Medved actually smiled.

'It's not getting worse, Lindsay. That's why I asked Bob to consult. Your erythrocytic count has jumped back up. To twenty-eight hundred.'

I gave a double-take to make sure I had heard right. That it wasn't some kind of wishful dream I was playing out in my own head. 'But the spells . . . the hot and cold flashes? The other day, I felt like a war was going on in me.'

'There is a war,' Dr Yatto said. 'You're reproducing cells. Fighting off bad ones. The other day, that wasn't Negli's talking. That was you. That's how it feels to heal.'

I was stunned. My throat was dry. 'Say that again?'

'It's working, my dear,' Medved said. 'Your red blood count has increased for the second time in a row. I didn't want to tell you in case it was an error, but as Dr Yatto said, you're building new cells.'

I didn't know whether to laugh or cry. I stammered back, 'This is real? I can trust this?'

'This is *very* real,' Medved said, with a nod.

I stood up, my whole body shaking with disbelief. For a moment, all the inner hopes and joys that I had suppressed – a chance at my career, running on Marina Green, a life with Chris – came tumbling through my brain. For so long, I had been so scared to let them free. Now, they seemed to burst out of me.

Medved leaned forward and warned, 'You're not cured, Lindsay. We'll continue the treatments, twice a week. But this is hopeful – more than hopeful. This is good.'

'I don't know what to say.' My body was totally numb. 'I don't know what to do.'

'If I were you,' Dr Yatto said, 'I'd bring to mind the one thing you might've thought you'd miss most, and go do that today.'

I wandered out of the office in a haze. Down the elevator, through the sterile lobby, into a flowered courtyard that overlooked Golden Gate Park.

The sky was bluer than I'd ever seen it, the air off the Bay sweeter and cooler and more pure. I stood there, just hearing the beautiful sounds of my own breaths.

Something crept back into my life that had been away, something I never thought I would embrace again.

Hope.

Chapter One Hundred and Ten

'I have something to tell you.' I phoned Chris, my voice ringing with urgency. 'Can you meet me for lunch?'

'Sure. You bet. Where?' No doubt he thought I had something important to break on the case.

'Casa Boxer,' I said, with a smile.

'That urgent, huh?' Chris laughed into the phone. 'I must be starting to have a bad effect on you. When should I come?'

'I'm waiting now.'

It took him barely fifteen minutes to arrive at the door. I'd stopped on the way at Nestor's bakery and picked up some freshly baked cinnamon buns. Then I popped a bottle of Piper-Heidsieck that I had saved in my fridge.

Never in six years had I bugged out on a case in the middle of the afternoon. Especially one of this magnitude. But I felt no guilt, none at all. I thought of the craziest way I could break the good news.

I met him at the door, wrapped in a bedsheet. His big blue eyes went wide with surprise.

'I'll need to see some ID,' I grinned.

'Have you been drinking?' he said.

'No, but we're about to.' I pulled him into the bedroom.

At the sight of the champagne, he shook his head. 'What is it you want to tell me?'

'Later,' I said. I poured him a glass, and began to unfasten the buttons of his shirt. 'But trust me, it's good.'

'It's your birthday?' he said, smiling.

I let the bedsheet drop. 'I would never do this for just my birthday.'

'*My* birthday, then.' He grinned.

'Don't ask. I'll tell you later.'

'You broke the case!' he exclaimed. 'It *was* Joanna. You found something that broke the case.'

I put my fingers to his lips. 'Tell me that you love me.'

'I do love you,' he said.

'Tell me again, like you did at Heavenly. Tell me that you won't ever leave me.'

Maybe he sensed it was Negli's talking, some crazy hysteria, or that I just needed to feel close. He hugged me. 'I won't leave you, Lindsay. I'm right here.'

I took his shirt off – slowly, very slowly – then his trousers. He must've felt like the delivery boy who had stumbled into a sure thing. He was as hard as a rock.

I brought a glass of champagne to his lips, and we both took a sip from it.

'Okay, I'll just go with this. Shouldn't be too difficult,' he said huskily.

I drew him to the bed, and for the next hour we did one

thing I knew I would have missed most in the world.

We were in the middle of things when I felt the first terrifying rumbling.

At first it was so weird, as if the bed had speeded up and was rocking faster than us; then there was a deep, grinding sound coming from all directions, as if we were in an echo chamber; then the sound of glass breaking – my kitchen, a picture frame falling off the wall – and I knew, *we* knew.

'It's a goddamn quake,' I said.

I had been through many of these – anyone who lived here had – but it was startling and terrifying every time. You never knew if this was the Big One.

It wasn't. The room shook, a few dishes broke. Outside, I heard the bleat of sudden horns and triggered car alarms. The whole thing lasted maybe twenty seconds – two, three, four vibrating tremors.

I ran to the window. The city was still there. There was a rumble that sounded like a massive hump-back whale breaching underground.

Then it was still – eerie, insecure as if the whole town were holding on for balance. I heard more wailing sirens, the sound of voices shouting on the street.

'You think we should go?' I asked.

'Probably . . . we're cops.' He touched me again, and we melted into each other's arms. 'What the heck, we're Homicide, anyway.'

We kissed, and once again we were locked into a single, intertwined shape. I started to laugh. The list, I was thinking. The skybox at the Giant's match. Now an earthquake.

This sucker's starting to get pretty long.

My beeper suddenly went off. I cursed, rolled over, glanced at the screen. It was the office.

'Code one eleven,' I told Chris. Emergency Alert. 'Shit,' I muttered, 'it's just an earthquake.'

I sat up, pulled the sheet over me, called in on the phone next to the bed.

It was Roth buzzing me. Roth *never* buzzed me. *What was going on?* Immediately, I transferred to his line.

'Where are you?' he asked.

'Dusting off some debris,' I said, and smiled toward Chris.

'Get in here. Get in here fast,' he barked.

'What's going on, Sam? This about the quake?'

'Uh-uh,' he replied. 'Worse. Nicholas Jenks has escaped.'

Chapter One Hundred and Eleven

As he sat shackled to the seat of the police van on the way back from Napa, Nicholas Jenks watched the impassive eyes of the patrolman across from him. He plotted, schemed. He wondered how much it would take to buy him his freedom.

One million? Two million? After all, what did the fool take home? Forty grand a year?

He figured the steely-eyed officer was someone above reproach, whose commitment to his duty was unquestioned. If he were writing it, that's who he would have put in the car with him.

Five million, then, he smirked. If *he* were writing it. That notion possessed a cold, punishing irony for him. He *had* written it.

Jenks shifted in his restraints – wrists cuffed, torso strapped to the seat. Only minutes earlier, he had stood in the red brick courthouse in Santa Rosa, while the prosecutor in her little Liz Claiborne suit pointed her finger at him. Over and over, she accused him of things only a mind as cultivated as his would think up and do.

All he could do was stare coldly while she accused him of being this *monster*. Sometime, he'd like to lock her in the law library and show her what he was really capable of.

Jenks caught a glimpse of the sky and the sun-browned hills through the narrow window on the rear door and tried to get a fix on their bearings. Novato. Just hitting Marin.

He pressed his face to the steel restraining wall. *He had to get out.* If he were writing it, there would always be a way out.

He looked at the guard. So what was the story. Joe Friday? What happened next?

'You married?' he asked.

The policeman stared through him at first, then he nodded.

'Kids?'

'Two,' he revealed, even breaking a slight smile.

No matter how hard they tried to resist, they were always fascinated to talk with the monster. The guy who killed the honeymooners. They could tell their wives and friends, justify the miserable six hundred a week they brought home. He was a celebrity.

'Wife work?' Jenks probed.

The cop nodded. 'Teacher. Business Ed. Eighth grade.'

Business Ed, huh? Maybe he would understand a business proposition.

'My wife used to work,' Jenks grunted back. 'My first wife. In retail. My current wife worked, too, in television.

'Course now, she only works *out.*'

The remark produced a snicker. The tight-assed bastard was loosening up.

Jenks saw a landmark he recognized. Twenty minutes from the Golden Gate Bridge. There wasn't much time left.

He glanced out the window at the patrol car following them. There was another in front. A bitter resignation took hold. There was no way out. No elegant escape. That was only in his books. This was life. He was screwed.

Then, out of nowhere, the police van lurched violently. Jenks was hurled forward in his seat, directly into the guard across from him. For a second, he wondered what was going on, then the van lurched again. He heard a rumbling.

It's a fucking quake!

Jenks could see the lead police car swerve to avoid the charge of another car. Then it skidded off the road.

One of the cops yelled, 'Shit,' but the van continued on.

Jenks spun around in panic, trying to hold onto anything that was fixed in the compartment. The van was bucking and jolting.

The police car following them jumped over a sudden hump in the highway, and, to his total amazement, *flipped*. The driver of Jenks's van looked behind him in shock. Then suddenly the other cop in front screamed for the driver to stop.

An 18-wheeler was breached in their way. They were headed right toward it. The van swerved, and when it did, the road buckled again. Then they were out of control – flying.

He was going to die here, Nicholas Jenks was sure. Die here, without anyone ever knowing the whole truth.

The van crashed into the stanchions of a Conoco station. It screeched to a stop, spinning twice on its side. The officer across from him was hurled against the metal wall. He was writhing and moaning as he looked at Jenks.

'Don't move,' the officer panted.

How the hell could he? He was still shackled to the seat.

Then came this horrid, wrenching sound, and they both looked up. The towering steel light above the station split like a redwood and crashed down on them. It smashed through the door of the van, striking the officer sitting in the back and probably killing the guard on impact.

Jenks was sure he would be killed – all the smoke, the screams, twisting of metal.

But he wasn't. He was clear. The streetlight had torn a hole in the side of the car, ripped his restraints right out of the seat. He was able to kick himself free, even with shackled hands and feet, and push himself through the gaping hole.

People were running in the street, screaming and in a panic. Motorists pulled off the road, some dazed, others jumping out of their vehicles to help.

This was it! He knew if he didn't run he would replay this moment for the rest of his life.

Nicholas Jenks crawled out of the van, dazed and

disorientated. He spotted no cops, only frightened passers-by streaking past. He limped out, and joined the chaotic street scene.

I'm free! Jenks exulted.

And I know who's setting me up. The cops won't get it in a million years.

Chapter One Hundred and Twelve

It took about three minutes for Chris and me to throw on some clothes and head back to the Hall. In the rush, I never told him my news.

By disaster standards, the quake was nothing much — unless you had spent the past five weeks tracking down the country's most notorious killer. Most of the damage ended up confined to shattered storefronts and traffic accidents north of the city, but as we pushed our way through the clamoring throng of press in the Hall's lobby, the quake's biggest news crackled with the fierceness of a live wire:

The Bride and Groom killer was free.

Nicholas Jenks had managed to flee when the police van taking him back to jail flipped over outside Novato, the result of a chain of automobile accidents caused by the tremor. The policeman guarding him had been fatally injured. Two more, in the front seat of the overturned van, were hospitalized.

A huge Command Center was set up down the hall

from Homicide. Roth himself took charge. The place was crawling with brass from downtown and, of course, the press.

An APB was released, Jenks's description and photo distributed to cops on both sides of the bridge. All city exits and highway tolls were being monitored; traffic slowed to a crawl. Airports, hotels, and car-rental ports were put on alert.

Since we had tracked Nicholas Jenks down originally, Raleigh and I found ourselves at the center of the search.

We placed an immediate surveillance on his residence. Cops spread out all over the Sea Cliff area, from the Presidio to Lands End.

In searches like this, the first six hours are critical. The key was to contain Jenks in the grid where he had bolted, not let him contact anyone who could help his escape. He had no resources – no funds, no one to take him in. Jenks couldn't stay on the loose, unless he was a lot craftier than I thought he was.

The escape left me stunned. The man I had hunted down was free, but I was also left conflicted. *Were we hunting the right man?*

Everyone had a theory about where he might head – the wine country, east into Nevada. I had my own theory. I didn't think he'd go back to the house. He was too smart, and there was nothing to be gained there. I asked Roth if I could borrow Jacobi and Paul Chin, to play out a hunch.

I took Jacobi aside. 'I need you to do me a big favor, Warren.' I asked him to do surveillance outside Joanna

Wade's apartment on Russian Hill. Then I asked Chin to do the same outside the house of Jenks's former agent, Greg Marks.

If Jenks really believed he was being set up, those were two places he might go.

Jacobi gave me a look as if I were sending him out on another champagne lead. The entire corps of Inspectors was following up leads. 'What the hell, Lindsay . . . why?'

I needed him to trust me. 'Because it struck me as funny, too,' I said, begging his support, 'why Jenks would leave that damn tuxedo jacket behind. I think he might go after Joanna. Trust me on it.'

With Warren and Paul Chin in place, there was nothing I could do except monitor the wires. Six hours into the search, there was still no sign of Nicholas Jenks.

Chapter One Hundred
and Thirteen

Around four, I saw Jill pushing her way through the crowd buzzing outside my office. She looked ready to kill somebody, probably me.

'I'm glad you're here,' I said, grabbing her. 'Trust me, please, Jill.'

'Cindy's downstairs,' she said. 'Let's go talk.'

We sneaked out, and were able to find her amid a throng of reporters clawing at anyone who came down from the third floor. We called Claire, and in five minutes we were sitting around a table at a coffee shop just down the block. Jenks's escape had thrown all of my speculations into disarray.

'You still believe he's innocent?' Jill pressed the issue immediately.

'That depends on where he turns up next.' I informed them how I had stationed a couple of men around the homes of Greg Marks and Joanna Wade.

'Even now?' Jill shook her head and looked close to blowing. 'Innocent men don't run from police custody, Lindsay.'

'Innocent people might,' I said, 'if they don't believe the justice system is being just!'

Claire looked around with a nervous swallow. 'Ladies, it strikes me we're entering into very sensitive territory here, all right? We've got a manhunt trying to locate Jenks – he could be shot on sight – and at the same time, we're talking about trying to firm up a case against someone else. If this comes out, heads will roll. I'm looking at some of those pretty heads right now.'

'If you *really* believe this, Lindsay, you need to take it to someone,' Jill lectured me. 'Roth, Mercer.'

'Mercer's away. And right now, everybody's focused on locating Jenks. Anyway, who the hell would believe this? As you say, all I have is a bunch of hypotheticals.'

'Have you told Raleigh?' asked Claire.

I nodded.

'What does he think?'

'Right now, he can't get past the hair. Jenks's escape didn't help my case.'

'I knew there was something I liked about that guy.' Jill finally smiled thinly.

I looked at Claire for support.

'It's hard to argue your side of things, Lindsay,' she sighed. 'That said, your instincts are usually good.'

'So then bust in on Joanna, like Lindsay proposed,' said Cindy. The more I was around her, the more I loved her.

Things had suddenly gotten very sticky in the way of accountability. I turned to Claire. 'Is there anything we might have missed that could implicate Joanna?'

Chapter One Hundred
and Fourteen

In the dim light of the makeup mirror, the killer sat transfixed by soft blue eyes that were about to become gray.

The first thing was to smear her hair until all the blonde had been dyed away, then brush it back *smooth*, a hundred times, until it had lost its luster and shine.

'You forced me into this,' she said to the changing face. 'Forced me to come out one more time. I should have expected as much. You love games, don't you, Nick?'

With a cotton swab, she applied the base, a clear, sticky balm with a glue-like smell. She dabbed it over her temples, down the curve of her chin, in the soft space between her upper lip and her nose.

Then, with a tweezer, she matted on the hair. Tufts of reddish brown.

The face was almost complete. But the eyes . . . anyone could see they were still hers.

She slipped out a pair of tinted contacts from the case. Moistening them, stretching her lids to insert each one.

She blinked, well satisfied with the result.

The familiarity was gone. The change was complete. Her eyes now reflected a steely, lifeless gray.

Nicholas's color.

She was him.

Chapter One Hundred and Fifteen

C laire's call woke me out of a deep sleep.

'Come down here,' her voice commanded.

I blinked groggily at the clock. It was ten after five in the morning. 'Come down *where*?' I moaned.

'I'm at the damn office. In the damn lab. The guard at the front counter will let you in. *Come right now.*'

I heard the urgency in her voice and it took only seconds for me to come to my senses. 'You're at the lab?'

'Since two-thirty, sleepyhead. It's about Nicholas Jenks. I think I found something, and Lindsay, it is a mindblower.'

At that hour, it didn't take me more than ten minutes to get to the morgue. I parked in the circular area outside the coroner's entrance reserved for official vehicles and rushed in, my hair uncombed, dressed only in a sweatshirt and jeans.

The guard buzzed and let me through. He was expecting me. Claire met me at the entrance to the lab.

'Okay,' I said, 'my expectations are high.'

She didn't answer. Only pressed me up against the door

of the lab, without a word of greeting or explanation.

'We're back at the Hyatt,' she started on. 'Murder Number One. David Brandt is about to open the door. Pretend you're the groom,' she said, placing her hand on my shoulder and gently easing me down, 'and I'll be the killer. I surprise you as you open the door, and stab – *right-handed* – not that it makes any difference now.'

She thrust her fist in the space under my left breast. 'So you fall, and that's where we find you, later, at the scene.'

I nodded, letting her know that I was following along so far.

'So what do we find around you?' she asked, wide-eyed.

I made a mental picture of the scene. 'Champagne bottle, tuxedo jacket.'

'True, but that's not where I'm headed.'

'Blood . . . a lot of blood.'

'Closer. Remember, he died of a cardiac, electro-mechanical collapse. We simply assumed he was scared to death.'

I stood up, gazed down at the floor. Then suddenly I saw it as if I were there with the body.

'Urine.'

'Right!' exclaimed Claire. 'We find a small residue of urine. On his shoes, on the floor. About six cubic centimeters' worth, that I was able to save. It seemed logical that it belonged to the groom – voiding is a natural response to sudden fear, or death. But I was thinking last night, there were traces of urine in Cleveland, too. And here, back at the Hyatt, I never even had it tested. *Why would I?* I always assumed it was from David Brandt.

'But if you were here, crumpled on the floor, and I was the killer standing above you, and the pee was *here,*' she said, pointing to the floor around me, 'who the hell's urine would it be?'

Our eyes locked in one of those shining moments of epiphany. 'The killer's,' I said.

Claire smiled at her bright student. 'The annals of forensic medicine are rich with examples of murderers "getting off" when they kill, so *peeing* isn't so far-fetched. Your nerves would be on end. And good old compulsive me, obsessed down to the last detail, refrigerates it in a vial, never knowing what for. And the thing that makes this all come together is, *urine can be tested.*'

'Tested? For what?'

'For *sex*, Lindsay. Urine can reveal one's sex.'

'Jesus, Claire.' I was stunned.

She took me into the lab to a counter with two microscopes, some chemicals in bottles, and a device I recognized from college chemistry classes as a centrifuge.

'There aren't any flashing gender signs in urine, but there are things to look for. First, I took a sample and spun it down in the centrifuge with this KOH stain, which is something we can use to isolate impurities in blood cultures.' She motioned for me to look in the first scope.

'See these tiny, filament-like branches with little clusters of cells like grapes? It's candida albicans.'

I looked at her blankly.

'Yeast cells, honey. This urine's laced with high deposits

of yeast. Boys don't get them.'

I started to smile, but before I could say anything, she dragged me on. 'Then I put the other sample under the scope, and brought it up three thousand mag. Check this out.'

I lowered myself over the scope and squinted in.

'You see those dark, crescent-shaped cells swimming around?' Claire asked.

'Uh-huh.'

'Red blood cells. Lots of them.'

I lifted my head off the scope and looked up.

'They wouldn't show up in a man's urine. Not to anywhere near this degree. Not unless they've got a bleeding kidney, which to my knowledge, none of our principals show any signs of.'

'Or,' I shook my head slowly, 'unless the killer was menstruating.'

Chapter One Hundred
and Sixteen

I stared at Claire as the news settled in my mind. Nicholas Jenks had been telling the truth all along.

He wasn't in the room when David and Melanie Brandt were killed that night. Nor in Napa. Probably nowhere near the Hall of Fame in Cleveland. I had hated Jenks so much I couldn't see past it. None of us had been able to get past the fact that we wanted him to be guilty.

All the evidence – the hair, the jacket, the champagne – had been an incredible deception; Jenks was a master of the surprise ending, but someone had set the master up.

I put my arms around Claire and hugged her. 'You're the best.'

'You're damn right I am. I don't know what it proves,' she answered, patting my back, 'but the person standing over that poor boy at the murder scene was a woman. And I'm just as sure that she stabbed David Brandt to death with her right hand.'

My mind was spinning. Jenks was loose, hundreds of cops on the chase – and he was innocent.

'So?' Claire looked at me and smiled.

'It's the second best news I've heard today,' I said.

'Second best?'

I took her hand. I told Claire what Medved had shared with me. We hugged again. We even did a little victory dance. Then both of us got back to work.

Chapter One Hundred and Seventeen

Upstairs at my desk, I radioed Jacobi. Poor guy, he was still sitting outside Joanna Wade's home at the corner of Filbert and Hyde. 'You all right, Warren?'

'Nothing that a shower and a couple of hours' sleep wouldn't improve.'

'Tell me what's going on.'

'What's going on,' Jacobi recited, as if he were resentfully going over his log. 'Four-fifteen yesterday afternoon, target comes out, struts down the block to Gold's Gym. Six-ten, target re-emerges, proceeds down block to Pasqua Coffee, comes out with plastic bag. I suspect it's Almond Roast. Goes into the Contempo Casuals boutique, comes out empty. I gotta figure the new fall stuff hasn't arrived yet, Boxer. She makes her way home. Lights go on on the third floor. Is it chicken I smell, I don't know – I'm so fucking hungry I might be dreaming. Lights go out about ten twenty-five. Since then, she's been doing what I'd like to be doing. Why you got me out here like a rookie, Lindsay?'

'Because Nicholas Jenks is going to try to find his

ex-wife. He believes she's setting him up. I think he knows that Joanna is the murderer.'

'You trying to cheer me up, Boxer, bring meaning into my life?'

'Maybe. And how's this . . . I think she's guilty, too. I want to know immediately if you spot Jenks.'

Chris Raleigh came in about eight, tossing a surprised look at my bleary eyes and disheveled appearance. 'You should try a brush in the morning.'

'Claire called me at five-ten. I was in the morgue at five-thirty.'

He looked at me funny. 'What the hell for?'

'It's a little hard to explain. I want you to meet some friends of mine.'

'Friends? At eight in the morning?'

'Uh-huh. My girlfriends.'

He looked completely confused. 'What am I not following here?'

'Chris,' I seized his arm. 'I think we broke the case.'

Chapter One Hundred
and Eighteen

A n hour later, I got everyone together on the Jenks
case, hopefully for the last time.

There had been a few alleged sightings of Nicholas
Jenks – in Tiburon down by the Marina, and south
of Market, huddled around a gathering of homeless
men. Both of them proved false. He had eluded us,
and the longer he remained free, the greater the specu-
lation.

We got together in a vacant interrogation room that Sex
Crimes sometimes used. Claire smuggled Cindy up from
the lobby, then we rang down for Jill.

'I see we've loosened the requirements,' Jill commented,
when she came in and saw Chris.

Raleigh looked surprised, too. 'Don't mind me – I'm just
the token male.'

'You remember Claire, and Jill Bernhardt from the
District Attorney's office,' I said. 'Cindy, you may recall
from Napa. This is the team.'

Slowly, Chris looked from one face to another, until he

settled on me. 'You've been working on this, independently of the Task Force?'

'Don't ask,' said Jill, plunking herself down in a wooden chair. 'Just listen.'

In the cramped narrow room, all eyes turned to me. I looked at Claire. 'You want to begin?'

She nodded, scanned the group as if she were presenting at a medical conference. 'On Lindsay's urging, I spent all last night going through the three case files; I was looking for anything that would implicate Joanna. At first, nothing. Other than coming to the same conclusion I had before that, from the pronounced downward angle of the first victims' wounds, the killer was right-handed. Jenks is *left-handed*. But it was clear that it wouldn't stick.

'Then something struck me that I had never noticed before. At both the first and third crime scenes there were traces of urine. Individually, I guess neither the Medical Examiner in Cleveland nor I ever thought much of it. But as I thought through the crime scenes in my head, the *locations* of these deposits didn't make any sense. Early this morning, very early, I rushed down here and performed some tests.'

There was barely a breath in the room.

'The urine we found at the Grand Hyatt demonstrated large deposits of yeast, as well as atypically large counts of red blood cells. Red blood cells in that amount appear in the urine during menstruation. Coupled with the yeast, there's no doubt in my mind that the urine was a woman's. A woman killed David Brandt, and I have no doubt we'll find a woman was in the stall in Cleveland, too.'

Jill blinked back, dumbfounded. Cindy's bright red lips parted in an incredulous half-smile.

Raleigh just shook his head.

'Jenks didn't do it,' I said. 'Joanna must have. He abused her, then he dumped her for his new wife, Chessy, just as he was about to strike it rich. Joanna tried to sue him twice, unsuccessfully. Ended up with a settlement many times smaller than she would have gotten a year later. She watched him gain celebrity and wealth, and a new, seemingly happy, life.'

Chris looked amazed. 'You really believe a woman could physically pull this off? The first victims were stabbed, the second were dragged twenty, thirty yards to where they were dumped.'

'You haven't seen her,' I replied. 'She knew how to set Jenks up. She knew his tastes, his investments, and had access to his possessions. She even worked at Saks.'

Cindy chipped in, 'She was one of the few people who would've been aware of *Always A Bridesmaid*.'

I nodded toward Jill. 'She had the means, the motive, and I'm damned sure she had the desire.'

A really heavy silence filled the room.

'So how do you want to play this?' Chris finally said. 'Half the force is looking for Jenks.'

'I want to inform Mercer, try to get Jenks brought in without someone killing him. Then I want to go ahead and pierce Joanna's cover. Phone calls, credit cards. If she was in Cleveland, something will tie her there. I think you'd agree now,' I said to Jill, 'we have enough to authorize a search.'

Jill nodded, at first hesitantly, then with more resolve. 'It's just impossible to believe that after all this, we now have to defend that bastard.'

Suddenly, there was a loud rap on the glass window of the door. John Keresty, an Inspector on the Task Force, broke in on us.

'It's Jenks. He's just been sighted. He's up in Pacific Heights.'

Chapter One Hundred and Nineteen

Raleigh and I leaped up, almost as one, racing back to the Command Center.

It appeared Jenks had been seen in the lobby of a small hotel called the El Drisco. A bellboy spotted him, free of his cuffs. Now he was on the streets, somewhere up in Pacific Heights.

Why there? My mind ratcheted through the possibilities. Then it became clear.

Greg Marks lived up there.

I radioed Paul Chin, who was still sitting surveillance on the agent's apartment. 'Paul, be on the alert,' I told him. 'Jenks may be headed your way. He was seen in Pacific Heights.'

There was a beep on my cell phone. It was Jacobi. Everything was happening at once.

'Boxer, there's an All Available Units on Jenks up in the Heights about a mile from here. I'm headed up there.'

'Warren, *don't leave!*' I shouted into the receiver. I still believed Joanna was the murderer. I couldn't leave her unmonitored, especially with Jenks on the loose. 'Stay at your post.'

'This takes precedence,' Jacobi argued. 'Besides, nothing's happening here. I'll call a radio car to relieve.'

'*Jacobi!*' I shouted, but he had already signed off and was on his way to the Heights. I turned to Chris. 'Warren's left Joanna's.'

Suddenly Karen, our civilian clerical, shouted for me. 'Lindsay, call for you on One.'

'We're headed out,' I hollered back to her. I had strapped on my gun, grabbed the keys to my car. 'Who is it?'

'Says you'd want to talk to him about the Jenks case,' Karen said. 'Says his name is Phillip Campbell.'

Chapter One Hundred and Twenty

I froze, fixed on Raleigh, then I lunged back toward my desk.

I signaled Karen to patch it through. At the same time, I hissed under my breath to Raleigh, 'Start a trace.'

I waited in a trance; seconds could mean the difference. The breath was tightening in my chest. Then I picked up.

'You know who this is,' Nicholas Jenks's arrogant voice declared.

'I know who it is. Where are you?'

'Not a chance, Inspector. I only called to let you know, whatever happens, I didn't kill any of them. I'm not a murderer.'

'I know that,' I told him.

He seemed surprised. 'You do?'

I couldn't let Jenks know who it was. Not with him on the loose. 'I promise, we can prove it wasn't you. Tell me where you are.'

'Hey, guess what? I don't believe you,' Jenks declared. 'Besides, it's too late. I told you I'd take this into my own hands. I'm going to solve these murders for you.'

Jenks could hang up any moment and we'd lose him. This was my only chance. 'Jenks, I'll meet you. Anywhere you want.'

'Why would I want to meet you? I've seen enough of you to last a lifetime.'

'Because I know who did it,' I told him.

What he said next jolted me.

'So do I.'

And then he hung up.

Chapter One Hundred and Twenty-One

Sixth ... Market ... Taylor ... the streets shot by, the top hat on the roof of Chris Raleigh's car flashing wildly.

Ellis.

Larkin.

We shot up Hyde, climbing through the lights, then rocked over the bumps as we careened over Nob Hill. In a matter of minutes, we arrived in Russian Hill.

Joanna lived on the top floor of a townhouse on the corner of Filbert and Hyde. We were no longer waiting to flush her out. Jenks was loose; he had probably homed in on her. Now it was a matter of preventing more killing.

We slowed, cut the lights as we wove through the quiet, hilly streets. The house had been unguarded for maybe fifteen minutes. I didn't know if Joanna was up there. Or where the hell Jenks was.

Chris pulled to the curb. We checked our guns, and decided how to proceed.

Then I saw a sight that tore the breath from my lungs.

Chris saw it, too. 'Christ, he's here.'

From a narrow alley two houses away, a man in a beard and baggy sports coat emerged. He looked both ways as he hit the street, then he made his way down the block.

Raleigh pulled out his gun and reached for the door. I looked closer in disbelief, grabbed onto him. 'Wait. Look again, Chris.'

We both gaped in amazement. He had the same look: the short, reddish-gray hair, the same unmistakable beard. *But it wasn't Jenks.*

The figure was thinner, fairer; the hair slicked back hiding a longer length, not cut short. I could see that much.

It was a woman.

'That's Joanna,' I said.

'Where's Jenks?' Chris grunted. 'This just keeps getting creepier.'

We watched the figure slink down the block as a frenzy of possibilities ran through my mind. This *was* creepy.

'I'll follow her,' Chris suggested. 'You go upstairs – make sure it's her. I'll radio for support. Go on, Lindsay. Go!'

The next moment, I was out of the car, crossing the street toward Joanna's apartment. Chris eased the Taurus down the block.

I pushed random buttons until a woman's angry voice replied. I identified myself, and a gray-haired woman emerged from the apartment next to the front door. She announced that she was the landlady.

I badged her, got her to locate a key pronto. Then I told

her to get back in her apartment.

I had my gun out, took off the safety. A film of hot sweat was building up on my face and neck.

I reached Joanna's apartment on the third floor. My heart was pounding. *'Careful, Lindsay,'* a voice inside me said, then came a cautioning chill. Could Nicholas Jenks be here?

I had certainly entered enough hostile environments during my police career, but none worse than this. I inserted the key, turned, and when the lock caught, pushed the door with my foot.

It swung open, revealing the bright, stylishly decorated apartment of Joanna Wade.

'Anyone here?' I shouted.

No one answered.

There was no one in the living room. Same for the dining room, kitchen. A coffee mug in the sink. The *Chronicle* out and folded to the Datebook section.

No sign that I was in the home of a psycho. That bothered me.

I moved on. More magazines – *Food and Wine, San Francisco* – on the coffee-table. A few yoga posture books.

In the bedroom, the bed was unmade. The entire place had a relaxed, unforbidding feel.

Joanna Wade lived like any ordinary woman. She read, had coffee in her kitchen, taught exercise, paid her bills. Killers were preoccupied with their victims. This didn't make sense.

I turned into the master bath.

'Oh, damn it!' The case had taken a last, irrevocable turn.

On the floor, in her workout tights, was Joanna Wade.

She was leaned against the tub looking at me, but not really – actually, she was still looking at her killer. Her eyes were wide and terrified.

He had used a knife. Jenks? If not him, then who?

'Oh, Christ,' I gasped. My head was spinning and it *hurt*.

I hurried over to her, but there was nothing I could do. Everything had twisted again. I knelt over the dead woman as a final, shuddering thought filled my mind:

If it wasn't Joanna, who was Chris following?

Chapter One Hundred and Twenty-Two

Within minutes, two blue-and-whites screeched to a stop outside. I directed the patrol officers upstairs to the grisly body of Joanna, but my thoughts had turned to Chris. And whoever he was following.

I had been up in the apartment for ten, maybe twelve minutes, without a word from him. I was worried. He was following a murderer, and a murderer who had just killed Joanna Wade.

I ran downstairs to an open patrol car and called in what had happened to Command Central. A riot of doubts was crashing in my mind. Could it somehow have been Jenks, after all? Could Jill have been right? Was he manipulating us, right from the start? Had he set everything up, even the sighting in Pacific Heights?

But if it was him, *why* would he kill her now? Was Joanna's death something I could have prevented? What in hell was going on? Where was Chris, damn it!

My cell phone finally beeped. To my relief, it was Chris.

'Where are you?' I bleated. 'You had me scared to death. Don't do that to me.'

'I'm down by the Marina. The suspect's in a blue Saab.'

'Chris, be careful. It's *not* Joanna. Joanna's dead. She was stabbed a bunch of times in her apartment.'

'Dead?' he muttered. I could feel the frantic question slowly sinking into his mind. 'Then who is driving the Saab up ahead of me?'

'Tell me where you are exactly.'

'Chestnut and Scott. The suspect just pulled up to the curb. The suspect is getting out of the car.'

Somehow, this sounded familiar. *Chestnut and Scott?* What was down there? In the tumult of green-and-whites screeching up in front of Joanna's building and reporting in, I raked my mind for a connection.

'He's heading away from the car, Lindsay. He's starting to run.'

Then it hit me. The photo I had picked up at Jenks's house. The beautiful and unmistakable moonlit dome. The Palace of Fine Arts.

It was where he had been married.

'I think I know where he's going!' I shouted. 'The Palace of Fine Arts.'

Chapter One Hundred and Twenty-Three

I hopped into one of the parked radio cars and took off with the siren blaring all the way to the Presidio.

It took me no more than seven minutes, with traffic wildly shifting out of my way, to speed down Lombard over to Richardson to the south tip of the Presidio. Up ahead, the golden rotunda of the Palace of Fine Arts loomed powerfully above a calm, gleaming pond.

I saw Chris's blue Taurus pulled up diagonally across from the tip of the park and jackknifed mine to a halt next to it. I didn't see a sign of any other cops.

Why hadn't any backup arrived? What the hell was going on now?

I clicked my gun off safety and made my way into the park underneath the giant rotunda. No way I was waiting.

I was startled by people running toward me, away from the rotunda grounds.

'Someone's shooting,' one of them screamed.

Suddenly, my legs were flying. 'Everyone out! I'm San

Francisco police!' I yelled, as I bumped through the people rushing by.

'There's a maniac with a gun,' someone sobbed.

I ran around the pond alongside a massive wall of marble colonnade. There was no sound up ahead. No more shots.

Leading with my gun, I rounded corners until I was in sight of the main rotunda. Huge Corinthian columns soared above me, capped with ornate, heroic carvings.

I could hear voices in the distance: a woman's mocking tone. 'It's just you and me, Nick. Imagine that. Isn't it romantic?'

And a man's, Jenks's: 'Look at you, you're pathetic. As always.'

The voices echoed out of the huge dome of the main rotunda.

Where was Chris? And where was our backup?

Cops should have been here by now. I held my breath, straining to hear the first police siren. Every step I took, I heard my own footsteps echoing to the roof.

'What do you want?' I heard Jenks's cry reverberating off the stone. Then the woman shouting back, 'I want you to remember them. All the women you fucked.'

Still no sign of Chris. I was tight with worry.

I decided to go around the side of a row of low arches that ran down to the voices. I ducked around the corner of the colonnade.

Then I saw Chris. Oh, God! He was sitting there, propped against a pillar, watching everything unfold.

My first reaction was to say something like, 'Chris, get down, someone will see you.' It was one of those slow-motion perceptions where my eyes were faster than my mind.

Then my body was seized with horrible fright, nausea, and sadness.

Chris wasn't watching, and he wasn't hiding.

The front of his shirt was covered with blood.

All my police training gave way. I wanted to scream, to cry out. It took everything I had to hold it in.

Two dark bloodstains were soaking through Chris's shirt. My legs were paralyzed. Somehow I forced myself over to him. I knelt down. My heart was pounding.

Chris's eyes were remote, his face as gray as stone. I checked for a pulse and felt the slightest rhythm of a heartbeat.

'Oh, Chris no.' I stifled a sob.

When I spoke, he looked up, eyes glimmering as he saw my face. His lips parted into a weak smile. His breath wheezed, heavy and labored.

My eyes filled with tears. I applied pressure to the holes in his chest, trying to push back the blood. 'Oh Chris, hang in there. Hang in there. I'll get help.'

He reached for my arm. He tried to speak, but it was only a weak, guttural whisper.

'Don't talk. Please.'

I raced back toward the patrol car and fumbled with the transmitter until I heard Dispatch. 'Officer down, officer down,' I shouted. 'Four-oh-six. I repeat, four-oh-six!' – the statewide call for alarm. 'Officer shot, rotunda of the Palace of Fine Arts. Need immediate EMS and SWAT backup. Possible Nicholas Jenks sighting. Second officer on the scene inside. Repeat, four-oh-six, emergency.'

As soon as the dispatcher repeated the location back to me with a 'Copy,' I threw down the transmitter and headed back inside.

When I got to him, Chris was still holding on to small breaths. A bubble of blood popped on his lip. 'I love you, Chris,' I whispered, squeezing his hand.

Voices rang out ahead in the rotunda. I couldn't make them out, but it was the same man and woman. Then there was a gunshot!

'Go,' Chris whispered. 'I'm holding on.'

Our hands touched.

'I've got rear,' he muttered with a smile. Then he pushed me away.

I scurried ahead, my gun drawn, glancing back twice. Chris was watching – *watching my back.*

I ran in a low crouch all the way down the length of the row of columns closest in, clear up to the side of the main rotunda. The voices echoed, intensified. My eyes were riveted.

They were straight across the basilica. Jenks, in a plain white shirt. He was holding one arm, bleeding. He'd been shot.

And across from him, holding a gun and dressed in men's clothes, stood Chessy Jenks.

Chapter One Hundred and Twenty-Four

She looked like a bizarre disfigurement of the beautiful woman she was. Her hair was matted and dyed a shade of gray and red. Her face still carried the marks of her disguise, a man's sideburns and flecks of a grayish-red beard.

She was holding a gun tightly, pointing it directly at him. 'I have a present for you, Nick.'

'A present?' Jenks said, in desperation. 'What the hell are you talking about?'

'That's why we're here. I want to renew our vows.' Chessy took a small pouch out of her jacket and tossed it at his feet. 'Go ahead. Open it.'

Nicholas Jenks knelt, stiffly, and picked up the pouch. He opened it, the contents spilling into his palm. His eyes bulged in horror.

The six missing rings.

'Chessy, Christ,' he stammered. 'You're out of your mind. What do you want me to do with *these*?' He held out a ring. 'These will put you in the gas chamber.'

'No, Nick,' Chessy said, shaking her head. 'I want you to swallow them. Get rid of the evidence for me.'

Jenks's face twitched in apprehension. 'You want me to *what*?'

'Swallow them. Each one is someone you've destroyed. Someone whose beauty you've killed. They were innocent – like *me*. Little girls on our wedding days. You killed us all, Nick – me, Kathy, Joanna. So now give us something back. *With this ring, I do pledge.*'

Jenks glared and shouted at her. 'That's enough, Chessy!'

'I'll say when it's enough. You love games, so play the game. Play *my* game this time. *Swallow them!*' She pointed the gun. 'No sense pretending I won't shoot, is there, dear?'

Jenks took one of the rings, raised it to his lips. His hand was shaking badly.

'That was Melanie, Nicky. You would've liked her. Athletic . . . a skier . . . a diver. Your type, huh? She fought me to the end. But you don't like us to fight, do you? You like to be in total control.'

She cocked the gun and leveled it at Jenks's head.

Jenks put the ring in his mouth. With a sickened expression, he forced it down his throat.

Chessy was losing it. She was sobbing, trembling. I didn't think I could wait any longer.

'Police,' I yelled. I stepped forward, two hands on my .38, leveling it at her.

She spun at me, not even showing surprise, then back to

Jenks. 'He has to be punished!'

'It's over,' I said, carefully advancing toward her. 'Please, Chessy, no more killing.'

As if she suddenly realized what she had become, the sickening things she'd done, she looked at me. 'I'm sorry . . . I'm sorry for everything that happened – except this!'

Then she fired. At Jenks.

I fired, too – at her.

Chessy's slender body flew backwards, hitting the wall hard and crumpling against it. Her beautiful eyes widened and her mouth sagged open.

I looked and saw that she'd missed Jenks. He was staring at her in disbelief. He didn't think she could do it, didn't think she hated him that much. He still believed he controlled Chessy, and probably that she loved him.

I hurried to her, but it was too late. Her eyes were already glazed and the blood was streaming from her chest. I held her head and thought that she was so beautiful – like Melanie, Rebecca, Kathy – and now she was dead, too.

Nicholas Jenks turned toward me with a gasp of relief. 'I told you . . . I told you, I was innocent.'

I looked at him in disgust. Eight people were dead. The brides and grooms, Joanna, now his own wife. *I told you I was innocent.* Is that what he thought?

I swung, my fist catching him square in the teeth. I felt something shatter as Jenks dropped to his knees. 'So much for your innocence, Jenks!'

Chapter One Hundred and Twenty-Five

I was running and I realized that I no longer knew exactly what I was doing, where I was. Somehow my instincts brought me back to where Chris had been shot.

He was still up against the pillar in the same position. He looked as if he'd been waiting for me to return.

I rushed up to him, knelt down as close as I could get. I could see police and the EMS medical crew finally arriving. What had taken them so long?

'What happened?' Chris whispered. I could barely hear him.

'I got her, Chris. Chessy Jenks was the killer.'

He managed to nod his head. 'That's my girl,' he whispered.

Then Chris smiled faintly and he died on me.

I never would have imagined, or dreamed, that Chris would be the first to die. That was the most terrible and dreadful shock. It was unthinkable, impossible to believe.

I put my head down close to his chest. There was no

movement, no breath, just a terrifying stillness. Everything seemed so unreal.

Then the medics were working on Chris, doing heroic, but useless things, and I just sat there holding his hand.

I felt hollowed out and empty and incredibly sad. I was sobbing, but I had something to say to him; I had to tell Chris one last thing.

'Medved told me, Chris. I'm going to be okay.'

Chapter One Hundred and Twenty-Six

I couldn't go near my office at the Hall. I was given a one-week leave. I figured I'd take another of my own time on top of that. I sat around, watched some videos of old movies, went for my treatments, took a jog or two down by the Marina.

I even cooked, and sat out on the terrace overlooking the Bay, just as I had with Chris that first night. On one of those nights, I got really drunk and started playing with my pistol. It was Sweet Martha who talked me off the ledge. That, and the fact that if I killed myself, I would be betraying Chris's memory. I couldn't do that. Also, the girls would never have forgiven me.

I felt a hole tear at my heart, larger and more painful than anything I had ever felt, even with Negli's. I felt a void of connection, of commitment. Claire called me three times a day, but I just couldn't speak for very long, not even to her.

'It wasn't you, Lindsay. There was nothing you could've done,' she consoled.

'I kind of know that,' I replied. But I just couldn't convince myself it was true.

Mostly, I tried to persuade myself I still felt a sense of purpose. The Bride and Groom murders were solved. Nicholas Jenks was shamelessly milking his celebrity status on *Dateline* and *20/20*. Negli's seemed to be in remission. Chris was gone. I tried to think of what I would do next. Nothing very appealing came to mind.

Then I remembered what I had told Claire when my fears of Negli's were the strongest. *'Nailing this guy was the one clear thing that gave me the strength to go on.'*

It wasn't just about right or wrong. It wasn't about guilt or innocence. It was about what I was good at, and what I loved to do.

Four days after the shooting, I went to Chris's funeral. It was in a Catholic church, out in Hayward, where he was from.

I took my place in the ranks, with Roth, Jacobi. With Chief Mercer, who was dressed in blues. But my heart was aching so bad. I wanted to be up near Chris. I wanted to be next to him.

I watched his ex-wife and his two young boys struggling to keep it together. I was thinking about how very close I had come to their lives. And they didn't know it.

Hero cop, they were eulogizing him.

He was a marketing guy, I smiled. And then I started to cry.

Of all people, I felt Jacobi grasp my hand. And of all the improbable things, I found myself holding his back. 'Go ahead,' he seemed to be saying. 'Go ahead and weep.'

Afterward, at the graveside, I went up to Chris's ex-wife, Marion. 'I wanted to meet you,' I said. 'I was with him when he died.'

She looked at me with the fragile courage only another woman could understand.

'I know who you are,' she said, with a compassionate smile. 'You *are* pretty. Chris told me you were pretty. And smart.'

I smiled and took her hand. We both squeezed hard.

'He also said you were very brave.'

I felt my eyes well up. Then she took my arm and said the one thing I wanted most to hear.

'Why don't you stand with us, Lindsay.'

The Department gave Chris a hero's burial. Sad, mournful bagpipers opened the service. Row after row of cops in dress blues. A twenty-one-gun salute.

When it was over, I found myself walking back to the car, wondering what in God's name I was going to do next.

At the cemetery gates I spotted Cindy and Jill and Claire. They were waiting there for me.

I didn't move. I stood there, my legs trembling badly. They could see that if they didn't make the first move, I could break down.

'Why don't you ride back with us?' Claire said.

My voice cracked. I could barely utter the words. 'It was supposed to be me, not him,' I said to them. Then one by one they all came up and hugged me.

I put my arms around all of them and melted into their

embrace as deeply as I could. All four of us were crying. 'Don't ever leave me, guys.'

'*Leave?*' Jill said, with wide eyes.

'None of us,' promised Cindy. 'We're a team, remember? We will *always* be together.'

Claire took hold of my arm. 'We love you, sweetie,' she whispered.

The four of us walked arm-in-arm out of the cemetery. A cooling breeze was blowing in our faces, drying our tears.

At six o'clock that night, I was back at work inside the Hall of Justice.

There was something important I had to do.

In the lobby, almost the first thing you see, there's a large marble plaque. On it are the names and dates of all the men and women who wore the uniform of the SFPD and died in the line of duty. Tonight, a mason is working on the plaque.

It's an unwritten rule on the force, you never count them. But tonight, I do so. There are ninety-three, starting with James S. Coonts on October 5, 1878, when the SFPD was first formed.

Tomorrow there will be one more: Christopher John Raleigh. The Mayor will be there; Mercer, too. The reporters who cover the city beat. Marion and the boys. They will memorialize him as a hero cop. I will be there, too.

But tonight, I don't want speeches or ceremonies. Tonight, I want it to be just him and me.

The mason finishes up the engraving of his name. I wait

while he sands the marble, vacuums away the last particle of dust. Then I walk up, and run my hand over the smooth marble. Over his name.

Christopher John Raleigh.

The mason looks at me. He can see the pain welling in my eyes. 'You knew him, huh?' he says quietly.

I nod, and from somewhere deep in my heart, a smile comes forth. *I knew him.*

'Partner,' I say.

Epilogue

Coup de Grâce

Chapter One Hundred and Twenty-Seven

I have come to learn that murder investigations always have loose ends and questions that cry out to be answered. Always.

But not this time.

I was home one night about a month after we buried Chris. I had finished dinner for one, fed and walked Her Sweetness, when there was a knock on the door – a single, authoritative rap.

I hadn't buzzed anyone up from downstairs, so I went and looked through the peephole before I opened up. I couldn't believe my eyes. It was Nicholas Jenks.

He had on a blue blazer over a white shirt and dark gray slacks. He looked as arrogant and obnoxious as ever.

'Aren't you going to let me in?' he asked, then smiled as if to say, 'Of course you are. You can't resist, can you?'

'No, actually I'm not,' I told him. I walked away from the door. 'Get lost, asshole.'

Jenks knocked again, and I stopped walking. 'We have nothing to talk about,' I called loud enough for him to hear.

'Oh, but we do,' Jenks called back. 'You blew it, Inspector. I'm here to tell you how.'

I froze. I walked back to the door, paused, then opened it, my heart beating fast. *You blew it.*

He was smiling, or maybe laughing at me. 'I'm celebrating,' he said. 'I'm a happy fella! Guess how come?'

'Don't tell me – it's because you're a bachelor again.'

'Well, there's that. But I also just sold North American rights to my latest book. Eight million dollars. Then the movies paid four. This one's non-fiction, Lindsay. Guess the subject, take a stab?'

I wanted desperately to punch Jenks out again. 'And I'm the one you have to share your news with? How goddamn sad for you.'

Jenks continued to grin. 'Actually, I came here to share something else. And you *are* the only one I want to share this with. Do I have your attention yet, Lindsay? You blew it big-time, babe.'

He was so creepy and inappropriate that he was scaring me. I didn't want him to see it. What did he mean, I *blew* it?

'I'd offer you a drink, but I hate your guts,' I smirked.

He threw up his hands, imitated my smirk. 'You know, I feel exactly the same thing toward you. That's why I wanted to tell you this, Lindsay, *only you*.' He lowered his voice to a whisper. '*Chessy did what I told her to do*, right up until the very end. The murders? We were playing a terrible, wonderful game. Tragic husband and wife kill happy, innocent husbands and wives. We were *living* out the plot of a novel. My novel. *You really blew it, Lindsay.* I got away clean. I'm free. I'm *so* free. And now, I'm richer than ever.'

He stared at me, then he started to laugh. It was probably the most sickening sound I'd heard in my life.

'It's true. Chessy would do anything I wanted her to do. All of them would – that's why I picked them. I used to play a game where they barked like dogs. They loved it. Want to play, Lindsay? Ruff, ruff!'

I glared at him. 'Don't you feel kind of inadequate – playing your father's old games? Joanna told me about that.'

'I took things way past anything my father ever imagined. I've done it all, Inspector, *and I got away with it*. I planned every murder. Doesn't that make your fucking skin crawl? Doesn't it make *you* feel inadequate?'

Suddenly, Jenks was putting on plastic gloves he had in his jacket pockets. *What the hell?*

'This is perfect, too,' he said. 'I'm not here, Lindsay. I'm with this sweet little liar of a bitch in Tahoe. I have an alibi bought and paid for. Perfect crimes, Inspector – my specialty.'

As I turned to run, Jenks took out a knife. 'I want to feel this going inside you, Lindsay. Deep. The coup de grâce.'

'Help!' I screamed, but then he hit me hard. I was shocked at how fast he moved, and how powerful he was.

I slammed into a living-room wall and almost fainted. Martha instinctively went after him. I'd never seen her bare her teeth before. He lashed out and cut her shoulder. My poor dog fell over, whining horribly.

'Stay away, Martha!' I screamed at her.

Jenks picked me up and threw me into my bedroom. Then he shut the door.

'There was supposed to be another Bride and Groom murder while I was in jail. New evidence was going to slowly reveal itself. It would become clear that I was innocent – framed. Then I'd write the book! But Chessy turned around and double-crossed me. I never respected her more, Lindsay. I almost loved her for it. She showed some goddamn guts for once!'

I crawled away from Jenks, but he could see there was nowhere for me to go. I thought I might have a broken rib.

'You'll have to kill me first,' I told him, in a hoarse whisper.

'Glad to oblige,' he grinned. 'My pleasure.'

I crawled hand over hand toward my bed, the side facing a window on the Bay.

Jenks came after me.

'Stop, Jenks!' I yelled, at the top of my voice. 'Stop right there!'

He didn't stop. Why should he? He slashed back and forth with the knife. Christ, he was enjoying this. He was laughing. Another perfect murder.

I reached under the bed to where I'd fastened a holster and revolver, my home-security system.

I didn't have time to aim, but I didn't have to. Nicholas Jenks was stunned, the knife poised over his left shoulder.

I fired three times. Jenks screamed, his gray eyes bulged

in disbelief, then he collapsed dead on top of me. 'Burn in hell,' I whispered.

I called Claire first – the Medical Examiner; then Cindy – the best crime reporter in San Francisco; then Jill – my lawyer.

The girls came running.

Turn the page for a preview of the next compelling thriller in the Women's Murder Club series.

2ND
CHANCE

The Choir Kids

Chapter 1

Aaron Winslow would never forget the next few minutes. He recognized the terrifying sounds the instant they cracked through the night. His body went cold all over. He couldn't believe that someone was shooting a high-powered rifle in this neighborhood.

K-pow, k-pow, k-pow . . . k-pow, k-pow, k-pow.

His choir was just leaving the Harrow Street church. Forty-eight young kids streamed past him onto the sidewalk. They had just finished their final rehearsal before the San Francisco Sing-Off, and they had been excellent.

Then came the gunfire. Lots of it. Not just a single shot. A strafing. *An attack.*

K-pow, k-pow, k-pow . . . k-pow, k-pow, k-pow.

'Get down . . .' he screamed at the top of his voice. 'Everybody down on the ground! Cover your heads! Cover up!' He almost couldn't believe the words as they left his mouth.

At first, no one seemed to hear him. To the kids, in their white blouses and shirts, the shots must have seemed like firecrackers. Then a volley of shots rained through the church's beautiful stained-glass window. The depiction of Christ's blessing over a child at Capernaum shattered, glass splintering everywhere, some of it falling on the heads of the children.

'Someone's shooting!' Winslow screamed. Maybe more than one person. *How could that be?* He ran wildly through the kids, screaming, waving his arms, pushing as many as he could down to the grass.

As the kids finally crouched low or dove for the ground, Winslow spotted two of his choir girls, Chantal and Tamara, frozen on the lawn as bullets streaked past them. 'Chantal, Tamara, get down!' he screamed, but they remained there, hugging one another, emitting frantic wails. They were best friends. He had known them since they were little kids, playing four-square on blacktop.

There was never any doubt in his mind. He sprinted towards the two girls, grasping their arms firmly, tumbling them to the ground. Then he lay on top of them, pressing their bodies tightly.

Bullets whined over his head, just inches away. His eardrums hurt. His body was trembling and so were the girls shielded beneath him. He was almost sure he was about to die. 'It's all right, babies,' he whispered.

Then, as suddenly as it had begun, the firing stopped. A hush of silence hung in the air. So strange and eerie, as if the whole world had stopped to listen.

As he raised himself, his eyes fell on an incredible sight. Slowly, everywhere, the children struggled to their feet.

There was some crying, but he didn't see any blood; no one seemed to be hurt.

'Everyone okay?' Winslow called out. He made his way through the crowd. 'Is anyone hurt?'

'I'm okay . . . I'm okay,' came back to him. He looked around in disbelief. This was a miracle.

Then he heard the sound of a single child whimpering.

He turned and spotted Maria Parker, only twelve years old. Maria was standing on the whitewashed wooden steps of the church entrance. She seemed lost. Choking sobs poured from her open mouth.

Then his eyes came to rest on what had made the girl hysterical. He felt his heart sink. Even in war, even growing up on the streets of Oakland, he had never felt anything so horrible, so sad and senseless.

'Oh, God. Oh, no. How could you let this happen?'

Tasha Catchings, just eleven years old, lay in a heap in a flowerbed near the base of the church. Her white school blouse was soaked with blood.

Finally, Reverend Aaron Winslow began to cry himself.

Book 1

The Women's Murder Club – Again

Chapter One

On a Tuesday night I found myself playing a game of crazy-eights with three residents of the Hope Street Teen House. I was loving it.

On the beat-up couch across from me sat Hector, a barrio kid two days out of Juvenile; Alysha, quiet and pretty, but with a family history you wouldn't want to know; and Michelle, who at fourteen had already spent a year selling herself on the streets of San Francisco.

'Hearts,' I declared, flipping down an eight and changing the suit, just as Hector was about to lay out.

'Damn, badge lady,' he whined. 'How come each time I'm 'bout to go down, you stick your knife in me?'

'Teach *you* never to trust a cop, fool,' laughed Michelle, tossing a conspiratorial smile my way.

For the past four months I'd been spending a night or two a week at the Hope Street House. For so long, after the terrible bride and groom case earlier that summer, I'd felt completely lost. I took a month off from Homicide; ran down by the Marina; gazed out at the Bay from the safety of my Potrero Hill flat.

Nothing helped. Not counseling, not the total support of my girls – Claire, Cindy, Jill. Not even going back to the job. I had watched, unable to help, as the life leaked out of the person I loved. I still felt responsible for my partner's death in the line of duty. Nothing seemed to fill the void.

So I came here . . . to Hope Street.

And the good news was, it was working a little.

I peered up from my cards at Angela, a new arrival who sat in a metal chair across the room, cuddling her three-month-old son. The poor kid, maybe sixteen, hadn't said much all night. I would try to talk to Angela before I left for the night.

The door opened and Dee Collins, one of the House's head counselors, came in. She was followed by a stiff-looking black woman in a conservative gray suit. She had Department of Children and Families written all over her.

'Angela, your social worker's here.' Dee kneeled down beside her.

'I ain't blind,' the teenager said.

'We're going to have to take the baby now,' the social worker interrupted, as if completing this assignment was all that kept her from catching the next CalTran.

'No!' Angela pulled the infant even closer. 'You can keep me in this hole, you can send me back to Claymore, but you're not taking my baby.'

'Please, honey, only for a few days,' Dee Collins tried to reassure her.

The teenage girl drew her arms protectively around her

baby, who, sensing some harm, began to cry.

'Don't you make a scene, Angela,' the social worker warned. 'You know how this is done.'

As she came towards the girl, I watched Angela jump out of the chair. She was clutching the baby in one arm and a glass of juice she'd been drinking in the other hand.

In one swift motion she cracked the glass against a table. It created a jagged shard.

'Angela,' I leapt up from the card table, 'put that down. No one's going to take your baby anywhere unless you let her go.'

'This *bitch* is trying to ruin my life,' she glared. 'First, she lets me sit in Claymore three days past my date, then she won't let me go home to my mom. Now she's trying to take my baby girl.'

I nodded, peering into the teenager's eyes. 'First, you gotta lay down the glass,' I said. 'You *know* that, Angela.'

The DCF worker took a step, but I held her back. I moved slowly towards Angela. I took hold of the glass, then I gently eased the child out of her arms.

'She's all I have,' the girl whispered and then started to sob.

'I know,' I nodded. 'That's why you'll change some things in your life and get her back.'

Dee Collins had her arms around Angela, a cloth wrapped around the girl's bleeding hand. The DCF worker was trying unsuccessfully to hush the crying infant.

I went up and said to her, 'That baby gets placed somewhere nearby with daily visitation rights. And by the way, I didn't see anything going on here that was worth putting on file . . . *You?*' The caseworker gave me a disgruntled look and turned away.

Suddenly, my beeper sounded, three dissonant beeps punctuating the tense air. I pulled it out and read the number. *Jacobi, my ex-partner in Homicide. What did he want?*

I excused myself and moved into the staff office. I was able to reach him in his car.

'Something bad's happened, Lindsay,' he said, glumly. 'I thought you'd want to know.'

He clued me in about a horrible drive-by shooting at the LaSalle Heights Church. An eleven-year-old girl had been killed.

'Jesus . . .' I sighed, as my heart sank.

'I thought you might want in on it,' Jacobi said.

I took in a breath. It had been over three months since I'd been on the scene at a homicide. Not since the day the bride and groom case ended.

'So, I didn't hear,' Jacobi pressed. 'You want in, *Lieutenant?*' It was the first time he had called me with my new rank.

I realized my honeymoon had come to an end. 'Yeah,' I muttered back. 'I want in.'

3rd Degree

James Patterson and Andrew Gross

The No. 1 bestselling mystery series of the past decade comes roaring back with 3RD DEGREE, a shockingly suspenseful thriller featuring the Women's Murder Club.

Detective Lindsay Boxer is jogging along a beautiful San Francisco street as a ferocious blast rips through the neighbourhood. A townhouse owned by an internet millionaire explodes into flames, three people die and a sinister note signed 'August Spies' is found at the scene. Soon a wave of violence sweeps through the city – and it seems that whoever is behind it is intent on killing someone *every three days*.

Even more terrifying, the four friends who call themselves the Women's Murder Club discover that the killer has targeted one of them. And Lindsay learns that one member of the club is hiding a secret so dangerous and unbelievable that it could destroy them all.

Working with Andrew Gross, James Patterson delivers the breakneck pace and never-saw-it-coming plot twists that have made him the top-selling and most addictive suspense writer at work today. 3RD DEGREE is another searing and unforgettable thriller from this internationally acclaimed author.

'A novel which makes for sleepless nights' *Daily Express*

'A master of the suspense genre' *Sunday Telegraph*

'Unputdownable' *The Times*

978 0 7553 4928 9

headline